The Broad Arrow

The Broad Arrow;

Being Passages from the History of Maida Gwynnham, a Lifer

By 'Oliné Keese'
(Caroline Woolmer Leakey)

A critical edition by Jenna Mead

SYDNEY UNIVERSITY PRESS

First published in 1859 by Richard Bentley & Son, London

This edition published 2019 by Sydney University Press

© Introduction and critical apparatus Jenna Mead 2019
© Sydney University Press 2019

Reproduction and Communication for other purposes

Sydney University Press
Fisher Library F03
The University of Sydney NSW 2006 AUSTRALIA
sup.info@sydney.edu.au
sydney.edu.au/sup

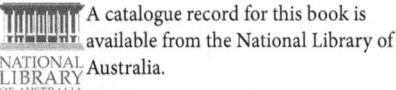 A catalogue record for this book is available from the National Library of Australia.

ISBN 9781920899745 paperback
ISBN 9781743324806 epub
ISBN 9781743324813 mobi

Cover image: Elizabeth Allport sitting on a hillside overlooking the River Derwent, South Hobart. Silver albumen print, sepia toning in oval mount (1856–1865), from the Allport Library and Museum of Fine Arts, Tasmanian Archive and Heritage Office (SD_ICS: 608136).
Cover design by Miguel Yamin.
Map of Hobart c. 1858 drawn and engraved by Richard Jarman (1808–1877), detail reproduced by permission of the Tasmanian Archive and Heritage Office (SD_ILS:573294).

Contents

Acknowledgments

This project has been conducted over a long period and I have incurred many debts of gratitude that I am pleased to acknowledge here. I could have had no more knowledgeable or generous guide for work in the Tasmanian Archives and Heritage Office than Dr Anthony Stagg and I am indebted to him for his sustained and skilful assistance. Working in the archives with Tony, encouraged and enabled me to reconceptualise both my approach to and the framing of this edition. I would especially like to thank Stephen Knight, (Honorary Research Professor, University of Melbourne) who first suggested I might be interested in Caroline Leakey's novel. Stephen's knowledge of nineteenth-century popular fiction, long praxis as a socio-historical critic and experience as an editor guided my thinking from the beginning. These colleagues read various drafts of the apparatus, correcting errors and making many helpful suggestions. Any errors remain my own responsibility.

Other debts include those to Harry Heseltine (Professor Emeritus, UNSW) and Paul Eggert (Professor Emeritus, UNSW) who were both generous with their extensive knowledge of nineteenth-century Australian textual editing and support. John Barnes (Professor Emeritus, La Trobe University) was an early supporter and encouraged my publishing work in progress. Graham Tulloch (Professor Emeritus, Flinders University) gave me tactful and accurate advice about nineteenth-century language for which I am especially grateful. Margaret Harris (Professor Emerita, University of Sydney), in her capacity as English Romantic specialist, solved a nagging problem; Wal Kirsop (Professor Emeritus, Monash University) kindly checked details of colonial readership in Tasmania for me. I would also like to acknowledge Dr Joy Hooton and the late Victor Crittenden for their contributions. I am very grateful to Laurie Hergenhan (Professor Emeritus, University of Queensland), whose life-long scholarly dedication to convict novels continues to provide the basis for work in this field. A more recent but no less important set of conversations with Dr Brett Greatley-Hirsch and Dr Katherine Bode have shaped and refined my thinking about editorial procedure. Dr Bode's work on the impact and meaning of digitisation marks a paradigm shift and she generously commented on my attempts to visualise digital data. Dr Greatley-Hirsch's work on digital editing, likewise, moves his field of early modern texts forward. For his comments on editing principles, as well as for his support and friendhsip, I owe Brett a special debt.

In Hobart, Dr Alison Alexander and Dr Hamish Maxwell-Stuart have been generous with their extensive knowledge of convict matters and I am grateful to both of them. Peter Chapman, the editor of the Boyes diaries, has also been helpful. The Reverend Stuart Blacker, erstwhile Dean of St David's Cathedral, gave me the benefit of his discerning biblical and liturgical knowledge without which, as readers will see, I could not have edited this novel. I have a very special debt to Ms Josephine Leakey of Newton Abbot, Devon, a descendent of Caroline Leakey with whom I have been in correspondence and to Ms Margaret Stafford, Hobart, who facilitated that exchange.

I am grateful to the Australian Research Council and the internal research committees of La Trobe University and the University of Tasmania for their generous support in funding aspects of my research and, in particular, the invaluable assistance I had from Dr Lucy Sussex, in Australia, and Hannah Kanter, in the UK, at an early stage of the project. Kate Walpole and Sandra Champion compiled an important database of records available at the Tasmanian Archives and Heritage Office as part of an ARC-funded project and I am grateful for their discovery of Leakey-related material.

I owe a special debt to the Australian Academy of Humanities for their generous support of the publication of this edition.

Like many researchers in the field of nineteenth-century Tasmanian history, I have benefited from the informative and enthusiastic assistance of the librarians at the State Library of Tasmania and, in particular, the custodians of the Allport, Crowther and Tasmaniana Collections. Tony Marshall and Sue Knopf were always informative and helpful—even with repeated requests. Gillian Winter, formerly of the State Library of Tasmania and a noted Tasmanian historian in her own right, assisted in the early stages of the project. I am indebted to Ian Morrison Heritage Librarian, Collection Department, for generously sharing his detailed and extensive knowledge of the TAHO collections. The librarians of the La Trobe Library, part of the State Library of Victoria, allowed me access to a unique diary in their collection that provides the only independent witness to Caroline Leakey. I have pleasure in acknowledging their assistance here and especially Jan McDonald for her gracious welcome. I am also very grateful to Helen Millar, former Librarian, Clinical Library, University of Tasmania, who solved an arcane problem of nineteenth-century medical practice.

I would like to record my special thanks to Elizabeth Ellis who, as Assistant State Librarian, Collection Management Services and Mitchell Librarian, State Library of New South Wales, granted permission for the use of Library's fine copy of *The Broad Arrow; Passages from the History of Maida Gwynnham, a Lifer* (London: Richard Bentley & Son, 1859) for this edition.

My sincere thanks to Judith Johnson, Hobart, who kept interest in this novel alive with her 1988 edition: it is this version that has provided many readers' only acquaintance with Maida Gwynnham's story. I would also like to thank the editors of academic journals in both Australia (*Meridian, Australian Feminist Studies*) and the US (*a/b Auto/Biographical Studies*) who published my articles on *The Broad Arrow* and thus helped to maintain scholarly interest in this text. I have been fortunate in having students at La Trobe University and the University of Tasmania who continued to ask me questions about *The Broad Arrow* and it has been their interest that has helped me to understand how the life of a novel may be reinvigorated.

Sheila Allison and Cate Lowry played a vital role in early attempts to publish this edition. Cate Lowry has my thanks—and that of the novel's readers—for a solution to the problem of formatting a complex text. Sheila Allison's faith in this novel gave me unfailing encouragement. I am delighted that Sydney University Press, under the leadership of Susan Murray, agreed to publish this edition. Denise O'Dea has been a determined and sympathetic editor and Hannah McFarlane brought real acuity to her role as designer.

Sylvia Yamanaka-Mead, Philip Mead and Rohan Mead have kept me focussed with indefatigable good humour.

During my years in Hobart, I had the pleasure of knowing Elizabeth Dean who worked hard all her life as a feminist, a reader, a writer, a business woman and a social worker. Above all, Liz was a person who believed in the continuing importance of preparing young people for their future lives and for this reason I have had Liz in mind as I worked on Caroline Leakey's novel.

My lasting debt is to Professor Peter Pierce and it is with great sadness that I record his untimely passing. Peter was a dedicated and enthusiastic supporter of this project, generously sharing his extensive scholarship, astute knowledge and unfailing good humour. The study of Australia literature is poorer without him. I am honoured, as a friend and colleague, to dedicate this edition to his memory.

Jenna Mead
Melbourne, Victoria
January 2019

Introduction

The Broad Arrow; Being Passages from the History of Maida Gwynnham, a Lifer was written by Caroline Woolmer Leakey and first published in London, under the pseudonym 'Oliné Keese' in 1859, and in Hobart in 1860.[1] The novel tells the story of Maida Gwynnham, a young and inexperienced middle-class woman lured into committing a forgery by her deceitful lover, Captain Norwell, and then wrongly convicted of infanticide. The novel's title comes from the arrow stamped as a sign of government property and thus an emblem of incarceration. The broad arrow is the pheon, a term in medieval heraldry, or the head of a mace-like javelin.[2] Henry Sidney, Earl of Romney, excerpted the symbol from his family coat of arms during his time as Master of the Ordnance (1693–1702), for use in denoting government ownership. In the Australian context, the broad arrow has particular resonances, first, as an ensign of eighteenth-century imperial aspirations that colonised the continent for white settlement. Second, the symbol appeared on every aspect of convict life, from clothing to leg-irons to registers to handmade building bricks and connoted not only loss of personhood but also criminality and epitomised carceral status.[3] It became thus an emblem of Australia percolating so far into the details of cultural practices that it came to be used, for example, as an element of book design: the first edition of Leakey's novel was stamped with a gilt broad arrow.

Maida's crimes are literal, in the forging of a cheque, and metaphorical, in maintaining a sexual relationship outside the legalised institution of marriage; in their intricate interaction, these crimes resonate throughout the narrative. Deserted by her lover, she is transported to Van Diemen's Land, where she becomes an assigned servant to the Evelyn family living in Macquarie Street, Hobarton (Hobart).[4] Maida is befriended by the family, which includes a pious minister, a snobbish colonial housewife, a retired magistrate who crusades for social justice, two young children who grow up nursed and educated by convicts, and two young women who are cousins and visiting Tasmania. Maida becomes their trusted confidante but, as a convict, she is also caught up in the underworld of convicts, petty crime and murder.

---

1   Oliné Keese [Caroline W. Leakey], *The Broad Arrow; Being Passages from the History of Maida Gwynnham, a Lifer* (London: Richard Bentley & Son, 1859; Hobart: J. Walch & Sons, 1860). Unless otherwise indicated, citations will be from the 1859 edition.

2   'pheon, n.', OED Online, December 2013, Oxford University Press. https://bit.ly/2D0hEje. See 1486 *Coote Armuris* sig. bv, in *Book. St. Albans*, 'Feons be calde in armys brode arow hedys.' Also Juliet Ash, *Dress Behind Bars: Prison Clothing as Criminality* (London and New York: Taurus, 2010) 10 in Sharon Peoples, 'Dress, Reform and Masculinity in Australia', *Grainger Studies: An Interdisciplinary Journal*, 1 (2011): 115–35 at fn 58.

3   John Frow, 'In the Penal Colony', *Australian Humanities Review*, April–June (1999) https://bit.ly/2AnrOHS.

4   Hobart is called both Hobarton and Hobart Town in the novel. Hobarton appears as an abbreviated, transitional form between Hobart Town, named by Lieutenant-Governor David Collins in 1804, and Hobart, officially confirmed as the capital's name in January 1881, *Mercury* 1 Jan 1881, 4.

The novel follows the vicissitudes of Maida's life across two hemispheres as a free woman and as a convict, from childhood, through motherhood, and then, for the largest part, as a working woman assigned to a family whose middle-class status registers all the expectations she might have had and all that she has lost. She is financially impoverished and struggles to survive both among her fellow convicts, where possessions are stolen and traded for cash, and among her former class peers, where financial independence signals credibility, dignity and social (and sometimes legal) power.

For Maida, there is no escape from the pain and degradation of convict life. A chance meeting with Bob Pragg, the convict who orchestrated her initial capture, leads to one of the novel's most terrifying episodes, and Maida eventually dies at the hands of a sadistic nurse just as her faithless lover, Captain Norwell, arrives in Hobart to plead for her forgiveness. Norwell ends his days mad and alone in the asylum at New Norfolk, while Maida, whose death is the inevitable consequence of the confrontation between her character and her status, dies steadfast—perhaps even triumphant—in the moral choices she has made.

The story of Maida's life unfolds alongside that of a colonial family and their convict servants through the daily business of running a household, looking after children, visiting friends, responding to the frustrations of local politics and parochialism, and talking about the important issues of the day, especially convictism and its social and moral effects, and attitudes to Britain as the source of social and political power—all treated with sustained and precise detail and often with considerable humour. Through the family's eyes readers witness the cruel system of secondary punishment in a visit to Port Arthur, experience the tedium of petty bureaucratic jealousies, and gain a rare glimpse into ordinary people's views on the extermination of Tasmania's Indigenous peoples.

Drawing on the styles and tropes of reportage, travelogue, social satire and exemplum, the novel offers a detailed, varied and direct account of life in Hobart across its social classes in the period just before the end of transportation, when political and moral tensions—between the penal colony of Van Diemen's Land and the free colony Tasmania would become—were at their most tense. Debate over the ethical, commercial and political consequences of transportation was vigorous from the mid-1830s onwards in both London and Van Diemen's Land, set against a background of trenchant comment, both for and against, in the colonial newspapers.[5] The *Penal Servitude Act* (1853, restricting transportation to sentences of more than fourteen years, and 1857, referring more generally to transportation) eventually passed the abolition of transportation into law although, in practice, cessation of transportation was achieved incrementally.[6] The change of name from

---

5   See, for example, the Report of the Select Committee on Transportation (1837–38), chaired by Sir William Molesworth and the House of Lords Select Committee on Execution of Criminal Law (1847). Another highly influential report though of a different political orientation and ethical position was John Thomas Bigge, Report of the Commissioner of Inquiry, on the judicial establishments of New South Wales, and Van Diemen's Land: ordered, by the House of Commons, to be printed, 21 February 1823. This was the second of Bigge's three reports and is marked by an approach unsympathetic to either colony. The report concludes that 'The operation of some [regulations . . .] may be modified; but as long as New South Wales and Van Diemen's Land contain so great a number of convicts, either suffering under their sentences, or subject to the terms of a conditional remission, most of the regulations to which I have alluded, and especially those that provide for the security and detention of convicts, and the identification of their persons, must continue to be strictly and unremittingly observed.' (n.p.) https://bit.ly/2yTFv07.

6   Penal Servitude Act 1857, Chapter 3 https://bit.ly/2AnrOHS 'II. After the Commencement of this Act, no Person shall be sentenced to Transportation . . .' CAP. III. ANNO VICESIMO & VICESIMO

Van Diemen's Land to Tasmania occurred toward the end of this period of profound change and conferred a new identity on the former penal colony.[7] The novel retains the name Van Diemen's Land and debate about transportation is heated, and so the action reimagines Hobart, Port Arthur and environs in the late 1840s and early 1850s.

Commentators have been critical of the novel's structure: an early reviewer complained, 'This is a tale of rough construction and rougher execution'[8] and, more than a century later, a leading scholar of convict literature empathised, describing the novel as 'a mixed bag, relying on fictional stereotypes and lumpy miscellaneous material not absorbed into a narrative flow.'[9] But Leakey's novel has an ambitious reach in which the two interlocking histories—Maida's and the Evelyn family's—give structure to a series of dynamic social, political, ethical and emotional exchanges, counterpointed one against another, that are all the more engaging precisely because their structure is neither neat nor argumentative.[10]

The material history of Leakey's novel offers an enlightening case study in the publication, distribution and reception of an individual book in the interlocking economies of commerce, geography and readership operating in the global nineteenth-century publishing industry that Alison Rukavina analyses in her exemplary study, *The Development of the International Book Trade, 1870–1895*.[11] First published in book form by Richard Bentley & Son, London (1859), by J. Walch & Sons, Hobart (1860) and subsequently reissued in various formats until 1997, *The Broad Arrow* never achieved the bestseller status of Marcus Clarke's *His Natural Life*, also published in book form by Richard Bentley & Son (1875).[12] The decisive moment in the book's long journey occurred in 1886 when, after the author's death, Richard Bentley & Son employed Gertrude Townsend Mayer to edit the novel's elaborate life history of a woman protagonist unfolding across two continents and an expansive emotional register from two volumes into a single volume in order to relaunch it as a colonial romance set among convicts in Van Diemen's Land. This was the commercially successful edition that was reissued for over a hundred and fifty years, beginning with Richard Bentley & Son's single volume in 1887, and ranging in formats from hardback to paperback to digital platform.[13] Tracing these components—the book's *histoire croisée*—reveals a detailed history of readership and circulation as well as production.

PRIMO VICTORÆ REGINÆ. An Act to amend the Act of the Sixteenth and Seventeenth Years of Her Majesty, to substitute in certain Cases other Punishment in lieu of Transportation. [26th June 1857.] Commenced 1 July 1857.

7   Order-in-Council 8 September 1855 approving replacement of the name 'Van Diemen's Land' by 'Tasmania' as the name of the Colony, Tasmanian Archives and Heritage Office [hereafter TAHO], GO1/97, 147–49; proclaimed 1 January 1856.

8   Anon., review of *The Broad Arrow*, *The Literary Gazette: A Weekly Journal of Literature, Science, Art and General Information*, 21 May 1859, 620.

9   L.T. Hergenhan, '*The Broad Arrow*: an Early Novel of the convict System,' *Southerly* 36.2 (1976): 142.

10   For an important reading based on the novel's own terms and acknowledging its ambitions, see John Scheckter, '*The Broad Arrow*: Conventions, Convictions, and Convicts,' *Antipodes* 1.2 (1987): 89–91.

11   Alison Rukavina, *The Development of the International Book Trade, 1870–1895* (Basingstoke: Palgrave Macmillan, 2007).

12   See Marcus Clarke, *His Natural Life*, ed. Lurline Stuart, The Academy Editions of Australian Literature (St Lucia: University of Queensland Press, 2001) is the definitive reference for this novel's intricate publishing history.

13   Hereafter, I will refer to Townsend Mayer's edited text as 1886; see bibliographic note, Macmillan edition (1900), vi. Richard Bentley & Son's publication of the edited version is 1887.

Townsend Mayer's technical shrewdness was to edit Leakey's intricate narrative at the level of structure, rather than sentence by sentence, or even page by page. Shearing off subplots, detaching characters, omitting political and ethical commentary, paring back local and specific detail, Townsend Mayer's approach to producing the second edition was steely, orderly and consistent. There are, for example, very few occasions where copy is added to smooth transitions across omitted material. The second edition achieved its aim of extracting a viable commercial product from Leakey's original novel as the novel's publication history amply demonstrates. After the publication of Clarke's acclaimed novel, *The Broad Arrow* was usually compared unfavourably with the heroic story of Rufus Dawes until it was eventually marketed (in 1989) as a companion convict novel with a tagline proclaiming the heroine's being sentenced for 'the term of her natural life'. But the effects of reducing the length by a third, editing out events, flattening dialogue and the repackaging of the second edition as colonial romance, as Tasmanian curiosity with selected photographs, as a female genre convict novel have as much distorted Leakey's original novel as shown the longevity of a niche product in the publishing industry. Readers have assumed, not unreasonably, that Leakey wrote some kind of 'convict novel' even though her book was published even before Marcus Clarke's novel appeared in serial form from March 1870. Then, too, the constant circulation of Townsend Mayer's edition has not only obscured the essential connections between the original and revised texts but also precluded the possibility that Leakey's novel explores another genre, *Bildungsroman* rather than convict novel.

This current edition restores the 1859 text for the first time and formats the text to show both the original edition and the 1886 revision and thus responds to the fluctuating history of the book. The rationale for this edition is neither antiquarian—to republish the lost first edition—nor modernising, seeking to produce a nineteenth-century novel for a twenty-first century reader; though there are, certainly, elements of both in the construction of this text. Rather, the present moment in the book's history creates an opportunity to read both versions of the text and develop a sense of the relationship between those versions by seeing them together on the same page: to read the novel's intertexts. Situating Leakey's novel within the century and a half of its history and paying attention to the progression of its material forms is not separate, though, from either an understanding of its literary ambitions or the imperative, once again, to develop an apposite editorial practice. The introduction details the book's *histoire croisée* to develop a nuanced understanding of the interlocking contexts in which readers have engaged with Leakey's novel and formed their own judgments on the life of Maida Gwynnham and the questions it raises. The principal editorial decision has been to represent the original and revised texts on the same page. Text edited out for the revised edition is marked with a light shadow rather than being codified through the conventional editorial apparatus that gives primacy to one text. It is in this respect that this edition is dynamic: readers may choose to read either the original or revised texts separately or in relation to one another. This edition also considers a number of theoretical questions about authorship, editorial practice, and the status of texts though only briefly where they are germane to the foremost task of putting Caroline Leakey's *The Broad Arrow; Being, Passages from the History of Maida Gwynnham, a Lifer* into circulation for a reading public.

The history of the book

The Broad Arrow is important as an imaginative work of fiction exemplifying particular workings of the genre of the novel in the mid-nineteenth century and thus it has a place in the literary histories of Britain and Australia and in the history of middle-class women's writing in both places. It is also a singular and useful historical source, though having the status of literature rather than archival record. Like Marcus Clarke's *His Natural Life*, which it predates by more than ten years,[14] Leakey's novel allows 'historians [to catch] some glimpses of convicts "from within," as it were' as they were enmeshed with other social classes and their values precisely because it reaches 'beyond the range of empirical history'.[15]

The novel is also a case-study in the connections between the book publishing industry and the changing tastes of consumption in reading cultures in Britain and Australia. In the publishing history of *The Broad Arrow*, the bibliographic identity of the novel undergoes a series of transformations as the book is published in London, Hobart and then Sydney by a number of publishers, between whom copyright is transferred (for example, Bentley & Son to Macmillan, August 1898) or lapses (for example, Angus & Robertson under the Eden imprint in 1988), and in a number of print formats between 1859 and 1988, most recently, in electronic form on the Sydney Electronic Text and Imaging Service (SETIS) platform.[16] Disentangling the commercial, cultural, personal and industrial pressures behind the appearance of colonial series, niche editions, fluctuating profit and loss, the effects of trade reviews and reviews in journals and newspapers, the exigencies of success and failure that characterise the history of this book presumes that such elements can be atomised and separately scrutinised. Perhaps this is a less useful approach than acknowledging the powerful relationships between those pressures as characterising *l'histoire croisée* of the emerging international publishing industry during the mid- to late nineteenth century.[17]

The publishing record of the book develops along two different, asymmetrical but interconnected commercial trajectories: one in Britain, where the novel was first distributed to the domestic and overseas markets and then repackaged for exclusive export to colonial markets, and the other in Australia, where the Tasmanian publisher recast it for local, domestic and perhaps tourist and antiquarian markets. The novel was published first by Richard Bentley & Son in 1859 as a two-volume work in post octavo format (or '8vo', measuring about 5 inches by 8 inches), with six steel-point illustrations, a gilt broad

---

14 Clarke, *His Natural Life*, ed. Stuart, xxxiii–xliii.

15 Michael Roe, 'Historical Background: Clarke and Convictism,' in Clarke, *His Natural Life*, ed. Stuart, 590; though Roe, himself, clearly misunderstands the boundaries between literature and history; see Postscript (590).

16 E. Morris Miller, *Australian Literature From its Beginnings to 1935*, vol. 2 (Melbourne: Melbourne University Press, in association with Oxford University Press, 1940), 601–2. Laurie Hergenhan, *Unnatural Lives. Studies in Australian Fiction about the Convicts from James Tucker to Patrick White* (St Lucia: University of Queensland Press, 1983), 177–8. Jenna Mead, '(Re)producing Caroline Leakey's *The Broad Arrow*,' *Meridian* 10.1 (1991): 81–8. On the SETIS platform, the text was SGML-coded under TEI.2 *Guidelines* (1997) and then converted to html and pdf formats for display (2003).

17 This discussion is indebted to Rukavina's fine study of archive sources in *The Development of the International Book Trade, 1870-1895*; for *l'histoire croisée* see 11 and ch. 4 'The International Book Trade.'

arrow on the cover, priced at 21 shillings[18] for the commercial market, perhaps on the advice of one of a group of women—often novelists themselves—whom George Bentley employed as publisher's readers.[19] Leakey had signed an agreement to publish using the pseudonym Oliné Keese in January 1859.[20] The following year, the two-decker edition was bound as a single volume, without illustrations, for the Hobart bookseller J. Walch & Sons, published under their own imprint and distributed to the Australian market at 10 shillings and sixpence. Bentley announced the publication under the heading 'New Works in Mr Bentley's List' in the London literary journal the *Critic* on 2 April 1859.[21] Walch advertised the book in the *Cornwall Chronicle*, a newspaper printed in Launceston, Van Diemen's Land, on 29 February 1860, noting its appearance in 'one thick vol.' and giving the bookseller's address as Hobart and Launceston. The new title also appeared in the publisher's own *Walch's Literary Intelligencer*, with the addition of the local detail that this edition was 'Specially got up for Tasmania'[22] by 'special arrangements with the author and publisher', with the added enticement that 'No work has ever yet been issued from the English Press in which Tasmanian scenes and Tasmanian doings (as they were) are so graphically depicted.' Within twelve months, the book had entered two books-in-print lists, one on each side of an already global market.

Twenty-seven years later, in 1886, Bentley prepared a revised edition of the novel, promoted as 'A New Edition'. It was printed in 8vo, with a broad arrow in black ink on the front cover, for the domestic market. At the same time, the English publisher issued this second edition (dated 1887) with '"Australian Edition" in a shield, surmounted by a kangaroo on the underside' and a note on the imprint page stating 'The Edition is especially issued by the Proprietors of the Copyright for circulation in the Australian Colonies only'. A two-page list of 'Bentley's Favourite Novels' was also included, maximising the advertising opportunity.[23] The publisher thus effectively split the market, and they confirmed the division the following year by including the Australian edition in their 'Colonial Series', which was comprised of 'restricted editions'. As the published list explains:

> The Colonial Series was confined to certain areas only: (1) Australia); (2) India; (3) Africa; (4) Canada. On the backs of the covers (to assist the stock-keeper) was the mark of each division in a shield or tablet denoting at a glance the area only for which it was available. Thus for Australia, a kangaroo; for India, an elephant; for Africa, an ostrich; and for Canada, a beaver.[24]

---

18   *A List of the Principal Publications Issued from New Burlington Street During the Year 1859* (London: Richard Bentley & Son, 1905), 909.

19   Royal A. Gettman, *A Victorian Publisher. A Study of The Bentley Papers* (Cambridge: Cambridge University Press, 1960), 193. I am grateful to Dr Norman Gardiner, formerly La Trobe University for advice on this reference.

20   Alison Ingram [compiler], *Index to the Archives of Richard Bentley & Son 1829–1898*, British Publishers' Archives (Cambridge: Chadwyck-Healey, 1977) L58, 195.

21   *The Critic* 2 April 1859, 316.

22   *The Cornwall Chronicle* 29 Feb 1860, 5. TAHO NS2849/1/1 *Walch's Literary Intelligencer*, May 1860, 199.

23   *A List of the Principal Publications Issued from New Burlington Street During the Year 1886* (London: Richard Bentley & Son, 1920), 2029.

24   *A List of Principal Publications from New Burlington Street During the Year 1888* (London: Richard Bentley & Son, 1917), 2133.

The Australian (or 'Kangaroo') series included

>Clarke.—For the Term of His Natural Life. 2s. 6d. July 1, 1885.
>Leakey.—The Broad Arrow. 2s. 6d. December 1, 1886.
>Nicols.—Wild Life in the Australian Bush. 2s. 6d. May 5, 1887.
>Maning.—Old New Zealand (Anonymous). 2s. 6d. June 9, 1887.
>Praed.—Longleat of Kooralbyn. 2s. 6d. June 14 1887.
>Nesfield.—Chequered Career (Anonymous). 2s. 6d. October 11 1887.
>Cooper.—The Islands of the Pacific. 2s. 6d. February 20, 1888.
>Macleod.—An Australian Girl. 2s. 6d. July 26, 1894.
>Pembroke and Kingsley.—South Sea Bubbles (Anonymous). 2s. 6d. April 9, 1895.
>Mackay.—The Yellow Wave. 22. 6d. September 10, 1897.[25]

This edition is marked as 'Australian' not only by the name of the series and its marsupial insignia, but also by its title page, which carries the headline 'Old Tasmanian Days', thus reiterating the novel's claim to historical authenticity and, perhaps, antiquarian interest. Paul Eggert has argued that, priced at 6 shillings for the domestic British market and 2 shillings and sixpence for a special 'Australian Edition', this new cheap edition made Leakey's novel a 'contender for classic status' and was edged out only by the competition from Marcus Clarke's *His Natural Life*, published by Richard Bentley & Son in 1875.[26] (This edition of Leakey's book was reissued in 1892; surviving copies of the 1892 print run are held by the State Library of Tasmania.) In 1887, seeming again to undercut Bentley's own colonial market, the English publisher issued the same edition of the novel with George Robertson & Company with the same identifiers—'Old Tasmanian Days' and 'Australian Edition'—on the title page.

Commercial as well as political pressure for Australian editions surfaced in an energetic editorial in the *Publisher: Australian Literary News*, 'A monthly record of the bookselling, printing, fancy goods, and stationery trades' produced by Turner & Henderson, 'Lithographers, Printers and Publishers' of Hunter Street, Sydney.

>It may be that the rising generation of Australians will be better fitted to judge, but with the present, we have often been painfully aware of the fact that Australian literature is not appreciated. Without rhyme or reason an Australian will tell you that he always goes to English papers and English magazines, when he wants to read anything, and yet we know that he frequently gets articles written by Australians under this English covering. As for a federated Australian literature, it is, we fear, further off than a political federation. Here in New South Wales we speak of Marcus Clarke not as an Australian but frequently as Victorian . . . We must . . . cultivate the national word 'Australians'. We must support Australian products . . .[27]

---

25   *Principal Publications . . . 1888*, 2133.
26   Paul Eggert, 'Australian Classics and the Price of Books: the Puzzle of the 1890s', *JASAL Special Issue 2008: The Colonial Present*, ed. Gillian Whitlock (2008): 140–41 https://bit.ly/2PMIJZN; and 'Changing Literary Tastes and the Blue Pencil: In-house Editing and Abridgement of Australian Colonial Novels at the House of Bentley in London', 8 (forthcoming). See also Susan K. Martin, 'She'll Rewrite Mate: Nineteenth-century Australian Women's Fiction and the Trials of Reprinting', *Australian Women's Book Review* 3.3 (1991): 12–14.
27   Anon., 'Federated Australia', *The Publisher*, 'Australian Literary News', 18 July 1887, 2.

This piece is followed, at the end of the issue, by a full-page advertisement for 'New Australian Editions' by 'the most popular authors . . . issued to the colonies' at 2 shillings and sixpence each. The list includes *The Broad Arrow* as well as Matthew Arnold's *Essays in Criticism*, Marcus Clarke's *Term of His Natural Life* and Charlotte Yonge's *A Modern Telemachus.*[28]

Eleven years later, in August 1898, Richard Bentley transferred the copyright in *The Broad Arrow* to Macmillan & Company. In 1900 the novel was reprinted without any Australian, Tasmanian, historical or series markers. This transfer of copyright was simultaneous with the takeover of Richard Bentley & Son by Macmillan; the *Bookseller* noted that Bentley & Son was 'a well-known and old-established house of business' and that the takeover was thus 'a matter of regret'.[29] Correspondence between Bentley and Leakey's literary executor, her sister Emily, 20 January 1887, states that the first edition made a loss for the publisher of £87 on an outlay of £274.7s.2d. for 750 copies printed; the title remained in print and on Bentley's list for forty-one years.[30]

Meanwhile, in Tasmania, J. Walch & Sons' 1860 imprint was followed, in 1886, by a new binding, again under the bookseller's own imprint. This binding comprised the revised 1886 text, a title page promising 'Illustrations of Hobart and Port Arthur', a 'Publisher's Notice' and six photographs. The Publisher's Notice was titled 'A Companion to Marcus Clarke's Famous Novel' and situated the story as 'not so generally known' but of exceptional interest dealing with '"life in Hobart Town and Port Arthur" during the 'forties', *written and published before Marcus Clarke's Book.*' It identified the author as 'a lady long resident in Hobart Town', thus guaranteeing the novel's authenticity and its special interest to local readers: 'To Tasmanians, and especially to "old" residents, this story has an added interest from the introduction, under slightly changed names, of real persons who cannot fail to be recognized.' The binding had a photographic cover in place of the broad arrow. Together with the photographic illustrations, this securely located the novel as 'Tasmanian' in both a geographical and historical sense. This edition foregrounded aspects of the novel that were likely to appeal to a domestic market: Tasmanian readers might be engaged by familiar times, places and people, while a national readership might buy the book as a record of recent colonial history. These images also attached the novel to a nascent tourist project that would have far-reaching cultural resonance and economic benefits. The effect was to historicise the novel, an impulse that came from the publisher and was motivated by commercial concerns. In marketing the title rather than the author, it gestured towards Sir Walter Scott's first novel, *Waverley , Or 'Tis Sixty Years Since* (1814), which had been published anonymously in 1814 and thus invoked an already established and successful genre.[31]

This issue was reprinted in 1900, together with the transfer of copyright notice, under the J. Walch & Sons imprint. One effect of this combination of additions—photographs,

---

28 'New Australian Editions,' *The Publisher*, 14.
29 Anon., *The Bookseller*, 7 Sept. 1898 cited in Michael L. Turner, *Index and Guide to the Lists and Publications of Richard Bentley & Son 1829-1898* (Bishops Stortford: Chadwyck-Healey, 1975), 1.
30 Ingram, *Bentley Archives*, L86, 134; ledger page L36, 68.
31 There is extensive scholarship on the historical novel and its development; see György Lukács, *The Historical Novel*, trans. Hannah and Stanley Mitchell (London: Merlin Press, 1962; 1955) and also Michael McKeon, *The Origins of the English Novel* (Baltimore: Johns Hopkins Press, c. 1987) and Michael McKeon ed., *Theory of the Novel. A Historical Approach* (Baltimore: Johns Hopkins Press, 2000); note too that this novel does not display the multiple temporalities, hybridity or mixed genre, or imitative form that characterise historical fiction.

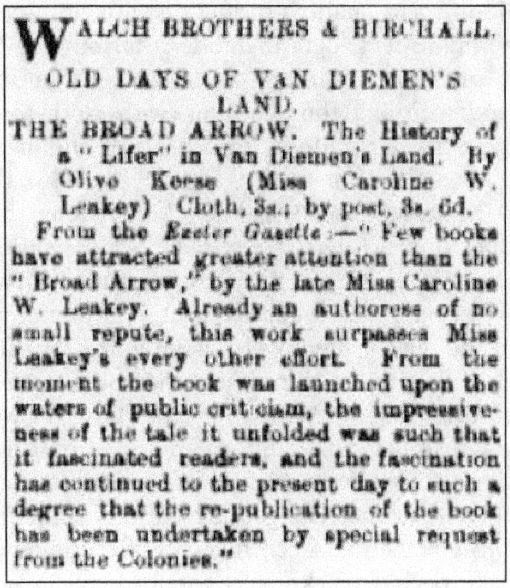

WALCH BROTHERS & BIRCHALL.

OLD DAYS OF VAN DIEMEN'S
LAND.
THE BROAD ARROW. The History of
a "Lifer" in Van Diemen's Land. By
Olive Keese (Miss Caroline W.
Leakey) Cloth, 3s.; by post, 3s. 6d.
From the *Exeter Gazette*:—" Few books
have attracted greater attention than the
" Broad Arrow," by the late Miss Caroline
W. Leakey. Already an authoress of no
small repute, this work surpasses Miss
Leakey's every other effort. From the
moment the book was launched upon the
waters of public criticism, the impressive-
ness of the tale it unfolded was such that
it fascinated readers, and the fascination
has continued to the present day to such a
degree that the re-publication of the book
has been undertaken by special request
from the Colonies."

Figure 1 Advertisement in the *Launceston Examiner*, 10 May 1887.

preface, national appeal—was to localise the novel. Where the original edition had played on the exotic appeal of colonial Tasmania for a British domestic market, the authenticating photographs, the assurance of the author's local knowledge and the appeal to local readers further set this 1900 edition apart from the Colonial Series that had been codified as Australian by the emblematic kangaroo. The terms 'Australia', 'Tasmania' and 'colonial' remained in circulation, but with each new edition they were repurposed for a new commercial context.

A snapshot of that complexity, *l'histoire croisée* on a micro-level, is revealed in a notice that appeared in the *Launceston Examiner* on 10 May 1887 (Figure 1).

This announcement promotes the newly revised novel, now 28 years old, to potential Tasmanian buyers by citing a review from the *Exeter Gazette*, printed in Caroline Leakey's home town. The review reveals the mystery of the pseudonym Oliné Keese (misprinted as 'Olive'), provides a biographical note, registers critical reception of the work, places the novel within the context of Leakey's other writings and acknowledges a rationale for the reissue in the 'special request from the Colonies' in breathless but economical prose. The language of the puff is clear enough but the tone of the last phrase is perhaps less certain: although the book has been reissued in response to the importuning of 'Colonial readers', a British review is cited, perhaps to reassure colonial readers of the 'fascination' of their own story.

Another asymmetrical aspect of the book's history—rather than its bibliographic identity—concerns its material production. The printer's name, usually given in a single line on the last page, tells another version of the exchanges between British and Australian or Tasmanian book publishing. The Bentley edition (1859) and the Walch imprint (1860) were printed in London by W[illiam] Cowes & Sons, Stamford Street; subsequent editions published by Bentley, Walch and Macmillan (1900) were printed by Billing & Sons in

Guildford. The 1859 edition was a quality production with cloth-covered boards, stitched binding, gilt device (the publisher's logo, in modern terminology), steel-point etchings and quality paper stock, priced at 21 shillings. The 1860 edition was a trade publication intended for a wider audience and thus cheaper, with cloth-covered boards, stitched binding, uncut pages and no illustrations, priced at 10 shillings and sixpence. Later editions vary but none shows the same quality as 1859: the 1887 Bentley and Robertson editions, and the 1900 Macmillan edition, had cloth-covered boards, trade binding, cheaper 'trade' paper stock and no illustrations. The Walch editions (1900 and 1918[32]) contained eight half-tone images 'tipped in' (that is, printed separately from the main text and then inserted),[33] paper-covered boards printed in monotone, trade binding, and trade paper stock. From the outset, the novel was intended for direct sale to the British domestic market and on consignment to overseas markets. The initial quality print-run gave way to cheaper printings, often destined for export, and it was not until 1988 that the novel was printed in Australia. That edition, published by Angus & Robertson, had paper covers printed using a four-colour process, perfect binding, cheap paper stock, and no illustrations. These details of material production are significant since they are the substance of the novel's *histoire croisée*. A central aspect for *histoire croisée* is its preference for a 'multidimensional approach that acknowledges plurality . . . Accordingly, entities and objects of research are not merely considered in relation to one another but also *through* one another, in terms of relationships, interactions, and circulation.'[34] So, the nature of the material object of the book, manifested here in the specifics of book production and distribution are active parts of its circulation through the global nineteenth-century book trade.

For over a century, supply of the novel depended upon its distribution via agents, packers, carriers, mail packets, shipping timetables and the clerical machinery that administered this system. J. Walch & Sons was the first Australian bookseller and distributor to establish a London agency in 1854,[35] and Charles Edward Walch (son of the founder) gives an account of this initiative in robust prose in his memoir.[36] The first problem was distance: 'a smart ship with good luck might deliver the mails in 90 days, but that was the exception, for it was oftener 100 or even 120 days.' The second was convincing British firms to deal with him: 'We had on previous occasions received [Thomas] Nelson's publications, but in those instances the orders had always been given through a merchant, and the invoices being made out in his name, we as a firm were not known in the transaction.' Equipped with his card, Walch approached the manager of

---

32 Morris Miller, *Australian Literature*, p. 602 cites 'Another edn. (J. Walch & Son.) 1918;' all editions citing 1900 in a bibliographical note on the imprint page have been sighted but not one dated 1918. It is noteworthy that Morris Miller had extensive Tasmanian connections and may have accessed archival material no longer extant.

33 One of these illustrations was signed 'C. Gruncell' and seems to have been the work of Charles Gruncell (d. 1930), a schoolmaster and keen photographer associated with the Southern Tasmanian Photographic Society. Chris Long, *Tasmanian Photographers 1840–1940: A Directory* (Hobart: Tasmanian Historical Research Association; Tasmanian Museum and Art Gallery, 1995). J. Walch & Sons published *Picturesque Tasmania* [n.d.] and *Tasmanian Views: An Album of Photographs* [19-?], both of which include a number of Gruncell's landscape photographs.

34 Rukavina, *Book Trade*, 12.

35 Rukavina, *Book Trade*, 33.

36 TAHO, NS369/1/26 *The Story of the Life of Charles Edward Walch with a Selection of His Writings.* Printed for Private Circulation (Hobart: Walch & Sons, 1908).

Thomas Nelson & Sons and, after using an atlas to explain where Australia was, set up a direct line of supply between Nelson and his own firm. His account captures a sense of how such business was transacted: 'I felt exceedingly glad that I had taken the advice of being dressed in a tall hat and frock coat and was wearing gloves.'[37] Walch consolidated the agency over four years and, in 1858, installed Arthur Holsworthy to run it. Arthur was succeeded by Joseph and later Charles Holsworthy.[38] In a letter dated 20 May 1897, Charles Holsworthy tells head office that 'Bentley could not send us full supplies of "Broad Arrow" but the balance of 39 will be sent in as soon as they come up from the binders.'[39] Some indication of the reliability of this supply chain, as well as of the accompanying commercial margins, is evidenced by the fact that even after J. Walch & Sons set up a printing works in Davey Street, Hobart, in 1900—'what we had long desired, ample facilities for turning out every description of work ENTIRELY ON OUR OWN PREMISES[40]—the latest format (with half-tone views of Hobart and Port Arthur) continued to be printed in England and imported. As London agent, Holsworthy's responsibilities included reporting on new titles and potential competition: on 3 February 1899 he reported that Macmillan, the new owner of Richard Bentley & Son, 'has no intention of placing either Bentley's Favourite Novels or Mrs Wood's novels in their Colonial Library'; on 19 May 1899 he writes concerning *His Natural Life* that 'Macmillan report that the 2/6 edition is out of print, but it is now done in Colonial Library.'[41]

In the twentieth century, the Australian trajectory moved onshore. Publisher Angus & Robertson reprinted the novel in 1989 under its Eden imprint to coincide with the 1988 Bicentennial celebrations. Angus & Robertson correspondence shows the role of Judith Johnson, a resident of Hobart, in suggesting the appropriateness of reissuing the novel in the context of Australia's national commemoration. Johnson drew the publisher's attention to the novel as 'a very much neglected companion to Marcus Clarke's *For the Term of His Natural Life*': 'no-one I have spoken to has heard of it.' She argued that the book 'should be available to the general Australian public as it gives a great insight into our history and the convict system' and noted that it is from a colonial woman's perspective.[42] The reissue comprised the revised 1886 text and an 'Original Publisher's Notice', that is, the preface to J. Walch & Sons' 1886 edition. Oliné Keese is given as the author, the title appears as *The Broad Arrow. Being the Story of Maida Gwynnham, a 'Lifer' in Van Diemen's Land*, and there are no illustrations or half-tones. The commercial driver behind this reissue may have been the market generated by the national celebration of white settlement, and the cover leverages Marcus Clarke's iconic convict novel, declaring:

---

37   Walch, *Story of the Life*, xli.

38   Walch, *Story of the Life*, lx.

39   TAHO, NS2857/1/4 Letters 294-347, Charles Holsworthy to J. Walch & Sons, 20 May 1897.

40   TAHO, NS2849/1/26 *Jubilee Number of Walch's Literary Intelligencer*, No. 608, May 1909, 111–13.

41   TAHO, NS2857/1/6 Letters 400-450, 01 Jan 1899– 31 Dec 1899, Charles Holsworthy to J. Walch & Sons; TAHO, NS2857/1/6 Charles Holsworthy to J. Walch & Sons.

42   Judith Johnson to Chief Executive, Angus & Robertson, 24 April 1987 (private hands). Johnson provided her own copy, inherited from her father's estate, to the publisher (23 June 1987); requested an acknowledgement, which was omitted (11 April 1989); provided advertising for the book in an interview, Ian Colvin, 'Rescue mission for lost literary gem,' *The Mercury* Saturday 30 1988, 23. The interview shows Johnson with her own copy of the novel (Walch edition, 1900, photographic cover and illustrations) and the Eden Imprint reprint (North Ryde: Angus & Robertson, 1988).

Sentenced at the Court of the County of Essex to be
TRANSPORTED
On the prison ship Rose of Britain to Hobart Town
Van Diemen's Land
For the heinous crimes of
MURDER AND FORGERY
She is to remain in that distant and terrible place
FOR THE TERM
OF HER NATURAL LIFE

The back-cover blurb adds more detail to the story of crime, misunderstanding and transportation, reiterating the links to Clarke's novel. The typeface, register and use of capital letters, combined with colonial imagery (a sprig of lavender, a cameo brooch and a torn parchment page), denote popular genre fiction for a local and national market. Whatever the impetus provided by the Bicentennial and the margins of printing the book locally, this issue appeared only once.

Nearly a decade later, in 1997 the University of Sydney, as part of a commitment to 'creating and maintaining a range of scholarly resources to support research and study', made the 1886 text available on an electronic platform, the Sydney Electronic Text and Imaging Service (SETIS), as part of its Australian Literary and Historical Texts series. In contrast to previous print editions, this electronic version (the text can be read online or downloaded as a PDF) is accessible to a global market.[43]

This moment in the book's trajectory marks its emergence within a new horizon that allows us to reconsider, not only editorial, critical and interpretative approaches and the national, international and world literature frames within which the book is located but also, the nature of the object whose *histoire croisée* is being conceptualised. In the translation from codex to digital format, *The Broad Arrow* is inserted into 'a volatile Internet environment' of 'non-copyright materials ... masses of commentary and associated information'[44] and thus the textual boundaries are dilated. But those textual boundaries are, at the same time, delimited since the paratextual materials that provided context and commentary in previous editions—the prefaces and publishers' notes, illustrations and advertisements, cover taglines and back cover blurbs—are all stripped away. Further there are effects following the translation to digital format that, although they might seem to be obscurely technical, change how we think about the ontology of this text. For example, digitally formatting the novel reproduces it as data or 'coded information ... marked by the syntax of its code' to which the addition of SGML tags 'assigns a given hierarchical structure ... to a linear string of characters' and thus this text can now be conceived as an 'ordered hierarchy of content object.'[45] In other words, since the content of this text—any text—is not usefully described as 'an ordered hierarchy' but rather one of 'overlapping and recursive structures of various kinds,' SGML operates to format a bibliographic entity rather than edit the text. This matters because the digital

---

43   Via http://purl.library.usyd.edu.au/setis/id/p00038.
44   Dino Buzzetti and Jerome McGann, 'Critical Editing in a Digital Horizon' in Lou Burnard, Katherine O'Brien O'Keeffe, John Unsworth, eds, *Electronic Textual Editing* (New York: The Modern Language Association, 2006), 58.
45   Buzzetti and McGann, 'Critical Editing,' 62.

text is not a representation of a semiotic system, a linguistic text; instead, it is a virtual representation of algorithmic processes and so this text of the novel is now a different *kind* of object. Not only is the status of this text ambiguous, so too is its proximity to any edition or issue of Leakey's novel. It will be fascinating to see how this digital aspect of the novel's trajectory develops, to see how the digital text reflects on its codex precursors, given that here is another instance of the asymmetrical history of this book. Digital and codex versions co-exist, neither one replacing or entirely displacing the other.

But in the print history of this book, the key event occurs in 1886 when, some five years after Leakey's death, the London publisher makes a decisive commercial move: to buy out the copyright and repackage the novel for Bentley's Kangaroo series on sale to the colonial market. The first step is to buy the remaining author's share of copyright for £30 as shown on her sister Emily Leakey's receipt dated 4 Feb 1887.[46] The next step is to rework Leakey's two-decker novel into a more commercial format and so an editor, Gertrude Townsend Mayer, is contracted to revise the book into a single volume that extracts a colonial romance from Leakey's multi-strand convict melodrama. Townsend Mayer had a long career with the publisher both as a book editor (payments are recorded from 1880–1893) and as editor of *Temple Bar* magazine after the Macmillan takeover, from 1898–1906. Townsend Mayer was also a writer herself: she published a novel, *Sir Hubert's Marriage* (1876), and a nonfiction work on the lives of women writers, *Women of Letters* (1894).[47] Bentley's ledger entry for December 1886 shows a payment for £11.8s; although this was a cash payment and the job is not named, the sum is consonant with other payments for editing.[48] Townsend Mayer's perspicacity as an editor is evidenced by the simple fact that it is her edited version of Leakey's novel that is republished repeatedly between 1887 and 1997.

Townsend Mayer's abridgement reduced the novel by 40,000 words, or approximately a third of its original length. She edited out narrative complexities and stripped out much though not all of the novel's political and ethical debates, foregrounding a simplified plot that conformed to the contemporary taste for Australian exotica,[49] while adroitly modifying many of the sensational elements of which readers have complained.[50] Miles Franklin, for example, having read the 1859 version, opined that 'Mrs [sic] Leakey fell short of Clarke's melodramatic fire in fusing improbabilities ... One does not accept Mrs Leakey's dramatics, nor all the sweetness of maids in decline, but her background detail is convincing.'[51]

All versions of the novel from 1887 to 1997, following Townsend Mayer, omit the author's preface, which situated Maida Gwynnham's history in the context of debates over transportation and 'fallen women', and formatted the novel to reflect readers' changing tastes and also to shape those tastes, thus, and very successfully, extending the market

---

46   Ingram, *Bentley Archives*, L63, 201.
47   See Virginia Blain, Patricia Clements and Isobel Grundy, eds, *The Feminist Companion to Literature in English* (London: Batsford, 1990), 727.
48   Ingram, *Bentley Archives*, L5, 122.
49   Paul Eggert, 'Changing literary tastes and the blue pencil in-house editing and abridgement of Australian Colonial Novels at the House of Bentley in London,' 10 (forthcoming). I am grateful to Prof. Eggert for allowing me to read this article; I share some of his conclusions about the editing of the second edition.
50   Anon., rev. of *The Broad Arrow*, *The Australasian*, 5 February 1887, 1.
51   Miles Franklin, *Laughter, Not For a Cage* (Sydney: Angus & Robertson, 1956), 46–7.

to produce new sales. Townsend Mayer's acute insight was that Leakey's novel, and the market for which it was being reworked, was a post–Marcus Clarke market. *His Natural Life* was serialised in *Australian Journal* between March 1870 and June 1872; volume 1 was published by George Robertson in April 1874 and the three-volume version published by Richard Bentley & Son in September 1875.[52] Tasmania as an historical location, a site of convict past, manifested in the mythic figure of Rufus Dawes, resonates across the reading public, especially for colonial readers. As I have already shown, advertisements, such as that in the *Publisher* for 18 July 1887, call *The Broad Arrow* 'a tale of old Tasmania', thereby historicising a previously contemporaneous novel. By 1900, J. Walch & Sons reissued *The Broad Arrow* with Townsend Mayer's text, subtitled 'With Illustrations of Hobart and Port Arthur' and authenticating the locations named in the novel. Half a dozen photographs were interspersed throughout the text and used on the front and back cover covers,[53] and a publisher's note identified the novel as 'A Companion to Marcus Clarke's Famous Novel'. Townsend Mayer's edited text then moves from niche colonial market to the mainstream. The 1988 reissue carries the subtitle 'For the Term of Her Natural Life' and correspondence between the editor (Judith Johnson) and the publisher shows no knowledge of the text's having been abridged.[54] The digital online version of the novel also uses Townsend Mayer's text, thus making accessible the popular text of Leakey's novel, with a bibliographic note acknowledging the abridgement but retaining the edited text.[55]

Repackaging the novel and reissuing only the edited text made visible the long shadow of Townsend Mayer's commercial insight and completed the tucking away of Leakey's novel as a minor variant of a standard on publishers' lists. *The Broad Arrow* disappeared behind Clarke's much more substantial novel, published in three volumes, and the 'passages of the history of Maida Gwynnham, a Lifer', to give the novel its full title, faded into an imitation of the gothic horror of Rufus Dawes. In this context, we might also note Eliza Winstanley's *For Her Natural Life: A Tale of the 1830s*, serialised between July and December 1876, that is, after both serial and book forms of *His Natural Life*.[56] Winstanley's two-part novel follows a woman protagonist, repeating *The Broad Arrow*'s central tropes of desertion, infanticide, transportation, whose life provides a narrative focus for an exposé of the unjust convict system. Winstanley's title situates her narrative as trading on Clarke's legacy rather than Leakey's: Rufus Dawes rather than Maida Gwynnham. The point here is that commercial decisions about the format of reissues of Leakey's novel or, more accurately, Townsend Mayer's edited version, extend beyond the physical object to

---

52 Clarke, *His Natural Life*, ed. Stuart, Chronology, xiv.

53 Attributed to J. W. Beattie in Gillian Winter, '"We Speak That We Do Know, And Testify That We Have Seen:" Caroline Leakey's Tasmanian Experiences and Her Novel *The Broad Arrow*,' *Tasmanian Historical Research Association* [*THRA*] 40.4 (1993): 151. Winter also references the abridged text fn 11 cf. fn 79 and describes Townsend Mayer's text as 'a slightly abridged version' (151).

54 Colvin, 'Rescue mission for lost literary gem,' *The Mercury*, 30 July 1988, 23; Judith Johnson to Angus & Robertson, letter, 24 April 1987 (private hands).

55 SETIS http://purl.library.usyd.edu.au/setis/id/p00038.

56 Eliza Winstanley, *For Her Natural Life: a Tale of the 1830s*, Bow Bells Weekly, July-December, 1876, vol. 25, No. 629-644; Dicks' English Novels No. 73 (London: John Dicks, 1876, 1881; reprinted Canberra: Mulini Press, 1992). Kate Watson notes parallels between Winstanley's, Leakey's and Clarke's novels in *Women Writing Crime Fiction, 1860-1880. Fourteen British, American and Australian Authors* (Jefferson, NC: McFarland, 2012), 157-158; see also Katherine Bode, '"Sidelines" and Tradelines: Publishing the Australian Novel, 1860-1899,' *Book History* 15 (2012): 10.

influence readers' apprehension of the text's genre, the status of the author and the value of the story the novel seeks to tell.

Author's biography

Caroline Woolmer Leakey was born on 8 March 1827 in Exeter and died in the same place on 12 July 1881. She was the fourth daughter of James Leakey, a painter of portraits and miniatures, and had six sisters and four brothers.[57] It was a family of fervent evangelical Christians: three brothers became ministers; at least one sister married a minister; two sisters, Leakey herself and her mother were active evangelists, and her father reputedly gave up painting to preach.[58] According to Caroline's younger sister Emily,[59] commitment to religious faith was the bond between forty-year-old James and his nineteen-year-old wife Eliza Woolmer when they married in 1815[60] and 'when by degrees he forsook his palette, the Bible, his cherished friend for so many years, became his sole companion'.[61] The Leakey household was modest without being penurious: James Leakey maintained a sufficient set of London and local connections to support his livelihood as a painter.

Some useful detail of the Leakey household emerges from the writings of Joseph Farington, the landscape painter and diarist:

> Mr Patch wished me to call upon a miniature painter of the name of Leekie [Leakey], who He said had practised in Exeter for some years, and also paints in oil small pictures of familiar subjects (figures). He has the merit of supporting a large family of relations, who are all very poor people of this place. He makes abt. £800 a year . . . Whilst I was in His room Leekie spoke to Mr Patch expressing a desire to paint my portrait . . .[62]

More than thirty-five years later, the diary of Caroline Yarde Scobell, a daughter of the Rev. John Scobell and his wife Eliza, for May to October 1846, records a sitting to James Leakey at Exeter for a portrait.[63]

Caroline Leakey regarded her religion as giving purpose to her life and offering a means of achieving that purpose in, for instance, taking over the headship of her late sister Mary's school in London in 1854[64] and in setting up the Exeter Home for 'our poor

---

57 J. C. Horner, 'Leakey, Caroline Woolmer (1827–1881)', *Australian Dictionary of Biography*, vol. 5 (Melbourne: Melbourne University Press, 1974), 71–2; https://bit.ly/2RadwQN.

58 F. M. O'Donoghue, 'Leakey, James (1775–1865)', rev. V. Remington, H. C. G. Matthew and Brian Harrison, eds, *Oxford Dictionary of National Biography* (Oxford: Oxford University Press, 2004); online edn, Lawrence Goldman, ed., https://bit.ly/2CXTiqh.

59 Emily P. Leakey, *Clear Shining Light: A Memoir of Caroline W. Leakey* [by her sister Emily] (London: John F. Shaw, 1882).

60 Leakey, *Clear Shining Light*, 107.

61 Leakey, *Clear Shining Light*, 53.

62 'Sunday 11 November 1810', 'Tuesday 13 November 1810', Kathryn Cave, ed., *The Diary of Joseph Farington*, vol. 10, July 1809–December 1810 (New Haven and London: Yale University Press, 1982), 3795, 3797.

63 Diaries of Caroline Yarde Scobell, 1845–1846, AMS5683 [n.d.], East Essex Records Office, https://bit.ly/2Piwg30.

64 Leakey, *Clear Shining Light*, 48.

fallen sisters' with a Mrs Stafford in 1861.[65] Leakey's commitment to the evangelicalism of her upbringing was contiguous with the 'muscular Christianity' associated with Charles Kingsley. After *The Broad Arrow* was published she wrote for the Religious Tract Society, bringing out one or two tracts a year—at least twenty-six can be attributed to her—with titles such as *Am I Safe? Or, Nellie's Dying Pillow* (1861) and *Aunt Tabitha's Charity Box* (1872),[66] thereby supporting herself as a professional writer.[67]

While Leakey was committed to Christianity, her poetry and fictional prose seek an imaginative connection to everyday life that transcends the evangelical. She wrote poetry that draws on religious belief and metaphor, publishing a book, *Lyra Australis; or, Attempts to Sing in a Strange Land* in London and Hobart in 1854. Her poetry ranges over a diversity of topics, including political events—'On Tasmania's Receiving the Writ of Freedom' and 'A New Light on Illumination'—as much as personal emotion.[68] *The Broad Arrow*, her first and only novel, draws much of its moral conviction and ethical framework from the balancing of Christian principles with the need to live one's life by making ethical choices. Although this edition focuses on Leakey's novelistic writing, we should keep in mind that she was first published as a poet, in some of the colonial newspapers of Hobart; her first published book was a collection of poems; and each chapter of the novel begins with an epithet, often taken from her poetry.

Leakey's novel was written out of her first-hand experience, a point remarked in contemporary reviews. In December 1847, aged twenty, she travelled in the company of the Rev. Dr Ewing and his wife to Van Diemen's Land, where she was to help her married sister. Her arrival as a passenger on the *Tasmania* was noted in *The Courier's* 'Shipping News' on 29 January 1848.[69]

Our knowledge of the details of Leakey's life comes almost exclusively from a memoir written by her younger sister, Emily P. Leakey (b. 1836), published in 1882, a year after Caroline Leakey's death.[70] *Clear Shining Light: A Memoir of Caroline W. Leakey* is dedicated

---

65 Leakey, *Clear Shining Light*, 65, 102, 116.

66 Jenna Mead, 'Caroline Woolmer Leakey,' in Selina Samuels, ed., *Dictionary of Literary Biography*, vol. 230: *Australian Literature, 1788–1914* (Farmington Hills: The Gale Group, 2001), 245.

67 There is extensive critical scholarship on this topic see, for example, Susan Sheridan, 'Ada Cambridge and the Female Literary Tradition,' in John Docker, Drusilla Modjeska and Susan Dermody, eds, *Nellie Melba, Ginger Meggs and Friends: Essays in Australian Cultural History* (Malmsbury, Victoria: Kibble Books, 1982), 162–75; Debra Adelaide, ed, *A Bright and Fiery Troop: Australian Women Writers of the Nineteenth Century* (Ringwood: Penguin, 1988); Margaret Bradstock, 'Unspoken Thoughts: A Reassessment of Ada Cambridge,' *Australian Literary Studies* 14.1 (1989): 51–65; Jenna Mead, 'Caroline Leakey: Body and Authorship,' *a/b Auto/Biography Studies Special Issue: Feminist Biography* 8.2 (Fall 1993): 198–216; Elizabeth Webby, 'Fiction, Readers and Libraries in Early Colonial New South Wales and Van Diemen's Land,' in David Garrioch, Meredith Sherlock, Ian Morrison, Brian McMullin and Harold Love, eds, *The Culture of the Book: Essays from Two Hemispheres in Honour of Wallace Kirsop* (Melbourne: Bibliographical Society of Australia and New Zealand, 1999), 366–73.

68 Caroline W. Leakey, *Lyra Australis; or, Attempts to Sing in a Strange Land* (London: Bickers and Bush, 1854), n.p. [94, 95].

69 *The Courier* [Hobart], Sat 29 Jan 1848, 2.

70 Emily P. Leakey, *Clear Shining Light: A Memoir of Caroline W. Leakey*. By her sister Emily (London: John F. Shaw, 1882). Cf. Margaret Giordano and Don Norman, *Tasmanian Literary Landmarks* (Hobart: Shearwater Press, 1984), 46–50 and Patricia Clarke, *Pen Portraits: Women Writers and Journalists in Nineteenth Century Australia* (Sydney, London, New York: Allen & Unwin, 1988), 46–50.

to the three Leakey brothers who became ministers[71] and their clerical brother-in-law, the Rev. J.G. Medland,

> with the hope that all I have written of her holy and guileless life may meet with their approval, and what I have left unsaid of her lovely natural and still more lovely spiritual character and of her eventful life, for the 'half is not told,' may rather be considered discreet than blameworthy.[72]

So, the tone is hortatory; the narrative is at least selective if not censored; and the origin of Emily's narrative—'a green and red bag ... marked "General Family Letters"'[73]—from which the biography quotes extensively has not, apparently, survived.[74]

Emily Leakey records her anxieties in writing such a memoir and names her model as the Rev. John Baillie's *A Memoir of Adelaide Leaper Newton* (1856). Newton had been a popular evangelical author perhaps best known for her *Song of Solomon: Compared with Other Parts of Scripture* (1850).[75] For all its limitations—a confused chronology aimed at highlighting her sister's trials and triumphs rather than giving a linear account of her life; undated letters and unacknowledged sources; fleeting characters and a vocabulary that modern readers may find uncongenial—Emily Leakey's memoir provides the lineaments of her sister's life story in language and form that speak to the sensibility, felt experience and concrete detail of a middle-class, mid-nineteenth-century family whose religious devotion is an empowering and decisive force in their lives.[76]

Caroline Leakey emerges from her sister's memoir as always having been in frail physical health; she may have been addicted to port wine[77] and laudanum,[78] and perhaps had a haphazard relationship to food.[79] She had suffered an injury as a child that left her permanently disabled. As her sister's memoir relates the incident, Leakey, who was educated mostly at home, attended school for a short time, during which one of the older girls

> caught her in her arms, saying 'You little fairy, I could squeeze you to death, you are so small; and as to your little hand, I could crush it to atoms.' And in showing how easily she could, the poor tender hand was terribly injured, insomuch that in a few weeks the family surgeon said it must be amputated ... The hand was saved, although maimed for life, and unsightly perhaps to strangers ... .[80]

---

71 Benjamin, the fourth and youngest brother (born 1833), was educated at Christ's Hospital and 'went to South America fairly young' (private correspondence, 9 December 2004).

72 Leakey, *Clear Shining Light*, vi.

73 Leakey, *Clear Shining Light*, 12-13.

74 Devon Record Office, 17 June 1991 (private correspondence).

75 Leakey, *Clear Shining Light*, 13.

76 Cf. Lucy Sussex, 'Mrs Henry Wood and Her Memorials,' *Women's Writing* 15.2 (2008): 157–68, https://bit.ly/2R4CmkT.

77 Leakey, *Clear Shining Light*, 63, 97.

78 Leakey, *Clear Shining Light*, 31, 98.

79 Leakey, *Clear Shining Light*, 96–97. For an investigation into this aspect of Leakey's life and her writing, see Shirley Walker, '"Wild and Wilful" Women: Caroline Leakey and *The Broad Arrow*,' in Adelaide, *A Bright and Fiery Troop*, 85–100. For a different view, see Jenna Mead, 'Biodiscourse: Oliné Keese and Caroline Leakey,' *Australian Feminist Studies* 20 (1994): 53–76.

80 Leakey, *Clear Shining Light*, 83-4.

We have another view of Leakey from the only other extant account of her: a shipboard diary kept by one of the other passengers, a Mrs Donald Cameron.

> October 1847 Miss L. looks a perfect child but is said to be five and twenty, 'not pretty, certainly not pretty,' very much marked with the small pox, little, bad figure, and makes devoted love to Mr Smith [another passenger] . . . [81]
>
> 11 November . . . We have Prayers morning and evening on Sunday, short Sermon both times. The sailors attend in the morning looking so nice and clean. Miss Leaky [sic] discovered one of them resembled Lord Byron, and took me to see the likeness. I confessed being very nearsighted, but, if she was pleased so was I . . . [82]
>
> I forgot to mention one of Donald's amusements, scolding Miss Leaky and Miss Palmer. Yesterday at dinner, Donald gave a lecture on the heinousness of ladies (particularly young ladies) drinking such a quantity of wine every day. Mr Ewing joined Donald, and supported him in all he advanced . . . [83]
>
> Friday 15 November . . . Fancy my amusement last night, seated on the deck, between Miss Palmer and Miss Leaky. Of course, moonlight, the young ladies turn about reciting their own poetry, pon my word, they surprised me. It was really very fair . . . [84]
>
> 24th December 1847 . . . Miss Leaky is a devoted admirer of Mr. Smith's, mends his clothes, gives him medicines etc. I think Miss L. is rather too unsophisticated. [85]

Leakey herself gives us something of the flavour of the ship's milieu in an anecdote recorded in her sister's memoir. A 'young officer' teases Leakey by calling her a blue stocking. 'The impromptu Mr Cameron' finds himself caricatured in 'a playful rebuke':

> If I am a blue sock, sir,
> I was not knit for you;
> Nor one inch of wool
> From your thin fleece I drew. [86]

Mrs Cameron's comments usefully temper those of Emily Leakey, suggesting the determination that motivated Leakey's own belief in herself as a genuine writer and her energetic involvement in the social world she would observe and turn into the material of her novel. [87] Cameron's references to Leakey's 'devotion' to Mr Smith suggest the nature of some of Emily Leakey's omissions from her memoir; [88] perhaps too, in her references to

---

81   State Library of Victoria, MS9124, *The Journal of Mary Isabella Cameron 1847*, 'Written on board the Good Ship Tasmania, being a narrative of facts, which occurred on the occasion of her visiting Van Diemen's Land. October, 1847', 4.
82   *The Journal of Mary Isabella Cameron 1847*, 7.
83   *The Journal of Mary Isabella Cameron 1847*, 13.
84   *The Journal of Mary Isabella Cameron 1847*, 15.
85   *The Journal of Mary Isabella Cameron 1847*, 29.
86   Leakey, *Clear Shining Light*, 23.
87   Cf. Winter, 'We Speak,' 135 for a different view.
88   State Library of Victoria, MSB454, Mary Isabella Cameron, 'Pages from the VDL Journal 3A-11,' [letter] 'My dear Father [nd], Miss Leekie I don't know much of yet, seems rather a funny person, she told Donald she had put him down in her Journal as exactly like Prince Albert, strange . . . You see she makes love wholesale . . .' (3)

the Rev. J.D. Rashdall,[89] the dedicatee of chapter four in Leakey's collection of poems *Lyra Australis*, and whose portrait, 'after Leakey', is held in the British Museum, we may have an instance of 'clerical' devotion that required some censoring.[90]

Despite Leakey's physical frailty, *Clear Shining Light* asserts that

> When she was twenty years of age the providence of God called her to leave home, and all its treasured love, that she might devote herself to her married sister in Tasmania, who entreated her to come and help her to train her children, otherwise dependent on the care (!) of convict nurses.[91]

Eliza Leakey had married the Rev. James Medland and this familial relationship was to provide Leakey with an introduction to the clerical hierarchy of Tasmania, a network of clerical families to visit and, in the course of a dispute between her brother-in-law and Bishop Nixon, a glimpse of the power of the church in colonial Tasmania. Once in Hobart, and between bouts of colonial fever and other ailments, Leakey established social connections with considerable breadth and reach, wrote and published poems in colonial newspapers, paid social calls on Government House, stayed at Port Arthur for as much as a year, sojourned with various religious figures—including the charismatic and highly influential Francis Russell Nixon, the Anglican Bishop of Tasmania, and his accomplished wife Anna Maria Nixon—and developed a thorough knowledge of colonial Hobart and its social and political milieu.

Hobart, in the five years of her visit (1848–53), was an energetic colonial city with the natural advantages of a deep-water port, a history of Dutch, French and English exploration, a rapidly changing built environment (as the current Tasmania Heritage Register records) and an emergent cultural identity complicated by the tensions between a penal colony and an ambitious immigrant population determined to make a new society in a beautiful place. Colonial newspapers from the mid-1840s and 1850s record thriving commercial and tourism exchanges between Hobart and Southampton, Hobart and Sydney, and Hobart and the west coast of America: mercantile and commercial ventures including whaling, wool and ship-building industries with all the regulation, deal-making and knock-on effects that accompany such development; and social events that reflected the frictions of a class system displaced and under pressure, and galvanised by the cultural legacy of previous governors and their wives, such as Sir John and Lady Franklin (1837–43).[92] The front page of the *Colonial Times* of Friday 8 February 1850 gives the flavour of all this activity: 'The well-known, first-rate, fast-sailing ship Rattler . . . will meet with every dispatch;' Walch and Son (sic) have received 'ex Anglia . . . Annuals for this year;' John Morgan 'respectfully solicit[s] your votes' for a position at the V.D.L. Mechanics Institute in competition with S.T. Hardinge, Secretary; James Sly is unpacking one case of Ladies' white satin shoes; and J.W. Mansfield will not be 'answerable for any debts contracted' by his wife, 'she having forfeited all claims to [his] protection'.[93]

---

89 E.g. Leakey, *Clear Shining Light*, 61.
90 'The Rev'd John Rashdall, A.M.,' Online Collection entry, http://bit.ly/2ErUU8o.
91 Leakey, *Clear Shining Light*, 17.
92 See Alison Alexander, *Obliged to Submit: Wives and Mistresses of Colonial Governors* (Hobart: Montpelier, 1999).
93 *Colonial Times*, 8 February 1850, 1. https://bit.ly/2Rb0na7.

Reference to public debate on the transportation of convicts comes in a letter to the editor on page four.

Two features in particular characterise the Hobart of *The Broad Arrow*: proximity and the past. In September 1850, according to *Clear Shining Light*,[94] Leakey stayed at Boa Vista, the home of Bishop Nixon, in upper Argyle Street, New Town (later part of The Friends' School), from where she wrote a letter to her brothers and sisters, dated 26 September. She makes no mention of meeting Thomas Arnold, brother of the poet and critic Matthew Arnold and second son of Dr Thomas Arnold, headmaster of Rugby, who arrived in Hobart in January 1850 to take up the post of inspector of schools and went on to have a role in establishing the forerunner of Tasmania's state education system. But Leakey could not fail to have known about Arnold's whirlwind marriage to the beautiful Julia Sorell, daughter of William Sorell, registrar of the supreme court.[95] They were married in St David's Cathedral on 13 June 1850 with Arnold's friend Lieutenant (later Sir) Andrew Clarke, Marcus Clarke's first cousin, as his best man.[96] The Arnolds subsequently established their household in a cottage in Stoke Street,[97] some 200 metres from Boa Vista, where the future and highly successful writer Mary Augusta Arnold (later Mrs Humphry Ward), would be born in 1851.[98] Such were the networks of social exchange in Hobart that, in November 1850, Arnold met Bishop Nixon's wife, Anna Maria, at a dinner in Longford during one of his tours of village schools.[99] Meanwhile, at a small evening party in Hobart, in the previous September, the Arnolds had met the

---

94   Leakey, *Clear Shining Light*, 29.

95   P. A. Howell, *Thomas Arnold the Younger in Van Diemen's Land* (Hobart: THRA, 1964) analyses Arnold's contribution to education in Tasmania. On Julia Sorell see Jane Sorell, *Governor, William and Julia Sorell (Three Generations in Van Diemen's Land)* (Eastlands: Citizens Advice Bureau, n.d.) and J. P. Trevelyan, *The Life of Mrs Humphry Ward by her* Daughter (London: Constable, 1923). Howell summarises Julia Sorell's reputation (43–4) and notes that Arnold was unmoved by any supposed whiff of scandal, citing a letter to Julia (28 March 1850) in which he writes 'the good people of Hobart are such capital hands at improving and embellishing, that I dare say you will not recognize . . . much of what you actually said' (44). Arnold is allaying Julia's fears about an alleged flirtation between Julia and a Captain Fitzroy; see Letter 51, James Bertram, ed., *New Zealand Letters of Thomas Arnold the Younger with further letter from Van Diemen's Land and letter of Arthur Hugh Clough 1847–1851* (London and Wellington: University of Auckland Press, 1966), 178–9.

96   See Arnold's reminiscence in his *Passages in a Wandering Life* (London: Edward Arnold, 1900), 129; for Clarke's relation to Marcus Clarke see *Australian Dictionary of Biography*. Available at http://www.adb.online.anu.edu.au/biogs/A030386b.htm; letter to Julia Sorell (Bertram, ed., *Letters*, 178, 179); Arnold describes his wedding in a letter to his mother, 18 June 1850, 'with Clarke as my "best man"' (Letter 53, Bertram, ed., *Letters*, 184). Cf. The peevish account of this marriage by Annie Baxter Dawbin in Lucy Frost, ed., *A Face in the Glass: the Journal and Life of Annie Baxter Dawbin* (Port Melbourne: William Heinemann, 1992), 137–8. Dawbin makes a social call on Julia Arnold, 29 June 1850, and finds her 'snug in her new domicile' (139).

97   An announcement of auction by Mr Elliston of Lot 8, 'On the New Town Road, near the Turnpike, a neat and comfortable cottage and garden, let to Thomas Arnold Esq., at £40 per annum', *Courier*, Sat. 24 July 1852, 1, confirms the Arnolds' occupancy close by Boa Vista.

98   And in one of those serendipitous coincidences that characterise nineteenth-century novels and attract much criticism, Arnold is surprised, in a letter (6 January 1850) to his sister Jane (called 'K' in the family), that when looking over the list of passengers on board the steamer *Shamrock* on which he is to sail from New Zealand to Hobart, he 'saw the names "Miss Grylls," "Miss E. Grylls" [and thought] can these be distant Cornish relative, who, unbeknownst to me, have settled in Australia?' (Letter 50, Bertram, ed., *Letters*, 170).

99   Letter 57, Arnold to Mary Twinning, 22 Nov. 1850, *Letters*, Bertram, ed., 197.

Rev. Ewing, with whom, accompanied by his wife and four children, Leakey had sailed to Hobart.[100]

If Thomas Arnold was emblematic of Van Diemen's Land's future, then in the person of Bishop Nixon, in whose house Leakey was a guest, she was proximate to one of the most powerful public actors in the colony's struggle with its pervasive convictism and the question *du jour* in the public domain. Appearing before the House of Lords Select Committee on Execution of Criminal Law in 1847, Nixon presented rhetorically adept moral arguments supported by personal evidence in the form of specific cases as to the effects of past government policy on the future of the colony of which he was spiritual guide. He expressed concern about the future of Van Diemen's Land once all its convicts had been freed:

> We cannot help looking forward to that hour with anxiety and dismay. What is likely to be the moral, the religious, and social condition of Van Diemen's Land some few years hence, when the 30,000 prisoners now in the island shall have become absolutely free, and scattered over its whole extent? I do not mean to say that they are all depraved, but they are convicts still . . .

Nixon presented a scathing account of women convicts: in reply to the question 'Why are female felons so bad?' he replied:

> Before a woman can become a convict at all, she must have fallen much lower, have unlearnt more, have become much more lost and depraved than a man. Her difficulty of regaining her self-respect is proportionally much greater.[101]

Leakey's novel would contest each of these claims to produce her own view on the relationship between systemic convictism, the wellbeing of an emergent social polity and the nature of Christian ethics, as exemplified by the case of the fallen woman.

Before turning to a reading of the 1859 text of Leakey's novel there is a caution we should note with respect to Emily Leakey's chronology. *Clear Shining Light* is uncharacteristically exact about the composition date of *The Broad Arrow*: 'From March, 1857, to March, 1858, my sister occupied her leisure hours with writing a two-volume novel, in which story she so well relates the trials of prisoners in Van Dieman's [sic] Land.'[102] These dates are inconsistent with, first, Leakey's own preface to the novel, in which she writes:

> So many attractive books on Australian and convict-life have appeared of late years, that I fear mine may be repelled as an unsuccessful imitation of other authors, unless I be permitted to explain that it was wholly planned, mostly written, and intended for publication several years ago.

---

100 There was, perhaps unjustly, some suggestion of scandal associated with his tenure at the Queen's Orphan School (Winter 140–1); see also Arnold to Mrs Arnold (mother), Tues. 29 Sept. 1850, Letter 55, Bertram, ed., *Letters*, 190–1.

101 [Report from] House of Lords, 11 May 1847, 'Minutes of Evidence Before Select Committee,' *The Hobart Town Courier and Gazette*, 5 January 1848, 4.

102 Leakey, *Clear Shining Light*, 54.

The same point is made by the *Spectator* reviewer, placing Leakey's novel in its contemporary context by citing the preface:

> It is only fair to say here, that this gentle minister [the Rev. Herbert Evelyn] is original, and not copied from Mr Charles Reade; for *The Broad Arrow* was 'wholly planned, mostly written, and intended for publication several years ago.'[103]

Second, Leakey left Van Diemen's Land in December 1853. In 1854, she took over the headship of her sister's London school for eighteen months. *Lyra Australis* was published in 1854; in 1855, her mother died; by January 1857, Leakey and Emily had gone back to Exeter, where 'for eight years longer we had the unspeakable privilege of attending to and comforting our aged father';[104] and in June 1858 their sister Sophia died of 'rapid consumption'. Oliné Keese's contract with Richard Bentley & Son is dated 2 January 1859; the preface is dated 9 February 1859; the first English review, in the *Athenaeum*, appeared on 30 April 1859.[105] This is a tight production schedule. We might also wonder how an unknown, provincial writer came to be accepted and effectively fast-tracked by one of the leading publishers of mid-nineteenth-century London, especially in view of the supposed hiatus in writing between 1854 and 1857.

We might speculate on these same traces of evidence and form a different picture: Mrs Cameron's diary shows Leakey already engaged in her writing in 1848, and sufficiently confident to read her work to others, indeed, to a pleasantly surprised audience. *Lyra Australis*, however we might judge the quality of the writing, is a substantial collection of poems. Leakey's publications with the Religious Tract Society suggest a capacity for sustained effort and a steady output, with at least twenty-six items between 1861 and 1882, and provided Leakey with 'constant employment'.[106] *Clear Shining Light* puts Leakey in London in 1854; Emily Leakey cites a letter that Caroline received from her mother celebrating her birthday in 1855, in which she is cautioned:

> Of these graces, my child, the Lord has give you a large measure, and I praise Him for you that He has so honoured you; but think not you shall escape from Satan's wiles. He will find out your weakness, and make use of your besetting sin to entangle you.[107]

These words are glossed by Emily with a note: 'I think my mother meant ambition for literary fame and society might become a besetting sin, as my sister had been introduced into a large circle of London *literati* by the late Mrs Jamieson.'[108] Later Emily Leakey reflects

---

103 Anon. rev. of *The Broad Arrow*, *Spectator*, 14 May 1859, 518.

104 Leakey, *Clear Shining Light*, 53.

105 Anon. rev. of *The Broad Arrow*, *The Athenaeum* No. 1644, 20 April 1859, 580.

106 Leakey's own phrase, 'constant employment,' in correspondence with Richard Bentley, 13 May 1879, Ingram, *Bentley Archives*, L 86, L1-L1a.

107 Leakey, *Clear Shining Light*, 50.

108 Leakey, *Clear Shining Light*, 50. Jameson has a notoriously common variant in Jamieson: Anna Brownell Jameson (19 May 1794–17 March 1860) corresponded with Richard Bentley & Son and published her *Memoirs and Essays* with them (1846); a Frances Thurtle (1779 -1870), afterwards Mrs Jamieson, published a range of religious and travel works. Jameson's late works are studies of religious art—including *Sacred and legendary art* (1848), *Legends of the monastic orders* (1850), *Legends of the Madonna* (1852), and *The history of Our Lord* (completed and published posthumously 1864)—and she is intimately connected to the leading intellectual and cultural networks of her day. See Judith

on her sister's literary status: 'Long before she died she thanked God for disappointment in worldly literary pursuits, and praised Him that she was led to write tracts instead of novels, and spiritual songs instead of merely poetical thoughts.'[109]

Perhaps; but Leakey's sustained sense of herself as a writer emerges in a letter she wrote to Richard Bentley on 13 May 1879, in which she seeks information as to whether 'Mr C.E. Mudie and his library are still in existence'; that is, Mudie's Select/Circulating Library (1842–1937). She is recalling a moment twenty years ago and a 'promise he [Mudie] made to me in the "Broad Arrow" time that if I published again he would "pay all honour" to my new work.' She has two new manuscripts—religious works which she acknowledges are not in Bentley's line—and is looking for Mudie to 'recognise them if I publish'.[110] Charles Mudie was still very much alive and in business. Richard Bentley, however, had died on 10 September 1871. Leakey's letter gives her address as East Southernhay, Exeter, now her home and also her place of birth. Clearly no longer a participant in the literary world of London, she is nevertheless prepared to seek out connections she regards as potentially useful.

My conjecture is that Leakey may have begun work on her novel during her stay in Van Diemen's Land (1848–53): the precision of, for example, the dialogue between characters may result from reportage, working perhaps from notes recorded during her stay. On the way home, she kept to her cabin for the whole three months, relying upon her own resources to pass the time.[111] Eighteen months in London presented an opportunity to make connections with the literary world—perhaps to find a patron—and an early result is the successful completion and publication of *Lyra Australis* in 1854. Leakey was now a published poet living in London, with connections and, just as valuable, the confidence to execute her literary ambitions in the form of a novel. However, the sequence of writing and publishing stalled with Leakey and Emily's return to Exeter in 1857 to care for their father. Even if Leakey were still in contact with her patron or friends in the literary world, she was no longer in London and no longer able actively to maintain those connections. This is when the progress towards publication faltered for 'several years', as she was to write in the preface. Hence the note of frustration we find in the preface and the determination to establish a chronology that would deflect any shortcoming on the author's behalf. Emily Leakey's chronology maintained the image of the dutiful daughter, respecting her mother's admonitions and writing in those spare moments between caring for her aged father. Leakey's own preface positions *The Broad Arrow* as no 'unsuccessful imitation' of other convict novels: her novel is not a belated work but an original one from a serious-minded writer.

It is a tribute to Leakey's perseverance that she was successful in being contracted to Richard Bentley & Son. The novel was produced in handsome two-volume format with

---

Johnston, *Anna Jameson: Victorian, Feminist, Woman of Letters* (Aldershot and Brookfield: Scolar Press, 1997). Mrs Jamieson, formerly Thurtle, published at least 12 works of history, travel between 1817 and 1859, including *Ashford Rectory; or, The Spoilt Child Reformed* (1820); she may have been in Bruges in 1850 where her husband is reported as having died. http://manifested-reveries.blogspot.com.au/.

109 Leakey, *Clear Shining Light*, 96.

110 Caroline Woolmer Leakey to Richard Bentley, 13 May 1879, Ingram, *Bentley Archives*, L 86, L1-L1a, emphasis retained. There is no evidence of a response from the publisher; letter reproduced in 'Caroline Woolmer Leakey,' in Selina Samuels, ed., *Dictionary of Literary Biography*, 248–9.

111 Leakey, *Clear Shining Light*, 45.

illustrations and was reviewed, for the most part positively, in London and in influential periodicals. The *Athenaeum* reviewer (anonymous but now attributed to Geraldine Jewsbury) compared it favourably to Charles Reade's '*It Is Never Too Late to Mend*': *A Matter-of-Fact Romance*, recommended it 'to all who are interested in the solution to the social problem', and noted that '[i]n the matter of mere interest and amusingness "The Broad Arrow" contains as much as half-a-dozen ordinary novels put together', although the last word calls the illustrations 'hideous'.[112] Nevertheless, sales were poor. Leakey must have been disappointed.[113] The J. Walch & Sons edition published in Hobart the following year had similarly poor sales;[114] a year later Leakey was publishing with the Religious Tract Society.

Genre and literary history

The Broad Arrow is clearly classifiable as a convict novel and literary histories of Australian writing have usually named it as an early example of the genre and the first with a woman as the protagonist.[115] Literary historian and bibliographer E. Morris Miller, in a paper delivered in Hobart on 10 April 1957, nominates Mary Leman Grimstone's *Woman's Love* (1832), a feminist novel set in southwest England, as the first novel written in Australia, during Grimstone's sojourn in Tasmania.[116] Hobart certainly made some claim on Grimstone; the March 1870 issue of *Walch's Literary Intelligencer* noted her death in an epitome titled 'Literary Table Talk', abstracted from 'a new and remarkably interesting publication called *The Literary World*'.[117] The Australian character of Leakey's novel becomes very obvious when we compare it to George Eliot's *Adam Bede*, a novel published in the same year (1859) in which a female protagonist (Hetty Sorrel) is also indicted and transported for child murder. *Adam Bede* shares a reference to transportation and in it too the effects of punishment are a primary concern.

Like *Adam Bede*, Leakey's narrative escalates through characters whose experience of sexual and romantic love goes disastrously awry. Unlike *Adam Bede*, transportation is a central thematic in Leakey's novel engaging the *The Broad Arrow*'s social, geographical, ethical and affective interactions rather than offering a convenient, if dramatic, narrative solution. It is transportation that, for instance, underpins Leakey's representation of labour, child-rearing and public morality, shifting the novel's English provincialism and stultifying class-consciousness to the frontier terrain of nation building.

---

112 Fn 105; attribution at 'Athenaeum Title Record' https://bit.ly/2PiI8Sw.

113 See Eggert, 'Changing Literary Tastes', 7.

114 Eggert, 'Changing Literary Tastes', 7. On the more general question of Tasmanian reception to convict fiction, see correspondence following Marcus Clarke's visit to Tasmania in 1870 to research *His Natural Life* (below).

115 Hergenhan, *Unnatural* Lives, 31–46.

116 E. Morris Miller, 'Australia's First Two Novels: Origins and Backgrounds', *Tasmanian Historical Research Association (THRA) Proceedings and Papers*, 6 (1957): 37–65; Miller considers Henry Savery's *Quintus Servinton* as 'certainly not written before 1829' (37) and points to Grimstone's Preface 'in which the author definitely stated [the novel] was written in Hobart, where she resided for five years' (37). Michael Roe also considers Grimstone's career in 'Mary Leman Grimstone (1800–1850?): For Women's Rights and Tasmanian Patriotism', *THRA Papers and Proceedings* 36.1 (1989): 9–25.

117 TAHO, NS2849/1/6, *Walch's Literary Intelligencer*, March 1870, 40.

While English reviewers drew a connection between Leakey's novel and the didacticism of popular novels such as those of Charles Reade, scholars of Australian literature, making an argument about genre, have usually placed Leakey's novel alongside Marcus Clarke's *His Natural Life* and followed Joan Poole's lead: 'But it was Marcus Clarke who really answered the questions [about the detrimental effects of the convict system] and it is interesting to speculate whether he had ever read *The Broad Arrow*'.[118] This speculation arises in the specific context of Clarke's dedication, in which he acknowledges the 'convict of fiction' in the works of Charles Reade and Victor Hugo,[119] and the appendix in which he lists the main historical sources for his novel.[120] The effects are, first, to locate *His Natural Life* within a specific and international novelistic tradition and, second, to substantiate Clarke's dependence on historical sources for the veracity of the novel's claims.

Clarke's novel gains its authority from its historicism; Leakey's depends upon her first-hand witness account; both engage the reader's mind and emotions through their imaginative power. Clarke visited Tasmania in January 1870,[121] his visit apparently producing mixed reactions, evidenced by a letter to the editor published in the *Mercury* on 19 April 1871, in response to the serialisation of *His Natural Life* in the *Australasian Journal*.

> Mr Clarke came to Tasmania unannounced; sojourned unnoticed; and departed unmissed. No fetes were given, no triumphal arches erected, and no banquets spread to do him honour. Can the remembrance of this oversight have anything to do with the origin of his false statements and ungenerous reflections? There must indeed be a sad paucity of material for the makers of colonial books to work upon, when they must needs rake from the vaults of the past those things which belong exclusively to it, and which had far better be forgotten.[122]

Anne-Marie Jordens carefully analyses the contents of Marcus Clarke's library from the catalogue, titled *The Well-Selected Library of Mr Marcus Clarke*, prepared by F.E. Beaver for the sale of Clarke's books following his insolvency in 1874, as part of her study of Clarke and history.[123] Ian McLaren reproduces the catalogue in facsimile in *Marcus Clarke: an Annotated Bibliography*, where Lot 97 comprises 'Molesworth v. Molesworth. A full report / The Broad Arrow; or, Maida Gwynnham: a Lifer. Tasmanian. 1860 / The Evidence of Accomplices: containing references to all the Reports on the subject from the time of Lord Holt, in 1696. 3 vols.'[124] Jordens notes the role of the bookseller C.E. Walch—of the Walch publishing family and a brother of Clarke's Melbourne friend Garnet Walch—in providing Clarke with Tasmanian books,[125] perhaps even of having retained some of C.E. Walch's own materials,[126] and she crisply summarises the problem: Clarke acknowledged a debt to Reade and Hugo:

---

118 Joan Poole, 'The Broad Arrow—a Re-appraisal,' Southerly 2 (1966): 124.

119 His Natural Life, ed., Stuart, 13.

120 His Natural Life, ed., Stuart, 567–71.

121 His Natural Life, ed., Stuart, xv.

122 'Letter to the Editor', The Mercury, 11 April 1871, 2 and signed S.H. Wintle. https://bit.ly/2u6lJdj.

123 Anne-Marie Jordens, 'Marcus Clarke's Library,' Australian Literary Studies 1.4 (1976): 399–412.

124 Ian McLaren, Marcus Clarke, an Annotated Bibliography (Melbourne: Library Council of Victoria, 1982): 342. Stuart, His Natural Life, also notes Jordens and McLaren, xxiv, fn 18.

125 Jordens, 'Marcus Clarke's Library,' 401.

126 Jordens, 'Marcus Clarke's Library, fn. 11.

but, he confessed, 'no writer—so far as I am aware—has attempted to depict the dismal condition of a felon during his term of transportation.' This is not true for he had on his shelves *The Broad Arrow* . . . by Caroline (Woolmer) Leakey, first published in 1859, thirteen years before the first serialized version of *His Natural Life*, and which, as H.M. Green says, 'has most of the faults of Clarke's novel and just a touch of its virtues'[127]

Moreover, the catalogue entry suggests that the copy of Leakey's novel that Clarke owned was, indeed, the edition published in Hobart by Walch & Sons in 1860.

Jordens makes a case for Clarke as an assiduous historical researcher and a serious bibliophile; he was also, as his biographer Brian Elliott tells us, sub-librarian at the Public Library of Victoria, 1873–81.[128] Clarke's unsuccessful letter of application to the trustees of the Melbourne Public Library (1880) asserts that '[f]or knowledge of bibliography, I may make special claim. My personal tastes and public circumstances have alike led me to make that branch of information my peculiar study,'[129] which suggests that Clarke would be unlikely to have remembered Reade but forgotten Leakey. Reading *The Broad Arrow*, as he is likely to have done, perhaps persuaded Clarke that the emotional charge of the convict subject, with its innate system of injustices and pathos, combined with the sublime gothic landscape of Tasmania's 'natural penitentiary' might be successfully written in the form of the novel he had begun to work with in *Long Odds* (serialised 1868–69).[130]

Setting aside the anachronism that comes with designating as a 'convict novel' one that preceded *His Natural Life*, which is usually regarded as defining the genre, there is another reason for conceding that a work rarely fits within the conventional confines of a single genre, that a genre is defined by one exemplar, or that literary history should only be read chronologically. The 'history of Maida Gwynnham, a lifer' follows a convict transported for life but we might also recognise the outlines of a *Bildungsroman* in the sense of a novel

127 Jordens, 'Marcus Clarke's Library,' 403.
128 Brian Elliott, *Marcus Clarke* (Oxford: Clarendon Press, 1958), ch. IX.
129 Elliott, *Marcus Clarke*, 266.
130 Clarke's connections to Hobart, the Walch family and J. Walch & Sons, publishers, are further evidenced by two extant letters from the Hobart publisher: TAHO NS2855/1/1 Letterbook No. 9, 2 Nov 1869, Letter 428, addressed to Clarke and NS2855/1/1 Letterbook 9, dated 2 Nov 1870, Letter 429 addressed to Clarson Massina. Letter 428 reports on Walch's failure to locate the Almanack for 1831; Clarke owned a copy but was searching for one with illustrations; Walch & Sons undertake to continue their search. The publisher has been successful, however, in obtaining a three-volume, illustrated edition of 'Wandering Jew' (sic) from a Mrs Hartam, of the Ship Hotel. Messrs Clarson & Co. requested this edition, on Clarke's behalf, and Walch is sending it to Clarson's Melbourne address. 'Mrs H at first declined to part with this book, but when she understood it was for you she most graciously requested us to send it to you with her compliments—at the same time saying that she would be happy to receive from you any modern novel you might send her in return for it—We have sent her with your compliments a copy of Long Odds.' Letter 429, addressed to Messrs Clarson Massina, 72 Little Collins Street, confirms sending 'Wandering Jew' and a note to Clarke; costs for shipping are debited to Clarson. Alfred Henry Massina is recognised as having been a strong supporter of Clarke's visit to Tasmania in 1869 ('Alfred Henry Massina,' Frank Strahan, *Australian Dictionary of Biography* [1974] http://adb.anu.edu.au/biography/massina-alfred-henry-4165). These connections deserve further thought but, briefly, while Clarke's dedication to his documentary historical sources is well attested, my suggestion is that CWL, likewise relied on documentary sources and, in particular, the *Hobart Town Directory and General Guide* (1852); see Explanatory Notes. I am indebted to Anthony Stagg for his guidance on these documents.

of education that follows the spiritual and moral growth of the protagonist from youth to adulthood, with 'the potential to provide an allegory of a particular trajectory within a national history'.[131] The nineteenth-century version of the genre is usually read as the story of a male protagonist through the phases of education from childhood to youth to adulthood. Early exemplars come from German Romanticism (Johann Goethe's *Wilhelm Meisters Lehrjahre*, 1795–96; Ludwig Tieck's *Franz Sternbalds Wanderungen*, 1798; Gottfried Keller's *Der grüne Heinrich*, 1854; Gustav Freytag's *Soll und Haben*, 1855; Adalbert Stifter's *Der Nachsommer*, 1857; Wilhelm Raabe's *Der Hungerpastor*, 1864); English expressions of the genre include Charlotte Brontë, *Jane Eyre*, 1847; Charles Dickens, *David Copperfield*, 1850; Thomas Hardy, *Jude the Obscure*, 1895.[132] Franco Moretti argues for the *Bildungsroman* as 'the symbolic form of Modernity'—and that would be a fascinating line to pursue in the context of this novel—but here it is the focus on youth as a primary stage and its inevitable dangers that is germane.[133]

If we allow a revisionist reading of the genre—a female rather than male protagonist in a carceral rather than Romantic setting—then aspects of the novel that overburden the convict fiction trajectory offer another narrative logic. For example, Leakey's novel devotes significant space to narrativising the phase of youth as formative: Maida, the protagonist, is motherless (Chapter 2, 'Maida') and despite the devoted love of her father, she is vulnerable to Norwell's predatory sexuality that is itself portrayed as jealous of the needs of Maida's own motherhood. The early lives of other important female characters exemplify the perilous consequences where the formative link between mothers and daughters is absent or distorted (Chapter 6, 'Mary Doveton,' who marries without a mother's advice; Chapter 12, 'Lucy Grenlow's Tale,' where the mother is weak and derelict). The raising of the Evelyn children by assigned convict nurses, exposes an intersection between class expectations, motherhood and a carceral underclass that jeopardises children's youth by normalising criminality. A connection to the project of nation building is dramatised in, for example, Chapter 13, when the Evelyns' little boy, Charlie, 'was puzzled to know which was the correct path — that commended to him by precept, or that chosen by the multitude. In fact, he had to decide between seeing and hearing.' Charlie's response after visiting a public work being completed by convicts, is to exclaim 'When *I'm* a pisner, won't I build a beauty!' and his chief objection to returning to England is 'Why, there are no lots of pisners in that country to do our work. How *could* I go?' The protagonist's spiritual education and maturity are constitutive of the narrative—rather than in addition to it—in the characters of the Rev. Herbert Evelyn, his daughter Emmeline and Mary Doveton, each of whom ministers to the incremental stages of Maida's spiritual wellbeing by providing compassionate exemplars of Christian discipline and, crucially, the moral incentive and resolve for her active intervention to expose the deceit of her former lover, Norwell.

These genres of convict fiction and a female *Bildungsroman* are not, of course, mutually exclusive, but they have very different narrative logics that are epitomised in three separate moments in the novel. The narrative trajectory of the convict novel is

---

131 'Bildungsroman,' *A Dictionary of Critical Theory*, ed., Ian Buchanan (Oxford: OUP, 2010), 58-59.

132 'Bildungsroman,' *Oxford Companion to German Literature*, 3rd edn, eds, Henry Garland and Mary Garland (Oxford: OUP, 1997; online 2005), 87-88.

133 Franco Moretti, *The Way of The World: The Bildungsroman in European Culture* (London: Verso, 2000; 1987), 5.

amplified in Chapters 20, 'H.M.S *Anson*' and 22, 'The Initiation—Within' and reaches its climax in Chapter 31, 'A Day Dream and a Night Vision,' where the protagonist confronts her nemesis, Bob Pragg, who engineered her arrest under circumstances that led to her conviction for infanticide and transportation for life. However, the resolution of this confrontation does not produce the dénouement of the novel or predict the fate of the heroine. Maida's fate depends not on her actions as a convict in forgiving the architect of her imprisonment—but upon her spiritual maturity achieved in her acceptance of the Christian imperatives of confession and the disciplining of her will. This moment is set up in Chapter 32, 'The Isle of the Dead,' when Maida, moved by the impending death of the Rev. Evelyn's daughter, Emmeline, accedes to the younger woman's plea to 'long for the peace of Christ'. In the following chapter, 'Accepted,' Emmeline's father passes his daughter's old room and, seeing Maida, approaches her: 'It is over, sir! Not almost, but altogether ... Miss Evelyn persuaded me, you have decided me. Her God shall be my God; her Saviour my Saviour!' And the point of this narrative is the spiritual—not romantic—union that requires her death.

There is a third generic trajectory in the romance plot, played out in the subplot of Bridget d'Urban and reaching its crescendo in Bridget's accepting Mr Walkden's proposal in Chapter 34, 'Bridget Again'. This motif of the romance plot ending in marriage is conventionalised in the lives of Mr and Mrs Evelyn, is disfigured in Norwell's marriage to Mary Doveton, and lies submerged in Maida's own story. The possibility that she might be 'saved' by marriage acts as a kind of narrative lure, drawing the reader in, seducing the reader while, at the same time, refusing the ending romance demands. Instead, this narrative lure surfaces as an allusion exchanged by main characters and takes shape as the butt of servants' gossip, until it emerges only to come apart when the Rev. Herbert Evelyn despairs—in a section omitted in the 1886 edition—'Would God that you did not love him [Norwell] *still*! Forget him, Maida, he is unworthy of you' (Chapter 27). Maida's death is a triumph: it represents her peace and the spiritual plenitude that stands in horrible contrast to the madness into which Norwell descends, leaving him a wraith in the last chapter of the novel.

Traditional literary history has usually subtended Leakey's novel to the generic imperatives of convict fiction, and reading that history otherwise depends upon a degree of scepticism about Marcus Clarke's own genealogy for his great novel; it would mean allowing literary history to operate in a more suggestive chronology than that described by the linearity of dates, and nominating genre as one possible paradigm of such a history. Perhaps the most compelling condition for this normative literary history is the availability of the revised second edition of the novel, rather than the more complexly structured first edition, and given the history of the book, this is not surprising. The current edition is an argument for reconsidering the genre of convict fiction and the place of *His Natural Life* as the dominant context for Leakey's novel.

Leakey herself, in her preface, provides a literary context for her novel, one which has long been ignored principally because the preferred 1886 revision. As we have noted, writing as Oliné Keese, and thus fictionalising herself, Leakey, writes, 'So many attractive books on Australian and convict-life have appeared of late years, that I fear mine may be repelled as an unsuccessful imitation of other authors.' This may be, for domestic and colonial readers, an allusion to Reade's '*It Is Never Too Late to Mend*': *A Matter-of-Fact Romance* (1856), in which there is sustained critique of the English prison system, dramatised in Mr Eden's triumph over the sadistic applications of the system by Governor

Hawes—'The gaoler had been out-witted by the priest'[134]—and an irresistible plot trajectory situated in Australia that counterpoints the English episodes. There is perhaps an echo of the title of Reade's novel in the penultimate chapter of *The Broad Arrow*: 'It's never too late to mend our ways and goings, I hope, Maida', although the phrase itself is proverbial.

If 'of late years' means the decade and a half or so up to 1859, the 'attractive books' may include John Boxup's *Life of John Boxup, Late Convict, at Van Diemen's Land* (1850), although this book was privately printed and probably limited in circulation) and Rev. Henry Phibbs Fry's *A System of Penal Discipline, with a Report on the Treatment of Prisoners in Great Britain and Van Diemen's Land* (1850, printed in London by Longman, Brown & Green) but this title would have made stern, rather than attractive, reading.[135] This allusion to recent books is unlikely to have included Henry Savery's *Quintus Servinton: A Tale founded upon Incidents of Real Occurrence* (1829–30) since it was rare[136] or Savery's *Hermit in Van Diemen's Land* (published under the pseudonym Simon Stukeley) rare in novel form and serialised only in the Hobart *Colonial Times*;[137] or John Howison's *Tales of the Colonies*, which includes 'One False Step', set in Australia, in volume 2, published by Richard Bentley & Son in 1830 and is thus early rather than 'of late years;'[138] or James Tucker's *Ralph Rashleigh; or, the Life of an Exile*, written circa 1845–46, as this novel was not published until 1929.[139] Charles Rowcroft's *Tales of the Colonies, or, the Adventures of an Emigrant*, though, while not a convict novel may have been in Leakey's mind as one of the 'attractive books.' The novel was serialised between October 1842 and June 1843 and then published in 3 volumes by Sanders & Otley later in 1843 and so it was certainly available to a London reading public and, as a review in the *Sydney Record* (20 Jan 1844) shows, also to an Australian audience.[140] Leakey may well have been conscious that Rowcroft's startling and exciting *Tales* proved popular, being reissued at least four times between 1843 and 1850 and then again in 1858. Or perhaps Rowcroft's earlier *The Bushranger of Van Diemen's Land* (1846) had fired readers' curiosity. If we do consider earlier works, then James Bischoff, *Sketch of the History of Van Diemen's Land* (1832) or Henry Melville, *History of the Island of Van Diemen's Land* (1835) might have featured in Leakey's perceptions of Van Diemen's Land among the reading public. More

---

134 Charles Reade, *'It is Never Too Late to Mend' A Matter-of-Fact Romance* (London: The Daily Telegraph, n.d.), 240.

135 John Boxup, *The Life of John Boxup, Late Convict at Van Diemen's Land* (Wetherby: W. Sinclair, 1850) in John Alexander Ferguson, *Bibliography of Australia*, vol. 4, 1850 (Sydney & London: Angus and Robertson, 1965), 365, F. 5301; Reverend Henry Phibbs, *A System of Penal Discipline, with a report on the treatment of prisoners in Great Britain and Van Diemen's Land* (London: Longman, Brown, Green and London, 1850) in Ferguson, 381, F. 5359.

136 Advertised as printed 'expressly for transmission to England, a very few copies only will be reserved for sale,' *Colonial Times*, Friday 21 Jan, 1831, 1. See entry in Ferguson, *Bibliography*, Vol. 1, copies are 'extremely rare,' 501.

137 On *The Hermit*, see 'Henry Savery,' Cecil Hadcraft, *Australian Dictionary of Biography*, vol. 2 (Melbourne: MUP, 1967) https://bit.ly/2q3Jh2e; also AustLit, database, entry on Henry Savery, https://bit.ly/2F5Xq9F.

138 1830 Geo. IV., *Publications Issued from New Burlington Street, during the last three months of the year 1829* (London: Richard Bentley and Son, 1893), n.p. https://bit.ly/2vnahOy.

139 Giacomo Di Rosenberg (James Tucker), *Ralph Rashleigh or the Life of an Exile*, ed. Colin Roderick (Sydney & London: Angus and Robertson, 1952), xii, xvi.

140 Anon., review, 'Tales of the Colonies; or the Adventures of an Emigrant. Edited by a Late Colonial Magistrate,' *Sydney Record*, 20 January 1844, 122–23.

generally on Van Diemen's Land, Leakey may have recalled John West, *The History of Tasmania* (1852) or Louise Anne Meredith, *My Home in Tasmania* (1852). James Fenton, *A History of Tasmania* (1884) provides, as an appendix, a 'List of Books Relating to Tasmania (compiled by James B. Walker)' which lists twelve titles from 1847-1852, including West and Meredith, and twelve more from 1854–59, including Major H. Butler Stoney, *A Year in Tasmania* (1854), John Mitchel, *Jail Journal; or Five Years in British Prisons* (1854), Colin Arnott Browning, *The Convict Ship; a Narrative etc. on board the* Earl Grey, *during a Voyage to Tasmania* (fifth edition by 1851) and Oliné Keese, *The Broad Arrow* (1859).[141] *The Cruise of the 'Beacon'* by Bishop Francis Nixon (1857), with whom Leakey stayed, is also listed.

In 'Reading in Colonial Australia: The 2011 John Alexander Ferguson Memorial Lecture', Elizabeth Webby draws attention to emergent trends in the development of reading culture in which convicts and convict literature feature, paying particular attention to newspapers, journals and public libraries.[142] These trends are given substance in contemporary Hobart newspapers and public library catalogues suggesting, if not the Australian context Leakey imagined for her novel, then the context in which readers located it as a work of fiction. The 1859 edition was advertised, as we have seen, in *Walch's Literary Intelligencer* (May 1860), having been reviewed in the preceding March issue, in the *Cornwall Chronicle* on 29 February 1860, and then later in the Hobart *Mercury* on 27 January 1879.[143] The revised edition was advertised in the *Mercury* on 24 January 1887, and in the *Launceston Examiner* on both 10 and 12 May 1887.[144] Sales of public and private holdings of books were regularly advertised in Hobart newspapers from the early 1830s, and on 23 November 1864 in the *Mercury* Messrs Burn & Co., booksellers, announced a sale of 'About one thousand volumes ... without one fraction of reserve, the proprietor giving up the business'.[145] The list includes 'Sir Walter Scott's Poetical Works, Byron's Works ... Prison Discipline, Broad Arrow, Chambers's Journals'. Here is an unsuccessful competitor to J. Walch & Sons, who is carrying the 1859 edition in either two-decker or single-volume format, evidencing the book's circulation outside the Bentley and Walch supply chain.

To this detail of Hobart booksellers' stock, slight though it is, we can add the witness of the borrowers' register of one of Hobart's circulating libraries and elsewhere catalogues of contemporaneous public libraries. These catalogues do not include bibliographic information or any indication of how frequently a book was borrowed, but the entries attest to the presence and availability of Leakey's novel. The libraries were also of varying sizes, catered to a range of interests, and acquired their titles from different suppliers, but there would have been some overlap between their memberships and each library

---

141 James Fenton, *A History of Tasmania From its Discovery in 1642 to the Present Time* (Hobart: J. Walch & Sons; Launceston: Walch Brothers & Birchall: 1884); James Walker's 'List of Books relating to Tasmania,' 447-457; titles listed here appear, 451-452. https://bit.ly/2PfGnpk.

142 Elizabeth Webby, 'Reading in Colonial Australia: The 2011 John Alexander Ferguson Memorial Lecture,' *Journal of the Royal Australian Historical Society*, 97.2 (2011): 119–35.

143 TAHO, NS2849/1/1, *Walch's Literary Intelligencer*, May 1860, 199; NS2849/1/1, *Walch's Literary Intelligencer*, March 1860, 169–70; *Cornwall Chronicle*, Wednesday 29 February 1860, 5; *The Mercury* [Hobart], Monday 27 January 1879, 2.

144 *The Mercury* [Hobart], Monday 24 January 1887, 2; *Launceston Examiner* Tuesday 10 May 1887, 2; and Thursday 12 May 1887, 2.

145 *The Mercury* [Hobart], 23 November 1864, 4.

contributed its own particular history to the culture of books in Hobart. The Hobart Mechanics' Library, for instance, had been influenced by a recent debate over the 'value of fiction and general literature' in a collection that aimed to 'improve' its readers.[146] William Westcott's library, meanwhile, drawing on 'Mudie's Select London Library', offered an exciting range and number of fiction titles.

Caroline Leakey's name does not appear in the borrowers' register of Walch's Circulating Library for January 1846–December 1851.[147] However, the register does provide an indication of the titles available to subscribers and an insight into their borrowing habits. A Miss Sorell (perhaps Julia, future wife of Thomas Arnold?) borrowed a popular work titled *Long Engagement* on 19 June 1849.[148] Since the register records readers' borrowing habits—sometimes a title goes out only once, while other titles are borrowed repeatedly— it perhaps provided one element in J. Walch's choices of stock from among publishers' catalogues in the following decade. Annals of Crime, 2 vols [part of *The Newgate Calendar*]; Chronicles of Crime 2 vols [later redacted by Camden Pelham (1886)]; [Charles Dickens's novella] Battle of Life (1846); [G. P. R. James,] *The Convict* 3 vols (1848), all appear as having been borrowed. Chronicles of Crime, 2 vols, is also listed as item 158 in *A Catalogue of Books* Contained (sic) in J. W. H. Walch's (father of the bookseller and publisher) Derwent Circulating Library Wellington Bridge published in 1846.[149] These titles evidence, for example, the popularity of a diversified genre of crime writing in fiction and non-fiction formats available through the circulating library that, itself, sustained social and commercial networks.

The *Catalogue of the Library of the Hobart Mechanics' Institute* (1860) lists, at item 1606, Broad Arrow by Oline [sic] Keese, 2 vols [i.e. 1859 Bentley edition]; item 1057, [*The*] *Convict*: by G.P.R. James; and another influential convict narrative, item 1452, [*The*] Caxtons [A Family Picture]: by Sir E.B. Lytton (first published 1849).[150] Here is Leakey's novel in its popular literary context, available to readers borrowing from the Hobart Mechanics' Institute Library just a year after its publication in London and in the same year as its publication in Hobart. The history of the Mechanics' Institute and its library provides an insight into the relationship between class and reading as a cultural paradigm that provides some further nuance to the placement of Leakey's novel on the library's shelves. Founded in 1827, emulating similar institutes set up in Edinburgh (1821) and London (1823), the

146 See Keith Adkins, 'Books, Libraries and Reading in Colonial Tasmania,' *Tasmanian Historical Research Association, Papers and Proceedings* [*THRA P&P*], 53.3 (2005):163; Stefan Petrow, 'The Life and Death of the Hobart Town Mechanics' Institute,' *THRA P & P*, 40.1 (1993):12; Adkins acknowledges the *locus classicus* for this topic in Elizabeth Webby, 'Literature and the Reading Public in Australia 1800-1850: A Study of the Growth and Differentiation of a Colonial Literary Culture during the earlier Nineteenth Century', Sydney: Ph.D Thesis, 1971.

147 TAHO, NS2864/1/1.

148 I am grateful to acknowledge Prof. Wal Kirsop for expert advice and for checking the register (personal communication 17 Sept 1991). I am especially pleased to acknowledge 'Selling books at auction in 19th-century Australia: The 2009 Ferguson Memorial Lecture' in which Prof. Kirsop discusses the place of Walch and Sons in the history of bookselling in Australia; published as 'Selling Books at Auction in 19th Century Australia,' *Journal of the Royal Australian Historical Society*, 95.2 (2009): 198-214 at 203.

149 *A Catalogue of Books* Contained in J. W. H. Walch's Derwent Circulating Library Wellington Bridge (Hobart: n. publ.; printed William Gore Elliston, 1846), 8.

150 *Catalogue of the Library of the Hobart Mechanics' Institute* (Hobart Town: no publ., printed by William Fletcher, 1860).

Mechanics' Institution (later Mechanics' Institute) promoted 'Scientific Knowledge among professional and practical Mechanics and others … By the aid of a Library, containing Books of Scientific Knowledge; and a Reading Room for the use of the Members'.[151] By 1858, the *Mercury* newspaper reported that 'the largest proportion of subscribers were those who joined for the advantage of reading the light literature contained in the Library; many others subscribe for the purpose of spending an hour in the Lecture Room, viewing it as a place of fashionable resort'.[152] The Library's *Catalogue* was, in fact, divided into two sections: the larger first section, pages 1-40, listed titles under the heading 'General Alphabet', including widely diverse works such as G[eorge] R[owland] Burnell's *Treatise on Limes, Cements, Mortars, etc.* (1850; item 1366) and S[amuel] Maunder, *Conversations on Geology; [Comprising a familiar explanation of the Huttonian and Wernerian systems]* (1828; item 1285) and C[harles] Hutton, *Recreations in Mathematics [and Natural Philosophy]*, translated from the French of Jacques Ozanam, in 4 vols [1840; item 1205]; the second section, pages 41-53, listed 'Prose Fiction: Novels, Romances, etc.'. While the popularity of the Library among middle class readers is only one part of the Institute's decline as an educational resource for working-class men and the *Mercury's* comment alludes to a vigorous struggle as the 'mechanics' attempted to regain control of the Institute, the *Catalogue* places Leakey's novel squarely within established social and commercial categories, operating with a significant degree of both cultural and economic capital.

The *Catalogue of Books in the Tasmanian Public Library*, compiled in 1871, lists Bulwer Lytton: The Caxtons (item 2114); Settlers and Convicts, by an Emigrant Mechanic (1847) (item 2253); Rev. John West: The History of Tasmania (1852) (item 1224).[153] This catalogue shows Leakey's novel, just over a decade after its publication, still listed with Bulwer Lytton's continuously popular novel and John West's important and influential history of Tasmania, both published twenty years or so before. In the same year, 1871, *A Catalogue of Books in Various Branches of Literature Direct from Mudie's Select London Library, also Magazines and Reviews Contained in W. Westcott's Circulating Library* lists at item 205 *Convict's Daughter* and *Convert's Daughter* (first published 1836); at items 985–94 'Eugène Sue, 10 works including Mysteries of Paris (item 982); item 1408 Broad Arrow, 2 vols; item 1714 Eliot: Adam Bede; item 1894 Two Convicts; item 2752 Convicts, 2 vols, Mary Carpenter; item 8444 History of Tasmania, 2 vols; item 2866 Reade, (Charles): It is Never Too Late to Mend; item 107 Bulwer (Lord Lytton): Caxtons, A Family Picture, 3 vols; item 179 Chronicles of Crime; item 1110 Woman's Love: M. L. Grimstone.[154] This catalogue provides the most detailed readerly context for Leakey's novel and includes English, French and Tasmanian titles, contemporaneous works (*Adam Bede* and *It Is Never Too Late to Mend*) and earlier novels such as *The Caxtons* and Grimstone's *Woman's Love*. Sue's serial would become globally popular and other titles were destined for narrower readership

---

151 'Laws of the Hobart Town Mechanics' Institute,' *Catalogue of the Library of the Hobart Mechanics' Institute* (Hobart Town: no publ., printed by William Fletcher, 1860) i; also 'Mechanics' Institution,' *Tasmanian* 23 November 1827, Number 39, [p. 1].

152 *The Mercury*, 15 April 1858 cited in Stefan Petrow, 'The Life and Death of the Hobart Mechanics' Institute, 1827-1871, *THRAPP*, 40.1 (1993): 11.

153 *Catalogue of Books in the Tasmanian Public Library*. Samuel Hannaford [compiler], (Hobart Town: James Barnard, Govt. Printer, 1870).

154 *A Catalogue of Books* in Various Branches of Literature Direct from Mudie's Select London Library, also Magazines and Reviews Contained in W. Westcott's Circulating Library (Hobart Town: no publ., printed by W[illia]m Fletcher 1871).

but all benefitted from the guaranteed stamp of approval in being 'direct from Mudie's Select London Library'. The usefulness of this catalogue is not so much as an index of literary merit, critical value or commercial success, though these factors influenced library holdings, but rather as an indication that Leakey's novel was recognised as belonging to a category of popular writing catering to a general reading public and made available through the pivotal institution of the lending library.

So, while English reviewers positioned Leakey's novel as a successor to Charles Reade's didacticism and the theme of the fallen woman, and Australian literary scholars have nominated it as a precursor to the putative category of 'convict novel' dominated by Marcus Clarke's novel, the evidence of public reading suggests other contexts might have included, for example, the popular line of crime fiction represented by Eugène Sue's *Les Mystères de Paris* (1846), an English translation of which was held in Westcott's Library; G.P.R. James, *The Convict* (1847) also held in the Hobart Mechanic's Institute Library and Walch's Circulating Library; the *Annals of Crime* (1833-34) and *Chronicles of Crime* (from 1841) both were held by Walch's Circulating Library; Westcott's Circulating Library also held a copy of *Chronicles of Crime*. A reader with such a taste might have found an attractive connection between Leakey's novel and Chapter CXCI, 'Cranky Jem's History' in George W.M. Reynolds's *Mysteries of London* (1846) with its vivid descriptions of convict life ('depraved — wicked — criminal'), spacious Hobart Town and Australian marriage customs and forgiven the incorrect geography for the action-packed pace, allusions to Dante and epic trope of the storm at sea, advertised for sale by auction as part of a lot by Mr Lewis Cohen at his rooms in York Street, Launceston in March 1860.[155] This suggestion is made with caution since, as we shall see, crime fiction in general also attracted a degree of opprobrium that suggests both class and national strictures of 'taste' and/or 'prejudice'.

There is no evidence to suggest that Leakey maintained connections with the reading public of Hobart after the publication of her novel, just as there is no record of her reading *For the Term of His Natural Life*, although the two novels are on consecutive pages in Bentley's ledger.[156] But it might have been pleasing for her to realise that the first edition of her novel was collected alongside the work of popular and successful novelists in these public, subscription and circulating libraries. The publishers, however, would have to wait for Mrs Townsend Mayer's abridgement to turn *The Broad Arrow* into a commercial success.

Two intertexts: the 1859 edition and the 1886 revision

The prior question to any reading of *The Broad Arrow* is which version of the novel is being read. Much of the narrative is found in both versions, of course, and the revision is recognisable as a version of the first edition. But there are significant differences between the two editions, and whereas as the first (1859) edition represents the novel Caroline Leakey contracted to Richard Bentley & Son, the second (1887) edition was not seen by the author, was not approved by her executor, and its copyright resided with the publisher. The second edition omits significant parts of the two-volume narrative, simplifying the

---

155 See Stephen Knight, *The Mysteries of the Cities. Urban Crime Fiction in the Nineteenth* Century (Jefferson & London: McFarland, 2012), 99. George W.M. Reynolds, *Mysteries of London*, https://bit.ly/2CA1zzt. The *Cornwall Chronicle*, Saturday 31 Mar 1860, 7.

156 Ingram, *Bentley Archive*, L42, 456

structure, abbreviating the role of three important characters and censoring segments of narrational commentary to produce a single volume colonial romance. Townsend Mayer introduced relatively few additions to the text—less than 20, ranging in length from a single word to a paragraph, across the 40,000 word abridgement—and in each case the addition facilitates narrative flow. This point deserves emphasis, since the revision relied upon Townsend Mayer's skilful editing of the structure, rather than rewriting of the content. The edited text, for example, omitting the author's preface, which had situated the work for Leakey's contemporaries, and instead targeting a specific, export audience.

Townsend Mayer's revision of the novel is radical, rather than conservative, and takes the form of structural editing—something usually done in collaboration with the author—to produce a work that resembles, but is not, the novel Caroline Leakey submitted for publication and that Marcus Clarke (probably) read in preparation for writing *His Natural Life*. At the level of the sentence, and sometimes the single word, Townsend Mayer normalises Leakey's linguistically accented and individuated prose and her characters' speech patterns. Her edit also successfully 'modernises' a text first issued in context with Charles Reade's, *It Is Never Too Late to Mend*, George Eliot's *Adam Bede* and Charles Kingsley's *The Recollections of Geoffrey Hamlyn* to produce a title issued *after* Charles Dickens's *Great Expectations* (1861), Mrs Henry Wood's *East Lynne* (1863), Wilkie Collins' *The Moonstone* (1868), Thomas Hardy's *Far from the Madding Crowd* (1874) and, crucially, Richard Bentley & Son's three-volume edition of Marcus Clarke's *His Natural Life* (September 1875), texts that had colonised a certain language, style and structure—a discourse—for the convict novel. Caroline Leakey wrote, and the London and Hobart publishers issued, a novel that scholars recognise as having articulated tropes and motifs in the emergent convict novel. Townsend Mayer's skill and acuity produced a commercially viable title that, as mainstream genre fiction, remained on various publishing houses' lists for a century. Reading these two texts in parallel we have the opportunity to explore these intertexts: separate from but implicated in one another in the same textual system constituted by reading them alongside one another.[157] While readers may read the first and revised editions separately, it is in reading them as intertexts that the literary effects of the book's *histoire croisée* are revealed.

The narrative structure of *The Broad Arrow* is one of the remarkable achievements of, so far as we know, the writer's first and only novel. As Townsend Mayer's abridgement demonstrates, the narrative mobilises around a single protagonist, the 'lifer' of the eponymous title. Maida Gwynnham's story unfolds in a forward trajectory supported by episodes of analepsis (flashback) and prolepsis (flash forward), locating its narrative logic in more than one time scale, and dramatised by a series of sometimes detailed, sometimes fleeting characters whose own stories—sometimes urgent, sometimes shadowy—interlock

---

157 I am using Julia Kristeva's formulation to describe the *textual* relations between the two versions; see her *A Revolution in Poetic Language* (New York: Columbia University Press, 1984), 59–60 and Kristeva, *Desire in Language. A Semiotic Approach to Literature and Art*, ed. Leon S. Roudiez (Oxford: Basil Blackwell, 1980), 15. For a different, though related, use of this term as '*authorial* intertextuality' (emphasis added), see Paul Eggert, *Biography of a Book. Henry Lawson's* While the Billy Boils (Sydney & Philadelphia: Sydney University Press & Pennsylvania State University Press, 2013), 332. Eggert argues that Lawson evolved as a writer (344) and thus a bibliographical account of the work needs to be expanded to include this trajectory. Editorial apparatus needs thus to respond to textual change, beyond simply recording such change, to record the feedback loop between publication and rewriting that Lawson's 'evolution' exemplifies (343).

with one another and with that of the protagonist. The narration is delivered by an omniscient narrator who manages the structures of event, place, and time and keeps control of shifts in point of view, narrative focus and transitions into and out of dialogue. Omniscient narration also works to focalise thematic elements in the narrative where dramatised action requires commentary, to produce economies of action or event, or to provide a perspective that is external to story without moving outside the narrative framework; there are some instances of free indirect discourse. This is the technical machinery of a full-scale novel of the times, neither collapsing back into the schemata of the eighteenth-century novel nor reaching forward to the sustained intellectualism and sheer sophistication of the narrative voice in the later George Eliot or Henry James. Leakey's novel shares with Reade's contemporaneous work an energetic pace, dynamic action, readily recognisable characters and a passionate commitment to the novel as a form of social thinking and ethical critique. In the second edition, the structure is not so much condensed—with the narrative packed into a smaller space—as curtailed and thus reduced in both quantity and extent. Townsend Mayer's blue pencil begins with the preface and maintains an impressively steady hand.

The first edition was divided into two volumes: Volume I comprising Chapters 1–21 and Volume II comprising Chapters 22–37. Chapter 1, 'The Festival', initiates the narrative; Chapter 21, 'The Initiation—Without', brings Maida to Hobart and the Evelyn family; Chapter 22, 'The Initiation—Within', opens up the domestic scene where much of the action will be located; Chapter 37, 'Norwell', leaves the narrative with Norwell in the insane asylum at New Norfolk. Of the first edition's 37 chapters, four chapters—5 'Bob Pragg' (with the exception of one paragraph inserted into Chapter 4), 6 'Mary Doveton', 10 'The Lie', and 12 'Lucy Grenlow's Tale'—are omitted. Nine chapters remain mostly intact, with abridgments of less than half a page at a time (Volume 1 Chapters 13 'Mulgrave Battery and The Lodge', 14 'The Paraclete,'; Volume 2 Chapters 23 'Being One About Bridget', 24 'The Post Office', 25 'A T.L.', 26 'The Conflict', 30 'Port Arthur—The Settlement', 34 'Bridget Again', 37 'Norwell'). Of the remaining chapters, some have relatively fewer excisions: Chapters 1–4 ('The Festival', 'Maida Gwynnham', 'Captain Norwell', and 'The Felon') omit between two and four consecutive pages of text; other chapters (9 'The Cousins', 20 'H.M.S *Anson*', 21 'Initiation—Without', 22 'Initiation—Within' and 28 'H.M. General Hospital, Hobarton') omit between four and nine consecutive pages in addition to excisions of more than 50 percent of a single page. In quantitative terms, Volume 1 is more heavily edited than Volume 2: the effect is not simply to tell a more economical story, but to tell a *different* story. The content of the narrative is altered, the technical range of narrational techniques is eroded and characterisation is simplified. It is in this sense that Townsend Mayer's revision is radical.

An indication of the dimensions of the edit can be visualised in selected quantitative data. These data are robust but I should stress that quantitative data are not to be conflated with qualitative data; correlation does not equate to causation; and a short chapter may be significant in the narrative sequence. Nor do these data distinguish between, for example, narration, description and dialogue. I have used word-count per page as the unit of data collection and then aggregated text edited from the first edition to produce the second as a percentage of the relevant chapter. This data-set is summarised in the bar graph (Figure 2), where the bar lines indicate chapter divisions in the first edition and the shaded area indicates material omitted to produce the second edition. In other words, the shaded area in the bar graph represents the shaded text in the present edition.

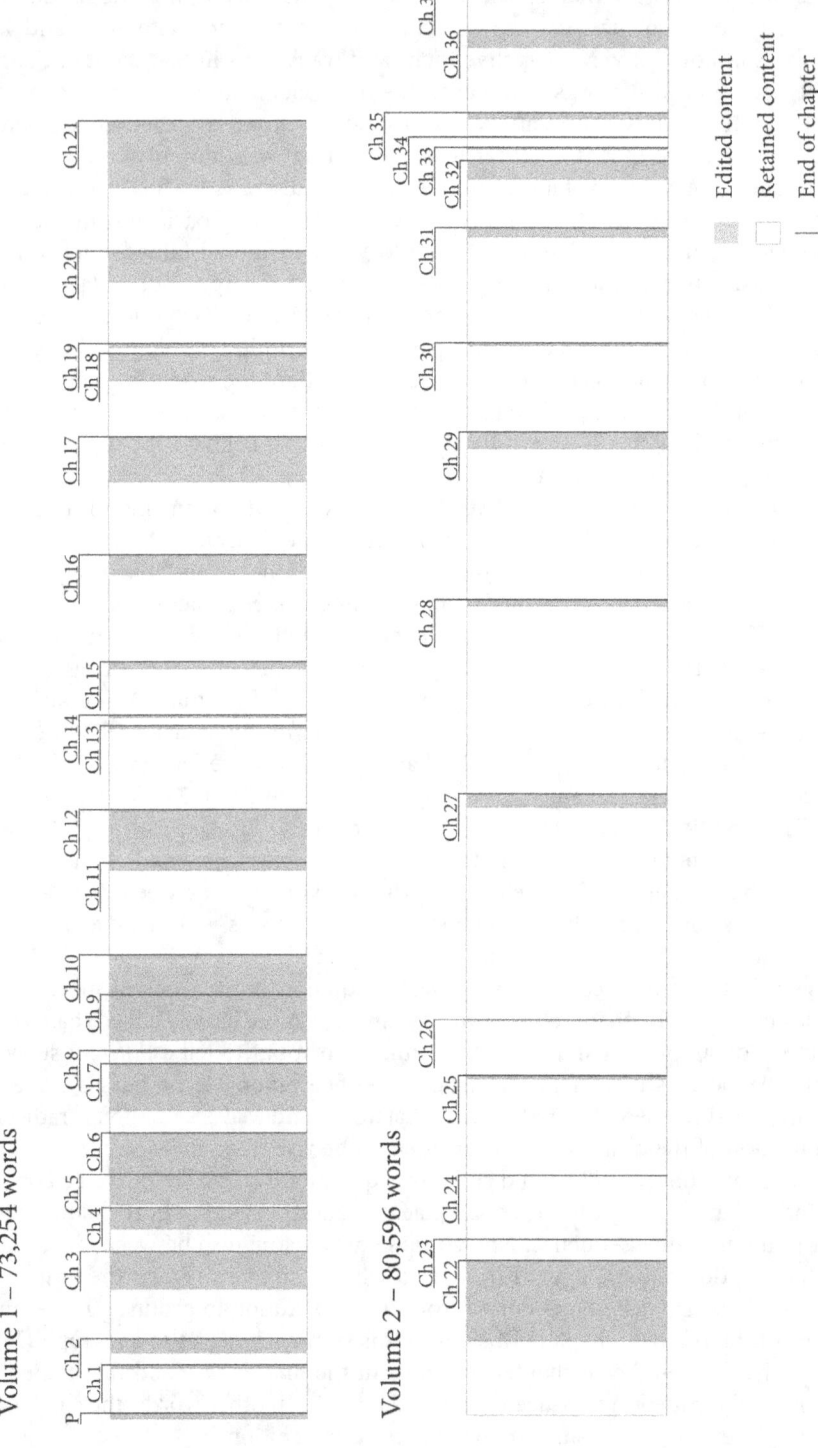

Figure 2 A visualisation of Townsend Mayer's edits.

Let's begin with the summative outline of these data. In total, the 1859 text comprised, in rounded sum, 153,580 words, while 1886 comprised 112,500 words. The bar graph shows the comparative lengths of the two volumes: in the first edition, Volume 1 is approximately 5 percent shorter than Volume 2. After the edit producing the second edition, Volume 1 is approximately 25 percent shorter than Volume 2. Townsend Mayer edited out approximately 27 percent of 1859's text: 42.5 percent of Volume 1's text and 12.4 percent of Volume 2's text. In addition to, in effect, four complete chapters being edited out—'Bob Pragg', 'Mary Doveton', 'The Lie' and 'Lucy Grenlow's Tale'—another five chapters in Volume 1 ('Maida Gwynnham' The Felon', 'The Reverend Herbert Evelyn', 'The Cousins' and 'The Initiation—Without') were abbreviated by more than half their length. By contrast, only one chapter in Volume 2, 'The Initiation—Within', is as substantially edited. Further, two chapters remained without any edit: Volume 2's second and third chapters ('Being One About Bridget' and 'The Post Office'). Nine chapters, across the two volumes, were abbreviated by less than 10 percent of their 1859 length: in addition to Chapters 2 and 3 just mentioned, these include 'A T.L.', 'The Conflict', 'An Old Acquaintance', 'H.M. General Hospital', 'Port Arthur—OPSO—The Kangaroo', 'A Day Dream and a Night Vision' and 'Bridget Again' in Volume 2, and 'The Rose of Britain' and 'Mulgrave Battery and the Lodge' in Volume 1. Townsend Mayer's edit changed the volume, weight and, critically, the pace of the narrative across the two volumes. The four chapters omitted altogether, for example, serve to shear off narrative subplots—the separate stories of Bog Pragg, Mary Doveton and Lucy Grenlow—retaining only sufficient detail to support the central narrative trajectory. Townsend Mayer's judicial understanding of genre fiction's narrative shape is evidenced by this editing in which, having cut away distractions from the central plot line, the narrative picks up pace and momentum before dilating for the two longest chapters—'An Old Acquaintance' and 'H.M. General Hospital'—both only lightly edited, where dramatic action and tight narrative focus provide emotionally charged story.

These data represent one aspect of Townsend Mayer's revision: the sheer volume of material edited out of the narrative. There are commercial knock-on effects here, of course: a shorter book is cheaper to print, bind and distribute. The shorter format, too, recalls the first edition while distinguishing the current one. Given the timing of the second edition, it is unlikely much of the market would have remained the same. But the title certainly remained an evocative one: three simple words concentrated into a single image, and that image itself, by 1887, immediately recognisable, thanks in part to Clarke's novel, as a marker of convictism.

The edit deserves closer scrutiny to unpack its effect on the narrative's content and meaning. This discussion will focus on the larger elements in the structural edit; other comments will appear in the notes to the text. The four whole chapters omitted include Bob Pragg's story in Chapter 5, which is deleted except for an awkward narrative hinge on the last page. Pragg is a lowlife who displays cunning and vindictiveness coupled with an unnerving ability to pinpoint inadequacies in the justice system. He sneaks into the narrative in Chapter 3 as a bystander who sees Maida on the omnibus, after she has passed the forged cheque, and in a single gesture manifests a sense of crude masculine threat, part way between simple violence and sexual innuendo: 'I've natural spite 'gainst that Grylls.' It is Pragg who, in Chapter 4 'The Felon', in a section revised out by Townsend Mayer, leads the police to Maida Gwynnham. Pragg will reappear in the crucial Chapter 27, 'An Old Acquaintance', when Maida is caught up in a graveyard scene of grotesque horror and then again at the climax of Maida's life as convict, in Chapter 31, 'A Day Dream and a Night Vision', where Pragg, now a starved and maddened escapee, seeks her out in the dead of night to plead for food and forgiveness.

The omitted Chapter 5 is analeptic: a flashback that holds the narrative trajectory in suspense to refocus the reader's attention on a character who will play a significant role in the history of the protagonist. The chapter opens with omniscient narration, turning back to pinpoint the failing of circumstantial evidence in convicting Maida of infanticide, then shifts to the present scene in the public house and closes narrative focus on Bob Pragg explaining the workings of circumstantial evidence to his gang in a public house, where they are drinking the proceeds of Bob's 'witness money'. The setting, characters and dialogue might have come from a chapter by Reynolds. This is Pragg's insider knowledge of the workings of evidentiary process:

> 'Beau-ti-ful! I say, man. Grylls herself couldn't stand such evidence. If the woman didn't look foul at herself 'fore 'ceedings was over I b'ant Bob Pragg. No one could resist it. The facts—there they was, cut out and fitted into one th'other for all the world as if they was true. There weren't one stretcher; not a single lump that could stick in his Lordship's throat. How glorious! The whole batch—judge, ranters, and humbugging twelve swallowed it smooth down without a wry mouth; and then to hear his Lordship's speech after gulping the dose! Grace after meat weren't nothing to it!'

But the narrator also maintains the ethical framework here, despite the intimate narrative focus on the criminal, by throwing out a rhetorical arc to the reader: 'We shall have much to do with Mr Pragg before we finish with him, therefore we may as well make his acquaintance now, as he is in a better temper than usual.' The reader is forestalled from sympathising with Pragg or assimilating to his sentiments: instead, through the first person plural pronoun, 'we' are made complicit with the narrator's position. In this context, the shift back to Norwell, in the last two paragraphs of the chapter, transitions the narrative back out of analepsis and restores the narrative to its main focus with a palpable demonstration of the horror to which Norwell's cowardice has exposed the rash and naïve Maida.

In this same part of the novel, we can see the effects of Townsend Mayer's revision through abridging at the structural level of the paragraph or page. In Chapter 3, 'Captain Norwell', the narrative stages the confrontation between Maida, now destitute and unable to feed her child, and her lover Norwell, who is badly in debt and has conceived of forgery as his only salvation; it is to lay out this plan that Norwell has sought out Maida. Among the paragraphs edited out, she admonishes Norwell and he responds by telling her, 'You are impulsive, Maida, and fastidious. You—you—there is more of touchiness than sensitivity.' Maida collapses: 'she could receive a rebuke. "Forgive me, Norwell! I fear you are right".' Norwell ratchets up the emotional pressure, 'He smote his brow, and more pale than haggard seemed his countenance' and delays telling Maida what she must do until, 'Henry, this suspense is cruel,' she says. Maida's words, edited out in the second edition, show that she is not ignorant of Norwell's plan; she pleads with him for another solution; he, though, is distracted by her sexual allure and motivated by his own narcissism. 'He was charmed to the spot; she had never looked more wildly beautiful; it was destruction to gaze at her . . .' The second edition edits out much of this struggle between the two lovers, and while the narrative has many more opportunities to disclose the complexities of Maida's character, much of the close study of Norwell's vanity disappears from the narrative with the revising of this chapter.

There are some important consequences here that are echoed elsewhere in the narrative, where similar excisions occur. First is an underestimating of narrative imperatives: Norwell needs to be more than a caricatured feckless lover. The logic of the narrative depends upon the value of Maida's commitment to her decision to remain loyal to Norwell until new knowledge she gains forces her to think and act differently. Second, on the face of it, Townsend Mayer is editing out a kind of melodrama that might not have suited either the genre in which she was recasting the novel or the market at which she aimed the book. But we need to recognise that '[j]ust as clichés express widely held views, if clumsily, so the themes of melodrama express real social problems, in headline terms.'[158] Norwell is a spendthrift and a gambler, irresponsible about money and the consequences of his actions. He creates a family only to desert them; crucially, the life of his lover is less valuable than his own. Leakey's novel insists, on every page, that the life of the female protagonist is valuable; that it may be represented in heroic terms; and that the character of a woman—her sexual desire as much as her emotional power—can mobilise an entire narrative and imbue that narrative with ethical worth. Third, having flattened out Norwell's character and made it normative, Townsend Mayer must manage the narrative machinery to ensure the coherence of the edited narrative.

Chapter 10, 'The Lie', essential to the first edition's portrayal of Norwell as vain, cowardly, full of charm and sexual guile, is misplaced in the streamlined, single-volume colonial romance the publisher intends to relaunch under the same title. This chapter begins with omniscient narration that dilates the narrative focus to set up Mary Doveton, whom we have seen visiting Maida in prison, as Norwell's next victim: 'It is to just such a spotless being as Mary Doveton that the sated worldling prostrates himself in unfeigned adoration.' The narrator calls out Norwell as a predator: 'So he spurns his victim at her own shrine, and departing, flings the ashes of her virtue in her face.' His victims are the fallen women deserted, shamed and then denied Christian charity, and for the narrator this is a social as well as a personal degradation. This chapter is structured, through its use of omniscient narration, to articulate the social problem under critique by identifying Norwell and his actions as part of this larger social dimension of the novel. The narrator then contracts the narrative focus to Norwell's accepting an invitation to a party where he hopes to meet Mary Doveton. Maida Gwynnham's story resonates in Mary Doveton's profession of love for Norwell: both women will have children who will not survive, and Norwell is implicated in the real and figurative deaths of both women. The repetition of this motif moves it from the level of an individual life to that of social malaise.

In the second edition, both Chapters 6 and 10 are omitted and so Mary Doveton enters the narrative as a name Maida overhears while serving dinner to visitors at the Evelyns' home in a chapter titled 'The Conflict'. Townsend Mayer needs to add a narrative link: 'Maida started; that name had been familiar to her in other days.' Really? The guests identify Mary Doveton as a former school friend of Mrs Evelyn from her time at school in England. So the connection is with Mrs Evelyn and not Maida. It is actually Norwell's name, mentioned a few lines later by one of the guests, as Mary Doveton's new husband, that is familiar to Maida in this version of the narrative. Later in this chapter, Townsend Mayer needs to amend the rationale for Maida's subsequent actions and so Maida's

---

158 Knight, *The Mysteries of the Cities*, 88–9.

personal loyalty to Mary Doveton—'but now that one, whom she [Maida] reverenced for her purity, had come unconsciously into her secret'—becomes 'but now that the happiness of other lives might be at stake'. Maida's letter to Norwell, and Mary Doveton's subsequent death, hangs off the weak modal verb 'might' and Maida's actions appear to be motivated by chance rather than certainty.

Editing out Chapter 12, 'Lucy Grenlow's Tale', has a different impact on the narrative in terms of structure, character and tone. Lucy's story tells of a young girl whose mother marries again and, with a new baby imminent, she becomes a nuisance in being another mouth to feed. Her stepfather beats her repeatedly; by implication, this beating is only one kind of assault that a girl like Lucy might suffer. Making a choice between her dead husband's daughter and her new husband's baby, Lucy's mother places her as a maid-of-all-work, calling her a 'dapper little maid'. This is a different kind of social problem: poverty, weakened family bonds, physical violence, youth and desperation combine to make Lucy vulnerable to the deceit of another servant, the monthly nurse, employed by the same family. Mrs Gullem entraps Lucy into embezzling money; when she is caught, Lucy is blamed for a series of shortfalls in cash. She is tried and convicted and transported on the same ship as Maida. As a child convict, Lucy becomes another kind of victim and Maida is her protector; later in the narrative, Lucy will come to Maida's aid and the relationship between them will mature as each character develops. Like the Rev. Herbert Evelyn, Lucy is a great supporter of Maida but, equally, she is the recipient of Maida's care, feeling and friendship. Lucy shows that Maida is capable of befriending and defending younger women: she is part of a network of such women characters—Mary Doveton, Wilcox, Emmeline Evelyn—who sustain genuine and unselfish friendships. Lucy's character gives the narrative access not only to the lives of young women convicts but also the possibility of making a life: Chapter 12 narrates the origin of such a life and the hopelessness over which Lucy triumphs. Instead, since the narrative needs Lucy Grenlow, Townsend Mayer adds a paragraph at the end of 'The *Rose of Britain*', where Lucy first appears, to explain her presence on the convict transport. This is an astute editorial judgment in that stripping out Lucy's tale maintains a simple focus on Maida and her crime, provides a clear hierarchy of major and minor characters, and facilitates the forward trajectory of the simplified narrative.

This edition displays Townsend Mayer's edit on the page and enables the reader to read both the first edition and the revised text, collating these texts *as* intertexts. The relationship between the two texts is foregrounded, rather than subordinated by an editorial decision to designate one text as primary and the other as ancillary. The first edition has the authority of primacy but the revised edition has the endorsement of being repeatedly reissued. In literary critical terms, Townsend Mayer's text is a reading of the first edition but the Oliné Keese's text is profoundly implicated in that revised edition: these are not easily separable texts although they are different texts.

The Broad Arrow, for all its structural complexity, was written to be popular and Townsend Mayer's edit foregrounds these elements. The revised edition shares a generic didacticism with novels such as Charles Reade's '*It Is Never Too Late to Mend*': *A Matter-of-Fact Romance* (1856) and Catherine Helen Spence's *Clara Morison: a tale of South Australia During the Gold Fever* (1854), sharing also with the latter its focus on a female protagonist. Such didacticism is now almost unthinkable in popular novels but it was an expectation deeply embedded in the consciousness of the middle-class readers who were the main consumers of such fiction. The revised edition acknowledges this readerly expectation but rigorously edits these sections of the novel.

The novel also incorporates aspects of sensation and melodrama—at times grotesque—that were popular in mid-nineteenth-century English novels. The death scene in the graveyard where young Sam defends Maida, Bob Pragg's death with Maida as his witness, Maida's own death in the hospital and the fate of Captain Norwell in the lunatic asylum all combine to produce the revelation of previously hidden detail that is common to melodrama with the extravagant emotion and action of sensational fiction. This aspect of generic fiction, at least, is familiar to readers now as a standard convention found in, for instance, the genres of horror and fantasy fiction. There is an important argument to be made about *The Broad Arrow*'s melodrama that falls outside the bounds of this Introduction. Drawing on a nuanced understanding of this mode, developed from readings of nineteenth- and twentieth-century Australian novels, we might argue that Maida Gwynnham anticipates both the 'real or supposed persecution and self-imposed victimhood' of later protagonists of melodrama as well as '[t]heir triumphalism that arises from the sense of their own suppressed virtue'.[159]

The narrative also draws on the taste for stereotypes, doubles and pairings familiar in the popular fiction of the day: Maida Gwynnham becomes, after her conviction, Martha Grylls, suggesting the 'maid' imprisoned behind a 'grill'; Mary Doveton, whose ideal Christian innocence is reflected in her name suggestive of the symbolism of the dove, is the counterpart of Captain Norwell, a play on 'ne'er-do-well;' Emmeline and Bridget are cousins and doubles of each other matched by Emmeline's father Herbert, who is the Reverend (known in the family as 'Uncle Herbert'), and his brother George, who is the retired magistrate (known as 'Uncle Ev'); the Rev. Evelyn is a saintly Christian while his brother is a pragmatic rationalist; Mrs Evelyn, George's wife, formerly the suggestively named 'Clara M'Rock', is the stereotypical middle-class colonial snob and she is doubled by Bridget's mother, who is a stereotypical middle-class English snob. There are also parallels in figures absent from the plot: Maida's mother is absent through her earlier death; the Rev. Evelyn's wife has died and so Emmeline, like Maida, is motherless; Lucy Grenlow is motherless on being transported to Van Diemen's Land; Mary Doveton marries without a mother's advice.

The convict characters too have names that match their status and suggest their nature: Bob Pragg rhymes with 'brag' and 'lag;' Lucy Grenlow is 'brought low,' Mrs Gullem 'gulls' or deceives the guileless Lucy, (Mrs Gullem sadly disappears from the revised edition); others are known only by their surnames like Pridham and Bradley. Sarah Grubb, Jane Dawson and Ellen Bracket are interred on the convict hulk HMS *Anson* where they are supervised by Mrs Bowden, the 'Lady-Superintendent', Mrs Deputy and Miss Perkins, whose name Uncle Ev cannot resist shortening to 'Miss Perky'; while Sam, the young convict simpleton who defends Maida and tells a pathetic life story that leaves him without a family, acquires a surname only when his death by hanging is reported. In names and attitudes, the structure of convict society is shown as mirroring that of settler society: both have their hierarchies and prejudices; in each the characters attempt to make daily life possible; everywhere individual characters show their capacities for good and bad thought and action more subtly than we might have expected in a consciously popular work.

---

159 Peter Pierce, *Australian Melodramas: Thomas Keneally's Fiction* (St Lucia: University of Queensland Press, 1995), 164.

The Broad Arrow and history

The novel is known as a *roman à clef*. The author's pseudonym is itself coded: 'Oliné' is the last syllable of 'Caroline'[160] while 'Keese' is a pun on 'keys', and many of the characters are clearly identifiable historical figures who lived in Hobart between 1848 and 1853 when Leakey returned to Britain. In fact, Leakey's portraits are so accurate that *Walch's Literary Intelligencer*, the journal of the Hobart book publisher, commented, in reviewing a reissue of the novel in December 1901, that

> [i]n such a book, where the principal characters are drawn from life, the slight change of name is too flimsy a veil to hide the real persons, and especially this is the case in three instances. In the benevolent, lovable Mr Washington, who that knew him could fail to recognise George Washington Walker; in the Rev. Herbert Evelyn, [a] picture of the Rev. Mr Medland [Leakey's brother-in-law]; while in Dr Lamb, who can fail to recognise the Dr Agnew of those days . . .[161]

Walch's reviewer continues the exposé by noting that 'Oliné Keese' was the *nom de plume* of 'Miss Caroline Leakey, who, during her residence here, had exceptional opportunities of acquiring a knowledge of things as they were as distinct from what they appeared.' The reviewer might also have noted that some other historical personages make an appearance in the novel: Mrs Bowden, Matron of the HMS *Anson*, Frances Russell Nixon, Bishop of Tasmania, and Colonel Arthur, formerly the Lieutenant-Governor.[162] These recognisable characters are one of Leakey's strategies for making her novel and its representation of colonial life credible; by contrast, Marcus Clarke's *His Natural Life*, as Andrew McCann persuasively argues, 'foregrounds some of the ways in which a Gothic literary sensibility, drawing upon the Romantic, the sentimental and the melodramatic, could be deployed in Australia as a way of framing colonialism's intensely ambiguous relationship to its own normative foundations and claims to legitimacy.'[163]

Readers' interest in using the key to solve the puzzle of the novel's characters has been a standard approach in readings of the text. In 1947, Wilfred Hudspeth, a Hobart lawyer, amateur historian and member of the Royal Society, was in correspondence with the State Librarian, J.D.A. Collier, and W. Wolfhagen (of the establishment Hobart family) seeking to compile a complete list of Hobart persona appearing in the novel.[164] One disadvantage of this mode of reading is that it diminishes the writer's skill in fictionalising the characters and the context in which the action is located. While, 'no-one could fail to recognise', for

---

160 Cf. Within her family, Caroline Leakey's nickname was, apparently, Tarvine. See Leakey, *Clear Shining Light*, 28.

161 TAHO NS2849/1/22, 186. And with a gesture of commerical self-reflexivity, *Walch's Literary Intelligencer* cites its own review of the 1860 edition, bound '[i]n one thick volume. Specially got up for Tasmania,' commenting further, '[s]ince that day "The Broad Arrow" has appeared in many editions, the latest and cheapest being the one we now offer, bound in Cloth at *Half-a-Crown*, with an additional *Fourpence* if sent by Post.'

162 See Winter (esp. 140–8) for a detailed survey of the Tasmanian persona.

163 Chapter 5, 'Colonial Gothic: Sensibility, Sovereignty and Settler-colonialism,' Andrew McCann, *Marcus Clarke's Bohemia: Literature and Modernity in Colonial Melbourne* (Carlton: Melbourne University Press, 2004): 185–219. https://bit.ly/2PKVm7S.

164 TAHO, NS690/1/98. W. H. Hudspeth's Historical Files. Notes on 'Broad Arrow' by Olina [sic] Keese.

example, the Quaker George Washington Walker, readers might fail to appreciate the deft sifting together of real and imaginative qualities in other characters by applying a template of Hobart society to the sweep of the novel.

The character of Clara M'Rock, who marries Mr Evelyn Senior (the Rev. Herbert's brother), appears in Chapter 18, although we have heard about her before then. She is a 'native, and had the fair skin, slender figure, and long limbs of the Tasmanian, with the not less characteristic, but more painful colonial feature—prematurely decayed and broken teeth'. Despite having being 'educated in England from her twelfth year'—intended to militate against her colonialism—her conversation is comically domestic, she is full of superior airs and her horizons are unimaginatively fixed on matrimony. Later, in Chapter 29, she displays an intransigent anti-Catholicism. Mrs Evelyn may be a gesture toward Julia Sorell: the names ending in feminine -a, both are native-born, and Thomas Griffiths Wainewright's portrait (1846), while conventional, also shows a disarmingly beautiful face.[165] Annie Baxter Dawbin records in her diary (1846, the same year as Wainewright's painting) that Julia Sorell 'is much fallen off exceedingly in her appearance, her two front teeth being decayed alters her very much'[166] and Sorell's anti-Catholicism is reliably attested.[167] Julia Sorell also attracted a certain notoriety: her mother had deserted the family; she had made and broken a number of engagements before her marriage to Thomas Arnold; she had a reputation for temper, willfulness and determined independence.[168] But Leakey's characterisation is more adept and ambitious than the simple transposition from historical figures that the genre of *roman á clef* may imply. It is the protagonist, Maida Gwynnham, not Mrs Evelyn, who is motherless, who commits a sexual and ethical transgression, who continues to attract masculine attention (Reverend Herbert Evelyn, especially in Chapter 27; Mr Evelyn Chapter 28; Captain Norwell Chapter 37) and whose 'intemperate,' 'wilful' 'tempestuous' and 'mysterious' nature is a powerful driver in the narrative.

Characterisation works by producing a kind of hybridity of historical data, generic convention and narrative imperative. The novel clearly distinguishes between the elements of affective complexity and intensity of persona needed in a protagonist and a lesser character who carries a subplot, provides social critique from a different angle (Mrs Evelyn is for using convicts as free labour, while her husband is pro-rehabilitation) and is a source of humour, thereby providing a foil for the drama of the major characters. The revised edition diminishes both the development of Mrs Evelyn as a comic character and the counterpoint between characters of different narrative magnitude by heavily editing Chapter 18—a hilarious episode about feeding geese is omitted—and so Mrs Evelyn survives simply as a caricature.

Among the minor characters, in Chapter 29 ('Port Arthur—O.P.S.O.—The *Kangaroo*'), the Rev. Evelyn is in conversation with a fellow cleric, Mr Harelick. Among the topics they canvass is that of seeking redress for perceived wrongdoings by convict chaplains within an acknowledged faulty system of convict administration. As the two clerics analyse their

---

165 Sorell, *Governor, William and Julia* Sorell, 122 (private hands).
166 In Frost, ed., *Face*, 93; Baxter Dawbin also confirms the unsatisfactory nature of colonial dentistry, 105–7.
167 Mrs Humphry Ward, *A Writer's Recollections* (London, 1918) cited in Bertram ed., *New Zealand Letters*, 233.
168 See fn 94.

difficulties in ministering to spiritual welfare within a penal institution, they dramatise one of the novel's pervasive thematics: the inevitable corruption of power exercised by hierarchised individuals. As Harelick asserts:

'Reports of us reach government only through its own agents … we are represented as the molesting party and not the molested party … "A dissatisfied, troublesome set, are the convict chaplains," were Turbot's very words of us, Evelyn.'

Evelyn's reply pinpoints the systemic problem: 'no improvement in convict difficulties and evils can be expected till a different class of men is chosen to work the system, nor while so much irresponsible power is vested in one man.' 'Now there's Turbot,' the redoubtable Harelick continues, 'except for severity of temper, what fitness is there in him to recommend him for the important position he holds?' Turbot, it emerges, is a 'third-class officer' promoted beyond his abilities.

Turbot is a play on the name of Sir John Eardley-Wilmot (1783–1847), a former jurist appointed lieutenant-governor of Van Diemen's Land (1843–47) who engaged Bishop Francis Nixon in a rancorous dispute over the power of convict chaplains, referenced here in the verbatim quotation from Turbot and directly impacting on Leakey's brother-in-law, Rev. James Medland, himself a religious instructor. Eardley-Wilmot's manner is recorded as marked by 'acerbity'; his relations with colonists 'sour'; his administration 'slap-dash'; his personal morals 'licentious'.[169] Between 1844 and 1852, the commandant of Port Arthur Penal Station, where Evelyn and Harelick are in conversation, was William Champ (1808–1892), a former soldier who succeeded Captain O'Hara Booth and was 'universally acknowledged [for his] talents, his zeal, energy and unflinching integrity, [and] his character for justice, even among the worst description of the convict class'.[170] The novel combines elements of these two influential figures, thus extracting the confrontation between the corruption of power and the efficacy of spiritual care from a local occurrence to a more general moral concern. Leakey's narrative technique, combined with the requisite tact on a matter with public and private implications, is further obscured by Townsend Mayer's edit, which omits Harelick's analysis of the system and the position of convict chaplains, culminating in Turbot's opinion, thus truncating a discussion that is initiated earlier in Chapter 18 and dislocating one of the thematic elements cohering in the novel's structure. The edit also obscures Leakey's ability to select and conflate character traits, as in Turbot, as well as to select and diffuse them, as in Clara M'Rock and Maida Gwynnham.

At the level of the sentence and the energetic beat of the narrative, Leakey's novel is full of authentic domestic detail about the preparing and serving of meals, the dress codes of immigrants and settlers, the management of households, the feeling of using bed linen stamped with 'B.O.' (issued by the Board of Ordinance). This same commitment to accurately observed detail underpins the descriptions of convict life that Leakey develops as a telling counterpoint to the life of her middle-class family. The novel gives graphic accounts of the conditions under which convicts travelled aboard ship as they were transported to Hobart and moved on to convict stations such as Port Arthur. There is precise detail about the conditions of work for various kinds of chain-gangs, the colour of uniforms worn by

---

169 'John Eardley Eardley-Wilmot,' *Australian Dictionary of Biography*, http://adb.anu.edu.au/biography/eardley-wilmot-sir-john-eardley-2015.

170 William Champ, *Australian Dictionary of Biography*, https://bit.ly/2J9t4kN.

convicts to signal their status, the various systems of secondary punishment, the changes that accompanied a convict's progress through his or her sentence, the different conditions for male and female convicts and, again foreshadowing *His Natural Life*, Leakey's novel considers a broad range of convicts across a diverse spectrum of crimes, types, classes, nationalities and individuals. Often, the power of the novel's description comes from its neat precision: the account of the convict-drawn railway at Port Arthur, for example, is striking because it is observed by a passenger who simply describes what she sees without, at first, registering the fact that men are substituted for animals.

This documentary realism was recognised as one of the novel's strengths in reviews of the first edition. *Walch's Literary Intelligencer* commented:

> [t]he most terrible problems of society and government [deriving from convictism] remain yet unsolved; and there have been terrible mistakes and inhumanities which must be avoided in the future. What these are can only be ascertained by the induction of facts … It is to a transcript of life and fact, and not to ideal speculations that we must look for the solvent of our difficulties, and the book therefore that honestly and intelligently attempts to contribute such material is doing right good service to humanity, now will it be scorned by the thoughtful reader because it comes in the garb of fiction and veils its earnestness of purpose in the lightness of a story.[171]

A review from another popular literary journal made a similarly pertinent comment from another point of view.

> As regards the pictures of Tasmanian life, they tally so exactly with all accounts which have reached us from those who have visited the country, that we have not hesitated to apply to them the title of photographs. They may be shortly summed up:—a glorious climate, a luxurious fertility, beautiful scenery, handsome houses, rich furniture, the last fashions from Paris carried, of course, to the extreme of gorgeousness, sumptuous tables, plenty of everything … but none of them all nor all together able to make up for the constant mistrust, the habitual precautions, the locked gates … This picture may be overdrawn, but it reminds us strongly, nevertheless, of an expression we heard dropped by an ex-Tasmanian: 'It will take two generations to make that atmosphere pleasant to be breathed by an Englishman.'[172]

The *Athenaeum*'s review made the argument for the novel's historical veracity:

> [i]t has left no doubt on our minds of being in its main features perfectly true; indeed, throughout the book there is a breadth and a vitality about the scenes and characters, which give the impression of their being transcripts from the real life described. The author has written from her heart about what she has seen and known and perfectly understands; the portions which she has invented fail, or, at least, do not ring full and true like the other parts.[173]

---

171 TAHO, NS2849/1/1 *Walch's Literary Intelligencer*, March 1860, 169.
172 *The Literary Gazette* (21 May 1859): 620–21.
173 See fn 105.

These reviews give us an invaluable insight not only into the realist tastes of nineteenth-century middle-class readers, but also into the sensitive balance readers maintained between fact and fiction. That consciousness of such a boundary is perhaps nowhere more evident than in *Walch's Literary Intelligencer's* assertion that

> *The Broad Arrow* does not pretend to regale us with the aroma of wickedness. It does not make crime either comic or romantic . . . Such abominations as the "Mysteries" of Eugène Sue with the whole pack of ribald imitators, are enough to sap the morals of a nation.[174]

The reviewer follows with an apology to Leakey for this disclaimer, made 'on her behalf': 'it was necessary, because somehow, this bad favour [sic] has become with all fiction that touches crimes, and we know that the mere title of the book has suggested misconceptions of its character'.[175] Then, as now, for 'abominations' of taste read cultural capital; for 'morals of a nation' read dominant ideology.

While *The Broad Arrow's* contemporary readers had a taste for realist detail, Leakey's outstanding strategy for authenticity and credibility comes from an aspect of her writing that has, to date, remained largely unremarked: the diversity and accuracy of the novel's language. Bruce Moore cites commentary on dialect in Leakey's novel to establish a cause for the development of pronunciation; one of the passages cited by Moore also appears in a discussion of the 'Australian twang'.[176] *The Broad Arrow* might stand as an historical record for the usage of different kinds of diction, accents, idiolects and registers in colonial Australia.

In his classic study of Australian language, Sidney J. Baker comments on Marcus Clarke's use of language to authenticate his vision of his hero Rufus Dawes's hell: Clarke used what he called 'the horrible slang of the prison ship' to underscore the gothic horror of his novel.[177] Leakey's goal is rather different: she aims to represent a broad cross-section of society, across social classes, as it is shaped by convictism and so her novel gains credence from the particularities of speech in characters who are socially, politically, and individually distinct.[178] The heroine, Maida Gwynnham, speaks the language of her middle-class upbringing and it is her speech, among other features, that marks her out among the other convicts. The speech of her fellow convicts, Lucy Grenlow, Robert Sanders, Bob Pragg, and Sam Tonkin, combines convict slang, underworld slang, flash talk, colonial phrasing and, at times, the slang of particular English counties, as in the speech of Lucy Grenlow's mother or Mrs Gullem, or that of particular nationalities, as in the case of Opal the Chinese convict.

---

174 For an essential reading of the relations between criminality, Romantic tropes, capital and the nation-state, see McCann, especially chapters 4 and 5.

175 TAHO, NS2849/1/1 *Walch's Literary Intelligencer*, March 1860, 169.

176 Bruce Moore 'The Dialect Evidence,' *Australian Journal of Linguistics*, 24.1 (2004): 22–3; Anon., 'From the Past: The Australian Twang,' *Ozwords*. 4.1 (1998): 6, The Australian National Dictionary Centre.

177 Sidney J. Baker, *The Australian language: an examination of the English language and English speech as used in Australia, from convict days to the present, with special reference to the growth of indigenous idiom and its use by Australian writers* (Melbourne: Sun Books, 1970): 24.

178 On the manners of colonial Hobart society, see the discussion of *The Broad Arrow* in Penny Russell, *Savage or Civilised? Manners in Colonial Society* (Sydney: University of New South Wales Press, 2010): 105–12.

Leakey had a very precise ear for language as well as a keen sense of observation. In her characters' speech there is none of the literary brilliance of Charles Dickens's idiolects. Instead, we hear a representation of ordinary speech that has been carefully selected both to persuade us of its authenticity and to advance the narrative. Uncle Ev remarks on the diversity of accents to be heard in Hobarton as he conducts Bridget on a walk about the town:

> The Irish brogue heard today is to-morrow changed for the broad Scotch accent; the Devonshire drawl is soon forgotten in the London affectation; the Somersetshire z's are lost in the Yorkshire oo's.

A number of words in Leakey's novel predate entries in the *Australian National Dictionary* while others, such as 'davvered' to describe faded flowers, do not appear. Elsewhere examples of the novel's dialect words are found only in Joseph Wright's *The English Dialect Dictionary*, Eric Partridge's various dictionaries of historical slang, underworld language and unconventional English, or are listed as rare usages in the *Oxford English Dictionary*. All dictionaries and glossaries have their limitations, of course, but it is also true that had Leakey's novel been available (as Clarke's has usually been) then our understanding of English as it developed through colonial times in Australia would have been extended. Inevitably, the meaning of some phrases has been pieced together from various sources and this remains a speculative process. Still other words and phrases (frustratingly) are apparently no longer traceable since entries are not available in early glossaries like James Hardy Vaux's list of late eighteenth- to early nineteenth-century flash talk, or more recent compilations such as Amanda Laugesen's study of convict words.[179] What does the phrase 'if she kicks up her guineas to the doctor' (Ch. 11) mean? In context, the sense is as a slur. Its use by a transported convict woman, on-board ship, suggests a British rather than Tasmanian idiom. If so, where is it attested? Is it specific to transported convicts or more generally prison talk? Why is the scent of eucalyptus trees described as 'catty perfume' (Ch. 29)? Against her usual practice of structural editing, Townsend Mayer omits this single word. Or 'bastely', in the sentence, 'Never fear, miss, it's too bastely for aught else; I've quite used 'em up' (Ch. 18) referring to a soiled kerchief. Although the adverbial form is not attested, perhaps this is a formation from 'baste', to thrash, flog, beat soundly and here suggesting the kerchief has been used repeatedly.[180] Such idioms appear tied to specific registers—slang, convict, dialect—but a phrase like 'She was never very famous, so they who knew her at home said' (Ch. 28) referring to a convict patient at the hospital who

---

179 *Australian National Dictionary*, ed W. S. Ramson, 1st edn (Melbourne: Oxford University Press, 1988), available online http://andc.anu.edu.au/node/13927; ed Bruce Moore, 2nd edn (South Melbourne, Oxford University Press, 2016). Eric Partridge, *Dictionary of slang and unconventional English : colloquialisms and catch-phrases, solecisms and catachreses, nicknames, vulgarisms and such Americanisms as have been naturalized. (With supp. material as Addenda)* 6th edn (London: Routledge, 1967). Joseph Wright, *The English Dialect Dictionary : being the complete vocabulary of all dialect words still in use, or known to have been in use during the last two hundred years : founded on the publications of the English Dialect Society, and on a large amount of material never before printed* (London: Oxford University Press, 1923). James Hardy Vaux, *The Memoirs of James Hardy Vaux: including his vocabulary of the Flash language*, ed and introduction, Noel McLachlan (London: Heinemann, 1964). Amanda Laugesen, *Convict Words: Language in Early Colonial Australia* (Melbourne: Oxford University Press, 2002).

180 Wright, *The English Dialect Dictionary*, 180.

has lost her reason, rather than being some kind of celebrity, seems too unexceptional to appear in the word lists of specific registers and yet, in this context at least, evades the usual semantic connections of 'famous' as an adjective.

Where the novel moves into political issues, such as the debate surrounding transportation, the language shifts into the register of morally informed public debate, again across a range of social classes. In the speech of George Evelyn, the retired magistrate and social reformer, readers hear the language of a middle-class person of moral conviction who is frustrated by the rigidities of colonial government—in which exasperation he was, surely, not alone. George provides a detailed account of the different effects of class in the home country and in the new world, and he does so in language that, later, becomes familiar in the expression of democratic politics in Australia. Arguments for and against convictism and transportation, and their injurious effects on a new community and, by implication, a new nation, are keenly dramatised by a range of characters whose individual moral and economic investments are faithfully portrayed—often in single phrases.

In George Evelyn's impassioned arguments against transportation and convictism we hear the same language and sentiments, including the analogy of slavery, found in, for instance, the final section of John West's historical account of transportation and its ethics (Section xxvii), first published in 1852.[181] By contrast, Aunt Evelyn, George's wife, makes the arguments in favour of transportation on account of the cheap labour it provides, in the same terms that may be found in Louisa Anne Meredith's *My Home in Tasmania*, published first as newspaper journalism and then collected in book form, also in 1852.[182] Uncle Herbert, the Anglican minister, and his daughter Emmeline voice the language of religious objection to transportation and in the horrified and often confused recoil of Bridget, their cousin, we hear the reaction of an ordinary middle-class Englishwoman for whom the whole experience of convictism is shocking. These voices are important because they represent the views and attitudes of a dominant political class, articulated in the public domain of the day; in fact, it would be difficult to underestimate the pervasiveness of connections between class and convictism in all its legal, economic, emotional and corporeal realities. Through media such as colonial newspapers, published histories, and the minutes of public meetings, these were the voices that brought pressure to bear on the official decision-makers on, for example, the Select Committee on Transportation (1837–38), chaired by Sir William Molesworth, in its enquiry into and eventual recommendation against transportation.[183]

At the other end of the social spectrum, Leakey chooses a working-class constable's wife at Port Arthur to comment on the extermination of Aborigines.

> I can't bear to know there's suffering going on; and 'tisn't only because they [convicts] are my own flesh and blood; I was just the same time back, when I was young, when the Aborgenes was served so shameful ... Oh Miss! They was shot down like rabid

---

181 *The History of Tasmania*, ed. A. G. L. Shaw (Sydney: Angus and Robertson, 1971 [1852]).
182 Mrs Charles Meredith [Louisa Anne Meredith], *My Home in Tasmania, During a Residence of Nine Years* (London: John Murray, 1852), 39-48.
183 See West, Part 9; *Report from the Select Committee of the House of Commons on Transportation Together with a Letter from the Archbishop of Dublin on the Same Subject and Notes*, Sir William Molesworth, Bart (London: Henry Hooper, 1838) includes 'Minutes of Evidence, Appendix, and Index.' Part 1: Evidence of James Mudie.

dogs; hunted on their own grounds just like kangaroos. I don't know the rights of it; I suppose it was needful, or 'twouldn't have been done: but, child as I was, I couldn't like it better on that account.

This image of hunted animals is taken up in the Rev. Evelyn's further commentary on this episode, when he laments '[t]hey [the Aborigines] bequeath us a legacy for which we shall have to answer when God makes inquisition for blood.'[184] We might compare this language with an analogue from contemporary poetry to gain a sense of the different effects that might be achieved. 'The Tasmanian Aborigine's Lament and Remonstrance', credited to 'Auster' and published in the colonial newspaper the *Courier* in 1847, begins:

Fair island of my birth, thy distant rocks
Call forth the tenderest feelings of my heart;
Although the sigh of thee my yearning mocks,
For cruel waves thee from thy children part.

Ah! White man, why—Oh! Why thy children's home
Dids't thou abandon, to drive us from ours?[185]

Even the language of the least dramatic of characters, whom we see usually only within the family—Charlie and Baby—is revealing in its intimacy. Young Charlie proudly announces that he is a 'gum-tree' rather than a 'silly English oak' in a comparison that draws on emblematic figures of nature from the old world and the new and is delivered with all the confident energy of a new generation. Baby's baby-talk recognises Maida's loneliness as a prisoner within a family; and there is a touching moment of paternal tenderness when George Evelyn remarks to his son that 'persons are not always sorry when they weep, Charlie, boy'.

Again, we might compare the language of the constable's wife with that recorded in a memoir set down in 1892 by S.B. Emmett in which he remembers seeing Aboriginal people in the streets of Hobart.

---

184 Cf. 'While I was in the colony the number of children under instruction was about two hundred. Nearly all of them were the children of convicts, and as healthy-looking as, considering their early upbringing, could have been expected. Amongst them were three children—all girls, if I remember rightly—whom one could not look upon without melancholy interest. They were as black as negroes, but the cast of features was not Ethiopian, but Australian . . . The colonial records show that they [Tasmanian Aborigines] were most cruelly treated, being for a long time shot down without scruple by the convict shepherds, on the ground that they stole and killed sheep . . .' (Arnold, *Passages*, 135–6). Cf. James Backhouse, *A Narrative of a Visit to the Australian Colonies* (London: Hamilton, Adams and Co., 1843); James Backhouse Walker, *Papers on Tasmania: Papers Presented to the Royal Society* (Hobart: William Grahame, Government Printer, 1884–96); H. Roth (Henry Ling), Marion E. Butler, James Backhouse Walker, J. G. Garson (John George), *The Aborigines of Tasmania* (Halifax: F. King & Sons, 1899), https://bit.ly/2CAdei4.
185 'Auster', 'The Tasmanian Aborigine's Lament and Remonstrance When in Sight of his Native Land from Flinders Island', *The Courier* (Hobart), Sat. 9 Oct 1847, 4; reprinted in *The Poets' Discovery. Nineteenth-Century Australia in Verse*, eds Richard D. Jordan and Peter Pierce (Melbourne: Melbourne University Press, 1990), 148–9. See also an important introduction to the section on Tasmanian verse (123–8).

In 1831 I went to school at James [Sprent's] in Liverpool Street. There were a number of blacks camped at G.A. Robinsons [sic] house in Elizabeth Street. I used to buy a two penny loaf & on my way home to Beaulieu where we then lived, used to stop to talk to the blacks & give the loaf to Eumarrah, who wd pat me on the head & say something in his own language by way of thanks. They use to put up a spade & standing 40 yards (?) off throw a [bulbrush] [sic] or thin stick at it, the object being to send it through the hole in the handle & hit a black who had his face behind it.[186]

Such a comparison between a novelistic representation of speech and the language of memory set down through oral transmission and written transcription discloses something of the speech rhythms, intimate details and ordinary meanings of the colonial imaginary in nineteenth-century colonial culture. Both these texts allow us to see, too, the ways in which personal details in individual lives become the material of literary and social histories, coming down to us in a process of interpretive translation or transition that is both tenuous and valuable.

The diction and phraseology of the Bible that surfaces continually in the novel not only authenticates the speech of the religious characters, but also shows just how deeply and practically that language suffused daily life. For middle-class characters like the Rev. Evelyn, his daughter Emmeline, his brother George Evelyn and his niece Bridget D'Urban, the Bible is not so much a sacred book—though it is certainly a source of wisdom—as a practical guide to daily living that gives moral shape to their conduct and ethical force to their decisions. It is a language that is so familiar as to be a natural part of speech. As Emmeline remarks to her cousin, 'Scripture language is so much more expressive than any other; it says so much in a few words, that one uses it without intending it sometimes.' For the convict characters, as the novel's characters remark, the words of the Bible are remote and unyielding and the novel recognises that those who most need its consolation have least access to it.

Elsewhere, in, for instance, those sections that rehearse the debate about sexual morality, readers hear the impassioned speech of those social moralists who argued the urgent need for compassion and support. One of the least obvious but arguably most powerful strands in the novel derives from this ethical debate: Maida Gwynnham is a woman who is brought up by her father after the death of her mother. But even his best intentions and abiding paternal love cannot prepare Maida for the experience of sexual desire and masculine deceit that will lead to her demise as a 'fallen woman', a forger and a convicted murderer. The tension is between the didacticism of the plot—Maida's conviction and transportation—and her refusal to deny either her sexual experience with Norwell or the strength of her own power for self-determination. One clear implication is that it is the role of women-as-mothers to educate young women in sexual politics, and the novel strives to find a language for such an education since, as the novel also makes clear, the language of religious conviction cannot resolve this tension. We might compare the language of Leakey's women characters in this respect with, for instance, that of Kezia Elizabeth Hayter, a twenty-four-year-old migrant to Van Diemen's Land in 1841, whose

---

186 Memories of S. B. Emmett (son of H. I. Emmett), who arrived as baby with his father by *Regalia* in 1819, as written down by J. B. Walker, 7 August 1892 (Inc. memories of aborigines, the old wharf, early settlers' homes). 1 mss. 7pp. plus letter, University [of Tasmania] Archives, RS131/16.

'morbidly guilt-stricken vision of religion' shaped her sense of being a wife and mother and is revealed in her diary:

> I am very discontented with myself . . . alas what a daily warfare a Christian's life is . . . I [am] much more convinced that I have much to learn to subdue in myself before I shall be worthy to be the most obedient and gentle wife to you I desire to be . . . [I yearn] to throw all my energies into the quiet . . . of woman's province Home oh how I love you.[187]

No character in the novel speaks in such a fashion.

There are many more detailed accounts of early life in Tasmania than Leakey's novel and historians of convicts in the colonial period from Lloyd Robson to Henry Reynolds to Miriam Dixon and Kay Daniels to Ian Brand, Hamish Maxwell-Stewart and Ian Duffield have drawn our attention to a wide range of contemporary documents ranging from colonial despatches to convict records, to individual histories like that of John West, produced at the time when Tasmania was becoming a member of the federation that would become Australia. Leakey's novel does not set out to give us a detailed and logical account of, for instance, the assignment system under which convicts were employed by settlers as cheap domestic and agricultural labourers or, in the later experimental probation system, contracted out to settlers to work in gangs.[188] Instead, Maida's 'history', as the novel is subtitled, dramatises the vulnerabilities of convict women on assignment. Maida is taken into the household of 'Mrs Patterley' of New Town (Chapter 31), who warns her against any 'improper conduct' towards her son: 'I've sent away ever so many Government women on his account, they're such a vile set; it's quite a nuisance to have them about.' The reason soon becomes obvious: young Patterley sexually harasses Maida, who, when she strikes him across the face, is convicted to be malnourished by

> skillet [a mixture of flour and water], wasted by severe labour, and worried by every species of indignity; but not all this until she had first been subdued by a protracted confinement in the dark cells.

Nor is the novel interested in settling disputes of historical detail: did convict women have their hair shorn as a punishment, as a matter of course, or of hygiene? Daniels argues that '[h]ead-shaving and hair-cutting present an interesting microcosm of the way attitudes to punishing convict women changed as policies came to reflect an increased concern with reformation and with constructing appropriately "feminine" behaviour' (112).[189] In Leakey's novel, the cutting of a convict's hair is a simple fact Maida accepts; she is more concerned to ask the Rev. Herbert to save two locks so that she may send one to her father. Later, the regrowth of her hair—'Your hair's a-grow'd butiful, my dear'—becomes a metaphor for Maida's progress from the female factory to the Evelyns' home.

---

187 Cited in Miriam Dixon, *The Real Matilda. Women and Identity in Australia 1788–1975* (Ringwood: Penguin, 1976), 68.

188 See Ian Brand, *The Convict Probation System: Van Diemen's Land 1839–1854* (Hobart: Blubber Head Press, 1990).

189 Kay Daniels, *Convict Women* (St Leonards: Allen & Unwin, 1998), 112.

The domestic reality of the Ticket of Leave system provides one of the novel's most humorous episodes. Chapter 25, in which Robert Sanders achieves his ticket, conducts 'the robing ceremony' to don his newly acquired clothes, and proceeds in to family prayers 'shaking from his head an overwhelming effect of bergamot and from his waistcoat a strong perfume of boy's love' is effective precisely because it parodies the affectations of the free settlers Sanders thinks to emulate.[190]

Leakey's novel is also a feminist novel, but not because it tells the story of a woman protagonist, nor for theoretical or abstract reasons. *The Broad Arrow* does not, for instance, promote a version of the New Woman who would emerge towards the end of the nineteenth century, nor does it offer legal or economic critique in the tradition of Mary Wollstonecraft or Elizabeth Gaskell. There is no feminist utopia here. The novel's feminism rests, first, with its insistence that social values have their beginning in the domestic sphere where women have primary responsibility. The education of Charlie and Baby in the home matters because, as the novel shows, this is where Charlie's ambitions for himself as an adult member of society are shaped. It is women who are responsible for providing the ways and means by which future citizens are produced: the ethics of women's work are not only personal but connect immediately and directly to politics and the ways that the policies and machinery of government shape a nation's citizens. Women and their work matter to the social polity.

Second, the novel recognises that women, like men, experience sexual desire, and promotes the view that Christian morality has a duty to show compassion towards 'fallen women': that is, the Christian who does not show compassion towards the woman whose sexual desire is betrayed simply betrays her once again. This is a complex point in the novel because it is not simply that all sinners deserve Christian love, although they do. Rather, in Leakey's novel, women characters are not simply the objects of Christian morality as it is pronounced by male clerics; the novel suggests instead that Maida is 'criminalised' precisely because she refuses to betray her lover. This makes sexual desire a powerful force, driving the narrative forward and underwriting many scenes, like those with young Mr Patterley. Thus, the novel eschews the entirely predictable and conventional happy ending in which a repentant Maida would become, upon receiving a pardon and forgiving Captain Norwell, the wife of the Rev. Evelyn.

A third aspect of the novel's feminism is its assumption that the story of a woman convict is a suitable way of dramatising one of the important political debates of the day. In her preface, Leakey noted that transportation had already ceased by the time the novel was published; 'the System' was no longer filling Tasmania with convicts. But its effects were still palpably in place and, for Leakey and her readers, it is the story of a woman's life that can hold up a mirror to society to expose its hypocrisies and inequities.

---

190 'A form of authority granted to mainly well-behaved convicts to allow them to work before the expiration of their sentence. Convicts could offer their labour for hire or be self-employed. They had to report at set intervals to local magistrates, and to inform them of any changes in employment. The ticket contained identifying information about the convict including physical marks and characteristics and details of their criminal history. Convicts could acquire property but they could only reside within a designated area. The system operated in Australia and similar schemes existed in other penal colonies.' *Australian Convict Sites. World Heritage Nomination* (Canberra: Department of the Environment, Water, Heritage and the Arts, 2008), 208.

While Leakey's novel, in the many details of its language, character and incident, is persuasive in its authenticity and its careful documentary realism, it is, nevertheless, a novel. 'Maida Gwynnham' never existed. Mary McLauchlan, the only woman convicted of infanticide in Tasmania, was tried at the Hobart Town Supreme Court on 15 April 1830, found guilty and hanged four days later. She had been a native of Saltcoats in Ayrshire, Scotland, a 'servant of all work; plain cook' and married with two children.[191] In the account of her execution published in the *Hobart Town Courier* on 24 April, the reporter draws attention to her dying 'contrite and resigned':

> [t]he mental agony which this wretched woman suffered is said to have endured previous to the execution, is described as truly horrible . . . when the dread hour approached, she was resigned and penitent . . . While pregnant she was often heard to wish that the infant she bore might not be born alive, and there appeared no other perceptible motive to incite her to the dreadful crime of murder, on the little innocent offspring of her own bosom, than that of malice towards the father. How awful . . .[192]

The Broad Arrow does not tell this story—powerful though it is. Nor does it tell the curious story of Mary O'Donnell, transported (with her two children) for larceny, whose shipboard conduct was recorded as 'good and orderly', not attached 'with the least fault' but on the contrary 'without exception quiet and well behaved and worthy of a good situation'. Yet, in September 1828, a jury found that 'a male child which had been found dead . . . had been wilfully murdered by Mary O'Donnell, its mother'. Edward Culley, allegedly the child's father, was held in custody but then released. Mary O'Donnell, pronounced 'not in a fit state to be removed', remained in custody at Lanhern, 'where she receive[d] the most humane treatment from Mrs Field and Capt. Cooling'.[193] O'Donnell was never prosecuted for this crime and, in September 1832, was 'Free by Servitude'.

Instead, Leakey's novel shows what Raymond Williams once called the 'structure of feeling' in a particular community as it struggles with its history at a particular time and place.[194] Leakey's novel aims to convey how the little community of free settlers and convicts who make up her version of Hobart Town in the late 1840s to early 1850s think and feel about the 'facts' of history that make up their daily lives at a moment when the dominant or official ideology of convictism was being resisted and moving towards change. This structure of feeling emerges from the individual lives of free settlers, convicts, adults, children, servants and masters as it is refracted through the lives of those characters. The novel is concerned not so much with the official system that institutionalised convictism in colonial society as with the thoughts and feelings of the individuals whose lives made up that society. Crucially, Leakey's novel aims to capture the feeling of lived experience, the interplay of attitudes and values, and a dynamic sense of action and belief that is the material of imaginative literature. To write such a novel, Leakey risks unsettling the separate trajectories of romance and *Bildungsroman* by working them together with

---

191 Phillip Tardif, *Notorious Strumpets and Dangerous Girls: Convict Women in Van Diemen's Land 1803–29* (North Ryde: Collins/Angus & Robertson, 1990), 1565–6. See also single line entry at TAHO, Conduct Records, CON40/1/5. McLauchlan's description is given at CON19/1/13, 30.

192 Tardif, *Notorious Strumpets,* 1758–9.

193 Tardif, *Notorious Strumpets,* 926–7.

194 Raymond Williams, *Marxism and Literature* (Oxford: Oxford University Press, 1977), 128–35.

the story of a convict woman. She offers readers a minutely observed and recorded, passionately argued and imaginatively conceived narrative. *The Broad Arrow; Being Passages from the History of Maida Gwynnham, a Lifer*, records a dynamic moment of convictism and the capacity of the novel form to think through the social and affective challenges of that historical moment.

A Note on the Text

Editing this text, in light of Paul Eggert's call for textual scholarship and editorial procedure that 'models our understanding of works on their material forms, their chronologies of production and in terms of the agents who originally produced them, in their successive versions,'[1] presents unique challenges that require some detail in developing a rationale. As Eggert also concedes, a rapprochement between literary critical approaches and the 'new material-cultural emphasis [that] has been a hallmark of the recent phase of book history'[2]— leaves some theoretical problems remaining. In addition, *The Broad Arrow* poses some challenges to existing textual theory and practice that are visible only now that an edition has been prepared. The first of those challenges is what sort of edition can respond to the particular elements presented by the extant texts?

This edition reconstructs the first edition of *The Broad Arrow; Being Passages from the History of Maida Gwynnham, a Lifer* (1859) [hereafter F] and displays abridgements to that text made by Gertrude Townsend Mayer (in 1886) for the second edition (1887) [hereafter R].

F and R are the only versions extant: together they represent all the textual variants. To date, no holograph or correspondence between author and editor for either edition or record of in-house copy-editing survives. The novel was not serialised prior to or in combination with publication in book form. Similarly, to date, no instructions, proofs or correspondance, in-house or between other parties survived for R. While the 'Preface' in F alludes to the chronology of writing the text, there is no inference made about authorial intention regarding the text. In the absence of an authorial manuscript, F represents the primary text.

Even more significant are the bibliographic data: R was produced and published after the death of the author, Caroline Leakey, but under the same pseudonym, Oliné Keese, as F. Thus, R does not have the status of an authorial revision: it is an editorial revision achieved by significant structural editing thus changing the length, shape, genre of the narrative in F. Reissues of the novel, however, follow the R text: F was not republished. In Eggert's sense of successive versions, then, R becomes the work known by the title and attains a kind of primacy.

The present text, thus, seems to evade D. C. Greetham's distinction between '*critical or non-critical*' where a critical text is an 'attempt to establish a text' and non-critical is 'simply to reproduce a text already in existence.'[3] There are no documentary witnesses on which to 'establish a text' that is, reconstruct the authorial text. While the present text

---

1   Paul Eggert, *Biography of a Book. Henry Lawson's* While the Billy Boils (Sydney: Sydney University Press; Philadelphia: Pennsylvania State University Press, 2013), 351.
2   Eggert, *Biography of a Book*, 350.
3   D. C. Greetham, *Textual* Scholarship. *An Introduction*, Garland Reference Library of the Humanities, vol. 1417 (New York and London: Garland, 1994), 347.

does 'reproduce a text already in existence,' this is not a parallel edition in which the two texts—F and R—are reproduced separately for the purposes of comparison. Instead, this text has required 'a subjective interpretation of the available evidence' to produce a single text that comprises F and R. Given that R was produced, almost entirely, through structural (rather than copy-) editing of F, occasions requiring a choice between textual variants are infrequent. However, where there are variant readings, critical judgment has usually preferred the F reading over that from R.

A similar privileging of authorial intentionality makes the term 'eclectic edition' inappropriate. 'The most systematic modern form of eclectic edition is based on *authorial intention* and derives from Greg's notion that textual authority should be divided between accidentals (punctuation, spelling, etc.) and substantives (the words).'[4] No attempt is made here to establish authorial intention: rather F is taken as a primary text, rather than an authorised or definitive text.

There are two further points: the unusual status of the novel as the first and only such work by the author, means there is no prose fiction context in which to locate the novel and so there are no other comparable works against which to make editorial decisions regarding, for example, emendation. Second, implicit in this process are two further assumptions: that a text—any text—reliably conveys an author's intentions that can be recovered and that some kind of evolutionary model may be invoked as a basis for preferring one (earlier) variant over another (later) one. In this case, even if comparison were made between earlier and later prose writings, that comparison would depend upon dissimilar genres (novel and religious tract), different modalities (fictional and hortatory) and different scales (the full-length novel and a kind of *petit récit*, a modest 'little narrative' that attests to singularities rather than the grand scale of major narrative).

In sum, this edition is a critical edition of the text; there is no attempt to discover authorial intentionality; the first edition [F] has the status of primary text; this edition collates variants from the revised second edition [R]; no attempt is made to imply an evolutionary model informing emendation.

The second challenge is how to formulate Eggert's nuanced relationship between literary interpretation and book history? There are three principles that have been influential in producing this critical edition. In *Textual Scholarship An Introduction*, D. C. Greetham observes:

> All textual criticism is conjectural at some point, for as soon as the decision to produce a critical text has been made, the editor is faced with critical choices which will depend not only upon certain technical data (e.g., information about the format or imposition of the book) but also upon a *subjective interpretation of the available evidence*. It has often been assumed that conjecture is involved only where editor reconstructs or creates a reading which is not extant in any of the witnesses; but *the choice between extant variants is just as critical*, just as ultimately conjectural, as the recreation of a form which happens not to be extant in any of the readings.[5]

---

4   Emphasis added; *The Oxford Companion to the* Book, eds Michael F. Suarez and H. R. Woudhuysen (Oxford: OUP, 2010; online 2010), https://bit.ly/2Cxau4Z cf. Greetham, *Textual Scholarship*, 333.

5   Emphasis added; Greetham, *Textual Scholarship*, 352.

A Note on the Text

This edition accepts that responsibility to exercise subjective judgment, to interpret the evidence and make choices between textual variants. This is the work of the editor just as it is the expectation of the reader. The apparatus documents the basis on which critical—that is interpretative—judgments are made.

This edition also confronts the problem posed by the process and apparatus of editing, even a text such as this one, where textual variation is delimited by the extant documents. Robert Dixon gives candid expression to this problem:

> Knowing as I do how much painstaking work has gone into the production of what [the editor] describes as the nine 'intimidating' pages of editor's emendations—which I confess that even I, another nineteenth-century 'specialist,' will almost certainly never consult—I remain perplexed and unconvinced about the wisdom of this form of scholarly editing. [6]

This comment was prescient: text encoding, electronic editions, digital archives, semantic web collaborations facilitate access to the primary sources, documentary witnesses, bibliographic entities and ancillary texts that the scholarly edition was designed to summarise in codex form. Web-enabled access is both constantly moving into the future tense as it changes with every software upgrade and nostalgically antiquarian as it gives users access to the previously inaccessible, for example, the manuscript treasures of custodial libraries and museums. Data mining technologies have made accessible data either previously accessible in print form only to the highly trained specialist or simply not available at all.

The problem is formal and material: given that extensive material is now available, how to give readers sufficient textual scholarship in a congenial format? This edition answers this problem by identifying the history of this book as the way to focus textual scholarship. Presenting both F and R—as intertexts—on the page allows readers to see two historical moments in the life of the book rather than a single moment [F] with later changes [R] accessible only through a separate, formal (potentially 'intimidating') apparatus.

The work edited here has a double history: as a literary work representing an imaginative social world of over a century and a half ago together with its commodified form as a book over the same period. Editorial and material changes over that period demonstrate the ways in which a text, as it survives in various formats, recedes from and catches up with its reading public. No reissue of the text edited here has attempted antiquarianism: each reissue has adopted a new format in an attempt to modernise the text for a new audience. Each of the two editions, each of the reissues, then, is historical. Or, as Stephen Knight makes the point in relation to medieval manuscripts:

> That historicisation of the recognized textuality of the [*Canterbury*] *Tales* interests me especially. It is the line along which I think editorial knowledge of the full variability of a text can be directed to useful purposes today. Those purposes can be partly to comment on its variability through history, and partly to edit the text with a consciously historical and socio-literary interpretation as the ultimate guide . . . I am

---

6   Robert Dixon, rev. of *Gertrude, the Emigrant; A Tale of Colonial Life* by Louisa Atkinson, ed., Elizabeth Lawson, *Coppertales: a Journal of Rural Art* 6 (2000): 115.

arguing that 'frendly' is the best reading because it is the most historically tense, the most weighted in a socio-literary way, the richest in historicity.[7]

This is an argument for the valuing of historicity: one of the primary values of a nineteenth-century novel for readers is, precisely, that it instantiates a history of the nineteenth century.

A decision between two (or more) variants in this instance is not one between a reading from F (1859) designated as 'historical' over against one from R (1887) which is not historical but rather a subjective and interpretative judgment about which reading is 'the most historically tense.' For example, R normalizes young Charlie's pronunciation *reading* 'prison' *for* 'pisson' and 'prisoner' *for* 'pisner; and so F readings are preferred. However, readings from R are preferred either as corrections of accidental errors (for example, literals) or modernisations that facilitate reading (for example, *reading* 'The gloomy flicker of the miniature lamp, hanging from the wall, serves only to show you the darkness' in R *for* 'outhanging from the wall' in F). This edition does not aim to reproduce every tic of the diplomatic edition nor to preserve either F or R as an artifact to be valued as antiquarian.

Choice of base text

The base text is F that has been produced by restoring text omitted to produce R.[8] Collating R against F aggregates all the textual variants since R represents the only source of variants.

---

7 Stephen Knight, 'Textual Variants, Textual Variance,' *Southern Review* 16.1 (1983): 48, 50. For a critique of this argument, see Stephanie Trigg, 'The Politics of Editing Medieval Texts: Knight's Quest and Love's Complaint,' *BSANZ Bulletin*, 9.1 (1985): 15–22.

8 Instructive comparisons might be made with modern editions of other nineteenth-century novels to clarify the effects of textual sources for this edition. Graham Tulloch, editing Sir Walter Scott's *Ivanhoe*, for example, selects the first edition (1820), emended 'in light of the manuscript [Pierpont Morgan, MS MA 440 1819] and proofs [Nat. Lib. Scot. MS 3401] and later editions published in Scott's lifetime' even though the Magnum edition (1829) 'is the latest version of the text . . .on which Scott himself worked,' since this later edition incorporates many changes that were not 'authorised.' Sir Walter Scott, *Ivanhoe. A Romance*, ed. Graham Tulloch, Edinburgh Edition of the Waverley Novels (Edinburgh: Edinburgh University Press, 1998) 444-445. Tulloch, again, editing Catherine Martin, *An Australian Girl*, for Oxford World Classics (1999), chooses the 1891 edition, published in single volume by Richard Bentley & Son, and produced after 'substantial' excisions from the first (1890) edition. Tulloch notes 'the excisions were not her [Martin's] work and were in opposition to her desire not to cut the novel' (xxxii). 'It must always be controversial to publish a text which has been abridged by someone other than the author,' Tulloch argues, 'but the 1891 excisions certainly produce a text which is more tightly focused . . .and shorten[ed] a very long text to a length which might be more acceptable to a modern reader' (xxxii). Rosemary Foxton, in her edition of Catherine Martin, The Silent Sea, for The Colonial Text Series (4) (1995), identifies 'three concurrent and authoritative type-settings and printings of the novel: newspaper versions in Adelaide and Melbourne [April – December 1892; April 1892 – December 1893] and the [Richard] Bentley [& Son] three-decker in London [1892]' (xxx). Collating the extant sets of proofs demonstrates that Martin had varying opportunities for revision: '*The Silent Sea*, as it existed in 1892, may be seen as a work in process — with its author prepared to allow publication in each of its phases of revision' (xxxiv). Foxton selects E1, the Bentley text, as the 'best available witness to the accidentals of the unrevised proofs;' arguing that, through reconstruction, 'the reading text of [the CTS edition] represents a state of the text which actually existed, and one which is the earliest recoverable state and the one closest to the author's manuscript' (xxxv).

R was the text reissued from 1887 (Bentley & Son) and use for the electronic text, SGMI-coded under the TEI.2 *Guidelines* (1997) and the converted to html and pdf for display (2003), available on the Sydney Electronic Text and Imaging Service (SETIS) platform.[9] R abbreviates F by approximately one third, including the omission of four whole chapters; thus, chapter numbers in F and R differ. Chapter titles and numbers follow F.

Appearance of the text

Material deleted from F to produce R, approximately one third of the full length, has been inserted into the base text. Excisions of 3 words or more from F are shadowed on the page and, thus, the abridgement is visually represented rather than being recorded in footnotes or tabular form.[10] This innovation allows the reader to read F but also visualise the abridgement that produced R. That is, F and R versions are given separate and identifiable status as intertexts, rather than being hierarchised into a primary text [F] with emendations from the secondary text(s) [R] marked in the apparatus at foot of page or in an appendix. The term 'intertext' is theorised from literary criticism and applied as editorial praxis: this usage aims to bring literary interpretation and book history together on the edited page.

The decision to vary the traditional editorial apparatus is motivated first, by the specific nature of Townsend Mayer's strategy of abridgement: curtailing the F text by approximately one third (40,000 words) through structural editing usually in units of a half to full page and including the excision of four whole chapters and second, by the potential for the traditional apparatus to become unwieldy. Using either superscript numbers, brackets or a text-based marker would have produced a mark at the beginning of an excision followed, often pages later, by the closing mark thus making it difficult to follow the process. The reader would be required to halt the reading in order to flick back through several pages to rediscover the opening marker. Another option—to use a single textual marker and tabular form in an appendix—requires the additional step of turning to the appendix.

Thus, a reader may ignore the shadow and read F; or, conversely, read only the shadowed R text; or read either intertext cognizant of the other. In addition, rather than using the traditional apparatus and needing to mark up an individual copy—a reader can immediately visualize the proportion and disposition of the revision that produced the R text.

Fourteen excisions of less than 3 words are listed in the Summary of Minor Variants.

Accidentals

Treatment has been conservative and the rule has been to retain the markers of a nineteenth-century text without compromising facility of reading.

---

9   http://purl.library.usyd.edu.au/setis/id/p00038
10   I am indebted to Cate Lowry, who typeset the first edit, for this innovation.

- Obvious literals in F and R, such as spelling mistakes and unambiguous grammatical solecisms, have been silently amended.

- Spelling variants in F and R have been standardised.

- Use of comma and dash is frequent in both F and R. F uses the dash to introduce direct speech; R uses the colon; each has been retained within the relevant text.

- Double punctuation in F and R, such as semi-colon followed by dash or colon followed by dash is simplified to a single mark; semi-colon followed by inverted comma has been simplified to comma plus inverted comma.

- Use of the exclamation mark in F and R has been simplified.

- Single inverted commas are preferred; double inverted commas are reserved for quotation within quotation. Inverted commas are retained for indirect speech (e.g. thoughts) only where there is possible confusion with direct speech.

- Hyphenation has been standardised; erroneous hyphenation silently amended. Hyphenation is retained to avoid ambiguity: no-one as the noun rather than no one suggesting an adjective.

- Capitalisation has followed textual usage (e.g. papa, uncle) and is retained for names (Rev. Evelyn) but elsewhere simplified (government, church, superintendent).

- In-text italics for emphasis are retained; use of upper case for emphasis has been simplified.

- Grammatical and orthographic variation (e.g. addition of capital letter in R following omitted text from F) has not been marked and may be assumed in R.

Substantives

- Spelling to represent dialect and accent is retained; use of apostrophe is thus frequent; unfamiliar words are glossed in the explanatory notes. Where R has omitted dialect or accent spellings, F readings are restored.

- Single usage, short-lived words, typically in F, have been silently amended: *for* antipodistical *read* antipodean; *for* dreamist *read* dreamer; *for* inly *read* innermost; *for* overplus *read* surplus; *for* photographost *read* photographer; *for* querist *read* questioner.

- Archaic prepositional constructions, usually single usage and typically in F, are simplified: *for* down-sittings *read* sitting down; *for* out-turn *read* turn out; *for* up-clearing *read* clear up; *for* up-gazing *read* gazing up; *for* upgrew *read* grew; *for* uprising *read* rising; *for* up-sprang *read* sprang up; *outspoke read spoke out.*

- Pleonastic verb formations, usually single usage and typically in F, are simplified: for forthcome *read* come; for pre-aged *read* aged; for up-throwing *read* rolling; for re-whispered *read* replied; *for* re-continued *read* continued.

- Idiosyncratic formations, such as 'tiraded' for 'spoken in tirades' or 'premonitarily' for 'as a premonition' are retained where meaning is readily inferred.

Style

- Style in F and R is characterised by long periodic sentences with paratactic grammatical constructions where conjunctions join independent clauses (rather than subordinating clauses) and the comma functions differently to modern usage. No attempt is made to modernise either grammatical constructions or use of the comma. Together with use of the dash, this syntax is perhaps most characteristic of nineteenth-century prose.
- Omniscient narration in F and R uses apostrophe and direct addresses to the reader; both are retain without intervention.
- F and R texts display five footnotes: one in Chapters 18, 20, 27 and two in chapter 29. These are retained; indicated by a textual marker; located at foot of page.
- There is frequent biblical reference *passim*, which is usually identified in the explanatory notes.

Additions to R

These are infrequent. Additional text is usually restricted to one clause or sentence and in one instance only, 'The *Rose of Britain*' (F Ch. 11 and R Ch. 8) comprises a short paragraph. In all instances except one, additional text covers omitted text where transitions are need in the narrative. Additions are given in the Summary of Minor Variants. In one instance, R takes over a paragraph from F Ch. 5 and relocates it as the final paragraph in Ch. 4.

A Note on the Illustrations

This edition reproduces the six engravings published only in the first edition of *The Broad Arrow* (1859). These illustrations were 'drawn and etched' by A. Hervieu, probably Auguste-Jean-Jacques Hervieu (1794–1858). Hervieu was born in Saint-Germain-en-Laye, France, and, having abandoned boarding school aimed at military training in Paris, studied with Anne-Louis Girodet de Roussy-Trioson and Antoine-Jean Gros (both pupils of Jacques-Louis David) and later, in England, with the Royal Academician Sir Thomas Lawrence.[1] As a young man, Hervieu was active in anti-monarchist politics and fled to England; tried in absentia, he was fined and, in effect, went into exile. He is closely associated with Mrs Frances Trollope, the mother of Anthony Trollope, who employed him as her sons' drawing tutor. Hervieu accompanied Trollope and two of her sons on a financially precarious visit to America (1827–1831) and later contributed satirical illustrations to Trollope's immensely popular *Domestic Manners of the American* (1832).[2]

Hervieu's personal friendship and professional relationship with Trollope continued after their return to Britain and Hervieu contributed some of the well-known illustrations for Trollope's exposé of child labour in the factory system, *The Life and Adventures of Michael Armstrong, the Factory Boy* (1840), having accompanied Trollope on her investigations in Manchester. During his time in America, Hervieu undertook various commissions including, with Hiram Powers, contributing to Joseph Dorfeuille's *The Infernal Regions* for Cincinnati's Western Museum; a grand work including a mechanical wax-figure descent into Dante's *Inferno*, part of a larger work representing the *Divine Comedy* initially suggested by Frances Trollope. Powers's famous statue, *The Greek Slave*, appears as a detail in Chapter's 13 and 21.

---

1   See John Francis McDermott, 'Mrs Trollope's Illustrator: Auguste Hervieu in America (1827–1831)', *Gazette des Beaux-Arts* 51 (March 1958): 170.

2   McDermott cites Mrs Trollope's 1830 letter to her son, Tom: 'I wish with all my soul you could see and hear poor Hervieu! He seems only to live in hope of helping us. He has set his heart on getting us home without drawing on your father's diminished purse . . .' (185).

Map of Hobart Town circa 1858, by Richard Jarman (1808–1877) detail. Tasmanian Archive and Heritage Office.

THE

BROAD ARROW:

BEING PASSAGES FROM THE HISTORY

OF

MAIDA GWYNNHAM,

A LIFER.

BY OLINÉ KEESE.

IN TWO VOLUMES.

VOL. I.

LONDON:

RICHARD BENTLEY, NEW BURLINGTON STREET.

1859.

Preface

After much hesitation, and with much doubt, I now send forth this work.

So many attractive books on Australian and convict life have appeared of late years,[1] that I fear mine may be repelled as an unsuccessful imitation of other authors, unless I be permitted to explain that it was wholly planned, mostly written, and intended for publication several years ago. With the circumstances which frustrated that intention it would be impertinent to trouble the reader.

As one reason why I should not publish this book, I am told that the subject is unbecoming a women's pen. If it be so, and if there be censure attached to a handling of it, I would face that censure, and deem myself happy in having written The Broad Arrow, if but one sister, now trembling on the brink of ruin, read it, and enter into my belief—that loss of virtue is (in *most* cases) the first and fatal impulse towards those depths of sin whose end it has been my painful lot to witness in Tasmania.

I am also told that transportation has ceased to be a topic of public interest [2]—an assertion I would not only doubt, but test, even though it be made by reliable authority. I would doubt it—fain to believe that so long as England has convicts to punish, the mode of punishing them can never be a question void of earnest, prayerful, and responsible interest.

I would test it—though feebly indeed—by placing The Broad Arrow in the reader's hand, leaving it to his consideration with this simple statement—

'We speak that we do know,
　　And testify that we have seen.'[3]

Lest any of my friends should be hurt at the publication of this book without their knowledge, I would apologise that I considered it best to act on my own responsibility, from an unwillingness to have any one but myself to blame in the event of an unfavourable reception of the work.

O.K.
London,
February 9th, 1859.

Volume I

CHAPTER 1

The Festival

> Oh! let the merry bells ring round.[1]

A JOYFUL clangour is rising from the tower of St. Judas[2] as the cold grey of the venerable cathedral warms itself in the afternoon sun. Our city is very gay. Bustle and excitement jostle one another in the streets. The shops display their rainbow assortments of finery with more than ordinary taste. Carriages throng the thoroughfare, and from the carriages fashion and beauty gaze placidly on the crowd making its way towards the Queen's high road. Placards announce a ball—and the newspapers hint that this ball is to be a nonpareil.[3]

But why is all this? Wherefore so highly beats the pulse of expectation? What may be the festival, and what this ball to celebrate it?

It is the festival of the assizes! And the ball the Assize Ball!

Doubtless you have hitherto mistaken the meaning of the word 'assize;' do not be ashamed—you know the old saying about the bliss of ignorance—consult Johnson. [4] Then, perhaps, this most solemn season of the year—this fore-glimpse of that awful time when man must face his Maker at earth's last tribunal—is being thus joyously welcomed, to antedate that mysterious spirit which shall prompt the saints to exclaim 'Alleluia!' as the smoke of the tormented goes up for ever and ever. Or it may be, that as the calendar proclaims an increase of crime, showing that a larger than usual number of our fellow creatures await their doom from the voice of justice, it is expected that the depression cast over the city will be of so deep and debilitating a nature, that the city must droop in hysteric weakness or sink in hypochondriac melancholy, unless a stimulant be administered. So present pain is quieted by a promised ball of unprecedented grandeur. The bells from St. Judas are made to outswell the prison bell; and, amid the hurry of preparation, the clank of the felon's chain passes unheard through the very midst.

The judges drive into the city. The stimulants take effect; the city does not faint, on the contrary, it never looked so blooming, never attired itself so gaily, as it does to-day. Oh, wondrous balm for bleeding hearts! Surely 'tis the balm of Gilead! [5]

No thinking person objects to pomp and state on all occasions calculated to impress the mind (especially that of the common people) with a sense of superior power. But is there not the pomp of the funeral?—funeral pomp. Does not the sight of the plumed hearse fill the breast with solemnity? Does not the crowd intuitively doff its cap before it? Do not the voice of laughter and the song of thoughtlessness involuntarily cease, or drop to softer tones, when the toll of the death-bell meets the ear?

Would the effect on the public mind be lessened were the judges to enter with more of such pomp and less of the present gaiety? Would justice lose one of her stern prerogatives were she to come robed in the sable of that woe of which she is so often the precursor?

Would she frown less terror upon evil doers were she ushered into her judgment seat with sounds betokening more of sorrow than joy?

Would the captive pining in his cell, or the broken-hearted parent tossing on his bed of blighted hope, watch with less horror for the dark consummation of his grief, were not its approach heralded by those cheery chimes, seeming to say: 'I will laugh at your calamity; I will mock when your fear cometh'?

Would the *cause* that brings our judges to our cities be less hated by the youthful heart were it taught to associate more of the funeral and less of the feast with the onroll of the carriage that bears sorrow, punishment, death in its rear?

We cannot answer for all children, but we know of one who, when hurried forward to see 'the judges come in,' shrunk behind the crowd to ruminate on some mystery, and, unable to fathom it, burst into tears, exclaiming: 'Why do they let those happy bells ring, the prisoners must hear them?'

The day for the ball arrives. You are invited to attend. Your particular attention is directed to a very elegantly dressed young man—Captain Norwell—as elegant in person and deportment as in attire. He is unanimously voted a fascinating man by the fair sex, and the king of the evening by the dark. He is surrounded by an admiring group of both sexes. Many a plotting mother opines that he will make an excellent husband, and many an anxious father pictures how well his jewel of a daughter would look in so brilliant a setting; while some elder brother apostrophises him—that is, Captain Norwell—as a 'lucky dog,' and lucky dog means a great deal in fashionable phraseology.

'What happy chance brought you to our part of the world at this season of the year, Captain Norwell—the ball?' The questioner is a lady old enough to have three grown-up daughters.

'No,' replies Norwell, in a tone nonchalant; 'but since I was here, I could not resist the temptation of mixing with such an assemblage of beauty as rumour said these walls would witness; and for once I find she has been very humble in her statements, and disappointment has not followed in her train.' A gracious bow to the blushing group around him accompanies this speech.

'You come to attend the assizes, I suppose?'

'Partly; I heard that a very interesting trial was to come on, and having a little time to spare, I ran down to hear it.'

Several voices ask:

'Oh! To which one do you allude?'

Neither fascinated ladies nor scheming parents observe that a slight shade passes over Captain Norwell's fine countenance, and a still slighter tremulousness into his voice, as he replies:

'I speak of Martha Grylls's.'

'You will put me out of love with dancing if you talk of that woman,' says an animated girl, whose merry laugh belies her words. 'I shall fancy I am dancing to the clank of chains, or waltzing to Pestal[6], if you talk any more such horrors.'

And the fantastic toe seems all of a fidget to whirl off the impatient fair one; but the pertinacious mother is not to be stopped. To stop Norwell in the vicinity of her daughters is the only stoppage she meditates.

'Which was Martha Grylls's? Not having the honour of such distinguished acquaintance, *I* do not know each prisoner by name.'

A quick, searching glance at the lady, and Norwell answers:

'The young woman indicted for forgery. I—I mean child-murder.'

'Oh! That beautiful woman? One would hardly think so lovely a face could belong to such a wretch: so calm and innocent, too, she looked.'

'*I* do not think she *did*, look so very *innocent*,' interrupts the animated girl; 'there was a flinty hardihood in her face that quite prevented me from pitying her, as I should have done *had* she cried. My heart was quite steeled against her; *I* felt no pity.'

'Flint and steel together should produce a spark, or one of the two could not be genuine,' says Captain Norwell.

'She stood so erect, and eyed the court so proudly, as if she would say, "Sentence me to death and I will thank you!" Once, though, I did think she was going to break down. Did you observe, Captain Norwell, about the middle of the trial, how she faltered; and then, when she turned toward the door, how she started as if she saw something which renewed her courage? She certainly saw some person or thing, for the hard look came back to her face. I wonder what or who it was. Perhaps she saw her father or mother.'

'That would have softened her!' replies a gentle voice, from a pale, interesting girl, whose diminutive stature has hidden her from immediate sight.

'Perhaps it was an accomplice then. The change on her countenance was unmistakable.'

Another in that ballroom had marked the change in the prisoner's manner as her faltering gaze fell on a certain corner of the court. Ay—he noticed it, but not to wonder at its cause. To his heart the change brought at once ease and pain—ease to the diseased part, and pain to what portion of it remained uncontaminated.

'Such stony hardness,' persisted the young lady.

'There is the stony hardness of despair—a breaking heart may lie behind a brazen wall,' replies the gentle voice from the corner.

These words are uttered timidly, but with great feeling, and the speaker, raising her eyes to Norwell, fancies that gentleman agrees with her, for she notes an expression of unutterable anguish momentarily distort his features.

The expression does not escape the vigilant eyes of plotting mothers and sanguine fathers. It goes far to the strengthening of the former's opinings, and deep into the jewelled picturings of the latter.

'Feeling sits so remarkably well on his handsome face,' remarks one parent.

It does indeed. An electric photographer could immortalise it.

You have been invited to attend the ball on purpose to hear this commonplace, out-of-place conversation—as out of place in a ballroom as a ball is out of time in an assize week. Fancy how awkward it will look to see in the same gazette, column by column—

The Assizes! The Ball!

Your presence is again required, but to a very different scene. Where you are now wanted there will be no festoon of blooming flowers wreathing a fragrant archway above you: no mimic suns making the decorated ceiling a lesser firmament of glory; there will be no radiant faces to greet you with the lustrous smile of excitement, no sound of music and dancing. Await you there a dark, stone archway, and an iron gate beneath it. There will be the relentless grating of its hinges, with the heavy sound of ponderous keys; and a coldness in the aspect of the building you are to enter will communicate itself to your soul, making you shudder to pass within its dreary portal. You must follow the guide along that narrow passage, where your footstep echoes cheerlessly through the dismal corridor. A doubly locked door swings itself solemnly back, and there is silence, darkness, despair. Pass on.

The heavily heaved sigh that just falls upon your ear, as the lock springs from its socket, only makes the silence deeper. Pass on. The gloomy flicker of the miniature lamp, hanging from the wall, serves only to show you the darkness. The look of apathy fixed on you by the occupant of the cell only reminds you that that despair is deepest which gives no outward sign. Pass on.

'Martha Grylls—a gentleman to speak to you.'

The hopeful tone and the earnest glance astonish you, as, energetically raising her hand to shade her eyes, the prisoner asks—

'Who is he?'

Pain succeeds your astonishment as you hear the utter hopelessness of the tone with which she answers:

'I don't wish to see him. I'll see no one.'

And the hand before shading her eyes, closes resolutely over them, as she drops her head, refusing to look at the clergyman, who is the gentleman announced.

It is Martha Grylls you look upon. You heard of her in the ballroom, and are prepared to meet her in the felon's cell. Her real name is Maida Gwynnham; but under the above alias she has been convicted of child-murder, for which crime the sentence of death was passed upon her at the assizes; since then, through the clemency of our lady sovereign, she has been reprieved, and now transportation for life is all she will have to bear. Listen awhile, and you may find that balls and prisons are not always unconnected. You may then decide that, after all, there was not *much* out of the way in that talk in the assembly room. We should never judge rashly; 'Things are not what they seem,' says one whose opinion is worthy. Listen! The clergyman who speaks is the Rev. Herbert Evelyn, not the chaplain of the gaol. He is admitted at this late hour by special authority of the powers that be.

'I am your friend, Martha; do not refuse to let me be so.'

'I have no friend; it is all false.'

'Martha, stop—stop and think. No friend?'

'None! None! Though once I madly thought I had.'

'And who was he?'

'HE! HE! Who said anything about he?'

There is an anxiety in Maida's voice, which tells Mr. Evelyn he has unwittingly touched the key-note to some part of her history—he wonders how to answer her. Then she continues half aloud, in a soliloquative tone, and absent air—

'Did *he* send you? Then he has not forgotten me!' And her hands unconsciously clasp and go with a tremble to her breast, as though she would hide some treasure there.

'No; he did not. One who loves you still better, bids me visit you with a word of comfort from Himself.'

Maida looks frightened, and with a bewildered air, asks:

'What do you mean? If *he* did not send, he cannot care for me; and there is no one else in the world to care for me or think of me!'

Mr. Evelyn goes towards her, and is about to lay his hand on her shoulder, but she waves him back, and he perceives that the blood has rushed to her very temples, and that passion quivers on her clenched lips; he has time only to remark this, ere she bursts forth:

'He never loved me! And now he is trying to win some other fond and foolish heart to its own destruction.'

She presses her hand to her burning brow, and proceeds:

'Ay! He will break some other heart when mine is sinking far away. Ay! He will tell the same lying tale to some unthinking girl, thoughtless and wayward as I was; and she, poor fondling, will believe him, and he will deceive her, and she will be left; and fear or pride will drive her from her home, she will fly to hide her disgrace; she will try to die, but death hates the wretched. She will steal to give her infant bread; she will be sent to prison, and thence across the seas; and we shall meet—two victims to his lies. Ah, how I shall love her!'

She abruptly stops.

'Was he at the ball last night?' Not waiting for an answer, 'He was in the court—I saw him. I was on the point of giving way when our eyes met—it was enough: that glance was fire to the dying embers—he understands *my* eye; he read its promise and seemed satisfied. There was—but was he at the ball last night? There is always a ball to commemorate the assizes. Was he?'

Mr. Evelyn answers not.

'Ah, you are surprised; you thought I spoke of a poor man. No—no! Such glories are reserved for the rich; they may sin, and hide their sin in a golden grave; they may break innocent hearts, and the world ignore the fact; it is these sins that fill these cells; it is these sins that will people perdition; and if God sees as man sees—'

But her voice fails, the blood leaves her temples, and faint from excitement and want of rejected food, she sinks insensible to the earth.

As Mr. Evelyn quits the prison, he sees a gentleman wrapped in a long loose cloak standing opposite the gateway, and gazing abstractedly at the grated window; the moonlight falls on his upturned face.

'If that index be true, all is not right within,' thinks Mr. Evelyn. As he looks on the uplifted face, a text unconsciously forces its way into his mind; you may find that text in Mark ix. 44. [7]

Mr. Evelyn cannot withdraw his eye from the manly figure before him; a strange fascination roots him to the spot; the text forces its way upward and upward—in a moment it will be on his lips. Mr. Evelyn does not wish this, but prophetic force is irresistible. Casting both eye and voice to the kerbstone, he murmurs, as though he had no choice of refraining—

'Where their worm dieth not!'

The stranger heaves a protracted sigh—the sigh disenchants Mr. Evelyn, and he moves forward—the stranger starts to find himself observed—and Mr. Evelyn is slightly confused, but Captain Norwell is never at a loss: touching his hat gracefully, in a sentimental whisper he says—

'He that would see Melrose aright
Must visit it at pale moonlight.' [8]

'We are agreed on this point I see, sir,' (again raising his hat). 'I wish you a very good night,' and Captain Norwell saunters down the street. As soon as Mr. Evelyn is out of sight he returns and rings at the gate.

'Confound it! What a row!—I only touched the bell, and here is noise enough to wake Lucifer on his throne.'

The bell swings, thrilling its sonorous voice far into the stillness of night, and far into the chaos of many a sinner's heart. Shall you start to hear Captain Norwell classed with those many sinners? Ay! The stern iron of conviction smote with that prison bell deep into his very soul. You may be sure persons do not confound things for naught. Many will long to hush in everlasting confusion the tongue which, at God's day, shall proclaim from the housetops the secrets of an assembling world—but as unable to stay one word of that resistless tongue as Norwell to stop the majestic vibrations of the bell—they will call on the rocks to cover them from its accusing voice.

'Can I see—Maida—I—Martha Grylls—'

'No, sir; past hours long ago, even if you'd a permit.'

'I leave to-morrow; cannot I be favoured as well as that gentleman just gone?'

'Parson, sir. Wonderful, sir, how the ooman treats the gentry. Can't indeed, sir. Gentry round her like bees—'tracts 'em wonderful.'

'Does she?' Norwell tries to speak unconcernedly—'She likes that, I suppose?'

'These creatures generally do, but *she* don't—*she* don't, and no mistake.'

Norwell looks relieved, and it seems the information is worth money to him, for he drops a crown into the turnkey's hand; that official jerks his cap in recognition of the palmy touch, but shakes his head at it.

'Can't, sir, indeed; it's as much as my place is worth to try on that game. If you was a parson now,' and the turnkey eyes him longingly, as though he would there and then put him into the priest's office for the sake of the crown; but he can discover no priest-like quality in Norwell's dress, so reluctantly holds out the money towards him.

'No, no, keep it,' cried Norwell impatiently; 'it's not for that; mind you gag your bell's mouth before I come again.'

The gate closes after him, and he mutters:

'I've done all I can—I wish she knew it. O Maida, Maida, where will it end?'

'Where will it end?' Would that the question could be sounded through the length and breadth of the land! Would that it could be whispered to the ear of every dissolute man! It may begin here—here in England—but its circles spread and spread until, as this book shall show, they reach far-distant shores. Would God it ended there! For we (that is you and I) know of another shore which binds with its fiery grasp that river rolling on in blackness of darkness for ever. O God! If its circles should reach that shore!

CHAPTER 2

Maida Gwynnham

W<small>AS</small> the only child of a gentleman possessing a small country property in Essex. She lost her mother at an early age.

To Mr. Gwynnham his wife's death was a blow from which he never entirely recovered. One singular effect of his grief was the indifference he exhibited to the society of little Maida. 'The world,' he would say, 'shall not find fault with me—Maida shall have all the comforts and luxuries my means will allow—she shall be educated to move with credit in the position of life to which she is born—she shall be my companion—she shall share everything with her father but his heart—*that* he cannot give.'

God have mercy on thee, poor father! There comes a time when thou wilt need comfort more than thy neglected child now pines for love.

A child of the most ardent affections by nature, Maida's love would have brought back light and warmth to her father's heart, had he sought to unite in her the sympathies which had been divided by death. But it was not until two years afterwards, when forced upon him by the disappointed importunities of the child herself, that he suddenly perceived he was rejecting the remedy his case required—the gentle offering of a daughter's heart.

Meanwhile the care of Maida's education devolved on others. She wanted nothing within her father's means; but she had already passed the age when children of sensitive mind begin to distinguish between benevolence and individual love. She had learnt that kind words are not always loving ones, and that kisses are not always the obeyed impulse of affection.

Her father's indifference became a source of sorrow which she could not resist, though she strove to hide it within herself.

Her proud spirit thought scorn of receiving mechanical attentions from her father, and once, when he had imprinted the usual kiss upon her lips, she raised her tiny hand and swept it hastily across her face, as if she would dash the offending token from her, exclaiming,

'I do not *want* his kisses, they are not *real*.'

It cost poor Maida an effort to reveal to her father that she sighed for love not freely offered. She long consumed her grief alone, and in the battlings of her yet infant mind, the reader may discern the foreshadow of a spirit that can suffer and be strong.

Mr. Gwynnham was one day sitting in a root-house at the bottom of his garden. He heard a child sobbing; he was not sufficiently acquainted with the voice to recognise it. On looking out, he perceived Maida seated on a grassy mound beneath a chestnut tree. By her side a dove-cage; she was pressing one of the doves to her bosom. Rocking herself to and fro, she talked to the bird in low, wailing tone.

'Happy bird! You have somebody to love you. Oh, Mamma! Mamma! Why did you leave me? Your little Maida has no one to love *her*.'

Drawn and Etched by I. Reeves

Maida Gwynnham as a child

The child stopped, struck by some sudden thought; she burst into a passionate flood of tears, rushed to the root-house, and facing Mr. Gwynnham, cried, clenching her fist, 'If *you* will not love me I will get some one else to! I *will* be loved! I *must* be loved!'

Mr. Gwynnham appeared thunderstricken. There stood his, as he thought, timid child, looking so wild, so beautiful, so like his wife in miniature, that for some time he gazed on her in speechless amaze; he then sprang forward and caught the small, trembling, form in his arms, and Maida felt tears, *real* tears, fall like burning kisses on her cheek.

'My Maida, you have been with me and I knew it not! Yes, you live again in the flashing eyes and indomitable soul of this neglected babe! How blinded have I been! My little one, you *shall* have love. All, all that was your mother's.'

'But won't you love me for myself?' said Maida; 'I do not want to be loved instead of any one else!'

Thus did Maida Gwynnham take her father's heart by storm.

From this time they were always together.

Maida resembled her mother in beauty, virtues, and faults. Affectionate, firm, truthful, ardent and generous on the one hand; haughty, passionate and impulsive on the other. She quite governed her father, who was not strong-minded, but kind, generous, and well educated. He very rarely controlled her in any thought, word, or deed; no wonder, therefore, that the change which the following conversation reveals was distasteful to her. On the day she attained her sixteenth year, Mr. Gwynnham said, 'Maida, love, are you willing to leave me for a short period? A year's instruction in music, French and drawing will finish what I have begun,' adding, with a timid and persuasive smile at his daughter, 'Papa reckons on his music, you know.'

'Go to school! No indeed, I'll not. Think of *me* going to be under baby rule—bed at eight, rise at six; no indeed! I say so once and for all.'

'You are too hasty, dear,' gently replied Mr. Gwynnham; 'I do not wish, or intend you to go to school. The plan I have made for you is a very pleasant one. In asking if you were willing to go, I had but this thought—the parting, and this question—can Maida leave her father?'

'Oh, papa!' was all the impetuous girl could answer, as she flung her arms around his neck and wept.

'You are going, deary, to a first-rate London school, to be a parlour boarder. There you will have a room to yourself, and unless you choose, you need have nothing to say to any person but the masters appointed to attend you. Mrs. Bentley will kindly allow you to take your maid with you.'

A month from the date of this talk Mr. Gwynnham took Maida to London. His parting words were, 'Let there be no secrets from your father, precious, our hearts have ever been one.' His daughter appeared astonished; to her truthful soul such words were incomprehensible. Ah, poor Maida! You will understand them by-and-by! With much weeping they separated.

Ay, there may well be weeping! Father, thou art sending a treasure from thy bosom; will it ever lie there more? The star of thy hope will set in a fearful eclipse. Was it in a spirit of prophecy thou spakest those parting words? Didst thou foresee that a creature so lovely as thy Maida would have temptations to strive with, and the tempter to baffle? And didst thou think to save her? Couldst thou look through time's far-seeing telescope, thou wouldst start at the blackened future before thy child. Thou wouldst see her noble purpose, her lofty heart, circumvented by a craft triumphant where strength had failed. We would fain hide from the father the sights this glass reveals. But you must peep in if you would know how Maida learnt the meaning of Mr. Gwynnham's words.

Look in. We cannot describe what the telescope shows, the task would be too painful. Look; there is Maida, beaming her loveliest. Her eyes are radiant with joy, as she listens to a gentleman who is talking to her: what he says you cannot tell; there are those who know; let them tell who have learnt how to overcome artlessness with art.

Look again.

As a dissolving view the scene has changed, but the figures are the same. Maida is weeping. *Her* face depicts great mental agony—his face just such anxiety as a person would feel on seeing a long-sought treasure within hand-grasp.

Now a few sentences do reach your ear.

'But why should not I tell my father? You are withholding a joy from him; you cannot know him if you think he would deny me—he never denied me anything; I *must* tell him, and *he* shall give me to you, Norwell.'

'No, he would not give you up, and you would be more miserable to do it after he had said nay. If he *is* so indulgent, he will forgive you. You shall have a letter written all ready to send directly the ceremony is over.'

You hear no more; the sound fades away with the view, which dissolves itself into a moonlight scene. A female in disguise leans on a gentleman's arm. They hurry by; you trace them to a railway station; they enter a first-class carriage. The whistle is loud, shrill enough to meet your ear; they are whirled off, and the station melts into an upper chamber. But one figure is there—a female; her black hair floats over her shoulders—her eyes glisten; you have seen those eyes before; they glisten, not now with radiant joy; there is a fire in them that you fancy must scathe the object it shall rest upon. A cup is in her quivering hand; you glance involuntarily towards a phial on the table; there is a label on the phial, and on the label there are cross-bones and a skull; beneath the skull is written, in large black letters, 'Poison.'

You shudder and turn to Maida; the cry of her childhood rings through your soul—'I will be loved! I must be loved!' and you long to say, 'I will love you, Maida; put down that fatal cup.' But she waits not your bidding. Her lips seem to tremble forth a prayer; she dashes the cup from her with 'I will be no coward; he shall see I *can* endure life!'

You must supply the blanks in Maida's history; the blanks which these scenes leave. Happy are you if you cannot do so!

There is a grief to which sympathy would be a mockery. We may not enter the present chamber of sorrow, and, going thence, reveal her confided secrets. There is but one voice that could console yon broken-hearted father; that voice will not humble itself to say, 'I have sinned against heaven and before thee.'[1] So it shuns that desolate room, and the lonely mourner is left to drink his bitter draught in the darkness of mental night. His heart is sundered like a staff of office over a great man's grave. Oh, wretched father! There was one who, like thee, had a cup of bitterness to drain to its last dreg. *His* agony fell as drops of slaughter to the earth. Raise thy spirit's voice, and join with Him in that earnest cry, and the cry will bring its own relief. Some angel wing will be sent to lull thy weary, tempted soul to repose, and thou wilt no longer mourn alone.

Three years have fled by. The sights that glass revealed as Future have for twelve months been the Past.

And Maida still lives on!

CHAPTER 3

Captain Norwell

AT the door of a humble lodging-house, in a country town, stood a gentleman in military undress. He seemed turning in his mind whether to enter or not. After a moment's hesitation he advanced, and ascending the stairs, gently opened the door of a small third-story room, where he perceived the object of his search—Maida Gwynnham, still beautiful—proudly beautiful, though in person the mere shadow of her former self. Captain Norwell soon found that sorrow had not dimmed the fire of her eye.

No word was spoken on either side. Maida seemed to ponder what course of reception to adopt; and Norwell, cowed by her haughty, unflinching stare, tacitly owned her superiority by waiting for her to break the unpleasant silence.

This while we will take the writer's and reader's privilege of turning past into present, and glance around the scantily furnished apartment. A cradle stands by the chair from which Maida has just started on seeing Norwell; and in the cradle sleeps a baby. On the floor, by the cradle, lies a heap of calico; a half-made shirt sleeve on the table explains this heap. In the farthest corner of the room is a loaf lying, as though it had rolled there by mistake, or had been made a plaything of. The cupboard tells us its own secret, by displaying, as the only occupant of its hungry shelves, an earthenware basin of tea-leaves.

But the silence breaks, we must go back to the past. Would that all such scenes could be the Past!

'Is *this* the way you receive me?' at length said the captain, perceiving that Maida chose to insist on the greater superiority of making him yield. 'Is this the way you receive me, when I have travelled from London on purpose to see you?'

'I did not ask you to come.'

'No!' replied Norwell, with a forced laugh. 'No, I know that; my lady Gwynnham never asks, she only deigns to command. But why is this, Maida? Why did you not let me know of your distress?'

Maida stretched out her emaciated arm, and shaking her fingers, cried—

'Look at these fingers—the skin just covers them. I have worked them to the bone in getting a morsel of bread for my child; for him I could do everything but beg.'

Breaking into a fearful smile, she added in an audible whisper:

'For him I could do everything but beg—for him I could even steal! Do you see that loaf *there*, in the corner of the room? My boy was crying for food, and I had none to give him; the baker's basket lay in a doorway, and I put out these fingers, worn to the bone (she shook them again)—I put them out and s-t-o-l-e! I rushed upstairs—my baby's cry was hushed. I could not break the loaf. 'Twas like fire in my hand when his cry no longer fell like burning sounds on my heart, so I dashed the cursed thing across the room; and there it shall lie until those who have lost it come to claim it, and take me.'

'But, Maida, you are rash and proud.'

'I know I am, both.'

'Do hear me. By telling me of your situation you would have avoided all this misery, and there would have been no begging in it.'

'Had you wished, Norwell, to discover my circumstances, you would not have awaited apprisal from one who hates to complain. Eleven months would not have elapsed since last I heard of or from you.'

'Don't scold, there's a darling!' said Norwell, in a coaxing tone; 'you love me still, don't you?'

In a voice of stern gravity, Maida replied: 'The hour of coaxing has passed. The last three years have written a bitter truth upon my heart. I am no longer young in anything but years. The storms—the passions—the impulses—the cares—the sorrows that have swept over me, have left no summer traces, but such as the winter blast leaves upon the earth, in withered mockery of what has been. There is no spot in my career on which memory could love to rest. The darkness of the past could only be out-darkened by the dreaded future I discern before me.'

Norwell started at the prophetic words, and in real distress.

'Do not—Oh! do not, Maida, say so. If I had only thought, I might have known that you would call, asking even *me* —a degradation—and—'

'Norwell, I am ashamed! Do you thus sum up my griefs? Do you suppose that the want of a few items of comfort has had to do with the lines furrowed on my cheek? Had hunger alone been my endurance, I had been a different person this day. You insult me in imagining that I condemn your unmanly silence, because—'

'You are impulsive, Maida, and fastidious. You—you—there is more of touchiness than sensitiveness in your feeling.'

Though Maida could not concede excuse, she could receive rebuke.

'Forgive me, Norwell! I fear you are right—I *do* become fastidious. Impulsive I ever was; would to heaven I—' She hesitated, and Norwell knew she stemmed the course of a pained thought rather than communicate the pain to him. Under the influence of a stirring impulse or provoked passion, Maida could lash the object of her anger with remorseless aim and almost cruel force; but let that impulse be unmoved, that passion unprovoked, and she could not hurt the puniest worm. Had Norwell been what her delusion even yet believed, he would have invited the confidence of her overfraught heart—not by making her finish her half-uttered wish, but by relieving her of it; for it was in his power to have supplied the words which would have at once eased her self-denying spirit, and showed her that he read those sorrows she sought to hide from him. No such thought, however, entered his mind; he congratulated himself on Maida's self-control, which spared him perhaps another lashing—certainly a scene. Like most selfish men he hated that which is emphatically called a *scene* , partly from an indigenous dislike [1] to all exhibitions having their rise in the holiest points of human nature, partly because he followed the usage of the day in scoffing at that regenerating flood which redeems half the world from savagery and egotism (witness a mother's tears!) and chiefly, to use his own elegant explanation, because he felt it so confounded awkward to know how to look, what to do, or what to say on such occasions.

Ah, Norwell, school lies yet before you; you have not only to view many scenes, but have to become an actor in them—be wise betimes and learn to like them.

'You love me still then?' at last sighed Norwell.

The tear glistened in Maida's eye, and he was answered. Once more her aching heart was soothed by perjured lips, whose specious words vowed lasting faith, and her parched spirit drank in the lying tale, surrendering itself to the cruel refreshment.

'But you are pale, Henry, very pale and haggard.' She gazed anxiously at him.

'I am not well, Maida; vexations of which you know nothing make my life a perpetual worry.'

'I *should* know them, then, Henry!'

A smile slightly reproachful and full of sadness accompanied this speech.

'Yes! The chief at any rate you should know; it for very shame has kept me so long absent from you, and still prevents me from publicly owning you. That alone is enough to account for my pale looks—other causes are spitefully superfluous. What say you?'

How beautiful did pale looks thus accounted for become to Maida! Trembling with suppressed affection, she replied—

'That must not fret you; I can wait till your father yields.'

'Bore it! That may be heaven knows when. My father isn't like yours, who'd forgive you if you'd let him, you little proud thing!'

A long time indeed must she wait if her union with Captain Norwell depends on the consent of a parent who exists not, save in the scheme of those perjured lips.

'But I *can* and *will* wait, on the oft-repeated condition, that until then you consider me only—' She stopped. Raising her eyes to Norwell, she exclaimed—

'O, Henry! Once have I fallen, need it be for ever? Can you not forget the past? Forget all except that one day I may be yours by holier vows—'

'Unless you wish to distract me altogether, don't begin that. I'll promise you anything if you will not forbid me to come to you, now I can again.'

'Except on that condition, I must and *do* forbid, even should I never see you again, Norwell. You hear?'

'I do! And suppose I must promise obedience, or my lady will extort it.' There was lightness in his speech, but none in his voice. He was too well acquainted with Maida to dispute her objections. As she was still necessary to his plans, he sought, by awakening her sympathy, to divert her from a subject which might end adversely to himself.

'I thought you wanted to relieve me of some of my troubles. I came here intending to unburden my mind; but once here I lose myself in you, and *my* troubles in *your* distress. I look ill? What does that face look?'

'Only what it deserves—never mind it. Tell me of yourself—let your griefs be mine, and if I can assist you—O, Henry, need I tell you how wholly I am yours?'

He smote his brow, and more pale and haggard seemed his countenance.

'No, no; tell me nothing, my own mad follies must bring their punishment. Why should I bother you who have already suffered so much for me?'

'By which suffering you are pledged to confide in me; there is enough in your face now to make all that I have endured seem mere play.'

'Ay, and there'll be more yet, unless I can procure help. Maida, my own noble one, will you believe me when I say that I have been innocent of neglect in leaving you so long? A struggle against a tide of misfortune has—'

'Henry, this suspense is cruel. Why torment me thus? You have dreadful news to impart; be quick—and tell the worst.'

The moment had arrived. The prey quivered within hand-grasp. He then told her that his position was precarious. Pecuniary difficulties pressed upon him so hardly, that where another week might find him, he would not harrow her tender feelings by hinting. He told of feverish excitements which sapped his life energies; of harassing vigils which might deprive him of reason. And when Maida inquired what assistance she could possibly render in adversities so hopelessly beyond her aid, Norwell answered that her affectionate participation in his sorrow was in itself an assistance; because it solaced his desponding spirits. On further inquiry he told her the most beggarly part of the trial was that a mere trifle would relieve him.

To one long accustomed to deal in pence, the trifle of four hundred pounds appeared rather Brobdingnaginal.[2] Yet, as she could remember the time when such a sum would not have alarmed her, Maida was disposed to credit Norwell for sincerity in so viewing the amount required.

'Is there no means of procuring the money, Henry?'

'There is the very nuisance! The exact sum is promised me, but it doesn't come. *Now* it would be salvation; by-and-by it will do more harm than good.'

A gleam of hope shone on Maida, before so dejected. Perceiving which, Captain Norwell exclaimed—

'Yes; it's only fair, since I have made you partaker of my trouble, that you should share the slight hope which preserves me from sinking.'

Maida was all gratitude and eager attention while Norwell explained that the old uncle, of whom she had so often heard, had promised to send a cheque for four hundred pounds; but that he would obstinately take his leisure in sending it, which leisure might be the ruin of his nephew if prolonged beyond three days more. There was just a chance that the cheque might arrive to-morrow, Norwell having written to hurry the old gentleman.

Maida was now in a fit state of conflicting feeling to be left to follow out the train of thought her betrayer had laid. Her heart, balanced with delicate exactness between the points of suspense—hope—fear—it can work on by itself, advantageously, too, to Norwell. He therefore bade her farewell, solemnly engaging to bring her the result of the next post before nine o'clock to-morrow morning.

'Remember, if there *is* anything I can do, Henry,' she said, as he quitted the little room.

'Yes, yes; I'm up to you.' He waved his hand graciously and descended to the street; and Maida set herself to watch for an hour, distant by a whole night's length. But to her surprise, ere nine o'clock of that evening, Norwell again showed himself. She saw immediately that something was amiss, for he looked more gloomy than ever. Throwing himself down on the only chair, he flung a letter on the table.

'Confound it! It is come, but it's of no use. I *must* have four hundred or I'm a ruined man.'

A dismal silence succeeded. Maida once tried to speak, but Norwell impatiently hushed her. At last he started from his seat, enlivened by a bright thought, which presented a way of escape.

'It is not without remedy, seeing it's only an old man's mistake. Yes; it can be done!'

Of course Maida brightened too: her smile was almost happy when Norwell said—

'You wish to help me; now is the chance for you.' Drawing a letter from his pocket-book, he handed it to her. 'Read this. You see he here promises me *four* hundred; well, now read that cheque, on the table there. You see it is only for *one* hundred. What am I to do? Am I to be ruined by the old dotard?'

'Certainly not; only don't speak so. Write at once and get him to rectify the blunder. It is an odd one, though, to make.'

'Not for a man of eighty, just in the flurry of starting for the Continent. As for writing to him, why, before I could receive an answer, I should be—ah! well, never mind where. At any rate, it would be useless to write: he has left England by this. We must act first and wake him up afterwards.'

Quite amused at the idea of waiting for his uncle's fidgets, Norwell burst into pretended anger.

'Oh! botheration take it. Wait for him, indeed, when I can remedy it myself.'

Maida asked how he proposed to do so.

'Nothing easier. We must alter the cheque to the amount intended. That's what I want you to do. A woman's touch is so much lighter than a man's. Look here.'

Taking the cheque, he seated himself at the table, and pointed with a pencil to the figures. 'As they are written, it will be easy to turn the *one* into a *four*: the distance readily admits it. See here; a little tail at the end of the one, a stroke through the tail, and it's done. The *spelt* figures are the plague.'

He scanned them thoughtfully, then continued: ''Twill do famously! See, the one is rather indistinct; put an *F* before it, there's room enough; and the tiniest touch to the *e*, and you have a pretty good four. The *n* is as much a *u* as an *n*, thanks to his penmanship.' He imagined Maida was following the pencil in its course over the cheque. Turning his head to make sure of her attention, he saw her standing erect, a look of horror depicted on her blanched features; her hand, uplifted, had stayed itself halfway to her lips, a passion worked beneath that stricken exterior, but not a passion to vent itself in wrath.

'Why, Maida!'

'Oh, Norwell! Do you too spurn me—and with such a request? This is misery.'

In well-affected surprise, Norwell put his arm around her.

'You silly child; what tragedy nonsense is this? Listen to me, Maida.'

All truth herself—strangely enough, through the dark experience of more than two years—she had not learned to doubt her deceiver. She listened to his perjured voice, and the rigidity of her features relaxed; her hand reached its destination, and in an attitude of warning she laid one finger on her lip. Norwell went on to say: 'You may depend it's all right, and that in his book uncle has placed four hundred against my name, or rather against this cheque. 'Tis not the first time he has made so doting a mistake. Excusable, too, poor old fellow; but that won't save me. If *you* will not help me, I must do it myself. I'm not going to founder for his forgetfulness. Of course *I* shall write at once and tell him what we've done, and he'll be glad enough.'

' *We* , Henry?'

'Not unless you choose; but if you will not, I must. Your hand would be better than mine, though; it would make the alteration more perfect.'

'If all this be true, I can discover no necessity for disguise. I understand you do not wish to keep it secret.'

Falsehood is ever petulant over if's. Truth alone can stand the test of the subtle monosyllable.

'It is more fun than I expected,' said Norwell, with a vexed laugh. 'Secret! no; but, you silly puss, however much my uncle meant four hundred, the bank will not pay a sum disagreeing with the cheque. His intentions must be in black and white, or they can't be cashed—they'd be cashiered if you please. Or if the figures showed signs of alteration, there would be an immediate fuss to be sure, though that would be of no consequence except for the delay. A word from Nice would stop their righteous qualms in a moment.'

'Well, but—'

'Now, dear, trust me, I know what I'm about;' (so does Satan when he plants thorns in God's narrow way) 'the only point to be decided is—will you do it, or will you not?—the money I must have; there is no time for debate.'

No, if he stay to debate, Maida's impulse may decline; he remembers she is impulsive.

'I do not understand money matters,' she sighed, resting her eyes trustfully on Norwell. 'If you assure me there is no harm, I will try my best.'

'What harm *can* there be, when it's from my own uncle? See, here is his name; he'll be annoyed enough when he finds what a trick he has served me. Under a similar error would you not do the same by your father, if you were hard up for money?'

'Doubtless—but he is one of a thousand.'

'And may not my uncle be one of a million?'

His voice was so earnest, his manner so open, Maida could no longer hesitate; the cloud that had transiently obscured her lover rolled off, and all was fair. Another trusting look.

'Mind, then, I lean on *you!*'

Poor Maida! Thy pierced hand too soon shall feel the rottenness of the reed thou dependest on. Would God thy hand could premonitarily smart to warn and save thy soul the barbed arrow there concealed. No, no; the reed is whole to sight—substantial, strong, and ready—it were wrong to doubt it.

Oh Norwell, Norwell! Canst thou let those confiding, loving eyes rest upon thee thus, without a blush thrilling thy very soul? Yes. Howmuchsoever his cheek may flush, a gambler cannot blush. The scarlet tide of anger or riot may flow, but it nears not that gentler stream ebbing from its home, the heart—to proclaim its existence by the outward and visible sign—a blush.

Maida sat at the table and Norwell bent over her, directing her pen.

'There—will that do?' she cried, pushing the cheque forward and herself back with the satisfied air of one who has accomplished a difficult task.

'Will it do, Henry?'

'Bravo! Old Rogers himself will be deceived.'

'*Deceived*, Henry?'

'Oh, any word you like will suit me.' His tone was cheerful—there was no deception in it—she was content.

'Now, then, you must sign your name at the back. No, what am I talking about? I am as much Martha Grylls as you. What a lark it is that he always will give a name of his own composure, as the clerk is said to have said—my name isn't fit to appear on paper, I suppose.'

Maida was puzzled until, taking up the cheque, she observed that it was payable to a Martha Grylls or order. Norwell explained that it was a whim of his uncle to trump up all the odd names he could think of; whether to make him laugh, or because he objected to have two Norwells on one paper, he could not tell.

'However, he never honoured me with the feminine gender before. I'm afraid I shall not do justice to the sex. Let's see, Martha Grylls had better write his or her name at the back; then I, Captain Norwell, shan't be the fair possessor of the melodious title in presenting the cheque for payment.'

Maida smiled, while he took up the pen, as if to write the name; he flourished his fingers a few times and then said:

'Well, perhaps you had better do it. I may not write Martharish enough for the personage. Here; just along there. You are more Martha Grylls than I.'

'The M.G. is *very* like your writing, Henry,' she remarked in handing him back the note.

'Now I have become Martha Grylls, I rather like it; it is so peculiar.'

This was spoken playfully. Why did Norwell gaze so sadly on her? Why turn with a face so full of misery as, folding the cheque in his pocket-book, he met her large eyes fixed fondly on him, and heard her almost gleeful voice:

'Now, thank God, you are all right! Now, naughty boy, go and renovate that pale face.'

But the face is perverse, it grows paler, paler still; more haggard draw the lines of care; she fears he is ill—his manner is so unwonted when he hurriedly bids her goodnight in a stifled utterance. 'It is the reaction of his sorrow,' she says, settling herself to a visionary watch of him who still possesses her heart's true worship. Ah, devoted woman, the wrench which tears thee from thine idol is one of crafty might, or it could not succeed.

When Norwell reappeared the next morning, his unrefreshed countenance and listless gait bespoke a sleepless night. Maida was grieved and disappointed. The money had not cured him. What else could she do for him? He was too unwell to ride to the neighbouring town. Would she object to go for him to get the cheque cashed at his uncle's bank? He would stay with the brat during her absence. She did not object—if they would pay her, she would be delighted to go for him. Might the shabbiness of her dress make them hesitate to give her the money? Dear no; who could doubt her authenticity as a gentlewoman? Or if they did, they dare not refuse payment at his uncle's own bank. She accordingly set off in the mail, and reached her destination just before the bank closed for the day. Some question from the clerk drew forth the reply that she had written the signature at the back.

'Then you are Martha Grylls, ma'am?'

Maida smiled, she could not help it; she was so amused at her new name. The clerk thought she smiled at his asking her if she was herself, so he politely said: 'We are obliged to be particular, ma'am.' And it passed off. Martha Grylls left the bank, and took her place in an omnibus, the only conveyance going to —— that afternoon. She anxiously watched for passengers, dreading to be alone with so large a sum of money. At last the door opened, and a hard-featured, red-visaged man plumped down by her, and he proved her sole companion. When they got into the high road this man began to talk to her in an unbecoming way, on which Maida insisted that he should remove from her side, and when he refused to comply, she called to the conductor, and requested his interference; which being lent, Bob Pragg was obliged to change seats, in doing which he vowed a vengeful oath at 'the vixen who couldn't speak pleasant to a fellow traveller.'

When the omnibus stopped at the little inn, a mile and a half from her home, a gentleman approached and spoke to the driver, who forthwith put his head in at the door, and asked Maida her name. 'Grylls,' she instantly replied, fearing to give her own name lest the inquirer should be an emissary of her father; but he was only a husband on the look-out for an expected wife. Grylls was nothing to him so he turned away. Bob Pragg, however, chose to comment on it, by remarking, 'That there name was ugly enough for such a spitfire as she there,' and then chuckling over the notion he repeated, 'Grylls—Grylls,' till he had got the word by heart. Unable to tell why, Maida felt sorry he had got hold of the name. 'Yet why?' she said; 'it is a mere freak. I may never hear it again.' Was it the malice of an evil spirit that persevered in whispering it into her ear? As the omnibus rumbled on, she could not deafen herself to an only voice which kept on—'Grylls!—Martha Grylls!—ah-h-h! Martha Grylls!'

They finally stopped at another inn, a half-mile distant from her lodgings. On descending, Bob Pragg offered her his arm.

'A feller's a catch this time o' night; better let me see you safe home.'

Maida thought it best to receive this suggestion politely, so she answered; 'I have only to go to ——, I am not afraid to walk alone, thank you.'

'You live *there*, do you? I'll call upon you when you're in a jollier temper—good-bye, Mrs. Grylls.'

Taciturn to sullenness sat Norwell. The yellow heap before him roused him not. Maida entreated him to tell her what further ailed him; but he shook off her importunities until the night was far advanced. He then sprang to his feet with a suddenness that made her tremble; turning upon her he cried:

'It is no use to hide it. Without a great sacrifice, I'm a dead man.'

'What sacrifice is there I would not make for you, Henry? My love has never failed. I could do anything but sin for you.'

'And you couldn't do that? What, then, if I tell you you have sinned already?' His eye rested piercingly on her. 'Maida, I am about to sift your love for me.'

A prompt smile would have signified her willingness to be sifted, had not the deep solemnity of Norwell's voice betrayed unusual meaning. She clasped her hands but spoke not: his voice increased in solemnity.

'Maida, the time has come! Do you love me, or do you not? must henceforth be answered in action. Do you know what you have done?'

'No! What? Explain, and quickly.'

'We—have—committed—forgery,' deliberately hissed Norwell; 'and it is too late to retract, unless you would hurl me into hell—for this pistol goes through my heart the instant you decide against me. There—Maida Gwynnham, I am in your hands; kill me if you choose.'

There was a fearful silence in that little upper chamber. The fiercest tempest of wrath, the keenest lightning flash—break forth, rather than that cold, dead stillness. Norwell quailed beneath the dilated gaze that moved not—yet fixed on him—while she who fixed it stood breathless, pale, and chill, as though her life-springs had been touched with ice.

'Speak, Maida! Oh, speak to me!'

No answer came.

A gradual change overspread her face—pitying scorn was depicted there. Another change—revenge sat brooding there. Again a change, and anger recoloured her pallid cheek. Yet once more a change. Her features compressed. The colour went back to the smitten heart, and firm determination was written on her face—her mind was resolved; her voice calm.

'Will it save *you*?'

'Why, why, it shall not get you into a scrape.'

'Do not lie; will it save *you*?' The same calm voice.

'Yes: if you choose it will save me; otherwise—'

The pistol clicked and supplied the blank.

'I am in your power, Maida.'

'And I in yours?' quietly and unwisely asked she.

But Norwell, too agitated to note the question in its advantageous view, merely replied: 'Why, no, hardly that, because you could implicate me.'

'I would leave that to Captain Norwell,' sneered Maida. 'Yes, to *you*, Henry. The scales have fallen from my eyes; I see it all too late, as, too late, I have discovered you. Detection is possible: your *hand* did not commit the forgery; your fame must not be touched, it stands too high; but Maida Gwynnham, that outcast! It matters not how low her fall: a meet resting-place is she for scorn and infamy.'

Norwell's agonized expression met her in its abject helplessness; it softened her, and tenderly passionate she pleaded.

'Oh, Henry! For you I have already sacrificed all that a woman's pride holds dear; for you I can go on with the sacrifice—yes, even to perdition. But *must* it be? Is there no other test wherewith to try my love? None but this, that will also embrace you in its scathing grasp? For, Henry, I love you enough to suppose that you could never more be happy were you thus to ruin a fellow creature. For yourself, your own peace, I plead; for myself I care not; to live to suffer for you would be to live to some purpose; yet cannot you destroy that fatal purpose? Destroy it, Norwell. I know the pangs of that gnawing worm, remorse, and would fain tear its ruthless fang from your bosom, even to plant it in mine own forever. Norwell! Dear Henry, be persuaded.'

He was charmed to the spot; she had never looked more wildly beautiful; it was destruction to gaze at her; he must yield to the impassioned pleader; another minute, and his guilty plan had been borne a blasted breath upon the wind, and his lips, eased of their load of sin, had promised repentance. He withdrew his eyes. 'Your debt, Norwell, your debt!' whispered the tempter. Still spoke the eloquent features: 'Dear Henry, reclaim your purpose.' 'Disgrace, prison, death,' urged the tempter. Still outspoke the eloquent features: 'Do, Henry; dear Henry, *do*!' There was a time when she would have added, 'For *my* sake;' but that time was now traditional. The mental struggle continued. The tempter laid an official tap on the shoulder of his imagination—he gave a startled cry; the purpose lay safe within his heart.

'Be it so,' cried Maida.

'Oh, Maida! Can you make the sacrifice?'

'If *you* can, Norwell; there lies the bitterness to me.'

'Oh! Do not, do not speak so! Pity, pity poor weak-minded Norwell, who cannot bear the finger of shame. *I* am the object of pity, not *you*. Your lofty nature may find happiness in vicarious suffering, but for me what is there?'

'It need not, *shall* not be.'

'It *must*, Maida; would you betray me?' His fingers played on the pistol.

'Not whilst I can suffer in your stead. Go, Henry; you have nothing to fear from me. The sin, mine by carelessness, shall become mine by substitution, for I see no other way to save you from punishment.'

'And from death. I would not live a second after disgrace. Oh, Maida! Be this your support—you save a soul from death.'

She shuddered; she longed to be alone, and beckoned Norwell to leave; he was not sorry to do so; it was hazardous to remain in her presence. Not venturing another look, he said:

'Then I am in your hands: my life is yours, to spare or slay.'

'*I* committed the forgery; let that suffice you, Norwell.'

The door slammed on him and he was gone.

I am a felon! thought Maida, and she recoiled from herself as though the brand of infamy already burned on her; then dropping on her knees, she cried, 'O God! Lay not this sin to my charge—it is to save one dearer than my life. Do Thou acquit me, and I can bear the lot of shame.'

We must do Captain Norwell the justice to say, his steps were lighter than his heart that night; and ere day broke he was striving to forget his compunctions in a hurried journey to London, whither we shall not follow him—we must return to desolated Maida, until he again shall force himself on our unwilling attention.

CHAPTER 4

The Felon

THE night seemed very long, yet all too swiftly it sped for the watcher, who sat silently counting the heavy sighs, which one by one doled out an infant's life. The heavings were fearfully audible—up, down, up, down, fainter, fainter, and the long night seemed longer still, yet all too short for the weary watcher. The clock had struck one; two hours more, and still that heaving breath alternately drew hope from the mother's soul, and sent a swift fear through it. There was a feeble smile upon the baby's parted lips; Maida listened; the world for another breath, though it snatch the last hope from her bleeding heart. But the little breast lay still, the snowy linen covering it heaved not; the lips were still disparted in a half-formed smile.

'He cannot be gone!'

Yes, poor Maida, henceforth thou art lonely. That smile was life's quittance-gate; the sigh that passed through it bore thy child to heaven. Lonely Maida!

The morning light shimmered coyly through the closed pane, and fell upon a lovely pair—death in its reality, cold, but void of mockery; life in its unreality, cold, and brimful of subtle mockery, drooped together on that couch. But for the low, tearless sob which broke at intervals from Maida, you would have thought that she, too, shared the kind reality of death. She knelt by the couch, resting her face on the baby's pillow; her hair fell like a pall over the little corpse, and strikingly the chill pallor of death looked up from the sable covering.

The clock had struck five—still Maida bent over the little sleeper, unconscious that she was watched by Norwell, who had ascended the stairs without noise. Horror-stricken he stood at the door. He came to impart direful news; but news and everything were forgotten as this sight of sorrow burst upon him. Gazing at the beautiful personification of solitary grief, he thought—

What have I done? Where is the bosom upon which this bereaved mother should be weeping? Can I be so base as to make her a further sacrifice? No, I will not! Every self-interest shall rather be sacrificed to *her* —my poor Maida!

Nay, turn thy pity on thyself, Norwell; save thy pity for that moment when thy just resolves, now really meant, pass not into effect, but into air with the first smile that shall pacify the accusing voice thus questioning within thee.

For some time Norwell remained a spectator only of the scene, so touching in its passiveness, so heart-rending in its reality. He then advanced on tiptoe to the bed, and stooping over the kneeling form, whispered:

'Maida, it is I; look at me, dear.' A tear sparkled in his eye.

Her lids languidly unclosed, and the purple depths which lay beneath fixed unknowingly on him. The tear that a minute before quivered on his lash rested on Maida's cheek: that tear was worth the world; to repay it she felt she could give a life of suffering. Oh, Maida Gwynnham, we remember not a tear, but tears, 'real tears', that fell like burning kisses on thy cheek; have they been blotted from thy memory? Oh, God, that they had, comes Maida's answer. Her eyes again unclosed. One flash darted, as if from beneath their dreamy depths, showing that the fierceness of their fire had been more than equal to the test of many waters. One flash they gave, but not the lightning flash which blasts: it was the kindling glance of love untold, triumphant over pain.

She remained seemingly unconscious for a time; then suddenly starting to her feet, and pressing her clenched hand on her heart, as if to keep down by force the choking emotion which was swelling there, she exclaimed—

'Norwell, what brings you—bad news?'

With the eagerness with which Maida spoke, Norwell gave his former resolutions to the wind. Not appreciating, or perhaps not recognising, that secret power by which a noble nature can turn from its own misery to assist another in distress, he thought that he had felt more for Maida than she felt for herself, and hastily replied—

'Bad news indeed for me, unless you stand steadfast.'

The old look of withering scorn shot across her, but she subdued it, and slowly and very calmly responded—

'Once more and forever I repeat I am yours for life. Oh, would it were for death!'

She stepped to the bed, and, with a delicacy lost upon Norwell, drew a fair linen kerchief over the corpse. Many women would have used the stiffening finger of death as a last means of pointing 'shame' to their deceiver. Maida covered it, lest it should even do so unawares. She would not occupy the vantage-ground offered her by the mighty champion. She stood upon a loftier ground, an unapproachable elevation, at which her opponent could only stare in impotent wonder.

Oh, Maida! How great had been thy power hadst thou occupied that eminence in the character for which Nature so nobly formed thee! Hadst thou shone thence a living invitation to the paths of peace, who could have resisted thine appeal? Still exquisite in ruin thou must crown the summit, but it will be as a haunted grandeur, on which men gaze with awe, and, hurrying by, hint of a darkened past.

Returning to his side, she very quietly asked—

'Bad news you say, Norwell? I am ready to hear and ready to act.'

'Then they are on us, Maida,' hurriedly returned the captain, the danger of his situation vividly presenting itself to his hitherto beclouded senses; 'it is all discovered, and,' wiping the large drops fast gathering on his forehead, 'I fear they have a clue to me; for *you* they are in full cry.'

'They need raise no cry, for I shall not lead them a chase; but you, oh! *you*, Norwell, must and *shall* be saved.'

Norwell's great anxiety seemed to be to talk on as fast as possible in order to prevent certain questions presenting themselves to Maida's mind—questions that, debased as he was, he trembled to face. As yet it was evident that she dreamt not of treachery. Her baby's illness had not allowed her to ponder the bearings of the case; it had never occurred to her that without some deep-laid scheme of cunning and crime her name could not be associated with the forgery. Had it occurred she would have discarded the thought as a horrible romance of imagination. Norwell had not prepared her beforehand for the blow he was about to strike, fully believing that it would be unnecessary to deal it. He made every arrangement for it, but at the same time hoped it might be uncalled for, the alteration in the cheque having been perfect. 'Why, then,' said he, 'alarm her and make her abhor me for a sin I may not commit?' So he trusted an explanation to the last minute, to the infinite peril of letting Maida hear, from the evidence brought against her, how she had been victimized. Her moral courage and presence of mind might bear her through; but Norwell doubted whether her indignant surprise or impulsive spirit would pass the cruel ordeal without revealing a discrepancy to the keen-eyed barrister.

'These hands committed the act,' quietly said Maida. 'I shall acknowledge *that* and no more.'

'Noble! Generous!— '

A scuffle downstairs arrested the captain's eulogy and Maida's impatience.

'We are lost!' feebly ejaculated Norwell.

Maida placed herself in a defiant position. The dismay was needless. A drunken man had reeled into the house and was inclined to dispute his ejection—this had been the noise. It had, however, the effect of arousing Norwell to the necessity of speed in bringing this interview to a conclusion.

'One word and I must be off; should I be caught with you it would be all over with me—it will be a pleasure to your noble dis—'

'Cowering coward,' murmured Maida, 'have done with flattery.'

'Well, then, be careful what you say—when you are apprehended be silent— when obliged to speak weigh well your words, or you—you will betray me.'

Maida shuddered.

'Now haste away, you have been here too long already. I am prepared for them;' and then, as if repeating her lesson, she whispered:

'*I*—did—it! They will only get those three words from me.'

Norwell was half down stairs when he returned, took Maida's hand, and looking anxiously at her, said:

'Maida, you will hear strange things. I have been hurried on to a point I never thought I could reach.'

'Go, Norwell—go.' He obeyed, but again came back.

'Maida, your punishment will be heavy—it may be—'

'Transportation for life!' calmly added Maida.

'And *I* a man—O Maida! Try, *do* try to escape. I will aid you. I will go with you.'

Again he descended and again he returned.

'Do you—can you forgive me? Can you think in any other way of me than as a cowardly wretch?'

'I can think of you as a martyr!'

Norwell understood the searching tone. 'Perhaps we have met for the last time,' he exclaimed, as the door closed upon him.

The reader will remember that they met once more.

Left by herself, Maida stood irresolute. The bare possibility of implicating Norwell was a poignant thought. She bit her lips as if already refusing to answer some wily questioner.

'What is it?' she cried, 'what is it? This feeling here that tells me I have a dreadful something to recollect?'

She started from a deep reverie with the air of one who wakes to a yet oblivious sense of an impending sorrow.

'What is it? Oh, what is it?' Her eyes fell upon the bed, and she was answered. She gazed wildly around the room.

'They will take my babe from me, and I have not even wept over it! No! The scalding drops are fevering my brain, but they will not come forth. My babe! My child!' she continued, in the thrilling accents of despair, 'the last comfort is denied thy wretched mother—she may not lay thee in thy grave.'

'Why not?' she quickly added, 'they are not here yet. The morning is yet early—no one is astir. Who will miss Maida Gwynnham's child?'

She stole on tip-toe to the bed.

Poor Maida! There is no creature near. No eye is on thee but *one*, and that is full of pity, erring and sinful as thou art.

She waited not for a second thought, but hastily descended the stairs, bearing her unconscious burden wrapped in the accustomed shawl. About half a mile distant lay a lovely unfrequented spot. Maida had often wished to rest her own weary head there. With a palpitating heart, thither she bent her steps: every sound made her start. The fugitive flying from the blood avenger could not have glanced more trembling behind. But Maida's fears were not for herself.

'Another hour and some rough grasp might tear thee from me, my precious babe, and thou wouldst have a tearless grave—now thy own mother will lay thee down, how tenderly!'

The morning was calm and bright—there was that mysterious silence around that is only made the more impressive by the faint sounds which occasionally disturb it. The very birds had hushed their cheery carols as though they knew that songs of mirth fall heavily upon a burdened mind. Was it the still small voice[1] which spoke to Maida in that gentle scene—the voice which she refused to hear in the stormy blasts that had desolated her haughty spirit? For she wept. Placing her babe upon the turf, she clasped her hands and, looking upwards, exclaimed:

'Oh, God! Thou hast made everything pure and beautiful. Canst Thou look on *me*, the only evil here? Oh, God! If this be sin, forgive it for the sake of Him whose name I have forfeited to utter.'

Courage, Maida! Thou hast breathed a prayer, and prayer was never yet denied, how long soever delayed the answer. It is stored for thee in heaven's golden treasury, and yet must yield its plenteous harvest. She knelt and tried the mould. It was soft and crumbly, readily giving to her touch. There was a rustle in the bushes. She peered cautiously around. Nothing was to be seen. She continued her labour—another rustle—she sprang to her feet—all was quiet again. She had removed the earth about a foot's depth when a shout was heard. A man leaped from the hedge and clutched her arm.

'Halloo, missus! I've a watched you this quarter hour—just to be *sure* what you're up to—if this yer an't seeing with one's own eyes, I'm blastered!'

Maida stretched her hand towards the child; the man laid his upon it.

'This yer's our article, if you please, missus. By jingo! You're an old hand. Here we've been after you for one thing—a bit o' paper business—and we catches you up to another that beats t'other all hollow, or I ain't Bob Pragg.'

Here two constables appeared, and with a look of disapprobation at the ruffianly man, desired him to desist. Then quietly taking Maida's arms, they requested her to accompany them.

'Take up the child, Watkins,' said the elder constable; whispering, as the other obeyed, 'any signs or marks of violence?'

Bob Pragg, who seemed in his glory, and most importunate to appropriate to himself a share in the arrest, replied aloud —

'None as *I* sees for, and nothing suspectible[2] about. Pizin, p'raps,' he winked mysteriously to the men.

'We'll thank you to mind your own business, Mr. Pragg,' returned Watkins; 'you've showed us the woman, and you've nothing more to do with her. Go forward. When you're wanted you'll be summoned. Go forward! Go forward!'

Bob Pragg, misunderstanding this 'go forward,' took it as a personal insult, and went forward with an air of injured prerogative, grumbling the while to his hobnails[3] —

'They gets all they can out of a feller, and then keeps the game to 'emselves.'

His eyes glistened when Watkins drew a pair of handcuffs from his pocket, and as quickly fell when the other constable beckoned.

'No, no, Watkins, she's quiet enough;' Then speaking aloud, as a hint to Maida,

'We only uses them for fractious parties.'

The hint, however, was thrown away. Maida heard it not; she was, as the senior constable had said, quiet, fearfully quiet. A ghastly disdain sneered from every feature.

Had her anguish been less, she had raved on them such a storm as her spirit alone knew how to raise. But could one word have created a thunderbolt to destroy her persecutors, no word would have formed upon those parched and paralysed lips. The men, Pragg excepted, were awed by the statue-like presence before them, and inclined to show her what respect they consistently could.

'Now, missus, we'll onways, if you please, and so long as you're biddable, we'll make you as comfortable as circumstances permits.' (A grin from Bob Pragg.) 'We never acts disrespectful before we're obliged. Now, Mr. Pragg, mind yourself, if you please.'

Watkins lifted the dead body, and, wrapping it in the shawl, carried it bundle-wise under his arm. Even this irreverence failed to attract Maida's attention. She was revolving some yet unfathomed mystery, or moulding some plan that yielded not readily to her wishes.

By an interchange of expressive nods, the constables had remarked Maida's start when they examined the corpse for marks of violence, and had noted it as a proof of guilt.

Ay, she had started, and with the start an intrepid thought had rushed into her mind—a thought whose purpose was to place Captain Norwell beyond reach of danger, because it should place her at the bar of justice in a different position of guilt.

'I have it!' she at last exclaimed; and a smile of triumph illumined her face. Then the old look of firm resolve stamped its awful though silent fiat upon her countenance. The mystery was explained, the plan moulded, the intrepid thought grappled with; that smile of triumph defied each one.

Arrested for forgery under the alias of Martha Grylls, Maida Gwynnham was indicted at the next assizes for the wilful murder of her child, the bill of indictment for forgery being held subservient to the more terrible charge of murder.

In Maida's cupboard was found a bottle that awakened vivid suspicions against the prisoner. It was produced in court, and a shiver ran through the audience as from the skull and cross-bones the dreadful word 'poison' with unmistakable distinctness bore witness to the alleged guilt.

Some laudanum found in the baby corroborated the testimony of the label on the phial.

Now comes the explanation of that smile that broke (a gleam of sunshine) from the disdainful gloom of Maida's face. A word to the wise is sufficient for them. The interpretation, therefore, shall lie in the facts—that the same exultant smile burst forth when the foreman of the jury gave the verdict:

'We find Martha Grylls guilty of the wilful murder of her child.'

And that, if possible, a still more victorious smile shone on the judge's declaration:

'Having been found guilty of the higher crime, which I shall sentence to the full rigour of the law, it were useless to urge the lesser charge against Martha Grylls.'

Then with solemn pathos, amidst the breathless hush of the court, the judge drew the fatal symbol on his head, and pronounced the death warrant, which was received by the court with one prolonged sob of smothered feeling, and welcomed by Maida Gwynnham as the benediction after a tedious sermon.

CHAPTER 5

Bob Pragg

A CASE of circumstantial evidence invariably creates a deep sensation in the public mind. The contest between opposing counsel is never so exciting, never is the battle so fiercely fought, so barely won, as when circumstantial evidence throws down the gage.

Not born and bred to the strife, juries hate a case of circumstantial evidence. There are so many sleepless nights after a 'guilty' verdict, so many dream-distorted sleeps, that they would rather buy themselves off the list fifty times over than incur a seat in the box.

Maida Gwynnham's trial aroused a far-spread interest. It was pre-eminent in every conversation. It was tiraded in tavern and tap, canvassed in coffee-room and club, and preached from pulpit and press. One clergyman made it a glowing fulfilment of the ancient prophecy [1] —'Be sure your sin will find you out.' Wonderful to tell, and contrary to usage in such themes of common interest, opinion unanimously agreed with the verdict. No one dissenting voice laid its useless veto on the judgement. The case was clear as daylight (Query, is daylight always clear?). The prisoner's guilt undoubted. The whole course of evidence had but one bearing. The most prejudiced could not question the decision. There need be no sleepless nights, no disturbed dreams, for the most fastidious jurist after this trial. Had but a solitary circumstance broken down, there would have been a gap for doubt. Had but one fact proved fractious, that one fractious fact would have kicked the whole evidence on the head, and triumphantly borne off the accused, giving the populace an opportunity of chorussing with a loud 'amen' the learned counsel's earnest admonition to the jury—

'If the prosecution has left a doubt upon your mind, in God's name give the prisoner the benefit of it.'

But as no circumstance broke down, as no fact proved fractious, the vox populi sent its 'amen' aloft, one-voiced, applauding the same learned counsel's solemn warning—

'If, on the other hand, the evidence brings conviction to your mind, let no earthly consideration prevent you from doing justice. Your country demands it of you. The rising generation demands it of you. Your God demands it of you. Justice is God's work, and you are His ministers to enforce it.'

'Amen!' shouted Bob Pragg, from the depths of his heart. He had been subpoenaed as witness, and now smoked the pipe of content over the satisfactory result of his witness-ship. He sat in a public-house of the worst description, and was surrounded by a set of men looking sufficiently suspicious to claim him as their chief. They were celebrating Bob's feats in the witness box with a treat of drink from the witness money.

We shall have much to do with Mr. Pragg before we finish with him, therefore we may as well make his acquaintance now, as he is in a better temper than usual.

Bob is oracular in speech, wink, and innuendo. His opinions will have more weight if we first learn that experience renders him capable of forming an opinion, and misguided talent of subverting one. It is not impossible that years ago he should have been what is called *good*-looking, now he is emphatically *bad*-looking. Unpleasant thoughts of apoplexy are suggested by his short, thick neck. He is a walking (not Walker's) dictionary,[2] with illustrated meanings of the whole list of words beginning with Hard. Hardiness, hard-hearted, hard-favoured,[3] line his forehead. Hardware is in every inch of the man, and all other hards are to be found in this living page. You can never cry, "Tisn't here!' with him before your eyes.

Pragg had given many mysterious winks, but they had fallen innocuous on the lethargic perceptions of his companions. At last, knocking out the ashes of his pipe with an energy that sent its bowl into the fire and a start into his sleepy mates, he enthusiastically exclaimed—

'It was the cleanest bit of business I ever seed!'

'After the old game again, Bob?'

'Eigh! I shan't forget it in a hurry. Clean slap off like *that* ain't everyday work, I'll promise you. I've 'tended 'sizes all my life,' (we know that, Bob, you needn't tell us in what particular character) 'and never heard anything to bate this.[4] I'm very curious in cir'stantial evidence—got a dozen cases pat at my fingers' ends—but this yer woman's takes the glaze out of 'em all. Nothing but cir'stantial evidence for *me* after this.'

'How so, Bob?'

Bob only answered by a wink, which he intended should mean a great deal, and proceeded. 'Be blastered, if it didn't convince Grylls herself a'most! Beau-ti-ful!'

And the amateur-like admiration of Bob was delightful, as, with upcast eyes and twitching chin, he repeated—

'Beau-ti-ful! I say, man. Grylls herself couldn't stand such evidence. If the woman didn't look foul at herself 'fore 'ceedings was over I b'ant Bob Pragg. No one could resist it. The facts—there they was, cut out and fitted into one th'other for all the world as if they was true. There weren't one stretcher;[5] not a single lump that could stick in his Lordship's throat. How glorious! The whole batch—judge, ranters, and humbugging twelve, swallowed it smooth down without a wry mouth; and then to hear his Lordship's speech after gulping the dose! Grace after meat wern't nothing to it!'

'To see 'en shake his hand to heaven and tell how vengeance always tracks a feller's secret steps, blastered if it wern't 'most a pity to throw away such a sermint.'

'What on earth be after, Bob, d'ye think they were all sold?'

'Head over heels, man!' chuckled Bob; 'there wern't no more truth in any of them blessed statements nor there is in *you*' (Bob was always sarcastic).

His hearers were fairly roused, and Stuckey suggested, 'That's only what you believes, not what you *knows*, Pragg.'

'Catch me,' winked Bob; 'b'lieving is knowing with me. Bob Pragg, Esq., don't easy b'lieve what he don't know.'

A skeptical shake of the head from Stuckey.

'Look 'e here, man, this is the go. They b'lieves a thing, and *then* sees it clear as moonshine. *I* sees a thing as clear as sunshine; then, and not till then, I b'lieves. Faith without sight ain't Bob Pragg's religion. They b'lieves that Grylls is a thumper—so pat before their blessed eyes facts goes to make her one—a ready-made murderer, caught in the very act, jumps up before 'em. But all the facts in creation couldn't make me see a murderer in that woman. So, as I don't *see*, I won't b'lieve.'

'An old sweetheart, eh! Pragg?'

The *subject* was an old sweetheart! Only answering the insinuation by a nod, Pragg continued—

'I learns by 'xperience. She an't the right sort for murder. She's pluck enough, but no natturl relish that way. You sees that in her eye, that looks straight out on a body; no this ways and that ways with her. She'd do for herself in a jiffy, if needs be, or she'd fight like a tiger for a feller in distress' (feller doesn't always mean a male); 'but she'd never lay a finger on a helpless mortal, much less on her own hincent baby. They're all wrong from top to toe, or I a'nt Bob Pragg.'

'Then shame on it, I cries! Why on earth did you stand there with your lies all 'gainst an innocent fellow creature; and she a woman, and a beauty too?'

'Not a lie in the whole blessed matter,' coolly replied Bob. 'There's the beauty of cir'stantial evidence. Truth every farthing of it; but every ha'p'oth confounded falsity. I stood there, man, to tell what I was paid for—telling facts, not to give 'em my thoughts, that wasn't wanted nor paid for.'

'I guess they were some which would have paid a trifle more for your *thoughts* than ever you gained by your *facts*; the woman's friends now?'

'Not a friend as could be heard of,' winked Bob. 'Trust me for *that*. 'Fore I used the facts I'd have sold 'em dirt cheap if I could have turned an honest penny by the thoughts.'

'Well, Pragg, *I* couldn't take a woman's life, with no provication, in that way. If I kills, it's 'cause I hates.'

'Nor me neither, Stuckey. I've natturl spite 'gainst that Grylls. For all *that*, I wouldn't take her life for any money. There'll be no hanging, take my word for it. 'Twill only be trans'tation for life.' Bob Pragg knew his ground; he wouldn't have allowed killing. 'Trans'tation I don't object to for her; 'twill cure my natturl spite and do the woman good herself. She *wants* change, as the doctors say.'

'Supposing you'm right, Bob, and she don't swing, what a spree [6] if the right one's took't at last, and is sent out to bring the other home!'

'Never, Stuckey; jist 'cause there's ne'er a real one to be catched. There's no murder in the case, tho' the evidence was brimming with it. The brat died natturl.'

This was uttered in a tone that offered no appeal; nevertheless Stuckey ventured one.

'What d'ye say to the poison found *in* the child? If seeing an't believing, finding is. Sure you won't object to letting another kill the baby, since you won't have it that Grylls did it. What can you say to the laudanum, [7] eh! Bob?'

'You've never heard of "Godfrey's," have you? [8] Then I have, and know that up north there's more babbies sent to sleep by that there stuff than you, or the wise wigged gents, thinks for. The brat's mortal bad; has a confounded stomick-ache, or some such squealing fit; Grylls gives 'en a drop of laudanum, and the child's quiet enough—more quiet than the mother meant for. It pops off 'fore the stuff's digested; so you finds it where Grylls put it—a mere c'incidence, as the judges says, that the discovery was made—a mere c'incidence (is that the word, Stuckey?) says I, that the dying and the pizin happed together. The one hadn't nothing to do with th'other, that's *my* evidence; but 'tan't *cir'stantial*, so goes for naught.'

'Well, Pragg, I say again, your spirit's admeerable, but I couldn't see a woman swing for a drop of laudanum, or "Godfrey's," or what's you call it, if that's the true go.'

'Curse your laud'num and your "Godfrey's!" Who said she'd gave either? 'Twas something mortal stronger that killed the brat. The same'll kill you one day. Do you know 'en? Death! As to swinging, why *you'll* swing before *she* does. Mark me, once and for all, I tell 'e 'twill only be trans'tation for life; and do you think just for *that*, I'd set 'em on a right track, to the lasting injury of the blessed cause? That ain't *my* religion. Show 'em their foolery now, and they'd think twice before they'd act another time; and who knows whose turn 'twill be next—perhaps yours, perhaps Bob Pragg's? Mind, as many rogues jumps through the trap of cir'stantial evidence, and runs clean off, as falls in and gets a hiding. If it's one man's enemy it's th'other's friend. Don't you thank your eternal stars if Jones pays your score and lets you off scot free?'

'Hurrah!' cried Stuckey.

'You can always make peace with yourself by guessing that tho' Jones is working out your debt, be blastered if he wouldn't have hundreds of his own to make good otherwise; so he may all as well give you a turn as not. When he only pays his own score, he saves nobody; but when he pays another body's, why, he saves another body without losing hisself, seeing he an't called on to do for more than one, hisself or not hisself.'

'Hurrah!' again shouted Stuckey.

'Hurrah for cir-cum-stan-tial evidence!' cried Bob.

'Hurrah for cir-cum-stan-tial evidence!' was echoed through the tap-room.

And straightway Mr. Pragg proposed the toast, 'The everlasting prosperity of circumstantial evidence.'

'And the rising generation,' waggishly amended Stuckey.

'And the justice's sermint—may it ever be written on our hearts,' added Bob.

So, amid the uproarious merriment of the party, were these three toasts responded to with three times three.

Norwell had not known what to understand by the unexpected charge brought against Maida. As one by one the proofs of her guilt were produced, he was staggered; they were unjustifiable. The dreadful crime could, without doubt, be traced. True—he had seen the child lying dead, and Maida moaning over it; but may not she have murdered it for all that? And may not the moan have been that of remorse? Thus pondering, he glanced towards the bar—loath, very loath, we must admit it, to believe any harm of Maida; when a slight curl in the corners of her nether lip—a look he well comprehended—convinced him of her innocence more than a verdict for her could have done. When he perceived the fatal termination of the trial, even in the distance—too sick at heart to remain—he hurried from the court; and turning at the door to draw in one long gaze of Maida, their eyes met, and the fuel was added to the fire of her constancy; and its smoke smothered the last thought of restitution which had lingered in his heart.

Assured by a barrister that the sentence would be commuted to transportation for life, Norwell pacified himself with the thought, '*That* will seem nothing after such a fright, she would have had that otherwise,' and gladly crept out of the loophole opened by circumstance (Providence, he said), and still wider opened by the fair law of England; he crept out into—

The ballroom! No harm either—it was the assize ball.

CHAPTER 6

Mary Doveton

> Form of beauty veil thy face,
> Worse my soul's deformity
> Showeth by thy godlike grace
> Form of beauty, gazing on thee
> Cometh there a voice within,
> Saying, 'She is sister to thee,
> Separate though by shame and sin,
> Thou amid the husks art lying
> She among the stars doth shine—
> Yet the spark is never-dying
> Which uniteth hers to thine. [1]

THERE was one of that gay group in the ballroom, from whom the history of Maida Gwynnham had not passed as an idle tale. Mary Doveton, the small, slight girl who had spoken so feelingly, could not forget the conversation. The subject of it haunted alike her waking and her sleeping thoughts, until she determined to visit the prison. A bold resolve for so timid and gentle a creature.

'What,' said she, 'if the woman would not see me, or should be abusive?' She shuddered. 'If the character they give her be true, I have no right to expect more than her indignation for my intrusion; but I must try; it would be a lasting joy to speak a word of comfort to the poor outcast. I will take some of my very best flowers, and if she will not speak to me, they shall speak to her. I will place them silently in her hand, and leave her.'

When the permit was obtained, Miss Doveton culled a choice bouquet—a not insignificant sacrifice—she loved her flowers—each one was a treasure. God speed thee, Mary Doveton, on thine errand of mercy; there is an angel by thy side, though thou seest him not.

As the gaoler drew back the bolt of Maida's cell, Miss Doveton unconsciously grasped his hand, as if she would fain delay. The stern ruggedness of his face softened as he met the beseeching gaze of those lovely eyes, and in a tone of would-be kindness, he muttered—

'Lord love your innocent face, she'm as quiet as a lamb, unless you raise the devil's own spirit in her; and you don't seem likely for that. 'Tis the parsons she hates.'

Have you ever seen a child brought to its parent for punishment? Have you noticed how the little truant stands abashed in the awful presence, its eyes fixing timorously on its father, as the golden head drops in frightened submission to the pending judgment?

If so, you may picture Mary Doveton inside Maida's cell. Her bonnet had fallen off, leaving waves of golden hair to float unrestrained over her shoulders. The only ray of light that made day in the dismal spot, fell full on her; and her hair, glistening in that solitary ray, seemed to give forth a halo.

Maida beheld in amazement the beautiful apparition. As it stood there so still, so saint-like, you might have asked with her, 'Is it an angel?' had you not known it to be an exquisite form of mortality.

Struggling to keep down the impulse which urged her to greet the wondrous stranger with tearful eagerness, Maida said—

'Do you want me?'

'They let me come to see you—may I?'

'If you are not come to read the Bible.'

'No, I never thought of it; but if you wish—'

'No, indeed, thank you. It angers me dreadfully to have people come palavering. Now I am a wretched castaway they come with their Bible, as though it were an instrument of torture, fit for *me* and such-like felons. Pah! This morning the chaplain read, with much unction, "The wicked shall be turned into hell." Sweet consolation, isn't it?'

'Dreadful! Only you would find many passages quite as true as that, only full of hope, if you read the Bible,' replied Miss Doveton, with gentle naivety. 'Whenever I am unhappy I read the Bible, and you cannot tell how it comforts me.'

'You, dear innocent! What can there be there not soothing to you? It is very delightful to read of peace, joy, happiness, and glory; but what if you read of remorse, misery, death, and hell; would it *then* be sweet?'

'Oh, dear!' the tears starting to her eyes. 'Here I came to console you, and I've made you worse! I do not understand these things; but I am very sure there *is* comfort in the Bible, though there *are* also such dreadful truths.'

'Truths?'

'Oh, yes! They would not be terrible were they not truths; there is the comfort.'

Poor Miss Doveton was thoroughly bewildered.

'Terror and comfort together? How? Where?'

'Dear, dear! I am so puzzled; I never came to preach, I mean,—what *do* I mean? The very knowledge that all the bad is true, tells one that the good is also true; so that there is sweet even in the bitter.'

'How do you know that either is true? Who ever came back to say so?'

'You mustn't ask me, indeed; I do not understand these matters. I believe, because I cannot help believing; every feeling in me says the Bible is all true; besides, I saw grandmamma die; she smiled through her shocking pains, and said she was so happy—and she could not have been happy about nothing.'

'No; trifles would not amuse in the solemn hour of death; but I do not like this kind of talk.'

'I had no previous thought of entering on it. Is there anything I can do for you? Any friend you would like me to write to? I should be so pleased to be of some service to you.'

A faint smile only replied to the kind questions. An inward struggle kept Maida silent for a few minutes. Mary had drawn close, and was now sitting by her side.

'I have not a friend in the world,' at last trembled from the prisoner's lips.

'No father? No mother? No one to weep for you? Oh! Should not I be wicked if I had no one to love me? You must have been very desolate!'

Maida Gwynnham hated pity, her proud spirit rebelled against it; but there was something in the low, sweet murmur in which Mary had spoken, that soothed rather than irritated. It sounded not as pity doled out, an alm to her suffering state. It seemed more like a thought that had strayed into speech without the thinker's permission.

'I have a father, but I have made him my enemy!'

'Oh! Where is he? I will go myself and implore him to forgive you; this very day—if possible.'

The old look of withering scorn was beginning to gather, and poor Miss Doveton feared she had been too hasty; but the look was not meant for her.

'He does not know I am here; it is *I* who will not pardon myself, not my father who refuses to forgive. I believe he—'

The tears were in Miss Doveton's eyes; she turned her head and strained her lids to the widest opening-point, in the vain endeavour to make the unruly drops be quiet; but pit-pat, pit-pat they fell softly on the hard floor. Maida leant forward, supporting her face, hands, and arms on her knees. Her breast heaved violently, as if acting the safety-valve to some tumultuous feeling that would otherwise break through every obstruction. Whilst so seated, she heard a timid voice—

'You have one friend.'

It was a touching sight, those two sister spirits blending, each one according to her own peculiar temper. The earnest, sorrowful gaze of Mary bent on the drooping, convulsed form of the convict. The sobs of agony, no longer to be checked, were easing one by one the o'erburdened heart of Maida Gwynnham—a storm-shower characteristic of her. The gloomy thunderous cloud shadowing her life could only find relief in so passionate an outbreak. While the purely sympathetic and scarcely perceived tears of Mary Doveton distilled like grateful dew. The heaven of her heart could never gather a cloud sufficiently dense to yield more than the soft rain upon the tender herb. She could not be passionate even in the two chief endowments of her soul—love and truth.

There was an unexpected witness of that scene; he never forgot it; it stereotyped itself[2] upon his soul, and opened a new era in his career. By some chance it had been forgotten that Maida already had company in her cell; so when Captain Norwell presented his order at the prison gate he gained admittance, and the gaoler, who waited outside the cell to re-conduct Miss Doveton through the corridors, was able to push back the door without attracting notice from the inmates. Norwell was about to enter when he observed that Maida was not alone. A glance sufficed to tell him who was the stranger. If Maida had thought her angelic as she paused in the doorway, how much more so did Mary appear in Norwell's sight; kneeling on the hard earth in that dark corner, her hands crossed upon her bosom, her eyes upturned in tender pleading, she seemed to him one of those bright beings sent forth to minister of the mercies of their God: the wings with which accepted belief invests those celestial messengers, imagination supplied in the flowing drapery of a morning dress, which fell in graceful folds around her. Except in adding to the effect of the exquisite *coup d'oeil*,[3] Maida bore no share in Norwell's admiration. He saw but one form, and felt he could almost become the habitant of a felon's cell if thereby he might earn a place in the affections of so fair, so pure a creature as Mary Doveton. Even his perverted perceptions failed not to discern that prayer was eloquent in those upturned eyes: though no utterance betrayed the hallowed secret, it was clear to even him that the spirit sought from its heavenly Master a fresh commission of mercy.

'Oh! Would that she prayed for me, and I should be sure of heaven,' mentally cried he who prayed not for himself, or he had not fallen so deeply.

Silencing the gaoler by laying his finger on his lips, Norwell retreated; the beauty of holiness was irradiating the prison; he dared not desecrate it by his guilty presence.

"Oh would that Mary Bowden prayed for me," exclaimed Capt. Norwell, "for then I should be sure of heaven!"

Thenceforward Maida bore but a very secondary part in Norwell's heart. In his conscience she lived—immortal.

'Maida!' at last said Miss Doveton.

'Maida! Where did you hear that name?'

'Is that not your name? Surely I was told it was.'

'Right—it was.'

'You are married, then?' checking herself as the remembrance of Maida's crime rushed through her. 'Of course—I had forgotten.'

'I am not married,' firmly replied Maida, 'or I should not be here; if you please we will not touch upon that subject—*the cause of all*!'

Miss Doveton looked puzzled.

Ah! Mary Doveton, there are more things in the philosophy of the wicked than are dreamt of in the paradise of your mind. [4]

'Tell me, how did you hear that name? I am not known by it here.'

Whilst Miss Doveton tells Maida that it was a gentleman who had inadvertently called her so, and that being an uncommon name it had fixed itself on her mind, we will revert to the alias. When the constable apprehended Maida as Martha Grylls, she had, with the penetration foreseen by Norwell, immediately allowed the disguise by silent acquiescence. As Martha Grylls, therefore, she was recognized in the prison, at Millbank, [5] on shipboard, and on the government books in Van Diemen's Land. But between us she shall remain Maida Gwynnham, until necessity obliges us to yield, or she herself allows us to throw off concealment.

'Who was the gentleman? I beg pardon, anxiety for my father makes me ask; he would soon trace me to this horrible place were that name spread abroad.'

'I do not think you need fear; it was a stranger, a captain, who mentioned you quite casually, and by mistake he called you Maida, confusing you, I suppose, with some one else.'

Maida thirsted to hear more; hoping to elicit further information, she inquired—

'How do persons talk of me? Tell me truly; I am past caring for opinion, which, if favourable, could little elevate me in my own esteem, as it could, if ungracious, thrust me into darker depths of degradation than my own opinion has already done. How do they talk of me, Miss Doveton?'

'I have not many opportunities of hearing; that gentleman spoke most feelingly of you; indeed, I was quite drawn to him, he seemed so touched with sorrow for you; men do not generally exhibit so much feeling. I must go now, Maida; may I come again?'

'Do; you *have* been a comfort to me; but pray do not use that name again, not even to myself.'

'No, I will not; I can't tell how it is that you seem familiar to me by it.'

Miss Doveton was leaving the cell when Maida called her back—

'Should you chance to meet that benevolent gentleman' (oh, the wormwood! [6]), 'would there be harm in giving my thanks to him? He might be gratified to know that his kindness had cheered a desolate woman.'

Simple-minded Mary perceived only feminine modesty in the uneasiness of tone in which Maida spoke; we, who are better acquainted with portions of Norwell's story, do not so utterly misinterpret the voice: but he for whom the message is intended as a caution will certainly construe it aright. His subtle selfishness will read it as truly as though it were written with a phosphor[7] pen on the dark wall of his conscience.

Again leaving the cell, Miss Doveton said—

'Then I have been a comfort to you?'

'You *have*,' repeated Maida.

But in what way chiefly Mary guessed not. The olive leaf had dropped into the troubled waters, and chance had guided it to the right spot. Love and sympathy had done much, but, lost amid the dark memories which crowded Maida's book of remembrance, they would have brought only temporary relief, had they omitted that whisper of glad tidings.

'He loves you, or why those signs of grief?'

And Maida sat down to dream as others have dreamt and as many yet will dream. There is no fonder dreamer than the heart, which returns verdict for itself on every paltry evidence of love which circumstance, not proof, may yield. Through all her keen perception in other matters, Maida lacked discernment here. She who was truthful, and, therefore, trustful, consented to act a lifelong lie to screen him who, with a few idle protestations, kept up the dream she fondly dreamt.

'The young lady that've just been here came back with this here cup for your flowers, and I've promised to see you in water for 'em,' said the gaoler, breaking in upon her reverie. He seemed half ashamed of his errand, and still more so of his promise.

He showed Maida a white china mug, with 'Mary' painted on it in golden letters.

'She'd been gone a half-hour 'fore she brought it, so I reckon she's been a pretty step for it; bless us, what next; a mighty ticklish trick[8] of the little dear. '

As Maida did not put out her hand to receive the mug, the man set it on the floor and departed, muttering—

'Won't so much as look at it! I could have told her that; she isn't a woman to be gammoned[9] with toys; but lor', she weren't no more than a child.'

No sooner were the gaoler's eyes off the mug than Maida's were fixed intently on it, and her soul, nursed into gentler mood by the late reverie, eagerly drank in all the delicate assurances, all the loving sympathies which lay with those golden letters on the snow-white cup. Tenderly raising it she clasped it in both hands to her lips, and pressed one long, fervent kiss upon the name. Then for the first time, remembering that the man had spoken of flowers, she looked around, and where Mary had knelt she saw lying a bouquet of pink and white moss rosebuds with a sprig of myrtle, and another small bunch of choice mixed flowers. Seeming to comprehend this arrangement at a glance, Maida put the buds only in the cup, and laid the other bouquet in her bosom, thinking aloud—

'She studies my peculiarity, and I will respect her taste; the roses shall be alone.'

The elegant instinct which led Miss Doveton, in the first instance, to choose a simple vessel rather than one of the vases which decked her luxurious home, and then, from a hundred others as simple, select one which bore her name, that instinct was not undiscovered nor unappreciated by Maida. None but a sensitive mind can read the true motive of the unobtrusive actings of another sensitive mind, and none but sister spirits can tell the pains, the disappointments, the reproaches a sensitive mind meets with in its intercourse with those who do not reciprocate its proffered attentions nor understand its unuttered yearnings.

As many days elapsed before the governor of the gaol could convey his prisoners to Millbank, Miss Doveton had permission and opportunity to visit Maida, and each visit but strengthened the bond of union which so mysteriously linked these two widely dissimilar characters into a relationship, rich with future interest, although a long blank for a time ignored its existence, save in the individual interests of each heart.

CHAPTER 7

The Reverend Herbert Evelyn

The secret of true eloquence is an eloquent heart.

STILL anxious to try what he could effect towards winning Maida's attention and confidence, Mr. Evelyn applied for permission to visit the prisoner again. Having received it, he presented himself at the gaol on the afternoon of the day on which Miss Doveton was introduced to the prisoner.

Remembering with apprehension the passionate ebullition[1] she had given way to before Mr. Evelyn, Maida was equally anxious to see that gentleman, in order to ascertain how far she had betrayed Norwell, and her own secret. Remembering also that Mr. Evelyn had spoken of a friend who loved her better than anyone else, and fearing that this friend could be none other than her father, she longed to ask her informant to whom he had alluded. But too proud to ask a favour, she incurred the risk of letting her doubts remain unsatisfied rather than seek an interview with Mr. Evelyn, through the kindness of the matron.

Pleasure was, therefore, plainly depicted on her countenance when the object of her wishes entered her cell.

'Well, Martha, I am indeed glad to see you more cheerful; how are you, my poor girl? I have thought unceasingly of you since the night of your conviction.'

Not noticing the question, Maida eagerly exclaimed:

'Oh, sir! Do tell me. What have I told you of my past history? I have been so miserable since you were here.'

'Then do not be miserable; you were so excited as to be almost incoherent. I only gathered from what you said that you had been betrayed by some villain calling himself a gentleman.'

'No names then?'

'None. I have not the faintest clue to any particular man.'

'Mr. Evelyn, though I was raving, I distinctly remember that *you* first spoke of a man. You said, "Who is he?" in reference to some speech of mine—you did indeed, sir.'

'Doubtless, Martha;' and Mr. Evelyn smiled sadly, 'but a hasty conclusion of your own aimed my words at an individual. I might have asked "Who is *he* ?" inadvertently, in *your* case. In *most* cases of crime I should have done so as one effect of my experience as chaplain to female prisoners, amongst which class I have found few who do not lay their misery at the foot of a seducer. That this theory has another proof in you, your impetuosity revealed only a few minutes after I made your acquaintance. The subject pains you; we will not talk further on it until such time as I shall have gained your confidence.'

An incredulous gesture—something between a smile and a sneer—was Maida's only answer.

'I am anxious to know, sir, of whom you spoke, when you said you brought a message from some one who loved me better than—than—*He?*' She at last added, with a flushing cheek and with a firm start of her whole frame—'Was it my father?—tell me *No*, and I care not who else it may be.'

'No, Martha! No earthly—'

'Thank God!' interrupted Maida; 'if he had sent you, he would soon be following himself' (hiding her face in her hands) 'and I could not—oh! I could not see him—it would break his heart to find me in these prison clothes. But perhaps his heart is broken already.'

She rocked herself wildly to and fro. Mr. Evelyn held his peace. Long experience had taught him that a chaplain's most favourable opportunity lies in the brief calm after a violent outburst of feeling. As he watched Maida, he hoped the storm was passing away. Not expecting that it was but gathering strength for a fiercer gust, he was unprepared when it broke forth.

'His Pride! His Glory! Let him come and see her now! His Beauty! Let him trace her claim to beauty now! Let him come and I will tell him what brought her *here*. How she came by these costly robes! What brought me here? Why should I be here? Why should I stay another instant, when—'

Mr. Evelyn arose, and, laying his hand gently on Maida's arm, said—

'Martha—you rave. Were you suspected of meditating an escape, the small freedom you now have would be taken from you of necessity.'

Thankful that her allusion had been misunderstood, and grateful to Mr. Evelyn for arresting that passion which might have hurried on a disclosure, she exclaimed with a long-drawn sigh—

'Ah yes! I must stay here—it is my place; but oh, my father—my poor father, sir; he has gray hairs, and should *he* be haunted to death by me? He knows not how deep my fall. Of my betrayal he heard—I have never seen him since. He would have forgiven me; he blamed himself—everyone but *me*; he offered the refuge of home to hide my coming disgrace, but—'

'Ah Martha, 'tis the old story—pride! pride!'

'Ay, cursed pride!—why did it not prevent my fall?'

'Stop, Martha! Do you give to pride that which belongs to the grace of God?'

'Grace! Why did it not come when it was most needed? Why did it let me go deep down into sin and then—?'

'You did not seek it, Martha.'

'Seek it! How seek it, when I knew not it would be wanted? I was a child—a mere child; what was I to know of grace against sin, of which I was in utter ignorance? I repeat in utter ignorance. Brought up in solitude made to suit my father's peculiar taste—reading only what books had first passed his approval—meeting only very occasionally with a companion, and that never of my own age, and always a guest of my father's—how was I to compete with a temptation of which I was wholly unsuspecting? If there be remedy in grace, why was it not sent to me in time?'

'Martha!' Mr. Evelyn spoke solemnly, almost sternly. 'Do not utter words not one of which you believe yourself. Have you never learnt at your mother's knee—"Keep us from temptation, and deliver us from evil?" Have you never had a Bible in which to read—"Christ is able to succour them that are tempted?" Have you never been to church to hear—"O God, the strength of all them that put their trust in Thee, mercifully accept our prayers: and because, through the weakness of our mortal nature, we can do no good thing without Thee, grant us the help of Thy grace," etc., etc.? Whilst I would cast every possible reproach upon your seducer, I would be faithful to you; and I must say, Martha—listen—you did not seek God's *special* grace, and refused his *natural* grace in rejecting the way of escape it offered.'

Unaccustomed to anything but scorn from her neighbours, and insidious flattery or abject servility from Norwell, the honest, manly, unflinching voice of truth, though full of reproof to herself, was attractive to Maida. It sounded to her ear as the thrilling bass of some long-forgotten tune, and she quietly seated herself to listen to it, whilst her face assumed an interrogatory expression, which seemed to ask—

'What way of escape?'

'Your father; why did you not confide in him, Martha?'

'Mr. Evelyn, you cannot be dealing truly with me in saying you are unacquainted with my history!'

Another sad smile.

'Poor child—I am acquainted with all this clause of your history, and can divide it into two heads—First. Destruction wilfully brought on yourself by disobedience to your father's commands in encouraging the man. Second. Destruction by foolishly keeping the pledges of his love to yourself, and so depriving yourself of the benefit of your father's judgment; he would have discerned for you between the real and unreal. I admit all you urge in respect to youth and ignorance, in all their unsuspecting trustfulness; but must repeat you rejected the natural remedy God's grace provided for that youth and ignorance, namely, the age and experience of a parent. I do not press the still higher remedy—the guidance, the counsel of your heavenly Father. You perceive, Martha, I guess that the latter was your case—am I right?'

A man that tells me all the things that ever I did, thought Maida, as she sat still, deliberating whether to affirm Mr. Evelyn's conjecture or not. 'Had my father laid commands on me, I should have obeyed them from love to him. Then I hated commands, now I consider them just and proper, though I have, I am sorry to say, no better inclination to follow them.'

'And so, Martha, because you hated commands, you avoided the chance of having them laid upon your actions?'

'Not exactly.' (Martha's mind wandered in the past, or she had not been so communicative.) '*He* told me no one was expected to tell love secrets, even to parents, and I partly believed him; especially as my father had never spoken in language that I understood of things likely to happen as I went through the world—now the fulfilment has passed; I read the prophecy; but when my father spoke it, it was a very dark saying—it was a foreign tongue—I understood not its vague cautions—ah! yes, I remember—' Her words lapsed into indistinctiveness.

'*Partly believed*, Martha? There began the evil,' said Mr. Evelyn. Maida aroused herself, and replied with energy—

'Do not let me deceive you, sir. I had a conviction that I ought to seek parental advice, but fearing my father would not consent to what I supposed were honourable proposals, because he would not like to lose me, I was glad to believe the propriety of keeping the whole matter from him until it was settled, and so I was led on until—ah! I was a child then! Oh, God! That my eyes then had been opened!' Suddenly checking herself, Maida looked up in suprise—she had been talking in a day-sleep. Mr. Evelyn continued for her—

'Until the fatal step was taken, and the wretched man told you, that having already lost all that woman cares to lose, you might as well continue an alien to your father's house. Poor girl! You have been cruelly wronged. Martha, will you kneel down and pray with me for that cruel man?'

Mr. Evelyn was generally sure of his ground before he ventured on it; he thought he was sure with Maida. He had found that many a haughty and wilful spirit will bend in formal prayer for others, when it scorns to do so for itself, and that many a depressed and burdened soul can venture that prayer for others it dares not offer for itself. Thinking that Maida partook of both these characters, he hoped that in listening to his prayer for Norwell, she might unaware send a petition for herself to Him who heareth alway. It was, therefore, with some disappointment that he received Maida's answer—a very decided and somewhat angry, 'No!' Then in a softer tone, she added, 'Mr Evelyn, if you would not raise a worse spirit in me than I have already, please not to pity me, nor speak so harshly of him; and as to praying for him, he needs someone better than I to do that—or little benefited will he be!'

'Then *I* will pray for him, Martha. I suppose as far as position goes, you will allow that I am better than you, and therefore permit me this privilege. In God's sight there is neither bestness nor worstness; what one is, that is the other—only excepting as the one or the other stands in relation to the Saviour of sinners. Martha, we shall understand one another by-and-by; in the meantime I will try not to pity you; but I have a trick of pitying persons, more, perhaps, to relieve myself, than to comfort them. We often pity others in order to let off a pain from ourselves,' said Mr. Evelyn, in a cheerful manner, that ill accorded with his voice and countenance. 'Before I go, Martha, you will not object to let me observe my usual custom?'

Maida gave no reply. Shutting his eyes, and clasping his hands, Mr. Evelyn repeated three texts—

'Come unto me, all ye that labour and are heavy laden, and I will give you rest.'

'Take my yoke upon you and learn of me; for I am meek and lowly in heart: and ye shall find rest to your souls.'

'For my yoke is easy and my burden is light.'[2]

Unable to resist the inspiration of these exquisite words, he broke forth into a most fervent supplication to Maida to consider the things belonging to her eternal peace; but whatever she felt, the arctic frigidity of her features did not relax, nor did the almost disdainful silence give way. Her spirit was beyond hypocrisy; neither by speech nor gesture would she say what she did not feel. She let her benevolent visitor talk on until he had preached a short sermon—when she stopped him. 'Sir, I know enough of these subjects to be aware that if there are degrees of punishment, mine will be the heavier for your visit to-day. I beg of you to desist. I appreciate your goodness in thus interesting yourself for me; but I must be candid and tell you that I am not yet sufficiently accustomed to my new position to feel pleased at being considered a lion of crime.'

'Poor Martha!' cried Mr. Evelyn, before he could prevent the unfortunate words. 'I will not make you add sin to sin. I will not continue my visits since they are distasteful to you. I will not come again; but, Martha, I will pray for you very earnestly. Your youth, your crime, yourself, have made a deep impression on me. There is a mystery in your history that I cannot fathom—there is something in your bearing so different from what I expected in one convicted of murder, that I would fain sound that mystery. I know that the law even is sometimes deceived.'

A satirical smile lurked in the corners of Martha's lips—a smile into which Mr. Evelyn gave a wistful and searching glance. He had spent a large part of his life in reading the smiles, nods, looks, and hearts of prisoners, but was baffled in his present attempt to read the meaning in that curling lip.

'Well, then, good-bye, Martha Grylls; we part in prison, why not meet in heaven? And we *shall* if prayer may take you there: but, remember, there *must* be repentance. Arise, go to your Father; He will behold you when you are yet a great way off—yes, as far off as Van Diemen's Land. Take this little pocket-bible , and read it for *my* sake, not for your own.' Then, looking upward, he exclaimed—

'O God, for the sake of the Sinless One, convince this poor wanderer of her guilt, that knowing it she may abhor it, and that abhorring it she may seek forgiveness, that seeking forgiveness she may find it through her only Saviour and Mediator Jesus Christ our Lord.'

Mr. Evelyn waited, but no 'Amen' came from Maida. He watched her face, but no 'Amen' was there. He then marked a slight tremor in her fingers as they entwined themselves more firmly in each other upon her breast; and with a faint ray of hope he was closing the door of the cell, thinking, with Mary Doveton, 'There may be a breaking heart behind a brazen wall,' when Maida called him back—she hesitated—then very softly said—

'Will you do me a favour, sir?'

'Anything—anything, Martha.'

'I shall have all my hair cut off when I am at Millbank; do you think they would give me two locks for a particular purpose?'

'Perhaps; it depends upon what person you ask: the matron would, I am sure; you must speak to her, and then?'

'Three months after I have gone—that is, left England—will you send one to my father, whose address you must promise not to discover until then, when, by a clue I will leave, you will easily find him—and the other—no, thank you, I will send that myself—will you oblige me, sir?'

'Willingly; but, Martha, you must write to your father.'

'Impossible, Mr. Evelyn! Should his own daughter's be the hand to sign his death warrant?'

'Yes, Martha! The warrant has to reach him—let it be through his child rather than through the public executioner. I have a daughter; I know a father's feelings. You have also yourself to think of and act for; you have to prepare your dying bed.'

'Oh, Mr. Evelyn! Believe me, you do not know my father; his pardon is as surely granted as though it were sealed, signed, and delivered to my possession. He would mourn, he would weep, he would bless; but never, never curse.'

'And so you would take advantage of your father's gentle weakness towards his erring child? I tell you, Martha, there is unworthy cowardice in this—yes—I say it—a cowardice unworthy of Martha Grylls, though the law has set its indelible mark upon her, making her in the world's view incapable of further unworthiness. Martha, I am God's ambassador of peace; but, in God's name, I declare I will never cry peace, peace, when there is no peace. I cannot speak peace to you on this solemn subject. I cannot flatter you with doubts as to what you have done; you have most likely brought a premature death upon your father, and without one sustaining hope you would let him totter to his grave; but I can and do implore you, in the name of God, and for the sake of your own last hours, to hasten to perform the very small duty which God's mercy still leaves open to you—to seek your father's pardon—'

'You do not know what you ask for, sir. Were I to write, he would come to me; and I would rather that he should see me in my coffin than here: it would finish the breaking of his heart; and, surely, you would not bid me do that! Besides, it would unnerve me—and then—'

'Would to God I could see you unnerved, Martha!'

Maida grasped Mr. Evelyn's hand, and fixing her eyes intently on him, whispered in beseeching tones—

'For pity's sake, do not talk so, sir; you will undo me—you will ruin me. What good would his pardon work upon a soul unforgiven by itself? For pity's sake, no more of this.'

'It is just for pity's sake that I would and must speak, my poor Martha; calm yourself, and listen to me:

'I have but lately come from that country to which you are shortly to be sent. For more than fourteen years I laboured there as a convict chaplain. I could tell you of hardships, of ill-treatment, of solitude, of homesickness, of loveless labour, and of unrewarded servitude—all of which you must undergo; but all I could reveal of these, in their every crushing misery, would be insignificant compared to what I could disclose of the unrelenting tortures inflicted under the sentence of conscience—the sentence of remorse—generally reserved for hours of solitary imprisonment, or the day of sickness and death, when its victims are unable to lighten it by toil, or elude it by flight.

'From one cruel phase of this torture I would rescue you, in imploring you to seek your father's pardon. That knowledge with which you *now* satisfy yourself will avail you nothing when once the great gulf betwixt him and you is passed. Too late you will then find that pardon, which exists only in your interpretation of his amiable nature, has no power to supersede that full, free promise of the heart flowing through the lip or pen. Many a soul, for whom I humbly hope mercy has been found in heaven, has gone out in utter darkness, unable to enjoy, or even to feel, the forgiveness accorded by its God, because no cherished voice, following from a parent's roof, echoed the glad tidings of reconciliation. Many an instance of the value set on parental forgiveness I could bring forward; one shall suffice. I remember a hard-featured, rugged-hearted man, who had laughed at my ministrations from the pulpit—defied my exhortations in the cell—a man who sneered at religion and denied his God—I remember him in tears, with heaving breast and trembling limbs, bending over a soiled and tattered scrap of paper on which was written—

"Mother's forgiveness and blessing goes with her boy."

"I'd strike that man dead, sir, were he the comptroller-general, or were he a third-class officer, who ventured to take that from me; except when I look at it, to make sure it's safe, it never leaves my person."

'Those were his very words, and *there* is that scrap of paper, Martha! As the best gift he could give me—as the surest proof that I had won his confidence and love—that hard-featured, rugged-hearted man, on his dying bed, put it into my hand, saying—"You'll value it on instead of me. If you hadn't been here I'd have got a mate to bury it with me."'

The little piece of paper fluttered slowly to the ground—and as Martha stooped over it longer than was necessary to pick it up, Mr. Evelyn watched her closely, but without result.

'Mr. Evelyn, you *will* not understand me—let me explain myself—but first, I pray you to believe that neither stubbornness nor pride is now at work in me. As we see an object for the last time, so do we picture it forever. We may hear a thousand tales of that object afterwards—and we may receive them all—but without altering the impression left upon our minds. Still mentally, looking at the object as it *was* when we *last* saw it, shape and form are the same, circumstance alone is changed, and we mourn over it as a ruined greatness, rather than denounce it as a subject of contempt. Mr. Evelyn, were your son drowned, would you rather be present to hear his dying cry, and see his struggling form float from your grasp, and so lay up for yourself a perpetual horror in the remembrance of the scene; or, supposing a choice between two terrors were imperative, would you rather have the tidings of his death brought to you, sparing you the haunting apparition, and leaving to your imagination your son as you last saw him—the bright, noble, intrepid youth? Your anguish might discover him beneath the sea, but could not taunt your sight with the distorted lineaments of death—it would but point to the own loved features of your boy, as undisturbed and beautiful as though you yourself had laid him there. I need not apply my words, sir; shall I in pity leave my father his only present consolation—the portrait of his child as she *was*? Or, shall I tear it from him to replace it with a lasting pain in the picture of his daughter as she *is*—Martha Grylls, the Felon?

It was a random shot; but deeply it wounded the target's centre. Mr. Evelyn *had* lost an only son at sea; *had* watched in agonised helplessness his unavailing struggles; *had* heard the stifling cry, and the solemn gurgle, as the divided wave closed over its lovely prey, and for evermore the struggle, the cry, and the gurgle, were in his heart and ear.

'You are ill, sir?' Maida advanced anxiously towards Mr. Evelyn, who, pressing one hand to his brow, supported himself by spreading the other on the wall.

'One moment, Martha!' whispered Mr. Evelyn, gently motioning her back; one moment passed, and a heavy respiration alone told of the contest from which he had come.

'I do not ask you to *see* your father, Martha. Under your circumstances, where there are all the finer feelings of the *gentleman* as well as the keen susceptibilities of the parent to be consulted, I would not advise a meeting; but you must write.'

A very earnest and steady look into Maida's face accompanied this boldly given, decidedly made assertion; but at the time, neither look nor assertion was noticed; the prisoner's thoughts were preoccupied, and her eyes fixed on the ground.

'You must write, Martha; and I will undertake to prevent a meeting; and also, if it would spare you pain, I would write to Mr. Grylls—(is that his name?)—break the dreadful intelligence, and prepare him to receive your letter.'

'Oh no! Thank you, kindly; if it has to be done, I will do it myself. I do not shrink from a penance as just as it is severe, for the news will break his heart. I have brought it on myself. The letter shall be written; but I must be allowed to send it according to my own arrangement, in order to make his coming impossible.'

'The matron will doubtless permit you this indulgence. I only ask you, Martha, to let me know when you send the letter.'

'You shall be informed, sir; and I thank you for showing me this duty. But, Mr. Evelyn, what did you say about my father's name—do not keep me in doubt—what do you know of him that you should say he is a gentleman? From whom did you hear it?'

'From *you*, Martha!'

'From me, sir!' An expression of more alarm than she had exhibited heretofore, warned Mr. Evelyn that he must be explicit if he would be merciful.

'I repeat, from *you*; what your father is I discern in every aspect of yourself, to say nothing of the information I have gleaned from an inadvertency of your own. Martha! You are not what you appear. Long experience has shown me that prisoners claim others in their rank than the poor and uneducated; it is not easy to deceive my practised eye and ear, how much soever you may wish it. Martha Grylls, you cannot hide from me the position in life from which you have fallen.'

To Mr. Evelyn's disappointment, a look of intense relief followed this reply. Ever dreading what her passion might reveal, Maida received with indifference a communication that at another time might have annoyed her. The disclosure was not important compared with some she could make.

'Farewell, Martha; I have already given you a parting benediction in that little book, and for my sake you have promised to read it. Be faithful to yourself in writing to your father. I will pray that you may be supported in the bitter trial, and that he may have strength to endure the impending stroke. God bless you!'

The key had hardly turned upon Maida ere a loud and touching cry vibrated through the stillness of the corridors.

'In one of her tantrums,' explained the gaoler.

'God be praised!' ejaculated Mr. Evelyn, almost simultaneously, to the complete mystification of his companion, who perceived no ultimate, much less immediate cause for thanksgiving in 'another of that woman's tantrums.'

Meeting the governor's wife in one of the passages, Mr. Evelyn made known to her the prisoner's desire respecting the hair. Mrs. Lowe engaged that the wish should be gratified as far as her influence with the superintendent of Millbank extended, but advised putting the possibility beyond all doubt by at once cutting off the two required locks.

'I should not like to be present, sir, when she has her beautiful hair taken off. I am glad to be spared the painful sight. It will be a great trial to her; so peculiar a creature.'

'She will not feel it, I think, Mrs. Lowe; there is no petty weakness in her grief. As a concomitant of her humiliating portion, she may receive it with a shudder, but the shudder would be for herself, not for her hair.'

Mr. Evelyn was right in Maida's case, but generally, convicts are more sensible of mortification in being deprived of nature's best ornament than in almost any other course of penal discipline. In Van Diemen's Land the convicts, especially the *men*, allow their hair to grow to an unbecoming length as an indisputable voucher of respectability. But we anticipate.

The gaoler, who had overheard Mrs. Lowe's remark, suggested to Mr. Evelyn, in a very confidential tone:

'That woman's hair'll fetch a mint o' money, sir; she wer'n't up to it or she'd never have brought it in with her.'

A stern frown reprimanded this very natural spirit of speculation, to which the gaoler, misunderstanding, replied apologetically:

'Yes, well, sir, you're right—it *is* fair it should go to government.'

But Mr. Evelyn's frown did not accept the apology.

CHAPTER 8

Too Late

A FULL half-hour before the —— station opened to the public, a closely shut vehicle drove to the gate, which immediately unlocked, and as quickly fastened, upon a decently dressed female, who seemed to conduct rather than accompany, three thickly veiled women that had alighted and entered the platform with her; but their presence was ignored by the G. W. R.[1] officials, and their existence only recognised in the person of her whom, par excellence we designate 'the female.' When she advanced to a carriage, the same secret understanding appeared there as at the entrance. The door instantly and quietly opened. She stood back, and let the veiled three precede her into the compartment, then, seating herself between two and in front of the third, she beckoned to a G.W.R. and he locked them in. This being accomplished, she heaved a gentle sigh of satisfaction, and leaning back to repose her exhausted energies, said mildly to the three:

'You may make yourselves as comfortable as you like, now.'

She should have said, and doubtless meant to say:

'You may make yourselves as comfortable as you *can*, now.'

None of the three availed herself of the permission. Indeed, their whole expression of dress and mien gave one the idea of discomfort too sure and certain to admit of the possibility of relief. Though assisted by 'the female' to surmount the stepping-in difficulty, each had displayed a peculiar awkwardness in the act that reminded one of the cramp. Afterwards, as they sat securely pinned in their shawls, one felt inclined to ask: 'What has become of their arms?'

But just then the carriage was made to back, and it had scarcely done so, ere the warning bell rang, and the express down train, snorting over the viaduct, ran into the vacated line.

Dexterously as 'the female' had contrived her entry, two other individuals had benefited by the premature unlocking of the station gates. One, a military man, had effected his entrance with a silver latch key; the other, a clergyman, by virtue of a lofty bearing, and an authority too marked for gainsay. Merely acknowledging his entrance by a slight inclination of his head to the wondering porter, Mr. Evelyn walked to a bookstall and purchased Bradshaw.[2] Turning its pages until he arrived at the down trains, he passed his finger rapidly through the hour list of London departures, then, hastily shutting the guide, he murmured:

'Yes—he can be here! Let me see: he received the letter yesterday morning—started for town by next train, and left by night express; he will be here presently, if I read the poor man's heart aright.'

Having thus inferred, Mr. Evelyn paced the platform with a sharp, uneasy step, and occasionally stopped short, to look earnestly out on the distance. In doing thus he knocked against a gentleman who was leaning on the further side of one of the broad pillars which supported the canopy. A glance of recognition passed between the two gentlemen, and as

Mr. Evelyn turned away from the pale and haggard countenance, the same text which on a previous occasion had applied itself to it, again intruded on his mind.

'Confound the man! He haunts a fellow when least he's wanted.'

With this surly salutation, Captain Norwell once more ensconced himself in his retreat.

Then it was that the down express snorted over the viaduct, and venting the remainder of its fury in portentous puffs, glided swiftly up the line, and stayed itself before the station.

In a moment all was hurry and seeming confusion.

'*This* door, porter, *this* door!' wailed a feeble voice from one of the first-class compartments.

The porter threw open the door. A tall, bowed figure issued from it, and stood in the midst of the bustle and packages as though all the bustle and packages in the world were nothing to *it*. With a helpless and almost imbecile expression, the figure raised its lack-lustre eyes and stared into the motley crowd, searching for someone who should be found in it.

A shrill whistle was the first sound that aroused the isolated figure to a consciousness that it must seek if it would find.

'Guard, isn't there a train leaving soon?' it feebly asked.

'Nour-and-half, sir.'

'Is that the one that is to carry some—prisoners to London?'

'Just started, sir; see it up the hill there.'

A piteous cry—a heavy fall—and two persons, drawn to the spot by sympathetic attraction, bore Mr. Gwynnham, a senseless paralytic, from the platform.

'Shall he be taken to my house, sir?' asked Mr. Evelyn, for mere politeness.

'If you please, sir; I am a stranger here,' assented Captain Norwell.

Anywhere! Anywhere! There is no spot on earth he now cares to call his home—that poor old man. Beggared amidst a pleasant competency. Insolvent while his credit is good. A traitor has presided at the treasury, and the bank of love has failed.

Anywhere! Anywhere! Let the bowed head find rest and the aching heart a corner to throb out its pain.

CHAPTER 9

The Cousins

> Upon thy laughter-loving lip
> Hangeth the ever-ready quip,
> Thou couldst not hide thy whereabout
> Tho' thou shouldst wing from tree to tree,
> Thy song, sweet bird, would find thee out,
> For long thou couldst not silent be.

AT the date of this story's commencement Mr. Evelyn had been one year in England, and six months prior to that date he had lost his wife in Van Diemen's Land.[1] The suddenness of the event preyed on his already impaired health; and listening to the solicitations of his brother and only child, he resigned his chaplaincy in Hobarton[2] in order to return to England to seek that repose for himself which his jaded energies so much required, and for his daughter those advantages which colonial education but sparely afforded.

The arrival of their Tasmanian cousin[3] was looked forward to with no small excitement by the D'Urban family. Bridget D'Urban, ever full of fun and drollery, had many a good-natured laugh in store for all the uncouth barbarities she expected in the young colonist; while her mother had secret misgivings that her girls would find no beneficial associate in one who must have imbibed a wrong view of things from unavoidable contact with the mixed and sometimes questionable society of Van Diemen's Land.

Both aunt and cousins were, therefore, sufficiently surprised when, late of a summer evening, Uncle Herbert (as henceforward we shall have to distinguish the Reverend Mr. Evelyn) introduced to them their cousin Emmeline, a young lady who, from ease of manner and grace of deportment, might have done justice to any English drawing-room.

Bridget, having made up her mind that Emmeline was as much her inferior in everyday proprieties as she was her equal in years, had determined, in the generous ardour of her heart, to spread the wing of her protection and hide from censure all her cousin's short-comings. She was accordingly disconcerted to find herself in the presence of a superior, who had no improprieties to shield and but few short-comings to pardon! It was from no exalted idea of her own social attainments that Bridget had thus pictured Emmeline—but unaware she had adapted the D'Urban mode of thinking, "Can any good come out of Tasmania?" and as her mamma's strictures on hoydenism[4] and boldness increased in fervour and number as Miss Evelyn's arrival drew near, she very naturally supposed that the surplus strictures were intended to warn against a worse hoyden than herself.

Neither had foiled conceit any share in her present discomfiture.[5] She was simply confused at having made so grand a mistake, just as you and I should feel discomposed on meeting a tall, stately personage, where we had entered, expecting to be pounced on by a little frisky body.

In a quarter of an hour Bridget was as proud of her cousin's appearance and manners as she had meant to be tender with her failings and faults. The contrast between the two girls was very striking—the more so, as they were of the same age—both on the verge of seventeen. The young English maiden was a girl in every sense—a good-looking, bright-eyed, rosy, laughter-loving creature. Showing a decided preference for the sunny side of life, and forever trying to shun the shadowy side; not by any means from a selfish indifference to the troubles of her neighbour, but because, in her own words, 'It's so horrid to see wretchedness without being able to relieve it;' unheedful of the jarring chords of less harmonious spirits, her heart seemed to beat time to a brilliant fantasia of its own: so with a song in her heart and a smile on her lip, Bridget D'Urban was rarely out of sorts with anything but misfortune that refused to yield to the sound of music and dancing, the only two remedies her jubilant mind could at that time suggest to the sons and daughters of sorrow.

She was the idol of the servants—ever ready to help them over a scrape, or to put her best construction on their worst action: they were never in fear of dismissal when Miss Bridget stood by them. Uncle Herbert told her that she would make a capital convict mistress, and advised her to try her alchymic powers of turning bad to good on a few of the Queen's specimens: on which she clapped her hands, and declared that nothing would be better fun than to go out there and cure a few kitchen rows; and then jumped up to cure uncle and cousin's grave faces by a hearty kiss and a second declaration that *that* was only her way of saying how delightful it would be to go to Van Diemen's Land. She knew she should be the last to think it *fun* and the first to call it *horrid* to see the poor, dear beings so miserable. Mr. Evelyn and her cousin believed her, for they were sure that *not* the bright, merry, dancing hearts are the selfish ones, though appearances are against them— but the cloudy, crabbed, slow-going hearts, they are the selfish sort. The former, placed side by side with affliction, soon are taught the best lessons it can teach—while the latter, as they approximate distress and care, become more moody, crabbed, and stagnantly *past* going.

Prematured by a southern clime, and aged by constitutional delicacy, Miss Evelyn had little of the girl in her, but all the appearance of finished womanhood in her gentle gravity of countenance and quiet dignity of carriage. She much resembled her father: to make her as like him as nature evidently intended, she wanted in her calm features and serene eyes a certain pained expression, remarkable in every line of Mr. Evelyn's face—an expression that had gradually stamped itself there during the holy man's long-continued warfare against a spiritual antagonist, who, with more than Goliath's effrontery,[6] daily, hourly appeared from the camp of sin and defied this champion of the cross.

A somewhat morbid tendency of mind early displayed itself in Emmeline. Her discerning parents immediately perceived the unhealthy predilection which, unchecked, would injure their little daughter's power of receiving and appropriating truth, and devoted themselves to effect a cure by a treatment at once skilful and lenient. They endeavoured on the one hand, by a nicely graduated scale of precept and by an unflagging course of judicious and illustrative practice, to teach her her responsible position in the world—and, on the other hand, to set beyond reach all that would increase her defective perception of right and wrong.

This was not easy to accomplish, surrounded as they were by an influence which only exerted itself for evil as a rule, and chanced to be harmless as an exception. It was only by that unceasing self-restraint and anxious vigilance, so prejudicial to the health and comfort of Tasmanian mothers, that Mrs. Evelyn succeeded in planting around Emmeline a system free from moral contamination.

Establishing herself in the nursery, she permitted no one to converse with the little Emmeline save in her presence, an old woman, who had been nurse in her mother's family, the only exception. Mr. Evelyn made it his particular care to guard against a spirit of conceit, which this exclusive education might induce in his daughter. Associating her, as she grew older, with himself in a few of his many projects for improving the moral condition of some of his penal flock, he sought, and not in vain, to enlist her sympathies for those who (he taught her) were still her fellow creatures, though debased to the condition of slavery.

There was no lesson he sought more earnestly to inculcate than that one so many are apt to forget; namely, that sin is to be hated as the great opposing principle of holiness, and not to be scorned because its effects are evil. He ever bade her remember that circumstance naturally, and God's grace specially, alone preserved her from being as those she saw around her.

When Emmeline attained her sixteenth year, she needed but a touch to make her all her parents desired.

That master-touch was given by God himself. This finger which laid the mother on her bier, and bowed the father's head in grief, aroused the daughter; and like the evening primrose, which raises its beautiful head only to the night, she stood in the midst of desolation as one sent by God.

Mr. Evelyn trembled to convey to her the news of the calamity that had stricken their hearth. He feared lest the old tendency, in spite of patient treatment and long quiescence, should break forth and vent itself in morbid lamentings over her mother's grave. Hence, with amazement, he beheld Emmeline arise from self and selfish sorrow, to perform, unbidden, those tender duties which are a right-minded woman's prerogative, and perform them with a delicacy rarely secured but by experience, and with a judgment ripened into maturity, with a suddenness that astonished onlookers—a judgment that might never have burst beyond latent existence, save beneath the scorching sun of affliction.

She appeared to her father a living rebuke to doubt—a voice as of old stilling the storm—

'Oh thou of little faith! Wherefore didst thou doubt?' [7]

Shall that seed which is sown in prayer and watered with tears, fail to bloom when the fulness of time is come?

During the long four months of homeward passage, Mr. Evelyn had leisure and opportunity for uninterrupted intercourse with his daughter, an enjoyment which active service in Hobarton had seldom permitted him. With humble gratitude he found, during the voyage, that Providence had reared a help truly meet for him in his own child, and it added not a little to his pleasure to know that he had been favoured to assist in the goodly work; and, much to his sorrow, to remember that she who had laboured with him in the unremitting toil of years was now deaf to the voice that had arisen to call her blessed.

One night they sat together on the poop. Above them the exquisite tropical sky was radiant with that calm loveliness that must be felt (we do not say *seen*) to be apprehended. Below, the wake of the vessel glittered like a molten glory rushing past them. Mr. Evelyn seemed to be gazing into an unseen world, through the medium of that rushing glory, associating the loved in death with the beautiful in life; for he spoke not, neither raised he his eye from the ocean.

Emmeline wondered at his silence. 'He is thinking of mamma,' she said to herself.

'Papa,' at last she whispered.

Mr. Evelyn turned, and read his daughter's meaning in her inquiring smile.

'Yes, my child, I was dreaming of your mother, but not exclusively. Emmeline, you shall share a secret that we laid up in our souls; by mutual consent we never spoke of it save once a year, when the day that gave it us came round.'

Emmeline did not reply, save by a gentle pressure of his hand.

'It is on this very day, at this very hour, sixteen years ago, that your brother was borne away from us by just such a stream as that!'

'My brother, papa! My brother? I never heard of him before.'

'Your brother, Emmeline. As you are sitting there, so he sat that night, sixteen years ago: when bending over the stern he fell overboard, and, floating quickly off, was beyond the reach of help ere help could be obtained. The captain and first mate restrained me by force, or I had surely followed him—his cry—but ah! These are bitter memories! Your mother was in the cabin, sitting with you in her arms at the stern port-hole, admiring the glowing path upturned by the rudder, when a swiftly descending object for an instant intercepted the light, and ere she could ascertain what that object was, her boy was distant from her. You were a babe not two years old.'

Then Mr. Evelyn entered on all the terrible detail, and explained why he and his wife had kept from Emmeline the knowledge of her brother's former existence and untimely fate.

After Mr. Evelyn had remained a short time in his sister's family, he determined on making a tour, partly with the view of renovating his strength, and partly to give himself ample scope for choice of a healthy locality in which to settle his daughter and himself. Emmeline stayed with Mrs. D'Urban, in order to share her cousin's lessons in the French and German languages, and in the use of the harp.

An attachment, that proved after a source of joy and sorrow to the girls, was soon formed between them. The introduction of these cousins to one another was one of the gentle ministrations of Providence, by which God anticipates the needs of his feeble ones, and prepares for adversities as yet a great way off. Emmeline made quite a pet of Bridget, who was content to be thought the younger, 'or anything,' so long as she might nestle her head on her cousin, and look up with those arch,[8] fun-loving eyes at the sweet face ever prompt with a responsive smile to meet the pleasant sallies on her ungirlish sedateness.

Once, when Bridget thus leaned on her cousin's lap, she exclaimed—

'I can't think how I came to be such a goose!' and then explained, by telling Emmeline all that she had pictured of her before they had met.

'You see, people have such stupid ideas about your country; they fancy the kangaroos are the only dancing masters, and the parrots the only singing mistresses. I wonder, Em, you have half the patience to answer such questions as the folks put to you; and yet I don't wonder, either, at what *you* do, or at what you don't do. Em, do you know I should be the first to scold if you turned madcap. I would not but have you as you are for all the fun in the world.'

A kiss on her sunny brow was the only answer Bridget obtained or wanted; she had a way of rattling out all her thoughts in the form of questions. Conformable to this way she rattled on—

'Tell me, Em, what made you so religious. Mamma says it's your delicate health, and that delicate persons are always more pious than others; and I don't like that: people have no business to be religious just because they can't be anything else; have they Em? I'll never believe that's your case. *I* think you were *born* religious.'

To her surprise, instead of the expected smile, she perceived a solemn sadness in Emmeline's face. She was up in an instant.

'Why, Em! I've vexed you; surely you are not angry with little Racket? It's only a fair question of ways and means.'

This was uttered with such comic seriousness that Em was obliged to laugh in spite of herself; when Bridget, being satisfied that she had not really mortified her cousin, sat down again, and in a more quiet mood, asked—

'Em, will you really tell me? I had a long battle with mamma and George about it the other day and though they silenced me, they could not convince me.'

'Which of your many questions am I to answer, Bridget?'

'Are delicate persons always religious?'

'Would God that they were, and we should not have so many prescriptions for hours of ennui, and nights of restlessness! I quite apprehend aunt's meaning, though. There are few persons so irrational, or so self-torturing, as to venture resistance to that which is irresistible. A politic acquiescence in an evil beyond control, is the least that can be offered; and too many are content to yield this least by sinking into a quietude of manner which again degenerates into apathy towards passing events, mistaken by themselves and others for a lowly submission to God's will and a religious disregard to the trifles of the time.'

There was unusual fervour in her voice, and a brighter colour in her cheek than Bridget had before observed, as she continued—

'But believe me, Bridget, true religion is not to be mistaken; you may think it is in a person in whom it does not really exist, but never—never can you be ignorant of its presence where it is truly to be found. There is as much difference between the apathy of unblest sickness and the resignation of piety, as between the unsteady flicker of a lamp and the clear light of day. True piety is never apathetic! Whether on a bed of death, or whether in a sphere of action, it is never oblivious to the interests of others. Physical weakness may disable it, circumstance may discourage it; but neither can touch its vital principle or change the unselfishness of its nature. With it, a setting of its affections on things above, does not mean a steeling of its sympathies to things on earth.'

Mrs. D'Urban entered the room at this moment, and noticing the brilliancy of Emmeline's cheeks exclaimed—

'If all Methodists [9] look as well as you do now, Emmy, I should not mind turning Bridget into one forthwith. What has sent all those roses to your face?'

'I fancy your entrance, dear aunt,' said Emmeline, rising and kissing her affectionately. 'I did not feel them, until now.'

'Oh!' cried the aunt, laughing, 'I hoped they were the fruition of Methodism, for which, I assure you, I begin to entertain a profound respect, seeing how much its influence has tamed my wild Bridget; she begins to have an occasional thought for others, now.'

'Oh, aunt? Bridget's charity is all set to music; but it is not the less charity, for that.'

She really is a lovely girl; one would not have looked for such a gentlewoman from those wild parts, thought Mrs. D'Urban, unable to divest herself of the D'Urban prejudices, and uncaring to discover whether that beautiful country she so designated were in reality as wild and incapable of producing flowers of human beauty as she supposed.

A few days after the conversation above related, on going unexpectedly into Emmeline's private apartment, Bridget found her cousin reclining on a sofa, suffering much pain in her side. She had time to mark how severe the spasm appeared, before her entrance caused Emmeline to disguise her pain beneath a smile of welcome, accompanied by the assurance that the attack was nothing; its frequency of recurrence had made her notice it but slightly.

'Emmeline, you are ill; that smile cannot deceive me; it means a great—, and goes for nothing with little Racket. Does uncle know of these attacks?'

'Why should I trouble him, love? Aunt says they are only growing-pains.'

'Growing-pains, indeed! I guess you had your last of them before you made mamma's acquaintance. Now I will turn tell-tale unless you promise to lie still until luncheon bell.'

With this threat, Bridget left her cousin, and proceeded to take her first voluntary step into the shadowy side of life. Entering her own sanctum, she locked the door, and seating herself at her desk, wrote to Mr. Evelyn—

My Dear Uncle Herbert,

I do not wish to frighten you, but feel constrained to tell you, that *I* (mind, nobody else) think dear Em is ill. I found her just now severely suffering in her side; and though she tried to laugh off her feeling, I could not help being much alarmed. You will best know whether or not there is cause for anxiety. If not, do not let this note worry you, and forgive

Your loving niece,

Bridget D'Urban.

The letter was written, sealed, stamped and despatched, before Bridget recollected that she should have sought her mother's advice and approval before sending it. All in a flutter, she ran to Mrs D'Urban, and told her how she discovered poor Em, and what she had, in consequence, done. But not the ingenuous confession nor the repentant tears of her daughter softened Mrs. D'Urban's wrath.

'What will your uncle say, miss, at receiving a sly warning from you, instead of a summons from myself? As if *I* should not be the *first* to remark a change in dear Emmeline. Sit down directly, you thoughtless girl, and tell my brother that I will watch Emmeline very closely, and inform him as to her health.'

So, with many sighs of sincere sorrow for having vexed her mother, little Racket wrote a second time to Uncle Herbert.

Thus did her first voluntary step into the shadowy side of life receive a check—one that was long remembered, not as a stone of stumbling but as a prudent waymark, cautioning her to *look* before she advanced into a path where she knew but little.

As was intended, Mr. Evelyn received both wound and balm together. He laid more stress on Bridget's extempore communication than on that which came from his sister's dictation. He placed more reliance on Bridget's report than on Mrs. D'Urban's, knowing, from experience of his sister, that those large, strong women who have never needed to coax debility in themselves, nor learnt to detect any one of its one thousand features in their children, are seldom quick to discern symptoms of incipient disease which may be wearing out the existence of less hardy subjects.

Two days from the despatch of the letters, Mr. Evelyn sat by his child, and his tutored sight read deeper meaning in the roses of her cheek and the lustre of her eye, than had revealed itself to Mrs. D'Urban. He saw in the enfeebled frame that bowed its head upon his shoulder more than the indulged relaxation of youthful indolence.

Three days from the despatch of the letters, Mr. Evelyn heard his fears realised by medical opinion, and decided to follow the physician's advice, and return with Emmeline to Tasmania, as much to give her the benefit of a sea voyage as to try what her almost native air might accomplish for her. On the evening of that day, Mr. Evelyn was closeted with his brother-in-law and sister for more than three hours, and when he came from conference with them, it was only to commence another with Emmeline, and then to begin a third with Bridget. We overheard the result of the three conferences when the noisy, racketing Bridget flew into her cousin's room, and exclaimed, ere the door had time to slam after her:

'I may go! They'll let me go with you!'

Then flinging herself into Emmeline's arms, she forgot the nearer prospect of rows in the kitchen in her joy at being companion-elect to the being she loved best in the world.

CHAPTER 10

The Lie

THE soul that has wandered from the path of rectitude and virtue, is fain to take refuge in borrowed excellence, and to receive by proxy that applause which conscience will not permit it to accept itself.

It is to just such a spotless being as Mary Doveton that the sated worldling prostrates himself in unfeigned adoration. It is her very retreating purity that attracts him. He has been behind the scenes of dissipation, and pulled the gaudy tinsel from the idol of his passion, and a laugh of bitter irony has mocked his disappointment when he beheld all false and cold within.

He gazes on the white simplicity of her spirit, and the transparency of its attiring affords no concealment. The inner loveliness is that of a perpetual childhood, and he longs to draw the veil of her unsullied innocence over his own misshapen heart.

He has drunk to the very dregs the purple cup of wantonness, which, while it palled his senses, has not allayed his thirst. The clear, taintless water of the fountain sparkles in the graceful crystal; it is so pure he can look through it and see the heavens beyond. He is maddened to remember his rejected birthright, and would give the world to stretch forth his hand and grasp the inviting crystal to baptize his polluted soul in the refreshing draught.

Norwell! Norwell! Where is *she* that would have been all to you that now you seek and need? Where is she, who, when you needed truth to hide your own falsehood, could have unbarred her own heart, and, with unflinching voice, bade you search there and detect one equivocating thought? Where is she, who for beauty could have outshone Mary Doveton—for innocence could have stood her equal?

True, you quailed beneath the haughty stare of the one; but never, never, Norwell, until you had learnt to fear its reproofs by teaching it your own base weakness. It could have been taught to look as lovingly on you as the large, soft eye of the other, beneath whose witching tenderness you now yearn to abrogate the past. Where is she who is now only what you have made her?

Was she not worthy of your confidence? Was she not willing to repay your counterfeit with love's true gold? True, you have need to shelter yourself within some shrine of sanctity; but ere you fell so deeply, was not *that* heart an altar meet to shield you? Or when you had fallen so deeply as to drag it in your fall, was it not supremely fair above the darkness of your sin? Was it not more noble in its faded glory than ever your deserts? No, no; the wretch who commits sacrilege upon the goodly altar, has no thought to screen his guilt beneath that altar. One free from his pollution can only suffice for him. So he spurns his victim at her own shrine, and departing, flings the ashes of her virtue in her face. And God gathers the ashes into his censer of vengeance. Woe the day when He shall pour the heaped wrath upon that mocker's head!

Call in the sisters of charity. Call in that sex to whom has been offered a common insult. Bid them that they chide, but not roughly, for the arrow of conviction already rankles in their sister's heart. Bid them look on her with a sadness in their eye, but let her not discover a loathing in their touch. She has fallen but *once*, and must that be forever? Though great her fall, may she not arise and stand upright—the arm of their pity assisting her in the effort? For effort, ay, struggling effort it must be. Her self-dependence is wounded, and refuses to let her lift so much as her eyes towards heaven. Her reliance is on *them*, those sisters of charity. Bid them but tell her she may arise, and she will be strong in their strength; or otherwise she must sink—sink—sink, until her ruin stare them in the face; for though at their bidding she may arise, she may not lie still at their behest. With her it must be either upward or downward, for sin has given the blow and there is cruel inertia in her case. For heaven's sake call them in, those sisters of mercy! They all have passed upon the other side; they have gone to feed the hungry and clothe the naked; they are sisters of charity *not* of sin.

Then, for heaven's sake, again go tell them that this is not a sinner of the hardened herd. Her heart is yet flexible, and may be moulded to their liking. Innocence has been wronged, and the villain has fled. She may be rescued from the less pampered ruffian who may shortly come by. Tell them she has but this *once* transgressed, and *that* this very moment. She finds it harder to forgive herself than ever they may feel it difficult to pardon her. Tell them that to-morrow it may be too late. There are those who will not shun her as a reprobate, but hail her as an associate. Shame may drive her to them to hide in their outlawdom her one act of lawlessness. To-morrow may be too late. Pangs of hunger have to be anticipated—prevent those pangs with tender mercies, or justice will follow them with punishment. Hunger may to-morrow prompt her to barter her soul for a mouthful of bread, or tempt her to stake her liberty on a stolen morsel.

Tell them, those sisters of charity, that not one of yonder blushless women but could once have looked them in the face; not one but has mourned her first sin, and that sin being branded on her drove her to hide individuality in a crowd, and to lose herself in a class.

Not one of those blushless women was born to accomplish the fearful story her life presents; not one was issued into earth an incarnated iniquity. But few have determinately gone over to the ranks of perdition. Many have gone over because they feared to be hooted over; and still more have been triumphantly borne over by temptation, the only Samaritan [1] that came by when they had dropped by the roadside. He bore them forward, but, reversing the good old story, left *them* to pay the reckoning.

They have passed on—the sisters of mercy; they are sisters of charity, *not* of sin, or, at any rate, of *that* sin which claims them as its special pleader.

One sister of mercy has returned: she would put a question—

'Is it not for the common good that we spurn that dark sin of woman? Were *we* to remove the life-long ban, the other sex would not be slow to second our movement. Then would that sin stalk barefaced in the sunshine, and what remedy could we produce?'

We are not careful, O sister, to answer thee in this matter. When the necessity upsprings, then Providence will suggest the cure; but millennial day will dawn ere then, ushering in a system so Christ-like in its forgiveness, and bringing its weeping Magdalens [2] to replace thy despair-made Rahabs, [3] flaunting in the gates of thy spurning system. Pass on, O priest and Levite! [4] Pass by, O sister of charity! On rideth one who will not be slothful to perform your rejected duty. The hostelry of sin lies over yonder, and his agents are abroad in the earth.

Norwell had no sooner caught a last glimpse of Maida's veiled figure in the railway carriage, and assisted in moving Mr. Gwynnham from the platform, than, weary, dejected, and self-loathing, he hurried to his apartment in the hotel, locked the door, and flung himself on the sofa, and there confounded himself unsparingly as a fool, coward, and every other name signifying evil. Then was it that, after thinking of Mary Doveton, he put those questions to himself recorded in the first page of this chapter; and very faithfully did he answer them—so faithfully, that, being without excuse, he started from the sofa with—

'Confound it! It's done and can't be undone—at least, it can't be undone without the sacrifice of myself, and that, of course, must never be. After all, poor Maida is the dupe of the law and not of me. The cheque has nothing to do with her present punishment, if it had—curse it—what a fool a fellow's thoughts make him! Who's there?'

'A note for you, sir.'

'Confound it—an invitation.'

Captain Norwell threw it on the table, and then, with a brightened countenance, caught it up again, exclaiming—

'It's the old hag of the assize ball. Ten chances to one I meet that angel there!'

He forthwith accepted the invitation, and then fell to thinking of that angel called by us Mary Doveton. Were it a possibility that from a corrupt mind could proceed one sinless thought, we should say that it was with such a thought Norwell stood afar, and worshipped Miss Doveton. He would have struck to the earth the man who dared to utter an impure word of her.

His impatience made him one of the earliest at the party. No Doveton had arrived, and he was beginning to change the ten chances into one, when, leaning on her father's arm, his angel entered. The simple morning robe had been changed for as simple an evening dress. The flowers at her bosom, and the wreath of real moss-rose buds looping her golden hair, were the only ornaments that significantly relieved the whiteness of her attire.

We leave to be imagined how intense was Norwell's delight when, after many fruitless efforts to gain Miss Doveton's attention, he observed a certain indication of pleasure in the smile of recognition that brought him immediately to her side to hear the delicious salutation—

'I am quite glad to meet you, Captain Norwell. I have for some time been wishing for this opportunity.'

The smile told him much that he had been anxious to ascertain. It told him that Mary could have heard no prejudicial report of his character; that her contact with Maida had not been injurious to a hope he ventured to indulge in; and it told him she had been thinking of him, and that, for some reason or other, she wanted to see him. Any reason that could induce such a wish in her was welcome to his heart.

'May I be honoured with Miss Doveton's commands?' bowed Captain Norwell.

The answer was a shock of pleasure, too exquisite but for silent enjoyment.

'I have a message for you, that I must deliver alone.'

And with a simplicity all her own, Mary Doveton walked towards the bow window, looking the while at Norwell, as much as to say, 'Will you follow?' an injunction he had obeyed ere he fully appreciated its worth.

Nestling in among the flowers with which the window was decorated, she looked up from their midst into Norwell's face, and said—

'I hope, as Miss Fletcher is not here to object to its dullness, you will not dislike to resume a subject we talked of at the assize ball?'

'No topic that Miss Doveton chooses can be dull,' replied Norwell, making a conventional phrase the sincere exponent of his feelings.

The message from Maida, as delivered by Miss Doveton, 'to the benevolent gentleman,' was at first rather uncomfortable in its effects on him. 'The benevolent gentleman' received it as though it had been a sting. But guileless Mary saw nothing remarkable in his uneasy manner of darting the question—

'What name did you say, Miss Doveton?'

Mary faithfully observed her promise to Maida, with regard to her alias, and therefore repeated—

'Martha Grylls; the poor woman for whom you expressed yourself so kindly—by gesture, rather than by speech, I should say—you remember?'

'Ah yes; that's the name—poor thing! It was very kind of you to think of telling her; and very touching that she should be grateful for so slight a sympathy—from a stranger too.'

'Ah, Captain Norwell, we never know where the benefit of a soothing word or look may end. Your pity found its way to ease a wounded spirit. Martha seemed to feel it deeply.'

'Not exactly as *my* pity. I suppose, Miss Doveton, she would hardly distinguish between one and another stranger's compassion?'

'Certainly not. I could not recollect your name; so merely spoke of you as an individual who had displayed sorrow for her suffering.'

'And to *that* individual she sent her thanks,' said Captain Norwell.

'Yes; and to that individual they will not be the less acceptable because they come unlabelled. The heart that can identify them is the heart to claim the thanks, Captain Norwell.'

There was a gentle archness in Miss Doveton's eye, as it rested on 'the benevolent gentleman,' in silent approval of his modesty; but it was unnoticed. The gentleman was watching a leaf, whose zig-zag descent appeared to absorb his attention, for only when it dropped to the ground did he turn to his companion with—

'Was Martha Grylls communicative? To most persons, I hear, she was very reserved; doubtless she warmed into confidence towards *you*.'

'I had no desire to learn her secret; in visiting her I had no intention of seeking to know her history; but think I gained her confidence, poor dear.'

'She volunteered her confidence, then, Miss Doveton?'

'Yes; and I value it more on that account,' naively replied Mary.

Confound her confidence! thought Norwell, as he sought in his forehead for a missing idea, which having found, he blandly asked—

'The confidence, of course, is sacred, Miss Doveton; without violating its sanctity, may I hear your opinion of Martha Grylls, founded on *her* version of her unfortunate case?'

Mary seemed perplexed.

'We misunderstand each other, Captain Norwell. I am ignorant of her story, excepting of that portion for which she is now in punishment. In saying I gained her confidence, I mean, that I induced her to talk freely of her feelings, and to tell me the thoughts of her heart. She was very guarded on the subject you allude to. Oh! Captain Norwell, I wish you had seen that woman. I know, of course, the law is right, and should not be partial; but it is hard to believe Martha capable of such a crime, unless under the influence of severe mental agony, which does not appear to have been the case.'

'Will you permit me to put a stop to this conversation? I am inefficiently fulfilling my duty as a guest in allowing a cloud to gather on a lady's brow. Shall we join the company?'

'It is easier to drive a cloud from the brow than from the heart, Captain Norwell;' and a half-heaved sigh gave emphasis to her words.

'Miss Doveton should have neither,' mechanically responded Norwell, as he shook hands with her father, who had advanced to meet him. Escaped from the severe mental flagellation which Miss Doveton had unconsciously inflicted on him, and convinced that Maida had borne him harmless, [5] Norwell was again at liberty to worship the lily of purity his imagination had deified. More than ever conscious of the disparity between himself and it, it seemed that this path of approach had been deceptive, and left him many paces more distant from the lily. While regretfully scanning this distance, he suddenly perceived an advantage offered him by his very sin. Maida herself disclosed the step by which he could reach the lovely presence. A well-continued show of sympathy and interest for the prisoner might gradually act on Mary Doveton's unsuspecting mind, and cause it to conceive an esteem for one who could feel so acutely for a fellow creature in distress; and this esteem being conveyed to her susceptible heart, might eventually change to love. This show of sympathy might be at once grateful to his own disquietude, which required relief in some form, and useful to disguise a certain troubled expression which his countenance assumed when his thoughts were left to prey on themselves.

But the task was more difficult than Norwell had anticipated. The difficulty lay not with Mary. Perjured as were Norwell's lips, he found it strangely hard to form upon them the lie with which he proposed to win Miss Doveton.

The assassin's blow is dealt in the dark, when the victim's back is turned upon his murderer. There can be few assassins relentless enough to strike death, where death is innocently welcomed with smiles and open arms. When Mary beamed a welcome upon Norwell, he deferred to repay that welcome with a falsehood; and when, at last, he could venture its utterance, it stumbled on his tongue, and fell—where do you think? To the earth? No; into Mary's heart.

His very difficulty subserved his cause; it endeared him to Mary, whose eye, being single, was full of truth.

There was only a maidenly blush upon her cheek, and love's own tremble upon her lips, when she laid her small white hand on Norwell, and whispered—

'I have loved you, Norwell, since that day.' And the eye, so full of truth, saw nothing to be ashamed of in thus giving answer to a love so humbly offered, so worthy of acceptance; but, with all its gentle power, it reflected her simple statement—'I have loved you, Norwell, since that day.'

His blanched features show untold feeling, as he receives the guileless troth.

Is it well, sweet Mary, to clothe thy speech with irony? Is it well to plant the secret thorn in thy surpassing gift? Thy God's grandest character is that of the upbraidless[6] giver. Be like Him.

'It *is* well,' says Mary; 'I have loved him since that day.' And there is wonder in her tone, as she would say—

Why deal in proverbs?

CHAPTER 11

The *Rose of Britain*

BECALMED on the tropical sea, two vessels lay listlessly lulling their weary passengers to a noonday sleep—a sleep that had anything but a soothing effect on the slumberers, who, ever and anon, would start, and in their uneasy rest implore, Dives-like, for a drop of water[1] to cool their parching tongue—a petition that would either never reach the steward, or else be answered with an aggrieved shake of the head.

'Can't do it—had your allowance;' and the steward gulps down a large cupful of cold tea which he has obtained by laying a toll on each dish of tea served at that morning's breakfast.

But steward has his favourites on board; and whilst his stewardship is inexorably faithful to some, he turns his pregnable side towards others, and this pregnable side holds his not deaf ear; an ear which quickly distinguishes whether the petitioner is one of his favoured few, or one who kicked up a bother about his tureen of soup, or told the captain that his cabin was only swabbed, and not holy-stoned.[2] Discerning the cry of a favourite, with stealthy movements he proceeds to quench the cry in a draught of some refreshing beverage; now it may be a glass of cold coffee—now it may be a glass of ale, left over from last night's supper—and then, oh, best of all, it may be a bumper[3] of cold, milkless, sugarless tea. None but those who have tried the delights of this draught in tropical extremities can tell how truly grateful above any porter or beer is this cold tea. Steward himself is a regular toper,[4] and yet he declares that give him your tea and he'll give you his tap. But even the pregnable side of steward rarely yields literal water; he will hardly risk detection, and the consequent charge of favouritism, by granting the letter of the petition. He has orders to draw only so much water from the tank, therefore he dares not disobey. 'A drop of something left from meals captain can't swear against;' neither can he swear at steward for generously giving that drop of something away. To steward's honour be it said, young ladies are always his particular fancy, for two reasons, namely, 'for their own dear selves' sake,' and because they don't give so much trouble as the gentlemen—they make their own beds, and keep their cabins tidy. Any young lady with a passable face and an amount of good nature sufficient to make her affable with steward, may have a pleasant voyage. For though captain governs, and mates sub-govern, it is the steward who holds the rein of comfort or discomfort; plague him, and you'll have a hundred annoyances which do not come under a captain's rule, or even knowledge—annoyances which can be so easily traced to natural causes, that of course steward must not be blamed for them any more than you or I.

All ye who value such alleviation as tropical miseries admit of, curry favour with the steward. All ye who appreciate winter consolations, in the form of hot sea-water bottles and aromatic caudles,[5] curry favour with the steward, ere the biting cold of the Horn[6] nip your very heart, and freeze your best feelings into one lugubrious mass of neighbour hatred.

All we have said of petitions, either gratified or denied, applies in the present case to but one of the vessels.

Both lay listlessly lulling their passengers—and the passengers of both were equally willing to be lulled—equally weary and feverish—equally anxious to snuff a breath of fresh air—equally tired of the ardent sky staring down upon them, relentless as the eye of conscience upon the bad man's soul. Here ended the similarity, save that both were outward bound. When the two vessels were within speaking distance, the master of the vessel of which we have been writing hoisted his signals, and displayed his black board, receiving in answer the announcement that the other ship was (from) London (to) Van Diemen's Land (with) prisoners.

Three words, which told a lifetime's tale of sorrow.

The vessels shifted still nearer each other, by lazy, who-may-care degrees, until an unusual state of excitement on board proclaimed that the two captains were about to exchange civilities through their trumpets.

The deck of the prison ship was crowded with prisoners—as a mass of brown serge distinctly visible; but from that mass to distinguish individuals required the help of the mate's telescope, looking through which was recognisable one figure whose tall and dignified form could be no other than Maida Gwynnham.

She stood at the bulwarks near the stern, and leaning on her was one who in the distance seemed a mere child, so small was she in comparison with Maida; yet, small as she was, she had on the prison serge and cap—this fact was discernible without the telescope's aid. On nearer view, her features were those of a young girl of fifteen years. She clung to Maida as an infant clings to its parent, following her with a quick uneasy step whenever she changed her position, and not seeming satisfied unless drawn close to her protector's side by the intertwining of her own and Maida's arm; then she appeared not to care how long she stood and watched the strange vessel.

In the free vessel was a group, which, as a group, was visible to the naked eye—to use an astronomical phrase—but to distinguish the individuals forming it, the captain needed his glass. There were three persons: a tall, slight gentleman, of an aspect decidedly clerical, a young lady, who sat on a camp-stool supported against the mizen, and a second young lady, whose clear, musical voice rang over the water as the trumpets conveyed their shrill messages backwards and forwards. So musical a laugh could only be Bridget D'Urban's. It rang right over to the poor child-prisoner, who, all against her will, laughed an answer to the merry voice; and Maida smiled a sad smile as she heard the youthful captive send back that miserable imitation, and yet she felt glad that the poor thing could laugh even such a laugh; the girl perceived the smile and feared it was a rebuke.

'I couldn't help it, Maida,' she said apologetically; 'it came so sweet and different from our women's great noises.'

Maida pressed her arm still more tightly around little Lucy. The Reverend Mr. Evelyn also heard Lucy's response to his niece's cheery heart-mirth, and an expression that Emmeline had learnt to interpret passed over his face; he turned from her and paced the deck for an instant, then, stopping abruptly at her side, he said, in a hurried tone:

'That was a child's voice! That ship is no place for so young a creature—they punish her soul as well as her body. They are teaching her sin by binding her to those who will instruct her well in their trade. And then she will get a series of severer punishments for proving an apt scholar in the school of vice to which she was only apprenticed to learn her own folly. She was put on board with a few years' knowledge of crime—she will come off with the knowledge of fifty years, unless some providence interfere on her behalf.'

Mr. Evelyn was short-sighted, or he would surely have recollected the figure that stood opposite him on the deck of the transport; had he looked through the telescope he could not have failed to discover Maida Gwynnham.

That Maida did not discover him is not to be wondered at, for never once did her eye stay its dreamy wandering into the fervid blue depths that lay, so tranquil, at her feet, until a rough hand grasped her shoulder, and a rougher voice demanded why she was later than her messmates—why had not she gone below with the other women; and it went on to say that she was no fit companion for the girl Lucy Grenlow, and that if she continued such doings she should be separated from her; at which threat the poor Lucy clung still more child-like to Maida, and Maida grasped the trembling form still more firmly to herself.

A breeze sprang up, and every stitch of sail was spread to atone for lost time. The two vessels, though bound for the same port, soon parted company. Shortly after the breeze had come to their relief, the news was spread that the log had been cast[7] and they were going at the rate of seven knots an hour.

Thus met on the broad ocean two ships bearing those who were appointed to an after blending of thrilling interests—interests of life, interests of death, and never-dying interests. Thus parted they, for the moment fixed by Providence had not yet arrived. Thus on the ever-varying yet never-changing sea of life are tossed together by storm, or drifted together by calm, mortal barques, who meet, exchange sympathies, commingle hopes and fears, report past successes, and mourn future prospects. The stormy winds lull, or the prayed-for breezes blow, and, bound for their diverse course, the mortal barques spread sail, and it is a wonder where has fled the lively interest each felt for the other; a transient glance, a slight watching of its disappearing fellow, and then, absorbed in its own career, each turns from each, and the horizon hides them both, and neither cares to ask, 'Shall we ever meet again? What is decreed in the chart of futurity for her who an hour since sailed side by side with me over this mighty deep?'

Maida had been on board the transport a fortnight before she was able to go on deck. The first morning that she took her place with the other women she noticed a small figure crouched up in a corner between two hen-coops on the leeward side. Her face was hidden low down in her lap; but by the jutting movements of the shoulder it was easy to tell that the little creature was sobbing violently.

'She'm gone to lo'urd[8] because she won't fall no further,' giggled a horrid-looking female, whose appearance was rendered more repulsive by a shock of grizzled hair, which had been cropped, and was now shooting up in perpendicular wires all over her head, making her look something between a withered grown-up tomboy[9] and an ex-lunatic. In defiance of rule she had taken off her cap. The matron was below, making up a recent quarrel with the surgeon-superintendent over a glass of wine, and simultaneously with her departure about sixty caps had disappeared from the multitude of shorn heads congregated on the deck of the *Rose of Britain*.

It was Lucy Grenlow who sat crouched up in the corner: she was one of the few who kept on their caps. As she bent her face more and more into her lap, she felt her cap twitched off, or, rather, an effort made to catch it off, but it was tied under her chin, so the twitch only raised her head with a jerk that let it fall more heavily into its covert.

'Let the maid alone, can't ye,' said the man at the wheel; 'she's a mere babby, and it's only right she should cry after her mother, the poor thing; darn my living soul if ever I'll come out with a prison-ship again.'

'You hold your —— tongue, or I'll give a point at the wheel for your insolence—a point that will set us spinning in a trice.'

With this the ex-lunatic or withered tomboy grasped the whole of Lucy's cap, together with the roots of her hair, and dragged her head up to the gaze of the herd.

'Here's a pretty face for you—lawk-a-me! Shan't she learn a thing or two from me before she leaves these precious boards? Yer, my dear, haven't you got your passage dirt cheap, that's all! Only paid five shillings for it, and here I've been working for this lift for nigh thirty year, and haven't got it till now. You'll have to bless your country to the end of your life for such generosity. My husband's been over there this ten year, and I've never been able to get over to un till now; he'll hire me straight away as soon as my probation's out. I suppose I an't been as brave as you, my little darling, for fortin favours the brave, they says, and her an't a-favoured me till now, goodness knows.'

All this while she held poor Lucy's head dragged backwards; the face was wet with tears, but the child tried hard not to burst out afresh; she even tried to smile, an attempt that destroyed her powers of endurance. By force she wrested herself from the brutal grasp, and with one loud wail, 'Mother! Mother!' sank upon the boards, cutting a deep gash in her forehead by the fall.

In an instant she was in Maida's arms, and would have been there much sooner had Maida known the cruel tyranny that was being exercised upon her. Absorbed in her own grief, and wasted by her own weakness, she had retreated to the further end of the deck, unwitting that a labour of love awaited her even in that den of infamy. It had not entered her mind that there was a possibility of a child-prisoner's existence amongst so aged a set of convicts; therefore, nursing her own sorrow, she was dreaming away the first morning of her deliverance from seasickness, when casting her eyes to leeward she saw the imbruted[10] woman drag back that youthful head. She started immediately to her feet; but, unaccustomed to the motion of the vessel, had to make several endeavours ere she could walk. During the last of those endeavours the girl's cry gave momentary strength to her limbs, and she almost darted to the spot. Her first impulse was to strike down the wretched creature; but by an instant perception of the more effective course, when the first buzz of excitement had died into that perfect hush which generally follows an accident brought on by foul means, she turned to the woman, and pointing towards Lucy, said—

'That child henceforth is mine; touch her at your peril!'

No one voice replied.

Maida waited a few moments, and looked with haughty quiet from one to the other of the scowling faces before her, to see if any would dare forbid the act of appropriation. But no resistance was made.

As she prepared to descend with her senseless burden, all feared she would tell the matron; and a deputation of women went forward to beg her not to peach.[11]

Maida listened with impatience to the odd mixture of oaths, petitions, threats, promises, by which the deputation beleaguered her; and when their vociferations let her get in a word, she said, with an air of dignity strangely unaccordant with the tumultuous manners of her rude audience—

'Telling will not recall the past; and until I perceive a danger of a similar act of cruelty, I shall not demean myself by punishing the offender.'

There was something so different to themselves in the speaker, that none ventured to gainsay her words to herself; but no sooner was she out of hearing, than hitherto repressed wrath broke out in fearful imprecations and vulgar jeers.

'*I*, indeed! Who's this mighty *I* come in amongst us all of a sudden, and all because of that little devil, Grenlow?' said one of the enraged throng, envious of a superiority she could not but award Maida Gwynnham in the depths of her heart.

'I guess this lady will have to swallow her gentility in the box one o' these days if she kicks up her guineas to the doctor,'[12] hoped a second.

A volley of curses from a third pretended to show her opinion of the intruder.

'I reckon we shan't be bothered much with her a bit, for the darned hypocrite 'll sure to be ill, and that 'ooman will sure for to scheme to get 'pointed her nurse; you see if she don't get the blind eye of the chap,'[13] (short for chaplain) exclaimed a fourth.

The ex-lunatic alone remained silent: her grizzled hair stood more perversely erect, like a forest of ill thoughts, from her head. There was a secret vowing of vengeance in her lowering brow and clenched teeth, as she shook her fist towards where the victim of her taunts had fallen. Turning sullenly away, she was about to go below, when the man at the wheel, just removed from his post, after assuring himself that no Argus[14] was near to detect his breach of rule—first mate being forward, second mate off his watch, and captain at his dinner, called to the women to hearken a moment to his advice, which he gave as follows—

'If ye be wise, all on ye, this is the thing ye'll do. That woman's a brick—a real, livin', rantin' brick;[15] and to prove it I'd marry her down straight away for the beauty of her two eyes, or else go down to Davy's locker,[16] if she wasn't a convict. Well, I'd have ye all keep in with her, or ye'll get the worst on it afore ye've done with her. You go straight away and elect her your queen, says I, and ye'll have some un worth standin' by; so good-bye all on ye, wise ones;' and with an admonitory flourish off made honest Jack, just in time to save his grog. Now as this advice coincided with the unexpressed feeling of each prisoner, all agreed that there was sense in Jack's sermint; and as there was no good in making an enemy where a friend could be gained, it was unanimously carried that Maida Gwynnham should be convict queen; though each voter privately hated her for the superiority which all were obliged to own, while they publicly abhorred Lucy Grenlow as the cause of the brawl which had exalted Maida Gwynnham to her honourable (?) position.

The fourth woman's prediction was correct. Maida had no sooner laid Lucy in her berth than she sought the chaplain, and asked him to use his influence in trying to get her appointed nurse; and the chaplain was successful.

The little convict had been ailing for many days; the morning's accident, therefore, was worse in its effects than might otherwise have been. She lay unconscious for a long time; and when, after a few uneasy tossings and half-sighed groans, she at last opened her eyes, it was only to look bewilderingly about and cry—

'Mother! Mother! I am so bad.'

'Are you, my poor child?' said the murderess tenderly, as she laid her hand on the sufferer's burning temples.

'That's nice; that's like you did when I had the fever, mother; I was feared you were gone. Don't go, don't go, oh, don't go!'

'I promised to tell the doctor when you awoke, dear; I will not be away an instant,' whispered Maida soothingly.

But the sick girl would not relinquish her hold of Maida's hand; so the convict nurse knelt down by the berth, and let her hand stay quietly in the fevered grasp of her poor young charge, whilst she kept the other hand on her forehead, now turning the palm, now the back of it, as its surface absorbed the heat from the parched skin of her brow.

'Mother, you b'lieve about the five shillings, don't you? Them gentlemen to court said 'twas all fibs; you b'lieve, don't you?'

'I believe every word you tell me, Lucy. But you must not talk whilst you are so poorly.'

'Will father beat me again if he catches me?' A shiver ran through her whole frame and lingered at her fingers' ends, until Maida pressed her hands gently between her own in order to stay the nervous trembling.

'No; father will never beat you again. There, lay your head on my arm; now you need not fear.'

'What's this?' cried Lucy, suddenly starting bolt upright, as something trickled down her cheek. She touched it, and found it was blood. She gazed at the crimson stain for a moment, and then asked, in a mysterious voice—

'Is that what I heard tell about to Sunday-school; the blood—what is it?—that cleanses from all sin?'

Maida wiped the trickling drops from her cheek, and said—

'I have heard of that blood; it will cleanse *your* sin, Lucy.'

'*You* haven't got no sins to cleanse, mother.'

'It will wash away *your* sins,' calmly answered Maida.

'Oh, don't, mother, don't! I know I've been very wicked; but I meant, indeed I did, for to put back the five shillings when I got paid.'

'I am sure you did, poor dear.'

Maida's heart was full to bursting; but no outer sign of sorrow was visible in the tutored features that bent over the invalid; pity, almost anguished pity was there, but no single token betrayed the mighty grief which lay buried deep, deep in the sanctuary beneath.

'Say it, mother, that what I heard tell about at Sunday-school—the blood, what is it?—my thoughts are all gone.'

'The blood of Jesus Christ cleanseth from all sin,' said the religious instructor solemnly. He had heard the latter part of Lucy's wanderings, and, more with a view to Maida than the delirious patient, seized the opportunity to proclaim the tidings of a Saviour's death to one whom he considered an *extra*ordinary sinner.

The old look of indifference immediately obliterated all trace of feeling from her face.

Would that I could see some expression there, thought the instructor, as he met the passionless marble of Maida's countenance turned towards him.

Did Maida read the thought, that her lips curled into a line of scorn? But only for an instant; the scorn changed into a smile, for Lucy seemed about to speak.

''Tisn't father, is it? Mother, don't leave go; it can't be father, he don't talk nothing about the blood. Who is it, mother?'

The religious instructor beckoned that he would answer. Drawing close to the berth, he repeated—

'The blood of Jesus Christ cleanseth from all sin.'

'No, no!' said Lucy, in the fretful accent of delirium; 'no, no! I want mother to say it.'

Maida trembled; there was expression enough in her countenance then.

The sick child looked imploringly at her; the murderess could not resist the silent appeal. Averting her head from the instructor, with thrilling distinctness she pronounced—

'The blood of Jesus Christ cleanseth from all sin.'

'Not yours, mother; you an't got no sin; you didn't steal five shillings.'

Maida did not answer—but delirious people *will* be answered; hence the difficulty in treating their whims.

'Not yours, mother! Mother, not yours?'

'*No*—not mine,' came the fearful reply.

''Cause you an't got none. Only me that's wicked;' and with a wild, shrill laugh the sick child clapped her hands, and sank back on her pillow, tired with the exertion.

'And why not *yours*, my poor woman?' asked the instructor in a very kindly voice. 'May not the *all* reach even your case?'

'As one of your charge, sir, I am bound to listen to you; but I do not prefer discussion; it only tends to strengthen the natural prejudice of the heart.'

'I have no wish to discuss, Martha Grylls; that is no part of my duty. I have but one desire, and that is to preach Christ to you and your fellow sinners. Oh, Martha! What would I not give to see you awake to the peril of your soul? The sinner's soul is always in danger; but in your case danger is increased tenfold. What if we had gone down in last week's storm? Where would then your soul have been? Where would it be now? Martha, you have a weight of guilt—unredeemed guilt upon your life. Should that life be snatched away, the guilt would sink your soul to hell—yes, nothing but hell is before you.'

'Very comforting!' said Maida, quietly folding her heart's secret still more securely to the innermost recesses of her bosom. 'The chaplain of the gaol had peculiar pleasure in this point of God's mercy, but it fails to win me.'

'"Because I have called and ye have refused, I will also laugh at your calamity."[17] Martha, should death overtake you unawares, this would be your case,' exclaimed the instructor earnestly. 'Look at that poor child; hers is a small sin compared with yours, yet see how it haunts her conscience. If she has such inward torment, what would yours be if you were laid on a bed of death? How could you face your Judge were you now to appear at His bar?'

'Does He measure sin by its amount, do you suppose, sir?' asked Maida, so innocently that the good man hoped he had at last aroused her interest; he did not observe the calm defiance in the eye that watched for his explanation of Divine purpose.

'That is dangerous ground, my woman; it is enough for us to know that all sin is hateful to God.'

'I beg your pardon, sir,' interrupted Maida, very coldly but very politely, 'it may be enough for *you* to know; my emergency being greater, I naturally wish to ascertain more of future probabilities.'

'Then go to your Bible, Martha Grylls; you will read there of all that the Lord intends we shall know. Have you a Bible?'

'I have, sir.'

'Then the greater will be your condemnation if you do not profit by it. Do you read it? Ah-h-h!—I'm afraid not—afraid not.'

'I do, sir, twice a day.'

'God be praised!' and the dear, zealous man rubbed his hands together as though there was yet hope for the murderess.

Maida's keen discernment perceived sincerity in the religious instructor's fervour, or she would not have deigned to reply as she had done, neither as she did, to prevent a misconception of her avowal.

'I do not read for my own gratification, but merely to fulfil a promise which I unfortunately made—I read the Bible for no other reason.'

'Poor, poor Martha!' said the instructor dejectedly. 'It is in that book that you would read Lucy's text. Ah! That blood is quite able to wash even your sin away, black and damning as it is. Do kneel down ere you read again and beg for God's blessing on what you read, and then—'

Maida was becoming irritated; she could not brook what appeared to her sensitive mind an indelicate pressing of an advantage offered by position, and with some abruptness she exclaimed—

'Whether a favour from God or man, I have a particular dislike to blessings which can only be obtained by begging. I cannot seek a favour likely to be denied me—to find acceptance with me it must flow unbidden.'

Her impulsive spirit gathered anger as she spoke. By the time she had finished this speech she had drawn herself to her full height, and stood surveying the instructor with flushed disdain.

Oh, Maida! Thy God was more compassionate to thee than thou wert to thyself, or those thy words had been written in the eternal page to thy lasting woe. Thou hadst decreed bitter things against thyself had the pen of fate been in thy power.

The antagonistic principle is strong in the human breast, so strong, that in our natural state we would rather walk to hell than be driven to heaven.

In addition to this principle, prisoners have the stimulus of revenge in refusing salvation. They have a notion that government wants them to be saved, therefore salvation is hateful to them; and did not God force it upon some of them, as He did upon Saul,[18] few of them would be saved. Not for himself, but as a salaried servant of government they dislike the religious instructor or chaplain. They discern the broad arrow[19] in all his pleadings, and accordingly detest them, and hope they are paying him out by marching on to perdition in the very teeth of his threats. There are of course exceptions to this rule—exceptions made by prisoners themselves in favour of heaven, and exceptions *in some chaplains*, whose correct judgment gives them irresistible power in spite of the government stigma so jealously regarded by the convicts. Such an exception was Mr. Evelyn, Maida's friend. Such was *not* the religious instructor of the *Rose of Britain*. (For their dignity's sake the women called him chaplain.) He was a truly pious, energetic man; but needed judgment and discrimination of character in discharging his important duties; for the lack of these two necessary items of a teacher's qualifications, he often brought about effects wholly contrary to his intentions. He failed as a pastor, whilst he did well as a preacher. From the desk, irrespective of idiosyncrasies, he erred not in shaking the quiver of truth over a body of persons under one condemnation; for the Spirit alone could guide the arrows—each to its appropriate mark. As a preacher he sought to turn a mass of sin, and on that mass brought to bear with great force the whole battery of Scripture denunciation, and none, save Pharaonic hardness,[20] could withstand the ably directed attack.

But when as a *pastor* he went from cell to cell, from solitary being to solitary being, and aimed the same power of attack on one poor sinner, the effect was to crush the timid, desponding soul, and to embolden the reckless, perverse soul with that daring which is akin to despair; that daring which rushes on because it cannot further exceed the bounds of mercy, and because it has already sinned the sin unto death, and reprieve is hopeless. Our instructor took the Bible for his text (so did the Zealots),[21] while he neglected to take it for his pattern. The voice of inspiration, whether from prophetic, apostolic, or divine lips, attunes itself to suit the case before it. It encourages and invites the timid—'Come unto *me*;' it reasons with the doubtful—'Come now and let us reason together, saith the Lord; though your sins be as scarlet they shall be white as snow, though they be red as crimson they shall be as wool;' it persuades the wavering—'Why will ye die?—Is there no balm in Gilead?' It comforts the broken-hearted—'I am he that blotteth out thy transgressions—I have found a ransom—Go in peace;' while it warns the careless—'The wages of sin is death—Fly from the wrath to come—What a man soweth, that shall he also reap;' it threatens the stubborn—'This shall ye have at my hand, ye shall lie down in sorrow—The wicked shall be turned into hell,' and finally condemns the determined—'And these shall go away into everlasting punishment—Whose damnation is just.' In his zeal for his outcast sisters, the instructor forgot so to deal with them; he indiscriminately shook the thunders of Sinai around them. As with the ex-lunatic, so with Maida Gwynnham. As with the stubborn, hardened Peg Lodikins, so with the little tender-hearted Lucy Grenlow. He would tell of the precious blood shed for the remission of sins, but not until such ones as Maida and Lucy feared their guilt was too deep to be washed out by it.

Then, again, he laid great stress on show of feeling; the maudlin tears of Peg Lodikins went for contrition, while the rigid features of Maida's stricken face were set down as obduracy. Mr. Evelyn had discerned at a glance that all the pride, defiance, calmness, or impetuosity of Maida were only props to the bruised reed within. He felt at once that not the irritating appliances of the executioner, but the tender though firm treatment of the surgeon, was needed there; and had he been her pastor, his ministrations would have tended to the gentle removal of those props by the removal of the cause which made them necessary. His anointing would have been to bind up the broken-hearted, only giving that pain which is inseparable from the healing process, how wisely soever dealt. We have already seen that whilst he lovingly entreated, he also faithfully reproved her. He despised not, in some cases, to follow St. Paul's example, 'Being crafty, I caught you with guile.'[22]

Had our religious instructor so managed with Maida Gwynnham, who may know what happy results had ensued? During those tedious months of comparative idleness, her tortured soul was left to its own resources; and these were a firmer planting of the props—pride, defiance, &c.—around the bruised reed, to guard it from the rough grasp that wrung the wound where it should have touched it delicately—that gave unbearable agony where remedial pain alone was wanted: what wonder, then, that Maida left the prison ship an unaltered, if not a hardened, character?

Before the women she listened with a marked deference to all the instructor said, and she made little Lucy reverence his teachings. She knew that though the driving system was repugnant to her, there were those who would never see the gates of heaven were they not scared thither by the whip of small cords, and, accordingly, admired the man who had sufficient nerve to inflict the stripes, whilst she repudiated his indiscreet mode of administering the lash alike to all within his reach. When alone she shunned him in every possible way. She preferred the box, irons, cells,[23] any punishment, to meeting him; but the more she shunned him, the more the dear, zealous man importuned her in every possible way; so that, brought to bay, she had often no resort but to assume an impregnable austerity, or to offer positive resistance, by which she incurred chastisement. In his mistaken zeal he once pronounced her an unfit companion for Lucy, and separated the friends for a season; and might have kept them entirely apart, had not the surgeon-superintendent wisely interfered, foreseeing no end of irons, cells, and box for Maida, and no end of persecutions, crying, and isolation for poor Lucy, in persevering in a course so distasteful to both.

Peg Lodikins had a facetious aside for the instructor's frequent interjectional comment—'It is my duty, ay, and my pleasure, "to be in season, and out of season," in my warnings to you.'

She would nudge the ex-lunatic with—'"In season, and out of season," pertickler the latter!' and then with sanctimonious glancing up she would silently laud the beauty of a word fitly spoken.

Lucy, in her admiration of Maida, fancied that the 'chaplain' dodged her from deck to deck, from sheer inability to keep out of her presence, and quietly determined in her own mind that—'The chaplain set a sight on that there Maida;' a conclusion that she stored away in her mental locker for future use, as we shall see.

We must return to the berth-side where we left Maida fulfilling the duties of nurse. For many days Lucy's life was despaired of. The doctor said her illness was not induced by the fall, but certainly hastened and aggravated thereby.

Maida dreaded the moment when returning consciousness should deprive poor Lucy of her new-found parent. 'Mother! Mother!' had been the constant cry of delirium. A long and tranquil sleep had gradually overcome the restless invalid, and Maida now knelt by the berth, anxiously awaiting the result. She quite expected that Lucy's dream of maternal proximity would end with the slumber, and was meditating how she should allay the disappointment and revulsion of feeling towards herself which must succeed, when she heard a suppressed sob.

It was from Lucy.

Whilst Maida knelt there absorbed in perplexity, little Grenlow opened her eyes without turning her head, and for many minutes surveyed the figure before her ere she could understand the mystery of the last week; and who shall blame that young creature, of scarce fifteen years, if tears from her very heart accompanied the recollection that she was a felon—being transported beyond the seas for the frightful crime of stealing five shillings!

She saw by the brown serge[24] that the figure was that of a prisoner, but what prisoner she knew not. She longed to read her future treatment in the face; but the face was buried in the figure's hands.

Lucy longed and longed for perhaps thirty seconds; and then, unable to bear further uncertainty, she stretched out her finger and touched Maida's arm, but the face moved not. Shall we say that Maida Gwynnham, the murderess, continued to hide her eyes because she had not courage to meet a look of disappointment from a friendless child?

But the touch was repeated, and there was an imploring motion in it that Maida could not resist. She withdrew her hands, feeling almost guilty as she submitted her face to the earnest scrutiny of the two widely opened eyes gazing up from the berth. The scrutiny seemed satisfactory. Though denuded of nature's best ornament, though surrounded by a badge of shame in the prison-cap, there was nothing in that countenance that the rarest beauty might not have envied—no point that the most fastidious critic could have desired to rectify.

Gazing on that countenance, Lucy again dropped off to sleep—again to awake; but this time with a smile—a smile that forced its way from her grateful heart through an avenue of inward sighs and regrets. She raised herself on one elbow, and extending her hand to Maida, whispered:

'Is it you that's been mother all along so kind?'

'I have tried to be, my child,' came the soft, meek answer. And that proud spirit that had fortified itself against all pity, reproach, or scorn, bent right down to meet a young girl's sorrow, and became child-like in its show of grief.

When the chaplain looked in at No. 107, to see how she fared, he saw not only her asleep, but close beside her, face to face, another slumberer, whose features, relaxed from their rigid coldness beneath the genial rest, had lost their wonted sternness, and were full of feeling. When Lucy had sufficiently recovered, she told Maida her story—a story of simple pathos—

Would that it were unique in the annals of youthful crime!

CHAPTER 12

Lucy Grenlow's Tale

LUCY'S mother had been a widow three years when she married again. Lover's promises did not merge into husband's fulfilments. When John Southwood wooed and won the pretty Mrs. Grenlow, he declared her children should find in him not only a father-in-law but a second father. He rejoiced to take her for better and for worse; the better being a comfortable little income in the form of a greengrocer's shop, the worse very decidedly consisting of three children, the present Lucy, aged thirteen years, and two younger sisters. But three months after his marriage he made another confidential declaration (not to his wife though), to the effect that, deny it who would, 'It was a beggarly hard thing that a man couldn't take a woman for better without being obliged to take her for worse, such worseness too as them there large-mouthed brats.'

Poor Lucy's chucks under the chin became less frequent, until one fine afternoon they came to a full stop, and turned into a severe beating. Lucy ran screaming to her mother; the mother flew to the father, only to be sent back weeping to her child, full of impotent fears that home was no longer home to her three orphaned girls. From that afternoon John Southwood threw off the paternal mask, and ill-treated or neglected his wife's children as best suited his purpose. One day after a terrible flogging, Lucy ran away, and did not return until hunger forced her to seek her mother's roof the following morning. John did not beat her again, but he clenched his fist in her face, and swore that the next time she played the running off dodge, 'he would tan her fit for the market,' an expression that Lucy intuitively understood.

The poor mother perceived she must adopt some plan to come between the girl and her father's brutality. So she bade Lucy dress in her best and come along with her. She led her from shop to shop in search for someone who might need an errand-girl or little maid-of-all-work. To her delight she at last obtained her young daughter a place in the latter capacity in the house of a small haberdasher. Lucy was to remain until she was fourteen without wages. At the expiration of that period, if proved wage-worthy, she was to receive five shillings a month.

Mrs. Southwood entertained no doubts of the promised remuneration, for she was sure of Lucy's good conduct, and did not mind, not she, telling as much to the haberdasher's wife in these words—

'Lucy's a dapper little hussy [1] when she has the life in her, but her life am easy put out of her. When she's tret well, she can do a'most anything.' And the mother heaved a sigh in memory of days when her girl was able to do well under kind treatment in her own home.

The very next evening Lucy entered on her maid-of-all-workship in the haberdasher's service; and with unblemished character and increasing reputation she worked out her wageless months.

Bright with hope, and radiant with expectation, she got up an hour earlier than usual on the day from which her five shillings was to commence. With extra alacrity she dressed the children, prepared her kitchen, and served the family's breakfast; and when, in answer to her brisk curtsey and exuberant smile, her mistress wondered—

'Why, Lucy, child, what ails you this morning?'

'It's my day for beginning, please, mem,' popped forth from her ready lips into missus's unready ears.

The five-shilling day in all its glory at last 'aksherly' arrived, as Lucy announced by the clapping of her well-worked hands on the morning her money fell due. And in the afternoon of that eventful day, she sallied forth in full bloom by missus's permission to spend her earnings. But having purchased a ninepenny pair of gloves, eight pennyworth of pink gauze ribbon, two sixpenny aprons, and one pennyworth of lollypops, her heart smote her, and she hastened home to give the remaining half-crown as a peace-offering to her father. Shame would not let him accept the gift in his own huge hand—that same hand that had so cruelly beaten the poor child: but having no intention to refuse the coin, he sent Lucy to her mother, at the same time telling her that next month she ought to bring the whole five shillings to help towards the coming baby.

Lucy loved her mother to her heart, and was nothing loath to obey her father in transferring the half-crown, nevertheless she had a grain or two of English in her composition which made her, young as she was, feel rather indignant at being told she must not do as she pleased with her own. When, however, she saw her mother looking so pale and tired, and heard her wish to goodness that there weren't another of 'em coming into this miserable world, her English heart relented, and she vowed over and over again, that mother should have every farthing of next month's money, and she thought all the praise and blessings she got in return for her vows a cheap five shillings' worth.

It was with a heart swelling with filial pride, that Lucy left her home that night, and it was with an aching, aching heart, that Mrs. Southwood watched her retreating step until she lost the last glimpse of Lucy's frock far down the street; and it was with a still more aching, aching heart that she turned from her little window again to wish to goodness that another of 'em wasn't coming for to make it still harder to know how to do, and how to please father.

Next month arrived. True to her vow Lucy carried the five-shilling piece to her mother; but father was not ashamed to receive it this time, seeing he had an additional call on his means in the very tiny person of a son and heir—a son to a brute of a father, and a poor sickly, woebegone mother; and an heir to what? To an inheritance of pain and care and trouble which the world is not forgetful to lay up for its progeny.

Next month arrived, and though Lucy was sorely tempted in the form of a smart pink ribbon—a particular weakness of hers and of her mother's before her—she kept faith with her vow and again deposited the crown in her father's hand. Next month had only in part arrived, when a son was born to the haberdasher, and a nurse was engaged to overlook the infantile interests.

Nurse took a fancy to Lucy, and in an evil moment Lucy repaid the fancy with her confidence; and divulging the family secret of the five shillings, sought advice on the propriety of spending one-half of the coming wage on herself. Nurse was decidedly in favour of such a step, and spoke not a little against John Southwood's rapacity, setting such rapacity down to the score of his step-fathership.

For a day and a half, Lucy remained in a doubtful state of mind. She longed to follow the pink ribbon bend of her inclination, and yet longed to give the whole sum to her father, in order to save her poor mother a row.

She looked in her kitchen glass and thought how a smart ribbon would become her plump shiny face, and thence into her mental glass, through which the pale, tear-marked countenance of her mother shook itself sadly at her, and then hesitated which of the two faces should have the benefit of her doubt. At this luckless juncture entered Mrs. Gullem, the monthly;[2] gruel-cup in hand she came. She perceived at once what turn the girl's thoughts were taking as she stood before the glass. Advancing to her, she exclaimed—

'I call it a monstrous mean shame that that pretty face should lose a lover all for a bit of ribbin. If I'm a woman, I know your mother'd rather see a yard or two of trimming in your cap and round your neck than she'd feel a few paltry coppers in her pocket a-jingling.'

'But father wouldn't,' was Lucy's quick rejoinder.

'The more shame he! Nothing in the world but an old step-father; and what d'ye get for your dootifulness? A few extra stripes on your back.'

'Oh no, Mrs. Gullem, he's never beat me since I was here.'

'But he don't thank you, you foolish hussy.'

'I don't want no thanks from he,' said Lucy, looking crestfallen. 'It's all for mother. Praps he'd beat her stead of me if he didn't get the money, and that would be worse than beating of me.'

'Come, come; you needn't peck up like that; what odds do you think 'tis o' mine? Why no more than *this*' (showing her little finger); 'all I want is to see a poor girl like you righted. A proper womanish feeling *I* calls it.'

'I didn't go for to offend you, Mrs. Gullem. I was only seeing how it felt like.'

'I know, I know; and admires you accordingly,' cried Mrs. Gullem, benignantly, as she walked out of the kitchen, leaving the leaven to work in the child's mind. Just from outside the kitchen door a sigh came back to Lucy—

'That pretty face to lose a sweetheart, what a pity! I'd manage it easy, just for the liking I've taken to her if she'd let me, and no one'd be the wiser for it.'

Not fifteen, and yet have a lover! What wondrous promotion for so young a girl! How delightfully old it made her appear! What maiden of fourteen could be proof against an insinuation so elevating? Not Lucy Grenlow.

The leaven worked more furiously.

Mrs. Gullem sat composedly in the nursery, chirruping to one of Leigh Hunt's[3] little pulpy masses, when Lucy beckoned to her through the partially closed shutter of the window.

'There, there, the pitty dear *shall* go to his mamma whilst nursey looks after the gruel,' intoned Mrs. Gullem, as she put the baby into its mother's arms, and obeyed the silent summons without appearing to notice Lucy's signal, and failing to remember that the gruel did not require her superintendence, having been already imported and partly demolished.

'I heard what you said, Mrs. Gullem. How do you mean you'd manage it?' asked Lucy.

'Heard what? Manage what, my dear?'

Mrs. Gullem spoke with the air of one who is charged with an unknown misdemeanour.

Lucy explained, and the nurse replied in a slow, recollective manner—

'Did I say that? Well, I must have said it right out of my heart, then, for I don't remember it now.'

Of course you did, Mrs. Gullem; it could not have come from any place less corrupt.

She continued for some minutes in an attitude betokening thought.

'Well, then, whether I said it or not, I'm quite willing to help you. Let's see; you wants to keep part of your money? Just nod *yes* or *no* as I goes on.'

Lucy nodded.

'Why not all? Bless us, five shillings an't much to trig you out as your pretty face deserves. Why not spend it all, says I?'

''Cause of mother.'

'Well then, spend half. Next is, you wants to manage not to let father know it, that's it, ain't it?'

Lucy nodded.

'And very right too, a nasty brute! But here's the mud,[4] and how to help you clean over I can't think all in a hurry.'

There is no hurry in the case, Mrs. Gullem; the plan is already formed in your crafty mind.

'How d'ye like this; spend it and give it to father too? I'd put you in the way of it.'

Lucy's face brightened.

'Borrow it; now to once;[5] and then when you gets your five shillings, carry 'em to your father all but sixpence. So you do each time till you have saved ten sixpences. Or may be, if you likes it better, when I get my pay I'll lend you a half towards it.'

Lucy shook her head, and thought the monthly did not know her master, or she would not propose a loan from him; but the nurse had no idea of borrowing according to Lucy's conception. The advance *was* to come from the haberdasher, but *without* his consent; in fact, it was to come from the till. Mrs. Gullem had interests of her own at stake, which made this necessary. What those interests were, let those tell who have gone to the brink of detection, and then to insure success to the last, have remorselessly pushed over one who has sufficient marks of guilt upon her to appease the cry of justice.

Carefully feeling her way, Mrs. Gullem told Lucy that she could easily borrow the money from the till, and pay it back again by sixpenny installments. The haberdasher was not a good accountant, having always depended on his wife's assistance in this branch; so she—Mrs. Gullem—said that the five shillings would not be missed; or if they were, would only be set against the *miss*-takes master always made in his reckonings; or, ten chances to one that any accounts would be kept during the husband's double work; he would have enough to do without fussing over trifles. Thus argued the old deceiver.

'Oh! Mrs. Gullem, that would be real stealing! What would mother say? She'd nigh to break her heart. I'd rather never have a ribbon, and I wish I weren't pretty.'

'Much obliged to your imperance![6] Talk of stealing to me—as honest a woman as ever nursed a baby—indeed, I think you must be mighty particular to show airs about a job that I'd do as soon as look. If I'm not scrup'lous and pious, I'd like to know who is. Catch me giving advice again to a thankless hussy.'

'But don't you think 'twould be stealing? How do I feel so queer about it like?'

'Because you pretends to be wiser than your betters. As to stealing, look here; don't you mean to be all fair and honest, and put it straight away back by sixpences at a time?'

Mrs. Gullem's voice gradually dropped to persuasiveness as she saw signs of relenting in Lucy's face.

'Yes,' nodded Lucy.

'Well, then, who's hurt by your loan? How can master be the loser by losing what he didn't know he'd got? For that's how I take it 'twill be. You'll get a smart ribbin round your pretty face, and he won't lose by your getting it. But whether he's the wiser or not, pay it back says I. My rule is, always pay your legal debts.'

But not your *il*-legal, was Mrs. Gullem's mental reservation; and many such debts has she incurred without either prior or after intention of liquidating them.

Lucy's head again shook, but not, as before, with a shocked motion; doubt seemed pre-eminent.

'Suppose it should be found out 'fore I'd paid, they wouldn't excuse me I'm feared.'

'Your intention's all right, you is in distress, and helps yourself to a few shillings that isn't wanted; that must satisfy your honesty, which is very great—as to the findings out, why, of course, that would be uncomfortable-like; but I don't think it *will* be if I guess right about master. If it is, why there's no help for it—you must tell a bit of a fib, and say you don't know nothing about it; this won't really harm, if you keeps honest and pays back the sixpences.'

Mrs. Gullem saw victory on her side, and without another word retreated to her nursery, and let off her secret chuckle in another hug of the baby, and another intoned endearment to it.

She had acted her part. She must now stand by to watch results, and guard herself. It was no part of her policy that Lucy should escape detection, therefore she refused to aid the child in securing the money. If the theft was clumsily made, so much the more advantageous to her (Mrs. Gullem's) aforesaid interest.

Following the advice of the adage, 'Give the devil his due,' we are compelled to say—that believing the generally accepted report of the haberdasher's character, she quite thought a private lecture, and parental flogging, would be the extent of punishment inflicted on the culprit. She, well skilled as she was in the deceitful twistings of the heart, had yet to learn that even Christians take a decided satisfaction in repairing their money injuries by the hand of judicial vengeance; even *they* forget to forgive as they would be forgiven. Not that we plead the possibility of carrying this divine and blessed injunction to its utmost in the public relations of life.

But surely if ever there was a case when a free forgiveness would have been as *possible* as *beneficial* in its issue, it was the present one, when sobbing as though each sob would be her last, Lucy Grenlow stood before her master, under suspicion of having robbed the till of five shillings.

Sob—sob—sob—was the only answer the haberdasher obtained to his questions, until he added—

'Lucy, you had better confess it; *then*, nothing more will be said about it.'

Lucy knew not that a policeman was in waiting, so wiping her eyes sufficiently hard to wipe them right out, she whispered a confession of her guilt; and then feeling immediate relief from the discharge of the dreadful secret from her breast, she stopped her crying, only enunciating her sorrow and contrition by convulsive noises which appeared like sighs jetted upwards and then pulled downwards.

No sooner was the declaration made than the policeman stepped forward and took Lucy prisoner. Mrs. Gullem who had been called in as a disinterested party to witness the search and note proceedings, also stepped forward, and begged the haberdasher to look over the offence just this once, pleading that it was very bad of Lucy, but then if she were forgiven now, she might be sufficiently warned for the future; that she was, after all, a mere child, and a good whipping would be best for her. But the haberdasher was inexorable; he said he was a public man and owed his country a duty, and if every one followed his example there would be fewer criminals. 'Nip crime in its bud, Mrs. Gullem,' (pointing to the bud Lucy), 'and we should not have so many full-blown, glaring flowers to uproot,' cried the patriotic tradesman.

A bold flaunting sunflower shining in the windowsill evidently supplied this illustration impromptu to his mind.

'I admire your kind, womanly mediation, but it would be weak in me to yield to it. Do your duty, policeman; sad, sad, though it be.'

And the officer bore off his prize.

Matters went hardly with Lucy. The five shillings was not the amount of the plaintiff's loss; sum after sum had disappeared from the till during some time past, until the old-fashioned expedient of marking some coin was resorted to. The very next evening more money was missing, a search was instituted, and it was found on Lucy, and recognised as *not* her property by a figure on the reverse side. The haberdasher at once charged Lucy with the former robberies, but she denied all knowledge of them, and, as we have seen, would not plead guilty to the sum found in her pocket until reassured by her master's promise.

Her story of meaning to repay the money was only received by a laugh from the court, and was discarded with a severe jest by the judge. It never occurred to Lucy to mention Mrs. Gullem as a party in the theft; neither did it occur to her childish mind that Mrs. Gullem had been a party in it. That worthy personage had studiously avoided Lucy since the time she had advised her to take 'the loan'. Having dropped her seed she wished to remain in ignorance of its progress. The first intimation that Lucy had committed the act, she received from the haberdasher; therefore, she could fairly display all due surprise when informed of the painful incident. This ignorance on her part had the desired effect on Lucy. If the girl had entertained any notion of joining Mrs. Gullem in the deed, her primitive train of reasoning, namely, that Mrs. Gullem, not knowing she had taken the money, couldn't have had anything to do with the wicked theft, would have non-plussed such a notion. As it was, her thoughts were by far too engrossed in the horrors of her guilt, position, and possible punishment, to spare one thought on Mrs. Gullem.

Nevertheless Mrs. Gullem had many to bestow on Lucy, and could not be easy until she had visited her in the prison, to ascertain what *had* been, and what had *not* been said. To her relief, the girl received her almost affectionately, and when she exclaimed, somewhat reproachfully—

'Why, Lucy, you never told me what you had done.'

The little prisoner burst out—

'Oh, no, no! I wish I had, and this wouldn't have happened. Oh, how ever came I to be so wicked, oh, *so* wicked, *so* wicked!'

'Ah, 'twas a pity; I could have advised you, poor child. I fear 'twill go bad with you, seeing there's been a lot missed—you may trust me, Lucy—are you sure now, you an't taken no more that's been lost?'

'Oh, no, no, Mrs. Gullem! I only took them 'orrid five shillings, and I meant to put 'em back, indeed I did.'

'Well, well, 'twas a pity, and I pities you, heartily.' She offered Lucy a pocket handkerchief full of child-comforts in the shape of gingerbread, apples, and sweets; but Lucy shook her head at the bundle, with an expression hopeless enough to have wrung any heart that had aught but selfish feeling left in it.

Mrs. Gullem was taking back the bundle when Lucy raised her eyes without raising her head, and said—

'Maybe the children would like 'em; 'twould help to keep 'em from fretting mother.'

On leaving, the 'monthly' kissed Lucy, and told her that she would never 'think no worser of her for them paltry shillings.' When she had gone, Lucy felt the door had closed on her best friend, and on one of the kindest and most upright of women.

The girl Grenlow, in whom the law recognised a practised thief, was sentenced to transportation beyond the seas for seven years.

'Pity you hadn't stolen *seven* shillers, and that would have made a shiller a year!' was a remark made by the ex-lunatic, on hearing Lucy's story.

CHAPTER 13

Mulgrave Battery and the Lodge

A gallant vessel towards our port
Makes on in stately pride,
Her sun-lit sails the breeze has caught,
And she doth landward ride.

'THERE'S a ship in sight, papa. Come, look at the flagstaff. Perhaps 'tis Uncle Herbert and cousins. Do let's go and see,' cried Charlie Evelyn, the only son of Mr. Evelyn, senior, of Macquarie Street, Hobarton, brother of the Rev. Herbert Evelyn, whose acquaintance we have already made. Two days before the above exclamation from Charlie, Mr. Evelyn had received a letter from England announcing the immediate return of his brother and niece to the land of their adoption. Since then Charlie had kept a keen look-out towards Mulgrave Battery,[1] whence reared up that herald of joy or woe, of hope or despair—the flagstaff.

Mr. Evelyn sprang to the window.

'So there is, my boy. Let us try to decipher the signal. There, now, the kind wind has blown it straight out for us.'

'From the south! From the south!' shouted Charlie, frisking from the window to the other side of the room, and thence back with a bound to the window, as the flag displayed the red cross on a white ground.

'That's one go, at any rate,' said Mr. Evelyn, patting the curly head of his little boy, who gloried in being a genuine 'gum tree,' and not a stupid British oak.[2]

Mr. Evelyn quietly reseated himself to a re-perusal of the *Courier*,[3] while Charlie remained faithful to his post.

In a short time a second shout brought Mr. Evelyn again to the window, and, with no less an interest than Charlie's, he watched the flag being hauled down from the top-mast, and the ball running up to the yard-arm.

'A brig; no, a ship!' cried Charlie, as the ball reached its destination at No. 1, on the right.

'Two goes in the right direction,' said Mr. Evelyn, patting his approval of Charlie's good memory.

A little more suspense, and down went the ball.

Charlie was too excited to announce the event, and Mr. Evelyn was too busy to observe it. The flag was hoisted in the place of the ball.

'A beastly, stupid old pisson ship!' exclaimed the child, in a tone of extreme disgust, as the prison flag proclaimed a fresh cargo of female convicts, *ex* the *Rose of Britain*.

'Charlie, Charlie, what will Uncle Herbert say when he hears you use such words? How would you like to have the vessel he comes by called such names, eh, naughty boy?'

'Oh, papa,' answered the curly-headed, petticoated urchin, 'his ship won't bring a lot more of those pests.'

Seeing a frown on his father's brow he apologised.

'Why, papa, Mr. Squire calls them pests. I don't mind 'em, though, except when they come instead of dear uncle.'

Mr. Evelyn looked uneasily at him, and then, humming a tune, walked backwards and forwards on the hearth-rug. He, as well as every other Tasmanian parent, had cause to feel uneasiness. His child breathed an unhealthy moral atmosphere, how could he fail to become infected? It was a constant strife between poison and antidote. Parental teachings were undermined by subtle nursery influences. Lessons of morality and piety, listened to with reverence on the mother's lap or father's knee, were contradicted by the practices of convict life, so that Charlie was puzzled to know which was the correct path—that commended to him by precept, or that chosen by the multitude. In fact, he had to decide between seeing and hearing. It was true, he was taught to look on the prisoners as transgressors, suffering the penalty of their sin; but when, instead of one or two individuals, he saw himself surrounded by them at home and abroad he was very naturally led to consider them a class born into the world to as inevitably fill its allotted position as any other great division of the human race. Free—bond—conveyed to his imagination only an idea of caste. Again, when he saw all useful occupations engrossed by this class, he was convinced that they were a very necessary and important people, without whose aid the world could not exist. Two interjectional remarks made by him on separate occasions will show his mental appreciation of this class. When taken by his father to see some public work, which was just receiving its finishing touches from convict labour, he admired in silence for a long while, and then broke out:

'When *I'm* a pisner, won't I build a beauty!'

And on being asked by a gentleman about to return to England if he would like to go too, he made several objections. He could not leave papa and mamma: there were no pretty parrots in England. But these objections were left in the background by the insurmountable climax:

'Why, there are no lots of pisners in that country to do our work. How *could* I go?'

These remarks were rewarded by a hearty laugh by all hearers save Mr. Evelyn. His brow contracted a frown peculiar to himself, as he heard in his child's voice the certain symptoms of moral disease.

'Oh, but he will grow out of such notions,' said one to the grieved father on that occasion.

'I have not the least doubt of it, sir,' bitterly replied Mr. Evelyn, choosing to take the words literally, 'even as the flower grows out of the seed. Notions produce the man, not man the notions, I take it.'

'You take it too seriously, then, sir. Convictism is a great nuisance *per se*; but, —— me, if I don't incline to that young rogue's way of thinking, and ask, What could we do without our convicts? Should we ever have been what we are without them? Blessings in disguise, eh, Mr. Evelyn? Blessings in government livery—ha! ha! ha!'

'King John gave us our noble charter; but I query whether a perpetuity of King Johns would be acceptable, Mr. Bruce.'[4]

'Oh, don't mistake me. I'm not taking the rascals' part. I'd much rather do without them; but, —— me, if I see how. And, after all, more is made of the evil than there is call for. I confess it's devilish disgusting when a man leaves his office with a ramping appetite, and runs home expecting a ready dinner, to find his wife sweltering over the fire, making a hash, where a roast goose was promised, and the cook lying drunk alongside her, or else gone off either with a constable to the watch-house or to the bush; but, to my mind, with such annoyances the evil ends. I hold the doctrine of original sin, and believe that wickedness don't wait for convicts to put it into our children's minds. The effects of the system are not so injuriously extended.'

'They do not extend to our pies and puddings, certainly, except in parallel cases to yours, sir; but there are dearer interests than those of the palate to be considered,' quietly answered Mr. Evelyn, unconsciously surveying the inflated paunch of his companion.

'Well, do you prefer immigrants? My wife says, "Give me fifty government servants before you bring home one immigrant;" that is, government despatches, of course; private comers are well enough. A viler or more useless set than the contents of an emigrant vessel can't be, in my opinion. There is no managing them: they turn up their noses at the convicts, very often their superiors, and give warning in no time if they are spoken to, or can't perform a certain amount of mischief unreproved.'

The speaker waited for an answer, but none came; and he proceeded—

'It is *my* opinion that government inflicts a no less evil in pouring on us shiploads of paupers than in filling our land with convicts. My wife's a witty woman, Mr. Evelyn, and she calls the one Prevention and the other Cure. Then, say I, this black dose of Prevention is worse than the yellow Cure; for in the former we have all the rascals without that badge of rascality on them, by which we are licensed to hold them in terror, eh, sir?'

'There is truth in what you say, Mr. Bruce; and when we remember that emigration is a nation's expedient to provide for those who might otherwise provide for themselves in a less respectable way, I do not see how there should not be truth in it; but I am disposed to think that much of our disappointment in emigrants, as a body, arises from an evil existing in ourselves. We have hitherto been much as slaveholders. We have had our fellow creatures under our thumb; without our leave they could neither turn, look, nor speak: to turn was to be refractory; to look was to defy; to speak was to be insolent; and each of these sins met its punishment. We have been served by slaves until we prefer their abject servitude, and our despotic masterdom to the servitude of men who have rights in common with us, and a strong will to assert those rights. Having been long accustomed to the unresisting obedience of the convict, we cannot brook the whys and wherefores of the free. I wish you a very good morning, Mr. Bruce,' and, raising his hat to the well-paunched gentleman, Mr. Evelyn passed up Goulbourn Street before his statement could be opposed.

Mr. Evelyn had fewer annoyances to complain of than many colonists. Since his marriage he had been blessed with five good servants, four men and one woman. Whether these men were 'good' from his treatment of them, or from laudable reformatory desires in themselves, is for future determination. One fact, however, is very sure, that neither of the four were 'good' from rate of crime, for all were desperate offenders. The woman had entered his service at sixteen years of age, having been transported for boot-stealing. She remained with him until she obtained her ticket;[5] then, obedient to the prisoner's universal yearning for his or her first act of comparative freedom, she gave her master warning:[6] the temptation was too inviting to resist. She changed owners, and in a fortnight, deprived of her ticket, she became the miserable habitant of a Cascades cell![7]

Little Charlie, a lovely specimen of infant Tasmania—a bright, glowing, bouncing boy of six years—had imbibed as small an amount of evil as possible from the moral contamination; but the amount was small only in comparison.

Interspersed with the five good servants had many scores of hopeless characters discomfited Mr. Evelyn's hearth and nursery. It was nothing rare to Charlie to have three new nurses on three successive days; it was no new thing for him to fall asleep under one woman's eye, and awake under another's guardianship. He was accustomed to these changes and chances, and thought slightly of them. He was accustomed to the prison petticoats and calico caps—they were nothing to him. There was no shudder when the constable marched off his nurse; he would skip to the window to see the 'fun,' as from earliest days he had learnt to designate the bearing away of some unfortunate convict. There was no shudder when a new *Anson* expiree[8] entered his nursery, clad in the brown badge of crime; he would run to her, and clasping his chubby arms round her legs, ask:

'What are you for?'

And then, if the crime did not equal his expectations, he would seem vexed, and say:

'That isn't very bad! Why didn't you steal a lot?'

The expiree would laugh, and, winking to her sister convict, pronounce the 'chap a regular shiner.'

Had not immediate influence been at work from prisoners who took a malignant pleasure in spoiling the handiwork of parental anxiety, there was in the daily contact with crime an indirect influence as baneful to the youthful mind. Moral sensibilities were imperceptibly weakened by the unavoidable and familiar intercourse.

As we have seen, in Emmeline's case, there was a possibility of so shielding a child, that it should grow up like a lily among thorns; but such growing up was only to be insured by an utter self-abnegation on the part of the parents, and a seclusion so strict on the part of the child, that but few could endure it for the long years necessary to ultimate success. The majority of Tasmanian parents, being young, feel it hard to make their marriage-life one of nun-like durance. Apt to look on the bright side, they trust their children to convict superintendence; they listen to the solicitations of the sunny sky or pleasure-loving friends, and go forth to those enjoyments which are considered the privilege of youth, and which are so alluringly displayed in such a climate as Van Diemen's Land. A mother of five-and-twenty, with six babies around her, is no uncommon sight. Such a young mother will look piteously at you, and ask:

'Is it to be expected, now, that I am to be shut up with these children all day long? I might as well be a prisoner at once.'

When you look at her witching eyes[9] and form, and contrast them with the careworn appearance of an anti-convict mother, you are disposed to decide in her favour.

But when you look at the nursery during her absence, and behold the six morsels of beings either terrified into unnatural quiet or learning lessons of immorality, you are in favour of the gentle parent, who, forgetting all but her offspring, wears out her prime of days in sheltering them from erroneous preceptors.

One sentiment with which the convict evil infects immature principle is one somewhat similar to that which intervenes between slaveholder and slave—a feeling that appropriates to the *Free* the first attribute of the verb, and throws the other two—doing and suffering—for the special use of the *Bond*. Children imbibe this feeling from their infancy; it grows with their growth, and strengthens with strength at rapid paces. Without having the actual abhorrence of crime, or without sharing the grievances which cause their elders to use the word 'convict' as a synonym for every opprobrious epithet, they apply to prisoners similar terms to those we heard from Charlie, merely as the parrot repeats 'pretty Poll' after its human teacher. The sweetest Christian in the island as unperturbedly announces that her woman has got 'three months,' as an English mistress informs her visitor that her servant has a holiday. A child hears, and draws his own conclusion from the matter-of-fact statement.

Weary of watching the flagstaff, Charlie had fallen asleep on the sofa, whilst his papa partook of an early dinner. Neither of the two, therefore, observed that the pantomime was again exhibiting on Mulgrave Battery; consequently, they were both taken by surprise, a few hours after, by a well-remembered voice—'Stop, coachman, this is it—the Lodge!' And in a moment more a cab drove up the gravelled path, and it was the work of scarcely another minute to bring Mr. Evelyn clean out of the window at a leap—and Mr. Herbert Evelyn from the cab, into each other's hand-grasp; and a grasp it was! Such a grasp as only those may know who have experienced what it is to have eighteen thousand miles of ocean rolling between them and their brothers.

By a natural attraction, Charlie bounded into Bridget's arms, exclaiming:

'This is Cousin Bridget, I know.'

And as Bridget kissed and over-kissed the curly-headed beauty, she felt she held a regular armful of roguery.

'This is cousin what I don't know, papa,' cried Charlie, glad that the prolonged operation of hand-squeezing gave him the opportunity of introducing Miss D'Urban to her uncle.

After a hearty kiss or two on her blooming cheek, Mr. Evelyn held Bridget gently backwards, in order to take a fuller view of the half-shy, half-smiling face that reciprocated his embrace.

'Why, Herbert, we haven't a rose that could beat this,' was the result of the inspection.

Mr. Herbert smiled sadly, and, pointing to the cab where drooped his daughter, he said:

'Ah, henceforward, I fear, we must exchange titles, and have the Lily of Tasmania and the Rose of England, instead of *vice versa*. My rose has faded! But, George, you go in; I have promised poor Emmeline that she shall be carried to her room to receive your welcome; here it would overpower her too much for after removal.'

As Mr. Herbert Evelyn assisted his daughter up the veranda stairs, the coachman came forward, and, reading permission in Bridget's good-tempered face, asked:

'Sure, never, that isn't the same Miss Evelyn what went home, come back in that unlikely fashion? The pride of her father as she was!' and a tear twinkled in his eye. 'Me and my mates has blessed her a thousand times, as she passed down along by his side; sometimes us thought whether he didn't get some of his lovesome ways out of her, only that he's natural good in hisself.'

'Who are your mates? Have you been a sailor?' said Bridget.

'Lord love you, miss! You'm a new hand, I guess. My mates is them what I came over with, and them what was ganged with me. I'm government,' he added, seeing that Bridget still looked mystified.[10]

'Ah, ah!' cried Charlie, clapping his hands; 'she don't know he is a pis'ner—they are all pis'ners;' and the little fellow seemed to enjoy his cousin's innocence, and so did the man, who chimed in, by way of comforting the fresh arrival—

'Ah! she'll know all about it by-and-by; won't she, Master Charlie?'

'Won't she, that's all!' shouted Charlie, capering with delight, and making a curious attempt to return the driver's sly wink.

'Just come from England, miss?' touching his cap.

'Yes.' Bridget hardly knew how to look.

'Somephin' in honour of Old England,' appealed the man, again touching his cap with one hand, while the other performed a series of gesticulations significant of giving and taking.

Bridget dropped a half-crown into his hand, which he received open-mouthed and open-eyed.

'By jingo, she'm a cracker!' he ejaculated, as he drove off.

'Oh, Charlie, how *could* you talk so before the poor creature? You won't be my Charlie if you are so cruel!' cried Miss D'Urban, as soon as the coachman was out of hearing.

'Oh! it's nothing being gover'm'et out here, cousin; everybody nearly is—I mean all the poor peoples; *she's* a pis'ner, only she's just got her clothes,'[11] he pointed by way of illustration to a maid-servant, who just then ran down the steps to relieve Bridget of her carpet-bag.

'Yes, ma'am, I'm government,' bobbed the woman, without the slightest tone of self-depreciation. 'I bought my clothes only last week, on purpose for the master's company.'

'And *I'm* a gum tree!' called Charlie, drawing himself to his utmost height, in imitation of that straight, tall tree as he stood at the top of the verandah, waiting for the others.

'Well, Bridgy, welcome to the Lodge!' exclaimed Mr. Evelyn, coming forward to meet his niece. 'Though I've never seen these blooming cheeks before, I think I am better acquainted with you than with any of my nieces. Miss Em has sent on before, and taken a place for you in my heart. A thousand welcomes to the Lodge, and all its honours, which have been accumulating for you since your aunt played truant, and ran up the country to pay her annual visit, and introduce Miss Baby to her maternal grandparents. The keys are waiting for you, and doubtless also a few "kitchen rows," which I hear you have a special gift in conciliating.'

'Oh, uncle! That's wicked Lionel! I'm sure dear Em would not have written you such nonsense.'

'Albeit, I am apprised of the wholesome fact, and congratulate myself that the remedy grows so near the disease. Now let me introduce you to Hobarton. Here, stand where you are, and look at the landscape. Could England give you anything more lovely? There is our pride, the Derwent, and there is our noble monument to our mother country's hero, Mount Wellington;[12] it generally has clouds on its summit, but this evening it has doffed them, to salute you, I suppose. There, straight across the harbour, how exquisite is the light resting on those hills retreating tier after tier, until the most distant seems to melt into the sky!'

Mr. Evelyn thought Bridget was listening attentively to him. On turning to her, he perceived her eyes were full of tears. Feelings she had hoped to smother, on being noticed, increased beyond control. Laying her head on her uncle's shoulder, she wept aloud.

Little Charlie slipped to her side, and, softly pulling her gown, whispered—

'Are you crying at me, cousin? I'm so sorry.'

Without removing her head, Bridget drew the little penitent close to her, while Mr. Evelyn replied—

'No, no, Charlie. Cousin Bridget is feeling very thankful to the dear, good God who has brought her over the long, long sea to a country quite as beautiful as her own England. We must let her cry a little bit; persons are not always sorry when they weep, Charlie boy.'

Bridget looked up, and repaid Uncle Ev with one of her genuine smiles, shining through her tears.

Mr. Evelyn also knew that many other emotions were working in her breast; all the strange sensations that crowd upon a newcomer's mind; all the recollections of the past and left behind, rushing with jealous vigour to assert their rights over the present and time forward, he well knew were contesting the ground of the English maiden's heart, as, for the first moment, she gazed on her future home, and found it fair to look upon, beyond her rosiest imaginings. Who that has stood on foreign shores has not felt these strange battlings of spirit? Has not felt a regretful pang through the heart, as in beholding the scene before him, he has been obliged either to shake the palm of superiority from his own land, or to share it with another?

'It is very, very lovely,' at last said Bridget, 'but it hardly looks foreign, or unlike England.'

'Nevertheless, it comes from forrin', as the sailor says. But what do you mean by like England? I suppose you, with all the rest of the folk at home, have always considered us a set of semi-barbarians. It is very odd that people having brothers, sisters, and relations of various orders in the Australian colonies, take so little trouble to ascertain the real amount of civilization in these islands.

'The notions formed of our mode of life are vague as those formed of Timbuctoo.[13] I answer for it, now, you expected a canoe rowed by savages would conduct you from the vessel to Hobarton, and then that you would be knocked down once or twice by bushrangers, or be carried off by boomers[14] before you could reach my house, eh, Bridget?'

'Not quite so bad, uncle, but I must confess I had no expectation of finding everything appear so English. I did not fancy you would all look like semi-barbarians, as you say, but must plead to a few misconceptions. I thought you would be dreadfully old-fashioned, and that—'

'And that you would blaze amongst us a very comet of fashion,' interrupted Uncle Ev, with a wicked smile.

Bridget blushed, too ingenuous to hide the girlish weakness. She said:

'I thought I should look better than other people, and be immediately recognised as a newcomer by my dress. Having read advertisements in the *Times* for cast-off clothes for Australia, I naturally—'

'Thought you might discover a few old friends out here,' again interrupted Mr. Evelyn. 'But I can tell you, Miss D'Urban, the young ladies out here make a fine to-do about those said advertisements. There has been serious talk among them on the propriety of petitioning the Home Government to introduce an Act, entitled "An Act for the Suppression of Offensive Advertisements." As to dress, no doubt you bring the newest fashion, seeing you are four months in advance of your sisters Vandemonian.[15] I query, though, whether you will not look the quietest bird in Hobarton until your home stock is worn out. Hyde Park cannot outdress our ladies! They learn to copy nature—unwittingly, perhaps, but not the less on that account. A style of colouring that would be inharmonious in England, blends with the ardent hues of the southern world. In England the sober little sparrow, or modest robin, teaches the befitting garment; here the parrot and firetail flutter by on a sunbeam, and lead the fashion. Everything here is bright and glowing, except the foliage.'

'The hills are not, papa,' interrupted Charlie.

'You have arrived at a happy season, Bridget. A month later, and the dust and heat would have done their work on all that now claims the title of verdant. The everbrowns bear jealous rule here; it has been jocosely said, to help out the government notion, that we are fated, even by nature, to have the badge of crime in our midst! But I doubt whether there is not a remedial aptness in the dusky foliage. Were the hills and trees to be arrayed in vivid tints, there would be no relief to the eye. Radiance above, around, and below would be oppressive. Yonder, how exquisite is the wattle! Were that shower of gold to fall upon a bright green, the effect would be to dazzle, instead of to please, as now. Yonder again, the silver wattle, how fairy-like is the delicate tinting; it gives more the idea of the pencil than the brush. But to see the wattle to perfection, you must see it in moonlight, when the beams shimmer through the branches, as though the feathery leaves formed a plaything, and not a barrier.'

'Oh, I shall like it very much, and should be very happy now, if it were not for poor Em,' sighed Bridget.

'Ah, poor Emmeline!' responded Uncle Ev, leading her into the house. 'How does Herbert bear it?'

'Like a Christian, Uncle Ev.'

'Very vague; there are two sorts of Christians.'

'Like Emmeline would if she were Uncle Herbert,' replied Bridget, with much assurance of voice.

'Ah, that is satisfactory. Now, then, you enter the Lodge—very barbaric, isn't it?' he quizzically asked, as the rich velvet-pile carpet and yellow damask curtains met Bridget's astonished sight.

'Oh, it looks like a dear old friend,' cried Bridget, running over to a small statuette of the Greek Slave[16] that stood, the simple and only ornament of a side-table.

'Why, uncle, you've everything, just as we have at home.'

'Ay, and rather more than you have at home.'

This was said with an emphasis that made Miss D'Urban expect an explanation; but uncle vouchsafed only a nod and a hem in reply, and he walked out of the room, leaving her to a quiet survey of the luxuries of a Van Diemen drawing room.

'Please, miss, the master said as you'd like to be showed upstairs. Everything's to sixes and sevens, as the mistress is gone up country; but then, after to board[17] anyhow that's on real ground's a blessing.'

The free-and-easy manner of the servant did not at all convey the idea of prison taint. Bridget took for granted that this domestic certainly was not a convict. Her dress was smart, and her appearance not subdued, as had been that of all the others. She did not know that a report had already represented her to the kitchen as a very proper young lady, before whom abject airs were unnecessary. She followed Nancy to an apartment that certainly displayed the want of a mistress's eye. The bed and the rest of the furniture were as English looking as could be, but there was an indescribable something in the whole aspect of the chamber that seemed irreconcilable with English comfort. The floor attracted her notice, perceiving which the sharp attendant immediately exclaimed—

'Never fear; 'taint dirt, miss; it's the natural look of them boards; all florses looks dark out here—it's the wood itself.'

Miss D'Urban, disconcerted at having her thoughts thus read, cast her eyes up far from the scene of her detection.

'Can't be helped, miss; 'twould be all the same if the mistress were home; 'tis them beastly flies, everywhere a buzzing and pitching,' again interrupted Nancy, as Bridget's sight involuntarily rested on two pieces of tape nailed crosswise through the ceiling—tape which had originally been white, but now was nearly black.

Poor Bridget! Where should she look from the Argus-eyed Abigail, who secretly enjoyed the stranger's discomfiture? On the wall? No, the same fly-marks were thickly dotted on the pink wash, and the same resolute observer exclaimed:

'It's the verminous beasts again, miss; there's no keeping the walls clean for 'em. Lor, miss, they drops into the very tea you drinks, them great, lazy, brown buzzers! And the milk, fay! You should see it! If it's left uncovered a minute, the vermints drops thick into it, so as you can't see what's under 'em.'

Bridget could not wear a disconsolate countenance long; so after a shrug of disgust she broke into a merry laugh which rang through the room and right downstairs, and, as the summons of a silver bell, brought little Charlie up to see what was the matter.

But it did not suit Nancy that the child should remain, so she unceremoniously turned him out, and on Bridget's looking—why— the servant's face drew to unwonted length.

'Why, miss, talking of them pests out here brings blessed old England to my mind, and natural-like I feel sad.'

'Oh, don't let us speak of England just yet, I can hardly bear it;' and Bridget's voice faltered in demonstration of the fact.

But the *effect* on Bridget was the *cause* with Nancy; a less softened moment might not further her views.

'Ah, if you can't bear it, miss, think of poor me, who's obliged to! Y*ou* came free to the colony!'

Bridget started, and, as if she had been guilty of a wanton reminder, crimsoned to her very temples.

The woman understood both start and blush, and determined to reap advantage from each. Shaking her head slowly and measuredly as the toll of a funeral bell, she answered—

'Ah, the likes to you may well start—yes! I'm government, been in the place five years come Christmas—I've seen better days at home—' Here she paused from emotion and Bridget, feeling cruel to her fingers' ends, went over and laid her hand on her shoulder.

'I am very sorry! I did not mean to hurt you; I had no idea you were—were—'

'A vile outcast!' finished Nancy. 'Say it out, miss, say it out—Nay-ver mind, nay-ver mind' (with a slow up-and-down motion of the head between each syllable) 'you can't hut me no more than I have been hutted already—you didn't go for to do it.'

Bridget was ready to cry. More advantage still! Suddenly starting from her apron, in which her face had been hidden, Nancy exclaimed, clasping her hands:

'And how was the blessed old country looking? Haven't you never a flower or token to give a poor prisoner to mind her of her home?'

'No,' said Bridget, uneasily scanning her packages as if she hoped some compassionate spirit might forthwith cause a flower to spring from the dry leathers.

'Ah, all these dear things came from home!' cried Nancy, spreading her arms circuitously over the heap of boxes, &c., as if she would pronounce a silent benediction on the lot. 'I could most fall down and worship 'em, one and all.'

Bridget was now fairly crying—the time had arrived. With a deprecatory smile, Nancy said:

'If you wouldn't think a poor prisoner bold, miss, I'd ask you if you'd any old trifle to put me in thinking of the blessed country, where once I lived as innocent as you—anything—an old dress you've done with on the voyage—ladies never wears their sea things to shore, the muggy feel of the vessel seems to cling to 'em; but they'd be treasures to *my* poor heart: to look on 'em and think where they come from would be worth a mint!'

In an instant Bridget had taken out and given to Nancy two gowns she had half finished with, right glad to offer amends for the wounds she had inflicted. The woman was making away with her prize when Mr. Evelyn, senior, entered to escort his niece to tea. In a loud angry tone he demanded:

'How now, Nancy! Have you been fooling this young lady? I guessed your work directly I heard you were closeted with her. Give those dresses back!'

'Uncle, uncle! Indeed I gave them her; let her keep them for *my* sake, do.'

'Let her *keep* them! Yes, for the next half-hour.' There was an inexplicable irony in the word *keep*, that made Bridget wonder.

Turning to Nancy, who stood cowed and lowly in the door, he nodded her away with:

'To oblige the young lady you may keep them; but mind you do, that's all.'

'I humbly thank you, sir,' dropped Nancy, denuded of all her former non-convict air.

Mr. Evelyn tapped his feet impatiently, but managed to say without impatience:

'Nancy, these tricks do not suit me.'

Bridget thought her uncle a most hard-hearted man. Why shouldn't the poor thing feel sad; wasn't it very natural a new arrival should elicit home tendencies? However, Mr. Evelyn's manner had frightened her, so that she forbore to speak out her thoughts.

But Uncle Ev guessed them in her vexed look, and said in a grave but kind voice:

'You must learn a few practical lessons before you will be ready to allow the necessity of scenes similar to that which has just passed between Nancy and myself; those dresses will procure her a dram or two before the night has expired, and by to-morrow you will have a chance of meeting them in Goulbourn Street: keep a look-out for them therefore—they are of so peculiar a pattern you cannot mistake them.'

CHAPTER 14

The Paraclete[1]

> O weary souls! ye shall be blest
> Eternally in God's own rest:—
> Outbursting from your night of gloom,
> How bright with day's unfading bloom
> Shall shine the star that bids you free
> From earth and earth's captivity.
> O pining souls! your God's dear peace
> Shall make your weary pinings cease.

WE have seen the signal hoisted on Mulgrave Battery—the signal that spread a universal dissatisfaction through every free breast in Hobarton. As floated from the flagstaff that announcement that another shipload of sin was about to disgorge itself on Tasmanian shores, a token also appeared to the captives on the transport. Yet no—though seen by all, two only of the prisoners accepted it as a token. To these two was it sent; to the others it was only a natural circumstance.

The convicts were assembled on the decks—every eye strained itself landward, every heart beat alternate throbs of hope, fear—fear, hope. The sun shone gloriously down, when very high in the clear air a pure white speck was seen floating on a long bright ray. It came nearer and nearer, slowly descending, until, poising over the vessel and gently fluttering its spotless wing, a silver-winged dove attracted the gaze of all, and a deep hush of admiration fell on the hardest heart there. Radiant in the sunlight, it seemed to rest a moment; then, gradually ascending, a cloud, that had almost suddenly appeared, received the wondrous creature out of their sight.

'It has gone into heaven,' mysteriously whispered Lucy Grenlow, as she clung to Maida.

Maida spoke not—her eyes had followed the heavenly visitant, and now that it had vanished from view she the more intently gazed on the point at which it had disappeared. She longed to pierce the cloud and trace the dove to its bright abode.

Not yet, poor Maida! The cloud must o'ershadow thee more deeply yet, ere thou mayst rend its veil and read the mystery of the peace of God. But surely as descended that silent messenger, so surely will thy God's peace come down to thee on the rich rays of redeeming love. As surely as ascended that dove-like form, so surely mayst thou ascend to the bosom of thy Lord.

Partly awed by the expression of Maida's face, and partly solemnized by the beautiful vision, Lucy remained silent for some time after her first ejaculation; then, feeling that her companion's eyes (withdrawn from the sky) were fixed on her, she said in a low voice:

'It seemed to come most on purpose for us.'

Maida blessed the kindly utterance which granted her a share in the message: her own pride or humility would have forbidden her to claim a part. Had she spoken she would have said for *you* and not for *us*.

'It's like the dove and peace of God that's on our church window at home,' said Lucy, very reverently.

'I'm going below, Lucy, for a little while,' was Maida's only answer.

Following her to her quarters, we see her look around to assure herself of solitude; we see her kneel and clasp her hands—one tear steals from the closed lid and bears a weight of sorrow with it to the ground. She takes her Bible from its shelf by her berth, and opens to the fourth chapter of Philippians, and drawing a pencil line through the margin of the seventh verse,[2] she shuts the sacred volume, replaces it upon the shelf, and joins her fellow prisoners on the deck.

It was a transaction between God and her own soul, but one rendered null and void by a long train of after events which made her life a perpetual conflict. Had she at once gone from that transaction to those who would have dealt with her as her peculiar temperament needed, it might have proved one of grand results. As it was, a temporary comfort alone was produced, and yet, unaware, she stored away the remembrance of the vision as a token for good.

CHAPTER 15

Uncle Ev and Uncle Ev's Notions

WE do not care to describe the persons of our heroes and heroines, for we deem a description superfluous. As the characters unfold an appropriate physical structure forms itself around them, affording a better habitation than we could devise.

Who that has heard of Uncle Herbert has not already pictured him a model clergyman in appearance? Who has not pictured him tall, slight, with a spiritual expression in his pale face and finely chiselled features? Who has not pictured him with a head whose partial baldness adds not age but dignity to his deportment? Or who has not discovered in his whole bearing a determination to follow his Divine Master whithersoever He may go, or whatsoever it may cost?

Who has not portrayed Uncle Ev the exact opposite to this picture in all save height? Who has not already invested in his person the following characteristics—good stature, robust make, an expression that means to be serious but more easily conveys an idea of hearty good humour, a sly lurk in his lip corners that belies the gravity of the lip itself, and a bushy head of black hair that can at once shake terror at convict servants or naughty children, and pass luxuriously through his fingers as he cracks his jokes with Bridget D'Urban?

Mr. Evelyn, senior, had been a police magistrate.[1] Disgusted with the duties of this office, he threw up his £500 per annum, choosing rather moderate independence and liberty of conscience, than wealthy dependence and slavery to the whims of every captious holder who chose to send his servant before him. He termed the appointment the 'Wash-tub Coveship,' once having heard himself called 'The Wash-tub Cove' by a party of female prisoners whom he had just sentenced to the Government Laundry. He had also been in the Executive,[2] but weary of the farce justice was obliged to play in dealing with men already sentenced to the utmost rigour of secondary punishment—weary of the solemn absurdities of judicial proceedings as then existing in Van Diemen's Land—weary of the oft-recurring joke of dealing law to outlaws, or of punishing convicts for falling into traps laid for them by the neglect of their officers or the short-sightedness of senators—weary of all these, Mr. Evelyn, senior, resigned his seat in the Council.[3]

Fond as he was of a joke, this gentleman abhorred practical jokes, a long series of which then formed the occupation of the Executive.

He had seen a woman, who was already transported for life for manslaughter, again committed amid the execration of the multitude for a similar attempt in Hobarton—and upon this woman, convicted of her second crime, he had heard passed the original sentence of transportation for life, so that while her former sin was still inexpiated,[4] her latter and aggravated guilt went wholly unpunished. Glad that the poor wretch had yet a space afforded her for repentance, Mr. Evelyn was not one to cry shame on the judgment, but, generous as were his feelings towards the murderess, he could not help casting a somewhat jealous eye on the ill-accorded leniency when he paralleled it with sentences he had known: sentences which, had they been pronounced by the injured party, had been set down as the result of implacable revenge—had they been passed by the voice of the people, had been attributed to excitement; but uttered neither by the prosecutor nor by the populace, Mr. Evelyn had only to turn with a blush from the bench where justice had dwindled to a heartless form.

Averse to his resigning a position at once respectable, remunerative, and responsible, his friends urged him to remain and use his influence towards reforming abuses, visible to all not blinded by the spirit of faction; but their persuasions were ineffective on Mr. Evelyn, as ineffective as would influence have been on a body of men who had but one feeling towards a member rendering himself obnoxious by opposition, namely, hatred; and but one mode of meeting his objections, namely, removal, through ways and means of their own.

But with his public life Mr. Evelyn did not abandon a career of usefulness. Disgusted with the errors of judicial administration, and deploring a system which could never be reformatory until reformation commenced with itself, he prepared himself to do what it would be well if every reflecting man would do when disappointed in the performance of acts of public benevolence, namely, to try how most effectually he could serve the little circle drawn immediately around himself. The result of such an effort could not fail to be happy in any homestead. In one chiefly peopled by convicts, whose eyes literally turned more anxiously toward their owner than the day watchers toward the east, the effort repaid itself in ways unthought of in English homes. Had each colonist followed Mr. Evelyn's example, and exerted his influence over the few convicts under his care, how materially had government been assisted in its weary plannings for the moral improvement of the prisoner, and how unnecessary had been made the constant change of system, which between the years 1838 and 1852 exhausted the patience of state secretaries, annoyed the free, and oppressed the bond population. Had each holder put his shoulder to this mighty plough, with what comparative ease had government directed it over the field of evil! How had the assignment system realized both to the assigned and the assignee the benefits it was reported to bestow; how had the terrors of the 'Worse than death' system been never needed, save to intimidate the incorrigible few; and how had the nation's treasury held yet within its purse the countless thousands wasted on the probation system.[5]

Mr. Evelyn did not advocate the influx of criminals to Van Diemen's Land; he was as anxious for the promised removal of the penal badge as any of his colonial brethren; but as a loyal subject and a responsible being, he determined, not, as many others, to shun bond labour and employ only free servants, but to take a willing share of the imposition whilst waiting the fulfilment of the long-cherished and oft-disappointed hope of every Tasmanian. He carried out his plan by becoming owner of a succession of pass-holders with whose vices he bore until they either yielded to his unflinching strictness, or drained his power of endurance, which power was of unusual stability for one who drew it rather from the natural source of innate superiority than from the fountain of all good and perfect gifts. As a bachelor, he was not allowed a female prisoner; a deprivation he only regretted for the pretext it afforded masters who, too indolent or too incredulous to adopt his course of treatment, asserted that his success in certain reform cases was mainly attributable to the absence of corrupt female influence in his household.

Strictly subject to the penal regulations of the comptroller-general's office, Mr. Evelyn was guided by a theory of his own in dealing with his bond-servants. In selecting his men, he chose from those who were reckoned 'The Troublesome Set.' Though not the worst by rule of sentence or crime, the convicts of this order had frequently blacker police rolls than their more guilty brethren. The latter with brazen front and dilated nostril displayed a comparatively fair page, whilst the former hung their heads before the words 'stubborn,' 'obdurate,' 'disobedient,' denoting the superintendent's opinion of them.

Mr. Evelyn chose from this troublesome set, not from private pique, as some supposed, nor from perversity, as was amiably hinted by others, but because, according to his theory, the men comprising it were, with exceptional cases, more objects of pity than of punishment, and fitter for penitentiaries than for prisons. He divided this set into two classes: involuntary offenders and contingent offenders. The troublesomeness of the former arising from an inability to abstain from whatever gratified their undeveloped moral appetites within the narrow scope of captivity; whose prison life was only a dumb show of what their free life had been; whose moral questionings extended no further than that point which led the child to ask, 'May I do *that?*' when her fingers were slapped for doing *this.*

Mr. Evelyn attributed the troublesomeness of the contingents to a still smarting sense of degradation incompatible with penal discipline. A round of punishments was, therefore, employed to coerce them into a proper state of indifference.

'It is hard for a feller that longs to be an honest man again to take kindly to things that comes easy to your born rogues, who tip their noses[6] and are at it again,' said one of this class found by Mr. Herbert in the cells. It appeared a strange oversight to Mr. Evelyn that such offenders should be confounded with the common body of criminals, and herded in transportation with felons who, but for an adroitness worthy of their calling, had years ago undergone the just reward of their sins.

To these two classes themselves, he by no means palliated their guilt, nor censured its chastisement; but in his heart, by action, and by official remonstrance, he charged with short-sightedness or blamed for indolence that system which branded in one indelible infamy the poor wretch pushed into evil by sudden temptation—the unthinking youth hurried on by the impulse of a fatal moment, and the bold outlaw who followed crime as his profession—mingling in one common condemnation the low moral perceptions of Sam Tibbins and the perjured conscience and guilty genius of Mark Knocklofty or Michael Howe.[7]

Having then no family ties to divide his time and labours, Mr. Evelyn engaged as many convicts as could find employment on his farm, the average number employed at one time being ten. In the same number of years, no fewer than two hundred prisoners passed through his hands. Several of the involuntaries, as unable to bear the kinder, though not less strict, surveillance of their master, as the rigid enforcements of the penal code, absconded at once from his service and that restraint which, in accordance with his doctrine of mental deficiency, he thought proper to impose. Oblivious of past suffering, and unthinking of the future, these miserable beings would go off, to be taken, perhaps, within a stone's throw of the farm; or, after a few days' fasting in the bush, to deliver themselves up to government for re-imprisonment and increased punishment. Discouraging as were these failures, they strengthened Mr. Evelyn's opinion of the irresponsibility of this class, and of their fitness rather for the mild coercion and competent control of the asylum, than for the vengeance of the law. With others of this class Mr. Evelyn lost all patience, and, after a few months' trial, he returned them to the barracks. To run and not be weary in the race of well-doing is only given to such a one as Mr. Herbert, who, starting not in his own strength, looks to Him who promises to sustain His servants in their moments of weakness and depression. When Mr. Evelyn sent these men back to government, he thought he had borne with them to the verge of human endurance. It was not until some years later, when he watched his brother's uncomplaining yet deeply tried patience, that he learned how far is the human standard of long-suffering beneath the divine rule, as laid down in Matt. xviii,[8] or that he perceived how valuable an ingredient is real and *judicious* piety in the administrative penal process. With a third portion of the involuntary delinquents, he was obliged to part for the benefit of his little community; they were so thoroughly weak-minded as to become the scapegoats of the flock.

With the fourth section he was successful, and though afterwards through temptation, or the negligence of less careful holders, some relapsed into trouble, many repaid his toil by turning out inoffensive and happy members of society; for not possessing sufficient sensitiveness to feel pain at loss of caste, they were only sensible of a superiority over their bond brethren still remaining on the government books.

With the contingent offenders was Mr. Evelyn's grand result. But this adjective must be taken comparatively (we do not pun on the degrees). By those who would use it only to express hundreds it must not be used; but by those who remember that the redemption of the soul is precious,[9] it may be uttered over the small band of prisoners rescued by their master's efforts from the moral wreck of transportation.

With the majority of this class he found the hardening process had far advanced—with some it had advanced beyond hope of recall: urged on by shame, ridicule, misery, bad example, and severity, it had left its victims 'as bad as they were made out to be.'

In a few the effect of indiscriminate treatment showed itself in mental disease, which yielded neither to genial influence nor medical advice. The moral energies could not arouse themselves from the shock of their fall. Restoratives came too late; had they been applied *at first*, when the whole head was sick and the whole heart faint, they might have proved beneficial. But the judicial means resorted to having been penal, and not suiting the case, had aggravated it into madness or sunk it to imbecility. With such cases Mr. Evelyn could do no more than see them safely housed in New Norfolk,[10] to rave or drivel out their life in the chief lunatic establishment of the island.

With the remainder of the contingents was the reward of his exertions, and the result before mentioned.

The moment they entered his service they were warned what they had to expect if they deceived or disobeyed their master; on the other hand, they were promised confidence, assistance, and forgetfulness of past misconduct, if they endeavoured to deserve such indulgence. And finding that neither warning nor promise was idle breath, an understanding arose between them and their owner which wrought advantageously to both. As servants, unless previously trained, or very young, they were not often accessions to domestic comfort.

After a year or two the ostler may become a tolerable cook, but, meanwhile, where shall the family dine? A ploughman in due season learns the duties of a housemaid, but who attends to bedroom comforts, or pays for breakages during the term of his scholarship?

The homely cottager who comes in to his rusty rasher[11] by his snug fireside knows nothing more of that rasher than that it once lived as a pig, and now has been cooked by his missus. He devours it, and the rancid taste is orthodox; were it less rancid or less rusty, he would be ready to cry out against witchcraft.

When a transported felon across the seas, that cottager is told to prepare his master's breakfast from the delicate sides of bacon hanging in the pantry, he shakes his head and supposes that 'that there bacon isn't tanned half enough for the master. See his missus's at home, that's all! Why, 'tis as yaller as though he'd never growed white!' And to the end of his servitude he shakes disapproval of the goodly flitches,[12] inwardly wishing that his missus at home could get 'a holt on 'em' to tan them so that a Christian could bear to look at them. The rust of home has worked as deeply into his heart as the touch of time into his wife's bacon; and he is too old to change his way of thinking to please even a convict owner, but, fortunately that holder is not one who will scarify his heart, to try if by that means the canker of home longings may be eradicated.

The former blacksmith yearns for the roar of the mounting flame. In his delight at again having fire beneath his rule, he sets his master's kitchen chimney in a blaze, and whilst others rush to stop the warm proceeding, he coolly answers:

'Never fear—'taint half a-roaring yet!'

But such extravagances were only sources of amusement to Mr. Evelyn in his bachelor days. He knew, that to get more efficient servants he must go to a worse class of convict. And (apart from his benevolent motive in hiring the contingents and involuntaries) he argued that the chief difference between them and other servants was, in their mode of dealing with their master's property. They spilled the ale, the others drank it. They spoiled the dinner, the others stole it. They smashed the china, the others sold it. They bruised the plate, the others melted it. Therefore, as in either case his beer, dinner, china, and plate were to meet an adverse fate, he would rather they should meet it honourably from a pair of stupid hands, than in the form of roguery.

But in after years, when gentler social interests demanded his first care, and the upspringing of a little family around him made it imperative that servants' capabilities should be equal to household requirements, he reversed his choice of convicts, and selected from those whose crimes were of the worst kind: such men could generally show the best police character.

Looking on punishment as one of the chances of their trade, they were prepared, not only to *bear* it, but to make the best of it; therefore, they passed their probation with fewer sentences than many who, as the poor contingent said, could not take kindly to these things.

These men were apt and clever servants. It was singular to mark how the extremities of London outlawry had sharpened their wits to encounter the emergencies of private life. Often, when the master turned in despair from some refractory item which refused to contort itself to domestic necessity, the convict factotum,[13] leering over his spit, would exclaim:

'Bless you, sir, that's nothink of a pass; hand 'em over this way, and he's done.'

Returning the refractory item, there would be a cunning twinkle in his eye, which said plainly as any words:

'There, thank my former craft for that.'

Could such men oftener fall to holders of Mr. Evelyn's stamp, they would not so often relapse into crime. Under such masters, it might be with them as with those four of Mr. Evelyn's whose reformation, commenced temporarily at first to save punishment, continued by way of experiment to prove how it would answer in a remunerative point of view; good sense deciding that it might be profitable to themselves, they launched into reformation as they would into any other speculation whose end was self-aggrandisement.

Had they tried the experiment under a master who only regarded them as engines of labour, it might have failed; at once disgusting them and strengthening their still secret opinion that 'honesty was *not* the best policy' for rogues.

But Mr. Evelyn was very careful that the profit should be clear to the sight of these arch speculators, or he well knew, accustomed as they were to the subtle calculations of knavery, they would not cast in their lot with honest men.

'How sordid a motive!' cries one; to whom we would reply—Examine thyself, cast not the stone of censure at thy brother, though clad in convict gray, until, having searched thine own mental world, thou canst pronounce it free from root of selfishness, and pure from unholy promptings; till then, lay by thy stone, and if heart may tell of heart, thou layest it by forever!

In saying that Mr. Evelyn chose his men from the worst set, the English reader must not suppose reference to be made to that *most* unhappy class of all unhappy offenders, too aptly designated, in colonial phraseology, 'Macquarie Harbour-dyed demons' and 'Norfolk Island-made desperadoes.'[14] With the Tasmanian reader there is no fear of such a misapprehension; he knows too well that between the worst set of the Launceston or Hobarton barracks, and the worst set of Macquarie Harbour or Norfolk Island, there exists a difference as distinct as between the spirits in Hades and the spirits in the place of torment. He knows too well that with a fearful significance, and not in a wanton waste of imagination, has the entrance to the former settlement been called 'The gates of hell,' and 'The devil's toll-gate,' whilst not less significantly is the latter still named 'The bottomless pit.'

These are places of which no one likes to speak, or only to speak in that whisper that expresses 'thereby hangs a tale!' No one dares to ask within hearing of a government officer:

'Why is it said of Macquarie Harbour, "Whoever enters here must give up all hope of heaven?" And of Norfolk Island, "Here a man's heart is taken from him, and there is given him the heart of a brute?"'[15]

While all agree to leave to the dread clearing-up of that day when the secrets of all hearts shall be tried by the man Christ Jesus, the answer to that long mystery of Van Diemen's Land, condensed in the question—

'How is it that these places, formed for special reformation, have not only failed in their purpose, but have been evil in their effect on the felon, changing him from bad to worse, from a state of furious resistance to apathetic despair, from fear of death to hatred of life?'

English hearers of the question cannot reply, 'Because you cannot expect men of such character to amend under any treatment'; or the Tasmanian inquirer, unsatisfied, will ask, 'To what purpose, then, is all this waste? Do we prepare for results which we do not expect? If we anticipate no amendment, why all these appliances to meet it?' The harvestman sends not forth his reapers into a field from which he looks for no grain. The implements of reform stare us in the face in these penal settlements; punishment, therefore, cannot be the only object of the mighty prisons.

Leave it! Leave it! In that day will it be seen whether these implements of reform have been faithfully wielded, or whether they have been allowed to gather rust amidst the rank culture of the moral desolation, or whether they have been misapplied and turned into weapons of torture. Leave it! Leave it! The throne shall be set and the books of judgment shall be opened. Inquisition shall then be made.

CHAPTER 16

Doubts on More Subjects Than One

SEE all that is to be seen at the earliest opportunity, was Bridget's practical maxim. She had no notion of waiting till ten o'clock, if her curiosity might be satisfied at eight or six. She had seen an evening in the antipodes; she now longed to see a morning. As yet no tokens of semi-barbarism had come under her notice; but might not the darkness have covered them? What might not the light of day reveal? She had marked the sun go down with his wonted glory, no peculiarity distinguishing his setting, save, perhaps, a deeper curtain of radiance drawn upon his exit. But then the sun—who expects peculiarities of him? Is he not the world's own sun, and not exclusively Australia's? She retired to rest, determining to be up at daybreak, in order to see how morning realities bore out evening impressions, and how evening impressions bore on morning realities.

She lay awake many hours revolving the events of the day, and pondering the mystery that had borne her to the uttermost parts of the earth. One minute she would close her eyes, and the sway of the vessel still seeming to lull her, she would fancy the outward-bound yet on its unaccomplished way. The next minute she would remember that the berth had merged into the bed; the sense of motion being only a vibration of the past. Complicated thoughts entangled her mind into a pleasant confusion she had neither power nor wish to put in order. The wonder of being in a new world, the doubt that she had ever existed in another, crossed and recrossed each other in her mind; and when she tried to decide between them, a long line of moonlight shone into the room and seemed to glide in between the wonder and the doubt, playing fitfully on one, and then upon the other, making decision still more difficult; then suddenly retreating, it left a question upon her soul, 'Is it all a dream?' and as the question came unallowed yet irresistibly into her thoughts, a silvery acacia waved its feathery branch, and cast a faint nodding shadow, which seemed in dumb show to answer, 'Yes, a dream, a dream! Dreamlike as this—vanishing—vanish—' and ere the word could finish, Bridget started up—her spirit full of wonders and doubts, moonbeams and shadows—to ascertain what was dream and what reality. The long line of light was not a dream, though withdrawn from her room, for there it lay upon the lawn; and the shadow? It was as much a reality as any shadow could be; for yonder grew the feathery acacia still sending it forth in the wake of the fickle beam. Her mental perplexity, nothing satisfied by the discovery, set itself to solve a host of other problems. What had wonders, doubts, moonbeams, shadows, and dreams in common, that they should all mingle in her thoughts? But problem brought on problem, until hopeless of fathoming the least, she exclaimed, 'It is so horrid not to know what anything means.' But the cry brought no good fairy with magic touch to arrange the tangled meshes into a fabric wherewith to clothe her ideas in a presentable form.

A moment more and one of Bridget's own laughs aroused herself to consciousness of being neither dream nor shadow, but a fair, well-proportioned substance lying snug and warm in a more comfortable bed than she had known for four months, whilst the self-same moon she had loved at home, and the bright cross that she had learnt to love since it had first looked down on her from southern skies, hung calm and beautiful just overhead, where she could gaze on them without raising herself from her pillow. She then bethought her of her laugh, and feared it had gone in to Emmeline; she well knew what a tell-tale it would be. So, determined to follow it on tip-toe to see what mischief it had done; noiselessly opening her cousin's door, she peeped in, and saw Emmeline sitting up with an anxious expression of countenance, as if listening to some uncommon sound.

'Did I frighten you with my nocturne, Em, darling?'

Emmeline only laid her finger on her lip in reply. Then beckoning Bridget to her, whispered:

'I feel rather uneasy. I have a vague sense of something wrong.'

'If it was a laugh that disturbed you, it was mine.'

'No, no; what I heard was hardly to be called a noise—it was more a feeling than a sound—there!' And Emmeline again hushed with her finger, and then pointed to a shadow which passed slowly across the window.

''Tis the acacia!' cried Bridget in a tone of feigned mirth.

But no one can make merry under the influence of midnight whispers and shadows; and though she firmly believed her assertion respecting the acacia, she by no means relished the few steps she took towards the window in order to prove the assertion. As she stood looking out on the moonlit landscape, she observed a figure dart from behind a tall, ghost-like gum tree, and spring over the slip rail into an adjoining paddock, where it vanished. She fancied she heard a window shut upstairs, and then a repressed footstep in the room in which the window seemed to be. With a presence of mind she would not have exhibited ere her intimacy with Emmeline, she turned quietly round, and said:

'You are nervous, perhaps, dear Em, after your fatigue and excitement. I'll sit with you a little, as I am not inclined to sleep.'

Em silently acquiesced, for she, too, had observed the figure dart away, her raised position giving her a side view of the lawn; but appreciating Bridget's intended kindness, she forbore to reveal her knowledge.

'It is all so new and strange, I can't sleep, Em. People aren't disturbed like this every night in Van Diemen's Land are they?'

'Like what?' asked Emmeline, smiling.

'Oh, fancying they hear noises and see shadows,' replied Bridget, recollecting herself. 'I hate noises in the night, and fancying one hears them is almost worse than really hearing; it makes one feel so warm, and cold, and horrid.'

'I am not alarmed now, Bridget, I guess what has been going on. Robbers take care not to leave their shadows behind them.'

A tap at the door interrupted her, and Nancy entered.

'A thousand pardons. I feared the dear lady might be affrighted if she heard the queer-like steppings about, as have waked me up. I heard you talking, so just came down to explain, that you needn't be frighted; the loss is all mine—them nasty blackguards have runned off with them two blessed gowns you gave me. I just hanged them up to get a bit of the fust out of 'em, and, sure enough, they's gone! I felt unaisy-like all to a sudden, as I laid in my bed. Fay, thought I, my blessed gownds! I jumped out, and looked from the window just in time to see 'em walked off—the shabby brutes!'

'I am glad to see you bear your loss so well,' quietly replied Emmeline. 'Mr. Evelyn will doubtless try to detect the thieves.'

'Thank you, miss; but I'm unwilling to fret the master about it. He's too good to be troubled with prisoners' losses and crosses. We won't say nothing to him, please, miss. It's the lot of all in this world.'

'Poor Nancy; I'm very sorry; perhaps I may be able to find you something instead,' sympathised Miss D'Urban.

'Fay! Miss, you're altogether a saint! To think of the poor convict having a friend like you in this troublesome world! But I won't break in no longer on you, ladies. I shouldn't have done so at all, only I heard you talking, and feared you were frightening yourselves, and might go and wake the master; and I hadn't the heart to let you do that.'

'Thank you kindly, Nancy. Now do go; good night,' said Bridget.

Emmeline only gravely bowed her head, with a significant and grieved expression.

'Then the master need know nothing about it,' whispered Nancy, putting her head in at the door.

'Why, Em, from the way you used to speak of them, I thought you would be a very champion for the poor prisoners.'

'Would that I could be! But, Bridget, you would not have me champion their falsehoods?'

'Now I hope you are not going to make out that Nancy's story is untrue. I shall hate this place if I have to doubt everyone's word. What end would the poor thing have in pretending to lose her clothes?'

'It seems she has gained one end already, in the promise of a second present; and I guess she has another; but ask Uncle Ev for enlightenment on this subject.'

'Very well; and in the meantime, Miss Em, I beg of you to remember your own favourite injunction: "Charity hopeth all things."'[1]

'Hoping against hope, dear Bridget. There is an apostolic injunction I can better follow in the present case, and in all moral emergencies: "Pray without ceasing."'[2]

'Ah! That *suits* you. I can better hope than pray: I hope because I can't *help* it; there is something so bright and sunny in it, that I naturally hope. Mine isn't, I fear, the sort St. Paul speaks of; in fact, mine is *nature*, and not *grace*. There now, don't look so grave, my sweet; I am not going to play on religion's holy ground—I did not mean to then. Scripture language is so much more expressive than any other; it says so much in a few words, that one uses it without intending it sometimes.'

'Give me a few of its precious words then, Bridgy, will you? I want a great deal said in a few words, for I am very tired—just a few words to fall asleep with—that, as good Bishop Ken[3] says, my dreams may be devout—the thoughts of God blocking up the avenues of sin—so that no evil may creep in to disturb my mind, whilst the will lies quiet with the body.'

'Why, I never noticed it! It is light enough to read without a candle; what glorious moonlight! Yes, positively.' And Bridget, having opened her Bible, commenced: 'There shall be no night there; and they need no candle, neither light of the sun; for the Lord God giveth them light.'[4]

'Think of that, Bridget! What an eternity of blessing expressed, but not explained, in that one short line: "There shall be no night there." Go and tell the weary labourer that henceforward there shall be no more night, and you proclaim his death warrant. No night! How, then, can he rest? Must it be toil—toil—without intermission? Then, indeed, will his days be shortened, and end prematurely in that long night, of which no one can deprive him. No night! Go, tell the man of sorrows so, and he will ask, despairingly, "Where, then, shall I hide my grief? Where seek a respite from my tears?" Tell the little child that is worn out with his play, he still must gambol on, for there is no more night, and he will hate the very thought of play, that must supersede his pleasant sleep. Where, then, the blessing, in the absence of night? Angels only could explain it; and the explanation would be a long list of heavenly joys, beyond our heart's conceiving—a list so long that inspiration has forborne to give it, but summed it up in that one whisper of heaven: "There shall be no night there." No sin needing the night to cover it; no sorrow, to seek the oblivion of sleep; no weariness, to demand a few hours' rest; no time for night, for the song ceases not; no place for night, for the light of eternity can find no dark mountains to drop behind, no sea of trouble to set beneath—it must shine on; no need for night, for the inhabitants shall no more say, "I am sick." There will be none to cry, "Would God it were morning!"'

Emmeline stopped short, and, fixing her eye earnestly on her cousin, exclaimed—

'Tired as I am, the mere thought acts as a foretaste of that cup of refreshing which the Lord God will put into his servants' hands, instead of the bitter cup which now—' But she checked herself, lest Bridget should think she referred to her own trial. Grateful as was the loving sympathy of her friends to her yearning spirit, she would never draw extraordinarily on it by complaints, nor exhaust it by continual demands, in the form of attitudes expressive of fatigue and pain. 'Now, then, if you will leave me, I think I can sleep,' she said, her voice of rapture sinking to a whisper; 'and I'm sure a vote of thanks is due to shadows and Nancy; for to them we owe this nocturnal visit, and I this kiss.'

Bridget buried her face on Emmeline's pillow, and a series of minor kisses, ending in one long, loud chirrup, told *how much* she owed to Nancy's disturbance.

She was rather pleased than otherwise to have had so queer a sort of night—it was next best to a decided adventure—and she was almost on the point of commencing there and then her V.D.L. diary, with a description of it, when hearing the watch-dog bark violently, she jumped into bed and, tired out with her long vigil was soon asleep, and awoke not until the bright sun shining in through her uncurtained windows startled her to the fact that she was already too late to see how morning dawned in Tasmania, while Uncle Ev's cheerful whistle on the lawn told her that the sun was not the only early riser.

Her first morning in another world! And *such* a morning! Full of fragrance, flowers, sun-smiles, and songs. Yes, *songs*; let who will say to the contrary. The heart that loves animation and mirth stays not to criticize the notes of the bird that gives life to the scenery. Unless the sounds be decidedly unmusical, they pass into and form a part of the loveliness which it admires, and from which it receives a mighty pleasure. Bridget stood in quiet admiration, looking out on the prospect—now on the distant Derwent, sparkling in its first moments of wakefulness—and then on the nearer beauties of her uncle's pleasure-grounds—attracted now by the thousand delicate tufts of the golden wattle, as it seemed to bow towards her for the express purpose of welcoming her with its earliest and freshest perfume, and then wondering if by any chance the tall, stiff gum tree could come down from its would-be stateliness, and bend with the graceful wattle, but at the same time feeling quite satisfied that the said gum tree should remain unchanged; there was something foreign in its gaunt, smooth, whitewashed-looking trunk, with its eccentric ragged leaves overhanging it from the top like an old-fashioned umbrella of doubtful colour, torn into shreds. Since she had come so far, it was only fair that some objects should reward her expectations, by giving a touch of foreignness to the country. In the midst of thus feeling and thinking, a commotion in the bushes, and a sudden flight of birds thence to the fence, and from the fence back to the bushes, aroused a home-yearning in her breast, and made her contradict her previous wish with a desire that nothing should be foreign, but that everything should look as much like England as possible. She then recollected to listen to the birds which, before unnoticed, had been most jubilant—ever since the first streak of light, and having listened, not critically, but as if entering into the spirit of their joy, she exclaimed:

'Why, they *do* sing! At any rate as well as most of our English birds.'[5]

'I was to tell you, miss, that Miss Evelyn sleeps, to prevent your going and waking of her up,' spoke a voice that rather unceremoniously disturbed Bridget in her dream of home.

'Who told you so, Pridham?' (The servant she had first seen.)

'The new Mr. Evelyn, miss; he said he'd peeped in and saw her fast asleep—at least he didn't tell me to tell you, but I thought I'd better—as I know'd you waited upon her like.'

'You are very kind and thoughtful, but you shouldn't say that my uncle bade you come if he did not,' replied Bridget, frightened at her audacity in venturing a reproof.

'I beg pardon, miss, 'twasn't meant; please not to mention it to master; really out here a poor girl gets into trouble 'fore she knows where she is. I've had a month at the suds[6] for less than that 'fore now, not by he, though' (meaning Mr. E., senior). 'I've not been here long enough to know his ways; but they say he's harder upon fibs than anything; so I'm 'fraid of my life at every word I speak to him—not knowing exactly what he counts fibbing—but *I* knows what suds are pretty well!'

'And what are the suds, Pridham?'

'One of the factory works; the women hates it next worst to doing of nothing.'

After a few moments' silence on Pridham's part, and uneasiness on Bridget's, the former said:

'I've forgotten now what I came for. I mean, miss, next to telling about the young lady; I wanted to put you on your guard against that there Nancy—she's the dangerousest woman ever I came across—and all the while she'd make a body believe she's innocent and after peacemaking. The deceit of her is worth hearkening to. Them blessed gowns! As she kept on about after you'd given 'em her—precious blessed indeed—if they was blessed when *she* took hold of them, they weren't blessed long after; but there, I don't want to set you up against her, only just to put you on your guard when next you gives away, to give where things will be valued. I don't speak for myself, for I have just worked out[7] a new gown for best, and be content with this here brown one till next month, when I've worked out another for mornings. The master isn't hard, though he's partic'lar.'

What does it all mean? I have got into a hornet's nest indeed, thought Bridget, and with her natural dislike to the shadowy side of life, she half wished herself home again: *these* were not the sort of 'kitchen rows' she professed to cure. With a mixture of real and pretended impatience, she said:

'Well, really, I am tired of hearing of those gowns; I shall think twice before I give any again.'

'Oh! I don't want to put you in that mind anyhow; we all admires your generosity, and hopes it won't be the last of it—it's only Nancy there we're 'fraid of—trouble always comes out of what she lays hands to; if trouble don't come out of them gowns, I'm— But there, I don't want to say no more about 'em; only if you will be so good as to mind if trouble does come, *I* haven't had a finger in it. I am so 'fraid what the master 'll make out, though he isn't hard, only partic'lar; and no wonder! Out here we're obliged to suspect everybody, and if I'm gover'ment and says it, what must them as come out free say?'

'Pridham, I'm very sorry, but really I don't understand all this; it's all strange to me yet. If I say or do anything to hurt any one's feelings, I shall be very grieved, and—'

It was now Pridham's turn to look mystified. What had she said about hurt feelings or grieving? She had only wanted to turn the tide of favour towards herself, by closing it to Nancy; and also by making a premature declaration of innocence to disclaim all share in trouble, which with prisoner instinct she foresaw in 'them two blessed gowns.' The convict always fears that which he cannot at once understand, lest it should embody some new evil to himself and always mistrusts that which he cannot immediately explain, lest it should be another means of extending his punishment under pretext of ameliorating it. Though the occasion was slight, this applied in the present case. Through the prisoner instinct, terror quickly followed Pridham's misapprehension of Miss D'Urban's words, and interpreted them into all manner of scoldings, deprivations, and perhaps even the dreaded wash-tub; so clasping her hands and bursting into tears, she besought Bridget 'not to tell on her.'

'Oh miss! I pray on you not to tell the master. I didn't mean for to offend. 'Twasn't insolence, indeed; no it wasn't! Poor girls like me gets into trouble 'fore they knows where they are. I knows I fibs dreadful; but believe me, miss, I never finds out I have fibbed until they tells me so, and punishes me for it. I will confess that I did hint for you to give me something, so please to forgive me; but indeed I never went for to grieve or hurt you like what you said. If Nancy gets a hold on this, she'll make fine work against me out of it.'

The look of penitence and fright in the girl's face was pitiable in the extreme. Bridget wondered still more what it all meant, and wished herself home again with increased violence. Since promise of secrecy seemed necessary to Pridham's happiness, she gave it her, though in utter ignorance of what she was *not* to divulge as of what there *could be* to divulge in the long addresses of the distressed damsel.

Thinking as despondingly of the future as it was possible for her hopeful mind to think, Bridget descended to the breakfast parlour, where sat Uncle Herbert, lost in reverie and the comfortable cushions of a large armchair. She had knelt by his side and kissed his hands ere he perceived her.

'God bless you, my child, and make you a blessing in this strange land! What think you of it? There is not a favourable report on your face. You have not your wonted sunbeam there.'

'Oh! Uncle Herbert; I've been sad and pleased twenty times over since I got up. First I was in raptures with the beautiful landscape over the water; then I was sad to remember it wasn't home; then I fell in love with that pretty yellow tree and with all the flowers—in fact with everything; and then, one of the prisoner-servants came in, and all my joy went in a moment. I hate seeing people miserable.'

'Where every prospect pleases,
    And only man is vile,'[8]

said Mr. Herbert Evelyn, rising, and drawing Bridget's arm into his.

'Your Uncle Ev has not returned yet; let us take a turn in the garden, and talk all about it.'

'Not about the prisoners; oh no! I vote we don't; it's so horrid! Really, whatever one says or does something comes out about those poor creatures. I didn't think it would be at all like this, and directly I arrived too.'

'Like what? Something has annoyed you, or you would not have had an opportunity of comparing likenesses.'

'You mustn't laugh at me, or I shall get in a flutter and not be able to explain myself.'

'I am in no laughing mood, my love. Go on, and tell me all you mean, and what has happened.'

'Oh no, you dear, good Uncle Herbert; you have too many real troubles to be vexed with my little nonsenses. I must learn to laugh at them.'

'God forbid, dear child! Anything but that; as all domestic trials you meet with here are likely to spring from the one great cause of this country, it would be as wanton to laugh at them as ineffective to rail at them. Rather let us weep and mourn; but still rather let us seek to allay them by means of the talents God has committed to our keeping.'

'I'm afraid I shall never be any use. When I think I've done something right, it proves just the contrary. If I hadn't been quite new yesterday, I am sure Uncle Ev would have given me a regular scolding about those stupid gowns.'

Uncle Herbert pressed her hand gently, and whispered—

'I remember something *very* right you once did. I may have to thank you for it forever.'

A quick, bright glance from Bridget, with a sigh—

'God's will be done, my precious Emmeline!' from Mr. Herbert; and, by a mutual understanding, that something very right was not discussed save in the heart of each.

Notwithstanding the sadness of their subject, the shadows were fading from Bridget's face. If not on the sunny side of life, she was in the light of heaven, and it was not in her to resist the beams that strewed a gilded path before her. It was not long before she loosened her hold of Uncle Herbert's arm, by several short, sudden skips, denoting the presence of intuitive gladness welling up from the sparkling fountain within through all depressing obstacles.

'But, Bridget, you have not yet confided your disappointments to me, nor told me where exists the difference between what you expected and that which you find.'

'Naughty Uncle Herbert; you are determined to make me ashamed of myself. As if I wasn't that long ago! Well, then, what I mean is this: I did not expect that prisoners would so mix with us as they do in everyday life, making us afraid to look or speak lest we should hurt their feelings or get them punished. I knew there would be hundreds of convicts, but thought they would be such dreadful creatures we should only be shocked at them; and I thought there would be dreadful affrays with them sometimes; but I never dreamt of such trumpery[9] annoyances coming out of the commonest sayings and doings, making one uncomfortable in such curious ways. It will be wretched if it is always going to be like this.'

'No, no; it is not always going to be like this. It will only be so whilst Miss D'Urban is learning not to give gowns in exchange for crocodile tears and Judas kisses,' exclaimed Uncle Ev, who, having stabled his horse, had just entered a path of the garden, divided from where his niece lingered by a tall hedge of sweetbriar and geranium, and he now stood opposite, yet concealed from her. Bridget did not yet understand him, and still harbouring suspicions of his hardheartedness, she felt half afraid that the suppressed scolding of last night might be forthcoming now. But doubt decreased an instant after his well-whiskered, smiling face nodded to her through a break in the hedge. He then jumped over a lower bush, and, coming to her side, gave her so kind a welcome that she began to think she had only just arrived.

'No, no, Miss Bridget; they are only trying it on. If nobody else obeys Scripture, prisoners out here do. They work while it is called to-day, before the night of experience frustrates their endeavours to get what they want from a newcomer. When you are more up to their ways, they'll leave you alone. In other words, when they've got what they can out of you, they'll forget all their home conceits and predilections.'

'But, uncle, it appears that so much is made out of nothing, just because they are poor prisoners. It seems so very natural to me that Nancy should be affected as she was, and—'

'Well, well, so it is; and something else as natural to convict principle will follow the natural gift of those gowns, or I'm very much mistaken.'

'Then you *are* mistaken. For they have both been stolen from her. Em and I heard a noise in the night, and shortly after Nancy came in and told us some rogues had taken them off the line and run away with them.'

'And how much of that do you believe?' asked Mr. Evelyn.

'Why, George, I think it is only fair that *she* should believe it all.'

'On the principle—let her believe while she can, and don't make a sceptic of her before her time? Well, there is something in *that*; but at the same time, is it not fair, for her own protection, to teach her the grand cautionary axiom of Van Diemen's Land: "Believe every man a rogue until you have *proved* him to be honest"—the antipodes of English etiquette: "Every man is honest until he is proved a rogue."'

'Thank you, uncle; the longer I defer learning that the better. But what you say reminds me of a question Emmeline bade me ask. She says Nancy had two ends in view in pretending she had lost the dresses; one was the hope of getting another present, and the other you are to tell me.'

'Well, the other I pronounce to be decidedly spiritual. Yes, no doubt she had a spiritual end in view, eh! Herbert, does that suit you?'

A look of remonstrance was the clergyman's only answer; and when Bridget's eye asked an explanation from Uncle Ev, he only nodded, 'Time will show,' and proceeded to conduct her to the house. When near the verandah, he stopped. 'A word with you, Bridget. I am very careful how I express my opinion of the convicts before my boy Charlie. He is a thorough little specimen of all ears and eyes. Any point you want cleared up, ask me when the young rogue is out of hearing.'

A loud bell rang as soon as Mr. Evelyn's step sounded in the hall. Mr. Herbert exclaimed, 'Ah! It's the voice of a dear old friend. Prayers, George, is it not?'

Uncle Ev nodded assent.

'Here, at any rate, we are one with England. The same hope unites us—one Lord, one faith, one baptism, one Father. Over this precious book all distinctions cease and distances diminish,' continued Uncle Herbert, laying his hand on the family Bible. 'Here we are told of One from whom neither height nor depth can separate us. No sea can roll its intervening wave between us and His love.'

'Shall I commence? Where are the servants? Are they not coming?'

'No; I don't choose it,' promptly replied the elder brother, in a tone which implied, ask no questions.

Prayers being over, Charlie followed his cousin into the verandah, to await the breakfast. As soon as he was beyond hearing, Mr. Evelyn said:

'The truth is, Herbert, in not permitting my people to attend prayers, I choose the less of two evils. During the ten years I devoted myself to the prisoners, though I didn't deem it necessary to carry the religious system so far as you, being a clergyman, are obliged to—'

'And wish to,' interposed Mr. Herbert.

'Well, and wish to—I allowed them all religious privileges that seemed expedient. *Now*, being surrounded by a different class of convicts, I find I cannot admit them to an indiscriminate use of the family's religious services. I've tried to forego prejudices, but each new trial only strengthens me in them; and I now think it little short of mockery to call in the servants to prayers, knowing as I do that most of them are living in open sin.'

'Papa, isn't breakfas' ready?' cried Charlie, peeping in at the window.

'What is the maid thinking about? It's a quarter to nine, and half-past eight is the breakfast hour. Ring the bell, my boy.'

The child's entrance put a stop to the discussion, and brought wholesome thoughts of physical requirements to the gentlemen's minds. But the bell had to give three increasingly loud peals before one answer could be obtained, and that came from Pridham, not from cook.

'Please, sir, it's no doing of mine. I've tried to rouse her; she'm reg'lar beastly down. I can't go nigh of her; she vows she'll see you blasted 'fore she gets the breakfast, and she says she'll crack me if *I* go for to get it.'

'Ah! ah! ah!' screamed Charlie, clapping his hands; 'what fun! Papa, let me come too.'

'Go back, sir!' sternly answered the father, as he prepared to descend to the kitchen; whilst a coarse song, in uproarious starts, sounded from below.

'What is the matter, Charlie?' eagerly inquired Bridget, feeling frightened enough to be glad of even his small company.

'Oh, nothing. I s'pose she's intosticated. Hark! There's such a row; I s'pose they're fighting.'

And off ran the little fellow to the head of the stairs. In a moment he ran in again, his cheeks flushed with excitement.

'Come, Bridget, come. I can't see them, but I can hear.'

Pale with terror, poor innocent Bridget clung to the back of a chair; but recollecting what Uncle Ev had said, she caught back Charlie, as for the third time he was running out.

'Darling, come in; 'tisn't fit for you. What would papa say?'

'I don't care; I will, I will!' shouted the child, trying to get free from his cousin's grasp.

'No, no; be my dear Charlie, and stay.'

'I won't; I don't want to be anybody's dear Charlie; I want to go down and see it.'

When the two Mr. Evelyns reached the kitchen, they found the cook sitting Turk-fashion on the floor, with a pipe in her mouth; a piece of white tape tied her stunted locks in one matted bunch on the top of her capless head; her dress was half on on one side, and from the other hung her prison jacket. Perceiving her master, she staggered to her feet, and squared towards him.

'Come on my hearty; them that wants their breakfist must fight for it—as the dogs does.'

Another step towards them, and down she flounced—but not so as to hurt herself; then came a torrent of abuse that made Mr. Herbert close his eyes with pain, and Mr. Evelyn stamp in disgust.

'If you move from your place I'll souse you, so please sit still,' at last said the latter, knowing that anger or disgust would be wasted on the miserable being before him.

Thump, thump, thump, went her thick boots, in determination not to be still, though she was obliged to keep her seat.

'I—s'pose—constable's coming?' she stammered.

'Presently,' answered Mr. Evelyn; 'and the less you rave now, the less will be your punishment by-and-by.'

Mr. Herbert had remained a spectator only in case of violence.

'Have you sent for one?' he now whispered.

Mr. Evelyn nodded, and in another moment in walked a constable. He went straight over to the woman, and began to drag her by her arms. She set up a terrible howl, and offered what resistance lay in her power.

'Leave her alone, sir,' commanded Mr. Evelyn in his sternest voice. 'How often have I requested that, when a constable comes to my house, he will perform his duty in a decent manner—fetch a cab; the woman does not go without.'

A cab having arrived, the man again commenced to drag the prisoner. Mr. Evelyn again remonstrated, and assisted the poor wretch to the vehicle.

'Now, remember: I'll never have a public spectacle made of such degrading sights when they come from *my* house.'

'Stay, I'll go with her,' said Mr. Herbert; then, in an undertone: 'It is not right she should be left to his tender mercies. I know him; he should not be in his present position at all.'

The constable's heavy brow contracted extra surliness as the clergyman stepped into the cab; but, unheedful of his anger, Mr. Herbert took his seat by the loathsome, and now almost unconscious, object of his solicitude, and, with his peculiar tact, commenced a conversation irrelevant to the subject before them.

'Well, Bradley, it is a long time since we met. I have been in England since then.'

No answer save a gruff—Hum.

'Have you received the news you were expecting from your wife, when I took leave of you all? How is she now?'

'Gone to the devil, for all I care!'

'Indeed! I am sorry for that; when did she go?' and Mr. Herbert turned his calm yet searching eye full into the rough, inquisitive, who-be-you? sort of face, that jerked quickly towards him in answer to this unexpected sympathy.

Let it work, thought Mr. Herbert; in a few moments he asked:

'Have you your ticket yet, Bradley?'

'No; nor never shall, if he can help it.'

'What, the old story! We must talk it over.'

Another silence, broken by Bradley.

'I have been in the boat's crew at Port Arthur since you went; got down there for heaving a log at Bill Scroggins. It missed him, or I should have swung for it, the magistrate said; but I'll have a heave at he yet, for all that.'

The malicious tone and grin which accompanied this speech prevented Mr. Herbert from noticing it; he knew it was said on purpose to annoy him. It had ever been Bradley's delight to 'shock the parson's fine notions.'

When Uncle Ev returned to the breakfast-less breakfast table, he found Charlie in a sulky fit, and Bridget trembling with the apprehension that her ill-fated gift had had somewhat to do with the morning's outbreak; she was, therefore, much relieved when her uncle told her that cook and Nancy were distinct personages.

'Oh, I am so glad! Then Nancy is all right, and it has nothing to do with—with—' She was too tired of the gowns to mention them even.

'I'm not quite so sure of that;' but seeing his niece's look of vexation, whatever might have been his thoughts, Mr. Evelyn forbore to say more. A fourth call of the bell brought Pridham, with a face full of alarm—for what might not that bell portend to her?

'Let Nancy do what she can towards the breakfast; we must content ourselves with toast this morning.'

'Please, sir, I can't wake Nancy—I've been tugging at her this long time; she'm dead asleep,' whimpered Pridham.

The storm burst!

'It's all a scheme, *you* are as bad as either of them; tell me all you know of this; hide anything at your peril,' stamped Mr. Evelyn, having controlled himself to the limit of his patience.

'I don't know nothing.'

'It's a lie, you do.'

'I don't know no more than that a man was here late last night a-talking with Nancy, and that he took away a jar with 'em, and left another.'

'You know a great deal more, and you will tell me, directly.'

'How should a poor girl know everything, when she's 'fraid of getting into trouble?'

'Nonsense—no humbug—go on.'

'When the man was gone, Nancy says, "Cook, them gowns smell awful fusty-like; I think a night's airing would fresh 'em a bit." I saw her wink to cook, and cook winked back to her; then when she came from hanging them out-of-doors she shrugs her shoulders, and says:

"'I feel awful creamy-like, and nervous to sleep alone—"

"'Shall I sleep with you?" says I.'

'You had no business to offer that,' parenthesised her master.

'No, sir; I know it was wrong, but—'

'No humbug—go on.'

'"Why, no," says she; "you sleeps with the young un, 'twouldn't do for you to change beds." She winked to cook and didn't think I saw her, so cook says, "My humble sarvices to you, Nancy, if you are ill. You'm welcome to me for a bedfeller if you think the master won't holler."

"'No, he'd say ne'er a word, when 'twas for sickness," and she winked again.'

'So they slept together?'

'I s'pose as they did, sir.'

'Nonsense, you know they did, and you know all the rest; but as I've heard enough for my purpose, you may go.'

'There won't be no trouble for me, please, sir?'

'If I find you have spoken truth, and have had no *further* share in the matter, I shall not punish you.'

'I haven't had no share at all.'

'Go—I don't choose to be answered; you took the share of not telling me that they were planning for drink.'

All Pridham's fears of being charged with, and chastised for insolence again bristled up, and she in proportion shrunk down. Humbling her voice and attitude to the very lowest depths of servility, she whined:

'I didn't mean for to say it; telling of them things would be getting into trouble, quite as bad as government trouble.'

'I repeat—no nonsense, Pridham; remember, wherever you have lived out before—you are now with a master who will not punish without reason. Now, go into Nancy's room and search about for the jar and bring it to me: don't touch the woman; then lock the door and give me the key.'

Pridham left to obey this order, feeling convinced of what before she had only quoted from hearsay, namely, that the master wasn't *hard*, though precious partic'lar.

'What, Charlie, you here? How often have I insisted on your leaving the room when you see me engaged with the servants?' said Mr. Evelyn.

He was just at that point of irritation which vents itself on the first object in its way; not even his child could escape. Mortification also had a place in his feelings. He had arranged a particularly nice breakfast to tempt Emmeline's sickly appetite, and to display to Bridget the amount of civilization attained in the colonial culinary department, and no meal at all was so Paddy-like[10] a substitute, that no wonder he was mortified. He had just sufficient self-control left to prevent his giving the last prick of pain to Bridget, who was already almost crying. He managed to say:

'I am very sorry, dear, that you should be so treated the first morning; it's a poor welcome, but one you will get accustomed to.'

Taking even this to herself, her handkerchief started to her eyes, and she rushed upstairs to hide her vexation in Emmeline's bosom, leaving Mr. Evelyn angrily striding up and down the room, and vociferating—

'I have borne it as patiently as any man! Believing the promise that the scourge would be removed, when we had taken our turn at it, I bore my part with energy; but when a man sees that faith isn't kept with him, why, he—'

'You are not going to turn Leaguist,[11] George?' asked Mr. Herbert, entering the room and guessing the subject of his brother's oration.

'Not I! I turned anti-convictist long ago, and shall not take a more opposing ground, until—'

'No untils!' cried Uncle Herbert, shaking his forefinger half playfully. 'Remember, I'm a minister of the crown.'

'Ay, ay, and of *another* crown that I fear I've not much to do with. You are beyond me *there*, Herbert,' said Uncle Ev, as, restored to good-humour, he placed his chair to the table, which at last showed signs of a coming repast.

'Remonstrant, but not revolutionist, is my title.'

'And mine too, though on different foundations,' replied Uncle Herbert.

The afternoon was far advanced when Mr. Evelyn unlocked Nancy's door, to see in what stage of recovery and repentance her long sleep had left her. She had not been heard to move, but Mr. Evelyn attributed her silence more to fear than to continued intoxication, and hoped that reasonably protracted suspense might be a wholesome discipline to her. He imagined her sitting most forlorn, and ready with flippant sorrow against he should appear to inquire into her conduct; but the draught which rushed on him, as he pushed open the door, extinguished at once his imaginings, and suggested a picture of Nancy under different circumstances, or rather suggested the thought that he was likely to find no picture at all; a glance round the room confirmed the latter suggestion.

She had bolted through the window!

A constable was immediately put on track for her; but when the evening closed in she had not been found.

CHAPTER 17

A Walk About Hobarton and a Talk About the Tasmanians

'THERE, Miss Bridget, how does your name look in print?' exclaimed Uncle Ev, throwing down the *Courier* before his niece, that she might see herself mentioned as one of the arrivals by the last vessel. 'Now then, no more retirement for you; make ready for the thousand and one visitors ever prone to avail themselves of glowing advertisements of prettily named young ladies.'

'Oh! I am longing to see the first people that come. Lionel made such fun of the folks in this colony. I can't fancy they will all be as nice as *you*. The Hills, who came home, said the men could only talk about cattle, so much so, that the bishop once preached on that text, "Whose talk is of bullocks."'

'You shall make your own observations, Bridget, before you hear my opinion. There! It strikes me that alarming rat-tat is from my good friend Dr. Lamb, so you have not long to delay your judgment; apropos of doctors out here, if they differ from the home faculty in no other respect, they do in treatment of their patients' nerves, inuring them to shocks by the free use of the knocker.'

'Dr. and Mrs. Lamb and the Rev. Mr. Walkden,' announced Pridham.

'Right glad to see you back—Oh, but he isn't here, though. I was expecting to see Mr. Herbert. How do, Evelyn? Not the less glad to see you. Your niece, I suppose? How do; welcome to Hobarton. Miss Evelyn! Now don't move, I insist now—dear, dear, I am sorry to see *you* back.'

All this was uttered before Mr. Evelyn could attempt an introduction, so that formality was spared; a warm shake of the hand having already taken place between Bridget and the company. Uncle Herbert entered, and caused a second round of congratulations, condolences, and sittings-down, which over, Dr. Lamb turned to Bridget:

'How is the duke?'

'Which duke?'

'That noble fellow's namesake,' and Dr. Lamb pointed to Mount Wellington.[1]

Bridget looked confused. She did not know that he had been ill. Uncle Herbert came to the rescue. 'He is failing, they say. I have the latest news in the *Times* of the day we sailed. The paper is at your service.'

'There has been a fresco found in Exeter Cathedral, I hear?' said Mr. Walkden to Bridget.

Fresco! She knew nothing about it. Exeter was so far from London too. 'I beg your pardon?' she answered inquiringly.

'I hear there has been a great excitement in consequence of a fresco recently discovered in Exeter Cathedral,' repeated Mr. Walkden.

Uncle Ev looked deliciously wicked, and watched for her reply; but his brother, more compassionate, relieved Bridget by entering on the subject with Mr. Walkden.

'How do you like what you have seen of this country, Miss D'Urban?' asked Dr. Lamb.

'Very much; but I do not think I shall like being here, everything is so different from home.'

Mrs. Lamb, who was sitting by Emmeline, here bent eagerly forward. Mr. Evelyn seemed in a fidget, and Emmeline manoeuvred to send her cousin an admonitory glance. Had not Dr. Lamb good-naturedly turned the subject, there is no knowing what offence Racket might have given.

'I suppose you have come out to take pity on some forlorn mortal, Miss D'Urban?' he asked.

'Oh, yes, my cousin wished to have me, and I was equally pleased to go with her.'

Uncle Ev beamed radiant towards Emmeline, and Mr. Herbert smiled quietly to himself, as Dr. Lamb answered—

'Indeed! But I can't say much for the forlornness of *that* case.'

Brigid perceived the laugh was against her in some way; so she joined in it with one of her merry laughs which gained her more esteem from the party than if she had been learned over frescoes or an able reporter of the duke's health.

'Oh, Mr. Walkden, isn't it wicked of them to make me laugh at myself?' she exclaimed, seeing that he alone preserved a steady countenance.

That gentleman thought no person could be wicked who called a laugh on Miss D'Urban's face; but of course he did not say so. Clergymen do not pay compliments.

'I like them amazingly,' cried Bridget, as the door closed on the visitors; 'and as for that Dr. Lamb, I'm in love with him. There is an un-English frankness about him, whilst there is no want of English politeness.'

'Unfortunately he is not forlorn enough for you!' said Uncle Ev, half shutting his teasing eyes at her.

'Oh! I hate forlorn folks; I like happy ones. Dr. Lamb, for instance; there is just the bright twinkle in his eye that makes one glad to look at.'

She stopped, and blushing, buried her face in her hands. Then jumping up she said—

'How stupid! Of course he meant that—as if nobody can come here without wanting to be married!'

She stamped playful indignation.

'The few must suffer for the many; but no person who knows my sunbeam will suppose it strayed so far for such a purpose,' replied Uncle Herbert, smoothing the glossy plaits of her hair.

'Well, Bridgy, I'm glad you approve of Dr. Lamb, he is physician general to this house; and next week he commences with Em, eh, Herbert?'

Mr. Herbert only answered by a look at Emmeline.

'As you please, papa,' she responded, as much with her sweet smile as by word.

'Mamma declared *she* would never trust a child of hers to a colonial doctor,' whispered Bridget.

'Your mother says a great many foolish things,' rapped from Uncle Ev, ere he was aware. On meeting his brother's look of disapprobation, he added: 'Well, I haven't patience with such foolery! I'd back Lamb with any living doctor. In surgery he is worthy of being called the Tasmanian Liston.[2] He has great advantage over his English M.D. brethren, for professional etiquette allows him free practice in all branches, surgical and medical, and his appointment at the Prisoners' Hospital affords him ample scope therein.'

'Is he a real M.D. uncle?' asked Emmeline.

'Yes, one of the few truly bearing the title. License, which I suppose we may call poetic, honours all practitioners out here with the Dr. prefix, from the proprietor of the Medical Hall, Elizabeth Street, to the senior physician in her Majesty's service. It's fair, too, perhaps, that the one sharing the profit, the other should share the title. But a word with you whilst I think of it, Miss D'Urban.'

Bridget was all attention.

'If you would avoid giving offence, you must be careful not to express too ready, unless a favourable opinion of the colony; and be still *more* careful not to draw comparisons between the mother country and this; and when in mixed company be *most* careful not to allude to convicts, lest there should be a convict's son or grandson present. Up country several of the most flourishing families are of doubtful origin. There is no published code; but I believe these, with a few others, are the accepted rules of polite society in Tasmanian, or indeed, in Australian life.'

'I shall accept them and be in polite life then, for I hate hurting people's feelings, whether they are free or prisoners,' said Bridget.

'It is a colonial supposition that prisoners have no feelings, and a government assumption that they ought to have none, save those known as physical.'

'Oh! Uncle Ev, you are joking again; now isn't he, Uncle Herbert? I can always believe what you say.'

'Not wholly, I fear. The supposition is practically expressed.'

'Then I shall hate to hurt them more than ever, that I shall.'

'I think, Bridget, I must parody the poet's sentiment, and say to you, "Thou hatest wisely, but too oft;" hatred seems a favourite passion of yours. What think you, Em?' [3]

'If words alone prove it; but there is a very paradoxical expression in those dancing eyes; hatred loses its pungency as it drops from her lips. However, we've discussed the hateful subject before, have we not, Bridgy?'

'Nevertheless, I love hating horrid things, and I always shall, for all the old poets or discussions in the world.'

'Speaking of hatred brings to my mind a fearful impersonation of that passion that I once saw in one of the Norfolk Island mutineers. I never hear hatred spoken of, but his awful form presents itself to me. You remember Macguire, George?' inquired Mr. Herbert.

'Much against my will, I do; but how is it every topic turns to convictism in some shape? The cloven foot is sure to peep out from every possible corner.'

'Out of the abundance of the heart the mouth speaketh. How should it not be so, when the evil is in our very midst, outraging our feelings, exciting our sympathies, imploring our energies, and inviting our prayers?'

'There, Uncle Ev,' exclaimed Bridget, who had been writing in her diary, 'I've made notes of your rules to send home to Mr. Lionel. You must take care how you behave, for everything goes down in this journal.'

'Let's see;' and Mr. Evelyn took the book, added a few lines to it, and gave it back to his niece, saying, 'There, read that.'

Bridget read:

'Rule Four—Never apply the term "colonial" to anything but produce. Example: Never say of a young lady—She is quite colonial; nor of any domestic arrangement—It is so colonial. Reason: Though patriotic to a high degree, all colonists aspire to English thoughts, manners, and habits. Whilst "colonist" is a title which makes the honest settler proud, "colonial" is an epithet obnoxious to his hardy sons, and one over which his pretty daughters pout.'

'Now then, Miss D'Urban, observe rule four, if you wish to keep a clear account with the natives (don't alarm yourself, I don't mean aborigines). When you wish to gain a crusty matron's heart or please a young husband, say of his wife or the mother's daughter, "Dear me! I quite thought she was English—she is not at all colonial!" and all crustiness will crumble into the confidence—"Ah, but my daughter has not been exposed to colonial influence;" while connubial bliss, beaming thrice blessed, will simper the assurance, "My wife, though born in the colony, is *quite* English in all her notions." The lordly squatter who only an hour before boxed his son's ears for calling England his home, vaunts to the stranger who claims his hospitality—"My place is so English you'll think yourself at home when I take you round it. There, sir, isn't *that* English?" The native who to-day raves against the tyranny of government in turning his beloved country into a moral pest-house, to-morrow mentions his cherished hope of laying his bones beneath British mould. Why, Charlie there, who now glories in being a genuine gum tree, will by-and-by fight the school-fellow that calls him colonial, won't you, Charlie boy?'

'What fun! But the colonists don't say such things amongst themselves, do they, uncle? But only when they are with what Uncle Herbert names Anglo-Tasmanians.'

'Don't they, though? Go up country with me, Miss Bridget, and hear two heads of families talk of some new family just settled near them, and you will find that "colonial" is an adjective as objectionably applied amongst themselves as in intercourse with us. In short, colonialism is a sort of national bogie, with which parents frighten their children into good manners, and themselves into domestic proprieties, as perpetrated in England. But you are not off yet, Herbert? You'll stay for lunch?'

'I have engaged to be at the comptroller-general's office by one o'clock, and at two the governor has promised me an interview. I long to get back to my work, and am, therefore, glad of an early appointment with Sir William.'[4]

'Had not Bridget better go with you, when you pay your formal respects to Government House? She can hardly wait for her aunt, or she'll miss the ball.'

Uncle Herbert seemed to think that would not be very much to miss.

'I shall not call there now. I met Lady Denman yesterday, and walked back with her to shake hands with Sir William. It was then that his Excellency fixed to meet me to-day. By-the-by, Emmeline, Lady Denman sends her love to you. She says she will not forget your penchant for strawberries, when hers ripen. She hopes to gather her first on Christmas day. Her ladyship was most friendly, and knowing of Clara's absence, charged me to tell you, George, to bring Bridget to see her, without the usual ceremony.'

'Nevertheless, I shall keep to the code, for fear Mr. A. D. C., not seeing Miss D'Urban's name, should forget the existence of such a person, and that would disappoint me as much as herself. I am quite impatient to see how she looks in the smart gown I know she has somewhere stowed away for this very ball, eh! Bridget, confess?'

'Be quiet, knowing everything, you Uncle Ev! Well, I do own to such a dress—and a beauty it is too; far better than any I should have had at home; indeed, all my things are prettier than any I ever had before.'

'Maternal forethought!' ejaculated Uncle Ev.

'Yes; I suppose mamma thought I should be vexed not to look nice among strangers,' answered Bridget, not remarking her Uncle's queer smile as he turned to Emmeline, who shook her head at him.

'Do you deny by that shake of your head, Miss Evelyn, that maternal forethought is a very bright thought?' And his smile was still more queer, whereon Emmeline pouted her lips into a beseeching form, as much as to say, 'Now don't, there's a dear.'

'We will not argue the point, then; but this I affirm, that if the end of this maternal forethought is to be realised as the object of its deserved, it need be very brilliant indeed. Do you agree ladies?'

Emmeline nodded approval.

'Oh you needn't ask me', laughed Birdget, 'If Em agrees I do. Whatever she signs to must be right. Get her signature, and you are sure of mine without ever reading the petition: I'm a bonâ fide petitioner in that respect.'

'Most fortunate! Your agreeance will be a necessary item in the end proposed. Now, Miss Fivewits, shall you be ready after lunch to pay your devoirs to the lady governess of the island, by writing your name in her vice-majesty's book? Having performed that ceremony, I don't know that we will not dispense with the further etiquette of *not* seeing her, and according to her own suggestion, find our way to her drawing-room. If you are a loyal subject, you will be in love with her; she is so like the queen; put her in a state-carriage, and drive her in Windsor Park, and she'd be our sovereign forthwith. I don't remember, though, whether her Majesty is shortsighted? Lady Denman is supremely so, for which interesting defect the opticians of Van Diemen's Land owe her a special debt of gratitude. Ah, yes! That's well recollected; you must have an eye-glass, my dear, out of politeness to Lady Denman. Good society has adopted one since her ladyship's sight failed her.'

'Good society! Wouldn't mamma laugh! She says society here cannot be worth much, because no one would leave England, unless obliged to.'

'Miss D'Urban, for instance. But your mother has made many mistakes in regard to this place. The present is only one of a whole chapter of blunders which she and a hundred other idle folk are content to remain in rather than trouble themselves to bring their opinion to the test of facts. My sister has made no greater error than that which you have just repeated.'

'Now, surely, Uncle Ev, you are not going to make out that society here is as good as it is at home?'

'That depends. When the Lady Geraldine Manners comes out, she may feel at a loss for a companion; or the Duchess of Sutherland might return for want of an equal; but Mrs. D'Urbans and Mrs. Caldridges may come without end; they will meet their equals, and very often their superiors, in everyday society here.[5] Place Hobarton by any town at home; canvass the inhabitants of each, and compare results; then see if we cannot fairly establish a claim for equality. In the English town, rolling by in their father's equipage, the daughters of a well-fee'd physician head the élite, and make the surgeon's daughter jealous. Here the young wife of a Government officer presides over the mysteries of the Government clique, while the banker's family shines pole-star to professional fashion. We must not include the military in either census, for they are the same everywhere, adding to the gaiety, if not to the glory, of a town. Here, though, the 99th has been so long settled, that it has married down into parental soberness, and so become bone of our bone and flesh of our flesh, that we shall feel it when they are ordered elsewhere.[6] In the English town the wife of a retired naval captain leads the decorums of the religious world, and stands placard pillar to all solemnities. *Here* the bishop's wife as ably, and far more appropriately, officiates for the piously inclined.'

'I think you are very hard on poor mamma, uncle.'

'I haven't patience with such idleness in persons who have had relations in the Australias for years; to sit still in contented ignorance of the state of their friends (ignorance which they would be ashamed to acknowledge of a foreign country) is unpardonable, I think.'

'But uncle, it is not only mamma who says such things. The Hills spoke against Tasmania, and the two Mr. Joneses, who came back just before we left England, spread an evil report. They said it was a horrid place, and that the people were rich and rough, caring for no one but themselves, and unable to appreciate quiet worth.'

'Well, well, I suppose we must plead guilty to the charge of the Messrs. Jones. We *were* unable to appreciate them according to the high standard of appreciation they set upon themselves. They, with hundreds of discarded claimants for British patronage, abjured their native land, thinking they had only to fix their colonial locality, and Caesar's message to the Roman senate would be their motto.[7] They arrived, and were disappointed. They found that the refuse of the professional roll, or the plucked candidates for academic honours, were not more acceptable here than at home. They learned the wholesome, though distasteful lesson, that Tasmania wants not such men as they, but earnest, intelligent men, who forswear England, not because they are too stupid to advance there, but because others have entered and won the field before them. The shipment of bad goods to the colony is a practical joke that Britain—legal, commercial, and parental—is very fond of playing. But ours is a case of Jones *versus* Tasmanian society in its generally accepted sense, and not of Jones *versus* colonial immigration. But I expect Miss Bridget regrets having brought forward those worthy gentlemen.'

'Oh dear no! I enjoy your lectures, Uncle Ev, when you don't get fierce.'

Uncle Ev put up his eyebrows, but somehow he could not manage to look formidable or wolfish, so he let them down again, and asked Bridget if he should continue his lecture as it still wanted three parts of an hour to lunch. Bridget said she would permit him to continue on one consideration, that he would allow he had as much pleasure in giving it as she and Em in listening to it. Uncle Ev was not sufficiently sure of this; therefore he would not allow any such weakness on his part. Bridget therefore excused him, declaring she felt pleasure enough to atone for all his shortcomings; but she begged him to be serious, for she really wished to know the habits of the people with whom she might live out her days, and when he spoke in fun she never understood him. However, Uncle Ev did not need a caution; he was sober enough for his sober subject; and sounding his usual ahem, commenced by saying—

'Society in the mother-country is a name given to a class claiming precedence of other communities, and arrogating to itself the power of electing or refusing members, according to its established rules. It has certain priveliges which it dispenses under the strict superindendence of its trustees: Fashion and Rank. Society in the child-country has, with a little difference, the same definition; but the difference, being only of circumstance, does not involve disparity. Society in the old country has the frost of age and the gray of experience upon it, and is consequently calm in its politeness, calculating in its preferences, and so exclusive as to be almost unwilling to admit additional members, though they prove themselves worthy of admittance by its own severe tests. Society here has the bloom of fresh-blown youth upon it, and is sprightly, generous, frank and ever ready to welcome newcomers who can stand the trials of its less critical, though not less strict formula. The faults of society here are the faults of youth; but to me they are more easy to bear than the prejudices of age. Specimens of the genus Jones, who think to impose on it by thrusting themselves, unintroduced and uninvited, on its attention, meet with a repulse as warm and demonstrative, as they would cold and punctilious, were they to propose a similar liberty with society at home. Persons bringing to the colony neither introduction not recommendation in mind, body or estate, may remain as long without the pale of Tasmanian society as they would beyond the recognition of English society; but let them come with letters from mutual friends, and they will be admitted with hospitable courtesy into the private circle. Let them come pleading auld lang syne, and they will be received openhearted; or let them claim the stranger's sympathy, or wayfarer's privilege, and the right of fellowship will be nobly extended; and if they not be ushered into the presence termed, *par excellence*, 'Society,' they will be warmed at the hearth of the inner shrine, and be cheered on their way by the kindly greetings of their host, and by the gentle ministrations of his family.

'The grand mistake made in England is that persons may come out here to *be* anything or *do* anything without loss of caste. There's poor Kingsby; you remember him?' (turning to Emmeline.) 'He read pleasant fictions of colonial indifference to position; and having been persuaded that here he might employ himself in any manner without disparagement to his position, he brought out his wife and family, and opened a grocer's shop. He was disappointed. "Friend, go down lower," was very plainly intimated to him when himself and Mrs. Kingsby proceeded to write their names at Government House. Calls abundant were made on him, but at his shop, and not at his private door. His wife—as lady-like a woman as I have met with—told me, with tears in her eyes, that she was willing to bend to her altered circumstances, but found it difficult to meet the butcher's and confectioner's wives on terms of equality. The chemist's and the ironmonger's wives considered it a condescension to call upon her.'

'What has become of Mr. Kingsby, uncle?' asked Emmeline.

'Oh, poor fellow, he found that folk who cannot keep grocer's shops at home cannot keep them out here. He did not understand business, and failed. He could not resume his profession, having at first appeared on the stage as a tradesman. He tried many trades, but succeeded in none. I secured him a position in the convict department; but he could not make the two ends meet. He got into debt, and, with the hope of bettering his prospects, re-emigrated. The last I heard of him was that he lay a-dying, broken in spirits and in health, whilst his wife plied out her life with the needle. It would be well if a few of these deterring cases were published side by side with the brilliant accounts that entice so many to leave well for worse.

'Now, then, Miss D'Urban, I think the fear of another such lecture will keep you from inveighing against us again.'

'No, indeed. I haven't heard half enough. I want to be wide awake to people, and I vote you continue your lecture until lunch really comes. I hear knives rattling downstairs, so it will be here presently.'

'That is after the fashion of the child who said tea must be coming because he heard the burnt toast being scraped; eh Bridget? As to continuing my address: I have only now to give you a caution on the application on what you have heard. You must be careful to apply my remarks to society as a *whole*, and not to individuals or families. I challenge the visitor only to a comparison of the number and eligibility of persons to exchange with him the cards, civilities, parties and socialities of polite life. I only assert that he has no right to complain of the want of companionable society. That the government officers, professional men, many of the merchants and landed proprietors, with their wives, are a class as worthy of the technicality "polite society," as any similar class is at home, is all I seek to maintain. When the visitor reminds me that all these have children, I cannot take him without the domestic veil, and bid him continue his comparison with England, where no baneful convict influence undermines infantile principle, or hardens the young heart into callous indifference to crime and its debasing consequences. Our drawing-rooms may vie with the luxuries of a British home; but whilst we are subject to such disturbances as those you witnessed on your arrival, the sanctuary of our inner life cannot compare with English comforts. The visitor who admires his smiling hostess, sees her not when she merges into the distracted housewife, finding one of her servants has absconded to save the penalty of an expensive breakage, and the other is lying drunk along the kitchen floor. When that gentleman in his turn becomes the host, he knows not that his lively guest will leave him to become the despairing mother, for during her absence her babe has been drugged with opium by her convict nurse, and it is doubtful whether it will ever awake from its profound sleep. The traveller notes with kindly pleasure the exultant air with which a handsome mother exhibits her offspring; but he hears not her after sigh when she discovers her little ones playing over a disgusting drama that convict actors have rehearsed before them.'

'Oh! now, Uncle Ev, I'm sure you are taking barrister's privilege, and making a great deal out of nothing.'

'You doubt me? What do you think of that rogue Master Charles? His favourite game is trying to simulate intoxication. After that affair with Nancy, I caught him going over it in the nursery. Pridham was acting Nancy; and there was he roaring it away in imitation of me. When I told him to stop he seemed quite aggrieved, and begged me to wait, 'cause the constable was coming in a minute, and then 'twould be such fun.'

Mr. Evelyn here walked abruptly from his niece—a courtesy that generally concluded all convict discourses.

'Well, I think Uncle Ev is a very funny man: he won't let me speak against the place, and yet he rails unsparingly at it,' said Bridget, proceeding to clear the table for Pridham, who brought in the lunch-tray.

'No, no, Bridgy; he rails neither at place nor people: he only deplores, as everyone must, the system which makes the latter unhappy, and the former an unsuitable abode for children.'

'Well, I think it is very wicked to hate the poor convicts. They can't help being here: they must go where they are sent.'

'No right-minded person does hate them.'

'You and Uncle Herbert, I know, don't; but I'm sure Uncle Ev does: he even gets angry when he talks about them.'

'You mistake, dear. No one is more truly kind and forebearing with them, whilst kindness and forebearance are of any use. He may hate, to use your pet word, the body of sin which the prisoners represent, but not the individual convict.'

'I think he is very hard upon them. He does not trust them as I'm sure Uncle Herbert would.'

'Papa is Christ's minister, and avoids having more to do with them in every-day life than I'm sure he can help; but when necessary he is as strict with them as Uncle Ev, and can assume as much severity.'

'Ah! I've caught out; for all that you won't allow me to speak against dear old Uncle Ev. *Assumes!* Yes, it may be that with your angel of a father; but severity is pretty real with Uncle Ev when he rates the convicts.'

' When it is *real* , Bridgy, it is always deserved; but his anger is more often put on than felt. Then, of course, between his and papa's manner there is the difference of character, and—'

She stopped. Her cousin perceived it was for some other cause than to sip her beef tea.

'Let's here the rest of the "and," Em darling. You had better now, for I half guess it.'

Em smiled, and shook her head.

'And besides, papa is a Christian. That's what you were going to say.'

Em shook her head, and replied—

'So is Uncle Ev.'

'Papa is a servant of God, then?'

'So I hope is Uncle Ev.'

'Then I don't know; and unless you tell me, I shall put some awful "and," such as—'

'Hush, hush Bridget, don't joke. I was only thinking that, perhaps, papa seeks special grace from God to enable him to manage his prisoners, and to subdue all angry feelings in dealing with them.'

'Well, I wish Uncle Ev would seek some too, for really I'm tired already. I haven't been here a week, and there have been no end of rows. Besides, it's so horrid to see people always wretched; it makes one feel almost wicked when one laughs. I don't wonder now that such a sad look has fixed into Uncle Herbert's face. There, again, Miss Em; explain why, if Uncle Ev cares as much for the prisoners as your papa, he has not got the same sorrowful countenance instead of that round merry one, so full of fun, that makes one laugh to look at it—when he doesn't grow savage at convicts, that is.'

She was delighted that she had at last puzzled Emmeline; but Miss Evelyn only waited until she became more serious to answer.

'It is easily explained, Bridget. Papa yearns over them as immortal beings, who may be saved while this life lasts, but who must be eternally lost if, when death comes, they have not turned to God through their Saviour. So he watches each moment of their passing lives as though they were all dying men, and as though each moment increased the mighty work to be accomplished before their death. When hope is over, and one poor soul has fled, papa turns soul-sick away; but his work is not done: he must watch on; he has hundreds to care for. No one could keep so perpetual a watch without showing it in his countenance.'

'Poor dear Uncle Herbert! I'm sure heaven would be full if he could save sinners.'

'What does Abraham say to Dives, Bridget? One who suffered more than we may ever know—one who now watches for the prodigal's return— *can* save, and is longing to save sinners, and yet heaven is not full! Salvation is God's to give, but man's to accept. Papa may take the precious offer to them, but he cannot make them accept it.'

'Don't let us talk anymore about it, it's so dreadful to think of people being lost, especially poor convicts, who haven't even happiness in this world.'

Emmeline's serene eyes looked out on the lawn. Bridget's were abstractedly set on the table as she took to her lunch: her brow was clouded over by some dark thought, that, passing over her spirit, excluded its radiance from shining through to give her countenance its wonted sunniness.

'Uncle is coming in, Bridget. I see him by the hedge of roses. Don't resume the convict subject, it always distresses him now.'

'Why *now* more than before?'

'I do not refer to a very present *now*; it commenced years ago, when he married, believing that transportation would cease. Before that time he gave himself wholly to the work of reforming prisoners for his share of the burden.'

'It is that which seems odd to me, from being so kind, to turn against them all of a sudden.'

'I wish I could disentangle that notion from your mind. Uncle Ev has *not* turned against them. I doubt he was ever what *you* would call kind to them. In those days of which I speak he was as strict and uncompromising as he is now. Before you charge him with undue severity, see and hear other owners!'

But Bridget still appeared to have her own thoughts on the subject. She nodded as though she would say, 'There is something wrong somewhere.'

'Come now, Bridget, I won't have you get out of love with dear good Uncle Ev.'

'Out of love with him! No indeed; his affection for you all will always prevent that, to say nothing of my own particular regard for him. All I am out of love with is the *rows*. Answer me one more question, and then I won't tease you further. Do you know I am quite ashamed of being such a goose to have come all this way to be puzzled with news of my native land. So before I meet other visitors, I want to learn all I can.'

She knelt down, and, resting her elbows on the sofa, looked up to Emmeline in her old English fashion.

'Tell me, before Uncle Ev comes in, why he expects transportation to this colony to cease; and if it isn't rather selfish to wish to turn over to another country that which he considers so great an evil to this.'

'You must seek information from a better source: you can hardly read a newspaper without meeting with a reply.'

'Oh! I hate newspapers; one has to read so much to find out ever so little. *You* can tell me why Uncle Ev always is so angry when he talks of convicts or transportation.'

'He is only one of a thousand who feel that it is time to relieve this beautiful country of a burden that it has quietly borne, and over which it would never have murmured had it been removed at the time promised by the government.'

'But that's just what seems so unfair to me. After you've got all the good you can out of the convicts, to want to send them away directly they are of no more use. On shipboard I used to hear the captain talk of all the buildings, roads and works they had done for the colony: from what he said, Tasmania owes to them her present position. Now, haven't you been the gainer by them for all that you cry out on transportation?'

'The benefit has been mutual. England gave us convicts to do our work, and we gave England's convicts work to do, and land-room in which to do it. Hush, here he is.'

Uncle Ev's quick step in the veranda, and he entered, beaming and bright as the day itself.

'What do you think of this for a fine December day? Rather too warm for wool, isn't it? Our Midsummer Christmases are charmingly defiant of Thomson's "Seasons," are they not?[8] And yet it's very odd; for all the evidences of the five senses you can't get folks to divest themselves of the mother-country's poetic associations. I suppose they won't, until the British blood becomes too infinitesimal for even homoeopathic discovery.'[9]

Bridget jumped up, and soon forgot the convict turmoil in the beauties of a large nosegay of roses, which Uncle Ev had thrown towards her.

'Now then, peer about for your gowns,' said Mr. Evelyn, as he shut the garden gate and offered Bridget his arm to escort her to Government House.

'Oh, Charlie, Charlie! come, quick, look at that funny man. It's a juggler, isn't it, uncle?'

Charlie came running back to see the funny man, but he looked about in vain, until his cousin pointed to a man dressed in a piebald suit of yellow and blue.

'Oh, you stupid! He's a prisoner: couldn't you see that in a minute? I s'pose he's a 'sconder, because the constable's got a big gun to shoot him if he isn't good. Ah! ah! ah! What a stupid, Bridget, not to know a pisner when he's got chains on his feet and hands.'

This little fact had escaped her notice, the grotesque dress and leathern cap having absorbed her attention. As the man passed by, the broad arrow on his back showed itself—symbolic alike of Government's claim on the body, and the Evil One's claim on the soul of the poor sinner. Bridget felt half frightened, and clung to her uncle's arm as the man raised his head and gave her a sullen side glance.

'Run on Charlie boy, and find out something better than that to show your cousin.'

Off ran the child, nothing doubting of his father's convict inclinations.

'Oh! I'll show her a lot presently.'

And, true to his word, on turning into the next street he exclaimed—

'There's a whole gang of them—everyone is pisners.'

He pointed to a party of men, chained and similarly dressed to the piebald they had just passed. Some of the men were working in the road, others drawing carts of stones, and others, more heavily ironed, were assisting their mates by various lesser services.

'Don't fear, Bridget,' whispered Uncle Ev, feeling her arm tremble; 'just follow me whilst I lift the child over this quagmire.'

She picked her path across the broken ground, hardly venturing to turn her head, lest the men should think she was staring at them; but no reciprocal delicacy possessed the gang, for they one and all rested on their spades to gaze at her, and two nearer to her than the others nudged each other, and then the nearest approached quickly yet stealthily, and muttered something which she could not understand, but she fancied it sounded like—'Give us a fig.' She hastened forward in spite of the mud; the gang dropped back demurely to their work, for the overseer came round.

Mr. Evelyn laughed as Bridget caught hold of his arm.

'Oh, uncle! They spoke to me,' she was too alarmed to say more.

'Well, they do not seem to have hurt you very much. What did they want of you? Something very innocent, I'll dare answer.'

'I couldn't make out what they said; it sounded like "a fig" something.'

'They thought your greenness betokened figs, or, in plain language, tobacco. "A fig of baccy" is the humble form of request; it is left to the donor's generosity to understand it more munificently. But do you know that you might get those men punished for speaking to you, if you were mischievously inclined? Had the overseer heard them, a few days of solitary would have been the consequence; it's astonishing what the poor fellows will risk for tobacco. Here we are at Government House; allow me to introduce you to the abode of vice-royalty.'

Bridget laughed as the lowly wooden building presented itself to receive her homage.[10]

'What a queen-like residence!'

'It's a pretty cottage; but as the allotted dwelling of his Excellency a scandal to Tasmania—a scandal that is kept in company by the handsome pension of twelve pounds a year wherewith government rewards Buckley for his valuable services to Australia. However, Government House is more comfortable within than stately without.'[11]

The call of ceremony being over, and Lady Denman not being at home to receive their friendly visit, Mr. Evelyn proposed a stroll through the principal streets.

'Do you perceive how the habits and arrangements of London are followed in public life here? The street-cries are perpetuated. The cabmen are so determined to carry out the usages of their fraternity that they even imitate their metropolitan brethren in a strike for higher fares. See that rank of cabs: there is no heavy country driver asleep on his box whilst the passenger gets into his neighbour's cab; all is animation and show of arms, as each one asserts his peculiar readiness to "take you in" in more ways than one. A wink would bring half a dozen babblers to your side.

'The incongruous medley of shops, rich and poor together, is London-like. Butcher, baker, grocer, all appear to have served their apprenticeship in the capital; the cut of the meat, the shape of the bread, the adulteration of the groceries, are in dutiful or unintended remembrance of cockney education.'

'Are all the tradespeople of London origin that it should be so, uncle?'

'By no means. Trades from every part of Britain have settled here. Every county has its representative, every provincial custom its follower. Every grade and every phase of English life meet out here. It is probably this very amalgamation that reproduces the English metropolis. Were each country to send forth a body sufficient to exist independently, that body might establish itself into an exclusive colony; in habits, provincialities, and dialect the counterpart of its parent. But as each district doles out its living gratuities to the colonial fund in ones and twos at a time, the result is a commingling of numbers into a family, who, having higher interests at stake than the cherishing of local identities, consent to forego, if not to forget their home peculiarities or only to preserve them where they add to the public good. Babel-like confusion would ensue from this general condensation were it not that man, individually or collectively, will have a leader, how much soever he affects to despise being led. "Nay but we will have a king to reign over us," is the universal principle of the human heart. Unaware to himself, a master spirit works his way upward; and, unaware to itself, the community yields to him,—adopting his habits, thinking his thoughts and seeing with his eyes. The Londoner has evidently been that spirit out here, as he will be elsewhere, until persons are undeceived of that notion, that the words "From London" on a country sign-board denote superior goods or able workmen.

'To the same cause may be attributed the freedom from peculiarity in the tone and pronunciation of the natives. As children they have no opportunity to contract the nasal twang or gutturals of any particular province; by the constant change of servants, and from an intercourse with a diversity of accents, they are preserved from fixing on any one peculiarity. The Irish brogue heard to-day is to-morrow changed for the broad Scotch accent; the Devonshire drawl soon forgotten in the London affectation; the Somersetshire z's are lost in the Yorkshire oo's. If you have not already remarked it, you cannot fail shortly to note how very well the common children speak, even where the parents set them no good pronunciative example.'

A party of children passed by, and as their speech was in bold defiance of Mr. Evelyn's assertion, Bridget looked up rather quizzically at her uncle, who said:

'Of course I do not refer to fresh importations; they have to unlearn home acquirements: I allude to the genuine born or bred Tasmanian. As yet the Australian colonies have given but few contributions to their mother-tongue; doubtless in time they will compile an appendix descriptive of their habits and modes of life. Already the characteristics of a new race begin to develop, and in another generation they will arrange themselves into distinct features. Well, what do you think of Hobarton? This is about the best part of the city. Look at these houses; they certainly want the substantiality of English buildings; but as to appearance, what could excel them? In some streets relics of the infant aspirations of the first settlers are still to be seen in the form of ground-floor cottages and make-do dwellings; but these only serve to demonstrate the fact that we have put away childish things. The architectural fault *now* seems to partake of that which is incident to youth. The houses uprear themselves with a speed that suggests instability: and too often a draughty door or shrunken skirting-board intimates that next time the timber might with advantage, be better seasoned. Whether from the elasticity imparted by the climate, or from the owner's hurry to have a roof over his head, it is certain that structures are raised from foundation to garret with an amazing rapidity. Here a house is planned, built, and inhabited before a similar one at home has passed from the mason's hands.'

But Bridget was tired, and did not appear to care about timber, seasoned or unseasoned. In answer to her repressed yawn, Mr. Evelyn said—

'Come then, let us home; to-morrow we will explore Newtown; its beautiful villas and tasteful gardens will repay research, and atone for the dulness of to-day's expedition.'[12]

'Oh, uncle, I'm only too surprised to express pleasure; I had no idea there would be such beautiful places here. And as to the shops—people wouldn't make so great a to-do about outfits if they could take a peep at them. That one, now, is almost as splendid as a Regent Street shop.'

'Almost, indeed! Every species of domestic need, comfort, and luxury, is amply furnished by the enterprising tradesmen, who at once make others comfortable and themselves rich. In *there* is a fellow making his fortune. He will spread a supper or dinner with any London cook. He is our Gunter; come in and test him, by way of refreshing yourself; an ice—or at any rate, *ice*—is as seasonable here in December as it is at home. An ice-house on Mount Wellington keeps Webb as popular through the torrid weather as his entertainments do through the winter. Literary supplies alone are inefficient; and yet I mustn't say that—small as they are, they meet the present demand. Doubtless, when literary yearnings increase, the means of satisfying them will also increase. A year or two ago, Longfellow's poems were not procurable in the colony; nobody knew that such a poet had ever lived. *Now* "Evangeline" has become a household deity, and everyone has learnt that life is real—life is earnest. [13] A few years since, parents were obliged to wait for the eligibility of a certain prisoner, of whose superior education they had heard, if they wanted a tutor or governess for their children. *Now* there is Bishopbourne for the boys; girls, I think with my wife, are still badly off for good schools. [14]

As they entered the garden gate, Charlie, who had run on in advance, came bounding back, panting with news he was eager to impart.

'She's found! She's found! They had such fun to catch her. Bradley says she fought like a tiger; she's bit his hand drefful. Won't she get a pretty sentence, that's all!'

'Charlie, Charlie, who have you been talking to? You forget papa's orders,' cried Mr. Evelyn.

'Nobody; only Pridham was waiting to tell us. Bradley stopped here to get a drink of water, and Nancy did nearly get away again—nasty beast!'

Pridham came forward, and the child continued—

'Here she is—such fun! Come and tell all about it.'

'Go back, Pridham; I will thank you to remember my commands, and not give Master Charles information of this kind. You will get into trouble if you're not more careful,' said her master.

The hint was sufficient. The air of importance vanished more quickly from Pridham's face than her person disappeared behind the kitchen-door. Whilst Mr. Evelyn spoke to her, Charlie drew close to Bridget, and winking a sly childish wink, he whispered—

'She gave Nancy something to eat, but mustn't let papa know; and Bradley got a drink of beer, really—not water—hush-sh he'll hear.'

CHAPTER 18

Aunt Evelyn and Family Matters

BRIDGET rejoiced in the prospect of Mrs. Evelyn's return. Curiosity alone did not prompt her joy. She longed to see what sort of an aunt she possessed under that title; but she longed still more to resign the honours of housekeeping. With girlish delight she had entered on those honours; her delight, however, soon changed into discomfort, when she found that more was expected of her as mistress than to jingle her keys, to weigh out the servants' rations, and to order dinner. Dinner-hour nearly trespassed on tea-hour, before the united muddlings of herself and Robert produced the desired effect in turning raw mutton into haricot, and an untrussed fowl into a roast.[1] After such a forenoon's muddle, it was with almost maternal pride that she watched the serving-up of the viands; and many persons will know how mortified even to tears she must have been when an unwitting blow from Uncle Ev struck down her pride. Shutting his eyes towards the dish at the bottom of the table, he asked—

'What, in the name of wonder, could be that smoky hodge-podge keeping this tough underdone joint in company?'

Emmeline saw the pain he was inflicting, but on her sofa she was too distant to stop further mischief. Pointing to the pease, Uncle Ev said—

'There Miss D'Urban, you see the hated badge, even in the face of nature, is doomed to twit us. She made those pease green, but art perpetuates in them the "colonial everbrown."'

Before Bridget had been a fortnight in the office, she determined that her aunt must be a being of mighty intellect and power, if she manages to call even a tolerable order from chaos so decided that, like the Egyptian darkness, it might be felt. [2]

Mr. Evelyn hired a man to supply one of the vacancies left by Nancy and her bacchanalian colleague. Robert Sanders had just become eligible as he applied at the barracks for an able servant. He knew it would be useless to inquire for one who could be recommended as a cook; such men being generally reserved for Government service, or pre-appropriated to families in whom the superintendent had private or politic interest. The list of 'eligibles' was not very startling. A man, willing-minded and sharp, was all Mr. Evelyn expected from it. Such a one appeared Robert Sanders. The brief dialogue which took place prefatory to his engagement will attest his willingness.

'Your name?' asks Mr. Evelyn.

'Robert Sanders, or anything your honour pleases.'

'Your trade?'

'*Hostler* - but I ain't partial; I can give a h'ist to aught that's wanted.'

'Do you think you can cook?'

His eyes glistened; he was fond of cookery if not of cooking.

Catching hold of his cropped hair, he says—

'Well, I b'lives I'll handle the wittels as well as most on 'em as don't know nothin' about it. Anyways, I'm willin' for it.'

'Your crime is burglary?'

''Es, sure, that's what they calls it; can't say I didn't lift the swag[3] when Sam Tomkins got in and pulled open the door; darned good her did me, though!'

'What is your religion?'

'I ain't partial; don't know as I've choice that way whatever your honour's a mind to 'll suit me. If your honour hires me out, you won't find me stick to trifles in nothin'.'

His eagerness to be engaged was so great, that there is no knowing where it would have hurried him; his willingness became alarming, and Mr. Evelyn hastened to put a stop to it by bidding him pack up his bundle, and follow him; on which Sanders gave a great gulp of satisfaction, and smothered his roots with his fingers, as though administering salve to his closely-cropped head.

When Uncle Ev presented this new curiosity to Bridget, he told her he hoped she would get him into train against her aunt returned. She stood aghast; not observing the sly twinkle in his eye, she thought he really meant what he said. Turning to Robert, he said—

'Your mistress is from home, Sanders; you will therefore do this young lady's commands for the present.'

Then to Bridget—

'Remember, if Sanders is refractory, I am always at hand.'

'Very good, sir,' responded the man. 'I b'an't much of a hand with the leddies, seeing I've been brought up to hosses but I knows what *come* means, and I knows what *go* means; so the young leddy 'll find me willin', darned if she won't.'

'Well, well, let it be so; and I hope we shall not have to trouble Government much about you, except for the muster report.'

'Very good, sir; I'm willin' as any feller goin'.'

'Give him something to eat, Bridget;' (in a lower tone) 'I'd rather *you* should than Pridham, or he may overeat himself the first time;' (then aloud) 'there is plenty of cold meat; carve him some, for he missed his dinner at Tench.'[4]

So she cut a plate of mutton, which, with a hunch of bread, and the remains of a gooseberry pudding, she set before him. How his eyes did expand as he sat down! To Bridget's horror, he mixed meat, pudding, and bread into one mess and then commenced to eat it with the iron tablespoon, only giving himself breath to ejaculate 'bootiful!' 'rare!' between the huge mouthfuls. When he had finished he pushed the dish from him, and exclaimed, 'Thank'ee, miss;' then, starting back in his chair, he arose with a suddenness that overwhelmed table, its contents, and all the fire-irons.

'Oh, dear! that wern't a lucky hit. Go up, yer ginger,' cried Robert. 'Never mind, I bain't hurt, miss;' broken crockery was of no consequence at all.

With this man began Bridget's domestic trials. She refrained from worrying Emmeline with many tales of distress; but every now and then even her elastic spirit would be overstretched, and confide in her cousin she must. Had Robert's powers been equal to his willingness, he would have done well, and Bridget's task would have been less irksome. We do not insinuate that he was what is emphatically called *deficient,* either in mind or body, but he needed a certain power of discernment in the daily proprieties of life. For instance, when his young mistress found him wiping the dinner plates with a used up pocket handkerchief, he took her remonstrance as directed against the use of his *own* property on his master's china, and replied—

'Never fear miss, it's too bastely for augh else; I've quite used 'em up. What if I hadn't? I ain't one to set store on my things, beyont fetchin' ' em out when they's wanted. I'm willin' to do my best for the master.'

No argument could persuade him that *disgust*, and not dislike to incur an obligation, caused the young lady's protest against the blue kerchief. The 'never fears' were repeated with an increased willingness, with an addition that made Bridget shudder whenever after she thought of dish clouts.

Another time, when the meat should have been on the spit, she found not the *sirloin*, but Robert roasting before the fire. His trousers were tucked above his knees, and he was chafing his stockingless feet, his legs luxuriously expanded to the two chimney ends.

'Robert, what will Mr. Evelyn say if dinner is late again?'

'All right, miss, was just a-thinking if 'tweren't time to handle the wittels; a pretty bit of eatin' in that j'int. I'll be after 'en when I've got a bit of the torment out of these darned legs.'

In one item of domestic service, however, he was particularly expert, and particularly delighted. In the boot and shoe department he was at home, there fondly dreaming the leathern array before him into so many horses awaiting professional attendance. He could not have too many pairs to clean, and the muddier they were the better was he pleased. At the sight of a boot or shoe, down would drop the basting-spoon or saucepan, and off would rush Robert to the prize; and it was no matter who should attend to the cookery so long as he seized the opportunity of flourishing away over an imaginary steed, now admonishing it with a 'Y'up there!' 'Ho here!' 'Still, you beggar!' as the shoe might slip from his hand; then consoling both himself and it with the prolonged sis-s-s peculiar to his trade.

Miss D'Urban's troubles also arose from her own ignorance of household matters; a thousand times she wished that a little instruction from Mrs. Rundle had taken turns with a lesson from Monsieur de Tiptoe, and a hint or two from the housemaid had alternated with the music master's raps. She then might have committed fewer of those blunders which, when they were harmless, were as good as nuts to Uncle Ev. One of these blunders left so painful a recollection behind it, that she quite dreaded the appearance of a certain dish on the table, lest it should call forth a sly allusion to the unfortunate affair that has passed into the bye-word, 'Bridget's geese.' With other charges she had received thirteen geese, the special pets of Mrs. Evelyn. The steady bipeds did not require much of her time; when she had given them a feed of oatmeal, turned them out into the paddock, and then again housed them for the night, that was all she had to do for them. This she faithfully performed, every evening the punctual creatures hissed for admittance, and every evening they were admitted; and all went on well. But as summer advanced the heat proportionately increased, and, to the signal discomfiture of grazing animals, the herbage proportionately decreased; consequently the thirteen found but small nibbling work in the paddock. Yet it never occurred to Bridget to deal out a larger or second ration. She observed that the grass had withered, but with that observation she connected no supposition of hunger on the part of the geese. One day the whole flock stoutly refused to be shown into the field, and when Bridget insisted with the joint power of her mouth, hands and apron, the thirteen put their necks together in consultation, and then, with a deafening clatter, they mounted and flew into the neighbouring paddock. Driven thence the poor things came back, and disconsolately wandered about their own domain for the rest of the afternoon. Day after day this scene was repeated, still Bridget never suspected the cause, and the only light Robert could cast on their erratic propensities was: 'He didn't know nothin' about *geese*, sein' he was brought up to hosses, but he sposed 'twas cos their wings wasn't clipped.'

Uncle Ev was up country to bring home his wife and baby, so he could not solve the daily migration. Uncle Herbert no one ever dreamed of disturbing with domestic perplexities, and out of love, Bridget rarely disturbed Emmeline with them. Glowing were the accounts Bridget wrote to her aunt; she begged not to be accused of vanity in telling how very fond the dear geese had become of her; indeed, they never caught a glimpse of her without cackling *such* a welcome, and it was quite ridiculous to see how they all rushed to meet her, and twicked her dress with delight. Mrs. Evelyn should judge for herself; and true enough, when that lady returned and went into the paddock to view the miracle, the thirteen flew open-winged towards her niece, and set up so outrageous, so eventful a greeting, that two dropped down dead at her feet.

'Starved to death!' cried Mrs. Evelyn, examining the feathered skeleton. 'Those rogues have stolen the food from the poor things.'

'Oh no dear aunt, I assure you I fed them myself every morning.'

'And no more?' cried Aunt Ev still more shrilly.

'No, I thought they grazed.'

'Yes, when they have the opportunity,' replied Uncle Ev, who unobserved, had followed them to see the prodigy of affection. Two more victims perished; the other nine recovered under the happier auspices of Mrs. Evelyn's tendance.

Aunt Evelyn was exactly the opposite to all Bridget had pictured her. She was a native, and had the fair skin, slender figure, and long limbs of the Tasmanian, with the not less characteristic, but more painful colonial feature—prematurely decayed and broken teeth.[5] *Now* thirty guineas refill a mouth with as ornamental, if not as useful, a set as that provided by nature. *Then* Mrs. Evelyn had to bear tooth-ache and tooth *want*, until some years later, when an American dentist settled in Hobarton, affording the inhabitants a chance of transferring their gold from their pockets to their mouths.[6] It was from this clever artist that she gained, not only her *third* teeth, but her first thoughts of the millennium. He was wont to alleviate the pain it was his profession to inflict by holding sweet talk on the blissful subject. 'Do you believe in the millennium?' he whispered to her, as faint from the extraction of three long roots she leaned back to yield a fourth to that cruel instrument. She nodded assent with a silent hope that there might be either no teeth or no dentists in the period so called. Others, to whom he put the same question, shook their heads either at *it* or at his mode of exhibiting it; whilst one gentleman, less refined or more tortured, was heard to roar. 'Hang the millennium sir! What has it to do with my tooth or your forceps?'

Mr. Evelyn had always declared that he would neither marry a colonial, nor a woman younger than himself; but men are quite as apt as the other sex to mistake their minds on subjects matrimonial. For all that, Clara M'Rock was a colonial, and not nineteen: for all that, he felt so safe in her society, because he was so old and she such a child to him: for all that she walked, talked and rode with him without compunction, because he was old enough to be my father—one day the gossip went round that positively Mr. Evelyn's declaration was about to split on the Rock Clara. And he did not deny it; but strove hard to prove that, though a native, Miss M'Rock could not be fairly considered *Colonial*, she having been educated in England from her twelfth year, a fact over which the lady herself was most scrupulously careful, lest it should be forgotten when the ornamental reminders of such an education lost themselves in the homely duties of married life. Whilst quick to resent charges brought by strangers against the colony, she felt herself privileged by her

English training to animadvert all that in public or private life could be termed colonial. When her first little girl was born into the world, she became eloquent on the subject of female education, inveighing against the manner in which girls were brought up, and the limited means afforded for teaching them the way they should go; whereas boys were well provided with schools and tutors.

'Schools!' she would ask, 'where are they? There is plenty of puffing and advertising, but there is not that one in the place to which I would send a daughter of mine. Every dissenting minister's widow or unfortunate speculator's wife opens a school, *fitness* for the post being the least consideration. Everyone recommends a pet teacher, but then superiority in *need*, and not in ability, dictates the recommendation.'

Towards such private governesses as were then she was equally hostile, and determined that no child of hers should ever be instructed by a colonial governess; and when Mr. Evelyn remarked, 'Give me a daughter dutiful and affectionate, and I will not ask her many questions in geology,' she replied that he would have to refrain from much more simple subjects if he did not send the youthful Clara to England, or engage a lady whose mind did not run on marriage in connection with her visit to the Antipodes.

It was at the age of twenty that Mrs. Evelyn entered on the duty of mother to a little girl, who, after four years, resigned in death her place in her parents' affection to Master Charles, the bouncing rogue of the present volume. To him succeeded another girl, whose acquaintance Bridget has just made, and who, as she lies crowing in her cot in answer to her papa's whistle, numbers seven months to her brief existence; but brief as her existence is, it has not escaped the evils incident to convict proximity. There is no such happy fortune for even the youngest who dwells within sound of prison bells. From the hoary grandsire to the latest addition to his race, all must feel the effects of a system which strikes immediately at the root of that tree called olive. Then why should exemption be urged for Baby Evelyn, the tiniest offshoot of the tree? If parental fondness did plead it, it was not granted; for she was scarcely five months old ere a perilous mischance befell her as follows.

Betsy, the nurse, had been so steady for eleven months that one Sunday her master thought he might venture to send her out alone to give the babe its usual airing. Mrs. Evelyn was unable to accompany her, and the air was too balmy and health-giving to be missed even for once. So Betsy was despatched with strict injunctions to return by noon. Proud of this first proof of a confidence for which she had long waited, she set out, determining to obey the command and be punctually home by twelve o'clock. Had temptation under any form but that through which she had previously fallen presented itself, she might have stood morally safe; but on that fatal morning the snare was irresistibly spread. The old temptation produced old longings.

She had not proceeded far before she encountered a shipmate, whose shabby attire was a certain indication that she had not kept out of trouble for long together. An exchange of questions and comparison of lucks ensued, and ended in an opinion on the stranger's side that one who had lived in so good a situation, had such smart clothes,* and well-grown hair, could not fail to have a few spare coppers in her pocket. Such coppers evidently had not vanished in spreeing, or Betsy must have been in Cage (short for Cascades), and as

---

* The dress of the better description of convict cannot fail to attract the attention of strangers, who, not knowing the peculiar significance attached to 'clothes,' may censure the master or mistress for permitting so unseemly a display on the persons of their servants. The finery is a signboard of convict respectability – i.e. freedom from trouble.

they must be somewhere, there was no place more likely than her own person. This train of reasoning the stranger pursued in silence for some time; she then startled Betsy with the inquiry:

'Will you sport an odd copper to old times?'

Betsy replied that she had taken the pledge, and hadn't tasted 'a drop of nothing' since she'd been out, and hoped she never should again.

But her companion said a glass out here wasn't like at home, 'twas more genteel; the best—what hadn't known trouble—wouldn't be ashamed of a glass of wine; the best lady in the land would be in trouble if there was harm in that sort of liquor.

Still Betsy refused.

'Well, then,' cried her tempter, 'it shan't be said that two mates met and wouldn't be friendly to past times and luck to come. I'll go and sell this bonnet off my head to fetch a sip between us, though it isn't the perlite thing to do, as them what's most respectable generally treats the other.'

Betsy's pride and convict vanity were touched, and she said she would willingly stand the treat so long as she was not pressed to drink. The friend agreed—not caring who should go without, provided she did not—and conducted Betsy to a house of the worst description, where, looking upon the wine whilst it was red,[7] Betsy's moral courage succumbed, the cup was taken, the liquor tasted, and further power of resistance gone. Other shipmates came pouring in; the time passed merrily, and when Betsy rose up to go, she promised to return on the following Sunday. She reached the Lodge only just as the clock struck twelve; the master's anger, therefore, was averted. He noticed her flushed cheeks, but accepted the explanation that she had taken the *wrong road*, and her dread of not being home by the appointed hour had 'flustered her a bit.'

Next Sunday she was again sent out, and it was deemed safe to let Charlie accompany her. During the week she had, in imagination, gone through former scenes of dissipation until her mind became inflamed, and bent on once more giving itself to those unhallowed pleasures which had caused the crime she was now atoning. She promised Charlie all manner of sweetmeats if he was a *good* boy; a peculiar meaning attached itself to this condition, and he was as good a boy as she could desire—seeing all, but repeating nothing. She was again careful to be back before the family's suspicions were aroused. The third Sunday arrived, and brought the same permission; she who had been so steady would surely not disappoint them the third time. Baby alone was confided to her care.

On Mr. and Mrs. Evelyn's return from church, no baby was to be found; however, Betsy might still be home before dinner, they only felt a little uneasy. Dinner was over and uneasiness increased into alarm. From watching at the windows and looking down the road, the parents proceeded to active measures. Tea hour passed, and alarm increased to anguish. Mrs. Evelyn now remained in the house, in case the infant should be brought in famishing for maternal care. Her friends, Dr. and Mrs. Lamb, who had hitherto been assisting in the search, sat with her, while Mr. Evelyn accompanied by a constable, went off in one direction, and a band of his friends in another.

Charlie was neglected in the general commotion; his existence was only remembered when he came in, cross and hungry, to ask where 'tea had gone to.' But crossness and hunger were both forgotten when he saw his 'own beautiful mamma' in tears. He sat quietly down, and slipped his hand into hers, until, on the point of crying himself, he slid over to Dr. Lamb, and whispered, 'Who's made her cry? Nasty people, I'll shoot them!'

Dr. Lamb whispered in return, 'Naughty Betsy hasn't come back, so mamma is afraid poor little sister is lost.'

With an appreciating nod, Charlie reseated himself.

An English child would have commenced calling up 'Children in the Wood' stories as applicable to the present case; not so this young colonist.[8] He lapsed into a thoughtful but not mysterious mood, as though he knew as well as anyone what sort of being lost this was; and how to get back baby was more the doubtful point than what had become of her. The dreary silence was at last broken by his very demure voice.

'If I could have a constable, p'raps I'd find her. I'd know it by the large pussy-cat on the wall.'

His voice became confidential.

'Only don't tell Betsy; she wouldn't give me any more lollies, and the bogie will fetch me away when it's dark.'

The result of an eager interrogation was a conviction that if only Charlie's description of 'down a nasty street, and up a nasty place,' could be defined, the lost one might be found in the Sunday rendezvous.

'Should you know the house if you saw it, my boy?' asked Dr. Lamb, determined to scour the length and breadth of Hobarton

'Oh yes! I'll peep into every door till I see the pussy, then there'll be plenty of prisoners, and fun, and baby lying down inside the other room.'

A cab was hired. Dr. Lamb's simple direction to the driver was:

'Take us to the worst place in Hobarton, then set us down and slowly follow.'

Without a comment the man drove them to——street, turned down ——street, and then silently opening the door, he gave Dr. Lamb a wink which said, 'Here or nowhere.'

Charlie was quite alive and proud of his mission. He peered into cottage after cottage, until he arrived at the fifteenth whose door alone was shut.

'Stupid!' cried Charlie; 'if 'twas open I think I'd see pussy, and then I'd know.'

Dr. Lamb rapped and entered.

'There's pussy!' cried Charlie, clapping his hands.

'Now then, my boy, jump into the cab, and wait for us; you mustn't go in with the bad people.'

Happily, the scene of vice which met Dr. Lamb's sight is hidden from us. We need not follow him, as pushing his way into an inner room, he discovered the object of his search lying asleep. From the heavy sob which disturbed the babe, it was evident that the slumber had succeeded a fit of unsoothed crying. The tears still rested on its little cheek, and as Dr. Lamb stood over it, it burst out afresh into a piteous wail, unable even in sleep to forget its wrong.

Perceiving that Betsy was not in a state to attempt escape, he hurried off with his tender burden, merely telling the woman of the house that if Betsy was not forthcoming when the constable arrived, she would stand a chance of being taken in her stead.

Relieved of her weight of domestic anxiety, Bridget again became Emmeline's chief attendant, and the happy, unclouded maiden of English days. And as, under the genial influence of summer, her cousin appeared to regain a degree of strength, and a respite from suffering, her happiness increased to merriment, and her uncloudedness into positive sunshine; and save when convict disturbances broke on the family peace, or she heard of prison miseries from Uncle Herbert, or they came under her notice in the form of chain-gangs, recaptured absconders, or the prison van conveying a load of females to the *Anson*, the flow of her joyous spirits rarely met with obstructions, for all in the house were too well pleased to have so unfailing a spring of gladness in their midst to stay one ripple of its refreshing course. This lightness of heart was a source of satisfaction to Aunt Evelyn, who gloried in stores of all kinds. Her storeroom was her particular pride; it had never yet been found deficient in yielding its weekly rations in what amount soever demanded. In Bridget she discovered a supply of good temper and vivacity likely to be as unceasing as her own bags of crushed sugar and kegs of Port Philip beef. She prized and respected her niece accordingly. Setting a utilitarian value on those qualities which made her the life of the party, she calculated that from Bridget's repository could be furnished ample assistance in household and other cares, together with a sufficient quantity of *fun* to keep the family in that pleasant article through all vicissitudes of temper.

The children loved Bridget for a not more laudable reason. Her appearance in the nursery was a signal for crow-and-caper dance to baby, whose little legs and arms set vigorously to work in anticipation of the treat.

Charlie valued her more in proportion to the races she ran with him than by proportion of the hugs she inflicted upon him. After a chase round the garden she would be 'the best Bridget in the world,' while she would be 'such a great stupid Bridget for kissing a big boy.'

Uncle Herbert experienced unconscious relaxation in his niece's society. To Emmeline he turned as to a second self, confiding to her yearning sympathies the tales of disappointment, sorrow, and sin, which each day's visit to the Penitentiary too surely afforded. Her sweet and gentle smile encouraged him, her hands clasped with his in commending to a father's care some widely wondering prodigal, her faith aspired with his, until the flame would glow, more fervent, and spiritually comforted, he again went forth to the same round of ministerial toil. This communion, therefore, was not relaxation, it was a preparation for renewed warfare. His daughter's smile but bade him forward, her prayer but regirded him for conflict, her faith but promised ultimate success; his mental energies still needed rest and an object on which to passively recruit. This object Emmeline no longer could be; her father's eye in resting on her conveyed a swift and poignant message to his soul, which stirred his jaded energies to a response full fraught with the sad surmise that through all imputed improvements she might yet be fading from his view. Emmeline felt this, and she knew that neither her cheerful countenance nor unobtrusive attentions could divest him of his misgivings. His smile was reciprocal and his eye grateful as he acknowledged her affection; but she perceived that anxiety was in the smile and pained inquiry in the eye. It was a mutual understanding, therefore, that when Mr. Herbert returned overcome by his depressing duties, too weary to seek Emmeline as a friend, listener, or sympathizer, she merely met him with the wonted caress, and then, retiring to her sofa, left the spontaneous music of Bridget's voice to soothe the worn-out mind into repose.

You must not imagine that he was given to spend his evenings in an easy-chair; an evening so spent was exceptional. When his prescribed government duties were over, he still employed himself in different ways on the prisoners' behalf—now writing to the Home Government to expose some abuse, then to the comptroller to pray for the mitigation of an unusually severe sentence. Now he would write to the English friends of a convict lying under sentence of death in the condemned cells, and who had, perhaps, that day begged him to break the dire intelligence to a fond mother or a pining wife. Then he would reply to a letter from some prisoner's relative at home, asking him to seek out such or such a one, supposed to be either dead or lost. Or else an annoying correspondence with the heads of the department would occupy his time. Such correspondence was necessarily frequent, while low officials were permitted to lay before interested secular powers charges of neglect or *excess* of duty on the part of the chaplain, and while such secular powers (of no very high standing) took on themselves the exercise of episcopal authority over him, seeming to delight in circumscribing his prerogative to the smallest possible bounds, and in making him feel himself as much under their control as was any overseer or constable.

The Bishop of Tasmania nominally reckons the convict chaplains among his clergy.[9] They are expected to show themselves at the visitations, and at public meetings convened for special clerical considerations; but here ceases the benefit of relationship to their diocesan. Not from unwillingness on his lordship's part to admit them to closer intimacy and to the full privileges of their order, but from inability to redress their grievances without an appeal to the local government, a step his lordship is naturally averse to, because it cannot fail to cause unpleasantness between himself (as the head of spiritual authority) and the colonial representative of supreme temporal authority. Therefore of all undefined positionists, the convict chaplain is the most unfortunate if he be not '*in* with the comptroller' or the superintendent of his station.

One would think that all parts of a moral machinery formed for the noble purpose of human reformation should work in unison. And does it not? asks the mere looker on, who has been admitted to inspect its able construction and varied movements. He is filled with admiration at the wondrous adaptation of each part to its peculiar end, and eulogizes the grand renovator, opining that some obstinate resistance or organic incapacity to receive improvement must exist in the object worked upon if the anticipated aim be missed. He expatiates on the exquisite order in which wheel rotates within wheel, but not having heard, he cannot be shocked by the grating of each as it turns upon its axis, for discord sets the primary wheel in motion, and its jarring is felt through the whole machine. Nor when he imputes to the object worked upon a heart hardened beyond relenting, a mind too set upon evil to be shaken by even the concentrated force of this wonderful machine, is he aware that the force is *rarely concentrated* the separate portions of the system being too divided among themselves to join their strength for the long pull, the strong pull, and the pull all together; while on that section immediately intended to act on the criminal's heart so heavy a clog is placed that its solitary endeavours are comparatively useless. The stranger knows not of these things. But to speak plainly—Is it not strange that one of the most important coadjutors in the reformatory work—one whose position is the most laborious, whose task is the most depressing, should have opposition from every official quarter instead of the assistance and sympathy he expects?—and *that*, too, where his adherence to the penal regulations is so nicely strict that not the most overbearing superintendent can charge him with irregularity or the most vigilant favourite spy out a fault. Private annoyances of the most petty kind are contrived to draw him into a quarrel.

If the chaplain be a man who would go down with the department stream, not caring into what depths of servitude it might drift him, nor into what abuse of duty it might hurry him—if he be content with the *name* of first-class officer, and suffer himself to be treated as an inferior—if he *see* all, hear all, *do* all, and say nothing—and chiefly, if he be not over godly nor too demonstrative in his life, then will he be a man after the superintendent's own heart—then, and not till then, will he find but few drawbacks to embitter his professional career, even though he be a gentleman by birth and education, even though he be unfortunately guilty of an M.A. to his name.

If you could transport yourself to a penal settlement, and there dwell for six months in the clergyman's quarters—you would perceive that Mr. Herbert did not exaggerate these strange matters. You would perceive that the convict chaplain, if he be what he should be *(not else of course)*, has unthought-of vexations, which in print would seem mere frivolities, and would be regarded as such by him, were they of fortuitous origin. But when he knows that these vexations are not occasional accidents, but occurrences planned by pique, and worked out by paltry jealousies and official resentments, he learns to regard them as a warning of concealed animosity, and they assume a power (destructive to his peace) to which adventitious misfortunes could never pretend.

CHAPTER 19

Being Nothing Particular

IT is now eighteen months since the arrival of the transport and passenger vessel. Of the living freight of the former we have lost sight, but anon we may hear of it again when occasion leads us to Restdown Ferry, and thence on board H.M.S. *Anson*.

Meanwhile visiting the Lodge, we find the family there going on just as we left them—Mr. Evelyn, according to colonial usage, taking the breaking in and keeping in order department—Mr. Herbert still devoted to the prisoners—Mrs. Evelyn alive and housewifely as ever—Emmeline varying from better to worse, from worse to better, but always patient and cheerful—Bridget acting the affectionate, untiring nurse, learning that even the shadowy side of life has pleasures for those who are not forced into it by indigence or crime. Though no better reconciled to the species of kitchen row peculiar to the colony, she is decidedly more pleased with the colony itself. She has been invited to the numerous parties and picnics for which the pleasure-loving Tasmanians are famed, but she has refused them all except the government ball (to which she not only received a formal invitation through the Aide-de Camp, but a friendly one from Lady Denman) and a scramble to the summit of Mount Wellington. Emmeline has greater attractions for her than all the young officers of the 99th, or a chance of being lost in the bush.

That eighteen months should witness no change in the servants' quarters is not to be expected. We find that Sanders no longer polishes imaginary horses in the form of boots and shoes, but, promoted to the stable, wields a veritable currycomb over living horse-flesh. His willingness has not diminished, though now his kitchen probation is over he does not mind acknowledging it was the hardest pull of his life to get through all them things he hadn't been brought up to; but this no one ever guessed, his cheerful 'Very good ma'am'—'all right sir,' having continued to the last. The poor man was in such dread of losing his place that he concealed his feelings. Pridham has been dismissed. She fell so violently in love with Sanders that trouble was foreboded, and the only mode of dealing with her was to send her away. Mr. Evelyn asked Robert if he would like a recommendation to marry her, but, shaking his head sidewise, Bob said that 'unless his honour was partial to it he'd rather *not*; he'd all so soon bide with his hosses as marry a gal he hadn't much mind to'—he supposes when he has his ticket there will be no difficulty in getting a wife to his mind, but there might be some difficulty in laying hold 'on such a pair of hosses as them again.' In Pridham's place another servant has been hired from the *Anson*. She is called Lucy, and has made an odd impression on Uncle Ev, by having positively shed tears on her leaving the hulk.

'Why, Lucy, most prisoners are delighted to get into service; be grateful to the gentleman,' commanded one of the officers.

'I'm not crying for to go, but for she to go too,' replied Lucy, choking down her sorrow, and throwing a farewell peep at a tall figure that watched her from behind a grated door.

A ring at the Lodge will convince the most incredulous that the present Lucy is the little Grenlow of the transport. She is budding into womanhood, but still retains her childish face—she drops a quick curtsey, and blushes furiously as she thinks her prison clothes attract other notice than her own—she gives a beseeching look that seems to say, 'Please not to stare at me.' She has drawn her hair down to its utmost length over her cheeks, but every now and then a disobliging lock whose ends can rarely reach her ear, falls forward, increasing her confusion and blushes; she hurries it back, and, hoping no one has observed it, curtseys herself out of sight.

CHAPTER 20

H.M.S. *Anson*

'WELL, Bridget, I must go to the *Anson* this afternoon. I have been to the watch-house, and there found our lady; she will have three months. As we feared, she made her way to the 'Labour in Vain' instead of to the orphan school.[1] I have refused to appear on her behalf, believing that the punishment will do her good, this being the third offence. Now don't look so vexed; steel that tender heart of yours, or you will never do for out here. You may go with me. Are you a clever physiognomist?'

'Pretty well; but I shall not have much choice on which to exercise my talents, shall I uncle?'

'Every bad lot has its best.'

'Well, I should like to explore the *Anson*. I suppose it is one of the colonial sights.'

'Ay, ay; I thought so. It's very dreadful, but I must just see it. That's the way with womankind. At half-past two, then, the cab will be at the door. Very tiresome to have to change servants whilst your aunt's away.' (Mrs. Evelyn had gone up the country to pay her annual visit.) 'We always happen to pick up some beauty during her absence.'

'There's poor little Lucy peeping in, uncle; come in.'

Half anxious and half frightened Lucy entered.

'If you please—mem—sir—is it true that Janet isn't coming back?'

'Yes, Lucy; how did you hear the news?'

'The constable, sir, promised her to call, and told me—and, and—sir—and—'

'And what, Lucy? Speak out, if you please.'

'And to beg you'd please to keep the place for her 'gainst she's out of trouble. She knows 'taint a every-day house, sir, as all the rest of us does, sir.'

'There will be time enough to think of that by-and-by. Let this be a warning to you, Lucy: you will find me a kind master if you deserve kindness, but—'

Here Lucy burst into tears, exclaiming between her sobs: 'Oh, sir, if you please, sir—you don't think I'd go for to drink the filthy stuff—indeed, sir, I wouldn't, nor nothing else.'

'Well, well, we shall see, Lucy. I did not mean to vex you; you ought to have learnt by this time that, in this colony, we suspect all persons until they have proved themselves beyond suspicion. I tell you plainly, Lucy, that you have lately appeared more friendly with Janet than I approve of.'

'Oh, sir! sir!' said the girl, almost choked with tears. 'I were afraid of her, indeed I were, sir; and it's lovely to think she's gone! I'd a sight rather do all the work myself than have her back.'

'Take care, take care, foolish girl; how do you explain all that anxiety to have Janet's place reserved for her, eh, Lucy? Do not attempt to deceive me.'

'It's easy explained, sir.' Lucy drew nearer to Mr. Evelyn, and glancing around the room to assure herself that she was not overlooked by malignant eyes, she continued in a low tone:

'You see, sir, I were obliged to give you Janet's message; and p'raps, if you see her in factory, you'll be so kind as to tell her I spoke for her, sir.'

'Why, Lucy, what is all this about? I will thank you to be straightforward.'

Lucy drew still nearer.

'When Janet got leave to go out, she says to me, sir, "Now, if I gets into trouble, which is as like as not, I'll send and let you know; and if you don't speak a word to the master for me, I'll give you a keepsake, you little sneaking hussy;" and she put her fist to my face, and says "Mind that: I'll find you out by some of my mates." You may think I were frightened, master.'

Mr. Evelyn, giving a long ahem, turned to his nieces—'In this, our good-tempered Janet, we have harboured a respectable reptile;' then to Lucy, 'Did she ever ill-treat you, that you fear her?' A second timid search about the room—

'Yes, sir; you remember that black eye I got? She gave it to me; and because I wouldn't promise to tell a lie about it, she went and broke a lot of soup-plates, to make believe that I'd tripped in carrying the tray, and so got the bruise; and as she managed to get first word with missus, I weren't asked no questions; and I were very glad, because she swore she'd pay me double if I told true. She made fine fool to you, sir, and missus, for heeding her lies: she said you was a sweet, peaceable babby, not to know more about fighting than to believe I got my black eye by a fall.'

'Enough, Lucy Grenlow; you were very wrong to let me keep that woman, when you saw such wrong doings.'

'Oh! please, sir,' sobbed Lucy, 'you don't know how dreadful 'tis downstairs when they hates a body; and they always hate a body that's better than theirselves. I've well-nigh cried my eyes out sometimes when I've seen things as shouldn't be in a respectable kitchen; but what were I to do when Janet swore she'd make a hell for me if I peached.'

'It is over now; I can excuse you: but, another time, remember your duty to your master; the innocent have nothing to fear. I never encourage one prisoner to tell tales against another; but where matters are visibly wrong, the case is altered. Now that will do, Lucy; for your comfort, I will tell you that at present we have all a fair opinion of you.'

Lucy looked her thanks, and dropped a profound curtsey.

'Have you any charge to make against Janet?'

'I don't believe, sir, that she'd ever a child to the orphan school. 'Twas only a make out to get leave sometimes; but please, sir, do not tell her, or there'll be no end on the mischief she'll do me.'

Mr. Evelyn made no reply. Emmeline asked Lucy—

'Then when you looked so anxious you were afraid that your master would agree to take Janet back?'

'No, mem,' said Lucy, brightening vastly. 'I wanted to mention to the master that I'd been reckoning about Martha Grylls, and thinks if she hasn't got into trouble again, her time will be up on the *Anson*; and if you please, mem,' Lucy stopped, and, colouring up to her temples, looked from Mr. Evelyn to Bridget, and from Bridget to Emmeline—as much as to say—'*Do* understand, without giving me the pain of speaking.'

'I guess what you wish to say, Lucy. This Martha Grylls is a friend of yours, and you want to speak for her.'

'Thank you, mem—Miss Evelyn.'

'Come, then, my girl, let us hear something of this Grylls: what can you say in her favour, eh, Lucy?' said her master.

'If you please, sir, she's a 'orrid temper,' commenced Lucy.

'Very satisfactory,' nodded Mr. Evelyn.

'Shockin' to manage, sir.'

'Better still—go on, Lucy.'

'But such a noble creature, sir; and I can't never fancy she's a common prisoner like me. If you only please try her, sir; she was quite a mother to me coming out; the chaplain set a sight on her, and all the women feared her like. She was so grand to 'em, without ever meaning it.'

Mr. Evelyn gave a sly glance at Bridget.

'We'll think about it; where all are alike strange, and all have a character to gain, I would as soon choose one servant as another.'

'Oh! no; if you please, sir: if you'll excuse me, sir, there's as much difference between they on the *Anson* as between night and day, sir; there's some as never scarce keeps out of the dark cells, sir; and there's they what never gets in.'

'Has your friend ever been in the cells, Lucy?'

'Oh! if you please, sir; if you please, that ain't a fair question.' Then flushing deeply, and seeming frightened enough to cry, she apologised—

'I didn't mean it rude, sir; indeed I didn't: but I'd as soon tell on myself as she, sir; I'd have broken my heart right away coming out, if it hadn't been for she, sir.'

'Has your friend been in the cells?' repeated Mr. Evelyn, in a voice that implied—'I mean to be answered.'

'Well, then, she did three time, sir; but it weren't no fault of hers, sir; they broked a little white mug she set a sight on; and then they called it kicking up a row, because she was a bit rombustious; and then then 'cused her of insolence. Martha, you see, sir, hasn't no respect of persons (beg pardon, I forgot that were Bible); if she thinks a thing ain't justice, she'd as soon tell a first-class officer so as one of us; and when she's up, 'tisn't easy to put her down.'

This harangue was delivered with so much naïveté and generous warmth, that her hearers exchanged glances of astonishment—they had not imagined little Lucy capable of showing so large an amount of feeling—her general demeanour being quiet in the extreme.

'But, Lucy, you cannot suppose these tempers will suit me?'

'Oh! she'll have nothing to worry her here, sir, I'm tretted well, and that's all she cares for now her mug's a broked; she don't seem to care for herself. Sure, thinks I, sometimes, Martha Grylls likes all them hard things and punishments. She goes about just as if she took a pride in them.'

'All very fine, Lucy; but won't do here. If I hire her, you must talk to her.'

'I talk to Martha!!' The very thought was profanity to Lucy.

'But before I make any promise,' continued Mr. Evelyn, you must tell me what this great friendship of yours and Martha's is. I do not approve of these prison attachments. 'Are—you—sure—Lucy, that she is not *your mother?*'

'Lor', no, sir!' cried Lucy, in unfeigned surprise. 'I wish she was, and I shouldn't be out here. She ain't nothing to me in flesh and blood. 'Twas all her kindness coming out that did it. I were the youngest on board, sir; and the women used to make mock on me: so, one day Martha, who didn't sociate with none of them, rosed up and took my part, and said, 'twas only because I was better than them that they tret me so bad; so then they hated me, but she stood for me all the voyage, and the chaplain was very good to me, because he set a sight on her.'

'Well, well, Lucy, go to your work now; we'll see what can be done.'

'If you please, sir, you won't listen to anything they says 'gainst her? P'raps they'll make her out bad.'

'Never you mind, the officers are the best judges of her conduct; do not presume on my leniency.'

Utterly unwitting of the meaning of the two grand words—presume, leniency—Lucy imagined them the superlative to all former degrees of promise, and dropped a befitting curtsey. 'Thank you, sir!' She hesitated—'Please, I don't know if she'd be angry; but I don't think Martha Grylls is her real name; they call her so—she let's *me* call her Maida.'

Mr. Evelyn nodded, and Lucy left the room; in a moment she peeped in again—

'If you please, sir, if her time isn't up, I'd gladly do all the work for a few days, if you'd wait for her?'

'That will do, Lucy, shut the door.'

'The little puss!' exclaimed Bridget.

'What do *you* think, ladies? Though I was obliged to put in a full stop now and then, I rather like her the better for all this,' said Uncle Ev, turning to his nieces.

'Poor little creature!' sighed Emmeline. 'How old is she, Uncle Ev?'

'Seventeen years; hers is a sad story—you must ask her to tell it you some day.'

'I'm quite curious to see this Martha Grylls; I hope she'll let us call her Maida, it is so much prettier a name than Martha—by-the-by, Uncle Ev—I vote we don't have any dinner to-day,' said Bridget.

'Thank you kindly, Miss Bridget, I'll excuse *you* with much pleasure; but perversity unusually prompts *me* to dine to-day; what says Emmeline?'

'I join dear Bridget in wishing to give Lucy as little to do as may be possible, now that she has double work. Ah Bridget! You see your thoughts can't conceal themselves.'

'Oh, if that's it, let it be lunch only; you won't object to that too, eh, Miss Bridget?'

'Not if you are good, and will promise not to tease Lucy; I will do all I can to assist the poor girl. Now sit still, Em, I insist on your being quiet; do you think I would let these dear hands meddle with heavy blankets? I'll manage the beds.' Bridget gently reseated her cousin.

'"Duty," Miss Em, is your watchword; your duty is clear, sit still!' With a sweet smile Emmeline sat down. A scarcely perceptible sigh escaped her as she watched her light-hearted cousin depart. When left alone, she pressed her thin fingers to her eyes, and one bright drop oozing thence coursed slowly down the transparent palm. Then looking upwards she whispered reverently, clasping her hand—

'O Christ—but give me Thy grace, Thy strengthening grace to say, "Thy will be done!" then *where* and *when* Thou wilt, direct Thy chastening hand.' As if the answer had already come, a holy calm overspread her face, and all trace of suffering was lost in an almost angelic smile that kindled from lip to eye on her wasted countenance. It was at such times as the present, that Emmeline felt with extraordinary keenness the trial which rendered her a helpless looker-on; where every energy—physical, moral and spiritual—was needed. When in the latter and last cases, she beheld the scenes of sorrow, strife and sin, which form an awful item in the daily routine of life in Hobarton—scenes which are regarded by the majority of the initiated with complacent indifference, or ignored with the philosophic axiom, 'What can't be cured must be endured,'—she yearned to go forth another Phineas, [2] and stand betwixt the morally dying and the dead. In her sweet humility, she thought herself laid aside in utter uselessness. But is that useless which prepares a soul for glory? The searching rays which ripened this goodly fruit for early transplantation from earth, reflecting from so willing a recipient, lost all their scathing power, and fell gently on the household with an irresistible influence. Received so meekly, betrayed so slightly, only they who had learned to trace the line of suffering beneath the unruffled surface of Emmeline's fair brow could tell how severe the individual pangs one by one completing the process which should, ere long, leave her meet for the Master's presence. If for a moment the serenity of her features was startled into a gesture expressive of her pain, it was only that they might look more lovingly, and smile the oft-repeated assurance—'It was nothing, taking me by surprised, the spasm made me start.'

Wielding the palm of example effectually before her family, how could she be useless? She moved as a Messiah in their midst, silently, but surely beckoning to heaven. The most ignorant or prejudiced doubted not that to follow her steps was to tread straight on to glory.

Her religion partook of no gloomy exclusiveness nor ascetic austerity. Hers was a religion of cheerfulness and kindly sympathies; for this reason particularly attractive to Bridget, over whom her influence fell as a chain of roses, leading her an enchanted captive. Bridget's character had not changed beneath her cousin's 'reign,' as she laughingly called Emmeline's almost magnetic capability of guiding her. Each original element still existed; but by a skilful rearrangement each one blended so harmoniously with the other that its presence might well be questioned. Her character was fast becoming one lovely whole, instead of a glittering mass of irregular brilliants. She had still the song in her heart, and the smile on her lip; but the smile was no longer one that smiled in ignorance of sorrow, and, therefore, repugnant to the heart of sorrow; it was a smile ready to shine through the gloomy chinks of grief upon the heart within, and whisper, 'We can hope for brighter days; the sun is even now behind the clouds—it will burst forth anon.'

The song was no longer that wild, jubilant gush, that awakened admiration in every breast save his, who pining in trial, felt aggrieved, almost insulted by the trilling notes of mirth. It was a rich, harmonious flow, that whether it reached the ear of kindred spirits or bruised hearts, could never fall amiss; no shrieking sensitiveness could be wounded by its inaptness, nor bereavement be mocked by its ungenial gaiety. It was a song listening to which, sorrow forgot her wail, and apathy consented to be pleased.

It is a grand mistake to suppose that identity is lost in submitting to the renovating influences of time, circumstance or religion.

Bridget D'Urban, the laughter-loving, mope-hating girl, will be Bridget D'Urban, the laughter-lover, mope-hater to the end of her days, unless some mighty unforeseen calamity arise and quench her spirit's light. It would be impossible for her to mope in the important responsibilities and interests of life, as in the trivial enjoyments of her youth.

'Because I preside over responsibilities, need I look solemn? They are solemn enough in themselves. Why not enliven them with smiles? she would ask, when moody mentors, fain to repress her manner of treating difficulties, lectured on her levity. She still hated the shadowy side of life, but she no longer shunned it; she would cross over to the weary beings, dragging out their life in its darkened corners, and smile her smile, and sing her song to them—or if needs be, mix her tears with theirs—but still she was Bridget D'Urban.

As if in silent prayer, Emmeline remained some time without altering her position. She then arose, and moved feebly to the window to tend her pet geraniums. A merry laugh reached her ear. Looking towards the garden, she perceived Bridget trying to shake a large drugget,[3] but each useless attempt only sent a cloud of dust into Lucy's eyes. At last, flinging down the unmanageable cloth, Bridget threw herself on the grass, claiming the young servant's commiseration by a comic pout of distress, followed by a hearty peel of laughter, in which Lucy half timidly joined.

Catching a glimpse of her cousin's figure between the well-filled flower stand, in an instant Bridget was up over the verandah steps and in through the window.

'Oh! such fun, Em; that horrid drugget—poor Lucy—but let me see how I look?'

Suiting her action to her words, Bridget danced over to the glass and complacently surveyed herself. Her ringlets were put back and twisted around her plait. On the top of her head was perched on of Lucy's neat little caps. Her dress was pinned up, and over it she wore a housemaid's stomacher apron.

'Don't I make a capital housemaid? Do you think I should get twelve pounds wages, out here—eh, Em?'

'Forthwith, if you would take them out in kisses,' said Em, fondly laying her cheek on Bridget's. What a contrast did those faces present!

'But dear, you have learnt that uncouth "out here," do not say it, there's a good one.'

'Have I? Then it is quite unconsciously. I hate to hear it; it sounds as though we were out-lawed in some dreadful, outlandish place. Better call Tasmania "out here" at once. But Em, I want to consult you. There is but a mere picking on the mutton-bone. Shall we have some chops for uncle?'

'No, Bridget, dear; Uncle Ev will not object to a vegetable lunch—poor little Lucy has enough to do.'

'Oh! I'll cook them.'

'Ah, Racket! I thought it was more of what you call fun that you wanted; but your presence will only disconcert Lucy.'

'How you *do* find out what is likely to vex people; you must have been a regular Pickle[4] in your time to have found out such secrets,' said Bridget, whirling out of the room.

She discovered Lucy standing in amazed disgust over a tub drawn from beneath Janet's bed.

'The—beast! and the master's too!' she slowly articulated, as Bridget approached.

No bandicoot or wombat had harboured in the tub as Miss D'Urban at first suspected. But a more anomalous medley met her sight. In a foul pool of putrid soap-suds, lay dish-cloths, pocket-handkerchiefs, floor-cloths, collars, dusters, some of Mr. Evelyn's socks, two shirts, and one of Charlie's pelisses; all rotting together in the corrupt, mud-coloured fluid. The articles of clothing had been given to Janet to wash at the period of Mrs. Evelyn's departure from home, and had been huddled by her, with some of her own things, into this 'respectable,' as Lucy called it,[5] until a convenient season, which, in Van Diemen's Land kitchen parlance, signifies a season of partial soberness.

'The beast!' repeated Lucy, emphatically. There's I hunted high and low for Master Charlie's pelisse, and I heard the master my own self row the laundress for losing of his shirts and socks, and says Janet—"Oh, these washers are a 'orrid careless set when missus ain't home to look after their things." Then says she, looking pitiful-like, "'Tisn't to be s'posed poor Miss Evelyn could poke after house matters, and Miss D'Urban, she don't like them things," and she goes and locks her bedroom door, and says, "Master won't relish the smell of the gutter; pah," says she, "ain't it bad, Lucy?" and so I said, "Yes, it's been dreadful long past, Janet; we shall get fever if master don't mind it;" "Lor, mercy," says she, "fever not, I don't want no workery rumpussing out here."' [6]

'Don't be disheartened, Lucy; you'll mend matters before your friend arrives,' said Bridget, soothingly, as the poor girl surveyed the unpleasant task she must accomplish ere she could continue her tidying operations. The kitchen was in a state of exquisite disorder preparatory to a grand reformation.

At the mention of her friend, little Lucy jumped to her work, and speedily became a very opossum of activity, leaping about from one branch of labour to another, while Bridget proceeded to lay out the cloth for luncheon. By keeping the mutton-bone in countenance with a nice salad, some English cheese, and a few sweetmeats, a repast was set to which Uncle Ev deigned to give a nod of approbation.

'Was that nod for me or the lunch, Uncle Ev?' asked Bridget, slyly.

'To an unexpected guest, Bridget. I didn't anticipate seeing the *bone* to-day, at any rate until after another meal. Janet laid in double stock yesterday I suppose—eh?'

At half-past two, Mr. Evelyn and Bridget set off for Risdon Ferry,* in sight of which the *Anson* lay. From Macquarie Street they reached the ferry at half-past three; there a boat awaited parties going on board the ship.

'Now then, miss, hold on, and I'll keep close behind you.'

And Miss D'Urban ascended the companion and stood on the hulk. Her uncle beckoned her to follow him below.

A female standing at a high desk by the open door of the first cabin raised her head and bowed a business-like bow as they advanced. She was evidently the monarch of all she surveyed.

'Is that Mrs. Bowden?' whispered Bridget. [8]

The question was overheard and answered by the ruling spirit.

'No, Mrs. Bowden is in England. *I* act in her place.' Another, and still more official bow followed. Accompanied by one of the officers, Mr. Evelyn and his niece arraigned themselves at Mrs. Deputy's bar.

'I want a servant-of-all-work; can you recommend me one, Mrs. Deputy?'

'We do not recommend; there are several people eligible, but they will not afford much choice, Mr. Evelyn.'

'Except to friends!' dryly suggested that gentleman.

Mrs. Deputy bowed, at once dignity and indignity, and repeated, 'There are several prisoners eligible.' True to the daring contradictions of Tasmanian words and their meanings, 'eligible' is not intended to signify aptness or suitability. A woman eligible for service is rarely fitted for service; the adjective only informs the master or mistress that she is ready to be hired.

'Is one Martha Grylls eligible, Mrs. Deputy?'

'Grylls, Grylls, Grylls, let me see,' drawing her finger down the list before her.

The attendant officer chimed in:

'Yes; she becomes so this very day.'

'Thank you, Miss Perkins,' bowed Mrs. Deputy, with an air that plainly said, 'I will thank you not to interfere.'

---

*   Corrupted from *Restdown*. [7]

'Grylls, Grylls,' and her finger travelled on.

'You cannot know whom you ask for, if you want her, sir!' whispered the cowed Miss Perkins.

'Thank you, Miss Perkins, perhaps you will leave the arrangement of this matter to me,' again bowed the commandant.

'Martha Grylls is at your service, Mr. Evelyn; shall I send for her?'

'I will trouble you, if you please.'

'Would not you prefer my calling several women, sir?' asked the attendant officer.

'I will thank you, Miss Perkins, to call Martha Grylls,' responded Mrs. Deputy.

The little officer had no choice but to obey; so bowing obedience, she sidled to the grating which divided the prison from the officers' quarters; and then standing on tiptoe, desired a Miss Snub to send forward 'That Martha Grylls.'

'Ordered forward, Martha Grylls!' shouted a female stentor; and, rising from a distant rank, immediately appeared a tall, elegant woman, who, passing Miss Snub with a curtsey, came into Mrs. Deputy's awful presence.

She had on the usual brown serge skirt (so short as to show a masculine pair of half-boots), a jacket of brown and yellow gingham, a dark blue cotton kerchief; and a prim white calico cap, whose narrow border was kept in frill by help of a thread run through it, completed her dress. The grotesque coarseness of this attire could not *hide* the inherent grace of the prisoner. Still dignified and beautiful, before her future master stood the wearer of those rough knitted blue stockings and clownish shoes.

Her cap was untied.

'Tie your cap, Martha Grylls,' commanded Miss Perkins.

Martha mechanically obeyed.

'It would better become you, Grylls, to curtsey the same as your mates, than to try to imitate your betters,' continued the little woman, conscious that Martha's obeisance surpassed her genuflecting capabilities.

'The curtsey was meant for *me*, I think, Miss Perkins,' said Mrs. Deputy.

In consideration of Martha's presence, the rebuked attendant darted daggers at Mrs. Deputy.

Mr. Evelyn put a few questions to Martha, all of which she quietly and satisfactorily answered.

'I will hire this Grylls, if you please, Mrs. Deputy.'

Preliminaries having been settled, Martha was sent to tie up her bundle, and business being over, Mrs. Deputy came down from the tip-top of dignity, and seemed not wholly disinclined for a talk.

'The appearance of the woman decided me at once, Mrs. Deputy; to belie *that* countenance, she must be a monster.'

'With a good master she will not belie it, Mr. Evelyn. Wise management will do much for her. Her police character is against her, and her crimes you are aware—'

'Yes, yes; but I do not heed the amount of crime: indiscriminate association generally makes it theoretically equal amongst prisoners. It is my opinion that both men and females come out of these probations worse than they went in. Reformations rarely, if ever, commence within prison walls; and reformation the more tardily begins in proportion to the length of durance. We have an extra task to perform on a probationer.'

Mrs. Deputy looked much hurt, and exclaimed, '*Here* on the *Anson* surely, Mr. Evelyn, you do not call it indiscriminate association: we have distinct classes—bad, better and best. Surely nothing can be superior to Mrs. Bowden's excellent system?'

'Than Mrs. Bowden I know no more gifted and prudent lady-superintendent; were all officers selected with like discernment, it would be well for the prisoner. Mrs. Deputy, may I take my niece through the wards?' asked Mr. Evelyn, anxious to avoid a discussion.

The lady only bowed assent, for she was deeply affronted at an attack on a system of which she was representative in place of the highly respected Mrs. Bowden: perhaps she was the more deeply wounded, because a conviction of the fallacy of the system already worked in her own mind. It is a natural weakness with many persons to be angry with a scruple they can no longer conscientiously resist. She just deigned to say, 'Miss Perkins, this gentleman wishes to see the *Anson*,' and turned to her desk. The little creature came hopping over with a sort of sidewise movement, not unlike that of an impudent cock-sparrow which can scarcely hop for pertness. Pecking to Mr. Evelyn's side, she whispered, 'Though I pity you, sir, I am downright glad to get rid of that woman. The trouble I have had with her!'

This was only meant for Mr. Evelyn; nevertheless, it reached the vigilant deputy's ears. 'I am sure *I* shall be glad, Miss Perkins. Often have I been pained by the foolish complaints made against her and poor Lucy Grenlow, when she was here. You know I am obliged to take my officers' part before the convicts; you ought therefore to refrain from bringing such nonsensical cases for me to judge. Had my duties allowed me time to pay particular attention to Martha, I should not have had reason to punish her so much.' As Mrs. Deputy was thus properly delivering herself, Miss Perkins stood a deferential listener; she just hopped off in time to hear a mutter that sounded very like—'I have as much trouble with the officers as with the women.'

Bridget clung to her uncle's arm as they passed through rows of prisoners, who were variously employed in working, reading, and learning, it being their school-hour. Each file arose and curtsied as the party passed.

Ever and anon Miss Perkins issued orders to some unfortunate.

'Mary Gull, tie your cap. What, Mary Pike, yours off! The next offence you'll go downstairs.' Mary understood the allusion, and hastily put on her cap.

'Sarah Gubb, you are talking there. Jane Dawson, where's your curtsey? Why don't you rise, Ellen Bracket? Muggins, I shall complain of you. Would you like to walk through the cells, sir?'

They went below. In one cell was a captive, kicking and stamping violently. Miss Perkins thought fit to soothe her by rapping at the door.

'You don't think that's the way to get out, do you, Stooks?'

''Twas you got me in, you *did*, you beast!'

'If I wasn't very indulgent, Stooks, I should get you double for that,' said the maternal Perkins.

'Is the devil indulgent? I should like to know, you old cant!'[9] cried Stooks.

With a deprecating smile at Bridget, Miss Perkins stopped at Number 10, whence issued an imploring voice:

'Do beg for me; I'm quite subdued, indeed I am, Miss Love. Oh! It's Miss Perkins. I beg pardon, ma'am, I thought 'twas Miss Love,' the prisoner was heard to sigh.

Passing on, they came to stalls where different trades—cobblery, bonnet-making, &c.—were being carried on.

'Do let us go, uncle; it is so dreadful to have these poor creatures made a show of,' whispered Bridget.

'They are accustomed to it,' answered Miss Perkins to the second clause of Bridget's speech.

'As the eels are, eh, Miss Perkins?' asked Mr. Evelyn.

'Oh, they keep each other in countenance. We look at them as a lot, not as individuals.' Here her eye fell on Martha Grylls, who was waiting, bundle in hand, at the grating.

'Follow us, and don't be talking there, Grylls. I don't wish to lose sight of you.'

'Come along, my woman,' said Mr. Evelyn kindly.

'*No*; walk before us, if you please, Grylls. I don't wish to lose sight of you, I repeat.'

Martha obeyed without a word.

All the women tried to give her a nod on the sly; and many anxious eyes followed the party as the grated door closed, and an audible sigh was simultaneously heaved by those whom it imprisoned. Each prisoner envied Martha and wished it had been her lot to fall to so sweet a looking lady as that bright-eyed girl who smiled on her in passing.

What lay beyond those gates not one could tell. They were as the gates of death—all doubt and mystery beyond. None ever returned to tell of the untried world to which they led.

Strange and vague are the mental picturings the prisoned female forms of the land of her exile, which she knows lies little further than a stone's throw from her. Some think, on leaving the *Anson,* they are to be turned adrift to all the horrors of an unexplored region; others that they will be driven to market for sale. The cunning and malicious amongst them delight in filling the minds of their less gifted associates with the most terrible apprehensions of the barbarities awaiting them on their departure from their probation. It is with a thrill of cruel suspense that such prisoners first plant their foot on Tasmanian ground.

In this respect the male convicts do not suffer so acutely. Their doubts, hopes, and fears are answered, realized, or crushed almost immediately on arriving at the colony. Their probationary course does not add suspense to sorrow. At once formed into gangs, they learn the worst, and are sent to labour in the roads, or work on public buildings. The torture of suspense is not added to it.

Miss Perkins accompanied Mr. Evelyn and his niece to the deck, where she mysteriously beckoned Bridget aside:

'I hope you do not mean to employ Grylls about children.'

She gave a significant wink. 'Of course, though, you don't. You guess why? It is not usual to tell the crime; but really I think it my duty to break rule to you. Do you understand me?'

Bridget looked a negative.

Martha had drawn near enough to hear Miss Perkins's friendly caution. Casting a glance of unutterable contempt on little Perkins, she stepped to Miss D'Urban, and herself solved the significant wink.

'Miss Perkins wishes you to know that I am sent out for murder. She would suggest the impropriety of making me a nurse.'

Bridget turned very pale, and cast an imploring look on the little officer, who, boiling over with injured prerogative, was on the point of reprimanding Martha's audacity, when Mr. Evelyn called them to be quick—the boat was waiting.

'Good morning, Miss Perky. We are much favoured by your civilities.'

The officer was hurt at the inharmonious name bestowed upon her, and vented her spite by exclaiming, as Martha was on the first step of the companion:

'I hope you'll behave better *now*, Grylls, or you'll soon learn the difference between factory and here.'

Martha turned abruptly on her. A second move, and she had been on her way back to the cells, instead of on the road to Hobarton. The crimson cheek, flashing eye, and quivering lip, a second more had met their chastisement; but Bridget's beseeching gesture once more prevailed. Quietly turning from her persecutor, Martha descended the ladder.

'Good morning, Miss Perky,' waved Mr. Evelyn abstractedly, as though his voice mechanically embodied his opinion in a *name* expressive of the little upstart, pecking at him from the deck.

'That horrid woman!' cried Bridget.

A quick nod and frown from Mr. Evelyn stopped what further she would have said.

A slight smile spread over the prisoner's face; but it soon faded into a look of anxious sadness. It mattered not to her whether the coast was beautiful or barren; whether the landscape was rendered vital by the upward wreathing of the blue smoke from pleasant homesteads or whether its desolate grandeur was made more dreary by the long blank masonry of penal life.

She started as from a dream when the boat jerked against the jetty. A ghastly pallor struck her every feature as she stepped ashore. For an instant she covered her face; then, gradually withdrawing her hands, the Maida Gwynnham of olden days discovered herself in the unabated dignity of that upraised head, and in the strength of purpose shining from the purple depths of those undimmed eyes.

A strength of purpose that even now was to be tried; and if the trial, surprising an unguarded post, be victorious for a season, who shall exult?

She was prepared to confront the hardships of convict existence. She was prepared for taunts, for jibes, for suspicions, for enemies, and felt that she could face them; but she was not prepared to meet any of these as they were now about to assail her.

CHAPTER 21

The Initiation—Without

THE cab was waiting for them at the ferry.

'Get up on the box, Martha. Coachman, help her.'

But she had mounted ere the driver could proffer his assistance.

'A likesome un,' winked the man to Mr. Evelyn. 'You've always got your eye-tooth about ye, sir.'

Now begins my public martyrdom. Now shall I feel the blighting breath of scorn, thought Maida. Would God that it would smite me down at once!

With an eye of impatient curiosity she viewed this new sphere of future suffering looming in the distance. She longed to hasten it, but with the longing of one that craves to know the worst. She longed to meet the first eye that should witness her disgrace. She longed to hear the first word that should break the fearful silence of this strange phase of life, but with the desire of one who yearns to learn her fate.

She was soon satisfied.

The coachman, a good-tempered, ruddy-faced old man, looking at her full of wonder, jerked a sentence from the side of his ample mouth.

'Got in a good berth, young 'ooman—that you has!'

The familiarity of this congratulation was worse than scorn, and Maida involuntarily shuddered.

'Your hair's a-grow'd nicely.'

He seemed mystified at Maida's tacit non-approval.

'The women likes a bit o' gossip general,' he muttered. A bright thought occurred to him. She don't hear me for them rattling wheels.

'Your hair's a-grow'd butiful, my dear,' he repeated, with a more sidelong and emphatic jerk.

Worse than three days in the dark cells! thought Maida.

'You feels queer like, my dear, don't ye?' he persevered, seeing she had turned very pale. 'Never mind! I knows ezac'ly what you feels. You fancies all the folks will stare at ye, so you feels sheepy-like. No such thing, my dear. They sees hundreds of you every day. They won't take no more notice of ye than if you was a leg of mutton. I'm a man, my dear.'

Here Maida ventured to peep at him, and perceived she had mistaken rough kindness for brutal officiousness, and her better sense accepted the civility, so honestly offered.

The old man seemed pleased, and went on to say:

'I'm a man, my dear: yet when I fust came out of Tench with the gang, blast me if I wasn't nigh to fent. Thinks I, every mother's son on 'em 'll be gaping at me. No such thing, my dear; nobody tookt no more notice on me than if I'd been a brisket o' beef. Lots on us is just equal to *none* on us. Now *you* feels like me; but there's no call for it. Cheer up! says I. It's fine out here; worth a while to get out anyhow. Ah! ah! ha!'

Tench and gang were Greek to Maida; yet she fancied they referred to prison days, and that her commiserator *was* or *had* been a convict. She wished to ask, but, judging by her own sensibility, feared the question might be offensive; so she merely replied:

'Thank you.'

'Kindly welcome, my dear. A-u-h! You'll get on fine. You don't seem like to get into trouble very often. Them what takes a drop gets oftenest into trouble out here—and home *too*, I'm thinking' (he added thoughtfully). 'Anything that way, my dear? Now keep heart; don't ye mind: they won't look at ye no more than a loin o' lamb.'

A party of ladies passed.

'There now, did 'em gape? Look over yonder; d'ye see that fine dressed 'ooman? She'm government. I remember bringing her in from *Anson*. That gentleman there, what pretends to be—he's convict, came in last load after I; so you've got fine company. The girls marry like mad out here.'

Maida could bear no more; her brain grew dizzy; she grasped the rail on her side of the dicky, and the man's arm on the other.

'That's right, my dear; 'old tight. I loves to purtect ye. Old Hawkins is known out here; he's been a government man, and knows all about it. 'Old on, you'm queer like.'

Mr. Evelyn called from the cab:

'Hawkins, I'll thank you not to talk with my woman.'

'All right, sir.'

The vehicle suddenly stopped.

''Old on, my dear. I wants to speak to the master.'

Off jumped the old man, popping his bright face into the cab. He whispered:

'The 'ooman takes on uncommon; she'm nigh to fent; never see'd sich; more acute than most on 'em. She'll drop off the box any minute; excoose me, but 'tisn't safe there.'

'Shall she come inside, Bridget? Do you object?'

Bridget looked as much as to say, 'Is it likely I should?'

'Here, my dear, you goes in there 'long with the quality.'

Maida hesitated, but only for an instant. Her overloaded heart could not brook the weight of importunate kindness Hawkins would heap upon it.

'That's right, my dear; keep a good face on't. You're nothing to them mor'n a fillet of veal,' winked Hawkins.

Glancing her thanks at him, she sank into a corner, and the grateful relief induced another, still more potent, still more needed.

She burst into tears.

That was enough for Bridget. It was a very Bochim within that coach.[1]

Following the impulse of her spirit, Bridget's hand had unconsciously worked its way from under her shawl, and found a resting-place on Maida's, where it lay so lightly, withal so significantly, that it gave the prisoner to understand more by one of its thrills than I could write, or you could read, in an hour. Suddenly remembering her uncle's presence, and peculiar strictness with convicts, she withdrew her hand, turning her head, at the same time, to meet the dread frown of reproof she expected; but Mr. Evelyn was watching the race-running trees with an interest rarely displayed by sober middle-aged men; his fingers were tabouring[2] on the glass, instead of motioning displeasure to her, and Bridget was very glad to escape the tokens of an incipient scolding.

'Oh, these blessed tears! But for them I should have gone wild. Since I left England I have only once experienced their power,' said Maida, after a while.

'Do you feel better now, Martha?' asked Bridget, ready to give over her cry directly it suited her for whom she wept.

'Yes, thank you, I am greatly refreshed.'

Uncle Ev, being anxious to prevent another scene, asked Maida if she had any question she would like to ask.

'I thank you, *none*, but shall be glad of your permission to drop my present name.'

'Oh yes; any name you prefer will answer my purpose; to the comptroller-general you must remain Martha Grylls. What do you wish to call yourself?'

'Maida Gwynnham.'

Mr. Evelyn's opinion was not discernible on his face, but Miss D'Urban's shone in every dimple of her blooming cheeks.

'I'm so glad! Lucy said so; won't she be pleased, uncle?'

'Lucy Grenlow?' earnestly gasped Maida.

Mr. Evelyn saw that his dignity was at stake; so wisely lost no time in granting a permission that was evidently not about to be sought.

'You can explain to Gwynnham where she is going, Bridget. Maida, my niece, Miss D'Urban, will talk to you.'

'We heard of—of you from a nice little thing,' (Mr. Evelyn frowned)—'our housemaid, I mean,' stammered Bridget, correcting herself.

'Lucy Grenlow?'

'Yes; it seems she has been counting the very hours to your release, and she reckoned you would be ready to-day.'

'Dear child!' adding slowly, as if in thought, 'she needs a protector.'

Bridget knew this would not agree with her uncle. She turned towards him half timidly. The trees were racing again; *perhaps* he was betting on them; *certainly* he was too busy to notice either of his companions.

'Here we are,' cried Bridget, as they drove into sight of the Lodge, Macquarie Street.

With a pardonable vanity, Lucy had decked herself out in her Sunday best. It would be such a glory to surprise Maida, who only knew her in prison clothes. She had on a neat blue mousseline de laine[3] gown; a smart white apron; the everlasting knitted collar, fastened with an old bow of Miss D'Urban's; and a jaunty little cap, trimmed with pink tarlatan, set off the whole most becomingly.

She was standing at the door, awaiting the expected arrival; but no sooner did she espy Maida through the cab window, than she darted into the house, just as a child which, in the coyness of its delight, runs to hide from a pleasure it has been anticipating. Not all the rings at the doorbell could bring Lucy back from her retreat behind the staircase recess. Mr. Evelyn tried to look severe. Bridget tried to look amused, and would have succeeded but for Maida, whose vain attempt to look calm was painfully portrayed in an effort of countenance that reminded Mr. Evelyn more of a grimace which he had noticed on the features of death, than of an expression indicative of pleasure.

Coachee was the only one of the party who contrived to look what he meant to look, or to feel what he intended to exhibit as his feeling. His rubicund face became more jolly, and a broad grin of satisfaction distended his ample mouth to its utmost width of elasticity. He *felt* pleased, *looked* pleased, and *grinned pleasure* at having set his protegée down at so promising a home. The old man knew every house in Hobarton that had the power of hiring a female prisoner, and he could foretell the fate of any likely woman by her master or mistress. According to the place at which he was directed to draw up, he could prophesy of her future prospects; and many were the kind words of encouragement, caution or sympathy, he would offer, as the case of his woman needed. Now it would be—

"Xcoose me, my dear, but if you bears with the mistress's twittings and suspicions to first, you'll be pretty comfortable after a bit."

Then to a less fortunate candidate—

'You'll think old Hawkins a rum block, but, says I, you may all as well know first as last. Do what you will, you'll *never* please the master. He'm one of them there sort as doesn't think government folks has any feelings of no kind; therefore, when you wants to go, if *scheming* won't do better, have a row to once; if it's a wise one, 'twill only get you a month (to most three months), and lop your ticket a bit; but that's better nor having the life eat off your very vitals, says I.'

To a third, as to Maida, he would prognosticate bright days. Having given her her bundle, he vouchsafed his capacious hand. As a lady, she would have been glad to condescend with that grace which discovers no condescension; but now there was a tremble in her hand as she submitted it to his grasp, for she saw that, as an equal, nay, as a superior, the coachman proffered this familiarity.

'Well, good-bye my dear. Don't ye mind a bit; keep out of factory and drink, and you'll be a T.L. [4] soon. The master don't give your clothes yet; but when you gets stays, blast me, if you won't take amazing; your figure's bu-ti-ful, and your hair's grow'd fine—hardly know'd you'd a-been cropped.'

Shaking her hand until the pain reached her very heart, he repeated—

'Your hair's a-grow'd bu-ti-ful!'

This assurance was intended as the richest balm to her wounded spirit; it was his infallible remedy for convict ailments of the mental order.

Hawkins had been a butcher, and from the dead or live stock of his former trade he drew his not overflattering similes.

'Well, Maida, it seems you must go to Lucy, since she will not come to you. Poor girl! I wonder her little brain has not addled by this: she has been in a state of excitement all to-day. This way, Maida; down those stairs, and turn to your left,' pointed Bridget.

Maida was on the last stair, when Lucy sprang into her arms. Great joy was in that meeting—as great as though the dramatis personae had been ladies, perhaps greater—they being captives in the captives' land.

There was a rap at the parlour door, and with a smiling face, and after a brisk curtsey, Lucy entered.

'What time will you have tea, please, mem—sir?'

Without waiting for answer, she continued:

'Please, sir, may I cook a chop for Maida? It'll be a bit of a treat. She's dreadful tired, and wearisome all over.'

'Yes, and whilst you are about it, cook a couple for us. We have had no dinner, you know, and three chops make no more trouble than one, eh?'

'Lor', no, sir, nothing's no trouble; but I thought, sir, to do Maida's right away now; she's faintish. You shall have yours nice and hot, done separate.'

The events of the day had given Lucy a dash of the champion and heroine. Last evening she would as soon have committed murder as have allowed anyone the preference to the master. When she brought in the tea equipage, a dark circle round her eyes told of tears, and she seemed ready for another cry.

'Well, Lucy, did Maida enjoy her chop and tea?' asked Bridget.

Lucy burst out—'No, mem; she tried for to eat it, and then when I went for to answer the door, I met Rover running out with it, the nasty brute! Lor, mem, I can't go for to tell the master, but I'd as soon see a lady doing of dirty work as she—she'm so grand like—without going for to mean it.'

It was indeed doleful work in the kitchen. Lucy remembered *her* first cup of tea and slice of white bread and butter, and what angels' food she had thought that meal. She recollected what a paradise the kitchen had appeared in her sight after the dreary scenes of prison—Millbank, the voyage, and the *Anson*. She remembered the first moment of comparative freedom when, set down to a cheerful *tete-a-tete* with her fellow servant, she had almost forgotten that she was still a prisoner. She had looked forward to go through all these pleasant surprises again with her friend, and in the warmth of her affection she had determined that, if the kitchen had been a paradise to *her*, it should be the third heaven to Maida.

Everything was set with scrupulous neatness. No relic of Janet's filthy administration offended the eye: all was snug. The little oaken round table, the small brown teapot, the dear old willow-pattern plates, and blue cups and saucers bore a decidedly English air: the white loaf, the pat of butter, were almost objects of reverence. No convict heart, long estranged from such sights, could be proof against so many accumulated comforts. 'Come back, poor wanderer, we wait to make thee human once again! Come back, we wait to re-civilize thee! We wait to make a home for thee!' these comforts have said to more prisoners than Lucy Grenlow.

But Maida Gwynnham was not a convict in *heart*, though crushed by convict *scorn*—though dragged by convict *chains*. In compassion to Lucy she tried to reciprocate the almost infantile joy of her blithe companion. She tried to smile between each of her apostrophes, glad that they followed each other too quickly to allow of a reply, for reply Maida could not make; her soul was full to overflowing, full of such varied emotions that, had they appeared on paper, they would have appeared a list of contrarieties.

'Here,' exclaimed Lucy, seizing her hand and leading her forward, 'here we are all alone! No more 'orrid Perkinses hopping after us, no more nasty Snubses a thumbing of us. Look Maida, look! Here's bread—real white bread! Butter! Cups and saucers—no more dreadful tin pannikins, and tea—real hot tea, and flowers, Maida, flowers! Oh! won't we be happy!'

She gazed wistfully and respectfully into Maida's face, and perceived that the smile she saw there extended not beyond the lip; even *she* could tell that a pained heart lay beneath the specious guise. The barbarians, watching when St. Paul should fall by the insidious power of the deadly reptile, were ready to deify him, as they saw the holy man, uninjured, shake the viper from him.[5] So Lucy, when the charms she had prepared failed to affect Maida, regarded almost with superstitious awe the wondrous being who could stand proof against such enchantery, and from that time a feeling of dread mixed with her worship of Maida.

Absorbed in apparent reverie, Mr. Evelyn sat in his armchair. Emmeline and Bridget from time to time glanced at him to see if his thoughts were dispersing sufficiently for them to open a conversation with him; but no, Uncle Ev was not in a mood to be disturbed. There was a contraction of his brow that they well understood, for when that sign of the starfish[6] appeared on his forehead, it was a sure token that his mind was not at home to the public. Both the girls were speculating on what might be the result of the rather sudden appearance of the starfish, when the timepiece warned for nine. Uncle Ev started up, chair and all, and came down with a bounce at the table; then, drawing himself into it by the arms of the chair he had brought behind him, he smoothed the cloth as though smoothing away a difficulty, and uttered the monosyllabic command—'Prayers.'

Bridget placed the family Bible before him.

'Ring the bell.'

'We are here, Uncle Ev,' gently suggested Emmeline.

'I know it, my dear—ring the bell, Bridget.'

A ray of delight crossed Emmeline's face as she heard the ting-a-tong of the bell, and she met Bridget's inquiring expression with such a smile as one could fancy an angel would give, when it had borne a message of glad tidings to some forlorn sinner.

Lucy appeared in obedience to the summons.

'Prayers,' repeated Mr. Evelyn, without raising his eyes.

'The young ladies is here, sir,' said Lucy, naturally supposing that since her young mistresses sat at the back of her master they had escaped his notice.

'Come to prayers; you, Gwynnham, and Robert,' nodded Mr. Evelyn.

She stared; why, what next? And left the room to proclaim the news in the kitchen, almost stumbling over the stairs in her eagerness to do so. 'There! We's to go in to devotions all in honour of you. I've only been in three times since I've been here, and that was when the master was out of the way, and Parson Evelyn called us in; he don't mind knilling down along with *we*, but the master says he won't have no such hypocritical doings.'

When they were seated in the parlour, Mr. Evelyn chose the advice given in the third chapter of Colossians,[7] and before kneeling down, he expounded, not the Scripture, which was too clear to need explanation, but his own intentions:

'I mean, Maida, Lucy, and Robert, to commence with you as I have not lately commenced with any convict. I mean to try you, and if you deceive me, as others have done, I vow in the sight of the Lord I will never kneel with a prisoner again. Do not flatter yourselves that I am prompted to this concession by anything I have heard in your favour; for you have to *work* for my good opinion. I permit you to join our family prayers as a last trial at an experiment which I have hitherto found unsuccessful, and not as a reward to any character which you may have brought with you. I never heed reports either for or against prisoners whom I receive from government.'

The half of this address was incomprehensible to poor Lucy. Had it been wholly directed to herself she would have been terrified, and her terror would have interpreted it into the first stage of a journey to the Cascades for the expiation of some unknown offence; but as it was for division between herself and fellow servants, her sagacity discovered that it could not be a *threat*, whilst her admiration for Maida turned it into a rhapsody on the coming glories of the Gwynnham reign. Maida lingered at the door at the conclusion of the prayer.

'No, not to-night, Maida; you can go to bed now. I will talk with you early to-morrow morning.'

She retired, and seeking Lucy, asked her—'Does Mr.—what is his name?'

'*The Master*,' replied Lucy, with delicious simplicity. 'I s'pose that's the language out here—so I says it.'

Maida faintly smiled, and continued:

'Does the master generally give orders the first night?—perhaps it is from kindness that he tells me to go to bed?'

'Sure to be to *you*! *He* always tells *us* straight away everything, and frightens us dreadful the very first night—he did me and Janet—and so he did Peg Walters and Susan.'

Maida returned to the parlour.

'If you please, sir, if it is in consideration to me that you do not give orders now, perhaps I may say that it would be a relief to me to receive your commands to-night.'

'Very well; come in—that will do—shut the door, and stand where you are.'

Bridget managed to stretch before her uncle to reach the snuffers; then, turning towards him, she syllabled:

'Let—her—sit—down—*do*.'

'No, Bridget,' responded Mr. Evelyn, aloud.

The prisoner stood erect against the door, her face directed as though looking at her master, but her eyes fixed upon the ground, as much from weariness as from inward depression; the long, dark lash drooped over them so heavily that they had no choice but to bend earthwards, unless they would close entirely. Just as she stood there she would have made a beautiful variation of the Greek Slave, had Hiram Powers[8] wanted to vary his immortal marble.

Mr. Evelyn was well accustomed to his present labour; nevertheless, there was an audible quaver in his voice that a prolonged 'Ahem' did not wholly remedy when he commenced:

'Young woman, there is a new life before you; it will be your own fault if it prove one of degradation beyond that which attaches itself to a convict. Such degradation you cannot escape; the stain of convictism can never be erased; but you may so far hide it that you may become a respectable and useful member of society *out here*— in the lower ranks of life, of course. Some masters advise their servants to encourage thoughts of return to their native land; *I* as strenuously advise to the contrary. Lay up your wages, *not* for your homeward passage money, but as a proof of your earnestness in making repentant resolutions. Let your best energies strive for the goal Freedom in *this* land, *not* in your own country—in this land which adopts *you* —a land that is generously willing, when you shall have earned its confidence, to share with you all the privileges of its free people—privileges which Britain will never again offer when once you have offended her by selling your birthright for the transient allurements of crime. I would have you cherish every fond, dutiful and remorseful remembrance of your parents and other relatives, whilst I would urge you to forget your *country* —not from want of love to her, not from enmity against her (God forbid that either of these should actuate you!)—but because you could never more be happy there. There would arise too many twitting memories, too many unavailing regrets, too many untimely reproaches, to make your return a *peaceful* one, or your dwelling a *home*. Where justice ends injustice too often begins. The demands of justice will be satisfied by your penance here; but there are other demands equally important, though less imperious, which will not be appeased by that which suffices the law. Such demands will querulously follow you to your grave. There have been more hearts broken, more hopes crushed in returning to England, than ever there have been in leaving it. Relapse into crime has not unfrequently been the bitter expedient adopted by those who, full of cheerful anticipation, have gone back to the home of their days of innocence only to lament their having left a land that promised to be nobly oblivious of the *past* so long as the *present* deserved its favour. Maida Gwynnham, if you have parents or dear friends, what I am about to say will sound with harshness on your ear, but in no harsh spirit I say it. To be warned of a painful possibility *now* may save you from a very painful certainty hereafter.

Therefore do I tell you, that those *very* friends who may now be so urgent for your return, who (impelled by the quickened pulse of affection) now hold out every bait that love can prompt to tempt you back to their embrace, when your sentence shall have expired—those very friends will be the first to remind you of your former guilt when you are again one with them. How truly soever it may *forgive*, it is the weakness of human nature to be unable to *forget*; should *your* friends, however, act a better part and scrupulously keep their compact with you, your *own* sensibilities would militate against your peace, by perpetually imagining insult where no insult was intended—by fancying taunts where none existed. My advice, founded on long observation, is, look on the *past* as left behind you on the *Anson*, look on the *present* as a precious boon by which a happy future may be attained. Keep your eye steadily fixed on that future, and, God helping you, you cannot fail of success. *Then* invite your friends to *you*. Distant from the scene of your fall, your disgrace will also seem distant. It is hard to harbour resentful feelings on a foreign soil; the right of precedence will be yours, and procure for you a respect which you would vainly seek at home.'

Mr. Evelyn had wrought himself into a pitch of fervour that he had seldom reached on similar occasions. His addresses to his servants were always solemn, and somewhat severe—always searching, and somewhat sarcastic; but to-night's speech was distinguished by a solemnity devoid of satire, a severity only severe by necessity of subject.

Whether it was a glimpse of the spirit that hid in the statue-like figure before him, whether it was the beauty of the woman or the enormity of the crime for which she was expatriated, that warmed him into so unusual display of energy, it were difficult to determine, but it is certain his voice assumed an emphasis which gave unwonted force to his words, and made an earnest impromptu of what might have appeared a stern formality.

'On the other hand, Maida, I warn you that vigilant eyes will ever be upon you, watching your actions. The slightest liberty taken with the indulgence now granted you in the comparative freedom of service will be as severely punished as honest endeavours and obedient conduct will be rewarded. The very arm outstretched to welcome you back to honourable society will be the one to unsparingly chastise the first breach of law.

'I have done—I leave these subjects to your serious contemplation and to your good sense. I shall be happy to converse with you on any part you may wish more fully explained.'

During this speech a ghastly pallor had gathered on Maida's face, her lips had fallen apart, not after the manner of one who listens intently, but with the listlessness of that languor which unhinges the frame after a long resistance to physical and mental fatigue. She leaned heavily against the door, whilst her knees smote against each other in seeking to support themselves.

By this Mr. Evelyn felt half afraid that he had appeared too interested in his charge to Maida and determined to atone for his weakness by an examination of unabated strictness.

Again sounding an admonitory ahem, he desired Bridget to resume her seat, and then asked—

'Is your health good, Gwynnham?'

'Yes, sir.'

'Your mistress is from home: until her return you will attend to Miss D'Urban's commands. You are to be general servant, and must be ready to assist wherever you are wanted. Your wages will be seven pounds a year, and I shall add a sovereign yearly for seven years, so long as you deserve it. What is your sentence?'

'For life.'

'A lifer! That is against your future prospects, but not so far as I am concerned.' Several shorter ahems not unlike grunts.

'You do not seem satisfied, Maida Gwynnham. Speak up—have you been led to expect higher wages?'

'Thank you, I am more than satisfied.' There was a bitterness in her voice that did not escape Mr. Evelyn; he stored it by for later consideration.

'Can you cook?'

Maida's lip quivered. No answer came.

Bridget put herself before her uncle, and whispered:

'Shall I question her? I know how to.'

Bridget also knew that she would manage it more delicately.

'No, Bridget! *I* am as much pained in thus talking to the woman as *you* and *she* are in listening. Is it not kinder to let her know at once what she is to expect as a convict servant, than to foster hopes which would mock her when she reached her kitchen? Your show of feeling is more distasteful to her than ever my remarks may be. I am not slow to perceive that Maida is endowed with a nature which will *double* all the sufferings inflicted by law, to say nothing of her former position.'

Maida aroused herself; it was enough for her to know that another was being rebuked on her account. In almost a cheerful voice she exclaimed:

'I pray of you, Miss D'Urban, not to vex yourself. It is kind of Mr. Evelyn, I mean master, to speak so plainly. I am tired to-night, but to-morrow, and I trust ever after, I shall appreciate his warnings.' Her whole manner changed; and, assuming the expression of an interested hearer, she awaited Mr. Evelyn's pleasure, which was to repeat in an undisturbed tone:

'Can you cook?'

'Not much, sir; I have not had practice, but I will do my best.'

'Can you wash?'

'A little; we washed for the officers on the *Anson.*'

'Are you a good needlewoman?'

'I am considered so. I worked a great deal for Miss Perkins.'

'Are you willing to be told? Your mistress will soon make a good servant of you, if you are obedient and willing.'

'I will try, Mr. Evelyn.'

'*Sir*, if you please.'

'I will try, sir.'

'Do you drink?—or rather, were you given to liquor before your sentence?'

No answer, but a flush on her cheek.

'Do you drink? I choose to be answered, Maida.'

Bridget was making her way out of the room, looking more flushed than Maida, and far more miserable.

'Come back, Bridget; do not be foolish.'

It was a happy interruption—the colour had time to fade from Maida's cheek, and we suppose Uncle Ev forgot he had not been answered, for he passed on.

'Have you any children?'

'I'm not married.'

'No consequence. Have you any children in the Queen's Orphan School?'[9]

Had this question been delayed a week, Maida would have known the dire necessity of putting it alike to married and unmarried, and that it is one as commonly asked by colonial employers as the everyday inquiries, can you cook? or can you scrub? As it was, she imagined the question an insult directed immediately at herself, and her eye burned, indignant, at the cruelty. What might have been the result of the fire kindling within, and darting from beneath her dark lashes, those best can tell who are learned in prison discipline. That the result was harmless we are glad to report. The imploring gaze of the trembling Bridget for a third time averted an impending evil, and Maida smothered her rebellious spirit in an abrupt 'No.' She dared venture no more.

'Are—you—sure?' Mind, I can ascertain beyond doubt whether you are speaking truth or not. I have only to walk to New Town.'

Here Bridget interposed.

'Uncle did not hear you say you were not married, Maida. She is not married, uncle.'

This recalled Mr. Evelyn to a knowledge of his niece's presence: with an annoyed nod he said, 'True, true. Now, Maida, I have done with you. I make a plan of saying *at once* all of a disagreeable nature; it will be your own fault if ever you hear of such subjects again. Do make me your friend, and take in good part those precautionary rules which may bear the aspect of privations. Doubtless Lucy has already told you of them. We never allow our women to go out alone, until such time as they have proved their trustworthiness beyond the fear that they may return intoxicated, or be taken by the constable to the watch-house. Our next rule is equally painful, but not so important. We make our servants wear their government clothes until their first quarter's wages become due. We have been cheated into this rule by prisoners who, having begged an advance in order to put off their badge of shame, have spent their money at the tavern, and then given government the benefit of the next three months' labour.

'One word more, Maida. Let me warn you not to renew acquaintance with any of your shipmates, except Lucy. Much of the misery of female prisoners arises from a continuance of the objectionable intercourse which, not being able to escape, they learn to delight in during their voyage and probation. You will need moral courage to remain steadfast in this turning from your former associates, for you will everywhere meet them, and everywhere be open to their importunities. They will invite you to spree with them whenever occasion offers, but—'

A smile of a very undefinable description forced its way to Maida's lip, and looking on that smile, Mr. Evelyn felt obliged to stop his exhortation, notwithstanding his dislike to succumb to a prisoner's feelings. Whatever he meant further to enforce, he let off in a third, shrill ahem, and then proceeded to tell Maida that she was to go into Miss Evelyn's room at seven o'clock to light the fire, the mornings still being too cold for an invalid—and that, having lighted the fire, she was to attend to any order given her by Miss Evelyn, and finally go down and prepare the breakfast.

On leaving the parlour, Maida tried to drop an orthodox convict curtsey, but that curtsey being a failure, it was followed by one of Miss Perkins's aversions.

'O, uncle, uncle!' sobbed Bridget, 'How could you! This dreadful place—I wish I could go back to England; if it was not for dear Em, I'd go home directly. I'm so glad she wasn't present.'

'Oh she's been doing more for Maida all this while than you and I, I answer for it.'

'Yes, she has been to the Fountain of Mercy,' smiled Bridget, through her tears. 'I wish Uncle Herbert were home, he would do Maida good.'

'Then you think she needs doctoring? I thought you were after seconding Lucy's adoration of the poor woman.'

'This horrid place! I am sure a crust in England is better than dainties out here,' muttered Miss D'Urban.

'I fear little Charlie would grumble over a crust; but I hope brighter days are in store for Van Diemen's Land. Politician or not, no one relishes government sauce to his bread—eh Bridget? But it's good Uncle Herbert don't hear me.'

Bridget did not hear him, either; and yet, as if her ear had received an impression of a somewhat jocular speech, she said—

'I don't think you are half so hardhearted as you pretend to be, Uncle Ev; you make the poor creatures all in a flutter, and fancy you a *monster*, while really you are very tolerably susceptible.'

'Mine is the hardness of necessity, Bridget; if I show them my teeth at first, it is only that I may not have to bite them by-and-by. If you could see what fools your aunt and I have been made by them, you would not wonder that my heart puts on an iron casing before it deals with prisoners; and of all prisoners, these probationers. I'd rather hire twenty raw, rough apprehensions fresh from the policeman's hand, than one of these p's from the schools of crime called Probation Stations.'[10]

Bridget lamented her question, for she saw it had raised the anti-convict principle so strong in Uncle Ev that she feared only a storm could carry it off; but a mere puff sufficed for the present. The well-worn simile of parent and child assisted Mr. Evelyn's ideas.

'It's all right and fair that children should help their parents in their old age; but that one unfortunate wight[11] should have so much of the bother and annoyance is abominable; 'tisn't Christian. The same Bible that says, "Children, obey your parents," says also, "Parents, provoke not your children to wrath."'

And provoked by his Britannic parent, very wrathfully strode Mr. Evelyn (the child representing Tasmania) up and down his handsomely furnished parlour, rendering, as he strode, sundry grunts, the result of undigested anger.

Bridget hated the anti-convict controversy; and fancying, in the depths of girlish vanity, that she was going to be made a party in it, she jumped up and managed to divert uncle by praising his oratory.

'Were you preparing that grand speech, uncle, when you retreated beneath the sign of the starfish during those solemn hours before prayers? If I had known what you were about, wouldn't I have disturbed you, that's all! Not Em even should have prevented me. Tell me, were you getting it up then?'

'No, my speech, as you call it, was an extempore: I felt quite eloquent over that splendid creature—a very Boadicea.[12] But when I say extempore, I must qualify my words. A prayer is not always extemporary because it is *unwritten*. The head of a family who daily conducts devotion without a compilation, follows by degrees as marked a formula as though he read each sentence from a book. The same set of phrases which a stranger thinks a beautiful impromptu, the children have yawned over from their earliest admission to the domestic altar. From having so often addressed prisoners on their entrance into service, I have, unawares, adopted a form which my mind uses on state occasions.'

'Well, Uncle Ev, extempore or not, it was an affair sufficiently awful; but the examination was worse than all.'

'And you, cruel child, tried to make me break down. When you have been here a little longer you will learn what sharks you have to encounter, and if you don't want every particle of feeling torn from your heart, you will have to hide it where shark's eyes can't detect it. In an instant they discover who *has* or who has *not* any feeling to throw away on them, and woe to him who becomes their victim.'

'You do not surely call humanity *thrown* away on them?' Bridget looked shocked, and awaited his reply.

'*Humanity* is *never* thrown away, Bridget; but that tender pity which you show, and which they designate either "feelins" or "greenness" is decidedly wasted, for two reasons, namely—'

'I don't want to hear them,' cried Bridget, stopping her ears, 'for fear they should come into my head the next time I'm green to the prisoners. I don't wish to be hardened before my time. I don't believe that feeling or anything else *good* is thrown away on them; nor do you either, really, only you like to find out their characters before you show yourself the dear uncle Ev that you are.'

'And you want to be cheated out of a few more shillings for snuff before you give over—eh, Bridget?' retorted Uncle Ev.

Bridget blushed to her ears, for she had been thoroughly deceived out of a shilling by Janet's long face and sincere sighs, which had grown deeper and oftener until they had ended in a hope that 'the dear young lady would *lend* her a trifle to buy a pinch of snuff to stop them tears from blinding her poor old eyes.'

'And you've a few more old dresses for the three balls,' persisted Uncle Ev, 'before you are ready to believe me?'

'I declare it's very shabby of you to bring my sins to remembrance,' replied Bridget, pretending to pout, and really vexed; 'as if 'tisn't horrid enough to be cheated, without being laughed at into the bargain. At any rate, I like the way Uncle Herbert treats prisoners; even the *bad* like *him*.'

'But Herbert does not make such good servants of them as I do. I have had no less than five good ones since I have been out here.'

'Ah! That is only because he never keeps them long enough. Em told me that when he had a house of his own he always took in those who needed a little care or training before they could get other places.'

'Poor Herbert! Both he and his wife made themselves slaves to a system than never rewarded their long self-sacrifice.'

The anti-convict question, thought Bridget, hastily changing the subject into—

'Oh, uncle! I mean to accept your challenge to Maida, some day, and hold a conversation respecting your speech. You can never be a true Englishman, and advise her to forget England.'

'It will be for her happiness to do so, and as quickly as she can, too. England is a kind friend but an implacable enemy. It is too late now, love, to commence another branch of this many-branched topic.'

Bridget fetched her bed-candle, and as she was lighting it said—

'How you *did* tease poor Maida about whether she had any children.'

'Well, well, if I was absent you took care I shouldn't remain so. Night, night, Bridget; take a peep at Charlie, and see that dear Em has her jelly before you go to bed.'

'Oh Em! I'm so glad you've not been downstairs; there has been such a fuss. If it weren't for you, I'd leave this horrid place: but I am not going to disturb you, poor dear tired one, with a history of it.'

'You cannot tell me more than I know already,' and Emmeline heaved a sigh from the very depths of her heart.

'Isn't Maida a lovely woman? I've formed a romance about her already.'

'I did not see her; I never once looked towards her where she sat at prayers; I dread to see her to-morrow; I suppose she will have to light my fire as Janet used to.'

'Emmeline,' said Bridget, in a low frightened voice, as she drew close to her cousin's bed, 'what do you think her crime is? I feel rather nervous to sleep alone.'

'Something very bad: a person in that station of life has no temptation to commit small sins; forgery, most likely. Has uncle told you?'

Bridget was unwilling to communicate her alarm to the invalid, but it was against her nature to have a secret (a dreadful one, too) and keep it a secret; so bending over the bed, she whispered—

'Murder!'

To her surprise, Emmeline only smiled.

When Mr. Evelyn left the parlour in order to retire for the night, he found Lucy sitting on a stair outside the door.

Though she had been patiently waiting there in the dark for the last three-quarters of an hour to speak to him, she seemed about to run off when she saw him.

'Lucy, what's this? My orders are—bed at ten o'clock. This is a bad beginning indeed; take care you and your friend are about.'

With a desperate effort, as though she would try though she should fail, the little housemaid said—

'Please, sir, may Maida and me change places. She ain't fit for the dirty work, and I can do it nice.'

'No, Lucy; she's a large woman, and more capable of hard work than you; or if she is not she will not do for me.'

'Please, sir, to make no remark on it, cause she don't know nothing to my asking, it were my own congesting,[13] sir. You'll have never a fault to find with her work, dirty or clean; but that don't alter her having to do it, noways it don't.'

During an extra long interval occupied by Mr. Evelyn in extracting a waster[14] from the candle, Lucy's round, shiny face looked up beggingly at him, whilst an infinity of quick curtsies seemed to bob out— 'Please, sir! *Do*, sir!'—between each fresh attack of the snuffers. The waster would not yield; its obstinacy afforded Lucy time to 'congest' an irresistible plea.

'Please, sir, she'd teach Master Charles manners better nor he has ever learnt 'em. Lor! The looks of her is right away lovely, and all on 'em says it is enough to make one grand to look at her—and I know Master Charlie'll soon set a sight on her, sir.'

Every muscle of Mr. Evelyn's mouth twitched with emotion, rather contrary to anger; it is a wonder, therefore, that he managed from such a mouth to evoke so formidable, so inexorable a '*No!*' Advancing three stairs towards his room, he turned.

'Once and for all, Lucy, let me hear no more of this nonsense; if Maida is a wise woman she'll take the punishment of her sin quietly; if not, she'll go to Cascades, and you'd better warn her.'

Lucy threw up her eyes to see if a thunderbolt were falling; then dropping to one of her old humble curtsies, she disappeared beneath the staircase.

We have followed Maida from the bar of justice to the scene of her expatriation. The family has retired to rest; one by one its members have dropped to pleasant sleep. But

Emmeline is wakeful. She is not aware that she has a companion in unrest in the occupant of the attic—one who, although morning has overtaken midnight, still stands at her little window, gazing out on what sky is visible through the narrow aperture. The candle has burnt out, therefore her figure is indistinct; but the dim light of heaven falls on her face, and discovers the features of Maida Gwynnham—features enigmatic in their calmness of expression, and singularly disregarding of wearied Nature's demands in the unabating vigil which absorbs them into death-like quiescence.

Save during the involuntary solitude of the cells, or the few moments snatched from the surveillance of the officers and the company of her shipmates, Maida has not been alone since she left England. When, therefore, she closes her bedroom door upon herself, she can scarcely believe she is unwatched, nor that from some unseen corner a voice will not command her to unbolt the door she has dared to lock.

Standing in the middle of the room with upraised hand and lamp, she explores every nook from which surprise is possible. Then feeling safe from the Misses Perkins's and Snub's persecutions, she sets her bundle on the floor, and kneeling before it, draws forth the Bible given her by Mr. Herbert, but not to seek comfort from its precious pages, as the earnest looker-on may hope; no, what comfort she expects lies not within that volume. With eager fingers she pulls off the morocco cover that preserves the binding and a letter falls to the ground. She seizes it and reads it through and through until its contents should be stamped upon her soul; the letter bears the date of nearly two years ago, and is one that Norwell contrived to forward to her just before the transport sailed. Once she suddenly dashes the letter from her and spurns it with her foot; then, as though the senseless paper were a thing of life, she takes it tenderly up and folds it to her bosom while her lips hastily murmur words inaudible, that have no effect on the senseless paper, though they seem to work in *her* a succession of emotions. She then stops short to think out a thought too sensitive to be continued, save by the undivided assistance of body and mind.

The candle is expiring in the socket and that intricate thought has not been traced; it still occupies her, until, determined to lay *it* and the letter by together, Maida disturbs the former with a sigh and replaces the latter in her Bible. She then remembers she has a master, the recollection brings a new succession of feelings, and she is rather pleased than otherwise with him. His inflexible will and tight-handed control will afford her a somewhat tangible burden to bear. It is the thumbing of the low-bred Snub, the petty malignities of the upstart Perkins that make her spirit writhe rebellion. As Lucy says, 'She goes about all them there hard things as tho' she liked 'em.'

She recalls her interview with Mr. Evelyn; she thinks of what is expected from her, and thinks and thinks till thought becomes impalpable, and merges into that one deep reverie from which we have aroused her.

Has the following of Maida to her room been a scrutiny too close? The telling what she did there, in answer to your question, 'Where is she now?' a detail too minute? Ah! *You* in English homes, *you* the master and mistress of freewill servants, *you* the honest reapers of honest toil, come with me to that land where captive exile hasteth to be free—where the sighing of the prisoner ascends from the small apartment in the roof—where dismissed from his master's presence the convict stands dejected, lonely, friendless; his sense of strangeness rendered more chill and dreary by the remembrance of chains which bind him to the land, how strange and loveless soever it may be. Come there with me, and, unless void of kindly sympathy, you shall learn that the record is neither trivial nor uninteresting, though it only inform you that a convict woman gazes out into the night; for, deeply folded in that information, you shall discern records past and prophetic, each full of pain and disappointment. And within that woman's tranquil exterior you shall discover a world of passions active unto tumult, of memories sorrowful to poignancy. How few amongst the multitudes attending a court of justice give more than a passing thought to their doomed fellow creatures removed one by one from the bar! There is a breathless silence while the sentence is being pronounced, and a murmur of applause or dissatisfaction as the case demands, when it has proceeded from the judge's lips; but how few analyse into definite meaning the legal form of sentence which has fallen on the ear of the poor wretch concerned; annihilating his life-long hopes, crushing his temporal, and too often his immortal prospects.

There is a vague conception that the prisoner will be taken back to prison and thence sent across the sea, and that, touching that country beyond the sea, he will forthwith become an object of terror, a ruffian, a bushranger, an excommunicate, against whom everyone's hand may be raised, and whose hand is raised against everyone, as though in the coasts of that distant land lay some horrible property potent to transform the man into a fiend; or else, stories of criminals who have raised themselves from penal servitude to luxurious mastership being current, there is an angry notion that crime is *rewarded* and not *chastened* in being banished to the Australian shores. Here ceases all surmise on the future career of the miserable being who a moment before stood, trembling and haggard, at the dock; and who in disappearing from the court has likewise disappeared from the stage of recognised existence; his name has been blotted out from the book of moral life, and henceforth the memory of him perishes. But his disappearance affects no one in the assembly, it is followed by no inquiry, he is not missed; few know or care to know that he lives on somewhere—that his life is ebbing in a routine of degradation embodied, but not perceptible, in the sentence passed upon him. Perchance to one more benevolent hearer may recur a thought of him whose anxious features arrested his attention as he listened to the learned counsel pleading in his behalf, and such a one may exclaim, 'I wonder what has become of that poor man whose trial we heard.'

But not all his wondering, questioning or replying can convey to his mind an adequate idea of what transportation is, nor convince him that it does not consist of heavy chains, the slashing whip, barren shores, murders and executions, though none of these are wanting amongst the accumulated items that make transportation a punishment more terrible to some than death itself, to many an award exceeding the offence, and to *all* an infliction far beyond judicial intention when it sends the offender from his home.

Volume II

THE

BROAD ARROW:

BEING PASSAGES FROM THE HISTORY

OF

MAIDA GWYNNHAM,

A LIFER.

BY OLINÉ KEESE.

IN TWO VOLUMES.

VOL. II.

LONDON:

RICHARD BENTLEY, NEW BURLINGTON STREET.

1859.

CHAPTER 22

The Initiation—Within

TO Emmeline it was nothing new to expect a strange face. It was not that expectation, therefore, which prevented her from sleeping, but an undefined sense of painful interest in the person who was to appear. She lay awake the greater part of the night, waiting for seven o'clock of the morning. No wonder, then, that when that hour arrived it found her asleep. Having been warned to do so, Maida entered Miss Evelyn's room without knocking at the door. Perceiving that her young mistress slept, she hesitated to advance; but the lovely countenance reposing before her attracted her to a nearer contemplation of the peaceful features, whose transitory shudder (induced by suffering) but showed to more advantage the calm into which they speedily relapsed.

Resolving that should scorn await her there, it should be repaid with scorn, severity with coldness, indignity with defiance, Maida had prepared to commence her life of public disgrace, and had entered the chamber full of proud and determined thoughts.

When, therefore, her eye fell upon the bed, and beheld there a face so sweet that it appeared incapable of scorn, so gentle that it could not assume severity, she felt as if she had done it grievous wrong by her previous supposition, while a keen pang of sorrow darted through her heart as she observed that death had laid unmistakable claim to the fair young creature lying before her. Emmeline moved her lips, and Maida, thinking she was about to awake, turned quickly away; but her own name, murmured softly and dreamily, reached her ear, and again she looked towards the bed.

'Poor Maida—would God—poor—poor—Maida!'

Emmeline opened her eyes with the last word, and slightly started as she saw a woman of graceful carriage, bearing a faggot[1] on her arm, and all the necessaries for fire-lighting and grate-cleaning in her hand, swiftly but stealthily cross the room, and kneel before the hearth. It needed not a second look to tell her this woman was the object of her dream; nor a second look to attest Lucy's statement that Maida was no common prisoner. It was with curious though mournful interest that Miss Evelyn watched her in this her first act of servitude; and yet she half doubted whether it could be her *first*, so adroitly and unhesitatingly did she begin and pursue her task. There was no token of helplessness and inability, by show of which, with pardonable vanity, superior convicts often intend their employers to discover that they have not been brought up to menial labour. As though she had been trained to it from her earliest years, Maida leant over the bars and plied the brush with unremitting energy, until the grate shone more brightly than it had done for a long time; and then, having lighted the fire, and swept up the dust and ashes, she gathered her apparatus together, and arose as quietly and unconcernedly, as would any housemaid who had done her duty, and nothing beyond.

Miss Evelyn hastily closed her eyes, hoping Maida would not know she had been awake; but the movement was not so rapid as to escape Maida. Though she did not turn towards Emmeline, she perceived it, and appreciated the delicate kindness. But, proud

165

and determined as she had entered, she could not leave the room without expressing her altered mood in a voluntary offer of her service. She stopped at the door, and asked, in a voice so gentle that no one would suppose it was a murderess who spoke:

'Can I do anything for you before I go downstairs?'

Miss Evelyn wanted nothing, but hearing in Maida's voice a desire to help her, she said she should like to be raised a little higher, and have her pillows beaten up. The request was a proof of confidence that touched the prisoner to the quick; it told her that, whatever indignities might elsewhere be heaped upon her, she would have none to fear from the gentle being whose head, now resting on her shoulder, dreaded no contamination from convict garments. She was again preparing to leave the room, when Emmeline, unable to refrain, stretched her long, thin hand to her, and exclaimed:

'Maida, this hand will, perhaps, ere long, be stiff in death; take it now, as a pledge of proffered friendship. Yes; do not start; distinctions made in *life* are useless on a bed of sickness. I repeat, take it as a pledge of friendship, which I offer from my very heart.'

Maida did not approach, and the hand dropped heavily upon the bed; emaciated as it was, it was too heavy for self-support. It rested a moment, and then again presented itself, accompanied by a look that overcame Maida's unwillingness to yield. Those who know Maida will not be surprised that, having once taken the proffered pledge, she clasped it with a fervency that satisfied Emmeline's most sanguine anticipation, but still she did not speak.

'You started at that word *friendship*, Maida; perhaps you thought I used it on the impulse of feeling: but no; I have lived in this country nearly all my life, and have found that one of the grand miseries of the convicts is having no friend to speak to, no friend to confide in; therefore, when I see one of my own sex newly arrived, I feel deeply for her, knowing what she will have to go through, even in a family where prisoners are kindly treated, and I long to become her friend, so that, when her heart is overwhelmed within, she may feel she has someone to whom to speak her grief; I *must* be your friend, Maida; something tells me I must be—'

Emmeline raised herself on one side, and, looking earnestly at Maida, continued—

'Tell me, do you disbelieve me still?'

'No, Miss Evelyn; neither did I disbelieve you. If I started, it was in hatred of that word, which has been profaned until it has lost for me all its hallowed meaning: it has been sounded in my ears until I loathe it; it has been abused until I forget its proper signification; and, when you used it, the word reached my mind not so much associated with your generous proposal, as with objects of vice, which I choose to call my inferiors. On shipboard, and on the *Anson*, I was daily either charged *with*, cautioned *against*, or punished *for*, intimacy with creatures I shudder even to think of. *Friendship* it was called—but that relationship cannot exist between fiends! For all that I so loathed them, if I only spoke *to*, or was *spoken* to, by one of them, an officer would reprimand me for endeavouring to strike up a friendship which could only be for injurious purposes or mutiny. If by chance two of us got together, either she was cautioned against making *friends* with a mate of such known bad character as Martha Grylls, or I was warned not to seek too familiar a *friendship* with her—pah!'

And as if the subject was one too disgusting to dwell upon, Maida stopped.

'That is past now; let its remembrance make you value more—'

But Maida interrupted.

'It is not past! Last night, in this house, the same caution was repeated.'

'For the last time, though. Mr. Evelyn will not mention those painful subjects again: nor will anyone in this family, except your mistress; and when you have become accustomed to her you will find that habit only, and not a desire to annoy, makes her speak as she does. Ah, Maida, you will have *many, many* things to try you; 'tis just for that I want you to consider me a friend.'

She laid her other hand over Maida's (which still held hers in a warm though tremulous grasp), and fixed an eye so tender, so beseeching on her, that Maida had much ado to hide the emotion which struggled in her bosom. But she *did* hide it, and that so well that Emmeline heard no trace of it in the calm voice that answered:

'Should I need a confidential adviser or friend, Miss Evelyn, I shall, with gratitude, avail myself of your kindness; but I am averse to promises, they have painful consideration with me, forcing me against my inclination. Were I to give the promise, I should fulfil it with as much reluctance as I should with unwillingness break it. It is not in my *nature* to confide in anyone.'

Oh, say not so, Maida Gwynnham! Thou art womanlike to thine inmost soul; but in the wreck wherewith adversity hath desolated thee, thy nature hath been so convulsed, that thou canst not discover thyself amid the ruins.

'As I said before, you will find everyone in this house kind to you, and disposed to assist your views for the future; but when your thoughts revert to home, and the chair by the chimney corner—when your heart is rent by misgivings, or wounded by reproach—you will want something more than *that*; it is *that* something I desire to be. I do not wish to draw a promise from you: what is your sentence?'

'Life.'

'A lifer! O, Maida! Then you have not even the small hope that buoys up other hearts; you need a better friend than I.'

'Amount of sentence is nothing to me; from the absence of all endearing ties or pleasant memories, locality is a matter of indifference. I have no one in England to wish me back; no one for whom I would wish to return; a despised creature I was sent thence, and a despised creature I remain here; ignominy is stamped upon me, and would be the same in any place. If I might fix on one spot beyond another, the one in which my heart would become the most hardened, and my mind the most forgetful of the past, should be the object of my choice.'

'Have you no parents—no relatives, Maida?'

'I do not know—I fear to know.'

An expression of anguish here compressed Maida's features, and pain was visible in the shudder that caused her to clasp her hand upon her bosom.

'Oh, my father! Poor old man! Was that letter his death?' burst from her lips ere she could control her words and bid the grief hide unuttered in her heart.

Though ignorant of Maida's history, Emmeline read the tale of sorrow concealed in that bitter cry. She knew that, the broad world over, heart answers to heart, and that the parent of the prisoner standing by her bed had passed through all the tortures that had stricken other parents to their graves; and if not sunk already, his life must be a prolonged dying, to which the article of death itself would be a state most blissful. A broken-hearted parent is one of the many untold calamities following the prisoner's career. During the brief silence which ensued, Emmeline opened her little Scripture portion-book, and when Maida appeared calm, she read the text for the morning.

'"I will be a father to you," is God's message to you this morning, Maida.'

'Oh do not, I pray you, Miss Evelyn, speak to me on that subject. I hate it; not from disrespect, but because the evil of it alone can belong to *me*. I have had it presented to me as something in which I have a fearful interest, having sinned against it, and awakened all its wrath. *You*, lying there with heaven's own peace on your very countenance, with relationship to God apparent in your likeness to Him, may revel in the sweets of religion. How should you not? What can *you* know of the dark side which makes it so terrible to me?'

'Is there anything very terrible in the promise of a Father to supply the want of an earthly one, Maida? Is there anything to alarm you in those tender words I have just read?'

'Everything is terrible to those beyond the reach of hope. The very joys of heaven beheld from afar will be a torment to the damned; so those parts of Scripture comforting to *you*, are to *me* so many messengers sent to torment me before the time; they tell me all I have lost!'

'They are *none* of them lost to you yet.'

'Our religious instructor thought differently; he seemed to see hell-fire already burning within me; happily safe himself, he cared not who else he consigned to the flames. I hated religion before I met with him, *now* I hate it tenfold, as an unnecessary addition to the miseries of a miserable existence. What an abhorred thing must religion be to *government*, since it deems it a fitting aggravation to prison discipline, and since *such agents* are chosen to administer it! I never met with but *one* who did not dispense it as a deadly drug—never but *one* who did not bid me drink and *die*. Were there more of such men as that one clergyman appointed, there might be less hypocrisy among us convicts.'

'That is very like papa; he will talk to you. Stay, Maida, stay; I am not satisfied. If you will not accept my offer, remember that it is not withdrawn: my stay on earth may not be long. Whilst I *am* here, consider you have one to whom to speak as to a sister.'

'Miss Evelyn, I had a father; in the days of my childhood he did not love me, but I *made* him. I could not exist without love. In after years I sinned away that love purchased by childish tears, and that with which I sought to replace it turned to wormwood in my heart, and embittered the principle of love within me. Since then I have lived on unloving and unloved, and will do so to the end. I am no longer a child. I can now exist without love, and I do not need a friend.'

'Maida, you *cannot* exist without love unless its absence be supplied by *hatred*, and the need of a friend by the presence of an enemy. In our natural state we all require a friend or a foe—something to love or hate; either passion *may* fill the heart, but one *must*; who would take the latter that might choose the former?'

'There is no might for me now, it is all *must*.'

'There is *no* must! The irrevocable decree of death alone can fix into certainty the possibilities of life. You do not know the condition of your heart, Maida. I am *sure* you do not; and am as sure that you *never* will, whilst you trust only to yourself to fathom its feelings, to analyse its motives, and to satisfy its longings. We are none of us capable of an unaided search into our own hearts. Such search must always be deceptive in its results. To know ourselves, we need assistance from a power superior to our own.'

'I would rather shun that assistance! It could only show me myself more vile than at present; to fathom my feelings would be to shock me with the depths of my depravity; to analyse my motives to discover pollution in them all. No, no, Miss Evelyn, the knowledge I have of myself is sufficiently frightful; spare me closer investigation for pity's sake.'

There was again a silence; it was broken by Maida, who with a slight sneer in her tone, said —'Supposing that I desired such assistance, could *your* experience afford it me? You cannot know to what a character you speak in me. You can know nothing of Martha Grylls, if you think there is aught in her experience that can bear comparison with yours; or that the dark meanings of her soul may be deciphered by the pure characters of your heart. What can she have in common with you?'

'God fashioneth *all* hearts alike. Maida, we have more in common than you suppose; were we to exchange the secrets of our hearts, we should start to see how many thoughts we deemed exclusively our own belonged to the other. There is nothing in *me* to prevent my being all that *you* are; there is no impediment to your being all that I am. *We* see each other and ourselves in the light of circumstance, and therefore never correctly see the true actings of the heart; but God—'

The door pushed open, and Lucy, unbidden, advanced. Not heeding Miss Evelyn, she exclaimed, with a frightened air:

'Oh, Maida, I'm in such a way; 'tis nigh to eight, and there's a sight to do yet; if the master comes down, and finds it ain't done, he'll be after you, and then there'll be a row, and p'raps trouble, if he finds I've been and doned them doorsteps for you.' (Dropping a curtsey to Emmeline.) 'I beg pardons, mem. I forgot you was here; you see, mem, I feels in a fritter like, 'cause it's her first day out, and the master'll be sharp on her.'

'And you feel responsible?' asked Emmeline, smiling.

Lucy glanced at Maida to see how she took this; to her delight there was no expression of annoyance on the latter's face.

'Why you see, mem, I told the master of she, and natural like I feels anxious. I wouldn't have them fall out for no amount.'

'Come then, Lucy, I will try to do you credit,' said Maida.

Emmeline gazed at her in surprise; she could not believe that the almost playful tone belonged to the person who a few minutes since had spoken so bitterly.

'Miss Evelyn, I thank you sincerely for your noble intentions, and regret that *mine* should disappoint them; you will not judge harshly of one who from long disuse has forgotten how to apply confidence or value a friend.'

'Lor', mem, don't she curtsey beautiful!' Admiration was in every line of Lucy's face as she turned to Emmeline for appreciation of Maida's exit. 'Lor', mem, you should have seen her 'mong our women on the *Anson*; she was as grand as Mrs. Bowden any day, and she was grand enough to frighten the wits out of the best of us,' lowering her voice.

'Lor', mem, now she's *come* I'm half afeared how she'll get on with the master. She ain't like one of us, to take it all natural, and the master won't put up with nothing from no one. Says he last night—"If Maida's a wise woman, she'll bear what she's got to bear, and if she *don't*, she must be made to;" and that's what she'll never do. I always says she likes bearing of things, but if she don't *choose*, nobody can make her to; not even Mrs. Bowden.'

Mr. Evelyn's voice on the stairs sent Lucy skittering away in search of Maida, who to her delight stood in the dining room enveloped in a cloud of dust sufficient to smother all dread of the master's anger. Order speedily followed Maida's steps, and the breakfast was duly laid before Mr. Evelyn appeared.

'I say, have you seen the new pris'ner?' shouted Charlie, pulling Lucy towards the parlour whence he had just espied Maida; 'wouldn't she catch it if mamma was at home, for sweeping the carpet without covering the pretty things!'

'Ought I to cover them, Master Charles?' asked Maida.

'Be sure! Bridget isn't half a missus; wait till mamma comes home, *then* you'll see. Our pris'ner women is all afraid of her 'cept when they's drunk—ah! ah! ah! It's such fun—do you like being drunk? This is the way,' and with a sleepy grimace, the child stumbled about the room.

'Poor little boy! If that is what you've been taught, no wonder we have become a byword.'

'You don't laugh, stupid woman!' Then checked by the serious look with which Maida regarded him, he said, sheepishly—'All the others does laugh at it. You mustn't look like that at me. Lucy said you were such a beauty; but you are an ugly old fright, and I hope you'll get into lots of trouble, and be sent to Cage; then we shan't have you back.'

Lucy flew indignantly at the child.

'Naughty boy! I'll tell your aunts!' But the little fellow was too sharp, he darted to the door, where, pointing his finger at Maida, he cried—'Crop-py! Crop-py!' and then ran off.

Maida turned in silence to her work. The finger of childish scorn touched neither her temper nor her mind, but it entered her very heart, and chilled her into a sense of utter desolation. She who had stood the taunts of vice, the sneers of virtue; she who had received in unflinching disdain the unmerited rebukes of inflated vanity, and had borne uncomplainingly the sentence of the law, now bowed her head in shamed sorrow over the reproaches of a little child. No wrathful thought against the young Shimei ² stirred in her bosom, but every thought and every feeling turned, poignant, on herself, revealing a mark of infamy so revolting and deep-branded as to arrest even childhood's careless eye. She leaned upon her broom, and groaned 'O God! My punishment is greater than I can bear.'

She heard a pattering footstep behind her, and, turning, beheld an infant toddling into the room. It stopped as she turned, and baby's two large bright eyes fixed intently on her, so intently that they did not move, though the little creature plumped flat down on the floor into a sitting posture. After scanning Maida steadily, the child thrust out a crushed flower, and said—

"No kye, no kye—pitty fow-fow—missie's pitty fow-fow—no more kye.'

Maida sprang to the child; and as the small, fat hand smoothed her face, and as the low, sympathising voice hummed—

'Poor, poor—poor, poor—no more kye,' she strained the baby to her heart, and forgot all she had been, and was likely to be, in the delicious respite of the moment.

Baby toddled off, and Maida descended to the kitchen. No one had witnessed the interview. The babe's innocence was not sullied by the embrace of crime; but crime, as personified in Maida Gwynnham, received a softening influence from the embrace of purity; and as she entered the kitchen, there was an expression on her lips that Lucy would have called a smile if she had dared.

'That's Bob,' said Lucy, as Maida glanced at a man washing at the pump-trough.

'Welcome, missus,' answered Sanders, turning with towel in hand and dripping face. 'I guess we sha'n't always be kept waiting after this fashion—a fellow wants his breakfast when he's been out with his hosses—howsomever, glad to see you clear of gover'ment for a while; I'm hearty glad it's *you* come instead of a free woman. The mistress vowed she'd get a migrate³ next time; 'taint many things I'm not willing for, but them free folks is one that I can't 'bide. I likes to have my equals about me; them as won't take airs because they've never been gover'ment; they'm always getting trouble on a feller, them others be.'

'What is this trouble I am always hearing of, Lucy?' asked Maida, anxious to turn the subject.

'Oh, everything is trouble out here that happins to prisoners.'

'Hang trouble! When a feller wants his breakfast and can't get it; that's trouble enough, ain't it, Madda?' said Bob. 'All I hopes is that *you* won't know it no more than *that*, for when trouble begins on a feller, the devil if it don't stick to him like mud. Come now, don't feel shy, Madda, or what's you called, we shall be fine together soon; we don't look to what our mates have done worse than we. Gover'ment mark 's the same on all on us, whether it's for murder or lifting[4]; and hang the gover'ment clothes, a hansom lass is an hansom lass, whether she've got on brown or blue; and the 'air ain't a consideration, seeing he grows in no time.'

And Bob, by way of illustration, drew his fingers through his long, greasy hair.

So the three sat down together, and the meal passed. Bob thought he had never devoured a better, for he had not only 'ate his wittels in peace,' but had been able to hear the sound of his voice in enlightening his new mate on a few points of penal etiquette.

'An't he handsome, Maida?' exclaimed Lucy, as he walked off.

Lucy arose, deceived into a hope that Maida had enjoyed not only her breakfast, but her introduction to Bob; the affectionate little being had forgotten to enjoy hers in the full occupation of watching the effect made by the two on each other. *Now* she listened to Bob with Maida's ears, but with none of her feelings; *then* gazed at Maida with Bob's eyes. The mutual impression would have been very startling could she have stamped it. Bob was a great person in her sight. He had nearly won his ticket, and his significant hints of what he meant to do when he really possessed it, had not been lost upon her.

'He didn't know that he shouldn't give the master warning for all that he'd two such hosses to look after; may be he'd sote[5] up for himself;' with various other large talkings, so worked upon her that the talker became an embryo hero. She admired the amount of courage that could, even in prospect, give the master notice; and as his long, grease-heavy locks flopped about in a manner most contrary to government notions of convict propriety, it seemed to her that the spirit of liberty, antedating Bob's partial freeedom, had gotten into each individual lock, and she began to doubt that government had ever taken the same liberty with his head that it had with other prisoner heads.

How Maida felt when she arose from that her first morning's meal, we gather neither from her countenance nor from what she says to Lucy; our previous knowledge of her character and case alone informs us of the torture, slow and subtle, which preys on her inner life. When we see her, calm and dignified, move to her menial duties—now sifting cinders, then scouring out the pantry, now following Miss D'Urban to market, then washing Bob's clothes—we discover by no outward sign that she is wrapped about with burning thoughts that wither up her soul into a hatred of existence. Day after day we see her move to those duties, clad still in her prison garments; and, perceiving not that pain is in each step she takes, we wonder how she can bear to do so. She goes abroad, and though under the protection of one of her master's family, the men in the chain-gang wink to her as she passes, recognising her relationship to them by the brown of the guilty sisterhood. We see it, and wonder she does not sink beneath that badge which, maliciously cruel, proclaims her shame in the public streets; but her power is greater than its malice, and though, unreconciled by habit, its cling to her is the cling of a serpent, it cannot cripple her dauntless tread, nor bow her erect form.

She enters a shop, and it is known to all there for what she comes or will shortly come; a young man leans over the counter, and enumerates the articles which he knows the probationer will first require. He tries to conciliate her with—'A stays, my dear? Must have it, you'll look a different figure when you've got a pair; get the master to advance for a pair, then.'

Drawn and Etched by A. Hervieu.

"Oh, Heaven!" cried Maida, "my punishment
is greater than I can bear."

We hear it, and, forgetting that feeling is deepest in its silence, and emotion, fire-like, strongest in its pallor, we wonder how blushes do not scorch her cheek.

A month drags wearily by, and Bridget uses the announcement of her Aunt Evelyn and Uncle Herbert's return as a plea for begging Uncle Ev to relax his rule for only *just once*, and let Maida put off at any rate her convict gown and cap: but Uncle Ev is inexorable; he abides to the letter of his declared intentions; he abates not his strict discipline one whit for all his niece's rhetoric.

Emmeline knows him of old, and expects no concession. Bridget gets warm, and charges the executors of the law with partiality; and on an explanation being demanded, she says that they pretend to have no respect of persons in dealing punishments, whereas they do very exceedingly favour the person of the poor above that of the rich, in awarding him only *pain* for the same crime of which *torture* is the award to his more wealthy brother. Explanation second being demanded, Miss D'Urban asks if there can be any comparison between the amount of suffering endured by the two classes undergoing the same sentence of transportation. She instances Maida, who, over and above the usual miseries of convict life, has loss of *caste*, subordination to her inferiors, association with coarse and uneducated minds, and daily, hourly degradation in a hundred points which are neither degrading nor annoying to Bob and Lucy, whose *moral caste* alone is lowered by transportation; who, in submitting to overseers and officers, have no fine feelings to be wounded; who, being born to serve and labour with their hands, would as soon, if well treated, work in Australia as in England, could they only forget the little fact that they 'did not come free to the colony;' who, being born to take their meals in kitchens with numberless Sams and Johns, Betsies and Annes, have memories no further taunting in convict association than such as the recollection of bygone Sams and Betsies may bring.

She then instances the case of one Quicke, who had been a physician. She repeats to Uncle Ev all she has heard Uncle Herbert tell of his sufferings on the peninsula,[6] where he got punished for not being able to do as much hard work as men who had been used to manual labour from their infancy; where heartbroken wretchedness was visited as sullenness, and what small show of manly pride he dared manifest was called refractoriness; he outstayed all his contemporaries, because he couldn't be recommended as a servant in any particular capacity, and because most kindly owners disliked to have their fallen equals beneath them; until degraded to a lower standard than those who were his inferiors by birth and education, he implored Uncle Herbert, who met him in the cells, to try to find him a situation when he was again eligible, adding, with tears in his eyes, 'I will do anything but cook; *that* I'm afraid I cannot undertake.' She then asks Uncle Ev if the punishment given to this Quicke is not a thousand times worse than that which (for the same offence) is given to his neighbour, though a beautiful equality of sentence is intended in passing fourteen years on each. After the fashion of Tennyson's Princess,[7] and by way of embellishing the effect she doubts not she has made, Miss D'Urban here taps her kid-slippered foot several times on the carpet. Construing Uncle Ev's silence into conviction, she waits for the result of her eloquence; but on perceiving that results are not likely to go beyond a 'humph' or two, she drops her air triumphant, and assuming a coaxing manner, begs him to agree with her that it is a downright shame to punish genteel prisoners in so many dreadful ways beyond common prisoners, making their misery *begin* again where that of the latter is nearly *over*. 'Now, isn't it? Just say *yes*, there's a dear, good man.' But Uncle Ev will not just say *yes*. He only replies that it is one of those upright shames which have puzzled wiser heads than hers, and will continue to puzzle those wiser heads until such time as sin and its penalty shall cease together. He reminds her of the saying, 'If you condescend to sin, you must condescend to its consequences.' Condescension being greater when a gentleman stoops to sin, Uncle Ev thinks that the punishment must, of necessity, be proportionably greater.

But Bridget is controversial. She says that whatever the gentleman convict *deserves* above another, his extra suffering evidently has nothing to do with his extra deserts; because the judge who sentences him has never been transported himself to try what it is like, and, therefore, knows nothing of the hundred miseries that form the extra punishment. In giving him seven years, he (the judge) thinks he gives the same as he gives the poor man, little thinking that to the *former* the amount of suffering to be endured in that time is equal to what the latter would endure in a fourteen-year sentence. Here her foot taps most princess-like, and she raises her voice bewitchingly—

'If he deserves, and is to have more punishment because he is a gentleman, let him have it fairly and openly; let it be known that there is so much more for him; and that he has double, because he is a gentleman, and then he will know what is before him. But do not, under cover of *seven years*, let him have the condensed wretchedness of a *life sentence*, bearing unthought-of degradations, whilst his country thinks he is only fulfilling a certain amount of sentence; all I say is, let it be *known* that he suffers so much. *Nobody* at home knows the horrid things the poor creatures have to bear! They don't! I'm sure they don't!'

Uncle Ev smiles, and she says she knows he is laughing at her, but she doesn't care; she knows she hasn't explained what she means, but her heart is so full of it, from seeing Maida, that she cannot help saying it all out, whether it be nonsense or not. She is sure these things *ought* to be looked into, and made known. She takes it for granted that she is the representative of the Universal Nobody before quoted.

Uncle Ev advises her to appeal to the home government on behalf of superior convicts, and state her belief that the over and above suffering of that class should not be so much regarded as *incidental* to their peculiar case, as *accidental* from some oversight on the part of the director, contractor, or whoever is the ruling power of the convict organ. He likewise advises her to suggest that, if the said over and above suffering be unavoidable, it shall be taken into consideration in passing future sentences; but he chiefly urges her to recommend that those who possess the power of transporting others, shall just make a trial of transportation themselves in order to better understand the punishment which they enforce, and to enable them to speak from experience, and not from mere cold formality, when they give their charges to prisoners at the bar.

Bridget does look so pretty, her cheek blooms so peach-like, her head tosses itself so becomingly, that Uncle Ev delights to see her in the controversial state, and (*entre nous*[8] he delights in hearing her too, notwithstanding that she rattles over an infinity of 'horrid shames,' 'poor dear creatures,' 'disgrace to humanities,' with other expletives, which generally supply the place of argument in young ladies' logic; for through all these superfluities he discerns much to prove that she has been neither a careless listener, an unfeeling spectator, nor become an hardened owner during her residence in Van Diemen's Land. He hears much that is a childish utterance of his own thoughts in regard to the wretchedness of superior convicts before they are debased below the hardened, care-nought point; and he hears much that is a simple expression of his own doubt whether such convicts do often emerge from their sentences better and wiser men, as the formal phrase hopes, or whether they do not more often sink into the lowest depths of convictism, clinging to their chains in the desperation of hopelessness, heaping degradation on degradation in order to smother, with every spark of moral existence, every capacity of moral feeling, so that their life-long punishment, falling upon a body insensate to finer pain, may be defrauded of its chief power of torment.

So Uncle Ev let his niece rattle out all her ebullition of genuine oratory, and when, as if out of breath, she stopped with a series of little pants, he exclaimed—

'Bravo, Miss D'Urban! You plead as one who has her subject at heart, if not her ideas at command. I shall recommend your appearing *in propria persona*[9] before the home government. I am sure those zeal-flushed cheeks will victimise the whole set, and make them grant your request, even to the half of their convict-punishing prerogative.'

'No, no; if I go to anyone, I'll go straight to the Queen. I don't believe she knows half that's done in her name. I got that from Dr. Lamb's servant. The other day I was talking to her, and she said something about the Queen, for which I reprimanded her; when she, poor thing, afraid, I suppose, that I should find some means of informing her gracious Majesty, drew a very long, humble face, and said, "I haven't nothing to say against the Queen. I dare say she's a very proper young lady. Very like there's lots of mischief put off on her that she don't know nothing about. Please, miss, not for to think that I've particular ill-will to her." By-the-by, Uncle Ev, speaking of her Majesty, don't you think it's rather odd to make the prisoners keep her birthday? They must celebrate it with a very bad grace.'

'It's rather a cram,[10] certainly: but it's curious how, with a few exceptions, repugnance to the object of the feast is swallowed in the feast itself. Extra rations cover a multitude of animosities for the time. An arch fellow once asked me for a fig to smoke her Majesty's birthday. On giving him a few pence, he put his finger pipe-like to his mouth, and said, mock reverently, "May she never want a feller to smoke[11] her, neither here or hereafter!" Another convict, of whom I asked what share he had taken in the birthday festivities, said, with a sly twinkle in his eye, "I'd got the ringing of the bells—a jolly sweat 'twas of it. It would have made me rather bilious if it had gone down alone, but I drove it down with other victuals, so I believe it digested; at any rate, it hasn't done no further harm than make me feel mawkish *hereabout*," laying his hand on his stomach. Well, Miss Bridget, away, and make your appeal. Her Majesty's ear is ever ready to bend to the cry of distress; and, notwithstanding all the convicts in this hemisphere, every colonist is ready to pray, God save the Queen! I am inclined to say, with Dr. Lamb's servant, I don't think she knows all that is done in her name, especially to poor Tasmania and Tasmania's convicts. But who is this?'

'Dear old Em, positively, come down alone! How did you manage it? By crawling on all fours?' exclaimed Bridget.

'No, I have had good assistance' (smiling towards Maida, who, on perceiving her master and Miss D'Urban, had relinquished her hold of Miss Evelyn). 'Don't you leave me until I am settled in my chair.'

But Uncle Ev, having kissed his niece, left the room, and Bridget followed him, fancying Maida would like to be a few moments with Emmeline.

Twining her arm around Miss Evelyn, so as to relieve her of her own weight, Maida led her towards her armchair. In answer to a look from Emmeline while they were crossing the room, she stopped in front of the window, one sash of which was thrown open, admitting the sweet November air, fraught with freshness, significant of coming flowers. No person but one of a refined mind would have understood the wish conveyed in the slight glance that arrested Maida. Some would have replied to it by hurrying the invalid to her seat; others would only have noticed it as a natural and unconscious movement;

but Maida, as she met the upturned eye, comprehended its meaning, and, supporting her dependent burden still more firmly, waited at the open window, that the refreshing breeze might fan the wasted cheek of the invalid, while her eye drank its fill of beauty from the surrounding prospect, from which the resurrective touch of spring had evoked an enhancing loveliness—spreading a gentle verdure down the slopes, and blending with the dusky hues of the distant hills lines of vitality that added animation to the scene, without depriving it of one of its native grandeurs or solemn characteristics.

From the little child, whose puzzled mental questioning cannot find relief in words, to the hoary hermit who, having devoted his life to the contemplation of nature, turns dissatisfied from the result, feeling that the something he would understand is a mystery, the 'open sesame'[12] of which has been lost in the ruins of the fall—from child to sage, all feel, in gazing on the face of nature, that there is a strange outgoing of soul towards it, and a reciprocal approaching of its beauties to the soul. There is a sensible communion, but a communion that mysticises, and does not satisfy the yearning of the spirit; it is all in sign and token, that, explaining nothing, makes the longing still more ardent: it is all the still small voice, whose low and scarce-breathed tone thrills through every nerve and awakens every attention, but melts away ere it reaches the spirit's ear, or if there is one breath that can be syllabled into meaning, it is the word 'eternity'. No one can turn from such a survey without a pang starting through his spiritual frame. In different minds the pang may arise from different causes; but, acknowledge it or not, be it *acute* or be it dull, the pain is there. To the soul of the sick girl, so near its loosening from physical thrall—so near taking to itself the wings of the morning and flying to a knowledge of that which it knows not now—to it may be vouchsafed a whisper of that Invisible shadowed forth in visible things—to it may come revealings of the unseen; links of that mysterious bond of union, felt by all, may discover themselves to her unveiling sight. The still small voice may reach her ear in audible tones; but its message can be nothing distressful, for a smile breaks the stillness of her lips, and, forgetting she is not alone, she murmurs as if in answer to that voice—

'I wonder where I shall be when next spring comes round!'

'Where you deserve to be, Miss Evelyn.'

The smile quickly vanished. Emmeline started; then, drawing up with a strength that was only instantaneous, she exclaimed—

'Oh, Maida, you would have me fix an awful doom upon myself. Give me my *choice*, and I shall be where every poor, self-weary, sin-weary sinner would be; but give me my *deserts*, and I shall be in that place, of which, as a sinner, I dread to think.'

Sinking into her chair, she continued—

'You *have* given me a theme for meditation! A moment since, gazing out on the pleasant scenery, I was filled with dream-like anticipations of the future, wondering at the fair beauty of a sin-stricken world, and by it trying to picture that land which is very far off, where the King reigns in his beauty; but you have now turned my thoughts into a different channel.'

Maida cast a scrutinising glance at her, and said—

'In speaking of *deserts*, I imagine that by virtue of them heaven is as much *yours* as hell *mine*. It is hard to look into your face, and believe you sincere when you call yourself a sinner; but I am sorry to have distressed you, Miss Evelyn.'

'Distressed me! You have inspired me with rapture and gratitude by bringing to remembrance the wonder of mercy that comes between our deserts and our fate. No, no,

Maida, my thoughts of that land so very far off will not be the less pleasing because they remind me it is not mine by claim of desert, but by right of inheritance. In our sure and certain hope of possessing it, we are apt, when viewing it by the eye of faith, to forget the mighty love by which it has become ours—the costly price by which the right of inheritance was purchased for us—the mystery of adoption by which it is secured to us, who are by nature children of wrath; but of all this you remind me in speaking of my deserts.'

'There is comfort in hearing you talk, Miss Evelyn; such comfort as may arise from the worst being known. When one is sure one's fate is fixed beyond chance of reprieve, one can settle into a calmness that is impossible whilst there is any degree of uncertainty about it. It is hope *deferred*, *not* hope *destroyed*, that makes the heart sick. When I hear you denounce yourself as a sinner, I feel, if *she* be a sinner, I must be one of so black a dye that no addition could make me blacker—no cleansing could lessen the stains. And when I hear you speak of *your* deserts, I ask, what, then, must *mine* be? Is there a corner of hell dark enough for me? A spot where the gnawing worm gnaws deeper and more relentlessly? Where the flames burn more fiercely? If so, that corner, that spot, is for Maida Gwynnham. You shudder—a ghastly comfort, is it not? But were you in my case, you would find it to *be* one. Were there a fractional chance of reprieve, I might wear myself out in trying to increase the chance into a hope; but seeing there is none, I can but abide my time, waiting for a fearful certainty with such quiet as despair can give: hope and endeavour are useless.'

'Oh Maida, not so. There is no such word as *useless* in this precious book; there is no such word as hopeless in this declaration of God's mercy. Love, unutterable love, invites poor sinners, such as we. There is no repelling voice; none to say "Forbid them."'

'But I do not deserve heaven, and I should not like to accept that which I do not merit.'

'When you love Christ, you will like everything which exhibits His lovely character, and proclaims His glory. The most winning picture of our blessed Redeemer is that which portrays Him the Forgiver of sinners. Every sinner that is saved is an added glory to His crown, another outdrawing of that divine excellence which can give gifts even to the rebellious. When you love Him, you will be *glad* that heaven is a free gift, so that all the praise, and honour, and glory which might otherwise be yours, may be given to Him, and Him *alone*.'

'I do not wish to love Christ. If I loved Him, I should wish to be with Him, and that is impossible. My doom is fixed, irretrievably fixed.'

'Promise me, Maida, that you will only try to love Him, and I will promise you that you shall be where He is forever.'

'Is heavenly love anything like earthly love, Miss Evelyn?'

'As like as the type can be to the antitype.'

'Then it is all pain and anguish! I will have nothing to do with it,' cried Maida.

She hastily left the room; then fearing she has retreated too abruptly, she re-entered to inquire if she could assist Emmeline in any way.

A livid paleness had spread over the countenance of the invalid, who had dropped back, almost senseless on her chair, as the door closed on Maida.

'Miss Evelyn! Dear Miss Evelyn! Oh, speak and say I have not killed you!' cried Maida, falling on her knees by her side. 'O God! Wilt Thou make me a murderer indeed, and of this sweet innocent?'

It seemed hours, but it was only minutes, ere Emmeline opened her eyes, and smiled on Maida.

'Yes, it is a great, great pain; but Christ's love is all enjoyment, and love to Him all peace.'

'Have you known the pain, then?' escaped from Maida, ere she could control herself.

'I have known the peace and enjoyment,' murmured Emmeline, and the blood shone brightly through her transparent skin.

Bridget entered the room, and Maida retired.

That gentle creature should know no traitor love, thought the latter, glancing farewell to Emmeline's frail figure, and yet that she *had* known it, she felt convinced, and the conviction awoke in the prisoner's heart a yearning tenderness towards Emmeline.

During the month which initiated her into Mr. Evelyn's service, Maida perceived that she had foes as well as friends in the household. The nursemaid had conceived a hatred for her from the very first, the cause of which hatred was twofold—jealousy and disappointment. In the simplicity of her heart, Lucy had confided to Rachel her hope that a match might come off between the hero of the stables and the heroine of the kitchen. This confided hope, together with Lucy's unbounded praise of her friend, inspired Rachel with jealousy, while the rigidity with which Maida enforced her master's rule, that nurse should not go into the kitchen after tea hour, disappointed her of meeting Robert, and supping in his company. In Janet's time, the chief rigidity had been in the constant watch kept for seizing opportunities of infringing this rule. The altered state of things Rachel set down to design on the part of Maida, who, she declared, had a purpose in view in thus shutting her out. In prejudicing Charlie's mind, she found one means of venting her jealous spite. Under her tuition, the little fellow's aversion had increased into decided animosity. Taught to associate Maida's name with murders and other horrors, he quite trembled if she happened to come into the nursery after dark. The story of a shocking murder, just perpetrated in Hobarton, served his nurse for an illustration of what would be his, or his infant sister's fate, if either offended that wicked woman; and Charlie was made to learn the illustration by heart, until he firmly believed that Maida would make as little of tossing him into the water-butt as of submerging a surplus kitten. On the contrary, Maida had so gained baby's heart, that the little creature no sooner found the nursery guard gate unlatched than she would toddle out with, 'Baby go see Midda,' and slide down stair after stair, until she reached the kitchen. Bridget often was privy to such an escape, knowing how Maida delighted in the child; and Uncle Ev himself, for all his scolding of careless Rachel, was once known to be guilty of not stopping baby from going any further when he caught her on the stairs. He excused himself by dwelling on the danger of frightening her when in the act of stair-sliding.

All interested in Maida's welfare rather dreaded Mrs. Evelyn's return. All had a misgiving that they would not agree; though could such a misgiving have reached Mrs. Evelyn, it would have astonished her beyond measure, for she prided herself on being an excellent convict-mistress; the excellence of convict-mistressism, according to her, commencing with liberality in rations, and ending with an unwillingness to get prisoners into trouble. Little etceteras—such as not reminding them of their fallen estate, remembering that they *had* other feelings beside those of hunger and bodily pain—did not enter into her list of necessaries. To the abject notions of most convicts she was a good mistress, for they reckoned by negatives after the primary considerations of appetite had been satisfied. A free servant, in recounting to a newcomer the advantages of her situation, mentions all that is therein done for her: 'Mistress allows me *this*, and gives me *that*; she lets me go there,' &c., &c. But the convict hireling tells his fellows— not all that his mistress *does* for him, but all that she does *not* do. In trying to cheer his mate, he says, 'This is a better place than you'll get again; she *don't* get us into trouble; she *don't* send us for punishment; she *don't* do this; she *don't* do that.'

But Emmeline and Bridget felt that Maida would require something beyond such animal kindness. In the desire of favourably impressing her aunt, Bridget wrote several eulogiums[13] on Maida and Maida's skill, intermingling them with a few expressions of pity for her fate, and hope that she would be happy in Uncle Ev's family. Mrs. Evelyn wrote back her delight that the new woman did her work well, and hoped of all things that she kept the doorsteps clean. 'As to pitying her, my dear,' she said, 'there is no need of that waste of ink and paper. These government people can't have much feeling, or they wouldn't be in their present position; what little feeling they *once had*, you may depend is gone *now*. I have been surrounded with them all my life, and never met with any who cared for being prisoners. With regard to her being happy, why shouldn't she be, my dear? I give my people plenty to eat, and I don't get them into trouble half as much as they deserve; in fact, when I meet with a man or a woman that suits me, I'd rather put up with anything than get him or her into trouble, for fear I should not be able to hire them back. P.S.—I hope, my dear, you are not making Maida think too much of what she does.'

In short, though Mrs. Evelyn would sign an anti-slavery document with heartfelt abhorrence of the system, she in habitual theory was as much a slave-holder as any 'Down Southern;'[14] we say habitual because the theory was not one of *heart* or *thought* — not one into which she had been drilled—but one she had imbibed: it was *not* a conviction, but a contraction. She did not carry the theory into unmerciful practice, because she was not cruel-natured; she would have been as kind to real slaves, as she was to the convicts—as kind to animals as to either. The casual observer might see little difference between her and Mr. Evelyn's treatment of the convicts, and might award that little in favour of Mrs. Evelyn. Both kept them up to the mark drawn for penal servitude; but the one was actuated by a desire to benefit the prisoner—the other was either actuated by *no* feeling, or by the supposition that those she kept up to the mark neither *had* nor had *any right* to feeling. In the same way that she applied the whip to the horse, so she stimulated her bond-servants to an approved pace. Both master and mistress exercised a tight control over their prisoners. But the latter did so in contracted accordance with the convict legal code, and with the convict traditional formula, which says, 'These creatures will do nothing without a bit and bridle;' while the former hoped that the restraining influence would hold them back from evil, and make them strive more earnestly for freedom.

Both were equally sorry to send them away for punishment—the one for fear the effect should work contrarily to the desired end, the other that she lost a good hard-working pair of convict hands; the one felt a pang in using the prerogative the law placed in his hand—he cannot bear to punish his brother man—the other was sorry because she disliked to punish animals, whether convict or quadruped. The one from satiric taint, (with which his former existence as a barrister infected him), could not abstain from exhibiting a few satires, in the form of improper nouns, even on the persons of those whose fate he deeply deplored. The other misapplied nouns in speaking of, or to them, because it was not much consequence what she called them; *one* name was as good as *another*, it did not make *her* less mistress or *them* less convicts. *Sister* or *brother* was the only name she hesitated to use, or deemed an *im*proper noun; whatever slight relationship existed before their sin, was wholly nullified by their present disgrace.

Both were equally anxious to keep temptations out of their servants' reach—but the one locked away his money, plate, and wine, from a sense of duty, the other for the safe-keeping of her goods. She declared stealing was a part of convict principle, and therefore it went as much against their conscience to miss an opportunity for dishonest action, as it was against her conscience to commit one. So utterly unconscious was Mrs. Evelyn of having contracted this mode of viewing the prisoners, that she was aware of no inconsistency in warning Charlie against abusing or ill-treating them. She was as earnest as her husband in teaching him correct behaviour towards them, but children are keen remarkers of their elders. Though Charlie could not explain *where*, he soon perceived something in his mother's feelings towards the proscribed race that ill accorded with her instructions to him. He intuitively understood that papa rowed them only when they deserved it, and mamma because they were only prisoners.

When mamma whipped him for kicking Lucy, and calling her a nasty beast, he had an undefined notion that he was punished under rule No. 5 of the Society for Suppressing Cruelty to Animals.

Mrs. Evelyn had not arrived half an hour before she expressed a wish to see the new woman.

'My dear, I wonder she did not bring up the tray on purpose to let me see her.'

'Perhaps, she would rather meet you first alone, aunt,' explained Bridget.

'Oh no, my dear, there's not the least occasion for that; I don't object to speaking to her before you. Ring the bell.'

Uncle Ev walked out of the room; Uncle Herbert had not yet entered.

'Let the new woman come up, Lucy; I can talk to her a little while I take my chop, it will save me time.'

Maida entered.

'Oh yes, she's a nice height—perhaps I shall turn you into a housemaid—and your name is—?'

'Maida Gwynnham.'

'That will do very well; I like to have pretty names about me. Maida sounds pretty; the other name's rather glumpy. What are you for?'

'I was sent out for murder.'

'Patience me! My dear; whatever was your uncle thinking of when he hired this woman? One would think her good looks bewitched him; he forgets that we may get killed in cold blood.' (To Maida) 'Does the master know what you are for?'

'He has never spoken to me on the subject.'

'How very thoughtless of him! I like him to bring home bad prisoners because they are always clever when they are very bad; but I never bargained to have a murderer about my heels. The idea is not at all pleasant—convicts are so apt to repeat the crime for which they have been sentenced.' (Turning again to her nieces.) 'There was Louisa Ferres, my dears, she tried to cut off her husband's head at home, and out here she tried to cut off young Turnbull's head, or something very like it.[15] What sort of a temper is she, Bridget?'

Bridget did not answer; Mrs. Evelyn, with a gesture of annoyance, turned to Maida with:

'Well, you are here, and I suppose must stay; but you must mind what you are about; I shall watch your temper, and if I see anything in it I don't like, I shall send you back to government, which is the proper place for such as you; *we* don't like having dangerous people about us any more than the English do. You'll be very foolish if you don't behave well, for this is an excellent situation, and the master and myself are very kind to our people. You'll have plenty of food—butter too, which you wouldn't get everywhere—it's eighteen-pence a pound out here, even in summer, and that's too much for convicts to eat—but we don't mind; we expect our government men and women to work, therefore we feed them well. You find she does very well in the house, don't you, my dear?'

'Yes, aunt,' murmured Bridget.

'What were you at home? You seem to be superior—a dressmaker, or something in that way, I suppose.'

'I have made dresses, ma'am.'

'Have you lived in service before?'

'No.'

'Who did you murder? Your illegitimate child, I suppose; that's generally the way.'

Maida replied not; a line of supreme contempt curled her lip.

'I don't ask for curiosity; but because I should like to know on what particular point to be on my guard; for instance, I should feel especially awkward if you had murdered a former mistress.'

'These are impertinent questions, and you have no right to put such to me! I shall not answer you, my mistress though you be!' Maida moved towards the door.

'There, now!' cried Mrs. Evelyn. 'Have I not need to fear? If the creature can toss herself into a rage just for a trifle, what would she not do for more than a trifle? Charlie, run and tell her to come back; I've no notion of letting her off.'

The child ran to obey his mother, when she stopped him.

'And yet, no; perhaps she'll strike you. Really, papa shouldn't put one's life in danger in this cool manner.'

'She's such a horrid creature, mamma: Rachel, and Lucy, and me, and baby is all drefful afraid of her.'

'My Charlie, you mustn't call anything horrid creature; 'tisn't a pretty word for a little boy to say; but you must keep out of that woman's way. It's a pity we talked so before him; 'twill frighten him, poor dear.'

When Maida closed the door, another on the opposite side opened on her, and she stood face to face with Mr. Herbert Evelyn. Both instantly recognised each other.

'Martha Grylls! Is it possible? Are you, then, the Maida Gwynnham that my niece has been writing so much about?'

He laid his hand on her shoulder; the touch thrilled through her, and, as if by supernatural power, surrounded her with images of the past. She dared not meet the penetrating gaze of those calm eyes. She bowed her head, and, as often is the case when one emotion is suddenly checked by the rising of another more potent, she wept aloud. She cursed the tears as they fell, but had no power to stay them; hide them was all she could do. Drooping so as to disengage herself from Mr. Herbert's hand, she rushed to the kitchen.

To us who have followed Maida from prison to Tasmania, it would seem strange that Mr. Herbert had never mentioned her to his daughter, or that during the month of his absence no inadvertency had revealed to Emmeline Maida's previous knowledge of her father; nor to Maida, that the Mr. Evelyn of England and the Mr. Herbert of the Lodge were one and the same person. So wondered all the party concerned, when a mutual explanation took place. But when we remember that Mr. Evelyn was summoned by Bridget to his daughter just after he had assisted Mr. Gwynnham from the platform to his house, and from his house had resigned him to the charge of an old servant, who arrived by the next train to meet and return with his master—when we recollect that by Emmeline's side it was likely he should forget all but the exertions necessary to bear her from England ere autumn merged into winter—we cease to wonder that the family had not become acquainted with the name of Martha Grylls before Lucy recommended the person who bore it to Uncle Ev's attention. And as for the second wonder, we must content ourselves with recollecting that we should never have wondered at all had the discovery not taken place. Maida had often questioned whether her young mistress might not be related to the clergyman who had visited her in prison; her quiet yet earnest manner of speaking often reminded her of him, and she fancied she could trace a likeness: but the fear of having her question answered affirmatively prevented her seeking a reply. Much as she respected the memory of that kind friend, she felt averse to meeting him, as, according to *her* view of things, pain only could accrue from such an interview; and also she wished to have no claim, beyond that which she should *win*, on the gentle invalid, whom she already regarded with a feeling that anyone but herself would have called love.

Mrs. Evelyn was not so pleased as Uncle Herbert when she found the servants had been admitted to family prayer. She considered the one Sunday service enforced by convict regulations quite enough religion for them; but she knew it would be useless to contend the point, so merely vented her disapprobation by a few sniffs and a loud whisper to Bridget when they were seated for prayers, 'My dear, don't you smell the stable?' On which Bob, who was not supposed to hear, replied, giving one of his peculiar sidewise nods—'Very like, missis; I was in along with the hosses when the bell twigged for prayers.'

Maida drooped over her little Bible when, in slow, sonorous accents, Mr. Herbert read the fifty-third of Isaiah.[16] As though it had spoken to her only yesterday, the well-remembered voice came back with its accustomed power; each word carried her along with it: she did not wish to listen—she did not wish to follow each tone, as it varied to suit the subject, but she had no choice—listen and follow she must.

Lucy informed her that she would hear Mr. Herbert, every Sunday, for he preached at Tench, where the servants were expected to attend; and when Maida asked how she liked his sermons, Lucy said—

'Oh! I am sure *you'll* like them; they hurts our feelings so much; he preaches so appleekable like to us.'

By which Lucy meant that Mr Herbert's preaching was what is generally called very *touching,* drawing many a repentant sigh and tear from the eye of the outcasts.

'The sermon hurt me uncommon to-day, Miss D'Urban,' was a popular saying with Lucy when she returned from the Penitentiary Church.

CHAPTER 23

Being One About Bridget

MR. WALKDEN had been in the dining parlour with Uncle Ev for more than an hour, when the latter left the room, and running upstairs, told Bridget she was wanted below. She tried to find out who wanted her, but Uncle Ev wouldn't satisfy her; nevertheless he made her promise to appease his curiosity when she returned.

'Oh! It's Mr. Walkden,' she exclaimed, on entering the parlour; 'and Uncle Ev told me that *I* was wanted.'

'And may not Mr. Walkden want you?' replied that gentleman, with a peculiarity of emphasis which Bridget could not but notice, though she did not marvel at it.

'Oh, yes! If 'tisn't about frescoes; I've been afraid of them ever since I first saw you.'

'Then you remember when you first met me, Miss D'Urban?'

'I've reason to,' said Bridget archly.

'And so have I,' answered Mr. Walkden, in the same peculiar tone.

Then neither knew what to say, and Mr. Walkden arose and shut the door; on which Bridget said:

'Oh! Do you like the door shut? It is so warm.'

Mr. Walkden went over to the window to see the state of the weather, and Bridget supposed he was very short-sighted, since he could not see the sky from where he sat. It only took a half-moment to look out, but that half-moment seemed long to Bridget, who began to feel uncomfortable lest Uncle Ev had been playing her a trick, so she followed Mr. Walkden and asked:

'Did you want me? Oh! I forgot; perhaps you are going to take me to see the Queen's Orphan School, I shall like that amazingly;' and a gleam of pleasure lighted her countenance.

'I will take you wherever you wish to go, Miss D'Urban.'

'You good, kind man! Suppose I say I wish to go back to England—what then? You see with me it is necessary to think twice before you speak once.'

'That has already been done; and I repeat, if you will go with me I will take you to whatever place you name.'

Whatever does he mean! thought Bridget: but only for an instant. Simpleton as she was, she could not doubt his meaning; her simple thoughts said to her, in words of plain language:

'He wants to marry you.'

Those who know Bridget D'Urban only as the light-hearted, merry-singing girl, will be astonished to hear how calm she became directly her thoughts said those simple words to her; with what womanly composure she listened to Mr. Walkden's proposal; and with what modest dignity she told him that she had left England on purpose to nurse her cousin, and could not, therefore, pledge herself to anyone; nor could all that Mr. Walkden urged make her say more.

Bridget hoped Uncle Ev knew nothing about it; she blushed as she met him on the stairs, but he only pinched up her face, and kissed her, as he had done a hundred times before, so she fancied her secret was safe.

'Where's Walkden?' he called after her, in a careless tone, when she had passed him.

'Gone,' she answered as carelessly; and that little monosyllable told Uncle Ev the result of the interview.

Mrs. Evelyn was very disappointed when she heard it; for whilst her niece had been with Mr. Walkden, she had employed herself in planning a wedding breakfast, and had just finished laying the last corner-dish on the ideal table, when Uncle Ev told her that he guessed his friend's suit had been rejected.

The morning's event had taken no one by surprise but Bridget herself. Mr. Walkden had frequented the house too often to leave the supposition on anyone's mind that he came without purpose. Had Emmeline been a less-condemned invalid, his great attentions to her might have created the suspicion that she was the magnet; but as the case lay, it would have been an injustice to her, as well as to Mr. Walkden, to suppose that his intentions towards her were more than such as any kind friend of a family would show to a sick member. Bridget, therefore, was the only accountable reason for his almost daily visits.

'Em, darling, I've got something to tell you in the evening, I can't tell you before, because I don't want you to *see* me whilst I am talking,' said she to Emmeline.

When the evening came she nestled down by her cousin's sofa, and laying her face in her two hands, her eyes peeped out from them with a more quiet brightness than usual.

'Em, I wish you knew what I've got to tell you: I'm longing to talk all about it, but it's horrid to begin. I am happy and vexed, and vexed and happy. I'm vexed because I'm afraid I've vexed somebody, and happy because—'

A luxuriously rosy tinting of her cheek, discernible through the twilight, was left to reveal the tale of her happiness.

'Did Mr. Walkden appear very grieved, Bridget?'

'Oh, then you know! How ever could you?'

'I have known it a long time.'

'How? He never told you before he spoke to me?' And without waiting for an answer she jumped up, saying:

'How very disagreeable! What a rude man! I dare say he asked everybody's leave; and now Uncle Ev will be teasing me.'

'Nobody told me, Bridget dear; but I have a pair of steadier eyes than you. Yours have been dancing about, lighting too slightly on every object to discover a fact embodied so plainly in *one* as to attract the notice of us all.'

'Ah! But, perhaps, if I'd liked Mr. Walkden, I *should* have noticed. I never once thought about caring for him.'

'That is just because you are Bridget.'

'What you say explains a great many things that I remember. It's so horrid that things only get explained after they have happened, and make one look stupid.'

'For instance: when a gentleman gives a young lady, with whom he is desperately in love, a choice rose that he has bought on purpose for her, and when she takes it, and says, after thanking him for it without a single *comprehending* blush, "Ah! It's a pity, because we have so many in the garden"—it would be far better if explained to the young lady that he had purchased the rose with silver, and presented it with painful hope—eh, Miss D'Urban?' exclaimed Uncle Ev's sly voice over her shoulder.

'You horrid Uncle Ev, do go along with you; I don't want anyone to be desperately in love with *me* unless I am with *him*, for I hate vexing anyone. I was delighted at first to think I had a real offer, the same as I have often heard of; but now I'm sorry, and feel as if I ought to marry him because he loves me so. I'm—' and Bridget burst into tears.

To this moment she had disguised deeply pained feeling beneath a playful manner; but now, too severely tested, she gave way.

Uncle Ev was truly sorry he had grieved her; so, kissing her tenderly, he left the two girls to talk out those feelings which it is best for girlish sympathies to exchange.

'I think it is very wrong to make a jest of these subjects—I do, indeed,' said Bridget, resuming her old corner by Emmeline. 'I'm fond of fun, but can never see what fun there can be in grieving others; and if these things are true, there must be grief on one side of the question.'

The cousins had a long and serious conversation on the proposal made by Mr. Walkden, at the close of which Bridget felt more composed, under the conviction that, sorry as she was for the gentleman, duty did not call her to engage herself to him for the sole purpose of what she termed 'unvexing' him.

The fervour of the benediction wherewith Uncle Herbert blessed his niece that night made her very happy; she felt that the only fact she had concealed of that day's event was guessed and silently appreciated by him:

'Yea and she shall be blessed!' he ejaculated, as he watched her light steps retreating for the night.

CHAPTER 24

The Post Office

ON the day in which Maida was sent out under Bridget's guardianship to exchange her first quarter's wages for articles of clothing, the latter called at the general post office to inquire when the next vessel would sail for England. Outside the office hung a placard giving a long list of prisoners for whom unclaimed letters lay within. Whilst waiting for her young mistress, Maida cast her eye partway through the list, when her attention was arrested by the name of Martha Grylls. She hastened to the post-door and demanded the letter; the clerk handed her one, saying:

'Sixteen pence to pay before you touch it.'

'I have not so much; do let me look at the address.'

'Martha Grylls, Post Office, Hobart Town, Van Diemen's Land. To be left until inquired for; or if not inquired for to be returned to,' &c., &c.—she read in characters that she well knew were from Norwell's pen.

'I am Mr. Evelyn's servant, cannot you trust me?'

'Mr. Evelyn's or not, we never trust prisoners, one day *here*, the next in trouble.'

'Miss D'Urban, will you lend me sixteen pence? There is a packet for me within and I can't get it, having spent all my money.'

'I could, but I dare not, uncle would be so angry; and yet if I know how you spend it, I don't see how he could object.'

'No, thank you kindly, I'll not risk his displeasure on you; with your permission I'll get the person at the shop to take back one pair of stockings; that will just give me the sum I require.'

To the shop they went, Bridget waiting without whilst Maida tried to accomplish her desire; but the attendant was obstinate: he pronounced it against rule to receive goods once removed from the counter. Maida pleaded in a way she would not have condescended to, but for so dear an object.

'What does the woman request of thee, James?' asked the master of the shop, who belonged to the Society of Friends,[1] and whose benevolent character, education, and gentlemanlike deportment made him an honour to the excellent fraternity he headed.

James informed Mr. Washington.

'Thou sayest truly that *thou* mayest not swerve from my rule; but thou canst not forbid *my* doing so, canst thou, James?'

And with a benignant smile he gave Maida one shilling and fourpence, saying:

'It is a small service, but I am well pleased to do it for thee. I hope thy letter will bring thee good news of thy home.'

Maida was leaving the shop, when she felt a gentle tap on her arm.

Mr. Washington stood behind her; he placed a little packet in her hand, at the same time whispering:

'It did not occur to me that these stockings may be necessary to thee.'

As though understanding Maida's look, he smiled. 'Receive it as a gift, or pay for it at thy convenience; I do not bind thee either to thanks or payment. Fare-thee-well.'

He had retired before she could reply.

It were needless to relate the trepidation with which Maida tore open the letter when she reached her kitchen; she trembled with eager suspense until she had read every word therein contained.

'My *precious* Maida!' she repeated slowly to herself, after she had read it through. 'How does he reckon preciousness? If by endurance, the amount must have increased since that time we sat together in the park, when he told me I was his precious Maida; *then* I had suffered nothing but those pleasant pangs they call first love. *Now*, ah! But he too has suffered, for he says: "I have not known a moment's happiness since you left." I am glad to hear it for your sake, Norwell; for mine I would it were otherwise—what is this?'

She picked up a bank note for five pounds that fell from the envelope.

She gazed at it, and then with a gesture of disgust thrust it into the fire. At that instant Rachel entered the kitchen. She had perceived the action during the moment she lingered outside the door, and now seeing Maida hastily put a letter into her bosom, she guessed there must be a secret going on, and determined to make the most of what she had seen, in serving her malicious purpose.

Assuming a very grieved countenance, she immediately proceeded to inform her mistress that she sadly feared the woman Gwynnham was not as honest as folk believed her to be; she recounted the story of the burning of the bank note, and then requested leave just to ask if it was likely that her going into the kitchen should frighten an honest body into burning honest money.

Mrs. Evelyn thought it most unlikely, and Rachel said, to her poor way of thinking, it was more 'suspectuous' still that Maida had bought neither cap, gown, nor bonnet, but had spent her money only in such things as would be useful to her anywhere, which seemed exactly as though she expected trouble, for, of course, nobody would buy finery if they were sure of being sent to Cage in a few days. Don't that look as if she'd done something she expected to be punished for?

But Mrs. Evelyn did not think so; she said Maida was so odd a creature, it was as difficult to know what she would *not* do as what she *would* do. 'However,' she added, 'I'll have no such freaks played by my convicts: they shall wear prison[2] as long as I choose, but not a moment longer. I don't choose to see the dismal brown about me after the first quarter.'

'Certainly not, ma'am; they's most as bad to see as to wear, especially for the quality.'

'Go down and tell the woman to come up and bring her purchases with her. It's all a part of the same impertinence.'

'It's after tea, ma'am; am I to go into the kitchen?' asked Rachel, innocently demure.

'How else can you call her?—don't pretend.'

With a glow of malicious delight off glided Rachel to send up Maida, and 'to get a trifle out of Bob's company' during her absence.

'What do you mean by not spending your money properly?' demanded the mistress, ere Maida had time to close the door.

'I have bought very proper articles, ma'am; however, you shall judge for yourself,' answered Maida quietly.

But three pairs of stockings, a pair of stays, a pair of boots, slippers, and a few yards of calico did not convince Mrs. Evelyn. She persisted that there should be print for a gown and some lace, with ribbons for caps. Maida said the money would not spread any further; on which her mistress declared that all those articles should be exchanged for others more suiting to *her* taste—she was not going to be annoyed by prisons after she had secured the first quarter's work. She asked Maida where her senses had strayed, that she should suppose her inner garments were of any benefit to her mistress.

Maida did not reply: after a dead pause Mrs. Evelyn burst out:

'And where did you get that bank note which you burnt when you heard Rachel coming?'

'It came in a letter I received from England.'

'You must let me see that letter, or I shan't believe you; it would never do for a respectable house to harbour a thief, for whom the constable may even now be searching. It is certain you haven't taken it from *us*, because we have not lost any money, but how do I know that you did not steal it from the shop this afternoon?'

'Because *I* tell you to the contrary,' replied Maida haughtily.

Mrs. Evelyn gave a little quick, amused laugh.

'Who is it from, then?'

'From one of whom I'd rather not speak.'

Another little laugh.

'You really are a *very* odd woman, Maida, but I must be satisfied when I wish to know anything about my prisoners.'

'Well, then, you *shall* know!' cried Maida bitterly. 'It is from the man who ruined me, body and soul. He sent me money which I flung in the fire since I could not fling it back to him.'

'No! Did you really? Well, you are a very odd creature; why, I would have kept it for you until you wanted another dress.'

'I would wear no garment of its buying, except a shroud; and yet, no! Not even that; death should not be so scandalised by me.'

Mrs. Evelyn gave another little laugh, and said between her teeth, 'Dear, dear!'

'Do you still wish to see the letter?'

'Oh yes, certainly; I have said so, and mean to be obeyed.'

Maida drew it from her bosom, and approaching the hearth, threw it into the fire, exclaiming, 'There let it burn! It could only fool me if I kept it.'

'You wicked woman! Is that the way you spite me? What will you do next?' cried her mistress.

Maida laid her hand on the poker, she only wanted to push the letter further into the grate; but the movement appearing to be a reply to the question, 'What will you do next?' alarmed Mrs. Evelyn, and suggested the prudence of leaving the matter for her husband's inspection; she quickly dismissed Maida, with the promise that the master should look into the suspicious business of the bank-note. The master, however, never did.

Open-mouthed listened Robert and Lucy to the tragedy of the bank note. The grandeur of the act betrayed the latter into an infinity of 'Lors!' while Robert appeared almost choked by it: he uttered 'Crinky me! The woman's a shingle short, or somethin' like it, to go stuffin' the fire with such blessed trade, and I so near my ticket too. I say, you see'd it with your own eyes, Ratchel?'

'I didn't with anybody else's, anyhow,' replied she.

'Lor!' murmured Lucy.

Robert was in close consultation with his greasy locks, which flopped and reflopped through and over his fingers.

'You seed nothin' harder than paper go in?' he at last asked.

The words had scarcely dropped from his lips, ere all three wonderers started as if by simultaneous impulse, and falling on their knees before the grate, began grubbing in the ashes, as diggers in a gold creek. In which act Maida caught them when she descended from the parlour.

They simultaneously arose. Rachel glided off to the nursery. Lucy stood in mute worship of the money-burner. Robert again appealed to his locks, and advised by them, muttered:

'I say, Madda, 'twas a darned shabby trick to go and fume that there money which would 'most have sote a feller up when he'd got his ticket.'

'I had too much respect for you, Sanders, to offer you such money; it would have brought a curse with it, had it been a hundred times as much I should have destroyed it.'

'Lor would she!' admired Lucy.

Bob flopped his hair, and muttering, 'A shingle short or somethin' like it,' departed to mourn the five pounds in the company of his only comforters, the horses.

Maida waited for an official inquiry into her conduct, and doubted not she should be severely punished; but none was made that night, and not until the next evening was she summoned to her master's presence. Mr. Evelyn stood with his back to the fire: she saw at a glance that he was ruffled.

'Maida, what is this I hear? Your mistress tells me that you have been very provoking about your clothes, and insists on your changing them.'

Maida explained, and then said:

'Having received no commands, sir, I was not aware that the money was not mine to spend as I pleased; I might certainly have laid it out differently, but not knowing that this dress annoyed anyone, save myself, I preferred to buy necessary articles.'

'Humph! Then you should have explained to your mistress, and not have been so insolent.'

'I am aware of no insolence about the clothes, sir: if the mistress complains of any I am willing to apologise.'

'Then she *does* complain. If you have not been insolent about the clothes, you must have been on some other subject. Insolence is punishable by convict law.'

'She made inquiries which I considered impertinent, and I answered her accordingly, sir.'

All the fire irons fell clattering down: the noise of their downfall fully accounted for the absence of the verbal storm Maida expected to follow her last speech.

When Mr. Evelyn had replaced them, he asked:

'What did you say, Maida?'

'Then I am to procure the things my mistress wishes me to have?'

'Certainly, if you have the means.'

'I have not, sir, but by changing my former purchases.'

'Bother the purchases; no, you must wear your brown for the next quarter; if you don't want to spare yourself the pain that I would fain spare you, wear it on, certainly. I shall not advance the money, for I clearly see that trouble will be the end of such constant hot water with the mistress.'

'I can wear the dress to the end of my sentence, sir, and that is to the end of my life,' said Maida, calmly folding her arms upon her breast; 'and as for that trouble which is always being sounded in my ears, I cannot conceive of what it consists worse than that which I already endure; standing at *your* wash-tub is no worse than standing at another; picking oakum[3] is much the same as picking over potatoes.'

'The cells, my woman, give a rather undesirable opportunity for thought.'

'Ah, there you are correct, sir; the sinner's misery must be aggravated by a prolonged retrospection of the past!'

'A retrospection I have no wish to enforce, Gwynnham. As to trouble being no worse than your present state, you must remember each sentence lengthens the period you have to serve to obtain your ticket-of-leave.'

'Death will grant me that before I am prepared to receive it, I fear, sir!'

'Nevertheless, I hope to see you a T.L. in life. Death can give your *conditional pardon*, of the conditions of which pardon you hear enough from Mr. Herbert. That'll do—go, I will arrange matters with your mistress, but let me have no more such rows, for I assure you I'm weary of them.'

After prayers, Mr. Herbert requested her to follow him into his study.

'You have had a letter from home, Maida?' he commenced.

'I have, sir.'

'I should much like to know if you have news from your father.'

'None, sir. I fear he is dead, or he would have found means to send me the pardon I so earnestly besought: there can be no doubt he received my letter.'

'He received it, I know that, Maida.'

'And it killed him! It is nearly three years since I left England: it were unfilial to wish him still to live, and yet, that he is gone I cannot bear to think. The suspense is horrible!' she exclaimed, after she had been in silent calculation of the possibility of his being yet alive.

'Maida, *I* can give you a short account of him. I have long sought an opportunity to tell you.'

'Is he dead?' gasped Maida.

'Ah, that I cannot say; my impression is that he must have died shortly after I saw him.'

'Oh! Don't, don't, don't say so: he must live to give me one word of pardon.'

'My poor girl, I think with you it were better he should in death leave a grief of which death only could release him.'

'No, no—yes, yes—Oh! Which do I mean?' she cried.

'Yes, better,' repeated Mr. Herbert.

'But then *I* gave him the grief, *I* gave him the death. Do not try to make my guilt appear less, it would not comfort me; though all your kindness might urge I should still see the haunting image of my father murdered by me.'

'Maida, I could not lessen the fact, if I dared to try; God forbid that I should try. I would have you view every circumstance of your career in the unpalliated light of truth, and God, of His infinite mercy, grant that the same light which shows you your sin may show you your Saviour.'

Had Maida reflected a moment, she might have known that Mr. Herbert was not the one to extenuate her crime in this respect.

'What have you to tell me, sir?' asked Maida drearily.

Mr. Herbert placed a chair, and insisted on her taking it; then standing before the fire, he fixed a penetrating look on her.

'You have had an exciting day, Maida: a letter from home is always exciting. Would you rather wait until to-morrow to hear about your father? I warn you beforehand it will give you pain.'

Ever ready to ward off danger from her soul's secret, had Maida been less absorbed in mental contemplation of her father, she would have been alarmed at the peculiar emphasis laid on the word *exciting*, in connection with Norwell's letter: now, raising her eyes heavily, she merely said, in the same dreary voice—

'Go on, sir.'

'You will remember, then, that your letter was sent so as to reach your father the day after your departure, in order to preclude the possibility of an interview, which we judged would be a trial too severe for his strength. I felt sure that, too late or not, he would make an attempt to see you. When I found on inquiry that your going had been delayed for a day, I felt as certain that the attempt would be successful, for starting by the first train after the receipt of your letter, I reckoned he would arrive at the station just as your company was setting off. Acting on the belief that he would come, I went to the station to lend any assistance which might be necessary, and to shield him from any publicity into which his parental feelings might hurry him. Thank God I went! His train was a few moments late, therefore the one which was to convey your party was in readiness to start simultaneously with the arrival of the other; consequently, when Mr. Gwynnham alighted, your train had just proceeded on its way.'

Mr. Herbert then recounted the scene given in the eighth chapter of this book, and Maida bowed lower and lower in her misery, until a few moans alone told that she was conscious of it.

'Here, here is the pain!' she at last said, pressing her hand upon her heart, and rocking herself to and fro. 'Here is the pain—large, cold, and heavy, too cold for tears.'

She sat a few moments longer in dreary silence, then turning suddenly to Mr. Herbert, she asked:

'Sir, why did you tell me all this; where was the cruel necessity?'

'It is right you should know it, Maida.'

'Yes, to fill up the heaped measure of my wretchedness!' she exclaimed with bitterness.

'And better that you should hear it from *me* than suddenly from the lips of a stranger some day,' continued Mr. Herbert, without noticing her interruption.

'Ah yes, forgive me! Forgive, Mr. Evelyn! All is confusion within me. I know not what to say, or think, or feel: I am only sensible of an indescribable weight of misery. I dread the moment when I shall awake to a clear understanding of my guilt and a full abhorrence of myself.'

Mr. Herbert only gave a look full of pity and kindness in answer to this appeal, a look that said he had nothing to forgive.

'If it would be any comfort to you I would write to England, and try to ascertain that which you desire to learn of your father.'

Maida shook her head.

'No, it could not be better; it could not be worse.'

There was something in her voice and incoherent manner that touched Mr. Herbert's heart, and yet he felt thankful that she showed her misery; he always entertained more hope of her when she bent beneath her fate, than when she stood boldly to bear it. 'Wait an instant, Maida; I shall return presently,' said Mr. Herbert, leaving the room.

'Clara, I wish you'd give me a glass of port for that poor Maida: she is so overcome with what I have said to her, that I fear she may faint.'

'Ah, I am glad you have been scolding her, she has behaved shamefully to me; however, she shall have the wine, and yet, don't you fear it may give her a relish for it? These creatures so readily regain their taste for drink.'

'I do not fear,' replied Mr. Herbert, taking the glass from his sister-in-law.

'Mind, I don't grudge it,' she called after him.

Maida sipped the wine and then set the glass on the table, unconscious that she had done either the one or the other.

'Should you like me to pray with you, Maida?'

'If you like, sir, anything you please.'

'A few moments then—'

And Mr. Herbert was not more; he commended her to God in a short earnest supplication; after which he took her hand, and shaking it kindly, said:

'Maida, remember I am not your *judge*, but your pastor and friend. I thank God for having placed you under my care; speak to me or to my daughter freely of all you suffer in mind or body.'

'Thank you, sir, and thank you for your kind attentions to my poor—poor—'

She could not get out the word 'father.'

'God reward you for it, when He punishes me for my aggravated crimes,' she stammered.

'No thanks are due, Maida: would that I had been able to be of more service to him! I wished to keep him at my lodging, but the faithful old servant who traced him from the station to my residence said he had received express orders to *fetch* his master, who, on leaving home, appears to have arranged for some catastrophe; old Roberts would answer no questions. I shall never forget the grasp he gave my hand, as he exclaimed, the tears flowing down his cheeks:

'The Lord Almighty bless you! It isn't because I am close I don't tell you all about it, but, because, when my master told me he was called on immediate business to ——, he said, "Roberts, follow me by the next train; my last words to you are, neither *ask* nor *answer* any questions about me or mine; many may be put to you, but remember my last words to you, Answer none." With that old Roberts took my other hand and said, "Sir, as I grasp your hand now so he grasped mine, repeating, "Mind! Keep your wretched master's secret." So how can I break my faith with him? But, sir, I will tell you *this* much, that the rich have their sorrows as well as the poor; when sorrow falls on the rich man's house it falls heavier than elsewhere. Maybe in spite."

'He would not so much as give me your father's address. I gave him mine, and he promised to let me hear the result of the attack; but never did; and shortly after, being called to my own sick child, I had no opportunity to seek further information. I should, however, have made opportunity had I thought of meeting again with you. I *might* though, and *ought* to have known that it was likely I should find her here!' continued Mr. Evelyn reproachfully to himself.

The unexpected mention of the old familiar servant overcame the obduracy of Maida's grief; it assumed a gentler aspect, and when Mr. Herbert turned towards her she was weeping. He therefore continued to talk in a low, soothing tone, to give her a longer opportunity to shed those tears he knew would cease directly they were noticed, but his tender care was useless; that instant Mrs. Evelyn entered and said, in her quick material voice, 'Oh, my dear' (she called everybody 'my dear'), 'I thought, whilst lecturing this woman, you might forget the time, 'tis past eleven. Ah, there you are, Gwynnham! I am glad to see you crying—I must send you to Mr. Herbert when I want you lectured to some purpose, I see!'

And she gave one of her little quick, short laughs, as if lecturing and being lectured were one of the most natural incidents of convict life.

Maida was hastily quitting the room: her mistress called her back, and said in the same matter-of-fact voice:

'Well now, I forgive you, so you need not cry any more; only mind, next time, really, I must send you to Brickfields;[4] good-night, you can take some supper.'

Then, as the door closed, she turned to her brother-in-law with another little laugh:

'Whenever these creatures get a row with one person they are sure to have a turn all round; there's you, George, and myself, have been at her to-day; poor thing! I'm afraid she won't like to take any supper, as it is so late. I'll just go and see.'

'I would advise you not to, Clara; she will not care to eat, she is in such deep sorrow.'

'Oh, I'm very glad of that. I dare say she won't behave so again; I hope she won't, for really I can't bear sending the poor creatures for punishment; when they can get a little sorrow at home it's much more convenient. Hark! That's baby crying, I must go; good-night, my dear.'

And off went the comfortable, happy wife, mother, and mistress; she tucked her babe back to the warm, snug bed into which she speedily followed, and in dream went through her routine of house duties. Once in her sleep, she broke out into one of her little laughs, and dreamily explained:

'Oh, it's only Maida; she's so odd!'

Off went the wretched daughter, prisoner, and servant and after feverish tossings to and fro, she fell into a restless slumber from which, with a deep, deep sigh, a dream of home awoke her, and she heartbrokenly exclaimed, 'My father, oh, my father!'

CHAPTER 25

A T.L.

NOT more brilliant the conceivings of the youth who, aspiring to the honours of majority, beholds for the first time the decisive 'Esquire' in enchanting relief upon a letter addressed to himself, than were the anticipations of Robert Sanders when he awoke one morning and found himself a ticket-of-leave. For some time he had vented his impatience for the glorious day in sundry contortions of his pen on numberless bits of paper. Though the contortions varied to every dimension of Rs and Ss, and Ts and Ls, the result was invariably the same, as Lucy discovered after she had spelled out a multitude of Robert Sanders T.L. from the confusion of characters presented to her; for Robert, not satisfied with merely seeing how his future title *looked*, found greater delight in hearing how it *sounded*. 'Lor', Bob, can't you write nothing else?' asked Lucy, tired of evoking her fellow servant's name from the chaotic penmanship.

'What else is there to write? A feller likes to see what's before 'en.'

And Robert's eye, falling on the array of T.L.s scattered on the table, saw a great deal more before him in those letters than we should if we looked until doomsday, unless—but never mind. A little nettled at Lucy's want of discernment, Robert set in to perform a second edition, which he perused in silent enjoyment, until she began to suspect that the scrawling and reading was some necessary process preparatory to the mysteries of T.L.-ism, and her respect for it accordingly increased. In a subdued voice she inquired:

'Do 'e want 'em read over again, Bob?'

Robert only gave a sidewise shake of his locks, which almost annihilated Lucy with its expressiveness; it said most plainly, 'Oh, go along—you ain't worthy;' and more than ever she believed the process one sacred to T.L.-ism.

But Robert had made other preparations. For more than twelve months his wages had disappeared without any visible reason in the form of wearing apparel. His mistress often inveighed against his shabby dress; but, willing as he was for most things, he evinced no readiness to spend his money; though, in answer to Mrs. Evelyn's scoldings, his 'Very good, ma'am,' 'All right, ma'am,' were as full of willingness as ever. Once, when she declared she would not have him wear that greasy hat any longer, he so far ventured on T.L.-ism as to reply—'Very like the master would fetch an old hat for the present.'

Where all his money had gone was a question that disturbed Mr. Evelyn; he felt uneasy lest it had been appropriated to an evil purpose. Robert's anxiety, on the contrary, was only to conceal, or rather to parry an answer to the question until his time arrived. He was creating a grand surprise for the whole family, and had, from quarter to quarter, been investing his wages in apparatus for working out this surprise, which was eventually to redound in a burst of admiration on himself. Now he added a gaudy waistcoat to the secret, then a pair of second-hand Wellingtons, which, by the help of new soles, had been made to creak an incredible amount of importance. A startling blue cravat was next added to his treasures; and, lastly, he purchased a pot of 'genuine bear's grease' for the due anointing of his anti-convict pate.

When Robert awoke and perceived that the sun shone no brighter than usual, he felt much aggrieved; he thought it 'a darned shabby trick of the sun to make no difference on Ticket-day, when a feller hardly knew what to do with hisself.'

The robing ceremony, however, soon covered every untoward circumstance.

'Robert Sanders, T.L.!' he ejaculated when, having finished his toilet, he surveyed himself as best he could before the small looking-glass in his room.

He was not disappointed; the sensation created in the kitchen realised his expectations. With slow, deliberate creaks he approached the door, then, entering, he gave a short, familiar nod.

'Good morning, gals.'

Lucy stood captivated, and Robert quietly received her admiration as the homage due to T.L.-ism, personified in himself; he applied his dazzling pocket handkerchief with becoming dignity. Maida's astonishment particularly gratified him; he saw no difference between it and Lucy's adoration; he doubted whether Madda could be a shingle short since she displayed such excellent taste, 'admiring of him in that fashion.' But the parlour was to be the grand scene of triumph. When the prayer bell rang, instead of being the first to obey the summons and to carry in the wooden bench for the servants, Robert lingered and lingered.

'Bob—quick—prayers,' called Lucy over the banisters. She was awe-struck by the answer:

'Can't come for a minute, Loocy.'

All the family was seated, and Mr. Herbert waiting to commence, when *creak, creak, creak* came Robert. Maida could scarcely repress a smile. Lucy and Rachel exchanged glances of captivation.

'It's the ticket,' whispered the former.

Mrs. Evelyn looked a thousand interrogatory 'My dears?' from her husband to Bridget, from Bridget to the servants, and at last, no one explaining the approaching creak, she exclaimed:

'Why, it must be a thief!'

Sublime and slow, Robert entered, and gave a sidewise nod to the whole room, shaking from his head an overwhelming effect of bergamot[1] and from his waistcoat a strong perfume of boy's love;[2] then, as if he had done for ever with wooden benches, he drew over a chair, and stretching his legs across one corner of it, bent forward over his Bible in a free-and-easy posture. Prayers over, he sent a significant wink to Lucy:

'Now you shall see what a ticket-of-leave can do'—then creaking up to his master, he said—'Please, sir, I am sorry for to leave you, but I'd be glad if you'd find some one else to look after the hosses.'

'Why, my man, what's gone amiss?' asked Mr. Evelyn.

Bob conferred with his locks.

'Nothin' as I knows on, sir, howsomever, I'm willin' for to stay to *oblige* you and the ladies.'

Oh, the chuckling delight with which he accentuated the word *oblige*!

'No, you have been here two years, and have conducted yourself to my satisfaction, Sanders; if, therefore, you desire to go I would not keep you—you being now eligible for your ticket; but I expect you to give me a reason for this abrupt notice.'

Robert conferred more seriously with his locks, and not being able to elicit anything better, gave answer in a somewhat crestfallen voice:

'My ticket, sir,' and it conveyed a more cogent reason for leaving than any other he could have assigned. It seemed at once to satisfy his master, who replied quickly and kindly:

'Ah—yes—yes—then you may go this day month.'

Mr. Evelyn knew it would be impossible to try to argue him out of his desire to avail himself of this the only method of exhibiting his partially regained liberty; he knew that not one prisoner in a hundred could withstand the pleasant temptation of choosing a situation for himself when his ticket gave him leave to do so; and he felt sure that to be that one man in a hundred needed more sense than Robert possessed.

On his way to the comptroller's office, Robert bought a yard or two of ribbon; on his return he cut it into two parts, and threw the one half to Lucy and the other to Maida:

'There, gals, is a bit of ribbin for you.'

He then threw himself back into a chair as though it were the easiest thing in the world to get tickets of leave and buy ribbon.

'Bless my 'art, I forgot Ratchel; I s'pose the gal 'll be wantin' somethin',' he suddenly said.

Lucy had taken her ribbon and carefully folded it back in the paper; Maida's portion lay untouched.

'You can give her this, if you please, Sanders. I can thank you for your kindness all the same.'

'No, no, you keeps it, Madda; I want to see 'e in it; a feller likes somethin' to show what's 'appened.'

'Shall I give her mine?' asked Lucy, fearful he might say yes.

'No, no, don't know for that—I'd as soon see you in it as her. You and Madda wear 'em; they'll last while I'm *here*.'

'Have you gave notice?' cried Lucy, with a little shrill screech of amazement.

'Told 'e I should; what's a feller's ticket for?'

'Lor'!' Lucy looked to see how Maida bore it.

'Come, Madda, take yer ribbin,' said Robert, in a tone of vexation.

'Thank you, Sanders.' She took it and set it by, and Robert gave a chuckle of delight.

'Where do you think you shall go to then, Robert?' asked Lucy.

'Maybe I'll sote up for myself—a keb,[3] now.'

And he fell a-thinking, probably on ways and means, for he suddenly looked up with:

'I say, Madda, do that cove what sends you tin[4] write often?'

Maida bent over her saucepan and asked, in the quietest possible voice, 'What cove, Sanders?'

''Im that send that five pound that you fumed.'

'He will never send me any more money, Sanders.'

But Robert seemed incredulous, and leaving the kitchen he went straight to his master.

'Please, sir, I'd like a recommend if you'd get 'em for me.'

Mr. Evelyn knew well enough what *for*, but he chose to ask, 'Why, Sanders, are you ill?'

Robert shook his locks sidewise with a knowing shake and muttered, 'Darned ill, that I be.'

'Oh, a recommendation to the comptroller!' exclaimed Mr. Evelyn, giving a sly smile at Bridget.

Mrs. Evelyn laid down her work and looked pleased; anything to do with marriage interested her.

'I'm thinking I'd like a comfortable gal; Madda, now, downstairs, she's a bootiful woman—or Loocy I shouldn't mind, but Madda maybe's the best - she's got friends as sends her a lift.'[5]

Mr. Herbert, who sat on the sofa by Emmeline, suggested that Robert should consult his master in private, but Uncle Ev enjoyed the joke too much to monopolise it, and Bob seemed by no means discomfited by the bright eyes that watched him.

'Well, Sanders, I have no objection to recommend you for marriage as far as your steady behaviour goes; but government will require more than that, or, rather, *I* shall require more before I can conscientiously sign your recommendation. What are your prospects—how could you maintain a wife?'

'A keb, I'm thinkin', sir. Madda maybe 'll get a lift from her cove again.'

Mr. Evelyn shook his head.

'Or I'm willin' for anythin'.'

'Remember, Sanders, a ticket is more easily lost than gained.'

'All right, sir, that's just it; I'm thinking a comfortable gal may keep a feller's wits about him. Madda, now, downstairs, I couldn't find nothin' better—she's a sharp hand—maybe you'll speak to her for me.'

'I can *do* or *say* nothing until I know how you propose to settle yourself; going from my house with only a quarter's wages in your pocket, how can you marry? When once you have your ticket, you have no claim on government unless you get into trouble again.'

Robert smoothed his locks in perplexity; he could not see an escape from his difficulty.

'Very good, sir; then there's no help for it; it must bide over for a time.'

'I tell you what I *do* recommend, Sanders, and that is, that you quietly work on here or elsewhere for a time—a prisoner is in more difficulty after his ticket than before. You have earned it well and honourably: I should indeed be grieved if you lost it, which you surely will if you hurry into temptation.'

'All right, sir, I b'aint in no hurry so long as I gets the gal to wait for me; this is a quiet place, and she don't see many chaps, but—' What else he might have been going to say, he dismissed with several shakes of his head.

'Which girl do you really want, Robert?' asked his mistress.

'Well, ma'am, I've sote my mind on Madda, but I ain't partial. I wouldn't say no to Loocy, she's a dapper little maid, but Madda would help a feller out of trouble best.'

'What does Maida herself say?' asked Mr. Evelyn, with a grave glance at Bridget.

'Oh, I haven't said nothin' to her. If the master's agreeable to it, 'tain't likely she'll object. I gived her a smart ribbin, and she took to it famous.'[6]

'I advise you to hear what she says before you think any more of it. I have my doubts on the subject' (another smile at Bridget).

'Gals is always agreeable to marryin'; maybe you'd tell Madda you'll recommend us when we've kept company a bit—she won't go against your wishes.'

'I'm afraid she will in this instance,' said Mr. Evelyn dryly.

'O darned! I ain't partial, so long as it's a likely gal—there's Loocy, if Madda won't.'

'Or Rachel?' added Mrs. Evelyn, laughing.

'I don't know as to Ratchel,' replied Bob thoughtfully.

'Well, Robert, you must speak to Maida yourself. I would much rather not—but I advise you to try Lucy first.'

'Very good, sir!' and Robert left the room.

'It is well to have two strings to one's bow, Bridget,' said Uncle Ev.

'Oh, uncle, what a curious way of getting married!'

'It is the orthodox way; but I assure you, Miss Bridget, Sanders has exhibited unwonted patience and decorum. To know anything of the woman he is going to marry is generally the last thing a convict thinks of.'

'Poor Maida!' said Mr. Herbert; 'I wish we could spare her this trial.'

'I only wonder it has been spared so long, Herbert; the sooner it is over the better. I shouldn't like to be in Robert's shoes when he proposes to her.'

When the servants appeared at prayers that evening, three parts of Robert's T.L.-ism had disappeared; there was hardly any discoverable in his voice when after prayers he said, 'If your honour won't take it amiss, I'd like to leave to-morrow.'

Bob had now some other reason than his ticket for wishing to leave.

'How now, Sanders! What has happened since the morning?'

'Why, it's darned awkward to bide with a gal what won't say nothin' to you. I've spoken to her, and she won't.'

'That is, Maida won't, I suppose, Robert?'

'Es, sure; she was very perlite tho'. I ain't said nothin' to Loocy. I'll let it bide over, maybe when I'm gone Madda 'll think better of it, and your honour could tell her it's the proper thing for her to do.'

'You are not *going*, Sanders! You must wait your month. Maida will not give it a second thought; she will not annoy you.'

'Dear me, what an odd creature!' said Mrs. Evelyn.

'I'll go without my wages—I'm willin' for to lose 'em,' urged Bob, in a tone in which T.L.-ism was again audible.

'Sanders!' cried Mr. Evelyn.

T.L.-ism vanished instantaneously.

Mr. Evelyn continued in a kinder voice, 'I have your good at heart, Sanders, in keeping you; if you are determined to leave this place, you can quit in a month. In the meantime I will see what can be done for you; many a poor fellow, with intentions as honest as yours at present are, has purposely fallen back into trouble, just to obtain from government that livelihood which he could not procure elsewhere. And as for your marrying, I will recommend you with pleasure when I can conscientiously do so. I won't have you say anything more to Maida, *mind that*; either Lucy or Rachel will suit you.'

This satisfied Robert. Restless to turn his ticket to some advantage, he was just in that state to be pleased rather than otherwise with an embargo that made decision less difficult. Mr. Evelyn had foreseen this, and under cover of authority did a real kindness to the poor fellow, who had only been waiting for such an aid. The ticket-of-leave lay in his pocket like a crown piece in the hand of a child. What's the good of money if it isn't to be spent? says the child. What's the use of a ticket if 'tisn't to be laid out in a few telling articles? says Robert Sanders. Who'll know that he is a T.L. if he doesn't sport a sign board and a wife?

'Very good, sir. Loocy's dapper; and when a gal's dapper it's as good as money to a feller. I don't know nothin' about Ratchel—Madda takes care that I shan't neither. Thank'e, sir, Loocy then, if you please.'

And flopping his locks, Bob withdrew to lay his ticket at Lucy's feet.

Lucy received his offer with unfeigned surprise; she had never dreamt of him for herself—the thought would have been profanation.

'Lor', Bob, I thought 'twas Maida!'

'So 'twas; but what's a feller to do when he can't get the gal he wants?'

It was so proper that no one should be chosen whilst Maida was in the way, that Lucy did not feel at all slighted by the question, and without any meant depreciation of Robert's offer, she gave the pat reply:

'Get the one he doesn't want, I suppose.'

The little maiden scarcely knew which most to wonder at—Maida's refusal of Sanders or her own good fortune. In her simple mind were mixed feelings of fear and pleasure—fear, that Maida resigned him on purpose for her; pleasure, that she, Lucy Grenlow, was actually the bride-elect of Robert Sanders, T.L.

Her fear would not let her rest until she had poured it into Maida's ear.

'Lor', Maida, I didn't go for to make him love me; 'twas all out of his own head. I'm afeard it's sore work to you to let him go for my sake. I'll give him up to you at any moment. Ain't he handsome, though, with his fine hair so long and smart?'

And she heaved a tiny sigh, as though *she* should find it sore work to let him go, even for Maida. But Maida quieted her alarm by saying, that loving Sanders was so novel an idea to her, it would take her all her life to get accustomed to it; therefore, in the meanwhile, she thought Lucy could not do better than make the poor man happy. She then kissed her plump, shiny cheek, and added:

'I am very glad to hand you over to someone who will take care of you. I do believe Sanders tries to do well, and means to do better.'

Lucy, mistaking Maida, replied, 'No, he hasn't done nothing so *very* bad, either.'

Then, understanding from her friend's grieved countenance that she had said wrongly, she apologised:

'I means that by side of other prisoners he isn't so bad; he's a decent man, and only—'

'Hush, Lucy! There are no onlies in sin. Remember *that*, and you will not fall into fresh trouble.'

Trouble, however, was far from the young convict's thoughts. The only drawback to her joy in accepting Robert had been the dread that Maida would break her heart for him. *Now* she was as happy a pass-holder as could be found in the island.

'Lor', Maida, fancy me Mrs. Sanders!'

And, late as it was, she flitted off to communicate the pleasant conceit to Rachel, who sat in the nursery, glum, solitary, and by far too disconsolate to think of going to bed. The news imparted by the unconscious Lucy by no means softened her glumness, but the former attributed to extreme weariness the gruff ill temper of the retort:

'Coming disturbing of a body at *this* time—'most ten o'clock; what odds who he marries? Precious gaby[7] that he is! I only wonder how he ever got out of Tench; and as to his ticket, that he makes such fool game of, it's nothing but a chance that any fool may have. I wish you'd shut the door after you.'

How dreadfully sleepy she must be! thought Lucy; but sleep was not in Rachel's eyes, for jealousy was in her heart. In the morning Lucy was more sure than ever that tiredness had caused her ill-humour, for *now* congratulations flowed, honey-like, from her lips. She had been rocked to rest by perturbations of jealousy, and had arisen pacified by the determination to supplant Lucy in Sanders's affections, or rather, *intentions*, for she felt sure that, whatever it might turn out afterwards, at present the match was one of convenience, affection having small or no vote in the matter as far as Robert was concerned. And she was correct. He wanted a wife, whether a particular Lucy or an unparticular Rachel or Anne was of no consequence. The particular Lucy known as Grenlow was only selected because she had come more in his way than another girl, and because he had noticed that she was sharp in her movements, and 'dapper with her sewin',' which accomplishments Robert highly prized, but then he would equally have prized them in any other Lucy.

Rachel's cunning perceived all this, and, notwithstanding her hatred of needlework, she determined to become a 'dapper sewer,' and with her needle's point to both vanquish Lucy and fasten Robert. He had a whim for white aprons. He had at first been made to wear them for his mistress's pleasure, during his kitchen probation; since then, he had adopted them for his own special gratification, and had, therefore, to purchase them for himself. The two he had now in wear had become very thin and shabby; he regretted one day to Rachel that he had not bought more calico instead of that there ribbins for the gals.

'I wouldn't regret that, Bob,' she replied; 'people mustn't never be sorry for the good they've done. I'll make you three new aprons, any day you please.'

'Darned, will 'e?' exclaimed Sanders; 'but I must bide till I've got the stuff for 'em.'

'That's all comprehended in the *making* of 'em, Sanders. I shouldn't offer to make them if I didn't mean giving of 'em too.'

She tossed her head in a pique; she was evidently much hurt.

Bob pulled his locks. Here was willingness! Here was 'dapper sewin'!' He pulled and pulled.

'Why, Ratchel, I ain't willin' for to put on you, seein' that I didn't give 'e a ribbin, and I'm downright backed by your kindness. I never guessed you was dapper up to sewin' of apurns.'

'I never, Bob! What's a nurse that can't sew?' And she fell to laughing at his innocence of a nursemaid's requirements. From this time she never entered the kitchen without work of some sort in her hand. If she only came down for an instant just to see how long before Miss Baby's broth would be ready, stitch, stitch went her needle, 'working at once with a double thread' her plans and Lucy's destruction.

Lucy skipped about the house full of brisk 'mems,' 'sirs,' and curtsies. Though no one had spoken to her of Robert, she took it for granted that every person possessed and rejoiced in her secret. But by degrees the brisk bobs and bright cheeks disappeared. No one could account for her altered looks. Her 'mems' degenerated into slow 'ma'ams,' her curtsies became drudgeries, only extorted from her by her mistress's reprimand.

'Why, what ails the maid, my dear? She's all in the mopes. I can't bear to have her about me,' said Mrs. Evelyn, when Lucy's wits had wandered further than ever.

'I think she's out of health, aunt; she has been so listless and pale lately,' replied Emmeline.

'Yes, she has been looking very tallowy; no doubt she's been making too free with dripping and suet pudding. You noticed that large piece of pudding that went down yesterday? I quite expected to see half of it again, well, when I went to the pantry this morning 'twas all gone. No complexion can bear that! I'll go and mix Lucy a dose of Gregory.'[8]

Uncle Ev seemed delighted; he turned to Bridget:

'Are you aware, Miss D'Urban, that the Gregorian Chant[9] is a great favourite in this house? Your aunt gives it us on all occasions. They say music cures the madness ensuing from a tarantula's bite, but your aunt cures every disease with the Gregorian Chant.'

'Now, George, my dear, don't be so silly; what *would* you do without Gregory? You'd be eaten up with bile.'

The dose was administered, but no amount of Gregory brought back the colour to Lucy's cheeks. It was painful to see the change that one short fortnight wrought in her. As Robert's month increased into two, three, and almost four months, so Lucy's health decreased until it seemed probable it would fail altogether. Both master and mistress questioned her, but she could assign no reason for her flagging energies, save that she felt 'low-spirited like at Robert's keeping on not going; she'd much rather for him to go.' Maida alone guessed the cause, and with redoubled vigilance guarded the kitchen from perfidious intrusion. She had seen nothing yet to give her a fair opportunity of taxing Rachel with her design on Sanders, but she watched with the determination to avail herself of the first that should present itself. Sanders was so open, and Rachel so cunning, that she might have waited until Lucy had pined into skin and bone, had not accident betrayed the secret of her malady by discovering Rachel's treachery.

Had Rachel come before her in any other character than that of rival in her lover's affections, Lucy Grenlow had been the last to use the secret for her overthrow.

Where is the woman, how kind soever her nature, that does not desire to rid herself of one of whom she is jealous—that does not long to tear away an image that comes between her and the object of her love?

Who will blame the dejected Lucy for experiencing a strange sensation of pleasure when she found herself under the painful necessity of informing her mistress that things were not going aright in the nursery? But having proceeded thus far, Lucy heartily wished she had never commenced the complaint; the first thrill of delight over, she blushed ardent compunction, and glanced at the door, fain to bolt from the keen eye of the master, and the complaisant interrogatory expression of her mistress. However, to withdraw the charge was impossible, therefore, plucking up all her courage, before Mr. Evelyn could utter a second solemn 'Well?' she darted out—

'Please mem, sir, I think she've been cutting of sheets to make aprons for Robert.'

'Well?'

'Please, sir, that's enough.'

'And too much! Well?'

Lucy was forced to tell all she knew about it.

It then appeared that Rachel had cut up and appropriated to Sanders's use two sheets which had been some time missing. A small half-burnt strip of sheeting, bearing the household mark, had been found amongst the nursery cinders, and had told the tale. Lucy was in a terrible state of alarm when her master ordered Sanders to come up. She wrung her hands and besought Mr. Evelyn not to say anything to him, for she was sure he had never suspected the origin of the gift.

After a strict investigation Mr. Evelyn inclined to her opinion, but Mrs. Evelyn would neither be convinced by the man's reasoning nor by the facts of the case; she gave it as her opinion that the knowledge of its having been stolen property had most likely enhanced its value; to most prisoners it would; why not, then, to Robert Sanders? Knowing that if his mistress chose to act on her opinion, no power could save his ticket, the poor fellow stood forlornly before his accusers, a perfect picture of prison lowliness; he pleaded willingness—he pleaded his love for the horses—he pleaded everything but his innocence—*that* as a convict he knew would be pleaded in vain if not believed by his employers.

Rachel's guilty appearance and examination, however, diverted Mrs. Evelyn from Robert, and with a sharp reprimand Mr. Evelyn dismissed him to his stable.

Of the nursemaid's guilt there could be no doubt, though there was abundant denial. She vowed she had cut up garments of her own to make the aprons; but search being made in her boxes, remnants of the sheets were found, and her falsehood proved. A constable was sent for, and Rachel commanded to hold herself in readiness to be taken away by him. She no sooner reached her room, than she hastily shut the door and hit herself violent blows on her nose, until the blood flowed; she caught the blood in a handkerchief, and then pulled the bell with all her might. Lucy ran to answer the bell; when she perceived Rachel sitting at the foot of the bed, covered with blood, which seemed to be oozing from the handkerchief at her mouth; she screamed—'She's killed! She's killed!'

Rachel beckoned to her, and said faintly, 'Go and tell 'em I've broked a blood vessel.'

Lucy was running off. Rachel beckoned her back, and whispered more faintly—

'Beg—'em—to forgive—me—and let—me—stay on—till I'm—a bit—better—'

The alarm was given. Mrs. Evelyn hurried up to see what could be done, forgetting stolen sheets, and everything but the opportunity of displaying her skill in quackery.[10] Mr. Evelyn followed, and also Lucy, who ran forward like a little dog which hurries back to the scene of danger when it has given the necessary alarm.

'What is it? What is it?' cried Mrs. Evelyn, rushing forward. Rachel turned up her eyes and shook her head.

'I will tell you presently,' said Mr. Evelyn, advancing. 'Get up, woman! That's not the way to break blood vessels. Get up—I will teach you.'

He took both her hands and tied them together with a strong piece of list.[11]

'There, now sit down; you are more likely to burst a vessel in trying to untie that knot, than in breaking your nose.'

Rachel saw that simulation was useless, and her faintness flowed forth in a stream of oaths that were more sickening to hear than the blood to behold.

'Now *mind*, I shall appear against you and have you severely punished,' said her master, when the constable arrived.

'Yes, they were two beautiful sheets,' parenthesised Mrs. Evelyn.

'Not so much for the theft as for your vile reason in committing it; the one is unpardonable, the other I could have forgiven,' continued Mr. Evelyn.

It never entered Lucy's head to harbour resentment against her lover; had she at first felt anger, the danger she had been in of losing him appeased every feeling of an uncomfortable kind; she even talked of her foe as 'poor Rachel' and hoped she wouldn't be punished 'very bad'; after all, 'twas natural like she should take to Robert, he was so handsome.

'She'll lose her 'air anyhow,' said Robert, smoothing down his own to reassure himself that his locks, lately so imperilled, were in safe keeping on his head. Lucy even vouchsafed a few tears when she learnt from Bridget that Rachel had eighteen months, part of which time was to be solitary.

Bright, blushing, and full-blown, reappeared the roses on her cheeks; smiles once more peeped out from her dimples; and mems and sirs, brisk to her heart's contenting, again dropped from her lips. More jauntily than ever sat the little cap on her head, when, peace restored to the servants' quarters, she again basked in the undivided light of Robert's countenance.

Mr. Evelyn had not been forgetful of his promise to see what could be done to enable Robert to set up for himself. He had now been nearly five months in possession of his ticket, and having given no further hint of his desire to leave the Lodge, Mr. Evelyn gladly permitted him to stay. Hearing that old Hawkins, Maida's first friend in Hobarton, had met with an accident which incapacitated him for his calling, Mr. Evelyn went to him and found him thankful to let out his cab to Robert. Mr. Evelyn became responsible for the first quarter's payment, but told Robert that he should expect to be repaid by the end of the year. Sanders was fairly bewildered with delight when he learnt that he was to be promoted to a cab and horse of his own; on the strength of the happy news he wanted to wed Lucy directly.

He seemed so to connect his ticket with marriage, that in his sight the one was imperfect without the other. He told Lucy and Maida that he meant to speak to the master about it that very evening; so after prayers to work he went, and with such success that, after an interview of an hour, he stalked into the kitchen, and, with a mysterious flop of his hair, requested Lucy to go up to the master. During her absence he acquainted Maida (whom he now regarded as a dowager, to whom love secrets might with impunity be trusted) that it was all settled; the recommendation was to be procured, signed, and presented; and that, according to his view of the case:

'There'd be fine doin's, for when the master said *Yes* to it, Miss Bridget jumped up and clapped her hands; and young ladies don't go clapping of their hands for nothin', do they, Madda, now?'

Maida heartily hoped there would be fine doings, and she promised to try her best to further any plans for celebrating the wedding.

'Now that's what I call 'ansome, Madda! And you have been disappointed too! I tell 'e what: whenever you likes to stop down to our house, you shall find what a feller can't get everywhere—that's a welcome, and hearty too.'

The recommendation was duly signed, and the banns of Robert Sanders, T.L., and Lucy Grenlow, pass-holder, were duly published in the church of St. David's.[12] One bright Tuesday morning a little procession issued from the Lodge, Macquarie Street, and entered the parish church. Passing up the aisle, it surrounded the altar, within which stood the Reverend Herbert Evelyn, who, having acknowledged the presence of the party by a kindly smile, commenced the marriage service. In his own rich voice he read the solemn charges ordained by the church, and then, no impediment being declared in answer to the searching glance fixed particularly on the bridegroom, he proceeded to ask the man if he were willing to take the woman in holy matrimony.

The question seemed to be worded to the man's taste, for he nodded a sidewise nod of approval, replying:

''Es, sure I will.'

The Prayer-book's answer did not half express his willingness.

When Mr. Herbert put the same question to the bride, she dropped a brisk curtsey; the small, soft 'I will' popped out only just far enough to reach the ear of him for whom it was intended.

Mr. Herbert then looked round and asked:

'Who giveth this woman in marriage?'

There was a moment's pause. Who should have given her away was evidently not in the group. No one responded.

Mr. Herbert repeated the question in a tone in which sadness seemed to blend with compassion, and a tall female of noble bearing stepped forward; taking the bride's hand, she presented her to the priest, saying, in a voice that had been distinct had it been less tremulous, 'I do.'

She then drew back into her place, and her large, deep eyes rested sadly on the floor.

'Those whom God hath joined let no man put asunder,' exclaimed Mr. Herbert; then, turning to the company and the few strangers who had wandered into the building, he said:

'Forasmuch as Robert Sanders and Lucy Grenlow have consented together in holy wedlock &c., I pronounce that they be man and wife together.'

The ceremony over, no one appeared to know what next to do. There was no spontaneous hum of congratulation; there were no fond parents—no tearful sisters—no gratified brothers to exchange affectionate wishes. The bride stood half crying, half smiling, working her little fat hand back into the white silk glove. The bridegroom uneasily flopped his long hair through his fingers. All were feeling uncomfortable, when on the constrained silence broke a voice full of benevolence and sympathy:

'God bless you, my child!'

Ere Lucy could believe from whom the benediction came, the clergyman, 'all in his robes and all!' as she afterwards wonderingly recounted, took both her hands in his and shook them with a warmth that could only have emanated from a father's heart. This was enough—the constraint vanished—a pleasant confusion of voices ensued, during which, forgetful of all convict proprieties, Bridget D'Urban threw her arm round Lucy's waist and gave her a kiss; and then, presenting her hand to Sanders, she said:

'I wish you happiness in your dear little wife.'

Charlie's hugs were profuse, and baby, who had refuged herself in Maida's arms, seeing kissing going on, stretched out her head to join in the celebration, and then pushed Maida's face towards Lucy, lisping, 'Midda kiss.'

When the wedding party returned to the Lodge, Mr. Evelyn himself opened the gate, and begged to congratulate Mrs. Robert Sanders. Supposing that refreshment might not be unacceptable after so much excitement, he announced that a table had been spread for the guests in the back parlour. Poor Lucy was overwhelmed with her unexpected honours; she burst into a flood of genuine bridal tears. Throwing herself on a garden bench, she hid her face in her handkerchief, and sobbed aloud.

Mrs. Evelyn, who had run down the gravel path in high good humour, gave a little laugh of satisfaction when she perceived Lucy in this plight—she thought crying so effective at weddings—'Especially, my dear, at convict marriages, because you know they must—'

'Hush! Oh! She'll hear you, aunt,' impatiently whispered Bridget.

'Oh, never mind, my dear, she knows she's a prisoner—besides, there's quite a pretty breakfast waiting for them. I want her to stop crying now.'

'Well, Lucy—Oh, I suppose I must say Mrs. Sanders now—and yet, *no*; Lucy Sanders will do best—Well, I'm very glad you are married. I hope you'll be a good girl, because you know government won't make any difference for your being married.'

'Clara, just come here a minute,' called her husband.

'I'm just congratulating the girl, my dear; I'll come presently,' replied his wife; but with her congratulations finished also his reason for calling her away.

Emmeline's sweet, pale face smiled its loving welcome to the happy pair, when at twelve o'clock they went together, by special invitation, to her room to bid farewell, and to receive a gift she had prepared for them.

'You must come and see me sometimes, Lucy,' she said. A faint 'mem' and a quick bob was the only reply.

'Maybe you'll fancy a drive in my keb once in a while—darned if I sharn't be proud to take you—darned if I wouldn't crawl down head foremost to fetch 'e,' at last delivered Sanders, who, having been in close conference with his locks, could find nothing else wherewith to ease his burden of thanks.

Mr. Evelyn had engaged a room in a respectable cottage in Melville Street.

Thither the wedded couple bent their steps, accompanied by Bridget and the children. On reaching the house they mounted the stairs, and as they approached the door of their room, it opened, and Mr. Herbert stood before them. He raised his hand and blessed them.

He then led them to a small, round oaken table on which lay a large handsome Bible; this he placed in Sanders's hand, saying:

'There, Robert, is something for you to begin life with. Commence with it, and when all things end, it will be your stay and comfort.'

CHAPTER 26

The Conflict

THE confusion consequent on Rachel's sudden discharge had been partly rectified by placing Lucy in the nursery, and by giving Maida the double duty of housemaid and cook. Any change involving novelty and activity was pleasing to the little housemaid, who entered on her post as *locum tenens*[1] with the utmost good will. Maida, long accustomed to fold away her feelings beneath an impenetrable depth of surface, exhibited neither displeasure nor satisfaction at the additional work allotted her for the next month. Her mistress's promise of ten shillings extra for the over-work put no unusual spring into her movements, nor did the extra duties abate her energy. When she had served her dinner, she as quietly changed her cap and apron to go into the dining room, as though to wait table were the express purpose of her existence. So ably and quietly did she accomplish her twofold service that Mrs. Evelyn began to think she might well continue in it.

'Really, my dear,' she said to her husband, 'I think Maida could go on as at present, and save us the bother of another government woman; she doesn't appear to feel the work too much, nor to mind doing it.'

'But I both mind and feel it for her, Clara,' replied Mr. Evelyn.

'Ah! But she is a tall, strong woman, my dear. I think if I allowed her a glass of beer once a day, she'd manage to keep up nicely.'

But Mr. Evelyn decidedly objected to Maida's continuing longer than possible in her present position. Maida had acted as housemaid, parlourmaid, and cook for about a fortnight, when one morning her mistress bustled into the kitchen and announced visitors to an early dinner. By way of thoroughly enlisting her servant's very necessary sympathies, she entered into a familiar gossip, telling Maida that the friends she expected were new arrivals in the colony, and that one of the ladies was an old schoolfellow of hers; after dinner the whole party would take the coach to Bagdad;[2] therefore Maida must make the best use of her eyes and ears while she waited at table, if she wished to hear the latest news, and see the last fashions from England.

One of the pleasant chances of colonial life is the unexpected meeting with old friends, and the unlooked-for mention of familiar names and family incidents. In olden days a family secret was considered safe when the person from whom it had to be preserved, or in whose keeping it was, wandered to foreign shores; the death of the party concerned could not render its position more secure. But *now*, all you who have secrets to preserve from friends distant on Australian shores, or a family misfortune to hide from happily unconscious and absent relatives, be *advised*—discover your secret, unfold your misfortune, for if *you* do not *others* will; you must haste to give the information, or you will not be the first to break it to those who justly expect to share your joys and sorrows. In these days of telegraph and steam, of gold-seekers and gold-finders, there is no spot in the earth except your own breast that can give safe cover to your secret. Everyone has a brother or a sister, a cousin or a friend, or an old servant in the colonies; any one of whom may circulate your news with additions of his own, making those angry whom you might have made pleased, sowing discord when you might have planted peace.

The company arrives; the dinner is punctually served; when, prompt in clean white apron and spotless cap, Maida attends behind her mistress's chair. A heated colour in her cheeks is the only token suggestive of her previous employment. But who cares to avail himself of the suggestion? Who wants to prove a fact concerning her? A servant behind her mistress's chair, what is there in that to need explanation? She is supposed to be there, and, under the supposition, demands are made on her by the pronunciation of certain unprotected substantives: bread—water—castors.[3] Her actual bodily presence is not ascertained, until one of the guests just happens to look at her in taking the mustard—then, struck by her beauty, he looks and looks again.

At an English dinner table there would be unpoliteness in drawing attention to the servants in waiting; but *here*, where most domestic sympathies settle around one point, and that point is O.P.S.O.,[4] there is no breach of etiquette in doing so; a guest as naturally asks questions about a servant whose superior manners or efficient waiting attract his notice, as he compliments his entertainer on a thriving rose bush, or his child's improved health.

Notwithstanding his only having just arrived from England, one of the party proclaimed his colonial extraction by an exclamation during Maida's absence from the room: 'What a decent-looking woman, Evelyn! Free or government?' All eyes in consequence were bent on her when she re-entered. The colour deepened on her cheeks as she received the gaze of a dozen pair of eyes.

'A splendid creature,' whispered the gentleman.

'And a dreadful one, too,' replied Mrs. Evelyn.

Significant gesticulations passed between them.

'No particular news from home, then, Sandford?' asked Mr. Herbert, in order to divert attention which he perceived was annoying to Maida.

'N—no—all very flat; *Punch*[5] can hardly strike a spark of fun out of the whole nation.'

'Talking of marriages and old school days, Clara, do you remember a pretty little girl called Doveton, whom we great girls used to pet,' continued the lady who had been calling over school reminiscences with Mrs. Evelyn, when Mr. Sandford's remark arrested her.

'Perfectly; you don't mean to say she is married?'

'Yes, she *is,* and very well married too.'

'What, little Mary Doveton!' cried Mrs. Evelyn.

Maida listened eagerly.

'She is a very charming woman, I assure you.'

'I don't doubt it; but it is difficult to imagine her a woman—a slight, fragile fairy as she is, to my recollection.'

'She has lost neither fairyhood nor simplicity: in womanhood she is as fairy-like as ever, and just as simple.'

'Who is the happy man, I wonder? Do I know him?'

'A Captain Norwell; such a handsome man: they make a most bewitching couple, and are all the rage.'

'Norwell! Norwell!' repeated Mr. Herbert. 'The name seems familiar, but I cannot recall the man. I should like to, for I well remember little Mary Doveton, though I have not seen her since Clara was at Mrs. Compton's school.'

'When you used to bring me notes from my friends in Hobarton, little thinking you were obliging your future sister-in-law, Mr. Herbert!' added Mrs. Evelyn, laughing.

'Norwell! Norwell!' exclaimed another heart in that room, as tumultuous feelings dragged the colour from her face and unsteadied her whole frame.

'Well, I hope he will make her a good husband.'

'There is no fear of that, he is a fine, noble fellow; his wife literally worships him,' answered Mr. Sandford. Mrs. Evelyn had for some seconds been giving telegraphic taps on the table in order to draw Maida's attention to the knives and forks, closing one by one on her guests' plates, but without success. Listless and inanimate, Maida's eyes rested on the last speaker, who continued to eulogise Norwell.

'Maida!' at last exclaimed the mistress, with a loud rap on the table.

Maida started—a deeper crimson rushed to her face, and then, departing, left a livid paleness.

'What ails the woman?' tapped Mrs. Evelyn, as Maida staggered beneath the weight of a tray not over-heavy. The rest of the dinner was a series of vexed taps and nods on the part of Mrs. Evelyn, and mistakes on the part of Maida. Her manner was perfectly calm and collected, therefore the more unaccountable to her mistress were the strange inadvertencies of her actions.

Maida hastened to be solitary. No doubt existed in her mind that the Captain Norwell with whom her fate so cruelly blended had been married to Mary Doveton.

She longed for night, which alone could bring her an uninterrupted review of all that she had heard, or afford her an opportunity for calm decision in the difficulty before her.

Night came. With a throbbing heart, as though she were going to an interview of which she dreaded the result, Maida sat herself down to a severe scrutiny of her own feelings, arraigning before her judgment each motive whose promptings she doubted. She remained for some time in deliberation, then looking about as if in search, she remembered she had neither pen, ink, nor paper, and all three were necessary to her purpose. What could she do? She wished not to wait till the morrow, lest opportunity should fail her. There was no book from which she could tear the fly-leaf. She thought of Emmeline—but *she* must not be disturbed; she then remembered that Mr. Herbert was often in his study to a very late hour. Slipping off her shoes, she crept downstairs; the action reminded her of that fatal morning, when, seeking to shield her babe from the stern grasp of justice, she crept away to give it loving burial.

The remembrance served to strengthen her in her determination.

A streak of light issuing from Mr. Herbert's study told her that she could get her wants supplied; she knocked, and he opened the door.

'You, Maida!'

'Yes, sir. Will you give me a few sheets of paper, and a pen and ink?'

'It is late for such a request.'

'I have no time by day.'

'Leave it till to-morrow, and I will try to procure leisure for you.'

'No, thank you; I require that concentration of thought which night only can give.'

'These are strange things to say, Maida, and a strange time to say them.'

'But you need not fear my purpose. Will you kindly give me the paper?'

Mr. Evelyn thought a moment, and then going to his desk took out a few sheets, which, with pen and ink, he put into her hand; at the same time, looking her full in the face, he said:

'I will give you them, Maida, but I confess I do so with much uneasiness. As *Maida Gwynnham* I trust you—but—'

'As a convict you are bound to doubt me, and correctly so, sir. I as much honour you for the one feeling as I thank you for the other; but, Mr. Herbert, you cannot know Maida Gwynnham as she knows herself, or you would trust her as little in *herself* as in her convict state. However, your *trust* shall not be misplaced, though I will do my best to displace your *doubt*.'

As Maida met the calm, reflective countenance before her, how sure she felt that in Mr. Herbert lay both ability and will to assist her. She longed to open her troubled and conflicting mind to his advice. She never so yearned for friendly counsel as in this predicament, when she perceived that a false move might ruin the gentle being she wished to serve, or an indiscreet word have the opposite effect to that which she desired. She could bear by herself all that only touched herself; but now that one, whom she reverenced in her purity, had come unconsciously into her secret, she longed to hear from other lips a corroboration of the opinion she had formed, and an approval of the course she was resolved to adopt; but neither friend nor counsellor dared she seek. Alone, alone, must she pass this fierce ordeal; alone, unsympathised with, and unadvised, she must tear from her heart her last, though unacknowledged, hope in life.

Placing the materials for writing on a wooden box, which served her instead of a table, she knelt before it and commenced a letter to Norwell; but she could not satisfy herself. Fastidious over his feelings as over her own, she destroyed sheet after sheet when she had partly written it. She wished to deal faithfully—to *warn, threaten, promise* him; but she would not reproach him. After many efforts she produced the following letter:

The Lodge, Macquarie Street, Hobarton,

 Van Diemen's Land

 To Captain Norwell.

 SIR

I was standing behind my mistress's chair to-day, when I learnt from the conversation at the dinner table that you had married Miss Doveton. Circumstances unknown to you have made me acquainted with that lady, and awakened in my breast a deep interest in her welfare—an interest that is much deepened by the report of her marriage to you. The surprise occasioned me an impulse of jealous displeasure, which subsided, on reflection, into the feeling which now induces me to write to you, though against my inclination.

I pass over the fruitless sorrow I feel for your poor wife. I even pray that her delusive apprehension of your character may continue, seeing that she has acted too far upon it to be benefited by discovering the truth.

My sole object in writing is to point out to you the moral difference created by your marriage in our respective positions.

From what I was obliged to hear at the dinner table, I deem it probable you may become informed of my having heard of your marriage, and I fear you may in consequence write to me to avert the effects of anger you may suppose me to feel, and in so doing run risk of exposing truths to your wife which would put an end to the enviable ignorance so necessary to her happiness. To anticipate your fears, and prevent their consequences, I engage by this letter to remain silent, as I have hitherto been; but to this engagement I attach, Captain Norwell, these solemn conditions (and I have the means of observing their performance by you): first, that you shall be kind and faithful to your wife; second, that you write *no more* to me.

Do not mistake my meaning, nor misinterpret leniency of expression into feebleness of purpose. I wish you clearly to understand that, if you again risk discovery by committing to paper things intended only for me, or if you fail to be kind and faithful to your wife, I shall no longer consider silence and suppression the best means I can employ for promoting the happiness of one who bears the name I once thought you intended to be mine. To Mrs. Norwell I henceforth ascribe the gratification I experience in bearing that part of my punishment which is your due. This being the last time you will hear from me, I will satisfy your inquiries before concluding, hoping that, at least as to a *part*, my replies will free you from embarrassment in the moral fulfilment of your marriage vow.

You inquire, first, whether I love you still? My answer is, *No!* This answer is not extorted from me by the knowledge of to-day. My love for you has been long since forbidden by the judgment of my conscience, forced into maturity by sorrow and reflection. I sifted with painful rigour the jealous emotion I felt on hearing of your marriage; and I discovered, with joyful truth, that it was due to surprise alone. Recollection returned, and the emotion was gone, leaving no trace of disappointment. You next ask whether I am comfortable. I do not suppose you know the bitter sarcasm attached to the word 'comfortable' in convict language, originating in an anecdote current in the colony, and which I give you as an appropriate explanation of the comfort in question. A gallows having been erected for the simultaneous execution of nine prisoners, was submitted for the approval of an experienced executioner, who gave it as his opinion that the accommodation was insufficient for *nine*, but that *seven* could hang there *comfortably*. Herewith I return the letters I have received from you during my transported life,

And remain, Sir,

Yours faithfully,

MAIDA GWYNNHAM.

The letter finished, the rigid discipline wherewith she had controlled her heart into obedience to her reason was laid aside. With a trembling grasp she seized the letter, and with an anxious eye she perused it aloud. She wondered how her hand had brought itself to pen the cold, stern characters before her. When she came to the question, 'Do you love me still?' her voice quavered, her long lashes fell and concealed the expression of agony that lay beneath. She could not form the round, cold 'No' upon lips so unsteady; it died away in an unspoken murmur. She was thankful that, secured beyond chance of escape, it would reach Norwell in a form betraying neither her regret nor her agitation. She was thankful it was not to be entrusted to *her*, but to be delivered in a letter. He will look on the answer, and see only in it the prompt and simple 'No'. He will know nothing of the pained power that has been put forth to pen that one short word: he will note only firmness in the deep mark that underlines it into emphasis, and will say, 'Ah, that is like Maida!' He has not witnessed the effort with which the undecided heart was made to draw that final renunciation to a claim that by right of justice was its own, so suspects not that that one short word is the token of victory after a severe conflict.

She was thankful, too, that the writing to him had not been practicable at the moment she heard the tidings; her impulsive nature might then have hurried her into reproach, despicable to her calmer mood; or might have impelled her to a display of those sufferings of which she scorned to complain.

Having read and re-read the letter many times, and being at last convinced that it contained no infliction which it would be prudent to spare Norwell, or no expression that could create a misgiving in his mind, or mislead him as to her intention or the state of her feelings towards him, she folded it, and enclosing three letters lately received from him, she melted together the wax broken from the seals of his letters, then dropped the burning liquid upon her envelope, and stamped it with the corner of the inkstand. The morning had scarcely dawned when she crept downstairs, and let herself into the garden through the verandah of the drawing-room window. Thence hurrying into the street, to the imminent peril of detection, and consequent severe punishment, she glided swiftly to the post office, and slipped her letter into the box; then, with a lightened heart and slackened step, she returned to the house, not caring by whom she might be met, or whom she might encounter.

When the family assembled for prayers, Mr. Herbert knew by her languid appearance that she had passed a night of unrest. He regarded her with a peculiar interest, for he, too, had endured hours of suspense and watch and all on her behalf. Of this, however, she was as little aware as that her haggard and yet determined countenance had seriously alarmed him when she presented herself at his door, and proffered her strange request. She was in ignorance also of the source from which, perhaps, she had derived strength and power to pen that letter to Norwell. She knew not that while she was pining for someone on whose judgment and counsel she might rely, even then that holy man, whose friendship she would not cultivate, whose advice she could not seek, was kneeling for her at the footstool of Infinite Love, and imploring that, though led into temptation, she might be delivered from evil.

She knew not that from behind his shutter he had watched her go out, nor that he had followed her in the agonised belief that she had gone to self-destruction; nor that the only rest he had taken for the night was from the time of her return from the post to the present hour. Believing as he did that Maida was the prey of some great mystery, and that the indifference she exhibited was only a mask assumed to hide the writhings of a spirit, every one of whose fine and complex powers of suffering were daily taxed to torment; and perceiving that, coexistent with this spirit, there warred within her a principle of freedom that detested the slavery she endured so uncomplainingly, Mr. Herbert continually dreaded to hear that she had sought the last resource of overburdened and unsanctified suffering, and exchanged the fetters of life for the illusive liberty of death.

When, therefore, so pale and ghost-like, Maida stood before him at that strange weird hour and asked for writing materials, he granted her desire, feeling it would be useless to deny it, and hoping that his concession might touch her into confidence. But when he saw her depart, calm and intrepid as she had come, his uneasiness increased into alarm. Connecting, as he did, her demand for papers and pens with a fatal determination to destroy herself, he feared what the morning light might reveal. He fancied he already discovered the explanatory document written in her firm clear hand, and indicted by her proud free spirit. From the peculiarity of her temper, he knew that to follow and charge her with a suicidal intention would only be to hurry her into the act, or to put the thought into her mind. He resolved, therefore, that all he could do was to pass the night in praying for her, and in watching her movements. Having committed his fears and suspicions to Him who alone can order the unruly wills of His creatures, Mr. Herbert retired to his room, and placing open the door, he commenced his anxious vigil, listening to every night sound, as though it was fraught with important results. Several times he went to Maida's apartment, and listened without until some noise within satisfied him that she was there.

When the twilight glimmered through his shutter, he prepared to take the rest so needed by mind and body. Wrapping about him his morning gown, he threw himself on his couch. He had scarcely done so when he distinctly heard a door unbolt, and a stealthy footstep on the stair. Then he heard the creaking latch of the drawing-room window. He sprang to his window, and in another moment saw Maida hurrying down the garden. By the same exit he followed her warily and at a distance, until he perceived that her errand, though mysterious, was harmless. With a thankful heart he retraced his steps, and cast off the burden of solicitude which had made the night one of weariness and distress.

CHAPTER 27

An Old Acquaintance

> Neither have ye brought again that which was driven away,
> neither have ye sought that which was lost: but with force and
> cruelty have ye ruled them.[1]

NO sooner had the garden gate closed on Robert and Lucy, than Mr. Evelyn instructed Maida to unlock the waiting-room and conduct thence to their several destinations the servants who had arrived to take the place of the wedded pair. There were one man and two women. John Googe she was to take to an outhouse which Mr. Evelyn had improved into a room for the use of all succeeding ostlers, whose love quarrels might not end so innocently as had the amours of Robert Sanders. Tammy Matters was for the kitchen, and Diprose for the nursery.

Diprose was an *Anson* expiree, and had been that morning fetched by Mr. Evelyn during the marriage festivities. She was dressed in the prisons, and had about her that frightened air so characteristic of the novitiate, and her eyes were red with weeping. As the door unlocked she started to her feet, and became so agitated that when Maida entered she stood before her as one palsy stricken.

Tammy Matters and Googe were old hands; they at once recognised in Maida a fellow servant; but the expiree, mistaking her for her mistress, bowed, lowly, before her, to the amusement of the others.

'Grab hold of honour whilst you can get it, mate; she won't be long a missus-ing you,' said Googe to Maida.

In leaving the room Tammy punctiliously observed the right of precedence. With a circular jerk of her elbow she edged Diprose back and herself forward: it was not to be thought of, that a new expiree should walk before her, who was almost due for her ticket. Casting a smile of contempt at the government brown, she smoothed down her own clothes with a smirk of approbation, glancing self-satisfied at the finery which apparelled her into a figure surpassingly grotesque. Every possible texture of material had been pressed into her bodily service. Her black bonnet had evidently been an apron; the silk, drawn tightly over a piece of shapeless pasteboard, revealed this secret by exhibiting alternate rows of tiny holes and greasy marks where the folds had lain. A whole nosegay of soiled, davvered flowers[2] of every sort hung loosely from one side of the bonnet, and flapped up and down with a constancy that reminded one of perpetual motion. Her gown of bright-coloured muslin barely reached her ankles: it could not have been lengthened but at the expense of one of the five flounces adorning the skirt—an expense that neither Tammy's love of finery nor hatred of needlework could sanction. A relic of the *Anson,* in the form of the prisoner's blue-checked neckerchief, pinned shawl-fashion on her neck, completed her attire. The convict petticoat, though looped up to suit the peculiarity of the muslin, was visible beneath the dress.

As Tammy professed to excellence in cookery, and to just the contrary in the house department, Mrs. Evelyn decided that she and Maida should exchange situations. The latter therefore became housemaid, and was consequently brought into more frequent contact with Miss Evelyn, for whom she had long entertained a deep but unacknowledged regard. All portions of her daily duty which had Emmeline for their object were regarded more as acts of pleasure than of servitude. The sweet low voice, so ever ready to greet her with a cheerfulness void of levity, and an affability void of condescension, had a sympathy in its tone that came more acceptably than sympathy expressed in words. And when, as was often the case, the gentle voice gave utterance to thoughts full of peace, and bright with the immortal hope that irradiated the inner life of the invalid, Maida would listen and linger, longing to hear more; then, when she could linger no more, she would gather all she had heard into her mind and bear it away; and often during the day, which to her was ever of toil and trial, she would dwell upon the words of peace and love, and bless the lips that had spoken them to her.

With what special interest watched the great Adversary of Souls the spiritual fluctuations of this tempted woman! How perseveringly did he try to hold her back from all that might benefit her! How cunningly devised were the hindrances he placed in her way! When, despite his endeavours, a grain of the precious seed of truth found access to her mind, how subtle in its commonplaceness was the means adopted to defraud her of it, or to destroy its fructifying power! A sharp and undeserved rebuke from her mistress, a degrading familiarity from one of her fellow servants, a threat, a provocation, were contrivances by which all Emmeline's example and Mr. Herbert's teaching were rendered useless. And yet, we know not why we should specify this as peculiar of *Maida's* career. A similar strife between the powers of light and darkness is everywhere being carried on. Whether in the person of the aged believer or in the young wavering disciple, whether in the bold confessed outlaw or in the timid youth hesitating over his first crime, Satan is awake the wide world over, everywhere arrogant over what he holds, and rampant for that which is beyond his reach. Imitating God, he despises not the day of small things. But with Maida, and with others in like condemnation, the strife is more apparent, the vacillations more striking, there not being the restraints and decorums of free life to hide them.

One afternoon, when Maida had occupied the situation of housemaid for three months, Mr. Evelyn determined to try the experiment of sending her out alone (hitherto he had adhered to his regulation, and only let her go out under the guardianship of one of the family). Bridget's bad headache afforded him an excuse for the experiment. Summoning Maida, and assuming that severity of manner which he reserved for state occasions, he told her that he was about to test the sincerity of her intentions, and try if she would be as trustworthy when out of his sight as he had yet had no reason to doubt she was within the immediate bounds of the household. He then cautioned her against shipmates and public-houses; and finally charging her to remain out no longer than necessary, and reminding her how pained he should be if she deceived him, and how unhesitatingly he should punish her if she disobeyed him, he dismissed her with a note and parcel to Trinity Parsonage,[3] bidding her stop on her way there to perform a few errands in the city. When she was ready to go, Mr. Evelyn himself conducted her to the gate, and, shutting it upon her, said:

'It is now three o'clock, I shall expect you home before *five*—now, mind!'

'I wonder how she feels, going out alone for the first time,' exclaimed Bridget, as her uncle returned to the drawing room. 'How she must hate me, as the poor unfortunate always made to follow her about; I'm sure I hate it for her.'

'She doesn't care *that* for it;' and Uncle Ev filliped,[4] to demonstrate the *that*. 'She is the queerest creature that ever came into my possession. I shall be right glad if Herbert does anything for her in the converting line, so as to bring down a little of her pride. Poor soul! I pity her to my heart. By-the-bye, Miss Bridget, you doubt that I have a *heart*, do you not?'

As five o'clock drew near, a perceptible though unexpressed anxiety pervaded the whole family. Emmeline and Bridget both tried to divert Mr. Evelyn's attention from the waning moments, but without knowing that their effort was perceived by each other. Each hoped she was succeeding to admiration, for Uncle Ev, standing with his hands tucked behind his coat, appeared to answer, or at any rate to acknowledge, by rapid 'hems', all that they told him of Charlie's precocities or baby's tricks; but as the clock struck five, the locality of his previous thoughts was at once determined; he pulled the bell with a loud click, and then, walking out of the room, called over the stairs:

'Gwynnham home?'

The fatal 'No, sir,' came back, and sent a cold shiver through Emmeline, who, turning silently towards her uncle, saw by his countenance that wrath was determined against Maida.

Bridget had already left the room, and, forgetting her headache, was putting on her bonnet to go in search of the fugitive. But Uncle Ev, who also seemed to be going out, met her on the stairs, and she knew, by the tone of the voice that bade her return, that resistance or inquiry would be useless. She looked at him; there could be no harm in that, yet it seemed quite the wrong thing to do.

'Go in to your cousin; there's no knowing when I shall be back,' frowned Uncle Ev; and he slammed the door after him with a force that threatened a terrible amount of trouble.

Meanwhile, where was she who created all this excitement? Having performed her commissions in the city, Maida proceeded to Trinity Parsonage and delivered the parcel. Returning thence by that part of the prisoners' burial ground which faces the town end of government demesne, she stood to gaze on that final resting-place for her captive brethren. Leaning on the fence, her eye wandered over the field, whose dreary aspect had naught to break its dull monotony save the ridges, which heaved its surface at careless intervals, giving it more the appearance of land prepared for the sower than of that already sown for the human harvest, of which the poet so touchingly writes: but it needed the symmetry of the husbandman's labour to make even outward resemblance to that rude picture complete. The inner picture— ah! who would dare compare? The contrast strikes too vividly. The husbandman ploughs his acres, and his heart goes with his work; each furrow receives his hope, his prayer, as well as his goodly grain. The grave is prepared with curses: the human seed is sown prayerlessly, tearlessly, for we do not call the formal, grudged service mumbled over the prison dead, a prayer—and tears, who expects them at a convict funeral? The eyes to shed them are across the ocean. The seed is sown, the earth is shovelled over it, and who cares to ask or think in what appearing it shall arise?

Maida leaned quietly for a few moments. The slow movement of her head from one part of the field to the other denoted rather a general survey of it as one object of sadness, than a search for a particular spot over which to feel a particular sorrow. She suddenly started, and, standing erect, gazed, intent, towards the furthest extremity of the field. Until this instant three men, partially hidden by the increased height of fence, had escaped her notice. With a quick cry of impatience, she sprang over the barrier and confronted two low-foreheaded, brutal-visaged prisoners, who were wantonly abusing their trust by kicking about and otherwise ill-treating two coffins that had been left them to inter. As

Maida now stood before them, one of the coffins was lying edgewise, having rolled off from two graves of unequal size on which it had been tossed; the other, almost raised to an upright posture, was supported by a heap of rubbish.

The younger man was a simple-looking fellow; he had been an obedient tool in the hands of the other two, who appeared to delight in the matter-of-fact manner in which the youth received and carried out their orders, whilst they spread it over the dead bodies. The burial service, of course, had been performed; but that invested the corpses with no sacredness in the sight of those who were left at once to fill up the ceremony and the grave.

'Who be you?' cried both men, and gaped the third, as, like an apparition, Maida rose up before them.

The fire of bygone days flashed from her dilating eyes, and, in a tone of haughty superiority, she exclaimed:

'I'll report you! What dare you do? I remain by you until I have seen them decently buried; cannot you let their mangled bodies rest in peace?'*

'Round away,[5] then, my pretty one! Round away on us! Who may you be? Remember we are alone together,' replied the elder man, in a voice of impudent raillery.

'We *are* alone, but I am safe. The wretch that could insult the dead, would fear to touch the living.'

She fixed her eye steadily upon him, and as she read the brutal characters delineated in his face, she fancied one by one appeared features she had scanned before, but where, or under what circumstances, she could not recall.

'Is it so, my darling? Then how comes Bob Pragg out here? Giles Waddy there can tell to that—can't ye, Gi? He'll warrant ye I've touched the living 'fore now, and that with no chicken-heft,[6] I'll promise ye; a chinker[7] gied by Bob Pragg ain't a gift of every day.'

With an involuntary shudder and look of ill-disguised disgust, Maida, deeming it useless to interfere with two such men, and yet longing to see the coffins beyond reach of further insult, dropped her voice to a scarcely audible whisper:

'They are prisoners.'

'They *was*, but I reckon they free enough now. Forgery and lifting,' he continued, as if that had been their names.

'And *you* are prisoners?' said Maida.

'In the Queen's service! Government livery, blue and gold—no mistake. Can you sport a fig of baccy?'

Bob touched his cap, mock reverentially, and winked to Giles.

'Who may your graceship be?'

Another touch of the cap, and a wink to the youngest man, who had never withdrawn his gaze from Maida.

'*I*—am—a—prisoner,' said Maida, speaking slowly and distinctly.

The trio started in unfeigned astonishment.

'My eyes!' at last ejaculated the youngest.

'I wouldn't scarce believed it, if I'd seen the brown petticoat,' said Giles.

---

*   It is a common supposition among the prisoners that after death their bodies are handed to the doctors for the public good, and that, when the doctors had finished with them, the mangled remains are carelessly thrown into a coffin, without any regard to decency—and carried away to the burying.

Here Maida raised her gown an inch or two above her feet, and with the convict garment confirmed her statement. Bob Pragg stared with a mixed expression of incredulity and delight; then shading his mouth with his hand, he whispered to Waddy:

'Be blostered if 't ain't Martha Grylls! I'd swear to her all the world over! There's pluck enough for she, and too much for any else.'

'We are all prisoners, then,' proceeded Maida. 'Should we not, therefore, show more feeling towards each other? Fancy: to be so treated by their brothers in trouble, and that when they are unable to resist!'

Her eye again began to gather fire, and her speech animation. It was not in her wholly to control the indignation struggling in her breast.

'They have had a life of degradation and misery—surely in death, when the oppressor can no longer reach them, their own comrades should let them rest in peace!'

'Oh, they took't it easy—tisn't all takes on as very like you did. Most on us couldn't be worse off than we was in England. Most on us only turned rogue when we couldn't turn a bellyful from honest work. To them what don't care for the name on it, it's better to be here with full bellies and hard work than 't 'ome with empty maws and idle jaws—that is when a feller can keep blind eye of the government coves—they'm *mighty* partial where they pleases!'

'Then you'll bury them at once?' interposed Maida, but Giles had not finished.

'Tho' I says it myself, I'd never have been out here, if I'd got work at home. I was as willing to live by fair means as any man going; but honest thoughts won't fill a poor fool's belly, and, —— me if it'll stop his children's bawl. When I frisked a crib[8] the fust time, I'd no thought o' doing it again; but then I found a wideawake sort of feeling come out of the job—a feeling that seemed to put fresh life in me; so I went on till I'd no notion of toiling a *week* for what I could get in a *night*, and joined company with a cracksman, and got lagged[9] after a while—and now I'm your humble servant.'

The thoughtful tone into which he had lapsed during this retrospection vanished during the last five words, and he appeared, by a sudden and remarkable transition of manner, again to become Giles Waddy, the ruffian. Maida attempted to speak, but Giles again stopped her, on which Bob Pragg commented:

'Gi's on his pet fiddle-string now—scrape, scrape, he'll go, till you wish hearty you'd never meddled with sober folks in their occupation—there, scrape, scrape, he goes again.'

'Strikes me—or I'll be struck stone dead—if them wise heads don't one day find out there's something wiser to be done than paying police and building gaols. Men don't swag on full bellies, 'xcept when they's had a smack on it,[10] and finds it relishing. The *fust* time they steals, they steals for hunger—the *second*, the deuce knows why.'

'Hold your jaw, you confounded blockhead! Thank your blessed stars you're not one of them wise 'eds—any day I'd rather be one of the *drove* than the driver.'

'Anyhow, we'll all roll into hell together! But don't *you* talk pious there—*you'd* no call to turn rogue—you know *you* turned because you admired the trade.'

A loud gruff laugh sounded through the ground. Maida stamped impatiently, but speak with authority again she dared not—not on her own account, but for the sake of the dead. Any burst of anger would be visited on those who lay helpless at her feet, for, with the young man's assistance, she had laid the coffins in a proper position.

'Now, then, do let us bury them!' she said.

'Us! Heft[11] away, then; but no harm in being merry over the confounded job. Leave alone there' (to the young man)—'no use to try it; the hole's too small for two on 'em.'

'It shan't be for want of trying, then,' and Giles kicked the topmost off, and jumping on the under one, endeavoured to squeeze it down a few inches by stamping his full weight on it; then, with an awful curse, he called on the young man to help drag it out from the hole.

Maida could witness it no longer in silence:

'I'll report you, and shall glory in the punishment you get. Give me the spade!'

Before Giles could resist, she had snatched the implement from him, and in the strength of excitement had struck it deep into the tough mould.

Giles raised his arm to strike her, but a loud guffaw, and a meaning wink from Bob, arrested the blow.

'Gi, you'll be a fool if you quar'l with her for doing your work. Let her have a heft at it whilst we take a spell over yonder.'

Another wink in the direction of a distant part of the ground made Gi, though somewhat sullenly, let fall his arm, and follow Bob to the spot. The young man was about to join them, but Bob nudged him back with—

'Go on courtin' the ladies with them great gogglers [12] of yourn, Sam! I should think your lantern jaws had well stuck fast by the gapin' they've had. But she's an old hand for the gents, and maybe you'll do in want of a sprucer sweetheart.'

'Ha, ha, ha!' from Giles, and—

'Froggy would a-wooing go!' from Bob.

And then from Maida so fierce a dig of the spade into the earth, as made both men start, and the youth repeat his interjection—

'My eyes!'

The men were part way over the field when Bob Pragg called back—

'I say Sam, make much of her, for she's like one rosed from the dead. The grip was most on her neck [13] for that babby of hers. They was in a mighty good temper that day, or she'd have had a dance on the tight-rope! Be blostered if she wouldn't have cut a few capers worth seeing of.'

In the flush that dyed Maida's cheek and temple as the spade drew heavily back, Sam saw only the natural effect of unusual effort. We, who know more of Maida, discern pain in its fervour, and mighty mental conflict in that involuntary closing of the lid, as the inward fire shone lustrous crimson through the transparent skin. A few more desperate onslaughts, and resting, as any wearied delver might rest, one foot on the bottom of the spade and one hand on the top, Maida turned and took her first look at Sam. His eyes were riveted on her so fully that he was obliged to give a number of small twinkles before he could unfix them. It was now for Maida to gaze at him, which she did, in silence, for many seconds, and then, 'Poor lad!' burst from her lips. 'Sam, how old are you?'

But Sam did not answer; he seemed too busy replying to mental queries of his own.

Whatever the replies were, they finally converged into a focus in the form of a question, which, though couched in lowly phrase, appeared to give him infinite satisfaction.

'Let's take a heft on't. Like you'm sweatin', miss?'

'No, Sam, you are tired; let us talk a little.'

'With *me*, ma'am?'

Wonder added to their former admiration, the glassy blue goggles again took possession of Maida's face.

'Yes—why not with me?'

'Be you a prisoner, *sure*, ma'am?'

The 'ma'am' came so naively and so aptly from his lips, that Maida accepted it from the poor lad as a tribute of respect from which she had long been estranged.

'I am your fellow prisoner.'

'A sight o' difference 'tween us tho'!'

And Sam, as if referring only to personal disparity, deliberately viewed Maida and then himself from head to foot.

'You've got a whole back of fine clothes.'

'Ah, but there is *this* beneath them!' bitterly said she, again showing the convict brown.

'And I can't keep out of yellows no ways. When I think now for the greys and I am just on having 'em, something comes along to get me into trouble, and it's a sight o' time 'fore I gets out of the yellows; I haven't been out of 'em yet for more than two months to a time.'

The colour had now faded from Maida's face; the ashy paleness that succeeded could no more escape the earnest search of Sam's eyes than had the flush.

'Be sick, missus?' asked Sam, whilst the immovable goggles remained firm to their watch.

A faint and sad smile found its way to her lips, in spite of the aching load that dragged downwards all desire to smile.

'No, Sam; I'm sick in a way that you cannot understand. You don't seem very suited to those clothes; tell me how you came by them.'

The youth lolled his ample tongue in his mouth in quiet satisfaction that he had permission to talk—a comfort he seldom enjoyed in the crowded desolation of the Tench, where older and rougher voices—when any voice was allowed—asserted the pre-eminence both in pitch and in period; while younger ones, fearful the blame of the uproar would fall on them, found refuge from the strife of tongues either in self-enforced silence or sullen moodiness.

'Must I tell how I got lagged, or how I gets into trouble?'

'Tell me all you like; it does me good to hear of other persons' troubles. Tell me about mother, and father, and all.'

The prospect of an uninterrupted recital glistening before him, reflected a thin glaze of pleasure on his sickly face, and put a moment's life into the glassy opacity of his eyes.

'I never had no father, as I know on; and mother—the naybors all took shy[14] on her, cos she'd got me; and when I came nigh to 'em they shoved me off, and said I'd no b'isness to be born; I wasn't nothin' to nobody; and mother fretted, and said I was everythin' to her, because she hadn't got nothin' else.'

Here another loll of his tongue, followed by a thick swallow, stopped Sam for an instant; and when Maida glanced towards him the goggles had not removed, but their earnestness seemed subdued by a mist that had spread over them.

'The naybors said she was taking to bad ways, but she told me she wasn't; she used to tell me everythin', tho' I didn't know much what it meant *then*—but *now* sims to me I was a jackass for not knowing. Well, missus, one afternoon she'd sat crying—sims I see her now!—and I was nation[15] bad hungered. "Mother," says I, "shan't us get nothin' to ate to-day?" Then she gave me the first bad word that she'd ever gave me—sims I hear her now! Her says: "Mother me to-morrow, you young devil, if you can!" "Mother," says I, "never mind, I can bide;" then she fell to crying worse, and then she grabbed me like mad, and bawled: "If mother speaks so to un, who else should speak kind?" Then she threw up her hands to God Almighty as fine as any parson, and bawled out: —"Justice? Let 'en come! I lay this sin at his feet. *Yes,* at *yours,* Edward Moulston!" "What is justice, mother? Be it anythin' good to ate?" says I. Then she laughed like Old Nick,[16] and bawled: "I believe you! It's good for nothin' else; but it doesn't do for starving wretches—it takes too long a-comin.'" I was gettin' most afraid of her; thinks I, the devil's got hold on her. Well, missus, then she went out, and brought me back some rare grub, so that I got a rale bellyful; she looked on at me all the while. When I'd done, she took her bonnet, and said to me, "You won't want nothin' more to-day, Samuel. If I'm not back by dark, go to bed; and if I an't back to mornin', and the folks comes to ask for me, tell 'em I'm gone out to look for justice; perhaps I'll have to go t'other side of the water to find 'en." And, great jackass, I never know'd what she was up to; so I never see'd her again—and then the naybors said she had drownded herself.'

The mist condensed into large drops, which, passing over his high cheekbone, and through the hollow beneath, fell to the earth—the only tear that had moistened that loveless grave, yawning for the lonely dead.

'And you, poor Sam?'

'I was sent to the house,[17] and I ran away; and then *they* got hold on me, and said I'd do famous for 'em if I'd be a plucky chap, and never round on 'em; so they took't me for winders, cos I was slim as a black-worm—and warn't I glad to go with 'em! Jist suited me, for I bain't bright in my head. Winders is asy work, when they bain't stiff uns.'

'*Who* brought you up, Sam?'

'Them cracksmen—they was very good by me; I never got flayed for aught but blundering, and I was a sight happier *then* than I be now.'

Again could Maida scarce refrain a smile at his simplicity. He told his tale so utterly unvarnished by sentiment, or smothered by compunction, that it was evident the words 'right' and 'wrong' had no place in his moral dictionary.

'But, Sam, don't you think you are better off, even as a convict, than you were, living with those wicked men, and doing their wicked work for them?'

'My eyes—no!'

And Sam stared, as if the stare should say, 'You arn't half the one I took you for.'

Maida looked intently on him, to discern the source of this reply:

'*What!* Not be on the road to honesty, instead of in the way to certain ruin, as you were then, Sam?'

Figure was lost on him.

'I've *been* on the roads, ma'am; but I took't bad in my legs, so I works about Tench now.'

She must simplify. If the goggles could only take in half they tried, Sam would understand a great deal; but theirs was large attempt with small success.

'Sam, tell me now: don't you think it was very wicked of you to do what those men bade you, and to lead so bad a life?'

'I hadn't no other—'sides, I was brought up to it fust.'

'But why—why did you run away from the poor-house, Sam? That was your first wrong step.'

'I didn't like it.'

This reply was given in so decided a manner that Sam evidently considered it as much without appeal to others as it had been to himself; he therefore goggled double power (suspicion gaining on admiration) when Maida expressed disapprobation. The poor fellow seemed anxious to please his new found friend. What could he say? He longed to hear his voice, and yet he would rather lose that pleasure than vex her and involve himself. The convict fear and mistrust, although displayed in the widened gape and gaze, instead of the piercing glance and evasive response of intelligence, were as strong in him as in brighter specimens.

'Dunno that I'd do it again, missus. Parson Evelyn talks about it fine—he found me in cells one day, and he talked till 'most I cried; and then says he: "My boy, if you'd got your time over again, do you think you'd run away from the work house, now I've explained why it was foolish of you to do so?" "Drat me if I would!" says I; "sims I were a big jackass for rinnin'—but I weren't up to it *then*; but boys is boys, sir, and nothin' else."

'Then the parson—sims I see him now—rose up, and laid his two fingers on my shoulder; and sims he smiled—for his voice weren't like 'twas 'fore. Says he:"Why, what be now, Sam? You an't no more than a boy." "Sir! bain't I?" said I, "Sims I feels mighty old. A sight o' things comes by every day, though nothin' don't sim to happen out of 'em; so I feels like a man."

'Then he sat down again, and says:"What d'ye mean, Sam? Tell me all about it." But though I was full of it, I couldn't speak it out—so I only gaped at 'en. So then says he: "Ah, I know all about it, Sam; so you needn't set your brain a thinking—more things happen than ought to happen to such a youngster." This yer weren't said to *me*, for he gozzled[18] it out of his throat like; thinks I, I'm in for it! He's going to round on me, sure as fate! And I felt 'most dead o' fright. "When were you flogged last, Sam?" says he, all to a sudden. "Yesterday, sir, 'fore I came here," says I. "What for?" says he. "The bowl of a baccy pipe, picked up after the gatekeeper," says I. "What did you pick it up for, Sam?" says he. "'Gainst I got a fig," says I. "And how many lashes did you have?" "Twenty-five—lor', weren't they screechers![19] He said, when he tied me up to the triangle,—'I owes you a tickler,[20] and now I'll pay 'e.' "

'Parson bolted out when I told un this, and I set up a howl after un. Thought I, Won't I catch it if the parson rounds on me! But he came back quiet as a fool; says he, only talking half loud, "Sam, my boy, you'll get into worse trouble, if you make this row. Then he sheered[21] again, and I bawled after un,"Sir! sir!! sir!!!" And he comes again, and says,"Well!" "You got it out of me, sir; don't 'e go and tell 'em. I could not bear another thrashin'. Oh! don't 'e—don't 'e, parson," says I to un. Then he spoke so solemn, he made a feller shake: "Sam, I am God's minister. I tell no one but Him of anythin' that my people tell me. You may always speak out to me, my boy; but mind, I'll have no bad words, nor lies. I can always find out the truth." I pulled bob to 'un;[22] but, for all I wanted, I couldn't say;"Thank your grace." Then he comes in right again, and took't his seat as if he had never left it, and says: "Sam, why were you so foolish as to pick up the pipe, to vex the overseer?'"

'Were those his VERY words, Sam? Try to remember,' interrupted Maida.

'Yes, they were; I remember them 'tickler.'

Maida well knew that Mr. Herbert used no word idly. Repeating those two words, 'foolish,' 'vex'—she felt sure that they were meant as more applicable to the case than stronger expressions.

'D'ye like it, miss? Sims tellin' it out's done me good,' asked Sam, heaving a sigh of satisfaction. Maida felt there was not much to like in it, as she beheld the poor lean, lank, miserable youth before her; but she was loath to break the slight web of comfort that had unexpectedly wafted across his path; so she replied:

'I like to hear about Mr. Evelyn, Sam.'

'Don't 'e like all about mother and me?'

'We all like to tell our troubles, and I like you to tell yours; what more did Mr. Evelyn say to you?'

'A lot; but I don't mind much. He said, if I'd get out of trouble, and try to be a good boy, then by-and-by he'd get a chap he knows on to hire me out.'

'Well, and I hope you are trying, for Mr. Evelyn will keep his promise. *I* am sure of that.'

Here Sam's gogglers fell considerably, whilst an expression of moody hopelessness weighed down his lantern jaw to its utmost limit of expansion.

''Tain't much use trying along with they there; they's got a way of making a feller like the deuce hisself; when a feller gets into trouble for nothin', he might all so well do somethin' to make it worth his while.'

This is a sentiment too bright for Sam, thought Maida, and she had hardly thought it, before Sam continued:

'Bob Pragg told me that 'ere; *I* ain't clever enough, he's a sharp un; he knows a sight, and he bain't bad to me when I does what he wants; but, my eyes, when I don't! Parson warned me of he; but the parson nor nobody else don't know what a poor feller what isn't clever, and don't know what nothin' means, has got to bear from them sharp uns; be 'fraid of they, missus?'

He turned his head towards the spot from which, preceded by a loud, coarse laugh, the two men were issuing.

'I am not afraid of *anyone*.'

'My eyes! Could 'e fight 'em?'

'Women don't fight, Sam.'

But Sam gave a little negative-like shake of the head, as much as to say, 'Don't they, that's all!'

'They's comin', missus! And us ain't buried 'em.'

'I am not going to dig any more, Sam. I shall make those men finish.'

How the goggles expanded! Adoration more than admiration holding them firm to Maida's face. He was too rapt even to ejaculate his favourite note, so extra expressive as it would just then have been.

'So, my pretty one! I thought your flourishes[23] wouldn't last us t'other side of the ground. I guess you've been making the best of your time. Eh, Sam? No blushing, madam; ain't going to pry into lovers' secrets; tho' I swear 'tain't fair that son of an ape should have all to himself; what d'ye say, Gi?'

A nudge from Gi brought Bob to the remembrance of a waning afternoon, and the probability of interruption to the plan he had laid during his absence. When the two were sufficiently remote, by a whisper into Gi's ear, Bob dispelled the sulkiness that had lingered in his slouching movements across the field. A sharp whew-w! was Gi's only answer to the whisper. A consultation ensued for the next ten minutes, and then for ten minutes more the two squatted on the grass, and, chewing certain blades of it, gloated over their plan, and drank imaginary bumpers to its success; for whatever else these brethren disagreed in, they both cordially united in hatred of Bradley, the convict constable, who should now have been superintending their work. That he *deserved* to be hated is not to our point—that he *was* hated by the whole gang over which he had control, is a fact more to our purpose. He had a savage glory in mortifying such men as Bob and Giles, by evincing his power to the most annoying minutiae of convict rule; and a still more fiendish delight in dragging to (in)justice the delinquencies of such poor weaklings as Sam. If the reader be a colonist, he will already have asked, 'Where was the constable or overseer, that he was not with the men at their work?' And this very question Bob and Gi determined should be asked by the superintendent of the barracks, in order to incur the answer, 'Drinking a dram at the "Bird in Hand" over yonder'; an answer which would sound unwelcomely to the superintendent and comptroller, as they could not in conscience hear it, and let Bradley keep his belt and pistol: and then how grateful to the warm, brotherly feelings of Bob and Giles would it be, to hail him to their gang, and to share with him their parti-coloured clothes!

They gladly agreed to forego the fig, and taste of the tankard promised by Bradley as a reward of good faith; for they hoped to chew a more delicious morsel, and quaff a more refined dram by following their *own* counsel than in keeping *Bradley*'s.

'Why, man, you don't seem satisfied,' cried Bob, in the course of the consultation.

'Don't see why we can't peach ourselves without getting the woman to report; maybe she'll get us into trouble along with that infernal dog.'

'And wouldn't it be wo'th a spell at the wheel, or a dance in the dark, to get him plucked of his jackdaw feathers![24] I tell ye I'd bear a flogging without a wince to get him down; and you be—'

'No bullying of me now, Pragg; I bain't *he*—so keep your jolly thumpers to yourself, or try 'em on your own skull till you can on Bradley's.'

'Hold your humbug and listen to me; I've laid plans before now, and if they don't turn out admeerable, I'm not Bob Pragg.'

'I've heard you once, and I bain't no fool.'

But Bob, ever oracular, must again show forth his wisdom, and glut his vengeance with a concoction of malice. In spite of Gi's protest, he would repeat his scheme as follows:

'She'm quieter now, and don't seem likely to report—that won't suit us; nor Bradley—she *must* report—and then 'twill out that Constable Bradley don't look after his birds; in fact, 'twill be clear that he prefers a "bird in the hand" to three in the bush, for this ground ain't much more than bush appearantly.'

'Ha! ha! ha! That's in 'em—you'll be constable next Bob.'

'O fie, Gi, I ain't bad enough!' cried Pragg, with a comic-serious shake of the head. 'Must be more like my masters first.'

'Will be *soon* tho' with a little more of their doctoring.'

'Where was I, Gi? Well, she must report, and pop goes he out of the staff into—cells! The thing is—'

'How to get her to march to headquarters,' cried Giles getting excited over the rehearsal.

'That's the go, Gi! Like to see ye game. How to get her? Trust me for that! I've seen her 'fore now; —— me if I don't raise the deuce in her. Never heard Bob Pragg's music? I'll play devil's tattoo[25] on them precious boxes there till I make her fly mad to the governor; then sharp's the word, Mr. Bradley! Now let's off. When I begins you'll know—there's no mistaking Bob Pragg, always except when he *means* you shall mistake him; *then* there's all so much no not mistaking him.'

'But what shall we do with that gaping blockhead yonder?'

'He ain't wo'th a thought; he must come in for it long with us, 'twill do'n good—polish en a bit. When government condescends to notice such blackguard paupers, and place 'em 'longside of gents, why gents can't do less than condescend too, and train 'em up in the way they should go—*should*, meaning in the way they are *fossed*[26] to go; seeing when they'm once in, there's no gettin' out till their hedication's finished.'

'And then I s'pose they'm pretty fit for *somewhere*.'

'Right, man; the place where gents go—the proper place for used-up O.P.S.O.'s, and we'm all *that*, from comptroller downwards.'

The loud 'Ha! ha! ha!' which chorussed this speech was the sound that brought Sam's treat to an end.

Gi's admonitory nudge warned Bob to action. Stooping to one of the coffins, he turned it on its side, and swearing a fearful oath, exclaimed:

'Now I'll stand no more nonsense! If they won't get into the hole, I'll throw a spade of earth over 'em and leave 'em; and the devil may come and carry 'em off if he likes; now heave away, Sam.'

Sam raised it at the opposite side; when Bob, feigning mistake, let go his side, and down came the coffin, and tumbled over a grave.

''Twasn't me, missus!' almost blubbered Sam, as he, with the two others, noticed the pale passion that worked in every feature of Maida's face.

'Catch here, Bob,' cried Giles, approaching; 'catch here.'

And as if playing football, he gave the coffin a tremendous kick; before he could give a second he was lying prostrate, and that by a woman's hand. By a dexterous movement, Maida had collared and thrown him, whilst his foot was upraised to give a second kick.

Another movement, and stunned by a blow from Giles, Maida lay senseless on the ground; as Giles bent over her in savage fury, Sam thought he was about to murder her. Losing all fear for himself, he sprang forward, shouting:

'You shan't touch of she!'

'At him, Sam! At him! Show yourself a man,' cried Bob, forgetting all his former plan in prospect of a fight. 'At him, she'm yours; you must fight for her.'

Encouraged, bewildered, and hurried on by excitement, Sam did 'at' Giles. Wielding the spade with a force as unnatural to himself as unexpected to Giles, he struck the wretched man so heavily, that only his weight in falling disengaged the spade from the grip of the riven skull into which the iron had pierced.

Three heavy groans gurgled from the lips of the dying man, and then a strange solemn stillness spread over the field, chilling the horror-stricken group into a breathless silence.

Neither Bob nor Sam moved, until a shivering sensation in the latter increased to an almost audible quaking of his whole lank frame.

'B-o-b?' at last he quaked out in sepulchral tone.

Bob looked, but did not speak.

'Who—did—it, B-o-b?' The large glassy eyes were riveted on the corpse.

The question aroused Bob to a sense of self-safety.

'Who? *You*, and no mistake! But I'll stand by ye, Sam, cos you've never done me no harm; but mind, you say a word about me, and I'll do for you in no time.'

'Don't want nothin',' came mechanically from Sam, who had either *not* heard or not apprehended. He had sunk on his thighs, and now sat crouched up, resting his chin in his hands, and gazing on Giles as if he had neither power nor will to withdraw his eyes from the corpse.

'Sam, boy, rouse yerself! We must be doing something 'fore Bradley comes along; keep a good face on it, and let us be the first to make the row. Up, boy! Up! The woman 'll wake, and Bradley 'll be along presently; lend a sharp heft or two, and get them plagues buried, then we'll carry Giles to Tench; leave the rest to *me*; silence is all I wants out of you.'

This was all, the first shock over, that Pragg made of the death of his comrade. How the death might affect him was the only remaining point that engaged his mind.

Accustomed to fear Pragg, Sam tried to stand, but the violent trembling of his limbs made him sink again.

'Get up, lazy-bones, and be a man; you've got guilt in yer very phiz;[27] there's no go for you whilst you shows your game by the fright in that ——whitewash[28] of yours. Up, I say!' And he kicked him with his knee.

But Sam only raised his large lack-lustre eyes for a second to Bob's face, and then slowly returned them to their ghastly resting place. Seeing it was useless to waste the now precious moments on the poor boy, Bob turned to the pit with:

'Confound the blockhead; he's no true blood in him for all he gied such a mortal chinker.'

By dint of digging, dragging, pounding, and shoving, he managed to get the coffins interred; but it was a difficult task. He had barely stamped the earth upon them when Bradley jumped over the fence, bringing the promised bribe of tobacco and ale.

A revenge beyond even Bob's malice awaited the official, as, flown with insolence and wine, he swaggered across the field.

Brutal triumph gleaming from his hard features, Pragg watched the effect of the scene on Bradley. The hour was his; he was master of the field. Quietly taking the bottle from the latter, he drained it, and flung it in the air, crying:

'To your health and ticket, old fellow! Did you ever hear of a canary?'[29]

'I've heard of a laughing jackass, and sees one now,' snarled the constable, perceiving that there was something amiss. Glancing around, he quickly discovered *that* something, and how the case lay. Accustomed to mark tokens of guilt and degrees of crime in different characters, he at once acquitted Pragg, and discerned the murderer in the miserable figure crouching before him.

Had his own situation been less precarious, he would have proceeded with ferocious glee to hale his victim to judgment; but all dream of official consequence vanished beneath the threatening darkness of Pragg's malignant leer. One glance hastily cast from under his heavy brow sufficed to warn Bradley that wrath was determined against him. How to avert it was his troubled thought. Maida was the only unsolved portion of the dreadful puzzle. What part had she acted in it? How came she lying there? Had the fight been on her account? Could she be of any service in making terms with his enemy? were questions that hurried through Bradley's mind as, without moving his head, he surveyed the strange group.

It must be now or never, thought he; in a quarter of an hour the Tench bell will summon the men.

Assuming what mastery he could over his quailing voice, he asked Bob:

'Who's the woman? What had she to do with it? Speak out; don't be feared.'

There was a malicious twinkle in Bob's eye as he answered:

'She's only a missus that came along and fented (like all women does when they's wanted to lend a hand); so one can't say she had *much* to do with it.'

Bradley felt uneasy; he could not discover the drift of this reply.

'Will you swear to it?' he asked.

'Swear to it or anything else you pleases.'

The same twinkle, and Bradley inwardly writhed.

'Don't doubt you, Pragg; but excuse me as a constable if I ask that youngster a question just by way of c'rob'ation.'

'Hoa! Here, you scoundrel' (shaking him roughly by the shoulder); 'hoa, and tell us, did the woman faint?'

'Y-e-s,' said Sam, in the same low, mechanical tone.

'Tell you what, Bob,' cried Bradley, 'there's no use in shamming.[30] I see exactly how 'tis; there's no mistake that he's fixed and you are free; but that won't let us off—we are all in for it—*me* as well as *you*, so I'll be honest with you, man; give your hand here to a bargain, and with my word to it you're safe.'

Bradley thrust his hand to Bob, but Bob deliberately thrust his into his pockets, giving, at the same time, a side-catch of his mouth and eye, which the constable interpreted: 'Don't you wish you may get it?'

'I like that amazin'! How d'ye make out I'm in for it? *You* are in a jolly mess of it; but 'xcept I gets into trouble for what others does, Bob Pragg stands as clear as any man. Can I help the dogs from fightin' it out?'

'Don't doubt you, Pragg; but them government coves is such a ——set, one never knows when one's safe; white easy turns to black with them. Don't you reckon on *clearness*, but take my advice, as one who knows a thing or two about them twisters.'

'What's the dodge?[31] Out with it.'

Bob had no intention to relent; but the longer he could dally with his prey, the better for his spite, and the more certain downfall to his enemy, from the disclosures he might afford by way of bribing silence.

'Strike hands, then.'

'That an't Bob Pragg; he hears first, hands after.'

Bradley looked on every side, and then pointed to Sam.

'He?'

'Safe as a log; no wits to peach—no brain for lies.'

Bradley nodded; and drawing close to Pragg, whispered:

'Bolt! I'll make out a case to suit, and turn their noses the wrong way till you're beyond them.'

Bob started; the offer was audacious and tempting; but hiding his surprise, he exclaimed:

'Show my heels like a murderer? Jolly trick! So let yon fool get free, and me be hunted across the island like any brute of a dingo?'[32]

'No such thing, man; guilt's too plain on him; besides, take my word that he don't even deny it: bolting and running won't show *guilt*—'twill only be one natturl effect of the outrage. The story 'll be somew'at like this:

'"Constable's too busy with the rascal to notice you—opportunity offers—you bolt, as any one of us would if we got such a chance—constable, of course, 'll be in a decent fluster about it, and eager after you, *but* all in the wrong scent till you're safe as a wombat in his hole." Trust me! I've been after bolters 'fore now, and knows a few tricks of the trade!'

Bradley attempted a laugh, but he failed. As earnestly as he dared he watched from under his heavy brow the working of his proposal; but Bob's hard lineaments showed no working in any way save that the hard mouth rounded for a whistle, and the hard brow contracted a care-nought wrinkle.

Bradley again stretched his hand.

'There's no time to lose—now or never.'

'It shan't be *now*, but don't know that it shan't be *never*. When Bob Pragg bolts—he don't ask leave,' and he planted his hands on his thighs. 'I've got an account to settle before I can go: my compliments to the comptroller, and tell 'em so from me, Mr. Bradley.'

'Then go and be ——!' roared Bradley, shaking his fist at Bob. 'And if you don't hang for your insolence it shan't be my fault.'

'You'll be too snug[33] to get a peep at me, anyhow,' sneered Bob, who, looking forward to sure present vengeance, stored up Bradley's threat for future payment. Bob was a tutored ruffian; he could control himself when self-control served his purposes.

Taking handcuffs from his pocket, the constable clasped them on Sam, and, shaking him till he was sufficiently aroused to stand, bade him, with a kick on his spine, walk on, whilst he and Bob carried Giles to the barracks. At that moment the bell rang, and, from every part of the town, road and building parties were seen returning to their quarters. Bradley, his burden, and victim were quickly surrounded, when, resigning his charge to a brother constable and overseer, the former said he must go and report to headquarters. But report never reached headquarters through him, for, turning swiftly back, he caught what little money he had, and, hurrying through Campbell Street, made his way for Kangaroo Point. Rather than meet the disgrace that awaited him, he determined to follow the advice he had given to Pragg—and bolt.

Turning to the barracks, he clenched his fist towards the building as a farewell, and vowed, with a curse, that he would never enter it again alive: he might be taken, but not whilst he had strength to fight, or breath in his body. His official costume carried him to some distance without risk of detection.

Night fell ere Maida came to herself. For many minutes she lay in a dreamy state, wondering why the moon shone so unobstructedly upon her. She could rarely see more than its light on the two-paned window in her garret ceiling. The Centaurs,[34] too, large and bright, looked on her. What could it mean? She almost feared to move, lest the pleasant dream should break.

Comfort insensibly distilled from the long, clear, unbroken rays that stretched towards her. She raised her hands and passed them over her eyes, and then, letting them drop, they fell—not on her warm bed, but on the cold, damp grass. The spell was broken. With a shiver she started and remembered all; but the brutal badinage was hushed into a calm that seemed supernatural. She felt stiff and dizzy—so dizzy, that as she looked around, the graves seemed to advance and recede, and rise and fall. The ridges of uneven mounds became more uneven, as, beneath the trembling light, they appeared to heave, as if about to discharge their dead.

Having satisfied herself that she was alone, that no more ruffianly insult could arouse her anger or disturb the scene, she went to the new-made grave, and sat by it. She was already later than convict rule permitted; she had no pass, should it be demanded, therefore she could incur no further penalty by remaining a little longer to think over the strange encounter of the afternoon.

She thought of Pragg; she felt he was her enemy, but for that she cared not. It was only fitting that the man who had wrung her from her baby should be appointed to work her further woe; it was only to be expected that he should haunt her to this remote corner of the world.

Her baby! To what a stream of memories did those words give rise. Her home in Essex—her indulgent, ill-requited, and maybe broken-hearted father—Norwell—her life of shame and misery—her crime (the thin smile involuntarily moved her lips)—its punishment. Then, fiercely beating against the dreary reach of future that stayed its onward flow, the stream ebbed, lingering now at one point that awakened tender feeling; then bounding, scornful, from another, until it again sank into quiescence, leaving Maida no alternative but to meet the contingencies of a hopeless present.

She was near her master's house before she recollected that an explanation would be demanded, and that a satisfactory one must be given, or trouble would ensue. She knew that both Mr. Evelyns would credit her story, but she did not wish to tell it for a reason, which was the result of her ignorance of the fearful catastrophe that had put an end to the graveyard quarrel. Her wrath had kindled, not for herself, or against the two depraved wretches, but on behalf of the unresisting dead. The determination to report had been fixed in her mind the instant before she fell by Waddy's hand; but when, on recovering consciousness, she perceived, by the graves, that the offence had been atoned for, she annulled her determination on Sam's account, fearing he would get equal punishment with the other two men if she made a report of their misconduct. It did not occur to her to wonder at her having been left so unceremoniously on the ground, for she knew too well that selfishness had induced the men to leave her. To the watch-house only could they have taken her; and judging her by themselves, she concluded they had thought she would surely round upon them in return for the punishment dealt to herself by way of costs for government lodging, and had therefore determined to let her lie.

Neither did she wonder why the constable (who, she was sure, had hurried in to conduct his charges to the Tench, after having neglected them all the afternoon) had not paid her due official attention. The same fear that had made the others so ungallant, had also influenced him not only to a similar act of ungallantry, but to one of exemplary self-denial, in resigning his claim to her as a case illustrative of his constabulary vigilance. But the blow that was now smarting on her temple, did that urge no vengeful step in Maida, unaware, as she was, that it had been already avenged by a swift and eternal retribution?

No: as her finger withdrew from the discolouring mark, and as the slight start caused by the unexpected pain subsided, a firm closing of the lip, with a steadier planting of her foot upon the earth, was the only sign that the blow had smitten below the surface, and driven the iron yet deeper into her soul. The lip was firm to uncomplaining, whilst her mind set the indignity to the accumulated items that make prison life one protracted suffering unthought of, and maybe unintended, when the sentence of transportation is passed.

The foot struck upon the earth, not in the impatience of the steed that cannot brook restraint, and longs to rush to freedom, but to steady itself to accomplish the destiny that it scorned with bitter scorn, even while preparing to fulfil the cruel demands, and fulfil it to the utmost, though every nerve should be unstrung, and every power fail in the unequal strife.

Endeavouring to frame an excuse that would involve no falsehood, she wandered into Collins Street, one moment resolving to anticipate the fate she expected, by giving herself into custody; the next instant retracing her steps to go boldly to the Lodge, and meet her master's inquiries with silence.

Her ponderings were dispelled by two shadows that gained upon her.

She quickened her pace. Still the shadows advanced until they overtook and passed on before her, leaving by her side two men in the constable's garb.

She heard them whisper—'No; it's a lady. I'm sure of it. Dressed shabby, because she's out this time. We can't speak to her, Tom.'

'Oh, I've seen prettier birds than that. Ladies wouldn't be out, shabby or not shabby, at *this* time. I say, got a pass, missus?'

This was said in an undertone for his own amusement. Prisoner or not, Tom thought it fun to see the lady increase her speed.

'Don't fool now, Tom. Remember how Bates took the magistrate Joyce into custody.'

'Let's follow her a bit. If we could get a sight of the brown, then we should be sure.'

So the men followed her. Tom got impatient, being a newly made official, and eager for capture.

'Excuse me, ma'am, but must do my duty. Are you out on leave? It looks suspicious when ladies are out alone this time o' day.'

'Got a pass?' asked the more initiated constable,[35] on the principle—justice is no respecter of persons.

Maida thought it better not to notice, but let them draw what conclusion they might from her silence.

'Stop!' cried the initiated. Running forward, he laid his hand on her shoulder. 'Come along with us. You can't give no account of yourself; you're government for all your fine bobbery.'[36]

'You need not hold me; I am willing to go with you.'

'Don't seem in liquor, Tom.'

'Been fighting, though. Most got a black eye.'

Both men were now satisfied as to Maida's character, and doubted not they were assisting government in the suppression of convict vice in taking Maida in charge.

Their belief in the character of their prisoner strengthened, and their desire to further the views of government weakened, as they approached a public-house, which, like nearly all the one hundred and eighty taverns of Hobarton,[37] stood at the street's corner—the prominent ally of sin!

The men drew back and conferred together. They shook hands, and then said to Maida:

'Young woman, it's after hours; but that's no hindrance to the chap in here. The pass! Let's forget it over a jolly drop. We'll be tight about your being out; and, what's more, we'll see you safe home after we've spreed it a bit.[39] Under constable's care nobody 'll say a word to you. I often take the women to Brickfield, and they generally sport a swig at the "Eagle-Hawk".'

Mistaking the expression on her face, the initiated thought Maida suspected the sincerity of his offer; so taking her arm, and attempting to draw her towards the door of the house, he exclaimed:

'Come, my lassie; I pledge you in a dram. We are no better than each other, when once we get in here—*I* forget our *belts*, and *you* forget your *pass*.'

'She's up to a thing or two; she doubts you yet,' said Tom.

'I doubt nothing that comes from a convict constable,' replied Maida, wresting her arm from a grasp more hateful than the official one. 'I doubt no breach of trust from men who would never be in office could free men vile enough be found to do their masters' bidding.'

'She ain't government!' cried Tom, in a fright lest he had betrayed himself in his hurry to exercise his power.

'I *am* government,' said Maida; 'and I *am* out without a pass; and I command you to take me to the watch-house.'

'She's drunk, Tom; I'll swear to that. We'll get a glass, then —— me if I don't give her her wish, and something more too, to-morrow: make a note of what she said against government, whilst I touch up the chap here.'[39]

The initiated went round the corner, and, tapping at a little back window, whistled a signal.

The back door opened. He went in, and having stayed a few moments, returned with two glasses of liquor. Giving one to Tom, he offered the other to Maida, with:

'Now, come; you can't say nay to *that*, or you ain't government. Off with it, and about your business. You know you look deuced handsome humbugging us. We ain't the men to hand over a handsome woman when she'll make herself agreeable a bit.'

Maida took the glass and flung it and its contents into the road. The smash drew an exclamation from the men; and the exclamation reached the ears of a gentleman who was crossing at the top of the street. The gentleman stopped and gazed earnestly towards the spot whence the noise proceeded; and then hastening forward, came in sight of the group before the constables could move off in marching order.

'It's the parson!' cried Tom.

'He's been watching us; no use shamming with he,' muttered the other constable.

'It's my master!' cried Maida, moving as if to him.

The initiated pulled her back.

'You've humbugged us long enough, and now wait and take your luck. Jolly trick to bolt as soon as you know your game's down.'

Agitation was visible in Mr. Herbert's countenance as by the clear moonlight Maida distinguished each feature; but his voice was calm and masterly.

'Maida, where have you been? We have been seeking you since five o'clock, when we first learned that you had not returned from Trinity Parsonage. Poor Emmeline is very anxious, and your master disappointed.'

A searching glance accompanied these words. The smell of spirits was strong, and the swelling on her forehead indicative of a brawl.

But though these suspicious tokens puzzled Mr. Herbert, they did not mislead him. There was that peculiar curl about Maida's lip, of which he had learned the meaning since his more intimate acquaintance with her.

He felt thankful that his brother had taken the opposite direction in search of her, for his feelings, already irritated at the notion that he had been deceived by one in whom he had confided much against his will, were in no mood to bear the contest for which, by the cool defiance of her voice, Maida seemed prepared.

'Where I *have* been I cannot tell you, sir; but *now* I am going to the watch-house. I have desired these men to do their duty; as they refuse, I go to surrender myself to government.'

'She's drunk, sir.'

'And you would make her more so. I relieve you of your charge.'

'Please your reverence, I must take her on, for she's out without a pass,' interposed Tom.

'Leave her,' said Mr. Herbert sternly, 'and go learn what your duty is before you attempt to perform it. What means that broken glass lying there, and that bottle thrust into yonder window?'

'You won't be hard upon us a cold night like this, sir? 'Tis often cold here, sir.'

'Ward, I'm ashamed of you; if you forget your duty I cannot mine. I must report you; this is not the first time you have been guilty of betraying your trust in that shameless manner.'

'Please, sir, wouldn't you like to hear our charge against the woman?' persisted Tom.

'Go!' repeated Mr. Herbert, waving his hand indignantly.

'You had better hear it, sir,' said Maida.

'I will hear it from no one but yourself, Maida.'

Again waving his hand, he watched the crestfallen officials move slowly down Collins Street, and then, turning to Maida, he looked steadily at her, and asked an account of her strange disappearance.

The scornful smile had faded from her lip during Mr. Herbert's interview with the men; her judgment had had time to work, and it convinced her that wherever blame might rest, it could not on the noble being before her, who had done more than his public duty in going to seek her, and who would only be doing his public duty were he to arraign her for infringement of convict discipline.

She felt that this noble being regarded her not as a prisoner who had absconded, and must be found for the mere purpose of receiving due punishment, but as a fellow creature who was in danger, and therefore to be rescued. He had sought her, not vindictively, but sorrowfully; he was now anxious to hear her story, *not* that he might form a case for the police court, but to ascertain what had befallen herself. Generally she would prefer that the negative in each of the foregoing suppositions should be the case—her haughty spirit would choose rather the chastisement than the pardon, the anger than the sympathy of most persons. Not so with Mr. Herbert; though her impulsive temper often made her grieve him, and though the deep-seated sense of injury which burnt within, making her careless of results and scornful of pity, often caused her to reject his proffered sympathy, and turn coldly from his ministerial exhortations, yet she revered his earnestness, and her soul paid secret tribute of admiration to the unflagging zeal that remained steadfast and self-possessed in spite of opposition.

She sometimes found the thought, 'What will Mr. Herbert say to this?' exerting a restraining influence on her actions: she would imperiously shake the thought from her with the inquiry, 'Can my state be bettered or made worse by anyone's opinion of me?' But, to her infinite annoyance, the thought would come creeping back, when to fortify herself against it by turning more coldly from his kindness, and by increasing her rigidity of demeanour, was her only resource to again rid herself of it.

The time had not come for the bowing of Maida's soul before the cross borne so meekly, yet upraised so fearlessly in her sight. Courage, O man of God! Think not with the religious instructor of the transport that there is no hidden meaning in that compressed lip and haughty exterior—think not that within that icy surface all is cold and lifeless as it would have you deem. The troubling of the waters commences deep within, then upward, upward, till the whole leaps in trembling vitality beneath the potent touch. There may burst no response from the forbidding stillness of that spiritual night, but may it not be that all its powers are rapt in the mighty question, 'Are these things so?' and can find no space or mood to solve thy lesser importunings?

'Well, Maida,' gently said Mr. Herbert, having waited for a reply, 'can you not confide in me? I am anxious to hear what has happened, before you meet your master.'

Maida longed to tell him all, in order to ease the disquietude apparent through the gentle voice and calmly searching gaze; but poor Sam—ah, he was friendless!

The lean, pale visage, and the fixed, staring eye of the miserable lad came before her. She felt she was the more capable of enduring punishment—or worse than punishment, Mr. Herbert's and Emmeline's patient disappointment—than Sam of bearing an additional weight of sentence, stripes, and sorrow.

'Can *you* trust *me*, sir?'

'I *can* and *do*, Maida; but I hope this trust is not to be instead of an explanation of that blow disfiguring your brow. You will not keep my poor child in suspense?'

'Miss Evelyn would not wish to get a poor, wretched, friendless creature into trouble.'

'You are not friendless, Maida, if you are wretched.'

'I do not speak of myself, sir; I could not tell you what has occurred without getting a poor lad into trouble. *You* should know, sir, that chastisements are administered both hastily and indiscriminately on convicts: though the poor fellow had nothing to do with either my absence or this blow, he would doubtless be dealt with as a party in the offence which I should be obliged to report, were I to account for my absence. Can you trust me with my secret, sir?'

'I repeat I trust you, Maida, and half gladly; to have a struggle between duty and inclination is a disturbance to a minister, and your confidence might produce that effect in me; but my brother—your master—how will he permit your silence? He is strict where he considers convict discipline has been wilfully infringed.'

'He may send me before a magistrate, but he cannot force me to speak.'

'Maida, I must be plain with you' (Mr. Herbert's voice trembled). 'I fear my brother *will* do that. He is determined to take extreme measures, for he thinks you have deceived him; and how is he to know to the contrary if you persist in making a mystery of your conduct? You were sent out at three o'clock in the afternoon, and now it is ten o'clock at night.'

'Mr. Evelyn does not disbelieve me any more than *you* do, sir; but he will not own that he believes me, because he is a proud convict holder, and will not condescend to those whom the law places beneath his feet. He finds in me a spirit as proud as his *own*, and he delights in trying to wring a confession from it.'

'Maida! Maida!' cried Mr. Herbert, shaking his head sadly. 'Have you not too much delicacy to speak thus to me of my brother?'

'Delicacy! What delicacy? You mock me, sir. A debased, degraded convict, who daily adds to her debasement and degradation—what delicacy should be found in her? Would government allow it to remain in her? Would it be fitting, I ask?'

'Most unfitting! Therefore, as a debased, degraded convict, I command you not to speak thus of so kind a master, who bears with whims that others would punish as sins, and who never punishes but where punishment is deserved.'

The stern quiet of his voice struck into Maida's every nerve—she felt the justice of the rebuke—she wished she had not provoked it—she wished she could forebear to provoke it further, but she was aroused, passion quivered in her breast and formed itself into speech almost against her will.

'Then I am ready to bear my deserved punishment. Let him send me to court, there my silence shall be as unbroken as before my master; for not in opposition to any particular person, but because I choose it, I shut myself to inquiry.'

'Then I must leave you, Maida; I cannot become a party to your wilfulness. You must go to the punishment I begin to think you deserve, and on which I am sure Mr. Evelyn will insist, if you appear before him in your present state.'

'I shall rejoice to go to court and receive the infliction that will follow. I shall glory in the punishment as another means of concentrating to one supreme evil the mass of degradation that has accumulated in me. I yearn for the completion that shall leave me no possibility of further infamy—when there shall be no more convictions to stifle—no sharp compunctions to blunt—no more hopes to disappoint—no feelings to wound—no heart to suffer—no soul to save; when I am all this, *then* shall I be what convict law has sought to make me! Then, having *borne* all, *braved* all, and *become* all, its demands will be satisfied, and it will bid me go in peace to that place where peace never comes.'

Mr. Herbert shuddered. He remembered that she had worked herself to a similar frenzy on the occasion of his first visit to her in prison, and dreaded a similar result; but looking earnestly at her, he perceived that the pallor of her cheek was the blanching of fierce excitement, and not of approaching exhaustion.

He closed his eyes, and breathed an unuttered prayer to God that strength and wisdom might be sent him to cope with the spirit of darkness that almost overpowered the victim by his side; for wisdom especially he sought, that while battling with the tempter, he might not wound the poor sufferer herself.

He purposely delayed his movements, walking slowly, and occasionally stopping altogether, to give Maida more time to recover her equanimity, and himself longer opportunity to reflect how to act.

'You are impulsive, Maida; reconsider your words,' he said at last, as though he had only just heard her.

What magic in those words! She starts—stands still—and earnestly scrutinises the speaker of them; memory works busily, her heart beats furiously, and recollection snatches her away and dizzily sets her down in a little upper chamber, and a voice that she has watched for, and wept for, and prayed for, arises dreamily from an unseen somewhere, and repeats—

'Maida, you are impulsive.'

As though answering the voice with the self-same speech of the days of that chamber, she murmurs—

'Forgive me.'

She clasps her hands, her breast heaves tumultuously.

'Maida, you are faint.' Mr Herbert offers to support her; but with one hand she waves refusal of assistance, with the other hides her face, while her head shakes drearily as if in last farewell to a departing friend; then, with a sudden reclasping of her hands, with a wild rolling of her eyes as though she heard the door of fate snap on that friend's retreating form, bursts from her lips a bitter cry—

'Would God I had never loved him!'

The cry did not mysticise Mr. Herbert; neither did he mistake its import, or misappropriate its application. The secret of female prison life was in his possession, and he rarely failed to read its sad characters in the many tales of misery confided to his ministerial care.

'Would God that you did not love him *still*! Forget him Maida, he is unworthy of you.'

Ere this fervent admonition had passed from the clergyman's heart to Maida's ear, the truant flight was over; her feet no longer trod the painful though airy realms of dream, but the rough uncompromising earth of a very nether world; she was no longer the Maida of that desolate upper chamber, battling in scornful solitude a lot that treachery had cast; she was Maida, the transported felon, expiating by a scorned servitude another's guilt, and a crime of which she was wholly innocent.

Forget him! She remembered that she had undertaken to suffer for him; endurance was hers by plighted vow, shame by free acceptance. Forget him! Could she? Strength was in the mere question.

'I feel strong again, now, sir.'

Mr. Herbert turned wistfully towards her; the words expressed no more than he heard, but the firm, strange tone bore a significance of its own. More earnestly than ever he longed to fathom the mystery that plunged that erring, yet high-minded woman into extravagances so wilful as to create terror one moment, while the next it nerved her to heroism so martyr-like as to inspire admiration.

In confirmation of her avowal, she advanced many paces as if desiring to hasten forward.

When they reached the Lodge, Mr. Herbert held the knocker as a last delay before ushering her into his brother's presence; he threw an inquiring glance; she received it with a quiet smile.

'You need not fear, sir; I can meet my master now.'

'But can you meet the trouble which may ensue; or have you determined to avert it by satisfying your master?'

'There will be no trouble, sir; my master's displeasure will be *all* I shall have to bear.'

She laid a peculiar emphasis on the word *all*, an emphasis which Mr. Herbert understood. He knew that while meaner souls would slink away congratulating themselves that they had escaped so easily, 'master's anger' their only punishment, her proud spirit would suffer more in bending itself to conciliate that anger, than in encountering the active strife of bodily penance; and he believed that had not her will been stronger than her pride, and her purpose mightier than both, she would have chosen rather to take on herself the consequences of a continued resistance, than submit to her master's interrogations, which she knew would be at once austere and cutting.

'Is your master home?' asked Mr. Herbert eagerly, as Tammy opened the door.

'No, sir; he came home once with a constable, and then went straight out again and 's been out ever since.'

'Then make haste to bed, Maida; I will explain to Mr Evelyn to-night; since we have arrived first he will not expect to see you, and you are faint and fatigued.'

'I am neither, thank you, sir; I will see the master to-night.'

'No—I wish you to go to bed; I take all responsibility on myself.'

Maida retreated, but with no intention of retiring to rest.

'Won't you catch it! The master's ramping like a great mad bull; he'd bellow if his rage would let him,' was Maida's salutation from Tammy, as she entered the kitchen.

'Now for the fine airs, they'll suit the oakum *well* and the wash-house *better*; linen wants airing a bit once in a while—ladies always airs their clothes, Maida'll do it fine—save 'em the trouble.'

'Let the lass alone, can't ye?' interrupted Googe, who had taken advantage of the general disturbance to smoke his pipe in his master's kitchen instead of by his own fireside; 'Never mind 'em, Maddy, they's only jealous of you, 'cause the parson's courting of you; if matters go wrong with the old cove, tip his reverence a wink, and he'll stop proceedings with a tickle of his brother's ear that'll make him start ginger;[40] the old chap's had his blinkers on, or he'd have shied long ago at what *we* sees every day; cheer up, he won't get the parson's sweetheart into trouble—it would sound so bad!'

'But caging her'd be no stop to the courting, John. I fancies I sees the reverend gent, taking his Bible so pious and marching to the Cascades. Famous opportunity! Shut up there in the cells. No prying to stop their lovemaking; won't he read the lost sheep parable aloud and holy, and then expound it soft and tender to suit the case?'

A loud knock at the front door stopped the coarse merriment which succeeded this impudent sally.

The women started, Googe sheered off, and Maida seated herself to await in silence the event of that knock.

Mr. Herbert issued from his study to meet his brother.

'She is home, George.'

'Did she *come*, or did you bring her?'

'I brought her.'

'I wish you hadn't then! I'm tired of the pranks of that woman; punished she must be, and I'd rather she had got it from others than from me. I detest appearing against the poor wretches. I must send her though; she's riding it a trifle too high, and wants a little reminder.'

'When you have talked to her I do not think you will find it necessary; she is quite humbled now.'

'Heigh, heigh! That's nice; half-past eleven is a good time of day to turn humble— the humbleness should go before, and not follow after. A pretty chase she's led me; I've been round Newtown, back again, peeped into every corner of Goulburn Street, beaten round Battery Point, and lastly, given the alarm at the watch-house, and now I'm fairly done up; but I'll see her.'

'I sent her to bed.'

'Bother it, Herbert! I wish you'd leave me to manage my own people; if the night passes smoothly over her, she'll think she's going to be let off; so if she's in bed she must just turn out.'

He pulled the bell violently: all the household knew the meaning of that bell, and winks, with shrugs of shoulders, conveyed unutterable telegrams from one convict to another, when Maida herself arose to go and answer the summons.

'It is for me, I will go myself.'

'Send her up,' said Mr. Evelyn, as the door opened.

'I am here, sir.'

'Shut the door and listen to me. Do you remember I warned you that it would be your own fault if ever you heard more of what I told you when I hired you from the *Anson*? When standing just as you are standing now you promised obedience to my commands.'

'Perfectly, sir.'

'Now, don't answer in that manner, it is treating me with a disrespect I will no longer bear; for my forbearance harms you without benefiting me. You have deceived me, Maida, and I now mean to show you how I deal with those who abuse my leniency, and with what power convict law invests the master and controls the servant. I was unwilling to exert that power; you have defied it, and now you shall feel it; though still unwilling, I consider it my duty to exert it.'

Not a muscle of Maida's face moved.

'Two hours ago I should *not* have been unwilling, for I was irritated at your abuse of my confidence. Had you then come back, I should have handed you over to government without hesitation, and without compunction. I am glad you did not, for my sake as well as for your own sake.'

Still not a muscle moved.

'What have you to say for yourself? How do you account for this freak? Speak, Gwynnham—speak—'

'I have nothing to say, sir.'

'No nonsense, and no lies, Maida. Convicts don't run risks for nothing. I won't be made a fool of. If you can't give an explanation to me, you shall to the police magistrate.'

The large eyes that had till now been fixed calmly on his face sent a hasty glance to Mr. Herbert, and then dropped to the floor.

Mr. Herbert lounged on the sofa, hiding, in a careless posture, the anxiety he felt for the issue of the conference. From between the fingers that were pressed to his forehead, he was intently watching the struggle. He dreaded punishment for Maida. It might undo all that he hoped was working in her. It might ruin her, body and soul. He perceived that his brother inclined to clemency, now his first rush of anger and vexation had subsided; but if Maida should become impetuous, how might not her impulse hurry her to provoke her own destruction! With what thankfulness, therefore, did he see the large eyes again raised calmly, and hear her say, in a submissive voice:

'Will you spare me, sir, and hear from Mr. Herbert all I dare tell by way of accounting for my strange behaviour?'

Mr. Evelyn turned to his brother with a look that said: 'Well?'

'May Maida leave the room, then, George?'

'*No*, I am sick of such humbug. I am not going to be so tender over her. Anything that is not too bad for her *to do*, is not too bad for her to *hear*. She's got into trouble, I suppose, and now's ashamed of it.'

'She is so far in trouble that she cannot account for herself, without involving a poor creature, who is not guilty.'

'Lucy, I suppose, who abetted her attempt to escape. I must forbid her the house.'

'No, sir, Lucy had no part in it.'

Maida was really alarmed, and spoke quickly and warmly:

'What Mr. Herbert says is true, sir. If needs be, I'll bear any punishment, but cannot bring trouble on a poor friendless lad.'

'*Your* punishment will involve no one,' said Mr. Evelyn dryly.

'Then I am willing to receive it, sir.'

'No humbug, young woman! You are not more willing than I.'

'As a favour to me, George, if even you do not forebear to punish her, will you forebear to *question* her?'

'Supposing I oblige Mr. Herbert, Maida, by ceasing to inquire how you occupied yourself during your absence, you have still the *absence itself* to be charged with. Are you aware of the heavy punishment incurred by an absconder?'

'The punishment is great, but I had no intention of absconding.'

'A fair excuse, since your intention of not being found is frustrated! How will such pleasantry influence the magistrate? Out here we do not punish for intentions so much as for acts. Your intention might have been laudable, but since your act did not agree with it, we must give you a hint to let it do so for the future.'

'Your hint will be more easily given than understood, sir.'

'Go to bed now; you shall hear more to-morrow. I wish no uproar to-night.'

'There will be no uproar to-night, sir, beyond that which, I hear, has been already.'

'Go! Do not add insolence to your obstinacy.'

It was a fortunate dismissal. On both sides the elements were gathering for an outbreak.

'Strange, strange mortal!' exclaimed Mr. Evelyn, as the door closed upon her. 'There's no working her into a bona fide convict, try what you will. The deuce has hold of her, unless something much better has. She is either a masterpiece of conscienceless deceit—or—'

'She is a mystery, George, that neither you nor I can fathom.'

'Hang your mysteries, Herbert! They are plaguy hard to handle.'

'You will not give her in charge, then?'

'Not this time; but I think I shall send her to Brickfields just to frighten her. She must be taught submission before she gets other masters, or she'll never get her ticket—never be out of trouble.'

'If it be only for my Emmeline's sake, let me implore you not to send her away to the Depot. Em will quite fret to lose her, and the poor woman herself could never obtain so good a situation. As you say, endless miseries would ensue.'

'Oh, Wilson would reserve her.[41] I'd let him into the secret. Em shan't lose her; and as to the woman herself, I only wish to—'

Mr. Herbert shook his head, and Mr. Evelyn asked:

'Well, what would you do? I own I'm puzzled by her. During all the ten years I tried my hand at reforming prisoners, I never had such a difficult bargain! Cases handed over to me as desperate have become manageable, if not reformed. I abhor the government system of heaping punishment on punishment, and sentence on sentence, and have always resisted it as a hardening, debasing process; but a little well-timed severity, or judicious correction, I found beneficial in showing my convicts what they had to gain by reminding them what they had lost.'

'I quite agree with you, both as to the brutalizing effect of incessant coercion, and the impossibility of wholly foregoing stringent measures in convict treatment; but I doubt, George, whether in Maida's case of to-night judicial severity would be well timed, or correction judicious.'

'Your grounds of doubt?'

'Another doubt—namely, that severity *is* merited, or correction deserved.'

'Humph! Then you believe that her attempt to escape was not premeditated, but only induced by sudden temptation?'

'I believe that *no* attempt to escape has been made.'

'Does she deny the attempt? If so, I'm inclined to believe her. Somehow I cannot think she lies, though—'

'She neither denies nor asserts anything; she merely begs that her conduct may be punished or passed over without a confession.'

'Yes, but she begs after the fashion of a highwayman—"Give, or I'll take!"'

'Her spirit has not been trained by gentle influences. If I mistake not, it has been tortured into unnatural developments, and being of a temper too lofty to sink in mean submission, and too courageous to be trampled upon, it has sprung from its tormentors, and now defies with haughty scorn the fate it cannot vanquish, and makes a proud triumph of bearing that beneath which others would droop despondingly, or yield servilely. The effect of God's affliction is to subdue, not to crush; to break to meek contrition, not to drive to desperation. But man can rarely take punishment from his fellow man, and not be hardened by it; for man lays down one code of vengeance, and abides by it, irrespective of character, and unheedful of results. Man's judgments too often inculcate unrighteousness, because erring in themselves. God's judgments teach righteousness, because founded on righteousness. He knows the frame ere He deals the blow. The leprosy of Miriam is not as the leprosy of Gehazi.'[42]

'True, Herbert, true. Maida shall have the benefit of our doubt. I had her good alone in view in desiring to chastise her, and *that* I only meant to do by a good frightening. On my honour, though, I think we should try to prepare her for the exigencies of convict life. She does well with *you* and *me*, but any day she may change owners; then what would become of the poor thing? Who would brook her haughty manner and imperious replies? So soon as one sentence expired, she would get new trouble for insolence and refractoriness.'

'But if we patiently and prayerfully continue our work of forbearance with her, may not she gradually acquire the power of self-restraint, so necessary to her as a prisoner?'

'Ah, it's very fine for *you* to preach! It is your profession, and easy for you to practise, for *you* can control yourself.'

'It was not always easy, George; once my will controlled me, and not I my will.'

'I hope it will be once upon a time with me too, one day. I know your prayers drive that way; you can't wish it more than I do. But I suppose Miss Em would tell me "Idle wishes catch no fishes," eh, Herbert?'

But Mr. Herbert had left the room.

'Herbert,' called his brother, following him into his study, 'Maida is not in bed, I hear. I shall just have her down, and give her a caution, and so let the absconding mystery drop. She must have a touch or two on the subject of her supercilious speeches. 'Twon't do to let her off scot free.'

'Will you reprove the speeches of one that is desperate—which are as wind?' said Mr. Herbert, pointing to the twenty-sixth verse of the sixth chapter of Job.[43]

'Bother it! You've always Scripture ready to defeat me.'

Uncle Ev swung round on his foot, and out of the room.

He did not disturb Maida that night, or rather morning, for it was on the stroke of one o'clock; and when Maida should have appeared to receive her master's decision, it was found that she was too ill to leave her bed. The chill night air had entered her prostrate frame, as she lay unconscious on the earth, and the heavy dews had moistened her limbs, to stiffen them into the poignant cramps of rheumatic fever.

CHAPTER 28

H.M. General Hospital, Hobarton

> Here time so heavy dragged with strife
> On wheels of grief move slow,
> Bearing the wretched on through life
> Up paths of human woe.

DEAR no! Mrs. Evelyn cannot think of allowing Maida to be invalided in her house; the mere mention of so ridiculous an impossibility calls forth a whole breathful of little short laughs.

'Fever, too! Dear, dear! How very amusing George can be when he likes, or rather, when the girls put him up to such nonsense! Really, though, illness is too serious a matter to make fun of—it might come upon one of us at any time—George *should* know better.'

And that George does not know better Mrs. Evelyn soon discovers in looking at his forehead. His face is grave as grave can be, on perceiving which she puts the question to him as a man of sober sense. Is it reasonable, or does government expect holders to be bothered with sick convicts when there is a hospital expressly for their reception? This she *will* do if Mr. Evelyn likes—she will lend the blankets in which Maida has already slept (no others, on any account!) to wrap her from the air during the removal from the house; but even this she can only do on condition that he will faithfully promise to deliver them to a laundress on his way back, to have the infection washed out of them. She is sure that this is all that can be expected from her; why, even English masters and mistresses send away their servants when they are ill. Mr. Evelyn suggests that the poorest servant in England has her friends to go to, but the convict in sickness is desolate and friendless. To go back to government is the only resource of the unfortunate sufferer, and he considers that the objection to this resource is one entitled to respect and not to censure.

However, Mr. Evelyn does not insist that Maida shall stay; he thinks it is only right his wife's wishes should be consulted, as she would have the chief responsibility and trouble; at the same time he says he shall be very glad if she will consent to let the poor thing be laid up in the house.

Mrs. Evelyn dearly loves to please her husband, but really the present mode of pleasing him is so odd a one, that she cannot bring herself to adopt it. If the complaint were anything else, now, she might not mind so much; but rheumatic fever is so painful and disagreeable, she must have Maida taken away—and that at once.

Bridget thinks her aunt's reasons go exactly by contraries; to *her*, the very painfulness and disagreeableness of the disorder are reasons why Maida should not be sent among strangers. However, she holds her peace, having learnt by experience that Mrs. Evelyn's view of convicts will never be altered by means short of a new pair of mental eyes.

So Sanders's cab is fetched, and when it stops at the Lodge, and he is informed who is his passenger and whither bound, he declares:

'Lucy'll be darned sorry for to hear of it—most as sorry as I be.'

Followed by many kind wishes, the cab drives slowly down Macquarie Street, Sanders hardly daring to touch the reins, for fear 'the horse should jerk Madda, seeing he wasn't brought up to carrying of people to the hospital.' Turning into Liverpool Street, the handsome frontage of the hospital appears in sight, and relieves Sanders of a load of anxiety, which has oppressed his countenance as well as his heart; so much so, that had he been mounted on a hearse, he could not have looked more dolefully apprehensive of misbehaviour on the part of his horse.

The porter issues from the tall iron gates.

'All right!' says Sanders, preparing to drive past the man.

But all is *not* right, chooses to think the porter; he is not going to be so easily baulked of gratifying his curiosity, which, under the name of official inspection, he always pampers, to the annoyance of visitors.

Popping his head into the window, he quickly pops it back again; a nod from Mr. Evelyn has settled the difficulty. Without venturing a word he touches his hat, unlocks the gate, and admits Sanders, who has dismounted in order to lead the vehicle through the garden. The building before which he stops is the Female Hospital, the entry door of which stands open, displaying a broad staircase. From some invisible corner the matron comes forward, and is quickly surrounded by a bevy of brown-gowned, white-capped women, who have issued from equally invisible sources.

Orders are given to take Maida Gwynnham to ward No. 4, and put her into bed No. 10. Whereupon two women dive into the heap of blankets lying within the cab, but they can only draw groans from the heap.

Mr. Evelyn thinks he can manage to lift out Maida, if he may be permitted to carry her upstairs. The matron smiles assent, and Mr. Evelyn leans into the cab, and speaking in a kinder voice than many would suppose him able to produce, he says:

'If you can only get your arm round my neck, Maida, I'll carry you to your bed.'

Maida makes the effort, and her master raises her gently and bears her steadily to No. 4, then, whispering words that bring a faint smile of recognition to her lips, he bids her farewell; but ere he quits the ward he looks about him, and asks:

'Who is nurse here?'

A grizzly haired, middle-aged female curtsies. 'I am.'

Her disappointment is extreme when Mr. Evelyn merely says:

'Then remember that patient is my servant.'

'The poor dear creature shall be well minded, sir,' she answers, stowing away her disappointment where she hopes it will not be observed.

Mr. Evelyn knows there is no necessity to recommend Maida to the matron's special care, the kindness of that worthy woman being well known in the colony, and ever warmly attested by all who, in the misfortune of illness, have had the good fortune to find themselves under Mrs. Cott's protection.

The house surgeon visited Maida shortly after Mr. Evelyn's departure. He questioned her, and made notes of her answers; then, giving the nurse sundry directions, he left the ward. In the course of the afternoon a mysterious personage entered, and marching straight to Maida's bed, stuck into the wall above her head a ticket about three inches square; then conning[1] it through in mysterious silence, and nodding a mysterious nod, he marched straight out again, turning neither to the right hand nor to the left.

As soon as he was gone, the nurse stepped over to read the ticket, and having read it she gave a dissatisfied grunt.

From that moment, or rather from the combined moments of the fixing of the ticket and the grunting of the grunt, Maida became a part of the establishment. Several of the convalescent patients tottered across the room to elicit what small subject-matter of gossip the square white card might afford them; then gathering round the fire, they began to discuss the probabilities of the newcomer's career, in a suppressed humdrum voice, which irritated her nerves far more than a reasonable amount of sound would have annoyed her head.

It is known to all how unexplained trifles worry an invalid, even one who in health may be the last to be affected by extraordinary occurrences. Maida, though distracted by the racking pains in her limbs, felt a sensation of terror overcoming her as one by one the women crept over to her bed, read, and crept back again. She had just enough consciousness to suppose that the attracting object was similar to that which drew her attention to the heads of all the other stretchers in the room; but then, 'What is written on the square marks?' she asked, and 'What can mine be about?' Her thoughts perplexed her and her pains tortured her, until, being unable to bear both perplexity and torture, she tried to raise herself to find out what government could possibly have to say about her in connection with the hospital, but the attempt failed, and with a scream she sank on her pillow.

'Nurse, *do* tell me what's on the ticket,' she murmured, when, in answer to the scream, the nurse approached, and, as though anodyne issued from her fingers' ends, gave several small pats to the bedclothes, smoothing away wrinkles that only existed in her own brain.

'Tell 'e *what*?'

Maida repeated her wish.

'Trumpery!' and the nurse turned away.

Maida groaned. The square white cards seemed to enter into her as a part of her sufferings; her head ached in trying to explain the mystery; the cards grew larger and shrunk smaller as her bewildered senses watched those which were exactly opposite; and then, for a moment wandering altogether, she connected them with the ticket-of-leave of which she had heard so much, and stretching her hand to receive it, a sharp pain restored her to consciousness, when with feverish impatience her mind again set in to work out the problem of the card.

'Nurse, I shan't sleep to-night if you don't tell me what it is,' she at last said.

'Curse the ticket! You won't a-get any sleep otherwise, don't 'e flatter yerself.'

'I say, you might as well tell her, Nurse; it's mortal bad to be mazing over anything when a body's sick,' interposed a patient.

'Bad or good, I won't have her told! She shall learn that I'm missus here, as much as somebody *else* was coming out in the *Rose of Britain.*'

And the nurse clenched her fist, but whether at Maida or at an unpleasant recollection of her own, is a question open to dispute.

From the submissive air with which the pleader dropped her cause and herself into a chair, it was evident that the nurse was correct, and that whoever was mistress elsewhere, *she was* mistress *there*—in ward No. 4 of her Majesty's hospital.

Twilight dimmed the room and all within it into indistinctness, but with painful clearness the cards still loomed on Maida's distorted vision. They appeared to have drawn so close to her that she thought she had only to put forth her hand to grasp one, but the inability to put it forth was equal to the cards being at a distance.

There was now a general movement among the women: each went to her stretcher, and, sitting at its foot, prepared to take her place for the night; the last lingerer had just snugged herself within the bedclothes, when the matron's kind but careworn face shone in amongst them to take her third official survey of her family, as she called the patients.

The nurse went round with her, showering expressions of pity as she went—pity which she hastily scoured off the patients' minds the instant Mrs. Cott was out of hearing. Stopping in turn at Maida, she raised her hands.

'Lor' 'a mercy! This new poor creature suffers dreadful—and so demented too—she keeps on about her ticket.'

'Ah! poor thing.' And kind-hearted Mrs. Cott bent down and consoled her, thinking it most natural that a prisoner should be anxious for her ticket-of-leave.

'Don't you fret now; this all goes in your sentence; you are not losing time; so cheer up, there's a good girl. You'll soon be better.'

'Do tell me what it means?'

'Poor soul! I'll tell you all about it to-morrow,' replied the matron, passing to the next number.

Maida closed her eyes with an audible groan. All about her were equally cruel.

When Mrs. Cott and nurse were at the farthest end of the ward, the woman who had before pleaded leaned out of her stretcher—which happened to be next to Maida's—and whispered:

'Don't you fret; the ticket's nothing; it's only to say who you are.'

The nurse stepped outside with Mrs. Cott, and the woman, whom we shall call Baker, hastily snatched the card from its frame and showed it to Maida.

'Here, quick; this is all; I'll read it to you—"Maida Gwynnham, *alias* Martha Grylls, pass-holder 24; *Rose of Britain*; Protestant." '

'Is that all?'

'Yes, except a Lattern word, which means what's the matter with you; that's all, on my word. Nothing about your ticket, you see; you won't have *that* till you're half done.'

'I don't care about my ticket,' groaned Maida, almost fretfully. 'Are you sure my crimes are not written there?'

'Bless me, no! More like your doctor's stuff would be down. What's your crimes to do with what you'll have here?'

Maida's mind again wandered in a confusion of past, present, and future. In a dreamy tone she whispered:

'Norwell isn't mentioned, is he?'

'Nor—what? No; nothing's there, I tell you. That Lattern word, I'll spell it out for you to-morrow; but I know it don't mean more than what I say; it's the doctor's way of writing your sickness—rheumatics, I take it to be. She's coming, quick, down!'

But the caution was needless, Maida being already as prostrate as pain and fever could lay her. Baker had barely time to slip the card back into its groove, ere, Argus-eyed and suspicious, nurse walked about the ward, pulling at a large excrescence which disfigured her nether lip; searching meanwhile from stretcher to stretcher for traces of the treason that she doubted not had discovered itself during her momentary absence; until resting on No. 10, her eye seemed unwilling to search beyond. She stood still, and lapsed into a profound contemplation—alternately darting emphatic malignity at the new patient, and tugging energetically at the superfluous flesh, which always suffered more or less in proportion to the amount of suggestive aid required to mark out her plans.

But for this unsightly excrescence, Maida would probably have recognised in the nurse of ward No. 4 of her Majesty's General Hospital, her former enemy, the ex-lunatic of the transport. The alteration in her dress, too, may have served to obscure her identity. The shock of grizzled hair no longer stood erect from her head, but lay in heavy masses on her gaunt cheekbones, which seemed to protrude for the express purpose of supporting the burden imposed upon them. A convict in the midst of convicts, she alone was exempt from the prison badge. Grizzled and gaunt, therefore, as she was, she became the cynosure[2] of the sick world within the dreary precinct over which she ruled. If her movements were not worshipped, they were watched by two distinct classes incarcerated within those walls: the admiring, or prisoners who had never yet been out of government; and the aggrieved, or prisoners who, in accepting the advantages of the house, had been obliged to resume the abominated serge—an obligation which deterred many of the better disposed from availing themselves of medical treatment, as afforded in her Majesty's hospital, until the latest moment, when, perhaps, the symptoms of their malady had seriously developed, or had progressed above the power of professional skill. A cap of white net, with generous border, and a print gown, was the dress that at once distinguished nurse from her bond-sisters, and invested her with a superiority beyond the imaginings of a 'free' mind. The eyes that noted the changes of her cap from blue to pink, from pink to orange, were eyes long weary of the perpetual brown—eyes that had little to divert the sameness of their occupation. Sweet and fresh came in the air through the open casement; but the sweetness made yet more ardent their longings for green fields and flowers, to a sight of which the tallest of their community could not aspire, for hopelessly beyond the reach of all the prisoners were the windows that admitted the taunting message from the outer world.

Visiting days, that generally bring pleasant variety to the tenants of a hospital, here were rarely guilty of such kindness. Visiting-Thursday came: the utmost hope it raised was that a mate might look in, or an unusually indulgent mistress, who had expressed a wish to have her servant reserved for her, might drop in to know how much longer she would have to wait. Visiting-Thursday passed: the only disappointment it left was that such a mate or such a mistress had not come. Had the mate appeared, ten chances to one that she had been too drunk to speak, or that her visit had been delivered in haste, it being only one of necessity, the fag end of an outing which she had extorted from the master under pretext of a visit 'to poor so and so a-lying sick down there.' Here looks in vain the pining mother—no daughter, with tearful affection, appears to soothe her dying pillow. Never comes the sister to whisper words of love and comfort to her sister drooping on a bed of pain and death. Weary is the little child of watching for the kind, tender smile that erewhile made it forget its sorrow. It watches and wastes, but never more draws nigh the step it strives to hear; it wastes and wastes, and soon it is missed from its little stretcher.

Here, in solitude, frets the old man. He knows he is wished dead by the nurse, who throws her services at him as you would throw a bone to appease a troublesome dog. He dotes, and calls upon his daughter, but she answers not; he reproaches her, but his reproaches do not move her; all he gets for them is a sharp rap from the nurse's hard, dried lips; so he sinks into puling[3] silence; and when the last breath sets him free, the only announcement is to government, which gladly numbers one less to the living stock within its pale, and to the chaplain of the house, who, unless he be a Mr. Herbert Evelyn, grumbles that the old man did not apprise him of his intention to die, that he (the chaplain) might have arranged for his burial at a more convenient hour.

As we progress, we shall discover that nurse is wrapped about with attractions more potent than the net and print, whose changes have so great an interest for captive eyes. Grim as is her smile, we shall find that it has a peculiar value; while her frown, independent of that which is natural to so fierce a contortion, has a terror of its own—a distinct, substantial terror. By rule of the old adage, the intrinsic value of her smile is easily estimated; but her frown! Who dares to calculate the amount of evil consequences condensed therein? Woe to the unfortunate who has the experimental computing thereof! Woe to the ward and the inhabitants thereof! When a cloud gathers on nurse's brow, it is as if a thunderbolt threatened the whole community. None knows where the storm may burst, or where the shock will be most keenly felt, but all know that none can escape; the flood of vengeance sweeps along, scathing *all*, destroying *some*.

The rod of office becomes a snake within her hand[4]—a snake whose malice *all* must feel, whose subtlety *all* must dread, and whose fascination none can withstand.

When nurse stood, as we have seen her, contemplating the new victim that had come beneath her snake, how writhed that reptile within her grasp, eager at once to dart upon its prey! Its instinctive craft alone kept it back. How gloated its malignant eye on the prospect of malice lying with Maida on the bed!

But Maida was unconscious of its gloating eye. During the fortnight of pain which succeeded her admission, when sufficiently herself to connect cause and effect, she attributed the extreme discomfort she experienced wholly to her illness, which she knew to be one of the most distressing disorders. She suspected not the cruelty which, by every device, was heightening the tortures of acute rheumatism. When she implored to have her bed smoothed under her, because every crease gave her pain, nurse hastened to her help; but Maida knew not that her haste was the result of malice, glad of another opportunity to vent its spleen. And when, in the fretfulness of fever, she still complained that she was not more comfortable, nurse told her that the cause was in her own poor racked limbs, and not in the bed; and Maida believed her, not perceiving, though sharply *feeling*, the reason in a large, thick leather, dried into uneven folds, which had been slipped in between the under-sheet and blanket, for the fiendish purpose of turning her discomfort into positive suffering.

When the fever abated, and the pains gradually subsided, Maida began to look about her. Lying weak and silent, she made quiet observation of all that took place around. Then was it that she first beheld nurse with an interest, in which some past, though unremembered incident, bore a part. She felt sure the grizzled hair, the dusky brow, and uneven eyes, were not strange to her; but the excrescence puzzled her. She had never known anyone with a lip like that. How could she, therefore, have seen nurse before?—the fancy must be a freak. Quieted by this conclusion, she tried to forget the being who, without a definite reason, had become obnoxious to her. But nurse would not be forgotten. Her prim figure, like an evil genius, was ever on the dead march before her, and ever with it came back the thought to Maida that the face should be familiar, notwithstanding the conclusion, notwithstanding the lip.

'Nurse, surely I have seen you before; can you tell me where?' she asked one day, after a long endeavour to reconcile the excrescence with the face.

'The devil may care! All I know is, we've met once too often. Where I shall meet you *again*, I'm pretty sure of,' replied the nurse, getting uneasy under the perpetual watch of

Maida's eye, fearing what it might discover if its vigilance were not checked. The women only knew her as Anne Watts—her colonial alias—and could not, therefore, assist in the search for her identity with the vague someone of Maida's recollection. But Lucy Sanders, who came to see her friend on a visiting-Thursday, at once cleared up the doubt by exclaiming, the instant she saw the nurse, 'Lor! Maida, if that isn't she that 'most killed me coming out.'

A quick glance of recognition took place, and Maida wondered how she had failed to recall the ex-lunatic in the barbarous features now grinning before her.

'I shouldn't wonder now, if that there ugly lip isn't a judgment straight from Almighty God,' whispered Lucy, when she had taken in as much of the grin as she desired.

From this moment the animosity publicly revived, and warfare commenced. The women shrank into timid neutrality at the first resistance offered by Maida to some usurpation of the nurse. They were amazed at the temerity of their comrade in defying the grizzly bear in her own den. But power was on the side of the oppressor; therefore the friendless creatures were also obliged to side with her. Many did so from *choice,* being as corrupt as she: *others,* in the depth of their heart, ranged themselves under the standard of liberty, upheld with unassuming dignity by Maida Gwynnham.

The first time Maida was permitted to leave her bed, she became an object of general attraction. Prison clothes dared to rival the free habiliments that had hitherto borne off all regard; and yet Maida felt friendless and desolate. She experienced that worst form of desolation—spiritual loneliness. She was surrounded by human beings; sisters in flesh and blood were very kind in inquiring how she felt after her exertion, but she was lonely amidst them, for not one heart in all those twenty forms beat sympathy with hers. Weakened by her long illness, and exhausted by so unusual an effort, despite her self-control, a tear worked its way to her eye. Turning to brush it off, she observed a pair of large, lustrous eyes gazing intently at her from the end of the ward. The stretcher from which these eyes looked up was on the same side as her own, therefore she had never before been able to obtain a clear view of the woman who went by the name of No. 1, and whose tearing cough and laboured breathing had excited her tender pity. The lustrous eyes were evidently trying to convey a message to her, and when Maida sent back a smile in answer to their silent appeal, they closed, as if satisfied with the present result of the interview, and No. 1 leant back on the pillows which propped her. The card above her head, in the one brief word 'phthisis,'[5] told the story of her suffering; and what that story is, they best may know who have marked the slow fading of their dear one beneath consumption's sure decay. It was the doctor's name for her disease, but Maida, from her distant seat, could not read it; therefore she asked a neighbour what was the matter with No. 1, and received the laconic answer, 'Frettin'.'

A word as short as that on the card; but how descriptive in its brevity! How much it told of heart suffering and pain—of hopeless longing and craving for affection—they best may know who have heard the sighing of the prisoner, and watched the slow breaking of an anguished heart.

Seeing Maida's compassionate look, her informant continued—'No. 4, Crazy Sal, there, is another frettin' case: in one way or another, most of them that's brought in here is fretters, unless they's scheming.'[6]

Maida had often been disturbed by Crazy Sal's wild cry, which was so like the bray of a donkey, that, during her delirium, nothing could persuade her that one of those animals was not in the room; but being in a line with her also, she had never fully seen the poor creature, who now presented at once a pitiable and unsightly object. From the absence of hair, which had been closely shorn, every part of the broad, distended face was exposed to view; the thick frilled night-cap only half covered her head, and completed the deformity, by showing to what extent it had enlarged. As Maida turned towards her, Sally, with a horrible distortion of countenance, raised her upper lip over her large teeth and sent forth a series of brays. Maida shuddered, and asked if that cry was caused by pain. Her neighbour said she believed 'it was not; it was a noise somehow she had taken to make whenever nurse went near her—perhaps because she wanted something "out" of her, or perhaps because dressing of the wounds hurted her—but whichever 'tis,' she added, 'we shan't be bored with her no longer, for she's going to be removed to a closet handy, so that she may be nigh nurse, and yet out of the way of teasing us.'

Maida now remembered that nurse's approach and Sally's cry had always been simultaneous, and she turned again to take a look at the poor woman, over whom nurse was now bending. Another raising of the lip, followed by a piteous cry, drew tears from her eye; she quivered in her seat, longing to rush over to the suffering imbecile, in whose cry she alone of all the hearers heard a tone beseeching help. She attempted to stand, but weakness resisted the effort, and she could only listen in sorrowing silence. The large lustrous eyes perceived the attempt, and again manoeuvred to arrest her notice, and when they succeeded, they turned slowly and significantly towards Crazy Sal, and then the thin white hands of No. 1 clasped each other in a prayerful attitude, while the large eyes looked supplicatingly upward. Maida was perplexed, and happening at the moment of her perplexity to speak to a convalescent, No. 1 thought she was seeking an explanation of her signs, and, forgetting everything but her own terror, she called out as loud as her low voice would allow—'Oh don't—don't—I shall get—' She stopped short, and nurse turned fiercely on her, 'I know what you *shall* get, if you don't cease your bawl.' She moved her two forefingers so as to describe a square, and then nodding a savage nod, which seemed to mean, 'Yes, *that*,' she turned again to Sally.

Wilcox, as we shall henceforth designate No. 1, trembled; her long thin fingers worked nervously into each other, but without a word she laid her head sidewise on her pillow, where the tears coursed over the two bright spots which had darted to her cheeks, when her exclamation was hushed by the sharp voice of her tormentor.

How wildly did Maida watch those tears as one by one they fell and were absorbed by the pillow until it became quite wet! Wilcox then spread her pocket handkerchief to make a dry place for her hollow cheek, and still lying as sidewise as was possible in her upright position, she drew out a little book and commenced to read.

'Put away that book, trying of your eyes—you ought to be getting asleep. I hate such hypocrisy; if you'd been the saint you makewise to be, you'd never have been out here—fine Sunday scholar! Does credit to your teachers.'

'I don't feel inclined to sleep,' answered Wilcox, mildly.

'You shan't read for all that, making your head ache for me to cure. Put away your humbugging hymn book; I hate the sight of en.'

'Shall I read it to you Wilcox?' asked Maida.

Nurse drew back where Maida could not see her, and clenched her fist at Wilcox.

'No thank you, Maida.' But the tone very plainly said, 'How I should like it!' So Maida listened to *it*, and not to the poor faint voice. She had seen the frightened look towards nurse, and divined its meaning.

'I shall like to read it myself, if you will lend it me.'

The thin white hand held out the well-worn hymn book, and before nurse could forbid, a convalescent passed it to Maida, who took it, and, turning to her companions, said—

'I'll read it aloud if you all like.'

One and all gave an eager ' *Yes* .'

'Which hymn were you reading Wilcox? I'll go on with it.'

'My mark is at the one, I think it is 189,' she replied, trying to prevent herself from meeting the nurse's eye; but the fascination of the snake was at work. The eyes must meet. The trembling victim crept, unresisting, into the hands of the tyrant, who with a villainous leer again delineated the blister; and what flesh remained on the invalid's wasted frame seemed to creep in terror as she hastily said—

'Maida, you are so very kind, but perhaps I'd better try to sleep.'

'The reading won't disturb you, my dear,' chimed in the nurse; 'it's a different thing being read to and reading oneself; go on Maida.'

How ghastly the grimace she pulled at Wilcox, as, having given this permission, she left the ward to vent her rage on some miserable being doomed by the privacy of her situation to bear unknown cruelties from this official monster!

Maida found hymn 189, and read the last verse—

> Jesus can make a dying bed
> Feel soft as downy pillows are
> While on His breast I lean my head
> And breathe my life out sweetly there.[7]

'Do those words comfort you, Wilcox?' asked Maida.

'They are my only comfort,' sadly replied the former.

Unbidden, Maida read them again.

'A poor sinner like me has nothing else to cling to.'

'Than what, Wilcox?'

'Oh! than Jesus!' she replied, clasping her hands emphatically.

'Jasus!' repeated Crazy Sal; and having once pronounced that precious name, which seemed to come back to the imbecile like one long forgotten, no one could stop her. She repeated it louder, louder and louder—until she quite screamed it—'Jasus Ja-sus!'

Was it the mystic power of that wondrous name that exorcised the evil spirit within her? Had the spirit of unrest slunk for a while into shamed quiet? Sally fell into a sweeter sleep than she had known for weeks. No opiate had been able to quell her weary tossings, but now the poor tired one slept soundly.

Henceforward she always called on Jesus when her pains were great, or when nurse approached her.

Maida was soon able to get up a little every day. The first time she could walk across the room she went over and sat by Wilcox, for the gaze of whose lustrous eyes she now regularly looked directly she stepped out of bed. A secret understanding had sprung up between these two captive sisters. Maida longed for the moment when she should hear from Wilcox's lips the message that her eyes had long since delivered. But not more than Wilcox longed for the opportunity of speaking to one whom she could not but believe God's kind providence had sent to relieve her of the remediable portion of her sufferings. She felt sure that she should find in No. 10 a friend who would make the last few days of her life as easy as they might be made, by protecting her from the cruelties of the nurse; and she prayed God that her days might close before Maida's discharge again left her friendless, to what she was sure would be the redoubled malice of her enemy. She had been a silent observer of all that had taken place, and had determined, when Maida's convalescence permitted, to appeal to her on behalf of Crazy Sal and herself. She was certain the kind and fearless voice which had so often spoken cheering words to an unknown individual in the stillness of the night was one that would assert the right of a helpless idiot and dying fellow creature.

How fervent was the grasp with which she caught hold of Maida's hand before she had come quite close to her stretcher! How grateful became the lustrous eyes as, fatigued with her journey across the ward, Maida dropped into her seat—the edge of No. 1's bed.

'Are you only twenty-two, Wilcox?' asked the latter in surprise, as she read the card over her head.

'Barely that. Sickness has made me look old; sorrow, older.'

Maida pressed the hand lying within hers.

'But I deserve it all!' she added slowly; 'all, all—yes—and a great deal more.'

This was something new to Maida, so accustomed to hear convicts rail against their punishment, and term their crime the *error* for which they were sent out.

'You speak after my own heart, Wilcox. I like to hear of *just* punishment—its justice is so generally disclaimed.'

There was a bitterness of tone with great seriousness of manner in this speech. The latter only was obvious to Wilcox.

' Punishment is always just to the sinner, Maida; and to such a dreadful sinner as me, too!'

'I am inclined not to trust your judgment on yourself, you do not seem very guilty.'

Maida put a lightness in her voice which was very foreign to her heart.

'Oh don't, don't! You don't know all my guilt!' and, as if ashamed of the mere remembrance of it, Wilcox covered her face with her hands.

'This is a gloomy subject for you.'

'And yet I feel happy in the assurance of pardon,' was spoken at the same time, so neither heard the other.

'What did you say about pardon? Have you your conditional pardon?' asked Maida.

'I am not even due for my ticket; I shall never need it—perhaps before this month is out I shall be where there is neither bond nor free; where the convict will not be discerned from his master.'

'I hope you will,' said Maida, gently.

Wilcox gave a sweet smile, and then continuing her former train of thought, she said—

'Yes; my *pardon*, I have my pardon; but it is *un*conditional —signed with my Saviour's blood, and sealed with the seal of heaven.'

'Wilcox,' (Maida bent tenderly over her) 'I do not wish to mar your peace, or make you doubt; but I should like to know how you are assured of forgiveness? How do you know it?'

The question seemed to make her thoughtful: she did not reply for a minute; then, the lustre shone out more brightly from her eye. She looked upwards with an expression of rapture, and exclaimed—

'My Saviour died! Ask me no more; that is enough for such sinners as me! *One drop* of His precious blood would have done; but he gave *all*. How can I *help* being forgiven? Oh Maida! how could I help it?'

This simple faith at once surprised and pleased Maida, who longed to ask more; but feared to dim the faith, which was now the all of that dying girl.

Though herself unable to enter into the mystery of that hidden joy which the world can neither give nor take away, she was convinced of its reality, and her generous spirit rejoiced in the happiness of one who had found that pearl of price [8]—peace and joy in believing, as yet unfound by herself.

The nurse's entrance and grim stare of disapprobation enforced a momentary silence, for which Maida was not sorry. She wanted to think over what she heard. When they were again free to speak, Wilcox turned to Maida, and gently squeezing her hand, whispered—

'Dear Maida! How I *do* love you! My mistress was kind to me; but I could only be afraid of her, *you* I love—love—love!'

It was a warm gush of feeling, flowing from a heart to whom affection has long been forbidden; and however much it was against Maida to make a show of her feeling, she feared she should disappoint Wilcox if she did not; therefore, bending forward she kissed her tenderly, and then keeping her face so as to be heard only by her, she said, 'Wilcox, you will not be here long, I am going to tell you a secret—perhaps you will be able to assist me. *I* should like to obtain that pardon of which you feel so sure—no one knows how I long for it! How can I get it?'

'Jesus will give it you: He gave me mine.'

'But how can I be *sure* that He will?'

'Get it first and be sure of it afterwards.'

Maida shook her head.

'Jesus has pledged himself to give it. Oh, think of His suffering and death, and then you will be sure they could only be for a very great purpose; and then think of His love and pity, and you will be drawn to Him.'

'Ah, I believe all that—but only for *others*; I cannot for myself.'

'I am not able to explain. I can only tell from my own experience how precious Jesus is to the sinner; the saint loves Him, worships Him, and praises Him; but oh! it's the poor *sinner* that *clings* to Him. Dear Maida, don't look sad, Jesus will give you your pardon, freely, gladly—no one ever wished for it in vain—you *must* have it. I cannot bear to think of your going away from Jesus.'

'I am always going away from Him. Once I did so willingly— *now* because I can't help it. Perhaps, as you have been ill so long you don't know what a prisoner has to contend with.'

'Yes, I do; I was hired out eleven months, and though my mistress was as kind as could be, there was much to bear; but I told Jesus of it all, and that made me happy till I came here.'

'If it will not pain you, I should like to hear your story—it may teach me something.'

'Pain me, dear Maida! There will be so much to tell of my precious Saviour's love and mercy, that it will be a great pleasure to tell you—though—'

Her voice faltered.

'Ah! I know; there are dreary blanks in our lives that no one can fill up—blanks that no earthly pleasure can fill,' said Maida.

'Jesus can,' murmured Wilcox, wiping the tears from her face.

'You'm converted, b'ain't you?' sneered the nurse, who had drawn sufficiently near to hear the last words.

'I hope so!' meekly answered Wilcox.

'So do I; but all I know is, that if you'm convarted, I be too!'

'Leave us, woman,' cried Maida; 'we are doing nothing that comes under your power to hinder. I mean to sit by Wilcox every day.'

'Don't—don't,' whispered the invalid; ''twill only be worse for me.'

'I've an old score to pay you, Mrs. Martha Grylls; don't think I've forgotten it, I be only waiting,' growled the Excrescence.

'I have only one way of dealing with my foes,' said Maida, calmly; 'as for your debt, I'm willing to forgive it!'

'Fine! That's like the imperance of the woman; I tell you what, you had your day when we couldn't help ourselves—now I mean to have mine when you can't help yourself, for you'm a mere bantling [9] yet.'

But as far as personal injury was concerned, nurse knew better than to vent her spite on Maida; all she could do in that way had been inflicted when she lay helpless in bed.

'You had better go, Maida, I shall only get worse off by your staying,' said Wilcox.

'How? What do you mean? Dare she ill-treat you; let me know it, and I'll—'

'Ah, nothing; we are none of us in the same temper always.'

Maida was not to be deceived: she asked no further question, but determined to watch. She had long been disposed to the opinion that so much fear must have some other cause than the mere offensive manner of the nurse.

She arose to go, and then sitting down again, said—

'I thought you had something to tell me, or something you wanted me to do, Wilcox. I have always so interpreted your earnest lookings at me.'

'So I had; but I forget everything when I can get anyone to speak of my Saviour with me; and really, when I think of His love, and of my sins, I feel ashamed of caring for my sufferings; but when they come they are so very bad to bear, that I grieve to say I forget Him and all He bore.'

'If they are the sufferings from your disease, you do well to receive them patiently; but I fear they are not wholly that—tell me.'

'I'll tell you what I did want you to do—to keep an eye on poor Crazy Sal—she made me so miserable, but it's no use now she's removed. I'm sure there's something wrong there, the poor, harmless thing would never screech so for nought; and then if you could see nurse's face as I have when she stoops over her pretending to be kind! Oh! It is dreadful to think of. Poor Sal wasn't so when first she came; she could then talk a little, but now she doesn't speak only two words, the name of her home, and that name she caught from the hymn. I cannot but fancy she finds a comfort in calling it out. Poor Sal! She's a shipmate of mine.'

'Poor Sally, indeed! I shall be very glad to alleviate her suffering, and as soon as I can walk about I will find means to discover the truth of what you say.'

And Maida's eye gleamed. It was well the nurse was not near to see the flash that darted from it as she thought of the imbecile's wrongs.

'But was she always in that state?' she asked.

'Oh! no; it seems she pined away her reason. She was never very famous,[10] so they who knew her at home said. When first she was put on board with a set of women she looked like one struck; when the ship sailed she stayed upon deck watching the land, and then when it got out of sight she fell down and fainted right away; after that she did nothing but cry all the way out. The matron and doctor pitied her at first, but everyone got tired of her crying, and someone put it into the doctor's head that she was scheming, and one woman declared she'd seen her swallow soap pills to make herself ill, so the poor soul had to take an emetic; the doctor said that was always his cure for schemers; but she wasn't scheming, 'twasn't in her. On board the *Anson* they could do nothing with her, and one day a dreadful attack took her all at once, and she's never been better since. Her sufferings here have been more than the doctors know of!'

'Then they shall be so no longer! If I can get at her no other way I'll rise in the night and creep in on my hands and knees,' said Maida.

Wilcox shook her head.

'But you haven't answered me about yourself.'

'I have not more than I can bear and less that I deserve, thank you, Maida. Some things might be better, but I thank God that they are not worse—they might be like poor Sal's.'

'Wilcox, do answer,' said Maida; 'I am not strong yet, and the thought of what you may have suffered and may still suffer, makes me quite ill, and you know,' she added half smilingly, 'nurse will make out I want some more of that nauseous stuff if I look flushed, or tired. Do tell me in what way she has it in her power to annoy you.'

Had Wilcox been in a smiling mood, the word *annoy* would have drawn a smile from her, but as she was far too anxious to think of anything but nurse, she raised herself and looked around: no one was nigh, the convalescents were grouped around the fire; the bed next her was empty, and the oppressor had gone into the next ward.

Lowering her voice, she replied:

'She has ways that you would never dream of, and such natural things that if the doctor or Mrs. Cott find them out they only think it's all right. *One* thing, though, isn't so, but *that* has never been found out. When I've offended her very much, when all the others are asleep, she creeps over and shakes me—shakes me till I'm 'most dead—and then the cough comes on, and doesn't stop for the night. I dread this shaking most of all, for it terrifies me so; and then next morning the doctors come, and she says I've had a shocking night; hadn't I better have another blister?[11] And they say *yes*—and oh, my chest is most eaten away already, yet she gets me another whenever she's angry.'

'Wretch!' stamped Maida; 'where is she?'

But Wilcox's imploring face stopped her.

'And pray what have you done to merit all this at her hand?' asked Maida, in a haughty tone, forgetful in her anger to distinguish between the offenders and the offended.

'When first I came I resisted some of her wicked ways. She offered to burn the blister that was ordered for me if I'd give her my glass of wine, but of course I wouldn't; 'twas then she began, and ever since it's been dreadful.'

'I suppose she knew me too well to attempt such tricks, but I have suspected some foul play of the sort with some of the patients.'

'Oh, she carries on a regular trade; half the physic is thrown out; those who are not fond of drink gladly exchange their wine or beer for leave to throw away their medicine or escape a blister; those that *don't* yield she pays out by telling the doctor that they require something or other that they dislike. Oh, Maida, I feel very down sometimes when I think that I ought to do my best to stop these things. Satan puts it into my mind that I can't love my Saviour because I don't—but—'

'God knows what would ensue, and does not expect it of you, I should think. Is there not a text that says, "He knoweth our frames"?' interrupted Maida.[12]

'Ah, yes, thank you for remembering it. Now do go, and *mind—mind* not to speak of what I have told you; I've made up my mind to bear it—it can't be for long.'

'And it *shan't* either!' Maida answered indignantly; 'however, you may trust me,' and her voice and countenance changed, 'and *my pardon*! You'll remember that?'

Wilcox smiled; then very fatigued, Maida tottered back to her chair just as the rattle of pannikins announced tea.

One morning, shortly after her visit to Wilcox, as Maida lay waiting for her summons to get up, which was now always given at ten o'clock, she fancied she heard a stifled sob proceed from No. 1, over whom nurse was leaning to dress her blister. She sat up and listened—another muffled sob. Without a word she slid out of her stretcher and crossed the ward; she stood behind nurse, and saw Wilcox lying (so that she could only look at the ceiling) with a handkerchief stuffed in her mouth. Her chest was bared, and on it there was the sore of the blister from which the skin had been taken clearly off; the raw, irritated flesh beneath was laid open and raised in uneven lumps. Nurse was strewing salt over the fresh wound, and as the salt fell she asked in a whining voice:

'Does it hurt you, my dear? It's only the flour I'm putting over it just to suck up the water 'fore I put on the plaister.'

Another sob was the only answer.

At the same instant Wilcox felt the handkerchief drawn out of her mouth, and nurse felt herself dragged backward.

'Coward! Wretch! Tyrant! You shall leave this place.'

The nurse was bewildered for a moment, and then bristling up, she asked:

'And pray what's all this about? Go back to your place, you bad woman! Fine for a rheumatic patient to be out without socks or shoes!'

'Finish dressing that poor creature's blister; *then* you shall know what it is about. How will you get off that salt you've rubbed into her?' haughtily demanded Maida.

'Salt? You barbarous hussy! Don't 'e, for love's sake, talk in one breath of *salt*, and that poor mortal's sore flesh—it's enough to make one's heart leap out.'

'How will you get it off?' sternly demanded Maida; at the same time raising Wilcox on her pillow.

'What the deuce does she mean?' wondered nurse, looking from one to the other of the women, who, in the different stages of dressed, partly dressed, and not dressed at all, had gathered round the disputants.

'Very like she mistook the flour for salt,' suggested one.

'To be sure! Fool I was for not guessing that!'

Then turning to Maida:

'If 'twern't that that thought was *enough* to riz your bile, I'd make you beg pardon for your insolence; but I'll look it over—only *mind* your own business for the future. People that meddles is always in the wrong. Salt! Me—I can't get over it!'

'Was it salt or flour, Wilcox?' asked Maida imperturbedly.

'I only felt something cold falling. The sore always smarts, so I can't tell.'

'Here, woman, if you ain't satisfied, look for yourself—what's this?'

Without doubt it was flour that nurse displayed in her hand; she passed it round for the inspection of the crowd, who not only touched it, but tasted it. The verdict was unanimously given for nurse.

'Then I beg your pardon, nurse. I withdraw my accusation, but certainly my eyes never more deceived me,' said Maida.

'Well, now, just to show I'm not affronted, here's my hand.'

But Maida refused it, saying:

'Thank you; I have not done yet.' (To the women)—'You had better go and dress; the doctors will be here before we are ready.'

Her voice was that of command, and all, except nurse's allies, turned to obey her. She then demanded what explanation could be given of the handkerchief.

'Bless us! What's the woman after? What handkerchief d'ye mean?'

'I put it in my mouth, Maida,' muttered Wilcox, faint with terror.

'Did you, poor darling?' replied Maida.

'No patience with such cant! Fine pity yours is, keeping of a dying creature, 'most naked, in the cold! Here, my dear, let me finish you; you are starved, ain't you?'

Wilcox shuddered when operations recommenced, but this time without cause; for almost tenderly did nurse complete her task, for some reason or other substituting a piece of fine carded cotton for the sperm-plaister.[13] Though nonplussed, Maida was by no means convinced, and she determined to say something to the doctors which should make them ask to see the sore.

When they appeared, to her delight, Dr. Lamb was among them. He was a general favourite with the women. If any favour had to be sought, it was always reserved for Dr. Lamb's day.

She seated herself by Wilcox, so as to create less surprise by the remark she had prepared.

No. 1 was soon surrounded by four of the fraternity, and four pupils.

'How d'ye feel, my woman?' asked Dr. Lamb kindly.

'I had a very bad night, sir.'

''Count for it in any way?'

'She'd a blister last night, sir,' chimed in nurse, who, almost cat-like, watched Maida.

'This blistering seems everlasting work,' muttered Dr. Lamb to Mr. Ferris, the house doctor; 'I doubt whether one night's rest isn't worth a hundred of 'em.'

Mr. F. only clicked his tongue against his teeth.

'Why, Maida, my friend, you look as if *you* were longing for a touch-up,' said Dr. Lamb.

'Touch-up' was a favourite expression with Dr. Lamb, in connection with *blisters*; therefore Maida understood it, and rejoicing at this unexpected opportunity, so much better than her own plan, she answered:

'Oh *no*, sir! I saw poor Wilcox's dreadful chest this morning. The sight is enough to last my life. Oh, so shocking!'

'Let's see, my woman. I don't want to punish you in that fashion.'

And, in his own quick way, Dr. Lamb pulled down the bed-clothes, and opened Wilcox's chest, before nurse had time to do it for him; but the carded cotton had by this stuck in so tightly that, without inflicting great pain, it could not be removed; so Dr. Lamb did not attempt it.

'Whatever did you put that on for? I have always said I won't have it used,' said the house doctor.

'I think I could tell you, sir,' said Maida, now sure that salt had been used.

'Why, sir,' hurried in nurse, 'the flesh looked so sore and bumpy, I thought it couldn't bear much fretting, so I clapped on a bit of cotton to soothe it a bit. It looked *so* bad (didn't it, Maida?), that they thought I'd been a-putting salt on it.'

'And you *did*, woman!' ejaculated Maida.

Dr. Lamb turned quickly to her with:

'Here, I say, you mustn't rub up people like *that*. I've never found nurse in the wrong yet.'

'Thank you, sir,' dropped nurse. 'What should I want to put salt in a body for?'

'A breast of bacon, perhaps?' laughed Dr. Lamb. 'What does Wilcox herself say: *have* you been pickled this morning?'

Wilcox attempted a smile—how miserable a one!

'I don't know, sir,' she feebly articulated.

Maida clenched her teeth impatiently, with a slushing sound.

'"Let dogs delight to bark and bite,"[14] etcetera,' said Dr. Lamb, passing on, and creating a laugh, which, in his good humour, he meant should be *fun*, for he always tried to amuse his patients with some drollery. He knew not the bitterness that fell from nurse's lips in the form of that laugh.

Maida, baffled in one point, would not without another struggle resign her protégé into the hand of the enemy.

When Mrs. Cott entered the ward to hear the medical opinion of her 'family,' before nurse or anyone had time to put in a word, she stepped forward.

'Mrs. Cott, I have a favour to ask.'

'Well, my dear?'

'I am pronounced convalescent; and as I believe the convalescents are expected to take charge of a bed-patient, will you give me Wilcox?'

'What does *she* say to it?' said Mrs. Cott, approaching the stretcher, and taking No. 1's thin hand.

'Oh, ma'am!' was all she could reply: she had endured enough; that one drop of joy overcame her; she wept aloud.

'So she shall, then,' said Mrs. Cott soothingly.

'Nurse, Maida Gwynnham 'll take Wilcox; she must therefore change stretchers. You'll be No. 2 now, Maida. You'll be relieved of all your patients by-and-by, nurse; you must turn matron. Where is she? I thought I was speaking to her all this while.'

But nurse had vanished.

How smoothly now glided by the numbered days of the dying girl; how quietly did she enjoy her little library, which, before hidden beneath her pillow, now ventured into light of day; and, arranged on a little stool, over which Maida had spread one of her own pocket handkerchiefs, her Testament, Prayer-book, and hymns were always within reach.

The first time Maida arranged her bed, she found a new flannel petticoat tucked away behind the mattress. Inquiring why it was there, Wilcox explained that she had brought it on purpose to be buried in; but as nurse was always covetous, she had hidden it out of her sight.

'I'd have given it her, Maida, only it's so dreadful to think of being buried with no decent covering; but I'll gladly give it *you*—you may take it at once, or when I'm gone.'

'I will see it put on *you*, dear,' said Maida, as calmly as though only talking of dressing her the next morning.

'And you will close my eyes? Oh, I hope you'll be near when I die, or else you won't be let to do for me.'

'Maida,' she said, after a moment's pause, 'you'll think me very childish, but something troubles me. Do you think it's true that they cut up prisoners, and throw them any way into their coffins?'

'Yes; cut up as small as mincemeat,' called out nurse, who was passing at that instant; but Maida quickly answered:

'I know strange things are reported, but *I* do not believe one of them. In order to certify to government that the patients really die of the complaint stated in the books, the bodies are always examined after death, but that is all.'

'I hope so. A man who had been employed in Tench told me that once when he was carrying a coffin he heard the bones all rattling about as if they'd been loose in a box.'

'Wilcox, do you think when your soul is happy with Jesus, you will care what is done to your poor worn-out body?'

'Oh, no! Foolish me! Oh, blessed Lord Jesus! Forgive my folly; only let my soul go to Thee, and my body may be thrown anywhere: the meanest corner is too good for me.'

Next visiting-Thursday the ward was thrown into pleasant surprise by the entrance of a lady who asked for one Eliza Wilcox.

She could scarce believe that the skeleton called No. 1 was her former servant.

'My mistress!' exclaimed Wilcox.

'Yes, and I should have been to see you before but I've been too busy.'

She sat down and chatted a little; then rising to go, she looked round the ward.

'All very nice and clean here, and Mrs. Cott such a good creature, too; I dare say you are all very happy—eh, women?'

One and all curtsied, and the movement passed for a yes.

'Who is her nurse?'

'I am, ma'am,' replied Maida.

'No, ma'am, I am, said the nurse, guessing the drift of the inquiry; 'I do for this ward.'

'You are Wilcox's nurse, at any rate?' asked the lady, looking at Maida; 'well, then, this is for you;' she held out a half-crown.

Maida took it.

'I will buy her some tamarinds with it, ma'am.'

'You vile, sneaking jade,[15] cheating me out of my perkisites[16] in that way. May the money rot in your hand! I'd like to see the tamarinds you'll buy with it,' exclaimed the enraged official, when the lady had gone.

'Maida, don't,' whispered Wilcox; ''twill do me more harm than good.'

'Very well, then, I won't,' replied Maida, aloud; 'but I don't want the money; and if I give it to nurse, she'll spend it in drink; so it shall go to any poor soul who finds it.' With that she mounted the top of a stretcher, and raising her arm, flung the coin through the open window; and at the same moment the nurse flouted out of the ward.

'She's gone to spit her rage on Sal,' whispered the women to each other.

'God help her, poor soul!' ejaculated one.

'Maida, shall I tell you?' said Wilcox, softly, as her friend took her place again by her.

'Yes, dear, what you please.'

'Our Master would not have done that—He would have soothed the anger even of an enemy'.

'How do you know that?'

'Because it says He was meek and lowly, and did not strive.'

Maida became thoughtful, and then replied—

'You are right, I am wrong; I will go at once, and beg her pardon; I should have given her the money: my temper always hurries me into folly. But, Wilcox, you mustn't say our Master—I do not profess to follow Him.'

'Then why don't you? You don't know how it would help you, to profess it outright.'

'In what? I'm afraid you sadly mistake me.'

'No, I don't. I know you want to be one thing, and your temper makes you be something quite different. Maida, Maida, have I offended you?'

Maida shook her head; and then leaning towards her, said—

'Wilcox, I would gladly exchange places with you, and endure one hundred times over what you have endured, to be as near death as you are, with your hope and peace.'

'I would not exchange places with Queen Victoria!' exclaimed the dying girl. 'No! not with the Queen upon her throne. Hark! what's that?'

'Ja-sus! Ja-sus!' came in piteous accents from the closet outside the ward.

'It's poor Sal!'

'Jasus!—oh, Jasus!'

Maida started.

'Go, Maida, go; she is getting rubbed in the straw.'

'Oh! oh! oh! Jasus! Ja-sus!'

A fierce nod was Maida's only answer.

'There, you senseless beast; the sooner you're rotted away the better!' reached Maida's ear as she stepped into the closet. 'There,' and all covered as it was with wounds from long lying, nurse rubbed the body of the imbecile in the fresh straw beneath it, just as you would rub a rolling-pin into dough.

'Jasus! Jasus!' cried Crazy Sal.

'Leave her!' Passion and feeling would let Maida say no more.

'Leave her!' The words were scarcely articulate for rage.

'I tell you *what* now, Mrs. Martha Grylls, if you come meddling with me, I'll find a means to make you wish you'd never darkened my path, you—! You've sought the job, so you shall have it; come and see how you like it: sweet, refreshing, nice, b'ain't it?'

'I meant to take it, and I mean to be Sally's attendant for the future; if you say one word against it, you shall be turned out of your situation.'

Fury grinned in the woman's features, but she feared to obey its dictates; another complaint from Maida might be followed by worse consequences than was the former. With a daring oath she left the closet, slamming the door after her with such violence as to make the whole suite of wards shake.

When Maida approached Sally, the imbecile shrunk in terror, and cast at her a timid side-glance such as a dog, accustomed to ill-treatment, will shrinkingly cast towards some doubtful person who attempts to pat him.

'Never mind, poor Sally; I will not hurt you.'

She wiped the tears from the swollen face, and then, loathsome as it was in its cadaverous whiteness, she stooped kindly over it and kissed the scaly forehead.

'Jasus?' whispered Sally, almost in Maida's ear.

'Yes, Jesus, He loves you.'

'Loves me,' repeated the imbecile; then, yielding herself to Maida, she submitted to the painful dressing and cleansing operation, without further complaint than an occasional groan, as some very tender wound came in contact with the prickly straw.

Maida had just finished, and in clean cap and jacket, Sally lay back on a clean pillow, when with a tap at the door, Mr. Herbert entered.

'They said I should find you here, Maida.'

He shuddered as his eye fell on the imbecile, who, fatigued with the late exertion, had sunk back completely exhausted, looking more ghastly than ever.

Maida explained her case.

'She's faint! What a strange colour she has become; give her a sup of water, quickly,' said Mr. H.

Before it could touch her mouth the lip went up, and then, protracted to an unusual length, came the bray, discordant and soul-piercing.

The nurse, knowing that Mr. Herbert was there, ran in to tell him that the noise was nothing to be afraid of; Sally was a poor, harmless creature.

'Jasus, Jasus!' screeched the girl when she saw the nurse.

'Go out, woman! Your presence troubles her,' beckoned Maida.

Without signifying his intention, Mr. Herbert knelt by the stretcher, and looking reverently upward, said, slowly and distinctly—

'O Lord, thou Son of David, have mercy on her for she is grievously tormented.'[17]

He remained in silent prayer for a few moments, and then perceiving the swollen eyes of the imbecile fixed on him, he arose and stood by her.

'Does she not speak?'

'Only two words, the name of her home and that word you heard her call out.'

'That name, that is above every name! The name of Jesus, is one—'

'Jasus! Jasus!' cried Sally, catching up his words.

'Ay, He will hear you, poor stricken one! He despiseth not the cry of the destitute,'[18] sympathisingly replied Mr. Herbert.

'Jasus! Jasus!' she once more repeated, and then appeared to faint; but it was the faint of death. She opened her eyes and gave one look towards Mr. Herbert and Maida, then closed them forever upon her sufferings.

And who will say that when the Saviour of the world shall come, bringing His redeemed ones with Him, poor Crazy Sal shall not be seen among the lowly who have crept into Heaven by power of that name which is the only one whereby we can be saved?

Maida wished to stay and lay out the body, but Mr. Herbert would not allow her to do so: he bade her follow him into her own ward, where going over to Wilcox, he sat down on stretcher No. 2, and the lustrous eyes looked up gladly at him from No. 1. After a while he told Maida he brought what he feared would be bad news to her. He said Emmeline had expressed a strong desire for change of air, a request so unusual for her, that the doctor had granted it though doubtful of the consequences of the journey; but if *that* passed favourably, there was every hope the genial climate of Port Arthur might benefit her.

'Am I not then to return to the Lodge, sir?'

'Oh yes, Mr. Evelyn has left word that you are to be taken there when you receive your discharge. I thought,' he continued, smiling, 'that you would be disappointed to find my daughter absent; she longs for you very much.'

'Miss Evelyn is very good, I shall be sorry to miss her, sir,' was all Maida said, but she felt much more, and had a secret misgiving that she should not see her young mistress again.

'If we can get permission, we mean to send for you to come after us; you must not be too sanguine, though.'

'I am sanguine of nothing, sir. I am to be discharged in a fortnight; before then, perhaps, the master will make me acquainted with his wishes, which I shall be ready to obey.'

A fortnight, thought Wilcox; shall I be gone by that time? And she examined her thin hands to see how much thinner they must become ere she could reckon on her release—they had only a skin over them; as far as their emaciation could bid him, Death might come as soon as he pleased; disease could extort nothing more from her save a few sighs, a few more laboured breaths; a few more days of distress. Maida understood the action, and forgetting her own vexation, in beholding the anxious glance of her friend, said—

'Wilcox, ask Mr. Evelyn.'

'Sir, we are troubled with a question; we cannot decide it.'

Mr. Herbert looked kindly towards her, and then to Maida, who asked somewhat hastily—'Would it be wrong to pray that she may die before I go?'

'It were better not; trust to that Friend who loveth at all times. He will become more precious with the absence of your earthly friend, Wilcox.'

'It is not that, sir; were my absence all, Wilcox would have nothing to dread from my discharge; but there are things which your kind heart never, never dreams of, and which only a prisoner can know; these things make my presence very necessary to her, poor dear!'

'I dream of them more than you suppose, Maida, and my inability to prevent them is a sorrow only second to my grief for that blindness which perceives not the evil.'

A tear stood in Wilcox's eye.

'Wilcox,' said he, kindly, 'do you remember those lines—

"Sweet to lie passive in His hands
And know no will but His" [19]

'Trust yourself to Him who provides for the needs of His creatures. Be sure that the God who so studies the nature of the dumb animals as to appoint the rocks for a refuge to the timid coney, [20] will not desert you in your hour of trouble.'

'But He has, sir,' interrupted Maida.

'Hush, Maida, you know not what you say,' quickly said Mr. Herbert. 'Think a moment. Has there been no good brought out of the permitted evil of Wilcox's sufferings?'

He turned his eye as though he would read her innermost thoughts. A smile played on the lips of the dying girl; she exclaimed, 'Oh, sir! I will leave myself to Him. He will be with me when I pass through the waters; He will be more to me than mother, or father, or sisters could have been, had I been dying in my home. Sir, I forget I am a convict when I think of these things. Maida can go, for Jesus will be with me; but never, never can I forget her love and kindness. Oh, sir! when I am no more, do be her friend.' She caught Mr. Evelyn's hand, and, gazing earnestly, repeated—'Do, sir; will you promise me?'

Mr. Herbert gave the promise, and turned to ratify it to Maida, but she had left the ward.

'Farewell, Wilcox. I go to my own poor child, who is very ill, though not so far prostrated as you. Give me a message for her.'

'Make her promise to love Maida,' she promptly replied.

'Is that all?' said Mr. Herbert, smiling through his sadness.

'If I may make so free, sir, tell her—but it will pain you perhaps,'

'No, my child, I have long since resigned her.'

'Then tell her, sir, not to dread death. He is gentle as a lamb to those who are not his enemies. Maida is to have my Bible and hymn book; but will you give dear Miss Evelyn this little Prayer-book, and say that if she reads the last verse of the twenty-seventh Psalm, she will find a text that has often kept up the faith of a poor sinking soul—tell her the Lord's leisure is the best.'

She gave the little volume to Mr. Herbert; he pressed her hand, but spoke not a word in taking the parting gift.

From this moment the bitterness had passed. There were yet eight days to Maida's discharge; she strove to be cheerful, and her companion was so in reality; one Sunday more were they to spend together. That Sunday was to be a special one, for the bishop was to address the females of the establishment, or as many of them as could assemble in No. 4. A half hour before his lordship arrived, parties of invalids issued from all parts of the hospital, and occupied the extra benches. All free persons who could be spared from their duties attended to hear the bishop, who, precisely as the clock struck three, entered, fully robed, and followed by the superintendent and house doctor.

'Nurses at the beds, and all convicts at the benches,' said the doctor. With a malicious grin the nurse of No. 4 took her place by Wilcox, and pointed Maida to a seat at the opposite end of the ward. To dispute were useless. In silence Maida obeyed, and she had only just taken her seat, when his lordship's solemn voice commenced the service. But the service was nothing to her; she sat eagerly watching Wilcox. The sermon commenced; but not the touching parable of the Prodigal Son could divert her thoughts from No. 1. She saw the invalid put out her parched tongue and try to moisten her lips; she beckoned to the nurse to give her something to drink; but nurse was too intent on the sermon to receive the signal. So Maida arose, and despite his lordship's piercing eyes, which followed every step she took, walked to No. 1, and put a teaspoonful of liquid to her dry lips. She was about to return, when, casting a second look, she saw Wilcox raise her arms, give one smile—bright with anticipation—one breath, soft as the flutter of a tiny bird, and the soul of the convict was free. Hastily, ere nurse should perceive the event, dropped Maida by the couch; tenderly and reverently she bowed her head an instant, then, stretching forth her hand, she fulfilled her friend's last wish, and closed the eyes, which still looked upward, hopefully, longingly!

'Thank God!' she murmured, rising from her knees. The nurse turned round, and Maida pointed to the lifeless clay with an expression that would be triumphant through all the solemnity of the moment. She sat herself by the corpse, and strove to listen to the earnest appeal the bishop was making to the prodigals arranged in sombre brown before him; but the attempt was in vain; her thoughts wandered over that brief chapter of her life in which the dying girl had formed so striking a part. 'Yes,' she mentally exclaimed, 'Mr. Herbert is correct, good has worked out of the evil of this poor creature's suffering; it has taught me that which I craved to learn, that a convict can be saved—to doubt it were treason to the King of kings.'

This had long been a question in Maida's mind. She had listened eagerly, though unavowedly, to Mr. Herbert's and Emmeline's teaching; but she feared they who had never fallen could not rightly answer for the salvation of those who had yielded to sin, and she therefore yearned to meet with an example of convict salvation. In Wilcox she saw one who from equal condemnation, had been received into paradise.

'Hast thou but one blessing, oh, my father! Bless me, even me also,' she cried with her spirit's voice, as she watched the blessing that had fallen upon her who a few moments since was a captive pining for release.

She was aroused from her meditation by a pause in the sermon; it was over. Raising his hands, the bishop turned slowly round, at the same time saying, with peculiar distinctness, 'The peace of God, which passeth all understanding, keep your hearts and minds in the knowledge and love of God.' By this time he stood with his hands toward Maida, then he proceeded—'And the blessing of God Almighty, the Father, the Son, and the Holy Ghost, be amongst you, and remain with you always.'

It seemed that the bishop had read her thoughts. Maida sank upon her knees to receive the benediction; clasping her hands, she uttered a loud, fervent 'Amen,' as the last word fell. And the recollection of the incident which had once before brought that text to her mind, came with a comforting power, and she felt there was neither irreverence nor superstition in connecting it with the present occasion.

But the time had not yet come. The tranquillity she experienced vanished with the bishop. The door had scarcely closed upon his lordship, ere the nurse rushed over and thrust her arm into the stretcher where Wilcox lay. Thence she drew out the coveted treasure with so sudden a jerk that the head of the corpse bounced back with a heavy fall. Exhibiting the petticoat to the view of the women, she shouted—'This is mine!'

Maida, gently as she could, laid hold of the flannel, and said, 'I do not wish to quarrel, but I must have this. I promised she should be buried in it.'

'——if she shall; if you can *get* it, you shall have it: not else.'

Maida continued to hold on with a firm but gentle grasp.

'Matron's a-coming, better let her have it,' joined all the women.

'What'll 'e give me then, quick!'

'Nothing,' said Maida, quietly folding the garment.

Once in the dead-house, the corpse was beyond her care; so Maida could never ascertain whether the flannel formed its shroud. She feared not, for Mrs. Cott told her it belonged to the Queen. Now she cared not how soon her discharge might be. There were other cases of interest interspersed with the many that were only *schemers*—as the convict phraseology denominates a certain class of patients—but she did not wish to undertake another whom she must desert in a few days.

On the Tuesday she learned from Mrs. Cott that Mr. Evelyn's family had removed to Port Arthur, Mr. Herbert having exchanged duties with the chaplain of that settlement; but that Mr. Evelyn remained in town, having been unable to make suitable arrangements for leaving the Lodge, which was without a man-servant. Googe had been apprehended as chief party in an extensive coining fraud that for some time had baffled the police, and cheated the tradesmen out of their legal money.

Drawn and Etched by A. Kempel

"It seemed that the bishop had read Maude's
thoughts. She sunk upon her knees, and
clasping her hands uttered a loud, fervent
'Amen.'"

Mrs. Cott told Maida that she believed her master was waiting to put her in the place of a man; on which Maida said, that as far as guarding the house went, she should not at all mind the charge. Thursday arrived. Maida received her discharge, and bade good-bye to the patients. When it was nurse's turn, she offered her hand, but that worthy refused it, saying, she had only one hope, and that was, that she should still be in the hospital when Maida came in to die; wouldn't she make a frightful corpse of her, that's all! She'd stretch her eyes wide open instead of closing them like a Christian.

'I'll forgive you if you do,' said Maida, forcing a smile; 'I am afraid you would close them in self-defence after a while. I should look so frightful.'

Ere descending the stairs she peeped into the closet where Crazy Sal had lain; it was still empty. She pitied the next object who should be there exposed to the unchecked malice of the wretched being chosen as nurse for the ward and its dependencies.

Does the reader wish to ask any question ere Maida's departure shuts the hospital to his inquiry?

'Why did the convicts bear such persecution without complaining to the proper authorities?' In all politeness may we be allowed to suggest that you wait for a reply until you become a prisoner; then you will know why, far better than we can explain.

CHAPTER 29

Port Arthur—O.P.S.O.—The *Kangaroo*

HIS Excellency the Lieutenant-governor having duly and formally signified his approval of the admission of the Reverend Herbert Evelyn and family into the sacred regions of Port Arthur,[1] and the comptroller-general having promised to apprise the superintendent of the settlement of their visit, in order that the wagons might be in waiting for them on their arrival, one bright morning in the month of February, Emmeline, accompanied by her father and cousin, took her place on board the *Kangaroo*, the government steam-boat plying between Hobarton and the Peninsula; and shortly after, a second cab set down Mrs. Evelyn and her children on the jetty, when Charlie speedily found his way to his uncle, and became vociferously jubilant at the prospect of a trip down the river, as the water route to Tasman's Peninsula is denominated. The free passengers were ready to start. A young lieutenant just bearing away his still more youthful bride to the ungainly solitude of Eagle Hawk Neck, was fast increasing his impatience with the increasing moments; when tramp-a-tramp, chink-a-chink along the road, and chained two together a gang of second-sentence men drew near. Ere they could reach the wharf a band of armed soldiers drew up on each side of the jetty, and at word of command, as the gang approached, they pointed their muskets, forming a guarded pathway for the convicts, who two by two passed through it and hobbled on board the steamer, where crowded together they had to stand out the passage. Quickly followed a band of probationers, bound for the Cascades—and then the soldiers divided—part marching into the boat after the men, the others returning to Hobart. It was now half-past seven; the captain mounted the paddle-wheel, gave the signal, and in another moment the *Kangaroo* was off, pattering on her way, most unlike her namesake, which with a hop, skip, and jump, gives chase to the fleetest huntsman.

Not having been told that the vessel was a prison transport, Bridget had looked forward with much delight to the scenery which makes a sail down the Derwent a *sine qua non*[2] to the beauty seekers of our antipodean shores. With the sight of the felons vanished all her dreams of pleasure, for she could not with one eye view the misery of her fellow creatures, and with the other dwell admiringly on the landscape; she must look all, feel all, pity all, or admire all, or else shut her eyes altogether.

'Can we never escape from them?' she whispered to Emmeline, as winding round the wharf moved slowly onwards the alternate tramp and clank. There was a time when Bridget would have turned from the spectacle which the deck presented as one not so pleasant to behold as that which lay before her in the distant hills; but now in vain opened to view magnificent scenes from the coasts of Frederick Henry Bay; in vain reared up the Iron Pot its grotesque dimensions, it awoke in her no curiosity; nor did the surf which boiled around its base attract her attention. The grand tumult of Storm Bay, the quiet farm of Slopen Island, were nothing to her so long as chains dragged down the hands and oppressed the feet of those with whom she was forced into contact.

The day was fair and cloudless. The breeze tempered the heat into a bearable degree; so that when the glare of the sun was excluded by an awning, it was luxurious to sit yielding to the gentle sway of the vessel, and watching the ever changing, yet ever lovely, pictures which one by one disclosed themselves from unexpected nooks and windings of the river.

Mr. Herbert, Emmeline, and Bridget, unable to join in the hilarity of the free passengers, abstracted themselves from the general party and occupied the sofa on the lee-side of the skylight, where their seclusion was only occasionally disturbed by the onslaughts of Charlie, desperate with scraps of news, or colonial legends inflicted on him by the mate.

Irrespective of anxiety for his daughter's comfort, Mr. Herbert was little inclined to talk.

He had discovered among the second-sentencers several of his flock, who only the Sunday before had listened to his admonition from the Penitentiary pulpit. His spirit yearned for them; he was aware what they would have to go through in the fierce retributive process of which he knew Port Arthur to be the furnace. *Hard* they were sent down—but *harder* they would return; perhaps again to be sent down—again to be returned *hardened* and only fit for Norfolk Island, where the process would be carried on to a greater perfection, because detached from the public gaze, and more distant from the chief authorities, who were never known to approach the shores without timely notice, to afford opportunity for the hurrying into corners of all that might offend their judicial eyes, or call for their judicial interference.

Mr. Herbert was not long on board before his eye had scanned the gang, and selected thence two men, who, for desert, were more fit for the penal settlement than half who were condemned there.

The savagely sullen brow and heavy eye of Bradley, the constable, were unmistakable, for all that his hair was closely cropped, and his head covered by the leathern cap of the convict.

By some strange caprice or thoughtlessness, he had been chained to Bob Pragg, who, notwithstanding the discomfort of his situation, secretly gloried in being the means of annoying his enemy by sticking as close into him as possible. Every now and then, with a sudden shove Bradley would push him to the extent of the chain, when back would stick Bob with the tenacity of a bulldog. Mr. Herbert perceived this, and kept his eye fixed on the pair, hoping to stop a proceeding which he feared, though almost laughably trifling in itself, might end in a court of justice. The heavier gathering of Bradley's bushy brow increased his fears. But Pragg was out of the parson's parish—nothing was to be gained by hearkening to him—nothing was to be saved by not frisking his foe; so averting his head he continued to irritate Bradley. Mr. Herbert then asked an overseer to unchain the two and bind them to some other prisoners; but the overseer refused, supposing 'they were only sparring it a bit; maybe in fun, for it takes the deuce to get their tricks out of them—or more like in spite, which nobody expects to kick out of them.'

Mr. Herbert asked if any known spite existed between the men—and learnt that they were sworn foes, perpetually bent on worrying each other.

'The last offence between 'em,' said the officer, 'had something to do with that burial ground murder, for which Sam Tonkins is to be hanged. When Bradley was caught, he vowed vengeance on Pragg, and made out a case against him; but the evidence wasn't very clear, so the bench let him off with three months at Port Arthur. You see, sir, till the men have had a taste of down there, they don't know how to value Tench privileges.'

'It is a dangerous precedent to give a man a taste of poison to make him appreciate simple medicine,' replied Mr. Herbert, despairing of making an impression on the overseer, who was a devoted disciple of the stringencies of the penal code.

Bridget was very glad that her cousin required her attention, for brooding over the brightness of day was a mass of human suffering to which she could not choose but turn whenever her thoughts were at her disposal. It appeared to her an unnecessary strictness to keep the men chained hand and foot when escape was impossible; and she watched her opportunity to tell the captain so; for though she knew they were not bound by his command, she hoped he might have some power in giving them at any rate a temporary freedom of limb. Jocose and hearty the captain came round to pay his devoirs to the parson's daughter and niece, and Bridget, long in wait for his approach, came forward blushing for an attack on the humane principles of the well-proportioned sailor.

'Your servant, miss,' he bowed, laying his hand upon his heart.

'Oh! Captain Jolly, can't you let loose those poor creatures?' burst out from Bridget's lips ere she could acknowledge his gallantry.

'Well—don't see how; they might fly overboard, and that would be awkward, seeing they are paid for. Go down in the cabin if they annoy you, miss.'

'They don't *annoy* me—they make me sad.'

'Well, I never viewed it in that light, Miss D'Urban; it seems to me rather comfortable to hear them piping away like six o'clock; if they don't pipe us to supper they remind us of it, and that's next best. On my honour, I don't know what we poor sea-dogs would do without our poultry.'

'Oh, captain! I meant the prisoners.'

'Bless my heart alive, miss! Let them loose? *We* should be in Davy's locker, sure as fate, before we'd spun much farther and *they'd* be on their way to California.[3] Did you never hear how they overhauled the bishop's frigate[4]? And—ha! ha!—bless my heart alive, miss, as my name's Jolly, '*twould* be jolly to strike the darbies off[5] that precious lot: we might as well leap overboard at once.'

'Horrid creatures! Whatever is it, captain?' inquired Mrs. Evelyn, who, baby in arms, just crossed the deck in time to hear the last words.

'Nothing, madam; only miss proposes we shall change places with the gang; and, on my honour, I've no inclination that way.'

Seeing Mrs. Evelyn look mystified, he explained: 'Miss is begging of me to cut away their cables, and I tell her they'd overhaul us before we could cry "Mercy!"'

'Really, Bridget, my dear, you do make yourself very silly; you mustn't listen to her, Captain Jolly: she has the most romantic notions about the convicts. I do believe she'd set them all free if she could: yes, and I believe *you* would, too, Herbert,' added Mrs. Evelyn, as she observed a quiet smile on his face.

'I should certainly give liberty to a great many,' replied Mr. Herbert, very gently.

'On my honour, parson, you take the Queen's money to some purpose.[6] What would they do with their liberty if you gave it them?'

'Get into trouble again as fast as they could,' answered Mrs. Evelyn. 'In fact, it's my opinion they are never happy unless they *are* in trouble.'

Bridget looked into the assembled gang for one single sign of happiness: not one appeared; desolation, despair, or defiance sat on all the sunburnt, blistered faces.

Mr. Herbert noted his niece's silent comment on her aunt's observation, and involuntarily following her example, his eye also wandered through the human indices for some reference to the imputed happiness; but none was visible in the dreary blank of countenance, or in the darkly written page of crime, whose physiognomy was full of meaning; but of what sort?

'Well, now, parson, supposing you had government permission to uncage a few of those precious birds, which of all those now before you would you let out? Yonder are two likely lads—those there—that keep spurring it like game-cocks.'

'I should be cautious in giving liberty to any man who had once entered a penal settlement. I consider all who have *once* been to Port Arthur, or other places of second punishment, most dangerous characters; but I should be glad to arrest the progress of half who are on their way there.'

'Well, I don't know anything about that: I'm paid to take 'em backwards and forwards—the deuce *I* care how many or how few get aboard, so long as my pay don't shift to suit the rise and fall of 'em.'

Captain took a turn to and from the paddle-wheel, and then, coming to Mr. Herbert, asked:

'But I say, parson, if we locked our penal settlements, what could we do with our second-sentencers if we'd no place to send them to? A hang they'd care for the judge and all the bench: they'd point their fingers at us, and off again to their tricks. Without our Port Arthurs we should have a constant repetition of that jolly farce of Louisa Ferres.'[7]

'I would not do away with our penal settlements, Mr. Jolly, until some well-digested plan were formed for the better lodgement of our men; but I would have the settlements conducted under a different system. It is not wise to trust the best men with unlimited power; the heart's vanity cannot stand it. Abstracted from the inspection of the public as these settlements are, there cannot be too much care in the selection of fitting instruments to work the system. Where there are several hundreds of men all at the mercy of one free man, what is to be expected if that free man be one of ferocious temper or ambitious views? This man, though ostensibly under the supervision of colonial authority, rules supreme over his miserable dependents; for what can comptrollers or governors, not being omniscient, know of the daily occurrences of a place seventy or a hundred and fifty miles distant?'

'Oh! There's a regular correspondence kept up between them; everything is reported.'

'Yes; the representations which reach Hobarton present a fair account of matters progressing to the satisfaction of——, the superintendent! There is no *dis*satisfaction or maltreatment of the convicts to blot the seemly foolscap. The comptroller reads, approves, and applauds the judicious officer, who so skilfully manages to keep down five hundred rebels in subjection, at once *un-irksome* to themselves and beneficial to the colony in general.'

'But then the comptroller goes down to see for himself.'

'Truly! The authorities visit the settlement and examine the police reports, which are all entered by a paid and, most likely, convict clerk, who, if the latter, must obey the orders of his superior unquestioningly and willingly, or be turned into the chain-gang; or, if a free man, can only deviate from the injunctions of his master at peril of a nod of dismissal, procured for him from the official head by a single word whispered by the superintendent. The reports, duly examined and commented upon, display praiseworthy vigilance; for entries of all punishments inflicted have been conscientiously made. The comptroller reads that one man has been chastised for misconduct, another for insolence; but whether such misconduct or insolence was *provoked* out of them, or was a wilful fault, does not appear in the entry.'

'Ha! ha! parson, anyone can see you've been amongst convicts; you've grown suspicious; can't trust your neighbour.'

'Well, really, captain, we *must* be suspicious in self-defence; with rogues on all sides, what should we do if we placed confidence in our people?' said Mrs. Evelyn, for once agreeing with her brother-in-law.

'I speak of *free*, madam; Mr. Evelyn looks foul-eyed on all.'

'Do not misunderstand me, Mr. Jolly; I make no personal reference; the present superintendent may be an excellent commandant.'

'You only refer to them as a lot: well, they are a rum lot; but for all that, what fault can you find with Port Arthur?'

'No: I'm sure it's a delightful place, all so clean and nice; really it's like a fresh-scrubbed room. If it was a dirty place I couldn't take the children there if you'd pay me for it, my dear,' chimed in Mrs. Evelyn to Mr. Herbert.

'Nothing is fairer than a whited sepulchre,[8] Clara; nothing sounds better in the many books which have been written of travels in our island than an account of visits to the prison stations: the cleanliness is lauded, the healthful appearance of the place noted, until one almost longs to become a convict, to dwell in so delightful a spot, and to be under treatment of so kind, so hospitable, so humane a man as the superintendent of the book. The traveller is bewitched; he sees through a false medium, and notes accordingly. Not knowing that one of the strictest penal rules is that the convicts shall touch their caps to their superiors, he observes the simultaneous movement to the superintendent, and mentions it as a gratifying proof of the men's affection, or, at any rate, of their esteem for their governor. And I do not blame him; the rod is hidden from his sight; how should he discover it? All is fair; why should he not rejoice in it?'

'Well, parson, so long as I'm not meddled with I'm as willing as any man alive to have a change, but as to what *you* want, we may stick in the mud till kingdom come if we wait for it; the deuce knows when your well-digested plan *will* be formed, and I also guess his satanic majesty'll try to put it off as long as he can.[9] Government has been playing battledore[10] and shuttlecock[11] with their system for many a long year, and, for all I see, been making duck and drake and young ones with their money, excepting *my* salary.'

'I agree with you there, Mr. Jolly. I do not believe the well-digested plan will ever be formed, for while we have sin to battle with, the strife must continue. Colonel Arthur's words, "What God hath made crooked, man cannot make straight,"[12] appear to me the correct solution of the convict puzzle; however, let us go on availing ourselves of such improvements as experience shall suggest. Having seen that there is danger in giving to *one* man unbounded authority over his fellow creatures, let us circumscribe his power by placing others to share it with him. Having seen that transportation, as *now* carried on, is a punishment of *revenge* and not of *reform*, let us use our individual efforts to practically convince the prisoners that, in banishing them from their native land, government has their best interest at heart, that England sends her unhappy sons from her, not as outcasts so much as penitents.'

'Now, parson, tell us, would *you* be superintendent if you could?'

'I would not, sir. I could not trust myself. I might commence with every good intention, but unrestricted power would soon make a despot of me.'

A loud flop on the other side of the deck prevented the captain's answer: he went across to see what had happened, then returned, whistling till he reached his party.

'It's nothing; only one of the gang has fainted, tired of standing in the sun, I suppose, and, in falling, he's played the deuce with his mate, overhauling him head uppermost.'

Mr. Herbert hastily went to the unfortunate men. The overseer, seeing the commiserating expression of his face, said:

'Only scheming, sir, take my word for it; pity's lost on them; why should *one* faint more than another?'

'That livid countenance does not look much like scheming, sir. I insist on your unchaining him, and giving him the assistance he requires.'

Sulkily went the overseer to work, muttering:

'We shall have the whole gang a-fainting if *this* is what they get for it.'

Bradley, who was close by, and had marked the whole proceeding, made a note of these words and his heavy brow lowered portentously as he stowed them away in his imbruted mind.

It was not long after that a second heavy flop was heard, and looking to the spot, Mr. Herbert saw that Bradley had fallen and Pragg lay sprawling on the top of him.

'I s'pose we must undo them too,' grumbled the overseer, 'mustn't be partial.'

'*No*, just extricate Pragg from Bradley; but I would not have the chains removed from either,' said Mr. Herbert, who had heard the grumble, though it was not meant for him.

But just out of spite the overseer *would* release them: he had barely done so, than, with the roar of an uncaged lion, up started Bradley, knocked him down, caught up a handcuff and struck Pragg a blow that felled him to the deck and made the blood flow from his head. Bradley then flung himself on his hands and knees and lapped up the blood.

'I swore to hell I'd never rest till I'd spit your own blackguard blood in your face; now, here it is!'

All this took place in a moment, ere anyone could stop the ruffian or overcome the first shock of surprise. All free hands now rushed forward, the enraged overseer among them. Bradley, surrounded by his bond brethren, whose fettered limbs prevented their laying hold of him, kept his opponents at bay by hurling at them such missiles as he could seize hold of.

'Grace to the man that catches him,' shouted the captain.

'Conditional pardon to him,' out-shouted the overseer.

'Death to him,' growled Bradley.

And the men who had tried to raise their arms to clutch him let them drop with a clank that rang through the boat. There was a simultaneous click of musketry.

'Surrender, or we fire!'

A moment's awful silence.

'I surrender!' cried Bradley, dropping his arms to his side.

There was a general move towards him.

'But not to you!' And dashing through the crowd of prisoners he sprang overboard, and far splashed the waters into the air as his body cleft them asunder and lost itself beneath them.

All was commotion, but none dared venture after him. Up rose the body at a short distance—again to sink—the waters, gurgling, closed upon it, and the ripples spread as calmly onward as though no immortal soul had perished beneath them. Who dares that soul to follow in its dreary progress—downward—downward, ever downward—for the pit is bottomless, and the doom eternal. The voice of inspiration hath pronounced it so—downward, ever downward—who may stay the doomed spirits?—falling—falling—falling! They gnaw their tongue and look upward, but all too late comes the upward glance, for the eye of love beholds it not; the cry is bitter, and the torment cruel, but relief comes not; the ear of mercy is deaf. God forgetteth to be gracious for the day of grace hath passed.

Mrs. Evelyn declared she could not proceed, but, with the children, would be put out at the next settlement. Mr. Herbert was not averse to this, for Emmeline, though uncomplaining, suffered from the frightful shock that had shaken the stoutest set of nerves on board. He was anxious to get her ease from the excitement which it was impossible to escape whilst on the scene of the catastrophe. Though his feeling was only one of deep and awed solemnity, commingled with sorrow, and though he did not participate in his sister-in-law's fear of being murdered in cold blood if he remained on board, he considered it desirable to afford his child a respite from a fatigue, for the endurance of which the appalling occurrence had wholly unfitted her; therefore, when the steamer stopped at Impression Bay, he agreed to disembark and go with Mrs. Evelyn to the house of a friend, the religious instructor of the settlement, and there remain the week which must elapse ere they could proceed by the *Kangaroo* on their journey to Port Arthur.

Expected or unexpected friends are always welcome on penal stations. Isolated from the rest of the world, the officers are glad of any interruption to the monotonous routine of their stationary life. The inundation of the Evelyns was therefore an event productive of much enjoyment, both to the instructor and his wife, who managed to stow away all the family except Mr. Herbert and Charlie, who were obliged to seek shelter in the doctor's quarters.

Impression Bay is an invalid station where the incapacitated convicts pass out their lives in such rest or labour as their case demands or their strength permits. To Mr. Herbert there was nothing new either in the settlement or neighbourhood; but when Emmeline was well enough to be left, he made Bridget run out with him to take a peep at the densely wooded country around, or to look out on the bay as it appeared from land.

The gardens delighted her. Summer's bright flowers lay with a languid, luxurious ease that imparted, or would have imparted, to her a dreamy sense of pleasure, had she been any other than Bridget D'Urban. But there was no dreaminess in her pleasures: they were real, they were earnest. When her uncle preferred to stay with her cousin, she would snatch up the baby, summon Charlie, and be off to the gardens for a frolic amid the roses. One day a thunderstorm overtook them there. Baby had not yet learned to fear thunder; but as peal clashed on peal, Charlie clung tightly to Bridget to hide himself, and to wish 'that God's many drums didn't play so drefful loud.' Hurrying back with her young charge, the heavy rain obliged Miss D'Urban to stop under the roof of a deserted constable's hut. She had not been here long before she and Charlie were terrified by a howl that seemed to come from within a wall near by, and yet was despairing enough to have issued from the infernal regions. It was repeated again and again. The drenching rain was more endurable, so off ran Bridget, carrying baby under her arm. An overseer's wife, seeing her panting on, opened her door, and begged her to come in. Nothing loath, she entered. When Charlie promptly declared to the woman that they had heard 'all sorts of drefful wild beasts over there.' Thinking he only meant the thunder, she took him upon her lap and told him, though they had devils and wild cats in the island, they had not any lions or tigers, so he need not fear. But when Miss D'Urban told her that, wild beast or not, they had been alarmed by the most doleful wail that ever mortal heard, the wife began to wonder whence the noise could have proceeded, and wondered on until her eldest boy burst into a laugh.

'Oh! 'Twas nothing, mother; 'twas only from the Cranky Yard.'

Bridget asked what undesirable yard that might be, and was informed it was a portion of the station appropriated to the insane, and the cries thence were often heartrending.

'"It's nothing but the Cranky Yard" is what they all tell us, miss; but I'm for thinking that the nothing's a great deal, only we mustn't say these things,' said the wife.

Perceiving that her auditor appeared interested, she drew her chair over, and sending Charlie to play, continued, in a low tone:

'Twas only last week, miss, that one of these poor creatures behaved bad, and was put in irons. Well, he was taken ill, and died. When he was near death he begged hard to have his irons taken off, that he might die unfettered, as any one of us would naturally wish; but his keeper wouldn't free him, so he breathed out his soul, lying on his face, with his hands chained behind him. God have mercy on his poor dear soul!'

Bridget stamped with indignation.

'There's no help for it, miss; we mustn't speak out our minds on these things, only just to each other; then each of us pretends not to believe them—*but*,' she shook her head.

'Why are these cruelties permitted?' at last asked Bridget.

'They are not permitted. I doubt whether they ever reaches the superintendent's ear in a way that shows cruelty. 'Twas the officer of the yard that was to blame for that poor dear creature.'

A tear glistened in her eye; wiping it off with the corner of her apron, she said:

'Faith, miss, I call everything *dear* that's suffering. I tell my husband sometimes that my very bread chokes in my throat that goes down with such money. There's only two ways of getting on out here, and them are—to make one's heart hard as quick as possible, or to get out of government work altogether. My husband's been through nearly all the stations, hoping what *was* in one *wouldn't* be in another; he's tried this last, thinking as 'twas invalid there couldn't be anything against one's feelings here; but now—ah, there!—it's no use talking, and I shouldn't say so much to you only it's known the colony over that Parson Evelyn's family is all the convicts' friend; and I've heard say that if the convicts rose they'd be as safe as Goshen[13] in the midst of it, and Squire Evelyn, too, for all he holds on for discipline. Ah, miss, the men knows who's who.'

In her delight at hearing her uncles so praised, Bridget nearly forgot the Cranky Yard; but Charlie came running in to say, not only that the rain had ceased, but that the beasts were making their noises again:

'Come and hear 'em then.'

'There, miss, you'd hardly believe, though I hears them every day I'm not a bit better pleased with it; I can't bear to know there's suffering going on; and 'tisn't only because they are my own flesh and blood; I was just the same time back, when I was young, when the Aborgenes was served so shameful.'

Bridget, supposing rightly that she meant Aborigines, asked to what treatment she referred.

'Oh, miss! They was shot down like rabid dogs; hunted on their own grounds just like kangaroos. I don't know the rights of it; I suppose it was needful, or 'twouldn't have been done: but, child as I was, I couldn't like it better on that account.'[14]

Bridget resolved to consult Uncle Herbert on the subject, and thanking her hostess, she made hasty way to the religious instructor's quarters. Uncle Herbert and Emmeline were alone, the instructor having gone to his duties, and his wife being elbow-deep in culinary hospitalities. Bridget, therefore, still irate with her subject, rushed at once into the inquiry:

'Uncle, what has become of all the Aborigines? I haven't seen one of them ever since I have been here.'

'They are confined in Oyster Cove, and supported by government;[15] the *all* consists of but twenty-three; poor things! It is sad to behold them. They bequeath us a legacy for which we shall have to answer when God makes inquisition for blood. "Whoso sheddeth man's blood, by man shall his blood be shed,"[16] is a denunciation as true of nations as of individuals; and to them who mark these things, retribution is clearly discernible in national records. Thoughtful readers of Tasmanian history must tremble to think *how* and *where* the retributive stroke shall fall on England or her dependencies. When they read of barbarities disgraceful to a Christian people; of murdered women; of tortured children, they can only turn and pray the anticipating prayer—"Lord, in judgment remember mercy, and visit not these sins on the head of innocence."'

But the Wednesday again came round, and with it duly appeared the steamer, puffing its goods into the bay, there to exchange them after the fashion of Aladdin's lamp merchant. A few weak, miserable-looking men were delivered to an overseer, and Mr. Herbert's party embarked in their stead.

Captain Jolly hailed Bridget as an old acquaintance, and vowed himself her humble servant so long as she required no more chains struck off from his men. She informed him that last week's catastrophe had by no means lessened her inclination in that way.

'Bless your heart alive, miss; talk of irons! You should go aboard the *Lady Franklin* when she's on for Norfolk Island: you'd have double chains, cross chains, deck chain—chains enough to last out the term of your natural life, as the law has it; though what or where the other life is, the deuce knows, for I'm sure I don't. Yes, you must see the *Lady Franklin*, nothing complete without her; though it's a beggarly compliment to her living ladyship to turn out her name in such a rigging as that.'

Bridget was very glad when the garrulous captain was needed forward, for he was not her style of thinker. The day was fair and cloudless as the sky of a last week in February could make it. The *Kangaroo* pattered briskly on, stopping to take a short breath at Salt Water River, and a longer at Cascades,* in order to deliver some probationers to the superintendent, and to take in a few second-sentencers for Port Arthur. Then steaming round Expectation Point, and passing Woody Island, it soon brought its journey to an end in Norfolk Bay. Here fresh disappointment awaited Bridget, who, having watched the debarkation and marching off of the chain-gang, looked for some approaching vehicle that promised the safe conveyance guaranteed by the comptroller-general. She had heard so much of the wagons which were to be in waiting at Norfolk Bay, that in looking far ahead for the teamed bullocks, which she expected to see toiling up the hill, she failed to note nearer preparations.

'Come, my dear, come,' at last said her aunt; 'make haste and look here before your uncle returns; he mustn't see it. Take this and put it on the seat of the wagon behind you; and when you get in, just point to it and nod to the men, and then you'll be all right and safe. I wouldn't venture in without, or those fellows would of course upset us.'

She opened a little basket, and gave Bridget a half-pound of tea and some tobacco.

---

* This Cascades must not be confounded with the female house of correction, Hobarton.

'Why mustn't Uncle Herbert see it? He'd be delighted to give the poor fellows a few comforts.'

'Nonsense, my dear; as a government officer he couldn't allow us to break the rules, which are strict against rewarding the convicts, especially with tobacco; but I wouldn't go without giving it to please anyone; they make nothing of upsetting a person they dislike. Why, my dear, they pitched the comptroller over, and he trundled down the hill for ever so far.'

'Now then, we are ready,' said Mr. Herbert, stepping back to the jetty.

Bridget's wonder increased, for she saw no sign of readiness save in a number of low carts that looked like luggage-trucks with very long handles, and seats for more delicate parcels. Her wonder abounded when she saw Mr. Herbert lift Emmeline into the foremost cart. Thus, then, had her rustic wagons dwindled into a conveyance rough and dangerous; how she trembled as she remarked the small rickety iron wheels! Mr. Herbert then packed her in behind Emmeline, reserving the seat next his daughter for himself. Mrs. Evelyn and the children were stowed away in the second wagon, three other passengers in the third, and the boxes in the last three.

What an odd way of doing things, to get in *first* and yoke the horses afterwards, thought Bridget; but in the act of thinking it she heard a shrill whistle.

'All right! G'on there!'

'Is the sick lady easy before we start, sir?' asked a convict of Mr. Herbert, who with no slight anxiety was watching proceedings.

'Quite, thank you,' smiled Emmeline.

'Where are the horses?' said Bridget.

A queer grin passed from lip to lip as each prisoner spat into his hand and pressed a firm downward hold on the shafts of the vehicle. But one man turned on Bridget a face so full of shame and misery that she felt ready to cry for having asked the question. There was something in this man's appearance wholly different from the others; a low melancholy settled on his not unpleasing countenance, while his bearing was that of superior birth. A smart whack on his shoulders from the overseer's thong made him withdraw his eyes from Bridget, and sent a flush of indignation to his sunken cheeks; his fingers snapped audibly in the palm of his hands in their longing to repay the insult; but he must bear it in silence—nay, even with respect—for he is a convict and the other a free man.

'To your place with your impudence, staring at the lady,' cried the overseer.

The man again laid hold of the shaft; a bar was placed across it, and preparations were complete.

'He is not equal to the exertion,' whispered Mr. Herbert to the officer.

'Must *get* equal to it, then, sir; he knows where to look for pity, and finds it's no use to show off down here, where magpie is magpie whether it feathers a gentleman or a snob.[17] G'on here!'

Another touch of the human horses, and off they trotted; now down, then up, as the inequalities of the very unequal road required. Five miles of ground had thus to be run over; warm work beneath the heat of summer! The velocity with which the wagons rushed over the declivities by its reaction partly impelled them up the succeeding eminence, but for this assistance their progress must have been alike wearisome to the passengers, and exhausting to the runners. Now a nervous excitement supported the spirits of the former and a fierce excitement the energy and strength of the latter, while toiling, tearing on by the wooden rails, they guided the trucks over the tram-road, and that without stopping for nearly three miles, when the halfway station allowed the panting, perspiring steeds a rest. Here a relay awaited those who were too done up to run out the journey to Long Bay.

'Now get up your steam, and quick, for we're late,' commanded the overseer.

This order was unnecessary, for the men were steaming with a vengeance. Their respiratory organs worked vociferously. There was a general play of chests, and amid the loud, quick breathings of eighteen, it was difficult to hear the word of command as it bandied about from officer to officer. The eighteen pairs of hands could scarcely relax their clutch of the heaving sides to wipe off the perspiration streaming from under the leathern caps and over the blistered faces of the runners.

'Old hands take places—relays forward, new hands back,' shouted the overseer.

Six convicts retired and six others joined the twelve old hands. The man who had attracted Bridget's attention remained.

'You back, you haven't done steaming yet,' motioned the driver; 'back I say, you Forbes.'

Forbes refused by a gloomy shake of the head, and then laid hold of the shaft.

'Back!' repeated the overseer, raising his arm. 'You'll burst by the way, and that's what you're after I expect, making to be a martyr.'

'There are other means,' muttered Forbes, resigning his hold; and receiving a grin from his comrades, he turned morosely away, and Mr. Herbert followed him.

'Forbes! I am very grieved to meet *you* here.'

'I am sorry for nothing that helps to kill me.'

'For what are you here?'

'I declined obedience to a brother convict appointed constable over our set. Constable Bradley it was; but, sir, don't question me—my teeth are set on it *all*, and I am determined to bear on till—'

He pushed from Mr. Herbert ere the latter had time to reply. The overseer commented:

'Sour as a crabstick—you'll get nothing but vinegar out of he—he hasn't spoken a dozen words to anyone since he's been down here, and he won't look a body in the face. I tell you, sir, I'd rather have a gang of these here men than I'd have *one* such as him.'

'Undoubtedly,' replied Mr. Herbert quietly, but in a tone that silenced him.

'I should like to see how *he'd* bear it!' burst from Bridget's overboiling indignation, as the driver moved off. 'If that isn't giving double punishment to gentlemen, I don't know what double punishment is.'

'Hush!' whispered Emmeline.

'Well, *why* should he have more just because he's a gentleman—it is a great enormous shame, it is.'

'I don't suppose these things which make the punishment so severe are known at home; but *do* hush—see, the men are staring at you—and nothing is more displeasing to them than to hear a superior convict pitied above themselves.'

'I pity them too—yes, to my heart I do; but then they are all punished alike. Nobody agrees with me about the worse treatment of—'

'I agree with you,' said Uncle Herbert, looking over his shoulder, 'but it is easier to agree as to the disease than to discover a remedy.'

'Then it ought *not* to be,' cried Bridget; 'they ought not to go on tearing out one man's heart while they only cut a limb off another—maiming this man, but killing that one—such cruel, unequal treatment.'

'Ah! it's a theme full of doubt and difficulty,' thought Mr. Herbert half aloud, and his eyes unconsciously wandered to Forbes, who with folded arms, drooping head, and a despairing fixedness of countenance, leaned against a bark hut, yielding one leg to a convict constable who was preparing to clasp the cross irons upon it, now that freedom of limb was no longer required for the tram. The chains being fast set upon his legs, he was ordered forward to a carrying gang.

'What's the delay, my men?' asked Mr. Herbert, turning with a sigh from Forbes.

'Naught, sir, only there's a tug a-coming there that'll take the wind out of us; hold on, ladies, or you'll be flunked right overboard when we shies off the top.'

'But there's 'most a mile to get to it,' growled a second.

A steep ascent lay before them. Mr. Herbert placed his arm round Emmeline and drew her to himself; the overseer jumped up behind Bridget.

'G'on here!' and, with a desperate shove from the hinder men and a corresponding pull of the foremost, the wagons were again in motion, the snorting, puffing of the runners serving the wooden railway for the noise of an engine. The ascent was gained: the hill on the other side drew forth a universal shudder as the order, 'Steady!—jump up!—and away,' was given. There was a swift, simultaneous movement of the hind men. Without stopping, they sprang on the backs of the vehicles—where, tucking themselves up, they depended, drag-like, from the bar to which they clung; then with a shout from each overseer away dashed the loaded cars down over the frightful steep. As the danger increased with the accelerating motion, the runners one by one jumped on the sides of the cars, till all were perched up; and the wagons had nothing save these human drags to stay their headlong progress—then, heedless of all impediments, on dashed the rumbling train, now quivering on the brink of a jagged precipice, then seeming to gather speed to the music of children's screeches and frightened passengers' cries for mercy. One by one the men dropped off when, nearing the goal, the wagons ran on more level ground, shortly to stop at the jetty of Long Bay, where the penal boat's crew waited to row the tired party to the settlement beyond.

It was almost dark. The Southern Cross already faintly showed itself from the gray sky, and ere the three miles of water brought them to the last jetty every bright star was out, and the lights of the station blinked in the distance.

'My poor child, you are quite worn out!' said Mr. Herbert, as Emmeline leant upon his shoulder.

'Yes, I'm tired; but rest is near,' she pointed to the Isle of the Dead which they were just passing.

Mr. Herbert pressed her to his heart and whispered:

'He giveth His beloved sleep.'

The dark outline of the ponderous buildings loomed into sight. For all that it was summer, there was not one in the boat who would not have liked to be warmer. Mrs. Evelyn shivered outright, and exclaimed to anyone who chose to listen:

'My dear, I feel quite uncomfortable, just as if I were going into prison; really everything to do with convicts is so unfortunate.'

The party landed. Save in its own vicinity, there was not a sound to be heard. Mrs. Evelyn shivered, still less at ease; the *silent* as well as *solitary* system seemed to pervade the place, which, in the uncertain light of stars and glimmering windows, appeared little more than a village of unusually large substantial houses. It was difficult to know in what part were stowed away the five hundred prisoners existing under the darkest phase of transported life.*

---

*   Except Norfolk Island.

Mrs. Evelyn's shivers increased.

'My dears, I wish you'd all speak louder; there's not the least occasion for whispering so—really it's quite doleful, as though 'twas against the law to hear one's voice.'

'Comes *natural* down here, ma'am; astonishing how a feller gets to croon that's been here a while,' answered one of the boat's crew.

In spite of this unpromising assertion, a brisk, cheerful voice came pleasantly through the humdrum.

'Here at last! We had all given you up for to-night. Where is brother Evelyn?'

And the spare, elastic figure of an ecclesiastic hurried up to Mr. Herbert, and shook both his hands at once.

'Ah, Father Evermore, is it you? Your presence both alarms and pleases me.'

'All right, my good friend, all right at the parsonage; I am only here instead of Harelick—he has been called to Norfolk Bay.'

'Clara—Father Evermore, of whom you have heard me speak so often.'

Mrs. Evelyn inclined slightly and shortly; she owed the priest no debt of gratitude, save for his having broken the dismal silence; a bow was sufficient to liquidate that debt. But Bridget was already in love with the venerable man, whose benevolent countenance and long silver hair stamped him, to her mind, a veritable *bon père Raffre*.[18] The silvery courteousness of his voice enchanted her.

'I need not ask which is our sick charge; bless you, my child! No, no; I am stronger than I look. Your weight will not crush me if I may share with your father the pleasure of leading you up the settlement,' insisted Father Evermore, kindly drawing one of Emmeline's arms through his.

She was, however, too tired to advance a step; she fell together with the attempt. In an instant two of the boat's crew crossed their arms into the lady's cradle, and bending before her, said, 'If the master would be pleased to allow them, they'd shift her so easy as not to shake a breath out of her.'

Mr. Herbert thankfully accepted their offer, and when his daughter put one arm over each neck, their satisfaction seemed complete. They lifted her carefully, and trotting off, they only rested once; on which one of them took the opportunity to turn his head and rub his cuff across his eyes.

'Are you tired, my friend?' inquired Mr. Herbert.

The man shook his head, and again rubbed his eyes; then seeing that Mr. Herbert looked pained, he muttered:

'I left a daughter at home, just like this yer, dying away; I expect she's gone 'fore now, without a last look of her poor father. Ah, sir! These be the bitters such as *you* don't know the taste of.'

The tears, now licensed, flowed apace; but he would not leave go to wipe them off—he shook them from his face, and said he was trying to feel ''twas his own maid he was heaving of.' After trying thus for some time, forgetting everything save that he was a father, he turned to Emmeline:

'Be asy, my dear? Grab on tight as you plase, so long as you'm asy.'

'A second-sentencer has feelings, you see, Miss D'Urban,' whispered Father Evermore, as again the soiled yellow cuff sought the ferret eyes of the prisoner.

'Through the avenue or up the gates, your reverence?' inquired the younger man.

The priest advised the latter to avoid at once the chill of the heavy foliage, and the strong smell of the blue gum then exhaling to perfection its catty perfume in the still, moist air.

'How beautiful!' cried Bridget, when, having passed through the iron gates, all prison feelings vanished with prison reminders. To some purpose are placed there those tall gates, if to their sentinelship is due the quiet beauty lying onward and overwatched by the ivy-grown church, which, striking the eye of the party as they entered the long line of shrubbery, drew forth Bridget's encomium.

'Beautiful as it is, it was sown in blood, Miss D'Urban, as indeed we may say of the whole civilised structure of this island.'

'Really, Mr. Evermore, you are very complimentary. I don't know anything of this church; but I should be sorry to mix blood with my thoughts of my country,' said Mrs. Evelyn.

'It is nevertheless a very necessary diluent,[19] dear madam, though in great measure I speak allegorically. Where real life-blood has been wanting, the groaning of the prisoner, which we call *heart-blood*, has copiously flowed from every part of the colony.' Spreading his hands courteously to attest the fact, he added, 'But the foundation of yon church was literally the scene of murder, and the Port Arthur legend is, that the victim's blood still gurgles in the trenches, and causes your bishop to delay the consecration of the building.'

'Ay, and that isn't all, neither; the leads up there could tell something if they'd tongues; they'd tell how many dollars was pinched out of 'em by Jenkins a-sitting up there a-moulding of money,' joined in the younger convict unable to repress an active interest in the settlement traditions.

But tales traditionary were speedily forgotten in one more cheering to weary pilgrims—one that was English in its utterance and colonial in its warmth: a tide of little Harelicks rushed down the grove, shouting a gleesome welcome; and then, smiling and matronly, the chaplain's wife ran over the steps to conduct her friends to the parsonage, of which, together with the clerical Protestant duties of the settlement, Mr. Herbert had undertaken to relieve her husband for three months.

'I'm half glad you're too late for dinner, for not *my* means nor *Opal's* invention could have produced a more substantial meal than that you see before you, for even which you must thank the soldiers: just at the last moment, when I was despairing of anything but navy beef for your reception-feast, they brought in two fine trumpeters.'[20]

But the large kind smile of their hostess was a reception-feast in itself, as, presiding over the tea table, she dealt out the fish, which, fair, fresh, and solid, had not left the bay many hours before those who now preyed on its dainty flakes.

'Short commons down here in hot weather, Miss D'Urban,' explained Father Evermore, on seeing Bridget exploring with some curiosity what appeared a log of boiled wood, but which, on closer inspection, turned out to be a lump of navy beef, of age unknown.

'*They* don't look much like famine, at any rate,' she laughed in answer, nodding to the tribe of sleek, ruddy Harelicks shining around the board, and smiling, large, and comfortable as their delighted mother, who, in her turn, smiled, extra pleased at the compliment to her children.

'No; thank God we manage very well. When it's too hot for the boats to bring in any meat, we can always borrow fish, eggs, or fowl; then the store-beef is a never-failing resource.'

'But it's so nasty, mamma; the storekeeper told me the last piece was older than papa,' ventured to suggest the boy Harelick.

Mrs. Evelyn began to frown on the culinary probabilities; but Mrs. Harelick assured her that alarm was needless; the borrowing system practised by the officers subserved all necessary purposes, and rendered the absence of shops of less consequence. She showed that A., who keeps a cow, lends B. a pound of butter, and in return borrows a dozen eggs. C. borrows a bottle of rum, and lends in return a wallaby, which her husband has snared; while the soldiers are only too happy to exchange the fish they spend half their time in catching for any trifle the cupboards of their neighbours may afford. Bridget thought it would be much better fun to buy and sell in this primitive way than with money; on which her aunt said, really her niece was so childish in her notions that no one could suppose she was a young woman of twenty; but Father Evermore gave Bridget to understand by a kind smile that in such matters he approved of childishness even in young women; and to further signify his approval, he told her he hoped she would consider his quarters at her service whenever she required a nosegay or dish of fruit. When he left the room, Mrs. Evelyn expressed wonder and displeasure that Mr. Herbert should allow Bridget to talk so freely to a Roman Catholic, and that he should permit himself to be called brother by one.

'When you know Evermore as well as I do, Clara, you will deem it a privilege to be called sister by him; he is of the true Church of Christ, and that is all I care to inquire. An humble, earnest, hardworking member—still toiling on when others would rest—he only seeks to be approved of his heavenly Father, to whose kingdom he will find admittance before many who vaunt themselves on names.'

'But he is a Roman Catholic, my dear,' persisted Clara, with an unconvinced air.

'And my dear friend is a Protestant; yet, through our blessed Lord, I hope to meet him in heaven,' lisped the priest, folding his aged hands together and laying them on the back of Mr. Herbert's chair. Then turning to Mrs. Evelyn he said, 'And I hope I may still call you sister through our Lord Jesus Christ.'

He again left, having only returned for his stick, and Mrs. Evelyn exclaimed impatiently—

'Really, my dear, it's quite dangerous to have Roman Catholics about us in this manner.'

Ere Mr. Harelick returned, Mrs. Evelyn had gone off with the children, and Bridget with Emmeline. His countenance bore that peculiar, tried expression so characteristic of the convict chaplain, though in a slighter degree than that on Mr. Herbert's face.

'They'll worry me out altogether soon, Evelyn,' he said, after a brief comparison of grievances with his clerical brother. 'I wrote a resignation yesterday, but my wife made me destroy it; she wouldn't let me show them how they had annoyed me; she thinks we can watch how matters go during the time you are here, and then act when the way is clear.'

'They must worry me *quite* out, or I shall not leave the department,' replied Mr. Herbert.

'Oh! *You* needn't fear, you are a visitor down here, and will find everything to your liking.'

'The redemption of the soul is precious, and it ceaseth forever,'[21] murmured Mr. Herbert, following out to himself his train of thought.

'Yes; would we could think more of those poor fellows and less of ourselves! I always tell my wife, that humbly and weakly as I preach it, I know they have the Gospel whilst I am here, and therefore, not knowing who may come after me, we ought to bear on to the last moment: if *you*, now, Evelyn, would take my place, I'd leave to-morrow.'

Mr. Herbert shook his head—he had his own flock to care for. He encouraged his brother to endure in all patience the trials of his ministerial course. It might be distressing to have the rod of lay office so domineeringly shaken over them by uneducated, and, too often, irreligious men; but their eyes should be toward the chief bishop, who, wielding the pastoral staff, would guide them into righteousness and peace.

'To strive to hear that bishop's voice,' he said, 'and then to follow it, should be the aim of our lives. It is good to hear it, better to follow it.'

'Ah! So we say every evening, don't we, Julia? But the next morning, when I find some fresh petty annoyance prepared—yes, *prepared*—for me, I lose courage, and feel it's hard to set to work against wind and tide, and without knowing, too, how I have offended. The last time the comptroller was down, he was as cool as could be; *what for*, I've never yet discovered. Well, when he had gone, something he had said to the superintendent was conveyed to me as an order from himself. Being a first-class officer I refused to receive second-hand commands, so no more was said about it; but they found means to pay me out, by keeping me so short of wood that we could only have one fire in the house for several days. When I complained, blame was shifted from shoulder to shoulder, until it was made to rest on the poor carriers, who were threatened with cells if they neglected the parson again.'

'The apples, too, Tom, that was very shabby,' said Mrs. Harelick.

At mention of the apples, in spite of his former vexation, good-natured Mr. Harelick burst into a hearty laugh.

'Yes, indeed; these things are so ridiculous that persons who haven't daily to encounter them would think them too foolish to repeat.'

'Foolish or not, these things are only bearable as they are borne for the love of Christ. It requires great grace to bear small trials; natural heroism goes far in enabling us to support heavy troubles,' replied Mr. Herbert, gently but firmly.

'Why, Evelyn, surely up in town, within earshot of the comptroller, you have not to face any of these annoyances?'

An expressive smile was the only answer.

'Oh! you needn't fear my wife, she's safe, and awake to these matters; aren't you, Julia?'

A large, benignant smile at once rewarded his opinion of her, and brightened the dark subject which lowered over the trio.

Mr. Herbert said he had not thought of Mrs. Harelick as an obstacle to free speech; he considered that the more such grievances were talked of the more they withered up the heart's best feelings. He found them difficult enough to battle against in reality, without making imaginary attacks upon the enemy's camp.

No one who looked at his countenance would have thought that these things made any deep impression upon him, much less that he felt them so acutely; his friends were therefore taken by surprise to hear him say—

'My experience is, that it is far more difficult to receive meekly one such indignity from lay under-authority than to make a great sacrifice for our Lord; it is easy to be a hero, an officer of the cross, but how arduous to become a common soldier! Setting these trials of my position to the account of that love which beareth all things, I am able, through grace, to take them quietly—would God I could say joyfully! Otherwise I could not take them at all.'

'Stop, Evelyn, I only partly agree with you there; one may go on submitting until one licks the dust, trampled on by men who by right of office are only our equals—by right of education and birth often our inferiors. I would not quarrel, but I would object; and if that were useless, I would resign, and I shall, too, some day, Julia, for all that you made me tear up that letter yesterday.'

The comfortable smile disappeared, and the upper lip fell demurely over the large white teeth, while Mrs. Harelick shook her head at her husband. 'No-o-o.' She then asked Mr. Herbert his opinion of resigning.

'Had I consulted my natural heart and my wounded feelings I should have resigned long ago,' he replied, in a decided tone. Then throwing one arm over his chair, and leaning his head back on it he continued—

'But, oh, my friends, it is a dying, dying, dying world. The department worries me with some ungentlemanlike treatment, and I feel inclined to resent its conduct by tendering my resignation, since appeal is of no service. Then I go into the hospital, and find some poor dying creature eagerly watching for me: he grasps my hand and prays me, for the love of God, to warn his fellow sinners not to neglect their immortal salvation, as he has done; I go to another ward, expecting to see one whom last night I besought to fly from the wrath to come, but the screen is drawn around his bed, death is there, fixing his eternal state. I go to the condemned cells, and death is there—death, moral and spiritual. I return to my home, and there is my own child dying; and then all my resentment turns upon myself for having encouraged impatient feelings. Let us look upon eternity, and we must forget all, save that we are surrounded by dying men, ourselves in the same predicament.'

The earnest voice ceased, and closing his eyes, Mr. Herbert sat for many minutes in silence; then arousing himself with a long, yet scarcely audible sigh, he added: 'I am puzzled to know what to think of those men, who throw every possible hindrance in the way of God's servants, instead of helping them in a labour so wearing to mind and body; it must be that having only to deal with the bodies of their bond brethren, they know nothing of the obstinate, life-wearing soul strife *we* have to wage day after day, year after year. Death, which relieves them of their responsibility, makes ours the more terrible and laborious. What say you, Mrs. Harelick, must we set down their opposition to the sin of ignorance?

'But that neither makes it easier to bear nor exonerates government for permitting such a state of things,' answered her husband.

'I quite exonerate government, Harelick; I do not lay at its door one of the annoyances which fret the convict chaplain from heartfelt attention to his duties. Where I deem government is culpable, is in not better protecting its clerical servants from abuse, since their being under secular rule is unavoidable.'

'Perhaps it's the sin of ignorance there too,' said Mrs. Harelick.

'And I believe it is. Reports of us reach government only through its own agents, who colour the case according to their view, which view is nearly always a prejudiced one, giving colour prejudicial to ourselves; we are represented as the molesting and not the molested party.'

'It is my opinion, that from the way we are represented, we have been long since set down with the incorrigible. "A dissatisfied, troublesome set, are the convict chaplains," were Turbot's very words of us, Evelyn.'

Another quite smile was again the only answer. Wishing to avoid further exposition of 'stationary' grievances, Mr. Herbert asked, 'How is it down here between master and men?'

'Oh, the same as ever, and the same as it ever must be whilst—'

'Now, Tom, *do* take care what you say,' said his wife.

'*There*, you see she wants to pay you off, Evelyn, because you would not trust her just now.'

'Now, Tom, don't; I only want to put you on your guard. You never know what ears there may be about. That was why you stopped, wasn't it, Mr. Evelyn, and not because of me?'

'That which I have to say I would not stop for any ears. I would say it if called before government to-morrow.'

'Do let us hear what you *have* to say then, for I'm sure if you up in Hobart have cause to speak, we down here may fairly have more cause.'

'In finishing your former speech for you, I believe I comprehend all I have to say, and that is, that no improvement in convict difficulties and evils can be expected till a different class of men is chosen to work the system, nor while so much irresponsible power is vested in one man.'

'Why, you've been foraging in my paddock![22] Those were almost my words this morning, weren't they, Julia?'

'Would that I had been there trespassing, then there had not been two witnesses to the evil; but, unfortunately, my mind has gathered its sentiments from an original field of observation, widely extended and darkly diversified, and has long ago arrived at the conclusion, that half the systems which have been tried and found wanting, have been so, not so much from deficiency in themselves, as from some defect existent in their coadjutors; in other phrase, from an erroneous choice of *hands*; the *heads* of the system have generally been well chosen.'

'Take off the head, then, and there is nothing but rottenness below,' laughed Mr. Harelick.

'Oh, Tom!' His wife was thoroughly alarmed; hastening across the room she bolted the door.

But Tom would not be quiet, it was so great a treat to have someone to talk to.

'I think, though, the *heart* of the system is not so much amiss; it means well, and if it could accomplish its intentions our convicts would do famously.'

Mr. Herbert shook his head gravely and said:

'The remembrance that more than one hundred and nineteen thousand of our fellow creatures have been subject to the experiments and failures of systems in these colonies affords no matter for light words. To me, the remembrance is a fountain, whence my eyes draw tears, and my soul prayer and humbleness before God.'

'Too true, indeed. The delight of at last hearing my own thoughts echoed by others more deeply based, makes me appear light when lightness is far from my heart. We agree so well, Evelyn, that I feel I have a right to speak to you of the grievous subversion of power as practised in many of these stations. Ah! It's a responsibility from which, good Lord, deliver me.'

Poor Mrs. Harelick sat distractedly in her chair, alternately looking from window to door, from door to chimney, for the ears she dreaded. Because a government house, she fancied it must be full of not only ears but eyes, and her search for them continued, till, with a desperate gesture, she implored Tom to be quiet; however, he would go on.

'Yes, with few exceptions, it has always appeared to me that the *hands* of the system, from first to last, from first-class officer to convict constable, are ill appointed. Now there's

Turbot, except severity of temper, what fitness is there in him to recommend him for the important position he holds?'

'Severity of temper, perhaps,' repeated Mr. Herbert, with the least touch of Uncle Ev curling in his lip.

'One would hope that where the good of so many hundred souls was at stake, not even a third-class officer would be elected without an almost solemn scrutiny of the man; but how can appointments, resulting more from favour than from conviction, be otherwise than erring?'

'Dear, dear, when we know the power that such men, so chosen, have of making their prisoner subjects wretched to desperation, what non-importance falls on the little show of power wherewith they seek to intimidate us!' And Mr. Herbert arose to put an end to the distasteful question.

'Not if we view the show of power as part of the plan on which they have fattened into vanity! They have exercised uncontrolled authority so long over one class of their brethren that their minds pall, and they desire to stimulate their depraved appetites with a taste of the free.'

'Tom! Tom! *Do* mind what you say,' once more despairingly urged his wife.

A loud rattling at the door did more towards stopping her husband than all her 'Tom's.' It was with a redundant smile that the distressed wife welcomed back Mrs. Evelyn and Bridget, for now she was sure the dangerous topic would be discontinued; for the chaplain wanted not prudence when he was in unassured company.

'How is Emmeline?' asked Mr. Herbert.

'Tired out, poor dear; I've only run in to say good-night, and I'm off to bed before she goes to sleep.'

'Talking of bed, my dear, how unnecessary of the department to give us such very disfigured bedding, just as though government feared we should make away with their blankets. I really shall feel like a convict sleeping between those broad arrows, and great ugly B.O.s, too, all over the things in that manner,' said Mrs. Evelyn.[23]

'Alas, madam, all is B.O. down here! No one has a right to himself, nothing is its *own*. You'll see the O.P.S.O. written on every man's brow; even where the broad arrow is not visible on his back. The serpent himself, as well as his trail, is perceptible in this natural paradise.'

'No need, at any rate, to have him in the house, coiled up in such great black B.O.'s on my little Charlie's blankets; the poor child was quite frightened to get into his cot. He said—"Mamma, does B.O. spell bogie?" and feeling rather cross, I answered, "Yes, of course, my dear," when he set up such a roar that I have been ever since trying to quiet him; even now he is sobbing in his sleep.'

'I congratulate you, ma'am; he is a fortunate child to retain his horror of a bogie in sight of which he has lived all his life. My best wish for Master Charles is, that B.O. may always spell bogie to him. I fear it has long ceased to convey that meaning to *my* children,' replied Mr. Harelick, tracing out a large B with his finger on the table.

CHAPTER 30

Port Arthur—The Settlement

IT was many days ere Emmeline could leave her room. Her little modicum of strength had been so drawn upon by the journey that it required every tender appliance with perfect rest to restore her to her former position; and long, very long, to give her a semblance of improved health. But when the semblance did appear, it was so true to nature that even the father was deceived by it, and a faint shadow of a just possible joy cast on his heart a sensation long forbidden; and resting with grateful delight under this slight shadow from the wayside heat, he uttered a prayer that before he had not dared to breathe, 'O my Father, if it be possible!'

Then the joy became less possible—the shadow faded—once more it approached, again to withdraw; until the father perceived that it was a mere mockery flitting before his path to delude his steady progress from the well-beaten track of sanctified sorrow; and once more with stricken but uncomplaining heart he resigned his child to the unseen hand that was beckoning her step by step from this nether world. 'Nevertheless, not my will, but Thine be done.'[1]

Devoting himself to her, he was thankful when comparative strength and freedom from pain enabled her to enjoy the passing sweets of a softly passing summer, which, balmy and restorative, swept over the sunny region of Port Arthur, preserving it an Eden of fertility and luxuriant beauty; while other less favoured parts of the island drooped and withered prematurely into the dusky tintings of autumn.

To spare Emmeline the fatigue of a rather steep flight of stairs, Mrs. Harelick had devoted to her special service a large front parlour on the ground floor. It opened on the station, and had by no means the pleasant landscape which enlivened the upper apartments. The lovely bay, and the Isle of the Dead, were not to be seen; but some gardens intervening, beguiled the more immediate sight from the prison apparatus, inescapably conspicuous on a prolonged survey from the bow window.

A low verandah, covered with multiflora rose, extending the length and sides of the house, shielded the lower rooms from the scorching sun, and gave the parsonage (otherwise bare and unfinished looking) a rural, picturesque appearance.

The first few days succeeding their arrival, there was no tempting Bridget from her cousin. Not all the enchantery of the government gardens to which the young Harelicks invited her could entice her from 'dear old Em.' Let them bring her the rare flowers which in rich, if not in wild exuberance wasted their sweetness on the garden air; until Em could go with her she should not go in search of them for all the pink acacias and ixias in the world; not she! In vain smiled Father Evermore's courteous face, not even respect to his silver locks should draw her to see more than she could see from the window; and that was neither much nor pleasant, unless she sat very sidewise to get a peep at the church and avenue descending from it. For after she had watched the children playing in the verandah, there was nothing but the settlement before her. We all know that distant life attracts the eye more than nearer beauty. Whilst there is one living object moving on an eminence before us, we must look at it, in spite of more inviting objects. So it seemed to Bridget that she must overlook the cheerful patches of cultivation just outside the parsonage, to watch the ceaseless stream of yellow life clanging drearily either to or from the buildings beyond.

The first morning she was startled from her sleep at five o'clock by a loud, quick bell that, being rung from the prison, peremptorily sounded through the whole settlement, bidding all concerned hasten to their day's duty. Mr. Harelick was one concerned, and ere the loud, quick bell ceased, Bridget heard the front door slam, and a step run down the grove. She was not concerned, but for all that she could not return to her disturbed sleep; besides, she wanted to know what could be going on at that early hour. Twilight mists had long dispersed, leaving pendant over all a faint splendour that gave promise of a speedy outburst of dazzling glory. Her heart leaped within her, as gently pushing aside the shutter, she glimpsed the breaking sun. She felt as if something ought to happen on so bright a day; and glad thoughts fluttered within her, impatient to take rosy flight from their narrow bounds. How beautiful everything must look in this summer weather! Last night, in the darkness it was fair enough, she said to herself; and opening the shutter a little more, she peeped out. There hung the silent splendour, but over what?—a plain peopled with living misery—a surge of human suffering heaved the settlement into a life so slow, so heavy, that all the brightness of the day could not stimulate it into more than lethargic movement—still, slow and cold and heavy, it moved in one unbroken mass; the sun might shine or it might lower for all that dead vitality seemed to care. But slow movements neither suit prison stations nor penal servitude. What sun or cheerful weather cannot do, must be done by other means.

Once more a bell rang. Then louder, sharper, and quicker than it, several voices of command were heard. The mass of pied yellow separated into sections, and to the 'G'ups' and 'G'ons' of constables and overseers diverged to the four outlets of Port Arthur. The boat's crew passed to the water's edge; the wood-fellers to Opossum Bay; the road gang towards Safety Cove; the settlement servants to their several masters; and one party, harnessed to carts, was driven up the main road, through the grove, and by the parsonage, when Bridget, still peeping out, recognised Forbes in the last of the men. He could not go so quickly as the others; he was therefore assisted on his way by alternate bruises and shoves—these from his fellow prisoners when pushed against them by the cart—those from the cart when repelled by its onward movement.

Bridget hastily closed the shutters, and sighed:

'There's no good in anything beautiful! Oh how I wish—'

She stopped, remembering her cousin; but Emmeline was awake, and had been watching Bridget's varying countenance as she discovered wretchedness where she sought for happiness, and darkness where she had looked for light.

'Oh, Em—Em—if "Thy kingdom come"[2] means an end to all these things, I'm sure I'll cry it with every breath I have. Fancy, five hundred convicts, all miserable! I feel as if I had *no right* to be happy. It shows we are wicked, or we couldn't enjoy ourselves. Angels couldn't if they lived here; that's why they don't, I suppose.'

A sudden stop to the up and down clanking of the chains and rumbling of the carts, together with a sort of scuffling sound, brought Bridget once more to the window.

The party had drawn up just above her; she saw Forbes drop his hands, and lean resolutely back on the cart.

'I can't go on—I'm not used to it.'

'Go on, you —— schemer!' shouted the overseer.

'I can't—I shall drop if I move another step.'

'Go on there, and leave him to follow.'

Bob Pragg was the leader: he attempted to move, but the two men behind him, resisting his effort, pulled him back. They would not run down a fellow-creature and a comrade for all that he had been a gentleman; one of them turned and said, 'Sir, we shall pull him down, and we can't do that.'

Forbes tried once more to get on: he gave a few short steps, and again dropped, whispering to his fellows:

'I would if I could—don't mind me; go on.'

But not a man, save Pragg, would stir, and his attempt was futile against a dozen drawbacks.

Again Forbes made a desperate effort; his hands fell, his knees tottered, and then he sank to the ground between the shafts of the cart.

''Twould serve the —— rascal right if I drove you over him,' growled the overseer.

Pragg seemed to think it would; but a low curse escaped the teeth of the other men.

Forbes was unharnessed and made to stand, while Pragg, loosened from the party, was sent for a constable to take off the unfortunate man.

Mr. Herbert, who had also been aroused by the prison bell, having heard the scuffle, came out to inquire the cause, and just at that moment Mr. Harelick issued from the avenue on his return from morning prayers.

'This man should not have been sent out this morning; he had work enough yesterday to fatigue a stronger frame,' said Mr. Herbert.

'It's his own fault—he's scheming; of course he's weak to-day because he wouldn't eat his rations last night or this morning, so he's come out to look after his appetite; he'll find it on the road somewhere 'fore the day's out, I reckon.'

Mental pain writhed not only in every feature, but also in every muscle of Forbes's attenuated frame. Wounded sensitiveness seemed to ooze through his long, slim fingers, as, nervously twitching them, he worked them into each other. He once or twice tried to raise his eyes to the two clergymen; but the glance was so furtive in its haste that both hoped he would fix it anywhere save on them.

'Is this true, Forbes?' said Mr. Herbert.

'True, sir, true? Do you know it's against the laws down here to question an officer before his men?'

'I beg your pardon; I should not think of questioning *you*. I spoke to the prisoner, Forbes,' said Mr. Herbert, politely inclining his head, and then in the same quiet voice:

'Is this true, Forbes?'

'Sir, it's against our rules.'

'I follow no rules but those of humanity, Mr. Overseer. Is it true, Forbes?'

'I could not take my rations, sir. I've asked to go into the hospital, but they say I am malingering, and refuse to admit me.'

'The cell shall be your only hospital; take him off; these are my notes, give them at the office,' bellowed the overseer.

The constable bore him off, and he was arraigned at the bar of penal justice for insolence, refractoriness, and attempt at mutiny; his punishment was accordingly heavy. Those who had refused to stir on his account were likewise punished as mutineers—Pragg exulted; his praiseworthy support of the overseer met with its reward in the credit book.

But much had to be done that day. The family of Harelicks would leave to-morrow, when Mr. Herbert must enter on the external, and Mrs. Evelyn on the internal, duties of the parsonage; before then, both must be duly inaugurated to their respective posts. The latter were more novel to Mrs. Evelyn than were the former to her brother-in-law. Morning prayers at five, cells, prison, hospital, school, and evening prayer, formed his daily routine, weekly diversified by the Sunday services in the church, a ride to Eagle Hawk Neck for a service with the soldiers, and to Norfolk Bay for the same purpose. Mrs. Evelyn went round with her friend to learn the various modes of domestic existence in the unfeminine district of Port Arthur, where the total absence of female servants made the position of the lady of the house one of real work. The two eldest girl Harelicks had been the little housemaids, one going her regular round with pail, broom, and duster, the other making up the B.O. beds with all the gravity of an old nurse. Clothes washing, scrubbing, cooking, and such labours were performed by the men. The ironing and bread and butter making fell to the mistress, and woe to her in the summer heat if no friendly assistance was near to lend a hand at the heavy fortnightly ironing!

The store-room perfectly delighted Mrs. Evelyn; it was a spacious apartment intended for the drawing room; but as the withdrawing of stores was a more frequent occurrence than the withdrawing of company from the dining parlour, Mr. Harelick's predecessor had turned the said room into a victualling depot, where now Mrs. Evelyn's eye rejoiced over every imaginable supply, necessary to life if not to luxury, and that in a degree of abundance which made her think smally[3] of her own pride at home. Mrs. Harelick said she was fortunate in leaving her friend a treasure in the form of a cook, by the name of Opal—a Chinaman prisoner, whose present sin was that of absconding, whose former crime had been a passionate attempt to murder his master. He was a professed cook, and prior to his second conviction had received thirty shillings a week at the best confectioner's in Hobarton.

'You have only to give him the materials,' said Mrs. Harelick, 'and without further orders dinner after dinner will come up without your knowing how. It is wonderful to see the nice dishes he makes out of the roughest materials, and not a scrap wasted. Let us go into the kitchen to him.'

'Opal, here is your new lady.'

'All light den—Opal welly glad—hope she nice lady, no scold, no give poor chain-gang trouble.'

Mrs. Evelyn proceeded to open the cupboard, when, emitting a noise as if he had been driving pigs out of a potato yard, Opal hurried over, shut the door upon the shelves, and put the key in his pocket. Mrs. Evelyn looked both offended and surprised, but Mrs. Harelick only laughed.

'You mustn't pry into his mysteries! He won't do anything if you do. In there he has innumerable little plates full of what would only seem useless scraps to you; but wait and see. He'd as soon throw a scrubbing-brush at you as look if you meddled with his dishes; not out of disrespect, though, or anger, but because he thinks that is the shortest way of showing his disapprobation.'

This did not please Mrs. Evelyn; she thought a made dish by no means compensated for a scrubbing-brush at her head. But Mrs. Harelick pacified her, saying there was no fear, Opal was the gentlest creature so long as his cupboard was safe from intrusion. He never grumbled at his work, whether it was washing the clothes with lime, or digging in the vegetable garden. A few materials to turn into condiments always put him in a good temper and in capital spirits.

Mrs. Evelyn learnt that government allowed two servants; the other, therefore, was employed as nurse, walking about the settlement with the baby and younger children as demurely as any female. Mrs. Evelyn was thinking she should not like this at all, when the man in question entered the kitchen, and the babe clung so fondly round his neck, and kissed and smoothed his tanned face with such unmistakable tokens of goodwill, that she forbore to express her feelings, determining that her child might after all fare worse in a woman's arms.

The outhouses were visited in the evening, when the livestock—comprising three cows, three goats, one horse, some fowls, a cat, kitten, and three large dogs—were bodily delivered to Mrs. Evelyn. The goats' milk was dedicated to nursery use, the cows' to house consumption, butter, and barter. The parsonage being considered the second dairy in the station, the officers were too glad to borrow its delicious contents on any article they could produce; but Mrs. Harelick said she always reserved some of the butter for the soldiers, who in return gave her the choice of their finest fish. The cows and goats were daily taken out to forage near Safety Cove. Opal had merely to leave them at the government dairy at seven a.m., when the former, joining the cowherd's drove, and the latter the goatherd's, were led out to pasture, and no more was seen of either until the evening, when the low of the one and the bleat of the other at the back gate announced milking hour and tea time.

A stranger dropping into Port Arthur, and coming suddenly on the picturesque herdsman reclining under the shade of some flowering tree, dreaming away the long hours of the day surrounded by his seventy goats, may fancy he has alighted on some Elysian sanctuary[4] of the shepherd's which has escaped the general ruin of the Fall, or at any rate the destructive march of civilization. But, questioning the happy dreamer, his own dream dissipates before the everlasting O.P.S.O. of the herdsman's talk, and the broad arrow on his back. He finds that the man's thoughts dwell indeed on *love* and home, but not of a sweetheart whom the shades of evening will restore to him, but of one forever sundered by rolling miles of ocean and insurmountable depths of degradation. His Phyllis[5] never owns him more, and as for his home, he has a government lodging down there in the station; but hell may just as well be home as *that*. His home? Ah, where is it? The place thereof knows him no more.

The stranger may inquire, if all this be true, why does government trust you with so much unguarded liberty? When your home longings burn within you in your solitude, what is there to prevent your escaping through the tempting opportunity offered by the unfrequented bush before you?

The herdsman, sure at last that he is not being mocked, looks up and asks, with a grin of hopelessness:

'Do you know your maps? Look at Eagle Hawk Neck,[6] and if it isn't marked down, just ride over to it this afternoon, and you'll soon find out *why* they trusts me.'

The stranger may take the hint, and devote the afternoon to a solving of the goatherd's problem. After a ten mile ride he reaches the Eagle Hawk Neck, and finds it is neither falsely named nor a luring bait to the chain-weary captives of Port Arthur. He returns from the fiercely guarded bar of sand, which, stretching to the mainland, forms the only possible outlet from the peninsula; he returns, no longer wondering why the lonely convict does not escape, but more fearfully wondering that one is ever found so reckless of life, so utterly despising death, as to venture into the certain detection, if not destruction, awaiting him at the Neck, where, if he elude the military watch, or, more dread and vigilant, the ferocious dogs chained across the isthmus, he has still to fling himself on the mercy of the pitiless surf, and dodge the hungry shark. And yet he is told that many desperate men have thus attempted escape, and of them one or two have emerged from the jaws of death, and, landing on the other side, have become bywords in the annals of crime and infamy.

When the station gates closed on her friends, Mrs. Evelyn entered at once on her own plans and alterations; all traces of the recent turn-out soon disappeared before her mistressly touches. Opal was given fairly to understand that his cupboards would be subject to inspection, and that no scrubbing-brushes were to be thrown at the children. Danby, the nurse-man, was cautioned against kissing, or permitting kisses from the little girl (still the baby of the Evelyn family); then supreme and happy, Mrs. Evelyn moved glibly about, satisfied even with the B.O.'s peeping from every corner, for they served to remind her that she enjoyed the large house rent free.

The station gates had scarcely closed upon his friends, ere Mr. Herbert locked himself into the study and there passed the morning in earnest prayer for his penal flock, that a blessing might attend his labours among them. He then sallied forth to hold his first service in the new cells chapel. Returning thence to the parsonage, he went to his daughter's room, and seating himself by her, she soon discovered that some perplexity worked in his mind; he promptly answered her look of inquiry by saying:

'It has always been a surprise to me, that our church, having so tenderly provided for all estates of her children, should have overlooked the prisoner. Never have I more painfully felt the omission than this afternoon, when, holding a service in the cells chapel, I had to read the Liturgy as prepared for general worshippers, to a congregation, who, if they felt at all, must have felt how much of what they heard was inapplicable to themselves.'

Taking up Wilcox's Prayer-book, which lay on Emmeline's table, he turned over the leaves and read the titles of the different services.

'Here we have anticipated every position of fallen man, save that which is so painfully brought before us in these penal states.'

'It cannot be that our church rejects this unfortunate class?' said Emmeline.

'God forbid, my child! Not while she professes to be the messenger of Him who came to seek and to save that which was lost, nor while she re-echoes that blessed voice, "Come unto me, all ye that are weary and heavy laden, and I will give you rest."[7] But it appears that she has forgotten there must ever be a portion of her family excluded by sin from the family altar, and therefore requiring a separate ministration.'

He remained silent and in deep thought, then, shaking his head as if to negate some mental suggestion, he exclaimed:

'I cannot see a clear way before me. In my own church where the free unite in equal proportions with the bond, and parts inapplicable to the latter may be supposed to be addressed to the former, I do not so much perceive the necessity for a special service; but here the necessity must be obvious to all, and where I have officiated this afternoon, where the congregation is composed of outcasts from the *worst outcasts*, the necessity for a special service becomes paramount. It is a difficulty that increases on my conscience, and will eventually lead me to renounce the public cell service, unless the authorities permit me to compile from our Liturgy a form for the use of those prisoners and captives so touchingly prayed for in the Litany; and a very beautiful form could be extracted with but little trouble.'

'Beautiful, indeed,' said Emmeline, a bright recollective glance kindling in her eye. Then, folding her hands and shutting her eyes, in a low voice she repeated that exquisite prayer in the Litany, commencing, 'We humbly beseech thee, O Father, mercifully to look upon our infirmities,' &c.

'Yes, that, with the confession and a few other prayers, would be well chosen to express the feelings of those who have visibly and outwardly strayed from the right way. God knows, when we come to speak of that spiritual way marked out by the Saviour's blood, we have all need to look to ourselves and pray with redoubled earnestness those prayers we would put into our fellow sinners' lips.'

'But, papa, what is there to prevent your using your own discretion in selecting prayers for the convicts?'

'In visiting from cell to cell, of course *nothing*—I am at liberty to suit my teaching to the case; but in the public services, *much*; our position is as unfortunate as undefined. Any attempt at reform, even in our own province, is regarded with a jealous eye by the secular powers, and we cannot appeal to the bishop without giving an offence which I am unwilling to give—for a house divided against itself cannot stand. I have often thought of submitting to his lordship a compilation from the church Prayer-book for my prison use, but have hitherto refrained, hoping the necessity for such a form would present itself to the convict rulers; it has not however done so *here*, whatever improvements may elsewhere have taken place. You are weary, dear. It is naughty of me to come troubling you, is it not?'

'Very; and more naughty of me to wish to know what harasses my father's mind.'

'If I tell you what troubles me now, will you promise to assist me out of it?'

Emmeline smiled ready acquiescence.

'Bridget informs me you are thinking of going to church on Sunday?'

'Oh! That is unkind. I had made a nice little plan for creeping into the pew unseen by anyone; that is treachery, Bridgy.'

'Only to *you*, though, and in a right cause. I'm not going to let you kill yourself for all the churches in Tasmania.'

'It is only just outside the verandah,' pleaded Emmeline; but she quickly yielded on seeing her father's anxiety, and Bridget undertook to be all attention in order to bring back a correct edition of her uncle's sermon, which he had told them was to be from the text, 'By the fear of the Lord men depart from evil.'[8]

On the Sunday morning the bells chimed out cheerily as though they called a free population to a Sabbath rest but the holy day afforded no respite, though it varied the weekly routine.

Very sorrowful was Mr. Herbert's face as, gazing around the church, he perceived how the insignia of crime and force darkened the sanctuary of God into another form of prison. Here, at his right hand, stood the armed guard of soldiers, pointing their muskets in solemn mockery of the peace that he should declare. The peace of God, he had to preach. What peace? silently sneered the musket's mouth. Bridget had not yet dared to look up, she feared what she should see. But when her uncle commenced the service, 'I will arise and go to my father,'[9] there was so sudden, so tremendous a rush of chains, that she had no choice to refrain from looking. She hastily turned and beheld some hundreds of her fellow creatures arrayed in the vast amphitheatre before her. There stood the hardened ruffian; there stood the heartbroken penitent; there stood the gray-haired criminal side by side with the mere youth; there stood every degree of guilt mingled into one dingy mass of yellow. Her heart sickened at the sight, yet she could not withdraw her eyes from the closely cropped sea of heads, until, with one simultaneous movement, down they all dived to the confession. Again they all rose. The hum of the responses blended with the occasional clank of fetters, or every now and then was wholly drowned in the combined rattle of the many hundred irons. Bridget no longer wondered that Mr. Herbert felt the impropriety of the service, it was a pain to hear it even.

'Holy! Holy! Holy! Lord God of Sabaoth,' devoutly exclaimed Mr. Herbert.

'Heaven and earth are full of the majesty of Thy glory,' replied the several hundred voices under dread of punishment, and several hundred chains prolonged the response in one dull vibration, which conveyed but a faint idea of the majestic glory spoken of.

'That it may please Thee to bless and keep the magistrates, giving them grace to execute justice and maintain truth,' prayed Mr. Herbert.

'We *beseech* thee to hear us, good Lord,' one-voiced responded the men, glancing, with peculiar earnestness, towards the magistrates' seat, as though grace would fall acceptably in the direction of that large green pew. The service concluded. While Mr. Herbert changed his robes, the hymn was given out and commenced. It was adapted to a Hallelujah chorus. Just as he appeared in the pulpit, the first verse finished, and the leader of the choir began the chorus; then from those hundred convict lips burst forth that lofty strain wherewith angelic hosts sound their great Creator's praise—louder—still louder—and yet more loud at each new breath arose the Hallelujah, but louder than the loudest chorus outpealed a deafening clangour of chains, as in their energy to outvie each other the men threw back their heads and shook their ironed limbs. Outswelled the heavy clangour, and a fearful mockery of the enraptured song smote upward, lingering in the roof like the rolling bass of distant thunder. They were about to begin the second verse, when Mr. Herbert raised his hands, saying, 'Let us pray.' The chains clattered down and once more arose. Mr. Herbert waited till the last rattle had died away. Then instead of the text Bridget expected, came a deep, rich voice, as delivering a message from another world:

'The spirit of the Lord is upon me! He hath sent me to bind up the brokenhearted, to proclaim liberty to the captive, and the opening of the prison to them that are bound.'

Swift with a message from his God, the iron of those chains had entered his heart; and who should stay his lips that he declare it not?

Once launched in settlement life, no variation broke the wearying sameness of Mr. Herbert's ministerial routine—cells, prison, hospital, sin, sickness, strife, and he had gone through his work for the week. Monday morning brought the same list of duty, the same cheerless ground to be trodden, the same tale to be told, the same difficulties to battle, the same discouragements to bear up against, but through these all there was the same God in heaven, saying, 'I am thy strength and thy shield;' the same Jesus whispering, 'Lo, I am with you always;' the same Holy Ghost the Comforter, invisibly refreshing the streams of grace; the same bright crown o'erhanging, 'Be thou faithful unto death;' and—alas! that he must drop from the mount of glory, (but so it is ever in this fickle world)—the same immortal souls living in death and dying in life, sinking, sinking, sinking. So, how should not the cloud oppress his brow, for all that his own eternal prospect is clear as the morning without clouds?

The family, too, had few interruptions to its quiet monotony—churning and ironing days were the grandest changes; these, however, occurred so regularly that they were hardly to be recognised as changes. The disappearance—or, rather, the non-return—of Danby, the nurse-man, from the muster ground caused a little excitement, and afterwards a great deal of extra work, for it was found that his absence was involuntary, being occasioned by an award of three days' solitary, amount due for five minutes' lateness at the muster. In like manner Opal disappeared for a week, one of his cows having chosen to break through penal rule and run home through the government garden instead of through the appointed road: she, of course, would not have understood cells, so the Chinaman became her substitute—both were B.O., bodily distinction was unnecessary.

These excitements involved creature suffering, therefore they were not agreeable to the parsonage family. Once a reported shipwreck really did bring some earnest blood into the pale face of the settlement; all was hurry and bustle when the screeches of the unfortunate crew were pronounced to be audible to everyone except the individual speaking. All the available males of the station turned out for Safety Cove, the scene of the catastrophe, and the boat's crew was sent off to assist the foundering wretches. Meanwhile, the vessel, quietly rounding Cape Pillar, was wholly innocent of the imputed wreck: the cries of her crew could only be traced to a set of station urchins, who were concluding a spree among the ruins of Point Puer,[10] by exhibiting their voices in the form of echoes amid the deserted buildings. And they who had ridden out to the cove one mass of benevolent feeling returned singly to the station, dropping in at slow intervals with feelings no longer benevolent, but such as it may be supposed possessed the fox which was invited to supper and sent supperless away.

At last, however, a substantial surprise came upon the family—a surprise that made them feel somewhat in the position of prisoners. One steamer-day, Charlie ran in with the unwelcome tidings that the boat's crew had just brought word from Norfolk Bay that the *Kangaroo* was laid up and unfit for service.

'How ever shall we get back then?' cried Mrs. Evelyn.

The answer could only be—'Here you are, and here you must remain, unless you brave the Neck, or venture in an open boat.'

'How shall we get Maida down?' thought Mr. Herbert and inquired Emmeline and Bridget.

Answer not more hopeful—'She can't come unless she go the land route with the postman, or except she turn horseman and make way over the bush.'

To Uncle Ev, all alone in Hobarton, the news was equally unpleasant. He wearied of bachelor life, and became impatient for the end of May, which was to restore his family to him. But to Mr. Herbert it came fraught with suspense and anxiety, crushing upon his heart—a weight for which he could not account. His daughter *seemed* to account for it, yet why he could not tell; there was no reason, the doctor said, that the winter of Port Arthur should not agree with her as well as the winter of Hobarton; the probability was that it would the better suit her.

'What makes you so sad, papa?' said Emmeline, as, leaning on his arm, she walked up and down the verandah; 'are you wanting to get back to your people at home?'

'No, my child; any part of my Master's vineyard is the same to me. A heaviness has fallen upon my spirit, wherefore I cannot tell.'

His eye unconsciously rested on the Isle of the Dead. Passing his hand quickly across his face, he appeared to dash away a distressing thought; his daughter, too, looked on the isle, and fancying her father only cleared his sight to obtain a better view of it, she said—

'It is a lovely spot,' and drew him gently on.

A few days after that, Mr. Herbert received a letter from his brother, and without assigning a reason to anyone but Emmeline, he signified his intention to start overland for Hobarton. Mrs. Evelyn declared it was a shame to leave unprotected women; she would not stay alone in the parsonage when it had been announced that absconders were out, and among them that notorious Bob Pragg, whose cold-blooded ferocity was known to all. Mr. Herbert told her that she need not be alarmed, Pragg having effectually escaped through the Neck to the mainland, whilst his companions had been recaptured. Though her fears were overruled, it was with no good grace she saw her brother-in-law depart; she foreboded that on his return he would either find them murdered, or stuck up by the absconders. Nevertheless, Mr. Herbert arrived in town, and thence back to the peninsula, without any notable occurrence having taken place, except we mention that Opal, out of pure love to Emmeline, had managed to spin one pound of gravy-beef into such a multiplicity of sausages, that every person connected their number with the loss of the kitten; but no confession could be extorted from him; he merely giggled with a cunning leer, and said *he* 'didn't tink nothing too fine for dat nice laddie wid de vely light face, what smiles so sweet on dis poor chain-gang'—his mode of pronouncing prisoner. He made no secret of his attachment. Much to Bridget's delight and Mrs. Evelyn's annoyance, he would frequently say: 'Opal luff dat plitty light laddie vely much.' His mistress would correct him with:'Love isn't a proper word for you, Opal;' on which, with troubled countenance, he would confess his ignorance of correct language, and apologize by explaining that what he felt was 'great, big, large, *there*,' laying his hand upon his heart to show *where*. Nor was his love all idle vaunt. Emmeline owed much of her enjoyment at Port Arthur to this her Chinese worshipper. One day when she was fatigued after a short stroll in the government gardens, Opal chanced to enter the room. He surveyed her in silence for some time, then, giving one of his peculiar grunts, he started off to the lumber-house—shortly returning to the verandah with four small wheels and the spring of a child's carriage. Presenting these to Mr. Herbert, he asked leave to make his lady a coach. Mr. Herbert assented, willing to gratify the poor youth. In the course of a week he produced a most primitive little vehicle, which was no less than a packing-case laid on the wheels; but, simple as it was, this original conveyance became a valuable accession to Emmeline's comfort, for with the help of shawls and cushions she made it an able means of moving from place to place among the beauties of the country.

Never shone Opal's ample gums and tiny teeth more brilliantly than when he was appointed to the honour of drawing his lady-love. He had a few set phrases by which he inquired into her state of ease; beyond these he never ventured on familiarity. A smile from Emmeline repaid him for the most elaborate journey or painstaking pull; a word was payment towards the next debt. He was at first disposed to regard Maida's subsequent arrival with suspicion; but after some days, on finding that there was room enough for both, he recovered his equanimity; and perceiving, by a sort of intuition, that her path, though parallel, was widely removed from his, he contentedly classed her with Bridget as a claimant on his young mistress's affection.

In fact, Maida was a myth to him; he kept at a respectful distance from her, and would persist in calling her ma'am, giving it as his private opinion that 'she was a bigger ma'am than the other ma'am,' which other was Mrs. Evelyn.

CHAPTER 31

A Day Dream and Night Vision

MEANWHILE Mr. Evelyn remained in Hobarton. The family had been gone just three weeks when Maida, having received her discharge from H.M.G. Hospital, was sent to the Lodge under a constable's care. Stephens, the new servant, opened the door and refused to admit her; he said 'he didn't know nothing about a government woman called Maida Gwynnham, and he wasn't going for to let anyone in while the master was out. If she'd like to wait till four o'clock to speak to him she might, but as he had gone to Kangaroo Point 'twas a chance if he'd be back; certain he wouldn't after four.'

So Maida was forced to wander about the garden under the constable's eye, while every now and then Stephens would peep out to see that she was a true woman, and no spy on the master's property. Four o'clock struck, and, no Mr. Evelyn appearing, he insisted that the officer should take her away to the Brickfields. The man argued that she might be let by the morning, and then Mr. Evelyn would kick up one of his rows which everybody felt from his excellency downwards. But Stephens said ''twas past hiring hours, and very like if the master was really minded to have the woman Gwynnham, he'd step over to the Brickfields and hire her out before she could be let to anyone else.'

So Maida was turned adrift in the Hiring Depot, and once more made to put on the prison clothes that she had only that afternoon exchanged for her own. In an instant she was surrounded by her old shipmates, of whom about twenty were congregated in the yard. Their bloated, hardened faces told her how much they had improved by transportation and association with crime. One extolled a spree she had enjoyed with the constable on her way to the Brickfields, and another shamelessly declared that she had been in Cage for two children, and she expected very soon to go in for a third, only she hoped to be hired out till it was quite time. Disgusted and fatigued, Maida asked if she might retire to rest, and, on plea of her having just come from the hospital, permission was granted. But there was no rest in the ward from either the filth or strife of tongues—the torrent of contamination flowed freely—the better disposed were obliged to hear what the vicious chose to relate. In the morning Maida was put to some labour, and then with the other women was turned into the yard. She retired as far as possible from her companions, and sat down on a stone to feel more vividly than ever the utter degradation of her lot; yet more calmly than ever to shut her feelings within her breast. Drooping thus, she was aroused by a sudden cry of pleasure.

'Why, Maida! You here?' and Lucy ran over to her. Sanders was with her; he approached, equally pleased to see his old mate.

'Well, Madda, 'tain't trouble I hope, that brings you here? Us is come to look out a woman!'

There was no small inflation of vanity in his voice and person as he made this declaration, same time making his locks to pass through his fingers.

Lucy explained:

'So long as one of us is T.L. you know, we can have a servant—Lor', Maida, think of me having one! But Bob says he will, and nothing shall stop him, and that, too, before baby is born.'

She suddenly blushed and looked so exactly like the Lucy of olden days, that Maida kissed her forthwith. What plunged her in so sudden a confusion was only confided to Robert's ear.

She beckoned him over to a corner of the yard and whispered something. Bob listened awhile and seemed to share his little wife's confusion: he consulted with his locks, and then told Lucy he thought 'twould 'do first rate—but darned if he could propose it.'

'Oh, Bob, I couldn't! You'll do it beautiful, you says everything so clever and nice; besides, you are Ticket and I'm not.'

So, flown with T. L.-ism, strode Robert Sanders over to Maida; Lucy following timidly and on tiptoe, for fear she should disturb her husband's grand intention.

'I say, Madda, we've talked at it, and if you've a will to it, we'll hire you out and give 'e just what the master did. Us'll get on fine together, darned if we won't!'

Whilst this was being uttered, Lucy peeped shyly from between her hands, but directly it had gone forth beyond hope of recall, she bent eagerly forward, and every bright feature said, 'Will you, Maida? Will you?'

Maida waited a moment, and then, smiling kindly, replied:

'Do you ask, or *command* me, Sanders? I believe I dare not refuse if you choose to hire me.'

Bob seemed enchanted! His T.L. was glorified beyond his fondest ambition; he stroked his hair in quiet enjoyment, and, nodding sideways, answered:

'Well, believe I could, but I won't foss you—don't like foss, it's darned hard to bear; if you don't like it, us won't ask up to the tepot,' as he called the depot.

'Then, thanking you for your very kind offer, I think I had better decline; but as for going with you, I would as soon be *your* servant as anybody's.'

Another stroke of approval, but Lucy exclaimed, her bright face clouding with shocked disappointment:

'Oh, Maida! Not our servant, I never thought of that; I meant you to come along and be one of us; we both love you, don't we, Bob?'

Bob only shook his locks, and uttered his expletive, 'Darned!'

A carriage drove into the yard, and the friendly talk was suspended, for an officer called for Maida Gwynnham.

A lady leaned from the carriage and surveyed her from head to foot:

'Are you a needlewoman?'

'I can use my needle, ma'am, but I am engaged; I believe my late master will be here for me presently.'

'We have nothing to do with late masters; if I choose to take you out, you must either go with me or to Cascades.'

Turning to the matron:

'The woman's insolent, I'm afraid she wouldn't do for *me*; that sort of nose is always a sign of impudence.'

At this moment Mr. Evelyn's loud 'Ahem' was heard, and turning round, Maida saw her master hastening up the path. He raised his hat to the lady.

'I beg your pardon, but this woman is *my* servant; I have come to fetch her out.'

'Not if I choose to take her, sir; she says the same thing, but it is entirely contrary to convict rule.'

'I'm afraid, sir, the lady is right,' whispered the matron; 'the more so as Gwynnham came in without even the pretence of belonging to anyone else.'

'I have paid for her at the hospital for two months, in order to secure her to my family,' replied Mr. Evelyn.

'No matter, sir,' bowed the lady, 'she came in here to be hired by the first comer.'

'I cannot contend with a lady; if, therefore, I renounce my *right* to her, will you *concede* her to me?' asked Mr. Evelyn courteously.

'It's enough to spoil the creature!' ejaculated the grandee, falling back in her seat.

She was selfish, and thought a servant worthy of so great a fuss must be worthy of her; she pondered a moment, and then inquired in a superciliously playful tone:

'Well, sir, who is to have the woman?'

'It is for you to decide; I would not disappoint a lady.'

There was more anxiety in his manner than he cared should appear; this was not lost either upon Maida or her would-be mistress.

'Well, then, since the gentleman declines you, jump upon the box, you Gwynnham,' said the lady with a forced laugh; 'and I suppose I must go into the hiring room and signify my wishes.'

She stepped from the carriage; Mr. Evelyn assisted her to the office door, and then firmly but politely said:

'Understand, if you please, that *I* have not declined the woman, but that you have taken her from me.'

A haughty bow was the only answer.

'And I must beg, if you do not find her what you wish, that you will favour me by letting me know before you dispose of her,' continued Mr. Evelyn.

'Anyone is welcome to a convict that leaves my house! Sure to be mere refuse if *I* send them off.'

She vanished within the depot, and Mr. Evelyn returned to Maida, who was now seated on the box.

'Maida, my woman, I'm sorry for this; you've slipped through my fingers.'

'Do not distress yourself, sir; I thank you for your interference, though it has been unsuccessful.'

The lady now appeared, and Mr. Evelyn hastily whispered, 'Remember you are mine, if you leave your present mistress.'

The carriage drove on—a last and sinister bow the only further acknowledgment of Mr. Evelyn's presence.

'Bother it; what'll Herbert and Emmeline say!' muttered Mr. Evelyn, as he rode from the Brickfields.

Maida was borne away to one of the many elegant villas surrounding New Town.

A footman opened the door, and Mrs. Patterley consigned her new servant to his care, saying:

'Take this woman, and after she has cleansed herself, send her up to my dressing room.'

Shortly after Maida went to her mistress, who abruptly commenced, 'You'll soon find out what your work is.'

'I understood I was engaged to be needlewoman.'

'I want sewing done; but that is only when you've nothing else to do—you are to be parlour-maid; in fact, you are to be anything I choose—I never allow any airs.'

Maida was retreating.

'Stop, woman; don't be so impatient; I've something to say to you—are you paying attention? Well, then—I've a son downstairs—mind I see no improper conduct towards him, or you'll go off to Cascades. I've sent away ever so many government women on his account—they're such a vile set; it's quite a nuisance to have them about—go—that's *all*, only mind what you're about. You don't bear a very good character in that way already.'

Maida hurried out, for indignation burned within her.

It was some days after this that her young master came into the dining room when she was laying the cloth; he whistled about the parlour for a minute or two, and then, standing at the other end of the table, said:

'I say, where did you get those splendid eyes of yours?'

Maida answered not.

'I only want you to look at me—you're so handsome.'

He went towards her, she laid down her tray and walked to the door; but it being nearer to him than to her, Mr. Patterley sprang over and placed his back against it, then tapping her on the cheek, he said:

'Now, give me a look, or you shan't pass.'

Maida *did* look; he did not wish for a second.

'Oh! I *say*, I don't mean like *that*; that isn't what a feller calls pleasing—look at me with those rare purple eyes of yours, the same as I've seen you star-gazing sometimes, enough to make a feller wild.'

'I warn you, sir, not to provoke me too far, for I am passionate, and might be tempted to strike you.'

'Strike away, then, pretty one!' said Mr. Patterley, bending his face forward.

And Maida struck him a real, good hard blow, sufficient to arouse both rage and redness.

'You contemptible wretch! I'll have you punished.'

As he uttered these words, his mother sailed into the room.

'The old story! Really these government women are the pests of one's life. Edward, surely you must give them encouragement?'

'Of course I do, mother; what man resists the—'

'What have you done to your face?' interrupted Mrs. Patterley.

'I struck him, ma'am; and I shall again if he comes near me.'

A loud ring at the bell was the only answer.

'Fetch a constable! This woman's going—'

'To the Brickfields, ma'am?' bowed the footman.

'No, to the police station.'

Maida was locked in a room until the constable's arrival, and then duly given into charge—she was marched off to the court.

'But, I say, mother, it will be awkward for me to appear against her: I must acknowledge that I teased her before she struck me.'

'Oh, never mind, my dear, you needn't appear; I'll go for you.'

So on the morrow, Maida was brought up, and Mrs. Patterley appeared against her, accusing her of insolence and improper conduct; on the strength of which complaint she was sentenced to a month's imprisonment with cells.

'I have nothing to say against the charge, except that it is all a lie—nor against my punishment, except that it is unjust!' exclaimed Maida, when the magistrate advised her to avoid trouble for the future.

In reply to which speech the magistrate thought it would take quite another month to cool the prisoner properly down; and, therefore, amidst the laughter of the court, he sentenced her to a second month with hard labour.

Mrs. Patterley was then driven back to her luxurious home, and Maida was conveyed in the prison van to the Cascades, there to be lowered by skillet, wasted by severe labour, and worried by every species of indignity; but not all this until she had first been subdued by a protracted confinement in the dark cells.

She had been in the establishment about seven weeks, when, for some distasteful answer to one of the petty officers, she was ordered three days' solitary; she was just at the end of the second day when the door suddenly unlocked, and Mr. Herbert stood before her—he could not at first see her.

'Maida, are you there?' he asked: his voice was low and tremulous. Maida did not reply.

'Why don't you come forward, there?' said the officer who accompanied Mr. Herbert; 'the light will shine in presently, sir, then you will see her; she's the most troublesome case we've got.'

Maida came forward, trying to look unconcerned; but the light caused her to close her eyes.

'Can I be left with her?' inquired Mr. Herbert.

'Well, sir, I suppose as you are a clergyman I must not object,' and the woman withdrew.

By this Maida had retreated to the end of her cell, and as she crouched up in a corner, her eyes looked like two large brilliants set in darkness.

Mr. Herbert entered, and, having closed the door, he said:

'Shut your eyes a minute, for I am going to strike a light.' He drew a little case from his pocket, ignited a match, and then lighted a wax taper. 'Now then, it will not pain you; look up, and tell me how you came here.'

'Pray, sir, tell me first, how you became aware of my being here.'

'Your master wrote me word, and I also saw it in the *Courier*.'

'And what brought you up from the peninsula, sir? No bad tidings, I trust?'

'Very bad, Maida; even your being here!'

She laid down her head, and groaned.

'For me, sir! All that way for me!'

'For you, Maida; and I mean to wait in town until I can either take you to Port Arthur, or see you under Mr. Evelyn's care.'

'Oh, sir; don't, I pray you! I can bear anything but kindness; that breaks what little heart I have left to me.'

'My poor Maida, none of us believe you guilty of the immorality assigned. We think, perhaps, you were hasty, and even violent.'

'I was both; but both were deserved, sir—I am weak and ill, and cannot bear your kindness—I am shaken in mind and body. If you talk so to me, I shall weep.'

Her voice became unsteady, and Mr. Herbert remained silent.

'All last night, sir, I was with my poor father, and that has unnerved me; as you speak words of kindness, I fancy I hear him. Oh, sir! You will think me a coward, when I tell you that I dread such another night, because I dread again to meet my father.' She covered her face with her hands, and then broke out in her old wild way:

'Hell is kinder than this, for hell has light! There was a time when I did not care for the cells; but now—I do not know how it is, I cannot endure them. Sir, do you think my reason is going?'

'Far from it, Maida; I think it is returning. You are, perhaps, accepting God's terms, offered in the first of Isaiah,[1]—and so Satan is doing all he can to terrify you.'

'Sir, I do not wish to put anything off on Satan, all I suffer is from my own wicked spirit and guilty conscience.'

Mr. Herbert smiled.

'Never mind what it is *from*, Maida; sit down and let me tell you about Emmeline and the baby—they both send their love to you.'

He talked to her some time, and then read the Twenty-third Psalm.[2]

'That is a strange passage to read to me, sir!'

'Why so, Maida? It is a sweet collection of thoughts, if nothing else, and I see no objection to your thinking them over.'

The overseer entered and announced closing hours, whereupon Mr. Herbert arose and whispered to Maida that she should not remain another night in the cells—he would appeal against further solitary confinement. He accordingly requested to see the superintendent, and to him stated his belief that it would be injurious to keep Maida longer in the cells.

The superintendent said she had but one day to accomplish; of this one day, however, Mr. Herbert would not hear; the prisoner's nerves being already irritated and disordered, he insisted on the necessity of releasing her, and was at last successful in obtaining a remission of her sentence. Having ascertained at what day and at what hour she would be free, he directed that she should be promised to no one, but be sent straight to the depot, where he or Mr. Evelyn would appear at the given hour to hire her out.

Six days from that period the brown van was again in waiting at the gates of Cascades, and amongst many other women Maida was conducted to it: the door was then locked, the key given to the constables in charge, and the dreary van drove off to the Brickfields. The women had scarcely been delivered to the superintendent, ere Maida saw Mr. Herbert descend from a cab and enter the hiring office. In another minute she was called forward, and in five more was on her way to the Lodge.

'Now, Maida, you are to have rest until your strength has returned; for this reason, I am going to leave you in Hobart. At Port Arthur you might be pressed into the general service; at home, there being only your master, you will not be required to work.'

Mr. Herbert tried to smile cheerfully, but Maida appeared listless and reserved. He continued:

'Necessity has partly decided me, for, except in an open boat, I do not know how I should get you down; the steamer is still laid up. Are you tired, Maida? You look so.'

'Do I, sir?' and she sat upright.

Mr. Herbert laid his fingers on her wrist.

'I must doctor you; you know my prescription? Miss Bridget calls it the everlasting quinine and wine.'[3]

'I have been plentifully dosed, thank you, sir. Government is generous with its medicines when there is any chance of losing a convict.'

'Here we are at the Lodge, we'll forget the prescription for the present. You will only find Diprose within; Tammy has been sent away.'

Mr. Herbert went to his brother, who lounged in the breakfast room.

'Is she come?'

'Yes, but in a weak, low state, poor thing! I can hardly venture a word to her.'

'By which you mean *I* am not to venture any. Ah! I'm up to you, Herbert; well, I'm not going to worry her, she's had enough, and too much already.'

Maida entered to learn her master's wishes. Mr. Evelyn arose, and Mr. Herbert left the room; his brother was always kinder to her when he was not present.

'Well, Maida, here you are at last! I think I may say I'm *glad* to see you back, but not in that doleful plight: look up, my woman, what ails you?'

'What ails me, sir? Should you wish information on that point I would advise a visit to the Cascades.'

'Well, don't let's rub up old grievances; all I can say is that I am sorry to my heart for you. I only wish I could lay hold of that young scamp, Patterley, and I'd teach him something, darned if I wouldn't, as Sanders says.'

But Maida was not inclined to laugh. Raising her eyes to her master, she said—

'I thank you, sir; by-and-by I hope to appreciate your kindness; now I feel cross and bewildered; to escape from observation is all I want—I shall only get into trouble again if I remain in my present state of mind.'

'Well, keep clear of me if you like, for I'm not in an over good temper either; I never am whilst there are pale faces about me, so go and get up your looks before you have anything to say to me.'

'As to the *rest* which Mr. Herbert promised me, sir?'

'The devil he did! Why, I've been waiting here this long time to be rid of some of my cares—the garden, for instance; there are all Miss D'Urban's flowers requiring attention: I wanted you to be after them; and there's Diprose upstairs, up to all manner of mischief. However, if Mr. Herbert promised you *rest*, go and take it, as much as you like of it. I don't think you'll ever get fat on it, though.'

Maida was obliged to smile in spite of herself; her master had never been so queer before.

'I was about to remark, sir, that I neither wish for rest nor need it.'

'Oh, humbug, yes, you do; you don't suppose I don't know what convicts want.' Dropping his voice to his natural tone—'I tell you what it is, Maida, if it will not be a comfort to you to hear, it is a relief to me to let you know, that I think your punishment a disgrace to everyone concerned. Yes! That's from *me*, late a police magistrate. Go and make what use you please of it.'

'I shall, then, make two uses of it, sir, the one to convict myself, and the other to force me to seek your forgiveness.'

Mr. Evelyn put up his eyebrows: his joking fit was over and he now viewed the case in sober sense as it stood before him in painful reality.

Maida did not understand the raised eyebrows to mean 'Go on,' so her master nodded 'Well?'

'Your kindness, sir, convicts me of deep ingratitude; you can never blame me on that point so much as I blame myself. Believe me, sir, I am not so by nature. I am proud, wicked, and resentful, but not ungrateful. I have been goaded into rebellion and perversity, until—'

'There now, that'll do; you need not tell me you are proud, that I've found out long ago; and as to your being wicked, you can grant that if you like, but as to your being resentful or ungrateful, it's not a true bill, or, by George—'

But Mr. Evelyn stopped with an ahem; he was on the punishment ground again, and therefore checked himself.

Mr. Herbert started for Port Arthur on the following day, and Maida was left to a season of genial quiet, for none in the house was disposed to interfere much with her. Her master purposely avoided her as much as possible; and her fellow servants had received secret commands not to seek her assistance. The man, Stephens, was an odd being, and would have had but little to say to her if he had not been laid under ban.

He seemed in so perpetual a flurry and excitement that he had incurred the sobriquet of Fussy.

From morning to night he was never still; it would be flurry, flurry to the last moment, when he would prepare for bed by dressing himself for the morning. Then, resting one leg on the floor and tucking the other under the bedclothes, he would ensconce himself in discomfort, ready to start at the first sound, or earliest sign of morning, again to go on flurrying until night. Whether he supposed he hurried on his freedom by this unceasing turmoil no one could discover. Silent and irritable he vented one favourite word on all occasions at all out of the usual course. He had a peculiar way of snorting out this word between two thick breaths, driven, smoke-like, from his nostrils.

'Fussy, the master's a-roaring after you,' would say one of his fellow servants.

Snort, 'Precious,' snort, his only answer.

'I say that there Sam Tonkins was hung up to-day.'

Snort, 'Precious,' snort. Fussy's sole appreciation of the fact.

He had also a favourite notion that the facsimile of everything pertaining to luxury or comfort had once been possessed by himself or his wife. When the lady governess of the island called, he would duly announce her, then banging the door, he would mutter:

'Shawl just like my wife's!'

Having the master's travelling cloak to brush, he would set at it with, 'Precious, not a bit better than the cloak I had at home, just the feller, b'lieve it's the same.' He had, too, a favourite dislike, and that was of the cicada, whose never flagging whir-r-r seemed almost to distract poor Fussy. He anathematised them more than twenty times a day.

'Why, what is it, Fussy?' asked someone, observing his uneasiness.

Snort, 'Precious,' snort, 'to think I've come out all this way to hear nothing but them critics a-whizzing their nonsense all day long; precious tongues they've got to keep on that way!'

No persuasion could make him call them crickets. No, no, he'd 'heard tell of critics at home, and knew well enough that they was famous for their keeping on when everybody else had done talking.' It was the master's peculiar delight to listen to his crusade against the 'critics.' Had he been a more educated man, Mr. Evelyn would have suspected him to be a disappointed author, but the poor fellow was, happily, innocent of letters.

Diprose, too, had no inclination to molest Maida; she was absorbed in her own sorrows. Though a convict, she was still a mother, and possessed the yearnings of a mother's heart. Day and night she fretted over her four children, dead or alive. She had buried two: one little child of five had been left in Scotland; the other, an infant, was in the Queen's Orphan School. When first she went to see her little son, she was doubly hurt; in the first place, because no one in the school seemed to know her baby from all the others.

'What! Not know my little Abel!' she exclaimed, bursting into tears.

'Get along with your Abel; who be he more than anybody else's Abel?' was the comfortable rejoinder.

And secondly, because little Abel himself did not recognise her.

'Come to his own mammy, then!' she said maternally, and straightway the child stretched his arms to a mother *not* his own.

She confided her story to Maida, whose ever-ready sympathy invited the outpouring of the deserted mother's heart.

She told her she had never known sorrow or a dishonest penny until the winter of 18—, when everything was scarce and work still more so; sickness fell on her children, and her husband emigrated to America to build a nest in which he could put his family. She never heard of him again, and was left to struggle with three children and a fourth expected. Two sickened, and in one day she laid them both in one grave; she said the neighbours came from far to see the bairns, they looked so heavenly in their coffins. After the first flow of pity had subsided, she was again left to poverty and misery; one night, when a half-crown would have saved her from immediate ruin, a bad man came round and tempted her with illegal money, which she passed, was detected, apprehended, and transported. This was her simple tale, and its truthfulness none could doubt who looked at her woebegone face and heard her constant sigh. She fretted on and on, until her master thought the hospital would be the best place for her.

As another case of 'frettin,' she was therefore admitted to that establishment, and never left it more until she was carried thence to the prisoners' grave yard, when her little Abel was cast on the world a despised child of a despised race.

A month passed, and still there was no chance of remitting Maida to Port Arthur. The *Kangaroo's* ailments were obstinate, and required still further professional treatment.

The family had now been four months on the peninsula. The winter had set in, it being the latter end of June, and in a week or two would be too far advanced to allow the possibility of sending Maida. One day when she had nearly given up all hope of being summoned, Father Evermore trotted up the lawn and left a note for Mr. Evelyn, requesting that an answer might be left at the vicar-general's before the next evening.

The note contained a message from Mr. Herbert, saying that Father Evermore, having occasion to go to town, had consented to bring back Maida if she were not afraid to venture in an open boat. Mr. Herbert added that there would be no other opportunity, the *Kangaroo* having been tried and found unequal to the trip, and another steamer could not be ready until the spring.

It needed no persuasion to induce Maida to get ready; she was as anxious to go as Emmeline was to have her.

But Fussy pronounced it very precious that he should be left to lock up the gates at night, a post of which he had entertained a decided dread from the time of the bushrangers' attack on the house during Maida's imprisonment.

Since her return to the Lodge she had always gone down to lock the outhouses and garden gates; for Fussy thought far too preciously of his brains to risk having them dislodged by venturing outside the door after dark; he considered that once in his life was quite sufficient to have a pistol held at his head. Now Maida quieted him by saying that she should see all right for two nights more, and then, perhaps, the master would either undertake it or let Diprose. It was her last night. Being engaged in preparations for her departure, Maida forgot the gates until ten o'clock, when she hastened down the lawn to close them for the night. The moon shone so gloriously that in spite of the keen wind she walked up and down the grove path, and was soon in one of her dreams of the past. Turning towards the thickest part of the grove, where a hedge of tea-shrub joined the trees into a continuous chain, she saw the hedge divide and a scarecrow figure approach her. It was that of a man whose famished look and tattered garments proclaimed him to be a wayfarer of no common order.

'Martha Grylls,' said the gaunt figure.

She started.

The voice was so hollow, and the eyes glared so spectre-like upon her, that for an instant she doubted it to be more than a phantasy, but it repeated, in yet more sepulchral tones:

'Are you Martha Grylls?'

'I am; what do you want of me?'

'To save me! There's no one else I knows of that will.'

'Who are you?' Maida felt a cold terror creeping over her; she imputed it to the bleak wind, and shrugged herself together, repeating, 'Who are you?'

'Bob Pragg. I'm *out*, and there's a free pardon offered on my head, and money to the bargain.'

'Pragg!'

'Yes! I knows no one but *you* that'll save me.'

'Me, Pragg! What do you know, then, of me, that makes you say so?'

'That you ain't the one to send off a poor dying wretch like me, to make gold of my blood.'

There was a dead silence, during which the chattering of Pragg's teeth, and Maida's hard, quick breathing, were the only audible sounds that interchanged with the wailing of the wind. A loud fitful gust swept down the grove, and by its suddenness forced Maida against Pragg; he stretched out his hand and clutched her; she shuddered as she felt the bony grasp that clung to her with the desperation of despair.

'I say, Martha Grylls, can you forgive an enemy? Can you? Can you?'

'I can, Bob—so help and forgive me, God.'

'Oh, those be solemn words,' gibbered[4] Bob.

'They are true words, Bob.'

'Give me your hand to it, then.'

He put forth a long claw-like hand, and it pounced on Maida's, grasping it, cold and deathly.

'Can you feed an enemy, Martha Grylls? I'm starving! I 'scaped from the Neck, and I've wandered in the bush till I'm 'most eaten up alive with the rot, and I'm 'most dead of hunger; I ate a dead guana[5] five days agone, and nothing but a sup of water's gone down since—I say, woman, can you feed an enemy?'

His claws almost pierced her skin as he shook her, repeating,

'Can you, woman, can you?'

'I *can*, Bob, but only by giving you money. I've no food of my own, nor could I get any without betraying you.'

'MONEY!' he laughed a wild shrill laugh. 'MONEY! Will that feed a starving belly? Curse your money and give me bread!' He lowered his voice, and glaring at her, muttered:

'Bread, for the love of God! *You*, the woman I've injured and would have injured more if I could, give me food—give me food!'

Maida clasped her hands in agony.

Pragg drew closer to her and hissed into her ear, 'A fine plea, ain't it? But I swear before—'

Maida laid her arm upon him.

'Bob, don't swear before anyone, for God is up there listening to you.'

'It is just before *He* that I'm going to swear, for it's the only true word of my life that I'm now speaking, and that is, I know that it's just the plea to go down with *you*. Ah, I know you, Martha Grylls, better nor you think! Ah, I know all about it.'

His teeth chattered beyond control; he could only mumble incoherent words that Maida could not understand, but her alarm was aroused. She shivered with fright as she said:

'Tell me what you mean; for pity's sake, Bob, tell me.'

'Give me food first, food, I say, food, and then I'll tell you that if I'm taken, I'll proclaim your hinnocence from the gallows—ah! that I will, or blast my living soul. Oh, Martha, Martha!' The tears rolled down his hollow cheek. 'Oh, Martha, when Bob Pragg's brought to tears the devil's out of 'en. I never thought to see the day when I'd blubber before a woman, and she *you*. I always swore I'd die game. But ah! There's no game in dying, no, not whilst there's *Hell!* HELL! HELL! Food, woman—food, I say!'

Maida recollected the little basket of stores, supplied for her journey. It was truly hers—she might give it.

'Bob, I *can* give you food; go back into the hedge and I'll run and fetch it; I must talk to you more by-and-by.'

She glided into the house; the light shone from the drawing room window, telling that her master had not yet retired for the night. She slipped up to her bedroom and was returning with her basket when Mr. Evelyn came out of the room.

'You, Maida! Where are you going with that basket? Fine preparation for your journey!'

'I'm going downstairs, sir.'

'Well, well, I'll wait till you come up. Why, how's this, Jags isn't brought in yet? Mind, if the rangers[6] come I shall declare you are in league with them.'

Maida rejoiced to hear him speak so, because it showed that he was in a good humour, so she laughingly replied:

'Very well, sir, I'll plead guilty; but if you'll trust the house to me, I'll ward off the rangers; my pistols are always loaded.'

'Well, then, good-night, I'll leave it to you, only don't come creeping up when you have done, but give a good, brave step that I may know you are safe.'

Therewith her master hummed himself upstairs; she heard his door lock, his shoes flung off, and then she knew *he* was safe. Having brought in Jags, the terrier, and let him loose in the hall, she barred all the front doors of the house and let herself out into the lawn by the back door, and, locking it after her, she put the key in her pocket. The two sunken eyes were glaring out for her from the thicket. She sat down by Bob and opened her stores; the long, bony palm snatched up the first eatable she drew forth. He bolted a few mouthfuls and then threw it down, shaking his head.

'I'm sick, woman—I can't eat now it's before me.'

'Try Bob; let me feed you.'

Bob shook his head, and a flood of tears extinguished the glare of his eyes.

'Oh, I say, woman; can you forgive a dying wretch? Can you? Can you?'

He laid down his head between his knees and moaned.

'Can you? Can you? This ain't Bob Pragg, is it? Oh! Can you? Can you?'

'Bob, don't torment yourself; I *can*, and *do*—and pray God to forgive you too.'

'Do you? Then, pray on, quick—for hell's a-gaping wide and I'm 'most gone down. There! What d'ye think of *that*? I pulled it off a tree where they'd stuck it.'

Bob pinched a soiled, torn paper from his breast, and threw it at her.

'There's money for this poor skinned carcass! Worth it, ain't it? You go and claim it, and the gibbet 'll be a happy death to me. Read it, woman, read.'

Maida opened the paper, when, distinct and horrible, three large black words appeared; the light was quite enough to exhibit them in all their horror.

'Murder! Murder! Murder!!! Free pardon and £30 reward.'

Every word of the fearful advertisement was visible. Then came a description of Pragg, with the above reward offered for his apprehension.

As Maida read out 'Round and ruddy,' he grinned a death's head grin.

'Like me, ain't it? Look here—round, ain't it? Ruddy? Ay, as the grave!'

'What am I to do with this, Pragg?'

'Go and get your pardon and your money home out of it.'

'Do you mean it, Pragg? I thought you said you knew me.'

'I know you; but I know myself better, and I know 'twould be a blessed relief to me to be delivered up by *you*. I want to feel paid out, I do, woman, I do. Pay me out—do, do, I say.'

Maida tore the paper into shreds and trod it underfoot.

'There, Pragg; I'll deliver you up to God, but to no one else.'

'To God!' shrieked Pragg. 'To GOD!'

The wind wailed down the grove, and his tattered garments fluttered on him like rags upon a gibbet.

'To GOD, woman! 'Tis He I'm most afeared to meet; if 'twern't for He I'd give my own self up, for death would be a grace to my rotted body. But, Martha Grylls—you that I dragged away from your own baby's grave—you that I swore on, save me from He, as you would save your own soul.'

'Oh, that Mr. Herbert were here!' groaned Maida.

'Don't fetch of he! He'd bring the very light of hell with him.'

'Bob, he'd bring his Saviour with him.'

'Ay, woman, ay; his Saviour, if you like—but where's mine? Oh, where's mine, I say? Where's mine?'

'There he is, Bob; look up!'

And Maida pointed up to where shone calmly down the bright, bright moon, untouched by the stormy blast.

Bob turned up his glaring eyes—a cloud drove past and hid the moon. Bob threw down his head and cried—

'You lie, woman—you lie; 'taint mine—he right hides himself when I look up.'

'Bob, I am a poor sinner myself, and therefore a bad one to talk about such things; but this I know—that Jesus came for sinners, and not for the righteous. He died for men and not for angels. He died for you and me, just because we are sinners—bad people—so He will save us.'

Bob moaned aloud, and once more looked up to the heavens.

'Bob, are you sorry for your sins?' asked Maida.

For an instant—through all his begrimed, haggard and fleshless form; through all his famished and sunken features—for an instant he looked like his old self; he winked a twinkling wink which came horribly from his glaring eye, and he said in his own familiar voice—

'That ain't the word! Sorry! I b'ain't sorry for them; but they be sorry for me—ay, sorry, woman! Shoving me headermost into the brimstone that I've heard tell of—Hell! I smell it nigh.'

Maida was bewildered; for all that she had heard the gospel so faithfully declared—for all that she longed to receive it herself, her tongue now seemed to cleave to the roof of her mouth. She knew that the Redeemer bled for sinners; but as she looked on the ghastly object before her, dyed in his fellow mortal's blood, she feared whether she had any right to speak comforting words to him; whether, by so speaking, she should not be deceiving by him to his double despair.

'Can you pray, Martha Grylls?'

'Yes, Bob; for anyone but myself.'

'Pray then—quick.'

Maida knelt, and commenced a few words—when Bob tore down her hands.

'Don't pray, I can't bear it; it's worse than hell, because it's hell before its time.'

But quietly, though trembling in every limb, Maida again clasped her hands, and uttered a short prayer for pardon for the wretched man before her.

'Oh, oh!' groaned Bob, and the wailing wind bore on and prolonged the oh—oh—oh!

The dogs set up a loud, fierce bark, which was snapped up and reverberated by the terrier within doors. Maida started.

'Bob, I must leave you; creep into the shed, and cover yourself over with this; I'll be out in the morning before it is light. Oh, Bob! I grieve to say it; but hadn't you better give yourself up? You *must* be caught, for you are weak and can't crawl far—poor, poor Bob!'

She burst into tears, and crouching down by him, said:

'Bob, I'd save you if I could; but I'm only a prisoner myself, I'll never give you up; but leave you I must, for I'm going to be sent away to-morrow.'

'Maybe I'll be dead of cold 'fore morning! Oh, it's freezing, ain't it?' and his teeth chattered and his whole frame shook.

The dogs sounded a second and louder alarm.

'Creep into this shed, Bob; the master 'll be getting up. Quickly as you can.'

Bob crept in, and Maida covered him as well as she could.

'Martha, is the gate free, 'sposing I makes up my mind to crawl away?'

He turned a look so piteous on her, that she wrung her hands.

'That little gate there shall be free. I can see it from a window upstairs. I'll sit up all night, and watch it that I may leave it safely open.'

Without venturing a second look, Maida glided into the back door, speaking low and soothingly to the dogs to keep them quiet. She passed swiftly into the nursery, and locking the door, took her station at the window to watch the gate. She heard her master go downstairs to make the round of the house—as he always did when the dogs were vociferous.

She also heard him fire off a pistol from the lobby window, and then all was peace again for the night.

She watched for two hours, when she fancied she perceived a slight movement of the gate; but the moon rays glancing about gave an appearance of motion to every object;

therefore, she looked long and steadfastly ere she could decide whether it opened or not. It did open, and just then the moon rode out from a cloud and a baptism of cold, clear glory fell around, making every dim outline give out distinctly the form it before had shrouded in uncertainty. It fell extra bright and clear over the little gate, when Maida saw a heap of rags crawling along the earth and pushing its way through the open gate. Softly as possible she slid up the sash. Bob heard her and turned towards the window; the large, white eyeballs rolled up and stared very ghastly towards her earnest face. Bob slowly raised his long arm thrice, he had not strength to wave it; but the shreds hanging from it fluttered his farewell. Maida threw up her hands in an attitude of prayer, and then closed the window. The moon again was overcast, and all once more was shadow and twilight.

In the morning Maida hurried down the grove; a vestige of Bob in the form of a tattered kerchief, together with the shawl with which she had covered him, was all that remained to attest the reality of that terrible night vision.

She heard no more of Pragg; but when on her way to the boat with Father Evermore—a cart, guarded by two armed constables and drawn by four chained convicts, drove slowly by her. The cart was covered by a rug—its contents were not, therefore, revealed. Yet, with a shudder, Maida turned from it, for the middle of the rug was arched pointedly, as though forced up by two sharp knees. There was an awed gloom in the countenance of each of the driven men, and a mysterious expression in the faces of the constables.

That night, when Maida was sleeping at the station, on her way to Port Arthur, the dead-house of H.M.G. Hospital was opened and a collapsed and stiffened corpse was laid there. The very doctors, accustomed to death in its most horrible appearance—turned, heartsick away as the wide, staring eye and distorted figure of Bob Pragg met their sight.

His body had been discovered by a road party, on its progress to the bush, behind Macquarie Street.

CHAPTER 32

The Isle of the Dead

> I went her lily hand to take,
> Its coldness made me start.

THE winter passed cheerfully. The mild climate of Port Arthur had only once or twice yielded to the stern control of winter. Snow had fallen on Mount Arthur, but had not dared to show itself further. Again had the sweet month of November opened on the imprisoned family. Again came the flowers bursting from their leafy folds. The afternoon was fresh and fair, and Emmeline said she had not felt so well for a long time; she should enjoy a little draw in her primitive carriage. Opal, therefore, was ordered to hold himself in readiness to obey his young mistress's pleasure, and brightly shone his olive face as from his full lips came the answer:

'Opal leady always for she; nice lady, me luffs her wely much; always got a smile for poor chain-gang.'

When asked where she would like to go, Emmeline replied:

'Let my little carriage be drawn in sight of the Isle of the Dead, and there let me rest and look out on the lovely spot.'

And there she stayed, Opal waiting reverentially at her side, until her father feared that, gentle as the air was, it might be too strong for her.

'Very well, papa dear, I will return. I have enjoyed my journey or my rest—which is it?—more than I can tell you.'

Mr. Herbert smiled, but how subdued, and softly inquired:

'Enjoyed it? That sea-girt graveyard always makes me feel sad.'

'Ah, papa, you think of the many poor creatures lying there, far from their home and friends. That *is* sad; but as I sat gazing on it, I only thought how peaceful a rest it would afford my aching frame, and how much, if you approved, I should like to be laid there.'

She pressed his hand fondly, and watched for when he should turn his face to her.

'My child's wishes are mine. What makes you speak so, my Emmeline? You just now said you felt better.'

'And I do; but still, papa, we won't talk of it; it makes you low spirited.'

'My daughter, I would not keep you one hour beyond God's time; His blessed will be done. I have resigned you, and only hold you from Him day by day, as His tender mercy grants me a longer delay. Time once seemed long to me. Now the Invisible and Eternal are near, and divided only by a veil so transparent that my eye beholds what lies beyond.'

'Then, dear father, you can wait calmly till the moment of the undrawing of that veil?'

'I can, my child! Thank God, for my dear ones are safe within it, once there no harm can reach them, no foe molest.'

Emmeline buried her face in her hands, and then suddenly raising it she exclaimed—

'Ah, papa, but is there not one still dearer within that veil? Oh, think that He is there, and then what sorrow your dear heart must still feel will all, all go.'

'My love, He is not within the veil, or we bereaved ones could not forget our grief, even knowing, as we do, that our treasures are safe. What says our blessed saviour?'

Emmeline looked; she did not remember.

'Lo, I am with you always; we are not with Him, but is He not with us?'[1]

By this the carriage had arrived at the avenue, and Charlie rushing out upon them prevented further converse.

Emmeline stayed up later that night; she appeared so unwilling to retire that it had struck nine before Mr. Herbert reminded her she had exceeded her usual hour.

As she bade him good-night she said almost lightly:

'To-morrow I shall be alive for a trip to Stuart's Bay!'

'To-morrow is God's!' replied Mr. Herbert somewhat solemnly.

There was something in his daughter's manner and appearance that perplexed him. He returned her long embrace fervently and fondly, but a vague sensation of near sorrow mingled with his farewell, as he clasped her in his arms.

'I shall like to sleep alone to-night. I am sure I shall require nothing. Maida shall sit up a little, and then I shall send her to bed.'

She looked over the stairs and repeated:

'Good-night, papa; God bless you.'

'And you, my precious,' replied her father.

Bridget assisted her to undress, and then sat by her until it was Maida's time to come in.

'Bridgy, when I am gone, which shall you do: go back to England, or stay here?'

'I don't know, Em—I don't want you to go, therefore I put off thinking of what it would be best to do; I hate talking about anything that has to take place when you are no longer here. I can't spare your dear face; it has become a necessity to me.'

She laid her head on her cousin's pillow, and by half playfully smoothing her thin cheek, tried to hide the emotion that made her voice unsteady.

'Has it ever struck you, dear Bridget, to be thankful that I'm not a prisoner?'

'How funny! No! Much they'd find to make prisoner of in you!' and Bridget started up, quite amused at the idea.

But Emmeline was serious. She continued:

'Instead of being what I am, a poor, helpless girl, waited upon by a cheerful, loving sister as you are to me; instead of having a tender parent to love and feel for me, with Uncle Ev, and all the other dear ones around me, I might have been not only helpless, but friendless and uncared for. Oh, what am I, that I should have so many mercies above my fellow creatures—above poor Wilcox and Sally?'

As Bridget listened to her cousin, and observed the holy expression of her countenance, she was puzzled to imagine, had Em been a convict, what sort of crime she would have committed. She was just going to say as much, when Emmeline turned on her a look so wistful that she could not help asking:

'What is it, dear?'

'There is only one question that troubles me—no, not troubles, that is not the word, for I cast my cares on the Lord, but only one point I should like to have settled, if it be God's will. Who will be with papa when I am dead?'

'Oh, my Em, can you doubt? I would never leave him if I would do for him, but—' she added sadly, 'I'm afraid I'm too giddy, too thoughtless for him.'

'No, Bridget, you are not giddy. You are happy and gladsome, and he loves you as his own, so be his daughter. *I* have given him only pain; you must try to give him pleasure.'

There came a gentle tap at the door, and Mr. Herbert entered to tell Bridget it was time she should retire to rest. She arose and kissed him, and the tears were in her eyes. He knew not wherefore, neither could he account for the extra warmth of her embrace, for he knew not of the compact that had just been made between his child and niece.

'The Lord love you, my daughter!' he said as he smoothed her hair.

A glance of surprise passed between the cousins; it was the first time he had ever so called her.

'Baby is rather troublesome to-night, therefore Maida will be delayed a little, so I am going to remain by you until she is ready. I shall return presently.'

'Good-night then, my sweet Em; I must be gone before he comes back,' said Bridget.

Why was that unwillingness to part? Why did they so cling to each other? Why did tears so blend with the farewell smile of the two cousins?

'Bridget, my own one,' said Emmeline, still holding her, 'I cannot tell you what you have been to me. My sister, my friend, my nurse, my everything that my father and my Saviour have not been, and yet they have been all these; you, then, have been my own, own Bridget.'

'What does it all mean?' sobbed Bridget. 'Everything is so strange to-night.'

'But still so happy—oh, happy, happy!'

'Happy things don't make people cry,' answered Bridget, for want of something else to say.

'Em, darling, tell me,' she at last exclaimed, 'you're not going to die, are you?'

'I think not; I never felt better.'

'Then don't talk of these horrid things.'

'You will be glad by-and-by to know what a comfort you have been. Oh! I must, must thank you. I feel as though I could not sleep without, nor without praising God for having brought us together. How little I thought, when we first met, that God had prepared you for me, you bright, happy one.'

'Em, *you* have made me all I *am*, that is better than what I *was*.'

'Whoso is wise [2] and will observe these things, even he shall understand the loving kindness of the Lord. That is the text I give you, Bridget. When you are in doubt remember it, and quietly observe God's ways; and though they may seem confused and intricate, watch, and surely as morning breaks out of night, so surely shall you find "that the end of the Lord is full of mercy."[3] Good night, darling, papa is coming.'

'I don't like to leave you.'

'Why not? No person shall stay to-night; I am sure I shall sleep soundly.'

But Maida entered with Mr. Herbert. The baby had fallen asleep, and she was free to relieve her master, whose frail strength needed all the refreshment that rest could impart to fit him for the early service with the men.

'Maida, you are only going to stay until twelve, and only that because I know you would be disappointed not to remain at all; but I need nothing, so lean back and sleep.'

Maida obeyed as to the reclining, hoping that Miss Evelyn would sleep if not spoken to. She closed her eyes; but opening them suddenly, found her young mistress gazing fixedly at her. They both smiled, and Maida raised herself.

'You see I am very obedient, Miss Evelyn, but I hope you will remove your injunction, and let me talk to you; I looked forward to it all day.'

'Dear Maida!' and Emmeline stretched her hand to her.

Ah! thought Maida, I little dreamt the time would ever come in which I should hear myself called dear.

And little, too, did she once think that she could ever again allow herself to be so addressed, much less that it would afford her pleasure, and that she should acknowledge that pleasure.

Emmeline seemed to read her thought.

'Do you remember when we first met?'

'Indeed I do, Miss Evelyn; heaven has gradually opened to me since that moment. Can you forgive me my evil treatment of you?'

'Of me! My dear, watchful nurse, what do you mean?'

'We will not speak of it, then, if you please; for all you may kindly say but shows me more what I detest to see. This much I will say, that in time my debt to you and Mr. Herbert can never be known, but—' she stopped short.

Emmeline listened in thrilling eagerness; Maida had never said so much before.

'But what?'

'I was going to speak hastily; I should say, it will be known if ever I am found in heaven. Your look of delight pains me, Miss Evelyn; there is too small cause for it: I am uncertain; in fact, I have not even yet decided for Christ, because I am such a torment to myself, perpetually wishing one thing, as poor Wilcox said, and acting another. I cannot decide for Christ until I can clear up my own misgivings, and reconcile my own inconsistencies.'

'Never mind yourself, Maida; thank God you have nothing to do with anyone but Christ. The victory is given, not won by you.'

'You excite yourself, dear young lady; we must not talk any more.'

A bright flush lay on Emmeline's cheeks.

'Oh, no, no! To hear you speak of these things does me more good than all the sleep in the world.'

'I who have been so vile!' exclaimed Maida, with some bitterness; 'to hear me speak so!'

'I have had one doubt happily settled to-night, and I forgot that I had yet another before I could say that the Lord had heard all my prayer. Maida, will you set that doubt at rest?'

An expression of pain was her only reply.

'Maida, only tell me one thing, and I could die this moment.'

'Do not torture me, Miss Evelyn; I cannot tell you what I do not feel. Would you have me lie? Would you have me say I possess that which I know I have not got?'

'Maida, I would have you say what you do feel—and that is, that you long, you crave, you thirst for peace, and peace is Christ. Won't you satisfy me? Maida! Maida! Won't you?'

There was almost a wildness in her energy, with a vivid radiance in her countenance, that was unlike her usual serenity. She waited a moment, and then softly said—

'Won't you, Maida?'

'What must I tell you, Miss Evelyn?'

'That you long for the peace of Christ.'

'I do: but that is not enough—it is not having it.'

'It is enough for me. I have heard sufficient to make me very happy. Go now, dear Maida; I can sleep sweetly on what you have told me. Good-night, Maida; won't you kiss me?'

'I have never done so, Miss Evelyn; why, then, to-night?'

The colour rushed to her cheeks as the old look flashed one instant across her features. It passed; and stooping, she printed one long kiss on Emmeline's brow.

A smile, so rapt that it might have lighted an angel's face, repaid her, and she yearned to fall on her young mistress's neck and there vent her feelings; but she arose, calm and quiet as ever.

'One word, Maida, and you shall go. Say what you will, I feel sure that there is some strange mystery in your tale. I have no inkling of it, so do not fear; but I am sure there is a something that should not be as it is. When I am gone, if ever you should need a counsellor, or be unable longer to bear your secret alone, remember my father is your friend.'

'That time will never come, Miss Evelyn. If I have a secret it is one that I can keep. But don't send me away—do let me stay, Miss Evelyn; I have given you pleasure, now repay me.'

'To-morrow you shall sleep here with me—to-night I wish to be alone: once more, good-night, dear Maida,' and the door closed.

In a few moments all was silent in the parsonage: all weary eyes were closed in sleep, and sleep, sweeter than she had ever known, hushed Emmeline in calm repose.

In the early morning, as was her wont, Maida entered Miss Evelyn's room on tiptoe. She still slept, so Maida, as she had often done before, crept over to look at her.

Last night's smile still lingered on her lips, which had fallen gently apart, disclosing two pearly teeth; one hand lay beneath, and partly supported her cheek, and the other lay upon the bed. Maida bent to kiss that hand—its coldness made her start.

She stood before Death disarmed of his terrors, for Emmeline was in heaven.

How long she stood entranced she knew not. The door shutting upon Mr. Herbert as he left the house for his duty aroused her.

'Dear creature! O God! I thank Thee that Thou didst give me power to place that smile upon those precious lips, now hushed for ever. I, who have given her so many pangs, am not worthy of a mercy so great.'

Bridget was dressing when Maida, with a faint tap, entered her room.

'How pale you are! What's the matter, Maida?'

'I am cold, Miss Bridget. You are up early.'

'Do you know, I awoke with such an uneasy feeling about Em, that, goose that I am, I was obliged to get up. Directly my dressing-gown is on I shall run up to peep at the darling; she was so extra exquisite last night that I can't forget her—*that's* why I'm up so early, Miss Curiosity.'

'I will go with you, Miss Bridget.'

What meant that trembling voice? Bridget looked at her. Involuntarily upturned the large eye, over which now quivered an undropped tear.

'Tell me, or I shall think she's dead!' exclaimed Bridget, catching both Maida's hands and shaking her.

'Tell me—I can't bear suspense—tell me, tell me!'

'She—is—not—dead—but—sleepeth,' came the slow and solemn answer.

'And I can't shed a tear,' whispered Bridget.

'Miss Bridget, let us go; one will be here presently who must go alone to that room of glory.'

Obeying the impulse of her heart, all unaware of what she did, Maida wound her arm round Miss D'Urban and led her upstairs.

'Oh no! She only sleeps. This cannot be death. Emmeline, my own one, look up and speak to me.'

But never answer came.

* * * * *

No weeds funereal lay scattered about—at once chilling the heart with their dreary aspect, and calling for energies which, though given reluctantly, relieve the burdened mind. There was no hurry of preparation. In the dim twilight, accompanied by an overseer, two convicts were seen approaching the house, bearing on their shoulders a plain deal coffin. Then, stealing in through the back door, they made their silent way to the chamber of death, where Maida awaited them; and ere the father knew what was taking place, Emmeline was tenderly laid in her last resting place, and smiled the pale face up from that simple bed, as sweetly and calmly as though it had been wrapped in costly cerements.[4]

But the men would not depart; they said they must see the parson, no one else would do.

'Well, my men, you wish to speak to me?' asked Mr. Herbert.

'It's gone abroad, your reverence, that the free is going to offer to carry Miss Evelyn. Your reverence will never take from us the last sight of her that's been the pride of the station. Sure, sir, you shall find us steady, and all so willing as them that's got wills of their own. There isn't a man in the gang that won't feel hurt if they sees her go by on other shoulders.'

'You shall carry her, for had she been asked she would have chosen you. I will see to it, and thank you.'

Mr. Herbert shook them by the hand.

'God bless your reverence, and them that's left! You won't say we've had a word with you, sir; it may go wrong with the gov'nor.'

Mr. Herbert bowed, for his voice failed him.

The man who had not spoken before now said:

'It's bad to our feelings to put that there rough timber over against her that should have the best of everything; but your reverence knows there is no help for it down here, where it's all for prisoners. I know the best in the store was picked out, but bad's the best.'

The father could almost smile: he had not observed the coffin—the gentle sleeper reposing in it absorbed his every thought.

A solitary boat, in which was discernible the convict yellow, returning from the Isle of the Dead, was the only other indication of an expected funeral. The last moment arrived, and yet no Uncle Ev appeared.

'He cannot be here now,' said Uncle Herbert, when a distant sound, as of a horse at fullest speed, was heard, and in another moment the well-known gray came dashing down the avenue, and Uncle Ev, alighting at the church, led his horse slowly towards the house. At that instant out struck the church bell, one, two—one, two. Mr. Herbert approached his brother, and in silence they grasped each other's hands.

'I can't see her?' at last whispered the elder brother, in choking utterance.

'Not until you see her *there*!' replied Mr. Herbert, pointing upward.

'Herbert, I have but one wish, and that is, that when yon dreary bell tolls for one of my children, that child may have your Emmeline's hope, and I may have your comfort.'

One, two—one, two. There must be no delay. The procession moved slowly through the settlement. As officiating minister and chief mourner, Mr. Herbert walked first, bareheaded, and in his surplice. Then, borne by six prisoners in white blouses, came the simple coffin, Mr. Evelyn, Bridget, and Charlie following close after, and then, forming a part of the procession, and yet isolated from it, succeeded a solitary figure, wrapt in a lonely grief that it was striking to behold; beyond her lingered Opal, his eye wistfully following the mournful band as it wound through the settlement and stopped at the bay, where three boats awaited it; one of which was empty, and attached to the second by a stout rope. In the other two sat the boat's crew in white jackets; they bent reverently on their oars as Mr. Herbert passed by them and took his place in the first boat. Mr. Evelyn, Bridget, and Charlie entered the next; then the coffin was lowered into the third boat, and the bearers retired to the jetty. There was no room for Maida—she must be left behind. She watched the signal for departure being given with a look of anguish, which Mr. Herbert perceived as he just raised his head from the folds of his surplice to take a last look at the coffin ere it was towed onward. He no sooner met that anguished eye than he motioned her to step into the third boat. What, with the dear creature herself! He cannot mean it, thought Maida; but Mr. Herbert beckoned again, and with a trembling foot she entered, and almost flung herself at the coffin's side. Plash! plash! With measured strokes the oars beat solemn time, and alternately with them out-swelled the full, deep bell. Save these, all else was silence—not a sound broke on the stillness. The station had hushed its many voices into one breathless tribute to her who had passed through it for the last time.

The plash of the oar has ceased; Mr. Herbert stands on the Isle of the Dead. His white robe flutters in the air as he turns to the death-freighted boat. Involuntarily, once or twice, his arms stretch forward when, tottering over the narrow plank, the boat's crew bear his child across.

Now all have landed; Mr. Herbert turns, and in the same order the procession threads its way up the narrow defile.

One, two! One, two! One, two! swings rapidly from the steeple rising from yon knot of trees. The vibrations die away, and all again is silence. When swept onward by the gentle breeze, a voice bursts from that solitary spot:

'I am the resurrection and the life; he that believeth in me, though he were dead, yet shall he live; and whosoever liveth and believeth in me shall never die.'[5]

At first the tone is tremulous, for it is a father who speaks; but lofty it swells, and yet more lofty, till, like sweet music from a distant shore, is wafted over the quiet bay that Christian hope and holy aspiration, triumphant over pain and death.

But now the funeral disappears, lost amid the foliage.

Unseen, it moves on until two chained prisoners waiting at an open grave mark the resting place it comes to sanctify.

Hitherto, in compassion to the father, there has been but slight outward show of grief; all have controlled their feelings; a very muffled sob has been the only audible indication of the heart's sorrow. But when the bidding word is spoken and falls the heavy clod upon the cherished form, one loud and bitter wail rings through the quiet of that desert isle, startling the wild goat from his rock and making the bird wheel, frightened, from his nest.

The cry comes neither from parent nor relative, but from that lonely captive, into the desolation of whose soul the fallen clod has struck and aroused a mighty echo of despair.

None tries henceforth to hide that sorrow it is a strife to hold within. The father alone weeps not. The bitter cry for a moment subdues his voice into a murmur; but it again breaks forth in holy rapture—'Blessed are the dead that die in the Lord!'[6]

All is over! The moment comes when grief may no longer feed its infatuated sight on the visibilities of death—when, as though it had never been, the joy of years is buried out of sight and death in fiction is all they may gaze upon. Oh happy they, who in this moment of darkest bereavement, of keenest woe, may look up from mortal to immortality, from corruption to incorruption, and behold life 'pre-eminent o'er all'!

All is over! Threading down the narrow defile the lessened band reappears, the measured plash once more is heard, and the three boats draw landward. But one is empty now and slowly as before is towed by the other two. Unbidden, Maida enters her master's boat, and unforbidden, sits there.

There have they left Emmeline alone in that desolate yet lovely Isle. There is she left surrounded by convict graves, from which hers is only distinguished by its flowers and freshness. Here and there a headstone peeps from a cluster of trees, announcing the grave of one who has never been galled with chains; yet these exceptions make still more pained the painful show of graves, unmarked, uncared for, and barely seeming more than the natural roughness of the mould.

Over one such a heap droops a withered branch of acacia, which, torn from a neighbouring tree, has there been planted in stealthy haste by some more kindly hand, who was fain to leave over his comrade's grave a token whereby to recognise it. Nor all in vain the rude memorial—life is within that apparently withered branch and is timidly budding from the lowest stalk. It is a wonder no overseer has discovered that *in memoriam*, and jealously pulled it from out the earth. But there it still lowly blooms, and when years have swept by, and that mound is trodden from view, it shall rise in its fragrant verdure, and none shall know the origin of that fair acacia. There shall it bloom an enduring memorial of that convict grave, a fitting emblem of that resurrection power which shall call beauty from ashes, joy out of sorrow, life out of death. Of the further secrets of this sea-girt graveyard few are known, and those few are, alas! too often the records of despair; but this is known, that many a convict stops on his path to cast a sigh towards the shore of the lonely island. Many a captive pines for its hallowed rest, to attain which some have laid violent hands on themselves.

All yearn towards this peaceful spot, for it is known of all that here is heard no more the voice of the oppressor. Here the prisoners rest together and the servant is free from his master; 'Here the wicked cease from troubling, and the weary are at rest.'[7]

CHAPTER 33

Accepted

IT was now the Sunday after the funeral. The congregation, free and bond, were surprised to see Mr. Herbert take his accustomed place in the desk, and still more surprised were they to see him enter the pulpit to preach his own child's funeral sermon. All waited for when the stricken father should arise from his knees and commence that lament over which all had prepared themselves to weep. All looked forward to experience a luxurious tenderness when the minister should merge into the parent, and yield himself to sorrowful recollections of the past. A sensation of astonishment, therefore, ran through the whole people, when in a voice loud, clear, and, if possible, more sonorous than usual, Mr. Herbert, looking calmly around him, thrice repeated slowly and distinctly, no funeral text, but Agrippa's words—'Almost thou persuadest me to be a Christian.'[1] Then dropping his voice into a low, earnest tone, he said:

'My friends, I thank you all for your kindness to my departed child. I am about to leave you; to your care I commit that grave lying in your Isle of the Dead. To your attention I commend her who lies within that grave. My bond brethren, you who are the same flesh and blood, heart and soul, I implore you to note that grave. I do not by this ask you to keep it in order, your own kind feelings will prompt you to do that unbidden; but this I *do* ask you, to attend to that grave as a voice from God, as a voice from heaven, bidding you go to Christ. And, oh, would God that the answer of your hearts might be, not almost, but "altogether thou persuadest me to be a Christian." Could but one such voice reach my ear, I should bless God for my child's death in this place. I should bless Him to eternity that in this far-off isle, on which mine eye may never rest again, I leave her to the stranger's care.'

An earnest appeal succeeded, in which he implored weary souls to pine not for the rest that island could afford, but for the rest wherewith the Saviour can refresh the heavy laden.

It was in the midst of this appeal that a tall, stately figure was seen to rise up, and with low, bent head to leave the church; her footsteps lingered near the door, and then Maida passed out; but not until the fervent voice had once more pleaded, 'Almost thou persuadest me to be a Christian.'

Mrs. Evelyn said it was like a prisoner not to care more for such an affecting sermon than to go out just for a little headache. But Mr. Herbert discerned more than physical pain in the lowly dignity of Maida's carriage; he knew it was no common feeling that could weigh down that head, so erect and noble in its bearing. He sought her directly after the service. The rest of the family had proceeded to take a quiet walk in the government garden; he therefore feared no interruption in seeking an interview with her, whom he considered one of his flock as well as one of his brother's family. But she was neither to be found in the kitchen nor in the outhouses. Opal said, 'He had seen dat leddie come in fast, quick, big, and go upstairs, but he hadn't seen her since.' (He would persist in calling her a lady, for that she was a prisoner could not be brought to his understanding.)

In going upstairs Mr. Herbert had to pass his daughter's room. He thought from within he heard a suppressed voice; he listened and entered; Maida knelt there. On seeing Mr. Herbert she arose, and approaching him, extended both her hands, exclaiming:

'It is over, sir! Not almost, but altogether. The moment of decision has come. With dying lips Miss Evelyn persuaded me, you have decided me. Her God shall be my God; her Saviour my Saviour!'

'Thanks be to God which giveth us the victory through Jesus Christ our Lord,' said Mr. Herbert, clasping his hands and looking upwards, his pale, careworn face bright as had been his dying daughter's.

'Sir! Those were Miss Evelyn's very words to me.'

'They are, and ever will be the Christian's words, Maida. Oh, Maida! I bless God for my child this day, I bless Him for the sorrow I have had, I bless Him for you, my daughter. Come, let us thank Him together.'

They knelt, and ere their praiseful prayer concluded, a third joined with them. Bridget had stolen back to weep in her cousin's room; entering on tiptoe, she beheld her uncle and Maida, and immediately bent silently beside them. They arose. Then was there joy in heaven. Then the glad shout of triumph proclaimed another heir born into the world of glory. And may it be that the shout passing from angel to angel, at last reached that Paradise where wait the gathered saints their entrance into the celestial regions, and there proclaimed the welcome tidings to one who through pain and disappointment had still hoped for Maida, who had yearned over her life and had prayed for her in death. These mysteries we know not of. But we do know that one sinner gathered into the bundle of life is worth a world-long trial, is a treasure beyond the toil of ages, and cost a Saviour's blood.

CHAPTER 34

Bridget Again

IS all of a fluster. Uncle Ev tells her that Mr. Walkden has once more found his way to Hobarton, and is waiting below to renew acquaintance with her.

Bridget hopes in her heart that he will make no allusion to days past, and the something that passed in them.

Mrs. Evelyn hopes he will, and that her niece will not make a simpleton of herself, for a real M.A. is not an everyday catch in the antipodes. Episcopal hands there rarely find true Oxford or Cambridge heads on which to exercise their ghostly function. Poor Mr. Walkden, too, has given so very decided a proof that, renouncing all other, he will either go without a wife or have Miss D'Urban, that really she ought to accept him. Her former refusal of him and his resignation of the comfortable living of Clarence Plains[1] had occurred together, or rather on one and the same day. But in resigning his living he had taken care to accept the wardenship of Bishopsbourne,[2] where to the present time he has been trying hard but uselessly to forget Miss D'Urban in the scholastic duties of the college. So uselessly trying, that yesterday the Launceston coach brought him into Hobarton; and he means to try how Bridget feels, or at any rate how she *looks,* now her former objection has for months been dead and buried. As she enters the room, he determines that whatever she *feels,* she certainly *looks* none the worse. Her cheeks, if possible, are of a richer carnation; and her eyes as full of light—less merry, though not less cheerful; in fact, they are more suitable than ever to a clergyman's wife.

However, she has not entered alone. Uncle Ev comes, too—for Bridget declared she would not go down unless he accompanied her. The visit ends in Mr. Walkden being invited to dinner—an early, friendly dinner—after which, by some 'horrid' chance, Bridget finds herself left alone with him. She gives an imploring look towards Uncle Ev, as she sees him strategising[3] for the door; but he only shuts his eyes wickedly at her, and departs, when Mr. Walkden asks her if any persuasion of his may prevail on her to change her mind, and revoke a sentence that makes him the most miserable of colonial clergymen.

She says she has undertaken to be Uncle Herbert's daughter, instead of Emmeline.

Mr. Walkden inquires if it may not be possible to unite the relationships of wife and daughter. But Bridget seems to think—no.

So the matter drops for that afternoon. Mr. Walkden, beseeching her to consider it, and let him know the result of her thoughts, dejectedly leaves the house; but not, as she supposes, to go to his hotel. He walks straight to the prisoners' barracks, and there watches for Mr. Herbert; whom he no sooner espies returning from his duties, than he joins him, and renews the matrimonial suit.

Bridget is out watering her plants after tea, when she sees Uncle Herbert approaching; she is quickly at his side; and then he tells her that, as far as he is concerned, nothing would give him greater pleasure than to marry her to Mr. Walkden; but he would on no account bias her against her wishes. Entirely off her guard, Bridget exclaims, 'Oh, uncle! I like him very much; only—'

She stops and looks vexed.

'Only you are divided between love and duty,' says Uncle Herbert kindly.

She, still more vexed, and somewhat hurt, replies, 'Uncle, if I am divided at all, it is between love and love. If it be a duty to fulfil dear Em's last wish, it is one of so much pleasure that I am loath to resign it.'

Nevertheless, she did resign it, and shortly became Mrs. Walkden, to the infinite satisfaction of her aunt, who, in kissing her after the wedding, said, with one of her little quick laughs:

'Of course, my dear! What else do you suppose your mother sent you out for?'

CHAPTER 35

The Awakening—More Victims

IN an elegant drawing room, in one of the West End houses of London, sat Mrs. Norwell, or Mary Doveton, as, laying aside the proprieties of wedded life, we are still fain to name her, for we cannot reconcile ourselves to her union with him whom she fondly and proudly calls her husband.

Now she arose and flitted about the room for some time, as if in search of something; and then she resolutely nestled into a couch, determined to patiently await whatever it might be that she expected—her fairy fingers pretending to diligence over a dainty heap of muslin and lace: now drawing forth a garment so small that it could only be meant for a doll or a baby, then ruffling it altogether back into the basket, she would raise her head and listen.

There came a brisk rat-tat in double-singleness at the front door; and we know for what Mary had been watching. She walked to the door, and, holding it open, wished the servants would not be so long.

Her pale face tinted with the gentlest rose as she took a letter from the silver tray handed her by the footman. She nestled back into the cushion, held the letter up, and then threw it down. 'Dear—! It is not from him. Naughty man that he is!'

But her pout of disappointment gives us pleasure not because her delicate lip peeps so prettily from its wonted line of beauty, but because it tells us that which we have been longing to hear, namely, that Norwell makes her happy. The letter lay unnoticed for half the evening. Mary was too engaged in accounting for her husband's silence to care about opening it. At last, she heaved a little sigh, and whispered, 'Ah, well! Now it's a pleasure to come; only I shall not sleep in waiting for the morning.'

She took up the neglected letter, and for the first time observed it was from abroad, and for Captain Norwell. Supposing it was from one of his Indian relatives, whose communications had always been equally intended for herself, and as Norwell invariably flung them over to her unopened, with, 'There, dear; it's more yours than mine,' she broke the seal; and in a few brief moments all Maida's care, pain, and tears were nullified. The shameful secret was in his wife's possession.

Mary withdrew the envelope, and her husband's own handwriting met her sight. She read, 'My beloved Maida,' and repeated the name over and over again, but could not remember where she had before heard it. Then came the name Martha Grylls—then Maida's own letter—when through all her sweet simplicity, through all her unwillingness, stared out on Mary a truth she would have died to make false—a lie she would have given her life to abrogate. But the awakening had come—there was no reprieve—no room for doubt—the accusation was from Maida—the confession from himself! Poor Mary! You must depart from your paradise, for the evil one is there. The canker is at the root of your gourd, and it perishes before you. Your sun goeth down while it is yet day.

She was not one to show either grief or joy by ecstasy. When the array of servants filed silently in for evening prayer, and when the butler laid before her the Bible and Prayer-book, she merely raised her eyes to him, shook her head, how drearily, and faintly articulated, 'I can't to-night!'

And more silently the servants glided from the room—each mystified and sorrowful at what should ail their gentle mistress.

There was the same dreary refusal of the refreshment tray, when it was wistfully presented her by her own maid—for all the others had feared to disturb her.

The maid waited; but Mary spoke not until looking up she saw tears in her servant's eyes; she then smiled a smile more touching in its misery than could have been the bitterest display of grief.

'My dear lady, are you ill?'

'Very, very!' and Mary dropped her head, but she shed not a single tear.

'Allow me, ma'am; you should not pass the night alone. The nurse was here to-night, and I gave her your message, saying you did not expect to want her for three weeks.'

''Tis not that, Fanny. I do not want *her*. My illness is all here.'

She folded her hands at once upon the letters and her heart, for she had resealed the former and laid them in her bosom.

'I would rather be left, Fanny; I shall go to bed presently.'

But her pillow brought no rest; her tortured mind could see but the one picture of her unmasked husband (in his threefold baseness), and Maida, beautiful and anguished, as she had appeared in the prison.

No sleep had closed her eyes, when she arose and descended to the parlour, again to await the post. The knock came; a thrill shivered through her, but not of joy; the paleness of her cheek became yet more deathlike as she received and mechanically opened the expected letter. Each endearing word called forth a desponding moan, and with each word the pain gathered more closely to her heart. She once more broke the seal of Maida's packet, and placing Norwell's within, she closed it again forever. Then putting the whole in another cover, she sealed it, and, after a few moments of anxious thought, wrote on it, with a trembling hand:

'For dear Henry, with Mary's love and—prayers.'

The struggle was ended; she flung herself into her chair and wept until she could weep no more. Faint and shadow-like she moved about all that day and the next. The morning after a second note from Norwell announced his return within two hours of her receipt of his announcement.

Not knowing that the servants had, after united consultation, agreed to send for their master, Mary wondered at his change of purpose; she had not expected his return for another week. Now one dull emotion of suspense numbed her into a cold quiet. She heard the loud rap at the door, and then her husband's voice sounded through the house; the well-known airy step was on the stair, but she moved not; another instant, the door flew open and Norwell entered. A glance at his wife's face sufficed to tell him that the alarm of her illness was not unfounded. He was shocked and startled, but the servants had begged him not to let Mary know that he had been summoned.

'Why, what ails you, darling? Are you ill? Surely not, or you would have sent for me.'

She had approached to meet him; he now folded her in his arms; but the form he held yielded itself so lifelessly to his embrace that he was terrified. He set her gently back on the sofa.

'Mary, love, what is it?'

He leant her head upon his shoulder, but she raised it again—not loathing, it was not in Mary Doveton to despise, but she felt she had no right to lie there.

'Mary, love, speak to me; what is it?'

She could no longer resist.

She fell upon his neck and wept piteously.

'Oh, Henry, Henry!' She said no more.

Could those tears have washed his guilty soul, Norwell had stood pure and spotless; but tears, crystal tears, what are they, though an angel should shed them, when it has taken the blood of Calvary to wash out the stain of sin?

That night the nurse and doctor were summoned, and ere morning they placed an infant in Mary's arms.

But all said the babe was dying. It feebly wailed throughout the day, and in the evening none could doubt that it fluttered its little wings for flight. The servant was hastily sent for a clergyman to baptize it.

Despite all remonstrance, Mary would have the ceremony performed by her bedside. Her husband asked what name she would like: she whispered—

'I—have—one.'

The clergyman came, the preparatory prayers were read, he received the child from the nurse, and said—

'Name this child.'

Norwell turned to Mary.

Looking fixedly at him she said—

'Maida Gwynnham.'

'Maida Gwynnham, I baptize thee in the name of the Father, and of the Son, and of the Holy Ghost.'

Norwell stole to Mary's side, and kneeling by her strove to read in her countenance some explanation of the strange proceeding; but the eyes were closed, and the pale features were mute; there was neither speech nor utterance in them; he only gazed on a sweet blank. He recollected, with poignant grief, the time when those same features, angelical and admiring, had sought into his face as he now sought into hers, and then he remembered, with a rush of pain, the artless words—

'I have loved you, Norwell, since that day.'

He observed that one hand rested firmly on her heart, as though it would arrest a pain. He laid his hand upon it, and Mary pressed it more firmly down.

'Mary!' he whispered.

She opened her eye; there was that in it which made a cold terror fall upon him.

'Oh, Mary! We are not going to be parted—are we? My life with you has been heaven upon earth.'

'Yes, Henry; and when I am gone, forget that you have ever loved me, and do your duty to—'

Norwell bent over her for the last word, but it was a mere breath that passed and left him desolate.

The hand relaxed, the letter fell, and he who should have received it earlier, all too late read his fate and the cause of his Mary's death.

That evening the fair fragile flower, with its tiny bud, folded itself into repose; both lay together in one coffin, the mother and the babe, for the Destroyer had breathed upon them.

It was but a few days after that that house in the West End was seen shuttered and disfigured with bills announcing a prompt and unreserved sale, the proprietor being about to leave England.

CHAPTER 36

Maida

Oh, sweet surprise of heaven,
Go forward, timid soul,
The Master's word is given,
No wave shall o'er you roll.
*****

Oh, sweet surprise of heaven,
One answer to all doubt,
'Come in, your fetters riven,
Why linger ye without?
Come in, ye free forgiven,
No hand may shut you out,
To you the kingdom's given,'
The joyful angels shout.

MAIDA had just entered the fifth year of her transported life, of which she had now to experience but two more changes—the ticket-of-leave and the conditional pardon. Both were still distant. According to the regulations then in force, she had to serve yet three years (together with the two months abstracted from the reckoning by reason of her punishment in the Factory) before she would be eligible for her ticket, and she must then hold that ticket a given period ere she could claim her conditional pardon. But all save her mistress had given up speaking to her of either the one or the other. To both these indulgences she displayed so utter an indifference that her master deemed it useless to encourage her with the hope of them, and Mr. Herbert considered it more a mortification than otherwise to her, to have either of these presented as incitements to good behaviour. Mrs. Evelyn would still threaten her with a protracted term of involuntary servitude, when the quiet curl of Maida's lip alone showed how little the threat affected her.

She had dropped into a peculiar position in the family—a position of her own forming, one on which her fellow servants dared as little to encroach as to question its existence, though to spite it they persecuted her in every possible way; a position which her master did not choose to molest, for all his wife's protestations against convict upstartism.

'Clara,' said he, on one occasion, 'the woman is quiet, orderly, and for work is worth two servants; so long as you have no fault to find in these respects I must beg you to have the rest left to me.'

'But she is *not* orderly, my dear; look at her now, when I'm sure she ought to be in the scullery cleaning her knives.'

Mrs. Evelyn pointed towards the garden with one hand, and with the other tapped violently at the glass; then stepping forward, she called out:

'What are you about there, Gwynnham, idling your time, or rather my time?'

'Bother it, Clara! I wish you'd let her alone; see, she is coming over, and there'll be a row, and I shall have to scold her, which you know I detest.'

'Oh, you needn't fear, my dear; she bears things a great deal better than she used to.'

'For that reason she should have less to bear; there, I shall leave you to finish what you have begun; but mind, I'll not be appealed to.'

Mr. Herbert, who had been reading at the table, looked anxiously up as Maida mounted the steps and stood in the balcony.

'Did you call me, ma'am?'

Mrs. Evelyn, annoyed at her husband's tenacity, snappishly asked:

'What business have you in the garden at this hour?'

'I was tending my flowers.'

'Then you ought to have been scouring your knives.'

'I have done them already, ma'am.'

'Then you've your master's boots.'

'They are also cleaned, ma'am.'

'Then your sewing.'

'I have none, ma'am.'

'Such nonsense! You know that's a story; there's always plenty of work in a large house.'

Maida's lip quivered and her eye flashed.

'Now I hope you are not going to be insolent. I haven't seen that face put up for a long time: I was in hopes you had left it off since you professed religion.'

Maida fixed her eye haughtily on her mistress, who went on to say—

'The thing *is*, I plainly see, we've been too indulgent to you; you forget what you are; and that'll never do: your own will mustn't be allowed as it has been.'

'I pray God that my will may never again be my guide, ma'am. To be left to my own devices would be to be given over to evil,' exclaimed Maida, the fire fading from her glance, and an expression of pain gathering on her countenance.

'What *does* the woman mean?' turning to Mr. Herbert: he arose and approached the window.

'Once, ma'am, my own will was the rule of my life, *now* God's word directs my actions, or I could not, in silence, hear you so speak, convict though I be!'

'I wish it would teach you not to be insolent.'

'It teaches servants to obey their masters in all things, and I humbly desire to do so.'

'Yes, indeed! Or you can soon be made to.'

Maida clenched her teeth and remained silent.

'You can go now; but really it's very hard a mistress can't speak a word to her own prisoner woman without such a to-do, and that after I have kept you three years and a half.'

'I am ready to fulfil your wishes, ma'am,' said Maida meekly.

'Go along, Gwynnham! I haven't patience with such nonsense, making a goodness out of your duty, which you either must fulfil or get into trouble; you know it's only because Mr. Herbert is listening to you that you talk such cant.'[1]

'I acknowledge it, ma'am. Had not my master's reproachful look reminded me of the solemn vow I made, I should not have borne with you, for grace has not changed my nature, though it has subdued my temper.'

The calm dignity of her voice and manner at once irritated and awed Mrs. Evelyn. She hastily replied:

'Well, I don't believe in convict piety; go and *act* it, then perhaps I may.'

'Where shall I find the needlework, ma'am?'

'If you can't get it without troubling me, leave it alone.'

'Then I may continue my work in the garden?'

'If the master chooses; but remember I don't choose to have you speak of the flowers as *yours*, it's a piece of insolence in a convict that I cannot stand.'

Maida stared.

'You did! You said you were tending *your* flowers. If the master allows you to work in the garden, that does not make them yours.'

'I beg your pardon, ma'am; the flowers I spoke of are mine.'

'You must have stolen them from us then?'

'I brought them from Port Arthur. They were dear—'

She stopped and cast a look at Mr. Herbert, who averted his head for an instant, and then, with a smile, inquired:

'My Emmeline's? I must go and see them.'

Mr. Herbert went out, and Maida prepared to follow him, but her mistress called her.

'Gwynnham, come back, you bold woman, I'm ashamed of you: do you think a father—'

Mr. Herbert turned, and, in a decided voice, bade Maida accompany him.

She hesitated.

'You permit her, Clara?'

'Oh! It's no odds to *me*.'

'Maida, I rejoice to see you steadfast in the path you have chosen. It is a perpetual struggle,' commenced Mr. Herbert.[2]

'It is, sir; but no more so than I expected. I, as a convict, have not the same comfort in it that a free person has, the contest being the result of my sins, and not of my being in the narrow path.'

'Your comfort, Maida, must not be in the struggle but in the victory.'

'Ah, sir, the victory being imperfect the consolation can be but slight.'

'The time of perfect conquest is not yet, Maida, nor will it be till we lay our bodies in the dust; not till then may we put off our armour. The conflict is one of flesh against spirit and only to end when our course is finished; then, Maida, may it be ours to triumph with the apostle, "I have fought the good fight."'[3]

'O, sir! Mr. Herbert, you?'

Mr. Herbert smiled sadly.

'Why not me, Maida? Do you suppose I have no warfare to accomplish?'

'Oh, yes, a mighty warfare, but for Christ, not for yourself.'

Mr. Herbert shook his head.

'Maida, my battle is with myself more than you know of, the last enemy to be destroyed is self.'

A look of perfect delight irradiated Maida's face, and clasping her hands, she cried—

'Oh! Then I well may struggle on: if you have conflict, how should not I?'

But the bright glow of pleasure vanished. She observed Mr. Herbert press down his eyes with two fingers, in a manner that indicated pain; his lips moved, then removing his hand from his brow he fixed his eye steadily on her—

'Ay, Maida, flesh and blood cannot inherit the kingdom of God.'

'I wish you could have a little rest, sir; your duties wear you out.'

But Mr. Herbert did not seem to hear her, he was deep in thought, and she hesitated whether to leave him or not. She stood still, leaving him to advance alone: this arrested his attention. He turned suddenly to her, and in a quick, earnest voice, said—

'Maida, one thing disappoints me. The impression you made on my mind the first time I visited you in prison has increased with my knowledge of you, until it has almost become a conviction, and I am disappointed, that with your open profession of religion, you have made no acknowledgment of *that* which, as a Christian woman, should trouble you—'

'Sir! What do you mean? Explain yourself.'

Drawn to her full height, she was the Maida of olden days, but only for a moment.

Grasping his arm, she exclaimed, hurriedly, 'Forgive me, sir; but, in pity, put an end to my distress.'

'What distress, Maida?'

'Oh, Mr. Herbert! Do not play upon my feelings! What acknowledgment have I to make?'

'Maida, listen to me, not to me as Mr. Herbert, your master's brother, not to me as your appointed pastor; but listen to me as one who has watched you, and prayed for you, and—and—and, *cared* for you; as one who would deliver his own soul by speaking faithfully to you.'

Maida trembled in every limb. Mr. Herbert laid his hand upon her shoulder, when, as though the touch had paralyzed her, she became rigid and statue-like.

'Have you no secret which, as a Christian woman, you have no right to keep to yourself?'

She stood speechless, dreading yet breathless to hear more.

'No secret for the preservation of which you stake your peace of mind?'

Maida tried to shake off her terror, but it was impossible; making a desperate effort, she exclaimed—

'Sir, you speak in parables. What right have you to try to frighten me thus?'

'I have the right of God! By His permission, and as His minister, I ask you, have you no confession which should long since have been made?'

'I understood, sir, our church had no priestly confession. I thought a confession to God was sufficient.'

There was a slight sneer in her tone.

'A confession to God without a corresponding action to our fellow creatures is useless—it is more than useless—it is a spiritual lie!'

'Are there no occasions, sir, on which we may throw ourselves on God's mercy without exposing ourselves to man's weak judgment?'

'Doubtless, God searches the heart; but you misapprehend me perhaps? Simply, I would say, it is no use to kneel to our heavenly Father, and say, I have sinned against heaven and in Thy sight, and then, arising, continue that sin we have just confessed—confession and restitution must succeed each other; I deal faithfully with you.'

'And you must be yet more faithful if you would have me profit by your candour, sir. I do not understand anything you have spoken, save that you are torturing me; yes, by cruel degrees.'

'Then I will be plain, Maida.'

She longed to say, Oh don't, don't, but she said just the reverse:

'I pray you go on, sir.'

'In the days of your rebellion against God and man, I perceived you hid some mystery in your heart; I perceived that, with a mighty power of self-control, you crushed your every thought, word, and deed, in subservience to that mystery; you appeared to hug a perpetual dagger to your heart; you smarted beneath its wound, and yet resisted help or alleviation, setting yourself rashly and determinately to bear it. No effort of mine has been spared to discover your secret.'

'Supposing I have a secret, is it necessary, sir, to you, or to anyone, to become acquainted with it?'

'As a Christian yearning for peace of mind, it is necessary to yourself, Maida! Believe me you can neither enjoy the peace of God nor communion with Him whilst you are not true to yourself. You start, but I have told you before, that much of my life has been spent in hearing tales of sorrow from my bond brethren and sisters. I have heard of miseries that have wrung my soul, of crimes which have revolted me. I have heard of infatuations and of fallacies that have excited my pity, of injustices which have called forth my indignation; but amidst all these, I have found that mystery is never used where it is not needed, that there is never mental (mind I do not say spiritual) conflict without a cause, a something yet undiscovered by law or unthought of by justice.'

'Sir, pardon me, I cannot let you proceed. I have never troubled you with my story, how, then, can you know either that I have wrapped myself in mystery or experienced mental conflict?'

She tried to speak calmly, but her voice shook.

'Maida, do not deceive yourself, your whole transported life has been one long conflict; eyes less watchful than mine have discovered that; I have seen far more.'

'Sir, give me but one instance, that I may know what you mean; this is very cruel.'

'So must ever be the piercing asunder of the soul and spirit, for the clearer discovery of the intents and purposes of the heart.'

A new light burst upon Maida. It was as the light which struck Saul to the earth, and from it came forth the question— [4]

'Is it a lie? Canst thou brave God with a lie?'

She could have fallen to the ground; a chilling sensation oppressed her, but she battled with it and repeated—

'An instance, sir?'

'Do you remember that night in which you came to my room for writing materials? Was there no conflict that night? No mystery of pain and grief that turned those few brief hours into an age of suffering, and ere morning added years to your appearance?'

'You must have watched me very narrowly, sir.'

Without noticing these words, Mr. Herbert drew a torn half-sheet of paper from his vest; slowly unfolding it, he held it towards Maida.

'Was there no conflict when this solemn adjuration was penned to that base man who worked your ruin, and who must have eternally destroyed you but for God's tender mercy—God's unceasing love?'

He held the paper towards her, but would not resign it.

She read part of one of the letters she had written to Norwell. It was the very one she had considered most violent and earnest—the very one that showed too much of her feelings and sorrows; fortunately it mentioned not his name; the cold 'sir' at the commencement alone told that it was addressed to a man.

The writing swam before her eyes; she had been pale before, now the pallor of her cheek was deathlike, livid; but suddenly a deep purple colour rushed over her whole face, and she clenched her hand upon Mr. Herbert's arm.

'Tell me, sir, how came you by that paper? I defy the right of anyone upon earth to interfere with my private actions, harmless to everyone but myself; by what means did you possess yourself of it? I insist on being satisfied.'

'I will satisfy you, Maida. The night referred to I could not rest, your whole appearance alarmed me; *now* I may tell you I feared you were meditating suicide; I passed the night in prayer for you. In the early morning I heard you leave the house; I followed you, and by the way I picked up this paper, dropped by you in your flight, and since carefully preserved by me as a proof.'

Maida interrupted him.

'Sir, you needed no proof; yourself first told me of a seducer, and I have never sought to hide my shame!'

'You are impatient, Maida. Shall I tell you why I preserved this paper? As a proof of what has long been established in my mind, that there is some grand mistake in your conviction. I do not believe you wholly guilty of the crimes for which you are in this colony.'

'Then why have you not made your thoughts public, sir? An endeavour should be made to clear an innocent person!'

There was a strangeness of manner and voice in the enunciation of this, that made Mr. Herbert look hastily at her.

'Because, Maida, the time has not fully come.'

'It has not!' (The same strange voice.) 'Sir, you would be deemed a mere enthusiast to found a plea of innocence on the ravings of a disappointed woman—a felon maddened by her punishment, as all felons are. But I must leave you, sir; I am in pain, great pain. My heart beats as though it would burst.'

'Then go, and may God assist you into a solemn duty!'

When Mr. Herbert returned to the drawing room, Mrs. Evelyn, still ruffled with what she considered the scolding she had received on Maida's account, exclaimed—

'Really Herbert, my dear, you shouldn't let that woman talk to you so. George and I have been quite amused, or rather annoyed in watching you walk up and down the garden. She really seemed to talk to you as her equal.'

'I beg to renounce all claim to either amusement or annoyance on the subject,' said Mr. Evelyn.

'Yes; but, my dear, don't you think it makes Gwynnham vain, and the others jealous? People will begin to talk by-and-by.'

'What do you say to that, Herbert?' asked Mr. Evelyn, putting up his eyebrows.

'Persons may talk of me as they please,' he answered quietly.

'Well, I don't know, when she gets her ticket,' laughed Uncle Ev, unable to resist an opportunity of quizzing. But his brother bit his lip with so grieved an expression, at the same time sending him so reproachful a glance, which seemed to say, 'And you too?' that he changed his manner and inquired—

'What were you talking about? I'm always glad to see you pitching it into that Maida, she gets on so well after!' (Then more seriously) 'There is a great change in her, the lion has become a lamb.'

'My dear, she looked anything but lamb-like just now. You should have seen her! A tigress—I should say,' replied Mrs. Evelyn.

Maida excused herself from attending prayer that night; and long after all the others were in bed, Mr. Herbert, who still read in his study, heard her moving about upstairs. The next morning, when she had removed the breakfast, she turned quickly to her master and said:

'Sir, I am ill; I must go to the hospital.'

'Oh, pish, pish, Maida;[5] get your mistress to give you a little Gregory, and you'll be right to-morrow!'

'I wish to go, if you please, sir; I am ill.'

'Well, then, put on your bonnet, and I'll take you to Dr. Lamb; he'll soon settle the point.'

'My dear, if Maida's ill she had better go to the hospital; I am quite pleased to see her so reasonable as to request it,' urged Mrs. Evelyn.

Mr. Evelyn nodded.

'Bonnet, Maida, bonnet,' and both mistress and servant knew it was useless to contend.

'Just tell me what you complain of, and then make haste and be ready.'

'I am only sensible of a strange fulness at my heart, sir, with a general feeling of indisposition. But I cannot be ready for half an hour. As I do not wish to return here, I must put up my things before I go to the hospital, for I am sure Dr. Lamb will order me there.'

Mr. Evelyn laughed.

'You've made fine plans for yourself, at any rate. Well; perhaps, though, you want a little holiday.'

Maida *did* want a holiday, and she was about to have one.

Leaving her master, she went straight to Mr. Herbert's study, and scarcely closed the door ere she said:

'Sir, do you mean to say that I cannot have God's forgiveness unless I confess my history?'

Taken by surprise, Mr. Herbert started.

'I dare to say no such thing, Maida!'

'What *do* you say then, sir?'

'That you cannot expect the Christian's peace while you do not act the repentant's part.'

'Then peace of mind is all I shall lose by telling my tale to no one but God?'

'This is not the proper way to talk of subjects so deeply important: if you wish to speak of these things, first seek the Holy Spirit's aid by prayer.'

'I have been praying all night, sir, and I am driven to distraction by the alternate light and darkness which follow me. As to propriety of way, opportunity must sanctify that; I may not have another.'

'What *do* you mean, Maida?' exclaimed Mr. Herbert, rising. 'Your words are strange, your manner stranger.'

'I am ill, sir; Mr. Evelyn is going to take me to the doctor, and then I mean to enter the hospital.'

'I'll speak to my brother.'

He went towards the door; she stretched her arms towards him.

'One moment, sir. If you will wait for my dying hour, then shall you hear all you seek to know; till then, since peace of mind is all I must forego in keeping my secret to myself,

I commit myself to God, and resign my present peace on your solemn promise that in so doing I shall not resign my eternal happiness, for *that* no mortal has a right to do, and I have no wish to resign it. Mind, sir! I rest on your promise that I shall not lose heaven by my silence.'

'Maida, Maida!' cried Mr. Herbert; but she had left the room. As she had her bundle to prepare, and as Mr. Evelyn was impatiently calling for her, he had only to return to his study to pray for his convict charge.

Dr. Lamb prescribed perfect rest with quiet; and strongly advised her to enter the hospital. He privately told Mr. Evelyn that she was in a very broken state of health; on the morrow he would see her at the hospital, and report further particulars.

The gates of H.M.G. Hospital once more admitted Maida Gwynnham. Once more her master consigned her to good, kind Mrs. Cott. On parting he shook hands with her; he had never done so before. Observing her gesture of surprise, he smiled.

'It's never too late to mend our ways and doings, I hope, Maida. If I never get hold of a worse paw than yours I shall count myself a happy man. Mind one thing, Gwynnham—just this: I shall be as glad to see you back as I am sorry to send you in. You know we married men can't be comptrollers-general, or you should have been laid up at my house.'

He shook her hand a second time, and walked down the path; then turning, he called out:

'I'll send Mr. Herbert to see you on Thursday; you'll like that, shan't you?'

She was ordered to Ward No. 4, there to behold the Excrescence still bearing the iron rod.

There was a grin of satisfaction in her teeth as she hailed Maida back to her clutches.

'Why, woman, what ails you? Death's in your very face; are you come in to die?'

She should have known Maida better than to suppose this apostrophe[6] would terrify her.

Seating herself on the bottom of a stretcher, Maida replied:

'Nurse, if you can tell me that you see death in my face, you will tell me better news than I have heard for years.'

'You don't b'lieve in hell, I suppose.'

'Yes, and in heaven too; and, nurse, I can say from my soul I hope to see you there.'

The Excrescence grinned incredulity and malice, and then sniffed.

'Yes! I think if ever *you* gets there, you'll find me there *before* you.'

During Maida's absence the nurse's ill-will had increased rather than diminished, the former having resolutely forbade her her master's kitchen, into which she had several times endeavoured to intrude under pretence of visiting her old patient. In this way she carried on an extensive traffic among the pantries of masters owning former hospitallers of Ward No. 4.

Maida tried to avoid quarrelling, but in vain; something occurred in the course of the evening that aroused her anger and forced her into a dispute. Nurse was a little the worse for drink (how bad, then, must she have been?), and, clenching her fist at Maida, she swore a fearful oath to the effect that, instead of closing her eyes and folding her arms if she died within her reach, she would make her a corpse so frightful as to make the devil himself take to his heels. She would stark[7] open both eyes and mouth as though she were 'a-calling for mercy that was never a-coming.'

In spite of herself a cold shiver ran through Maida as she heard the malignant threat. She dropped her head, and sent a silent prayer to God, and then, rising, prepared to undress for the night. She lay still for two hours, when the oppression at her heart became unbearable. She sat up in the stretcher, and begged the nurse to allow her to sleep semi-recumbently, and received the pleasant answer:

'She might sleep in hell if she liked.'

Mrs. Cott came round, showing her kindly face at the bedside of every poor, weary patient. When she arrived at Maida's she exclaimed:

'Go for the doctor; this woman's worse!'

The house doctor came and prescribed for her; he requested that someone should sit up with her, and that he should be called if certain symptoms appeared.

But sitting up with a convict is a dissimilar operation to sitting up with a free patient; there is an obvious want of that comforting confusion, of soft treadings, murmuring voices, and thoughtful appliances which love alone can produce. There may be muffled steppings to and fro, but then list slippers and not affection is the cause—list *must* be quiet. Surly and gaunt the Excrescence took her place near Maida. Then, throwing off her cap, and rumpling her grizzled hair, she became, in the dim light of the lamp, the ex-lunatic of the transport magnified into double deformity.

'Nurse, do you think Mrs. Cott would send for Mr. Herbert Evelyn?'

'I am not going to try; you must bide without the parson for to-night.'

'Nurse, I think I'm dying; I feel so strange.'

'The devil may care, I don't. He's more concerned in it than me or anyone else.'

Maida tried once more.

'Nurse, *do* send for Mr. Herbert; I'm sure he'll come. I must, must see him.'

'If you are worse I'll send for the doctor, and nobody else.'

All was silent for a while.

'I'm dying!' whispered Maida; but the nurse heard not: she was heavy with drink bartered from the patients; and soon her thick, bull-like snore was the only lullaby that soothed the dying convict to her last rest.

For Maida Gwynnham was dying! Had the nurse been awake she might have heard a low, gurgling sound working its way up Maida's chest; she might have seen her raise her hands and gently shut her own eyes; and then she might have seen her arms fold upon her breast. Ere long she might have seen the stream of life ooze, crimson, from Maida's mouth, dyeing her pillow in its fatal stain. But nurse saw none of these, and when, startled up by an extra loud snore, she took the lamp and held it over the bed, with a shriek she let it fall: the victim was beyond her power. Laid in the decency of death by her own dying hand, Maida Gwynnham needed not her services. It was as though an angel had descended and touched her with heavenly calm.

A vessel lies beating about in Storm Bay. God's ban seems on it. It has been signalised[8] since morning, yet cannot approach the land. The captain laughingly says there must be a Jonah[9] n board; and as he speaks, his eye rests upon a tall figure wrapped in a mourning cloak, standing aloof from all, gloomy and taciturn, watching the contrary sea. The deep-set eyes of the stranger in turn are raised, and fix on him a long, deliberate stare.

'No offence, I hope,' says the captain.

The eyes drop quickly back to their watch of the striving waves.

Well, now, I shouldn't like such a welcome as *that* every day, thought the captain, turning with a sense of uneasiness from the yellow of those bloodshot balls.

But Norwell knows not that he has turned such a look on the speaker; it came up from the darkness of his soul, and unaware wandered in the direction of the voice that had uttered the name of the miscreant prophet.

Norwell knows not that he has become a byword on board, nor that he is a marked object to all—not so much by his mourning garb, which proclaims him a desolate man, as by a forbidding investiture of countenance, which hints at a troubled conscience. He has been shut up four months with his fellow-passengers, yet has made no friend, formed no acquaintance.

The children have shunned him; the sailors declare he is bewitched. With one consent the wind side of the poop has been accorded him, and his measured tread has become an accustomed sound on board. It ceases not in storm or calm, in the tropical heat or the cold of the Cape; he seems to be walking out a penance, which he dare not stop at the peril of his soul.

✱ ✱ ✱ ✱ ✱

The next day Mr. Herbert sat at his seat, poring as usual over his book, when a large letter was handed to him. It was only O.P.S.O., and could therefore be nothing requiring immediate attention; he laid it down. When the tea was brought in he took the letter and opened it.

'Herbert, what is it?' cried Mrs. Evelyn. 'My dear, he's faint.'

But Mr. Herbert, waving his hand, signified *No*. Mr. Evelyn picked up the paper his brother had dropped. It was an official despatch from H.M.G. Hospital. The brothers exchanged glances of surprise. Tears suffused Mr. Evelyn's eyes as, walking to the window, he used his handkerchief with that doubtful sound that may equally serve for cold or emotion.

Returning to the table he threw down the paper before his wife.

'There, Clara; what think ye of *that*? Read it.' Mrs. Evelyn obeyed.

H.M. General Hospital,
5th February, 18—.

The Bodies of the undersigned now lie at this Establishment waiting interment.

Name.	Age.	Ship.	Description.	Religion.	Date of Death.
Mary Ann Crawford	17	Anna Maria	Prb.	Protestant	4 February
Eliza Brown ...	46	Do.	T. L.	Do.	4 February
Martha Grylls *alias* Maida Gwynnham	26	Rose of Britain	P.	Do.	5 do.

To the
Rev. H. Evelyn,
&c. &c. &c.

JAMES CURGENVEN,
Superintendent

'Well, who would have thought it, my dear? I'm quite sorry. I've lost the best servant I ever had.'

'Poor, poor Maida! Caught like a rapture[10] from our sight!' said Mr. Evelyn, dashing down into a chair.

'Well, George, my dear, how could one know she was going to die?'

'I *should* have known it, then!' exclaimed Mr. Evelyn impatiently. 'It was like herself to steal ahead of us in the dead of night.'

He dipped his teaspoon up and down a few times in his tea; then pushing the cup untasted from him, he left the room.

But Mr. Herbert had left the house.

CHAPTER 37

Norwell

An end is come.—The end is come.—It watcheth for Thee. Behold
it is come!— Ezekiel[1]

BUT the vessel is at last in harbour. The port officer has been on board, and all the
passengers are free to land. Boats in all directions push from the wharf to bring back their
living freight. The poop is quickly deserted of all, save one passenger, and that is Captain
Norwell. It seems he does not know his own mind, for more violently than ever he paces
the deck, until reminded that he must leave the ship, the cargo being about to disgorge
itself. A boat in watching for this last chance of an engagement is stoutly hailed by the mate,
and in another moment Norwell steps into it, and anon he lands on Tasmanian shores.

'Where shall I take you, sir?' asks the cabman, who happens to be Robert Sanders.

'Anywhere,' replies Norwell.

'Darned asy!' nods Sanders, mentally determining to set him down at the Macquarie
Hotel, which having done, he flops.

'Straight from home, sir? Fine country this for them that's free.'

Norwell shudders. Simple as are these words, they tell him he has reached his goal, and
is once more near Maida.

'Very like, sir, you'd find a drive round agreeable. I'd learn you up a bit of what's
worth—the gentry in general likes it.'

Anything is preferable to being left to himself, so Norwell re-enters the cab, and
Sanders drives slowly on, stopping occasionally to point out surrounding beauties.

'The gaol, sir. Rare wall that. Darned fool that would clim' 'em.'

The bloodshot eyes frown on the heavy wall.

'Canaries, sir, just fledged.'[2]

Norwell looks up, but the butt-end of the whip is pointing down at a road gang
clanking by in their yellow clothes.

'Do'e see the toppermost of them that's harnessed to the cart—he there looking
desperate bad of the weakness—he's a rale gentleman—a new hand; he takes darned shy[3]
to the pick apparently. He's he that frisked the Bank.'

Norwell looks, and the man exhibited shrinks agonisedly, perceiving that he is the
object of attention.

'Confound it!' mutters Norwell. 'Is that the way?'

''Es, sure—all alike—why, they'd clap them there irons and things on you, if you was
government.'

'G'up here!'

The harnessed men had stopped to take breath; at this word of command they trot off
again, and Norwell groans aloud.

'Prisoners' hospital, sir.'

'Go on, can't you!'

Sanders obeys, but again out goes the whip, as they turn up Campbell Street.

'Prisoners' barracks, sir—us calls it Tench.'

Another movement.

'Prisoners' burial ground. Darned ugly, an't it?'

'Confound the man! Can he show me nothing but prisons?'

''Es, sure; sure, sir. Over there, straight along's the female barracks.'

This Norwell stands up to see, and Sanders, delighted that he has at last interested his tenant, continues:

'Government women what's out of places, or from *Anson* or Cage, bides in there till they'm hired out. Drive 'e round if you like, sir, and turn back New Town way.'

But there is nothing in the low, scattered buildings that tempts Norwell. With an abrupt 'No,' he throws himself moodily back into the seat. Pulling the check-string shortly after, he asks where he must inquire to find any particular convict.

'Government books, sir; 'bliged to report ourselves once in six months; or mayhap you'll find your man at Tench. Can I assist you, sir? The new gentry's generally got a prisoner they wants to find out for somebody at home. I've helped out a lot.'

But learning that it is a woman Norwell is in search of, Sanders advises him to try first at the Brickfields. To that depot they accordingly drive, and are there told that Martha Grylls, under the alias of Maida Gwynnham, is at a Mr. Evelyn's, the Lodge.

'Darned! My old place!' cries Robert. 'Then it's Madda Gwynnham you'm after! An old mate of mine—a darned fine woman; but she's had no end of trouble. Her and my wife is fine together.'

They arrive at the Lodge, and to Sanders's perplexity, the gentleman will have him ring at the back door, notwithstanding that he is warned of the certain salute there awaiting every unfortunate interloper from the mouth of Jags, the terrier.

'Take your fare, and leave me. I'll find my own way back,' says the Captain, delaying to ring.

'If it's Madda you'm after, she's an old sweetheart of mine, and very like she'd be pleased for me to bide 'long with you, to ase the shyness a bit.'

'Curse the man! How he worries me! Go about your business.'

And aggrieved, though Norwell has given him half a sovereign, Sanders drives slowly off.

As the key turned in the gate, Norwell caught hold of the handle. What if it should be Maida herself? His heart sickened, and his brain swam dizzily. But it was a man who appeared.

'Round to the other door, sir.'

'No, I only want to inquire for a person called Gwynnham, said to be at a Mr. Evelyn's.'

'This is it, but Gwynnham went away from here sick yesterday. She's at hospital. You won't see her to-day, sir—to-morrow you may; it's visiting-day there.'

But Norwell could brook no to-morrows. Be his doom what it may, he must know it to-night. Inquiring his way to H.M.G. Hospital, he sought admittance of the porter. That official subjected him to a course of interrogations, until through the gloom of Norwell's countenance broke a fierce light.

'Confound the man! Will you admit me or not?'

A gentleman who had just entered without hindrance turned and looked on him, as from his clenched teeth hissed these angry words.

Who are you, haunting me thus? thought Norwell, when, meeting Mr. Herbert's eye, a rush of memory brought back to him the English prison and the scene at the railway station. That man blends with my fate. I hate the sight of him. I haven't been a day in the place ere he rises, like a ghost, before me.

He turned to the porter, and asked:

'Who's that just gone up?'

'Parson Evelyn. You can follow him, if you please, sir.'

The porter had taken Mr. Herbert's look as intended for himself, and hastily granted a permission that otherwise might have been forced from him; for twice again had Mr. Herbert turned, and each time the official appropriated the look.

Norwell waited and waited, but no one appeared to inquire his message. He did not wish to ring, for fear he should re-encounter Mr. Herbert.

At last a woman passed down the stairs. He beckoned her out, and made known his request. She pulled at an excrescence on her under-lip, and seemed to think he asked impossible things.

'Quite contrary to all rules, sir. If I'd ever such a mind to oblige you, there'd be no getting at the key—and at this time, too!'

'Key! Do they lock her up?' muttered Norwell.

'Stop where you are, sir, and I'll be back presently.'

There was something in her manner which gave him to understand that her services were purchasable.

'If it's money that you want—'

He said enough. The excrescence was his humble servant.

After a few moments' absence, she again appeared, but from a different door. She signalled Captain Norwell forward, and then whispered:

'Can't be a better time, sir. The key's in the door, and there's nobody about. Come along, sir.'

She laid her finger on the excrescence, and with a prolonged 'Hush-sh-sh!' led him through a narrow passage at the back of the house.

Stopping at a small door, she peered cautiously around, and then motioned to him to enter.

'It's as dark as night, woman!' started Norwell.

'Not when you'm in and used to the light, sir. I'll go round and slide away another bull's-eye.'[4]

A cold tremor ran through him. He could not advance.

'You don't mind going in alone, sir? I can't for my life go in too. If I was caught 'twould be certain trouble. That's her over there, right along by the wall. Shut your eyes a minute, and then open them, and you'll see famous.'[5]

Norwell did so. The outer day excluded, a long line of dusky light stretched athwart the room from the bull's-eye, and rested on a row of narrow benches. As his eye gradually accommodated itself to the misty twilight, a strange horror rooted him to the spot. Suspense and dread smote heavily at his heart. He scarcely dared to look to the right hand or to the left.

A flash of a terrible truth struck through him as a bench shaped itself into a coffin, and then another, and another, and another loomed out of the dim forms before him, until he found himself surrounded by coffins of every size; but they were empty, waiting for their prey.

In unconscious terror he advanced.

'Oh, God! Maida, are you here?'

He spread his arms wildly around, groping—for what?

From without, the nurse pulled back a second bull's-eye; another line of light rushed in, scattering the darkness before it, and made way towards Norwell. He need look no further, for Maida was at his side. His long black cloak swept over the coffin.

'Sir! Sir, do 'e come out, it's mortal cold in here,' at last murmured the nurse, tired of waiting for the gentleman. But he neither moved nor answered; she was getting frightened; the tall black figure keeping silent watch in the dead-house was enough to see; it aroused every superstitious feeling in her wicked heart; but more terrible to see was the speechless despair of that tranced face. She would rather look at the corpse than it.

'Sir, sir, do 'e come along out!' Her teeth began to chatter.

The dull yellow of his bloodshot eye turned slowly upon her.

'Woman, this is a foul trick to play upon me.'

But how guilty soever elsewhere, here nurse was innocent. Taking for granted that he knew of Maida's death, she had never supposed but that he had sought admission to the corpse. That voice, heaved up as from a sepulchre, was worse than all: vowing she'd never again let strangers into the dead-house, she fled from an apparition so fearful; she cared not who met her so long as she escaped the dreadful place.

Lost in his own dark thoughts, Norwell looked not beyond the second line of light, or in the remotest corner he would have seen a man intently watching; but Norwell saw nothing save the one object before him, every power of his soul was harrowed on it. Harrowed! Was there aught in those noble features to alarm?

The coarse envelopments that shrouded Maida disfigured her not. As she lay there she had never looked more beautiful; the loveliness of which pain and sorrow had deprived her had been restored by death.

'Could I but cry aloud, would she raise those lashes and speak forgiveness to me?' groaned Norwell.

No, no, closed, ever closed those depths so rare and dream-like in their beauty; so brilliant and quenchless in their fire; they may not bless thee now; rejected once, they mock thee evermore. The line of light was obstructed by an approaching figure that had emerged from the darkness of the remote corner. Norwell's thoughts were still at work too busily, confusedly, poignantly, to notice it. The figure stood by him; still he observed it not, till a calm, low voice thrilled through him, and made him start, again to meet Mr. Herbert's piercing gaze.

'Her first rest, sir!' he pointed to the coffin. Spellbound, Norwell had no choice but to face his adversary.

'Who are you, sir, in God's name?'

There was no defiance in the speech; it was spoken tremulously, almost beseechingly.

'As you will answer at the dreadful day of judgment, when the secrets of all hearts shall be disclosed, I adjure you tell me what you know of this woman,' exclaimed Mr. Herbert, letting his hand fall audibly on the side of the coffin.

'Sir, rather tell me what you know of her?' said Norwell, shrinking back a step or two.

'I know she died a victim to some base man! And I would seek that man, sir, and show him what a destruction he has wrought. Would God I could bring him here, and face him with his crime!'

'You have your desire, sir. Behold the man!'

There was a stern despair in his bloodshot eye, as folding his arms, he drew his cloak about him, and waited what Mr. Herbert should say; but there came no reply.

'I only wait for vengeance, sir. I have crossed these seas to seek my just reward. I can bear myself no longer. I crave the avenger's hand.'

'You can know no judgment swifter or more keen than that which those pale features pass on your conscience, sir. Let them declare your doom. They will be merciful if they dare.' Mr. Herbert pointed to the corpse. 'Would God that every dissolute man could stand where you do now; could look around this house and count the coffins yawning for their victims; for here, sir, are many who had been still in peace and health but for the seducer's art.'

'Do you know no more than that, sir? Tell me, what know you more of me?' said Norwell huskily; the bloodshot eyes loured[6] darkly, terribly, and he almost stayed his breath to hear the answer.

'I know where your crime commenced towards this woman, and there it ends. But what intervening guilt has helped to fill your measure of sin, I cannot tell, and now before the living God—before this murdered woman, I charge you reveal what more you know of her.'

Norwell laid his forefinger on Maida's hand, and murmured as if in a dream:

'She lived, she suffered, she died for me, and in my stead; go and tell them so, and bid them find in me, Captain Norwell, all they sought of guilt in her. Chains should never have galled these hands.'

The bloodshot eyes started wildly, and he broke into a low, hissing laugh.

'Were these hands made for murder? Then there is murder in heaven, and I shall go there as well as she.'

His voice gurgled in his throat and he fell unconscious to the ground.

*****

We would not have you follow him; his dark, despairing eyes would haunt you evermore. His oft-repeated question none can answer; he would ask it you, for his voice finds but one utterance, and that is full of woe.

'Is she coming? Maida, Maida, is it you? O God! O God! It was I! It was I!'

The door of his cell draws back, and he gazes out upon you as a spirit lost. One alone can soothe him; one before whose tall and solemn figure the raving maniac cowers into silence, until, reassured by Mr. Herbert's sad but kindly voice, the bloodshot eyes look up, and the lips utter a murmured wail.

'O God! O God!'

When Mr. Herbert secretly pleads that the wail may become a prayer in the ear of Him who willeth not the death of a sinner, no, not of the vilest. As he prays the eyes of the maniac fix earnestly on him, and the lips whisper confidentially:

'Did you love her? Did you love her?'

But ere Mr. Herbert can answer, the patient returns to his raving and breaks out:

'Is she coming? Is she coming? O God! It was I, 'twas I!'

Stories so strange are hinted of the patient known as No. 12, that visitors to New Norfolk Asylum are fain rather to hurry by than to enter his cell. It is said government takes particular interest in this patient and is most watchful over him: it is well it should be so, but, alas!

'Care comes too late when is the mischief done!'[7]

THE END

Summary of Minor Variants

Excisions—less than 3 words from F

1. F Ch. 1 p. 8 *reads* heavily heaved sigh; R *omits* –il-heaved
2. F Ch. 1 p. 9 *reads* and she, poor fondling, will; R *omits* poor fondling
3. F Ch. 3 p. 15 *reads* This while; R *omits* while
4. F Ch. 9 p. 57 *reads* We overheard; R *omits* We overheard
5. F Ch. 16 p. 102 *reads* Fay! Miss; R *omits* Fay
6. F Ch. 18 p. 130 *reads* It was at the age of twenty that Mrs. Evelyn; R *omits* It was; that
7. F Ch. 21 p. 162 *reads* and merges into that one; R *omits* that
8. F Ch. 22 p. 168 *reads* my very heart; R *omits* very
9. F Ch. 27 p. 215 *reads* nosegay of soiled, davvered flowers; R *omits* davvered
10. F Ch. 27 p. 223 *reads* but I weren't up; R *omits* but
11. F Ch. 27 p. 226 *reads* At him, she'm yours; R *omits* she'm yours
12. F Ch. 27 p. 231 *reads* Most got a black eye; R *omits* Most
13. F Ch. 29 p. 265 *reads* she must look all, feel, pity all; R *omits* look all
14. F Ch. 31 p. 301 *reads* 'Precious, not a bit;' R *omits* Precious

Additional text in R

1. F Ch. 2 p. 13 *reads* He rarely controlled her in any thought, word, or deed; no wonder, therefore, that the change which the following conversation reveals was distasteful to her. R *reads* But when she was sixteen her father took her to a first-rate London school, to receive finishing lessons.
2. F Ch. 2 p. 14 *reads* But you must peep in if you would R *reads* understand the history that will follow.
3. F Ch. 3 p. 22 *reads* good-bye, Mrs. Grylls' Taciturn to sullenness sat Norwell. The yellow heap R. *reads* She found Norwell in her room when she returned. He was
4. F Ch. 4 p. 25 *reads* face on the baby's pillow R. *adds* her face on her dead baby's pillow
5. F Ch 4 p. 25 *reads* He came to impart direful news; but R *reads* in this new grief for Maida everything was
6. F Ch. 4 p. 29 *reads* laudanum found in the baby R. *adds* in the stomach of
7. F Ch. 9 p. 54 *reads* After Mr. Evelyn had remained a short time in his sister's family, he determined on making a tour, partly with the view of renovating his strength, and partly to give himself ample scope for choice of a healthy locality in which to settle his daughter and himself. R Ch. 7 *adds* But his daughter's rapidly-increasing ill-health caused him suddenly to return, and on consulting a physician he was advised to take Emmeline back to

8. F Ch. 12 is omitted in R. At Ch. 11 p. 74 R. *after* simple pathos *adds* At fourteen she was a maid-of-all-work without wages, and was induced by an artful woman, as a screen for her own pilferings, to 'borrow' five shillings from her master's till, with the intention of replacing it by installments. She was detected, charged with the whole series of robberies, and, as we have seen, transported.

9. F Ch. 16 p. 102 *reads* 'Why Em, from the way . . .' R *adds* 'Why, Em,' cried Bridget, astonished at her silence, 'from the way . . .'

10. F Ch. 19 p. 136 *reads* concealed his feelings. R *adds* Except that

11. F Ch 21 p. 150 *reads* 'You're nothing to them mor'n a fillet of veal,' winked Hawkins. R *inserts from later in the chapter (p. 152)* Hawkins had been a butcher, and from the dead or live stock of his former trade he drew his not overflattering similes.

12. F Ch. 21 p. 158 *reads* Whatever he meant further to enforce, he let off a third, shrill ahem, and then proceeded R deletes these clauses and *adds* He proceeded

13. F Ch. 26 p. 208 *reads* The confusion consequent on Rachel's sudden discharge, was partly rectified by placing Lucy in the nursery, and by giving Maida the double duty of housemaid and cook R Ch. 22 *adds* The confusion consequent on Rachel's sudden discharge had been partly rectified up to the time of Lucy's marriage, by placing her in the nursery, and by giving Maida the double duty of housemaid and cook.

14. F Ch. 26, p. 209 *reads* when Mr Sandford's remark arrested her. R *adds* Maida started; that name had been familiar to her in other days.

15. F Ch 26, F p. 211 *reads* She could bear to herself all that only touched herself; but now that one, whom she reverenced in her purity, had come unconsciously into her secret, she longed to hear from other lips R *adds* She could bear by herself all that only touched herself; but now that the happiness of other lives might be at stake she longed to hear from other lips

16. F. Ch. 26 p. 211 *reads* hope in life. Placing the materials for writing on a R. *adds* Returning to her room and placing the materials for writing on a

17. F Ch. 27 p. 218 *reads* 'He'll warrant ye I've touched the living 'fore now, and that with no chicken-heft, I'll promise ye; a chinker gied by Bob Pragg ain't a gift of every day.' R Ch. *adds* The name horrified Maida. She knew too well now why she had recognized the face.

18. F Ch. 27 p. 218 *reads* With an involuntary shudder R *adds* With an involuntary shudder she dropped her voice to a scarcely audible whisper:

19. F Ch. 27 p. 226 *reads* Gi's admonitory nudge warned Bob R *adds* An admonitory nudge from Giles warned

20. F Ch. 27 p. 237 *reads* salutation from Tammy, as she entered the kitchen. R *adds* And as she spoke a summons was heard on the street door.

21. F Ch. 28 p. 254 *reads* her voice and countenance R *adds* softened

22. F Ch. 28 p. 258 *reads* came in piteous accents from the closet outside the ward. R *adds* 'What noise is that?'

23. F Ch. 30 p. 292 *reads* a weight for which he could not account. R *adds* When Mr Herbert had to return for a short time to Hobart Town

24. F Ch. 34 p. 316 *reads* Is all of a fluster. R *adds* Bridget is all excitement.

25. F Ch. 35 p. 321 *reads* as she had appeared in prison. R *adds* where, as Mary Doveton, Mrs Norwell had visited her.

26. F Ch. 37 p. 339 *reads* voice gurgled in his throat R *adds* ceased

Notes

Preface

1 'So many attractive books': see Introduction.
2 When CWL arrived in Van Diemen's Land in January 1848, a third of its population were convicts under sentence. By 1846, when Earl Grey briefed Sir William Denison on his appointment as Lieutenant-Governor of Van Diemen's Land (1847–55), there were 29,949 convicts in the colony (Robson, 442); by 1851 the population was 69,598 (20,069 convicts), 1852 63,456 (19,105 convicts) and by 1853 60,000 (16,598 convicts) (Robson, 467). Transportation to Van Diemen's Land ended in 1853, the year CWL returned to England. A detailed account of transportation and its abolition appears in Robson (483–512). The long-term effects of transportation and convictism, combined with economic decline from 1850 onwards, perpetuated the social and moral impoverishment that is CWL's concern in her novel; see, for example, 'Royal Commission into the Queen's Orphan Schools,' *House of Assembly Journal*, Paper 72, 1859 (Bolger, chs 6, 7).
3 John 3: 11.

Chapter 1

1 Epigraph: L'Allegro, Air, Prima Parte, Georg Friedrich Händel, *L'Allegro, il Penseroso ed il Moderato* (1740). Elsewhere, epigraphs not attributed are CWL's own.
2 St. Judas' Cathedral and the city may be based on Exeter, where CWL was born. Judas' name announces the motif of betrayal.
3 'nonpareil': 'having no equal' (*OED*).
4 The comment comes from 'Ode on a Distant Prospect of Eton College,' a poem by Thomas Gray (1716–71): 'where ignorance is bliss / 'tis folly to be wise.' 'Johnson' is Samuel Johnson, *A Dictionary of the English Language: in which words are deduced from their originals, and illustrated in their different significations . . .* , vol. 1 (London: J & P Knapton, T & T Longman, C Hitch and L Hawes, A Millar and R & J Dodsley, 1755), entry for 'assize'.
5 Jeremiah 8: 22 'The Lord asks "Is there no balm of Gilead; is there no physician there? Why then is not the health of the daughter of my people recovered?"'
6 'Pestal': perhaps a reference to the Swiss educationalist Johann Heinrich Pestalozzi (1746–1827), who 'laid great stress on the value of the school use of national songs and fully recognised the cultivation of song as a harmonising influence on character' (*Oxford Companion to Music*).
7 Christ depicts the pains of hell for his disciples: 'Where their worm dieth not, and the fire is not quenched.'
8 Sir Walter Scott, 'The Lay of the Last Minstrel,' Canto II, stanza 1.

Chapter 2

1 Luke 15: 18 'I will arise and go to my father, and say unto him, Father, I have sinned against Heaven, and before thee.'

Chapter 3

1 'indigenous': 'inborn, innate' (*OED*).
2 'Brobdingnaginal': i.e. exorbitant, out of proportion, after the land of Brobdingnag, whose inhabitants are as tall as steeples, in the second part of Jonathan Swift's satire *Gulliver's Travels*.

Chapter 4

1 I Kings 20: 12 'And after the earthquake a fire; but the Lord was not in the fire; and after the fire a still small voice.' Maida, like Elijah on Mount Horeb, has been distracted from hearing the voice of the Lord.
2 From 'suspectable': 'that may or should be suspected; open to suspicion'; now rare (*OED*).
3 'hobnails': 'a nail with a massive head and short tang, used for protecting the soles of heavy boots and shoes' (*OED*).

Chapter 5

1 Numbers 32: 23 'But if ye will not do so, behold, ye have sinned against the Lord: and be sure your sin will find you out.' The clergyman is misapplying scripture to Maida's case.
2 The pun refers to John Walker (1732–1807), an English actor, lexicographer and elocutionist who compiled *The Rhyming Dictionary of the English Language* in the late eighteenth century, revised and republished (1847, 1854, 1860, etc.) as *Walker's Pronouncing Dictionary*.
3 'hard-favoured': 'having a hard or unpleasing "favour", appearance or look; ugly' (*OED*).
4 'to bate this': 'to contend with blows or arguments' (*OED*).
5 'stretcher': 'exaggeration, story or yarn' (*OED*).
6 'spree': 'a lively or boisterous frolic; rough amusement' (*OED*). See later uses as 'spreeing'.
7 'laudanum': a derivative of opium, much used in the nineteenth century.
8 'Godfrey's': a proprietary laudanum-based preparation.

Chapter 6

1 Epigraph from Lyra Australis, CWL's book of poems (published 1854), 'To the Evening Star,' ch. 4, p. 132. http://purl.library.usyd.edu.au/setis/id/lealyra.
2 'stereotyped': 2. *Fig* 'To fix or perpetuate in an unchanging form, 1819' (*OED*).
3 '*coup d'oeil*': meaning a scene as its strikes the eye at a glance (*OED*).
4 An allusion to *Hamlet*, I v: 166, 'There are more things in heaven and earth, Horatio, / Than are dreamt of in your philosophy.'
5 A prison in Pimlico, London, from which convicts were exported to Australia, 1816–90.
6 'wormwood': 'the plant *Artemisia absinthium*, proverbial for its bitter taste' (*OED*).

7 'phosphor': i.e. phosphorous, 'one of the non-metallic elements, a yellowish translucent substance resembling wax, widely distributed in nature in combination with other elements; it is extremely inflammable, undergoing slow combustion at ordinary temperatures, and hence appearing luminous in the dark' (*OED*); figurative.

8 'ticklish': 'needing cautious handling or action; delicate, precarious, risky' (*OED*).

9 'gammoned': '1. Thieves' slang . . . 2. To engage (a person's attention) while a confederate is robbing him' (*OED*). Hence, to be deceived or diverted.

Chapter 7

1 'ebullition': 'a state of bubbling agitation' (*OED*).

2 Matthew 11: 28–30.

Chapter 8

1 'GWR officials' are Great Western Railway officials.

2 A railway guide, first published by George Bradshaw (1801–1853) in 1839 as *Railway Time Tables*.

Chapter 9

1 Abel Tasman named the island in 1642 after the governor of the Dutch East India Company, Anthony Van Diemen.

2 The capital of Van Diemen's Land was named Hobart Town in 1804 by Lieutenant-Governor David Collins (1804–10) and, in 1881, contracted to Hobart, after the Earl of Buckinghamshire and Secretary of State for War and the Colonies, Robert Hobart. CWL uses both Hobart Town and Hobarton, the transitional abbreviated form, interchangeably. R uses Hobart Town *passim*.

3 When convict transportation was abolished in 1853, the name 'Tasmania' (after the original European discoverer) was introduced on 17 December 1855, in part to suggest a moral renovation had occurred. 'Tasmania' and 'Van Diemen's Land' are used interchangeably in the novel.

4 'hoydenism': CWL's coinage from 'hoyden', 'a rude or ill-bred girl (*OED*).

5 i.e. Bridget is embarrassed by having assumed her Tasmanian cousin would be 'ill-bred'.

6 I Samuel 17: 4–58: Goliath, the giant Philistine warrior, defied the armies of Israel but was killed in single combat by David.

7 Matthew 14: 31, 'And immediately Jesus stretched forth his hand, and caught him, and said unto him, O thou of little faith, wherefore didst thou doubt?'

8 'arch': 'sly, saucy, pleasantly mischievous' (*OED*).

9 'Methodism' was the, initially derisive, name applied to the eighteenth-century evangelical Christian movement led by John Wesley (1703–1791) on account of their methodological study and devotion. The Wesleyan Methodist Church, the largest branch of nineteenth-century Methodism, first held meetings in Sydney and Windsor in 1812. In Hobart, meetings were held from 1820. A minister was appointed in 1821 and a chapel (which still stands) built in Melville Street.

Chapter 10

1 The allusion to the Good Samaritan (Luke 10: 33–37) provides a Biblical model for women to become 'sisters of charity' and support, rather than spurn, fallen women.

2 After his resurrection, Christ appeared first to Mary Magdalene, Mary his mother and his mother's sister, all of whom he consoled. See John 20: 11–16.

3 Rahab is the harlot who hides Joshua's messengers and, thus, is the only person not cursed when Jericho fell. See Joshua 2: 1–21.

4 Levites were the Old Testament descendants of Levi and had assumed priestly functions.

5 i.e. Maida has assumed Norwell's guilt; nor will she hold his guilt against him; thus Norwell is 'unharmed' by the crime.

6 'upbraidless': not attested in *OED*; perhaps CWL's neologism for 'one who cannot be upbraided'.

Chapter 11

1 Dives was commonly taken to be the 'certain rich man' in Christ's parable, Luke 16: 1, 19. Luke 16 also tells of 'a beggar named Lazarus' (v 20) who, when he dies, is carried to into 'Abraham's bosom'. When the rich man dies (v 24), he cries out from hell, saying, 'Father Abraham, have mercy on me, and send Lazarus, that he may dip the top of his finger in water, and cool my tongue; for I am tormented in this flame.'

2 'holy-stoned': 'a soft sandstone used for scouring the decks of ships' (*OED*).

3 'bumper': 'a cup or glass filled to the brim esp. for a toast' (*OED*).

4 'toper': 'one who topes or drinks a great deal; a hard drinker; a drunkard' (*OED*).

5 'caudle': 'a warm drink; thin gruel, mixed with ale or wine, sweetened or spiced, given to sick people' (*OED*).

6 i.e. Cape Horn; the more usual route taken to Australia was around the Cape of Good Hope.

7 'log had been cast': 'An instrument for measuring the velocity of a ship. It is a flat piece of wood, some six inches in radius, and in the shape of a quadrant. A piece of lead is nailed to the rim to make the log gloat perpendicularly. To this log a line is fastened, called the log-line' (*Brewer's*).

8 'lo'urd': 'leeward' towards to lee, or that part towards which the wind blows;' pronounced 'leu'erd' (*Brewer's*).

9 'tomboy': 'a bold or immodest woman; a girl who behaves like a spirited or boisterous boy' (*OED*).

10 'imbruted': 'to degrade to the level of a brute; to make bestial' (*OED*).

11 'peach': 'to inform against (an accomplice or associate)', from impeach (*OED*).

12 'This lady will have to swallow her gentility in the box one o' these days if she kicks up her guineas to the doctor': *AND* and Laugesen have 'box' as 'A moveable box-like shelter in which convicts were confined at night'; other entries are not apposite. But, given this use and a later one ('She preferred the box'), 'box' is perhaps slang for a form of punishment, as in 'being confined in the box;' thus, Maida will be brought down to the common convict level by being punished 'in the box'. 'Kicks up her guineas to the doctor' may imply an obscenity not listed in the usual references.

13 'get the blind eye of the chap': i.e. to earn a favour from the chaplain's turning a 'blind eye'.

14 In Greek mythology, a monster born of no agreed parents with multiple eyes; Hera has him guard Io, of whom she is jealous, but he is tricked by Hermes and killed (*Oxford Classical Dictionary*).

15 'a real, livin' rantin' brick', i.e. an outstanding person. Perhaps a slang expression from 'brick' = 'a good fellow' + 'ranting' = 'to be jovial, boisterous, gay or uproariously merry' (*OED*). But also see the association with Ranter = Methodist (*OED*) or dissenters more generally to refer to noisy, energetic or vociferous preaching. 'Rant' has an intricate set of connotations, extending to sexual licence (Farmer and Henely, *Dictionary of Slang and Colloquial English*, 368).

16 Usually, 'gone to Davy Jones's locker', i.e. dead. Jones is a corruption of Jonah, the prophet, who was thrown into the sea. 'Locker', a seaman's phrase, is any receptacle for private stores (*Brewer's*).

17 Proverbs 1: 24, 26, 'Because I have called and ye refused; I have stretched out my hand and no man regarded'; 'I also will laugh at your calamity; I will mock when your fear cometh.'

18 An allusion to the conversion of Saul, who became the apostle Paul, Acts ix: 3–26.

19 The convicts resent the reminder of their own status, in the chaplain's words, symbolised by the broad arrow printed on their clothing.

20 An allusion to Pharaoh's unyielding resistance to the plagues sent to secure the release of the Israelites, see Exodus 7–12. 'And the Lord said unto Moses, Go in unto Pharaoh: for I have hardened his heart', Exodus 10: 1.

21 This Jewish sect, which bitterly opposed the Roman domination of Palestine, inspired the fanatical resistance which led to the destruction of Jerusalem in 70 CE.

22 'St Paul's example', 2 Corinthians 12: 16.

23 'box': see earlier reference; 'irons' may refer either to leg-irons or the iron collar worn by women convicts as a punishment (*AND*); 'cells' may refer either to ordinary cells or 'dumb-cells' used for solitary confinement; 'dark cells' were windowless enclosures.

24 'serge': 'a woollen fabric'; rough, durable, used here for the convict's uniform (*OED*).

Chapter 12

1 'Dapper' is 'neat, trim, smart, spruce in dress or appearance;' 'hussy' is, originally, 'housewife' but also 'woman, lass.' (*OED*)

2 'monthly': a monthly nurse is 'one who attends a woman in the first month after childbirth' (*OED*).

3 Apparently, Leigh Hunt (1784–1859), writer of poetry, drama and essays on various subjects often published in journals of which he was the editor. Active and life-long supporter of John Keats, Percy Shelley and the Romantic poets (*Oxford Companion to English Literature*).

4 Perhaps a version of 'here's the rub' i.e. here's the impediment, the sticking point from bowls 'where "rub" means that something hinders the free movement of your bowl.' (*Brewer's*)

5 Perhaps a version of 'nonce:' A corruption of *for the anes* (for then once), meaning for this once.' (*Brewer's*)

6 While *OED* gives 'Imperance (obs)' as 'Commanding quality, commandingness,' here it is most likely a malapropism for 'impudence.' Nurse in Ch. 28, H. M. General Hospital, Hobarton will use the same locution.

Chapter 13

1 Built in 1818 on the point of Sullivan's Cove, it was intended to defend the port of Hobart Town.

2 'gum tree': synonym for 'currency', or native-born Australian of European descent (not in *AND*), cf. 'gumsucker': 'These colonial chaps, Gumsuckers as they are called', G. T. W. B. Boyes Diary, 1840 (*AND*).

3 The *Hobart Town Courier* was published on Wednesday and Saturday between October 1827 and May 1859. CWL's name appears in the 'Shipping News', Saturday 29 January 1848, as a cabin passenger who had arrived on the barque *Tasmania*.

4 A commonly held view, cf. the charter's being forced upon King John, as Magna Carta, by English barons in 1215.

5 'A permit entitling a convict to live and work as a private individual within a stipulated area until the expiration or remission of sentence' (*AND*). Under Lieutenant-Governor George Arthur (1824–36) convicts were organised into a system. Male prisoners were categorised:

> Class 1 prisoners granted tickets-of-leave which freed men from most restrictions and enabled them to work for wages and own property;
>
> Class 2 assigned servants were prisoners given to particular settlers who were responsible for clothing and food in return for performing whatever tasks were required;
>
> Class 3 prisoners employed on government works;
>
> Class 4 prisoners working in road gangs;
>
> Class 5 those sentenced to hard labour in chains;
>
> Class 6 second-offenders sentenced to severe labour and rigid surveillance in penal settlements like Port Arthur;
>
> Class 7 similar to Class 6 but served their sentence in chains.

Women were classed as:

> Class 1 those suitable for assignment;
>
> Class 2 those who had committed minor offences;
>
> Class 3 the criminal class, numerically the largest. (Brand, Port Arthur 7–8)

The novel shows male convicts in Classes 1–6 and female convicts in Classes 1–2.

6 i.e. gave notice of her intention to leave.

7 'Female Factory' or 'House of Correction' was established at Cascades in South Hobart, in 1828, for the punishment of secondary offences; also referred to as 'going to Cage' and going 'to Cascades.' The complex of buildings expanded to accommodate 1000 women and 175 children. Conditions were wretched and the site was subject to frequent flooding. In the 1830s, women sent to Cascades were divided into three categories: third or crime class for insolence, drunkenness or being absent without leave; second or probation class where prisoners performed lighter tasks and received comparatively better rations; first or assignable class where prisoners waited to be assigned as servants to private households. Female factories also aimed to teach women 'habits of industry' and so they were employed in various occupations, especially laundry, known as working 'at the suds'. The factories also housed women not employable elsewhere and operated as hiring depot, hospital and nursery as well as prison and workplace (*Comp. to Tas. Hist.*). Maida and other convicts in the Evelyn household will find themselves in 'a Cascades cell' for various offences.

8 HMS *Anson*, moored in the River Derwent, served as a female penitentiary in the 1840s, though by 1851 Lieutenant-Governor Denison recommended that it should be broken up.

Charlie's nurses are selected, by his parents, from convict women on the basis of good behaviour and recommendation and employed, in this case, in child-minding while living in the family home.

9 'witching eyes': probably a contraction of bewitching.

10 The coachman has been part of a convict labour gang, hence the sardonic use of 'government'.

11 The maid-servant has completed her probation in service and has used her first wages to buy articles of clothing to replace her convict issue of serge petticoats and jacket and cotton cap. See Ch. 24.

12 The river flowing through Hobarton was named after one in the English Lakes District. The imposing mountain behind the town was prosaically styled Table Hill at first but in 1824 was renamed Mount Wellington, after the victor of Waterloo.

13 Now in Mali, the town's name is a synonym for remoteness.

14 'boomers': originally a Tasmanian expression for a very large kangaroo, esp. an adult male grey kangaroo (*AND*).

15 Vandemonian: 'a non-Aboriginal person native to or resident in Tasmania', from Vandemonia, 'A name for Tasmania, esp. as a penal colony' (*AND*).

16 *The Greek Slave* by Hiram Powers (1805–1873); completed in 1844 and patented in 1849 in an (unsuccessful) attempt to control reproduction. Exhibited at the Great Exhibition, 1851, the statue was 'for a time one of the most talked about statues of the nineteenth century' (*Oxf. Comp. to Art*). Small-scale statuette versions were popular in middle-class homes as icons of good taste.

17 i.e. after being on board ship.

Chapter 14

1 The title, meaning 'advocate' or 'intercessor,' given to the Holy Spirit cf. John 14: 16, 26.

2 'And the peace of God, which passeth all understanding, shall keep your hearts and minds through Christ Jesus.'

Chapter 15

1 Governor George Arthur divided Van Diemen's Land into nine police districts, each with a magistrate in charge of constables and field police, dispensing a summary justice and acting as the local registrar. *Hobart Town Directory and General Guide* (1852) lists Hon. F Burgess Esq. as Chief Police Magistrate (26) and A E Wilmot as Police Magistrate (26). Mr Wilmot's address is given as Macquarie Street (49); Mr Evelyn's address, The Lodge, is given as Macquarie Street in Ch. 13.

2 The Executive Council of Van Diemen's Land was established in 1825 comprising the Lieutenant-Governor, the Chief Justice and the Colonial Secretary.

3 The Legislative Council of Van Diemen's Land was established in 1823; a partly elected council replaced it in 1851.

4 'inexpiated': 'not expiated or atoned for; unappeased' (*OED*).

5 These complaints refer to alterations to the system of probation for convicts and the increase in the numbers transported, especially in the late 1840s. The system was introduced in 1839, modified from 1846 and wound up with the cessation of transportation in 1853. Probation replaced the previous assignment system, regarded as

inconsistent; neither reforming prisoners nor acting as a deterrent. Probation represented the stage of convict progression, after confinement and subject to good behaviour, in which convicts might achieve a probation pass and be assigned to a settler's household. The next stage was ticket-of-leave or pardon. Probation failed, it is usually agreed, through 'poor planning and administration, inadequate funding, huge numbers and an unforeseen economic depression.' This failure undermined Lt Gov. Eardley-Wilmot's position and consolidated opposition to transportation (*Comp. to Tas. Hist.*).

6 Perhaps, a gesture of contempt; by analogy with 'thumb one's nose at'.

7 Evidently three celebrated bushrangers of Van Diemen's Land. Knocklofty is commemorated by the name of a hill in West Hobart; Howe (1787–1818)—the most famous of the supposed trio—by a march west of Oatlands. Robson (48, 83–5, passim) records the career of Howe but has no mention of the other two supposed bushrangers.

8 Here Christ teaches forgiveness, instructing his disciple Peter of the need to forgive a brother's wrongdoing not seven times but seventy times seven.

9 Psalms 49: 8.

10 The New Norfolk Hospital was located on the Derwent River 38 kilometres north-west of Hobart. A wing was added in 1833 to accommodate 'lunatics' and the hospital was given over entirely to the care of the insane in 1848. See Ch. 37.

11 'rusty': 'reasty, rancid'; now only a dialect word (*OED*).

12 'flitches': 'the side of an animal, now only a hog, salted and cured; a side of bacon' (*OED*).

13 'factotum': 'a man of all work; also, a servant who manages all his master's affairs' (*OED*).

14 'Norfolk Island-made desperadoes' From 1821–32, Macquarie Harbour, on the remote west coast of Van Diemen's Land, operated as a penal station for secondary punishment. A convict settlement functioned at Norfolk Island, also for hardened and recidivist convicts, 1788–1814, 1825–55. Two sections of Marcus Clarke's His Natural Life (1874) are set at Macquarie Harbour and Norfolk Island.

15 'Whoever enters here. . .' an allusion to Dante, *Inferno*, Canto III, line 9, 'All hope abandon, ye who enter in.' 'Here a man's heart . . .': an allusion to Daniel 4: 6, 'Let his heart be changed from man's, and let a beast's heart be given unto him; and seven times pass over him.'

Chapter 16

1 An allusion to 1 Corinthians 13: 7 'Beareth all things, believeth all things, hopeth all things, endureth all things.'

2 1 Thessalonians 5: 17.

3 May be an allusion to Frances Nixon, Anglican Bishop of Tasmania.

4 Revelation 22: 5.

5 Brian Elliott, in *The Landscape of Australian Poetry*, traces this commonplace that native birds were either raucous or songless to Dr John Dunmore Lang's Historical and Statistical Account of New South Wales (1834) in which Lang referred to 'the gaily-plumed parroquet chattering among the branches;' Elliott comments that such birds were 'brilliant but songless.' (20–21, 23) Elliott is clear in attributing this motif to Lang rather than Adam Lindsay Gordon's 'A Dedication,' published in Gordon's *Bush Ballads and Galloping Rhymes* (1870), which has the more well-known lines, '. . . In lands where bright blossoms are scentless / And songless bright birds', first appear (92–93). See also reference to 'songless birds' in 'Yarra Banks No. 1,' *Banner* (Melb.), 17 March 1854, 4.

6 i.e. working at the government laundry. See Ch. 13.

7 'worked out': 'to make (something consisting of such fabric) by means of needlework, to sew or knit; to embroider' (*OED*).

8 From Reginald Heber's (1783–1826) famous hymn 'From Greenland's Icy Mountains'.

> What though the spicy breezes blow soft o'er Java's isle;
> though every prospect pleases, and only man is vile?
> In vain with lavish kindness the gifts of God are strown;
> the heathen in his blindness bows down to wood and stone!

9 'trumpery': 'something of less value than it seems; hence something of no value' (*OED*).

10 'Paddy-like': i.e. meagre food to which the Irish, or Paddies, might be accustomed.

11 A reference to the Anti-Transportation League, established 1849, whose advocacy contributed to the abolition of transportation to Van Diemen's Land in 1853. CWL's support for the League's aims is evident in 'On Tasmania's Receiving the Writ of Freedom,' collected in her volume of poems Lyra Australis; or, Attempts to Sing in a Strange Land (1854).

Chapter 17

1 The Duke of Wellington had died from a stroke at Walmer Castle, Somerset, 14 September 1852 and CWL uses such details to authenticate the historical setting of the novel.

2 Robert Liston (1794–1847), a pioneering surgeon who demonstrated the use of ether as an anaesthetic.

3 Misquotation of Othello's description of himself as 'one who loved not wisely, but too well', William Shakespeare, *Othello* V: 2.344.

4 'Sir William and Lady Denman' are based on Sir William Denison (1804–1871) (Lieutenant-Governor 1847–55) and Lady [Caroline] Denison, who married Denison in 1838 when she was 'probably in her twenties'. She died in 1899 having followed Denison to various colonial appointments (New Zealand, Tasmania, Sydney) and given birth to thirteen children. (Alexander, 178). The second part of CWL's *Lyra Australis* is dedicated to Lady Denison.

5 A fictitious character representing the upper-class snobbish woman; cf. 'Mrs D'Urban', who is a middle-class character in the novel.

6 The 99th Regiment, commanded by Colonel Henry Despard, was settled in the colony during CWL's sojourn (1848–53). Of the complement of 18 officers and 700 men, 15 officers and 515 men were stationed in Hobart Town in 1852.

7 'Veni, vidi, vici' ('I came, I saw, I conquered'), recorded by Suetonius.

> In his Pontic triumph he displayed among the show-pieces of the procession an inscription of but three words, 'I came, I saw, I conquered', not indicating the events of the war, as the others did, but the speed with which it was finished.

(*The Lives of the Caesars*, 'Julius Caesar', 37). The comment here is ironic.

8 *The Seasons* (1726–30) is a long poem by James Thomson (1700–48): 'one of the most popular (and frequently reprinted and illustrated) of English poems' (*Oxford Companion to English Literature*).

9 Hom(o)eopathy: 'A system of medical practice founded by Hahnemann of Leipzig about 1796, according to which diseases are treated by the administration (usu. in very small doses) of drugs which would produce in a healthy person symptoms like those of the disease treated' (*OED*).

10 Refers to the original Government House of Hobart Town, which stood at the southern end of Macquarie Street. In 1812, Governor Macquarie expressed disgust at its condition. Work on a new building was begun in 1842, soon abandoned as extravagant and not recommenced until 1853. In CWL's time in Tasmania, Denison had a wooden annex added to the original building as a ballroom (Alexander, 198).

11 Presumably a reference to William Buckley, a convict, who lived with an Aboriginal tribe in the vicinity of the Barwon River in Victoria for some 32 years (Hirst, 104–05). Buckley prevented a party of Aborigines from attacking John Batman and his party in 1803 and, in return, Lieutenant-Governor Arthur agreed to pardon Buckley (Robson, 209); perhaps, Buckley also received a pension. Hirst has a slightly different account whereby Buckley was employed, at a salary of 50 pounds, as an interpreter for the new colony established at Port Phillip Bay (1835–37); though he left for Hobart in 1837, married a widow with two children and became a government storekeeper. (105–06)

12 Now New Town, the first suburb built when, from 1805, free settlers moved north of the initial settlement.

13 A narrative poem (1847) by the American, Henry Wadsworth Longfellow (1807–79); a popular and influential poet in colonial Australia.

14 A Church of England college at Bishopsbourne, near Cressy, in northern Tasmania, opened in 1846. Students were trained in 'Classics, Mathematics and Theology' (Robson, 391). For documents detailing the history of Bishopsbourne and its development into Christ's College, later affiliated with and absorbed into the University of Tasmania, see University of Tasmania, Ms UA, 17, Christ's College Records, eprints.utas.edu.au/18612/UA17.pdf.

Chapter 18

1 'haricot': 'a ragout (originally of mutton, now sometimes of other meat)'; as distinct from the common kidney bean or French-bean (*OED*).

2 Exodus 10: 21, 'And the Lord said unto Moses, Stretch out thine hand toward heaven, that there may be darkness over the land of Egypt, even darkness which may be felt.'

3 'lift the swag': 'to rob, plunder' (Partridge, *Historical Slang*).

4 The main convict penitentiary and barracks adjacent to the gaol in Campbell Street was 'typically classical' in style. Designed by convict architect John Lee Archer, the complex was built in the late 1820s and comprised the Tench (penitentiary, 1827–28), a chapel ('old' Holy Trinity') initially used by convicts and free settlers and a beautiful clock tower (1830–33). The whole site is usually recognised as Archer's masterpiece and exemplary in colonial architecture. Later, the chapel was converted to law courts and a 'new' Holy Trinity was built in Warwick Street (*Comp. to Tas. Hist.*).

5 CWL notes a disfigurement and persistent cause of pain that generally goes little remarked in Australian nineteenth-century novels but features in diaries of the period.

6 The *Hobart Town Directory and General Guide* (1852) lists three dentists: James Montague, James Emanuel and Thomas Hemsworth but does not identify any as American (45, 64, 69).

7 An allusion to Proverbs 23:31, 'Look not then upon the wine when it is red, when it giveth his colour in the cup, when it moveth itself aright.'

8 While this reference is to fairy tales of errant, endangered children CWL's account of the mislaid infant in Hobart is one of the earliest instances of the topos of the 'lost child' in Australian literature; see Pierce, *The Country of Lost Children*.

9 An allusion to Francis Russell Nixon (1803–79), appointed first Bishop of Van Diemen's Land in 1842 and arrived at Hobart Town in July 1843. Nixon was an energetic opponent of transportation and appeared before the Molesworth Committee (1837–38). He retired through ill-health in 1863. CWL stayed with Nixon and his (second) wife, Anna Maria, at Boa Vista, North Hobart, while she convalesced, during which time she wrote some of the poetry later published in *Lyra Australis*. Nixon was very influential in the colony as a religious authority (sometimes in conflict with his clergy as is suggested here) and social leader (Anna Maria was a formidable hostess and Nixon a noted painter). Emily Leakey's biography quotes a letter from CWL, in which she says:

> [i]t would be impossible to tell you of all the kindness I received from him [Nixon] and Mrs Nixon; but one thing more you must hear—the dear bishop used to site beside my bed, and put his cold hand on my burning forehead, and as the palm became warm it would turn it to the back, and then change again and again.' (27–28)

Chapter 20

1 A public house cf. references to other public houses: the 'Bird in the Hand', the 'Eagle-Hawk', and 'the 180 taverns of Hobarton'. In 1847, the year before CWL came to Van Diemen's Land, James Hearl (or Hearll) was proprietor of the 'Eagle Hawk', James Kennedy of the 'Labour in Vain', and John Mezger of the 'Bird in the Hand'. CWL's estimate of the number of taverns is accurate (see Ch. 27). Bolger, who estimates there were 150 taverns in the early 1850s for a population of 24,000, comments:

> Refuge lay in the taverns behind slab walls within sound and smell of the waterfront. Selling English and Colonial ale, small beer, and cheap Mauritius rum, the drinking shanties of draughty weatherboard and shingle roof were the focus of a way of life. Upon their doors were posted notices which were the means of communication between rulers and ruled; from their lintels hung the only forms of lighting in the streets (excepting the big lantern over the stocks at the gaol gate in Murray Street). (37)

Five years later, the *Hobart Town Directory and General Guide* (1852) lists James Hearll as the licensed publication of the Eagle-Hawk, George Easton at the Labour-in-Vain and Thomas Mezger and Christopher Basstian at the Bird in Hand (127–30). See also Ch. 27.

2 Numbers 31: 6, 'And Moses sent them to the war, a thousand of every tribe, them and Phinehas the son of Eleazar the priest, to war, with the holy instruments, and the trumpets to blow in his hand.'

3 'drugget': a 'coarse woollen stuff used for floor-coverings, etc.' (*OED*).

4 'pickle': a 'troublesome or mischievous child' (*OED*). Perhaps also an allusion to Tobias Smollett, *The Adventures of Peregrine Pickle* (1751), a picaresque novel; the hero's adventures provide ample opportunity for satire, misanthropy and parody.

5 'respectable' is Lucy's malapropism for 'receptacle'; see also Ch. 21, 'congesting'.

6 'workery rumpussing': rhyming jingle, cf. higgledy-piggledy and evidently meaning 'a disturbance to work' (*Brewer's*).

7 The ferry from western to eastern shores of the Derwent, where, at Risdon Cover, the original settlement had been established by Lieutenant John Bowen in 1803 (Robson, 35). CWL's etymology sounds plausible but 'Risdon' was named by John Hayes, on his 1792 voyage, 'after the second officer of the *Duke of Clarence*', one of his vessels (Robson, 9).

8 Mrs Bowden was an historical figure. In his *History*, West notes that 'Mrs Bowden, a lady of majestic presence and enlightened mind, who had acquired considerable experience in the management of the insane, was appointed matron' of an intended female penitentiary. HMS *Anson*, formerly a ship of war, was established as a temporary expedient (510).

9 'cant': 'affected or unreal phraseology; esp. language (or action) implying goodness or piety which does not exist'; 'one who uses religious phrases unreally' (*OED*). Cf. The 'secret speech or jargon of the vagrant classes' (*Dict. Hist. Slang*). Partridge gives 'cant' to mean 'food' and 'gift' (*Routledge Dict. Hist. Slang*). Attested in *AND* as a noun but not as an epithet. See Anne Cox Woodrooffe, *Shades of Character*, vol. 1 (1844) 'Mr J[udge]. You old cant! What do you mean by the old time? Why I am but a boy; not yet married. Don't talk of the old time to me' (74).

Chapter 21

1 Judges 2: 5, 'And they called the name of the place Bochim: and they sacrificed there unto the Lord.'

2 'tabouring': to 'beat as upon a tabour; to drum' (*OED*).

3 'mousseline de laine': '("muslin of wool") a dress-material orig. all wool, but later of wool and cotton, printed with various patterns' (*OED*).

4 A ticket-of-leave gave a convict freedom within the colony until the original sentence expired. Hawkins, coachman and ex-convict, may be modelled on William Hawkins, cart and dray licensee, listed in *Hobart Two Directory and General Guide* (1852), 133.

5 Acts 28: 3–6.

6 Evidently, the furrows of Uncle Ev's brow as he meditates on private thoughts.

7 Admonishes Christians to think on 'those things which are above, where Christ sitteth on the right hand of God' (v 1).

8 See Ch. 3, n. 16.

9 The first of several such schools in Hobart, established by Lieutenant-Governor Arthur in 1833 in New Town. It was intended as a place of education not only for orphans, but for neglected and illegitimate children, such as those born in the convict Female Factory (*Comp. to Tas. Hist.*). Reverend Robert Crooke (1818–1888), a sometime catechist for the Convict Department, spoke in 1843 of the conditions at the school as 'sufficient to make the blood run cold.' Further, 'the slightest offence, where committed by boy or girl, was punished by unmerciful flogging' (Hughes, 525).

10 'Probation Stations': see Ch. 15, n. 5.

11 'wight': archaic term for 'person' (*OED*).

12 'Boadicea': queen of the Iceni in Britain. In 60 CE she led a bloody rebellion against the Romans that was punitively suppressed and resulted in her death.

13 'congest': 'to gather together; to heap up' (*OED*), but perhaps Lucy's portmanteau, 'congesting' may derive from 'considering' and 'suggesting.'

14 'waster': 'a foreign body in the wick of a candle which causes it to gutter and waste. *Dial.* (*OED*).

Chapter 22

1 'faggot': 'a bundle of twigs, sticks or small branches of trees bound together for use as fuel' (*OED*).

2 2 Samuel 16: 5–13, The son of Gera who 'came forth, and cursed still as he came', casting stones at King David.

3 'migrate': Bob's malapropism for 'migrant' or 'immigrant'.

4 'lifting': i.e. shoplifting.

5 'sote': 'set up for himself' (dialect).

6 'on the peninsula': i.e. one of the convict stations on the Tasman Peninsula; among them, Port Arthur and the Coalmines.

7 *The Princess* (1847) is a poem by Alfred, Lord Tennyson (1809–1892) concerning the strong-willed Princess Ida, a devotee of women's rights who founds a university but eventually marries her betrothed prince.

8 '*entre nous*': between us.

9 '*in propria persona*': in your own person.

10 'cram': 'slang: a lie' (*OED*).

11 'to smoke her': 'v. To make fun of, to jest at; to ridicule, banter, or quiz (a person)' (*OED*).

12 'the open sesame': the key to the mystery from the phrase used to enter the robbers' den in 'Ali Baba and the Forty Thieves' from *The Arabian Nights, or, Tales Told by Scheherazade During a Thousand Nights and One Nights.*

13 'eulogiums': from 'eulogize', 'to speak or write in commendation of; to extol' (*OED*).

14 Someone from the predominantly slave-owning southern states of the USA. President Abraham Lincoln makes the Emancipation Proclamation in January 1863, making the owning of slaves illegal.

15 See Supreme Court Report, *Courier*, Hobart, 24 April 1852, 3, for a detailed account, and George W. Walker's letter to the editor, *Courier*, Hobart, 8 May 1852, 3. Briefly, George W Walker, the model for the Quaker shopkeeper, Mr Washington in Ch. 24, had been called as a witness in Louisa Ferres's trial as she had been in his service. Walker's letter to the editor sought to clarify his testimony with the intention of achieving the 'truth'.

16 Isaiah 53 foretells the sufferings of Christ, 'a man of sorrows', who 'bare the sin of many, and made intercession for the transgressors'.

Chapter 24

1 Also known as Quakers. Two visiting English Quakers, James Backhouse (1794–1869) and George Washington Walker (1800–1859), established the Society's first meeting in Hobart in September 1833. Walker had been apprenticed to a draper in his youth; Backhouse wrote *A Narrative of a Visit to the Australian Colonies* (1843), which became a significant primary source for colonial history (Oats xiii, 81). *Hobart Town Directory* lists 'George

Washington Walker, draper and Savings Bank' on the right hand side of Liverpool Street (75); 'Matthew Jackson, draper's assistant', is listed in the same street; the Society of Friends is listed at 111.

2 'wear prison', i.e. wear prison clothes.

3 'picking oakum': 'loose fibre, obtained by untwisting and picking old rope; used esp. in caulking ships' seams, etc. The picking of oakum was formerly a common employment of convicts and inmates of work-houses' (*OED*).

4 'Brickfields': site of a pauper asylum and a depot for hiring convict labour, situated in North Hobart.

Chapter 25

1 'bergamot': 'a tree (Citrus bergamia); from the rind of the fruit a fragrant oil is prepared, called Essence of Bergamot' (*OED*).

2 'boy's love': alternative name for southernwood or *Artemesia abrotanum*, also called garderobe; small, bushy plant with feathery leaves; volatile oil gives off pungent camphor scent used to safeguard clothes against moths and other insects. Also said to promote beard growth when prepared as an ointment and applied to the skin. See entry, based on nineteenth-century sources, in Mrs M. Grieve, *A Modern Herbal*, 754–55.

3 'keb': cab (dialect).

4 'tin': 'slang orig. thieves' cant' meaning 'fellow, chap, customer'; slang, money (*OED, AND*).

5 'a lift': 'an act of helping, or a circumstance that helps, to a better position' (*OED*).

6 'famous': '(chiefly *colloq.*) as an emphatic expression of approval' (*OED*); *passim* but cf. Ch. 28 'it seems she pined away her reason. She was never very famous for it, so they who knew her at home said', where 'famous' means 'celebrated in fame or public report' (*OED*).

7 'gaby': 'a simpleton' (*OED*).

8 'Gregory': a laxative 'compound powder of rhubarb' (*OED*); from James Gregory (1758–1822), Scottish physician.

9 'Gregorian Chant': 'Ancient system of ritual music, also known as plain-chant or plain-song (characterised by free rhythm, limited scale, etc.) which is founded on the Antiphonarium ascribed to Pope Gregory' I (reigned 590–600) (*OED*).

10 'quackery': Mrs Evelyn is a 'quack or charlatan; administering ignorant or fraudulent remedies' (*OED*).

11 'list': 'the material of which the selvage [or border] of cloth consists' (*OED*).

12 The first church in Hobart, St David's, was consecrated in 1823. The present St David's Cathedral was later erected on the same site.

Chapter 26

1 '*Locum tenens*': One who holds the place of another.

2 A town, 36 kilometres north of Hobart, named by Hugh Germain, explorer and former Marine private, who reputedly travelled through the Midlands of Tasmania in the early nineteenth century, carrying a Bible and a copy of *The Arabian nights, or, Tales told by Sheherezade During a Thousand Nights and One Night* and naming places.

3 'A small vessel with a perforated top, from which to cast ground pepper etc.; extended to other vessels used to contain condiments at table, as in "a set of castors"'. (*OED*)

4 Probably a joke and very much in the vein of convict humour with a pun on 'stamp:' here Maida is 'stamped' by her status as a convict as being inconsequential. 'On Public Service Only' is found on mail that, by law, was exempt from charges because it was posted on public service.

5 '*Punch, or The London Charivari*, an illustrated weekly comic periodical, founded in 1841; at first a rather strongly Radical paper, gradually becoming more bland and less political. (*Oxford Companion to English Literature*)

Chapter 27

1 From Ezekiel 34: 4, which begins: 'The diseased have ye not strengthened, neither have ye healed that which was sick.'

2 'davvered': from 'dav(v)er', 'to fade, droop, wither;' hence 'withered, faded drooping' (*Dialect*).

3 The context suggests the 'new' Holy Trinity Church, on Warwick Street to the north of the city, designed by James Blackburn and completed in 1844, rather than the 'old' Trinity Church, on Campbell Street, built as part of the Penitentiary Chapel. Maida delivers a parcel to Trinity Parsonage; Trinity Parish is shown on the Glebe; the Prisoners' Cemetery was located to the east side of Trinity Cemetery on the Quadrant. See map. Rev. Philip Palmer presided at Holy Trinity between 1833 and 1853; his address is given as the Glebe, part of the Domain, in *Hobart Town Directory* (93).

4 'filliped': 'a movement made by bending the last joint of a finger against the thumb and suddenly releasing it; a smart stroke or tap given by this means' (*OED*).

5 'round away': 'to turn on (a person) with reproach or rebuke' (*OED*).

6 'chicken-heft': perhaps from 'heft' = lift, lift up, + chicken = timid (*OED*)? Cf. later, 'Heft away, then.'

7 'chinker': 'a catch, a twist in a rope'; 'a sprain on the back or loins' (*Dialect*); in context, 'a hard or solid blow, perhaps to the chin'. Cf. later 'he gied such a mortal chinker.'

8 'frisk': 'to rob (a place) or steal (a thing)'. 'Crib': house (Partridge, *Underworld*).

9 'cracksman': a 'housebreaker.' (*OED*). 'Lagged': to lag was 'to transport for seven years or upward' (James Hardy Vaux); also 'to transport a convict a convict from Britain to a penal settlement in Australia; to sentence to a term of imprisonment' (*AND*).

10 'smack': 'a taste' (*Dialect*) here 'a taste of it'; another meaning, 'to drink with enjoyment' (*Dialect*), may be appropriate here.

11 'heft': to lift, lift up' (*OED*).

12 'goggler': 'slang: an eye' (*OED*).

13 'grip': attested as 'to catch, or lay hold of; to ensnare, catch in a trap'; also, 'to apprehend, to arrest' (*Dialect*). But here, with 'a dance on the tight-rope' meaning 'to be hanged' (*Routledge Dict. Hist. Slang; Dict. Slang and Colloq. Eng.*), by analogy with 'dance upon nothing' (*Dict. Slang and Colloq. Eng.*), grip perhaps means '[the hangman's] grip was [al]most on her neck'.

14 'took shy on': perhaps a version of 'to fight shy of', 'to keep out of the way, to abstain' (*Dict. Slang and Colloq. Eng.*); here, to shun.

15 'nation': 'used as an intensive: very, exceedingly, extremely' (*Dialect*) (Jennings). Also, an abbreviation of 'damnation', 'a vulgar term used in Kent, Sussex and adjacent counties, for very, nation good' (*Dict. Slang and Colloq. Eng.*).

16 'Old Nick': 'the devil'; from St Nicholas the patron saint of scholars and, perhaps, thieves. (Partridge, *Slang and Unconventional*).

17 'house': abbreviation of 'workhouse'.

18 'guzzle': vowel shift, 'to drink immoderately; to take by the throat, to throttle, choke' (*Dialect*); 'to choke.' (Partridge, *Underworld*).

19 'screechers': not in *AND* or Laugesen, *Convict Words*. Partridge (*Underworld*) gives 'screech = giving of information to the police'; Wright's *Dialect* has, among other entries, 'screecher' meaning 'to make a great outcry'. The context here suggests a stroke with the whip sufficient to make the prisoner 'screech' out.

20 'tickler': not in *AND* or Laugesen, *Convict Words*. Partridge (*Underworld*) has, among other entries, 'tickler', meaning 'a stick, staff or cudgel'; Wright (*Dialect*) has the perhaps related sense of 'a sharp stroke with a cane or whip'. But here, the reference to the 'triangle' (the frame to which prisoners were tied for whipping) suggests 'ticker' = 'a tickle' ('a pleasantly thrilling or thrilling sensation' (*OED*) and thus an instance of grim convict humour.

21 'sheered': 'to turn aside; to swerve' (*OED*).

22 'pulled bob to 'un': Perhaps a variation of 'To give the bob to anyone: To deceive, to baulk' (*Brewer's*).

23 'flourishes': 'an ostentatious waving about of a weapon or anything else; a showy movement' (*OED*); here referring to Maida and Sam's work with the spades.

24 Perhaps 'wheel' = 'treadmill' (convicts' slang). (Partridge, *Underworld*). 'A dance in the dark': *AND* gives the later *His Natural Life* (1874) as a citation for 'dark cell'. In this earlier reference Bob Pragg uses a colloquialism, presumably current some fifteen years earlier, for the form of solitary confinement where the prisoner is kept in complete darkness and fed on bread and water. Later, Maida will experience time in a dark cell in which she is terrified by recurrent fears and ghosts from her past and perhaps this experience suggests the 'dance' Pragg refers to, as in 'dancing around in terror'. 'Jackdaw': a bird 'noted for its loquacity and thievish propensities', applied figuratively to 'a loquacious person' (*OED*). This is a good example of CWL's sensitivity in recording the combination of idiolects that made up colonial speech.

25 'devil's tattoo': 'tapping on the table with one's fingers a wearisome number of times' (*Brewer's*).

26 'fossed': forced to go.

27 'phiz': 'face, countenance; expression of face'; abbreviation of phiznomy, i.e. physiognomy (*OED*).

28 'whitewash': perhaps from 'whitewash', 'a cosmetic wash used for imparting a light colour to the skin' (*OED*) and thus Sam's face, drained of colour, appears to have been whitewashed.

29 'canary': 'a convict (from the colour of the clothing)' (*AND*).

30 'shamming': to sham is 'to cheat, trick, deceive, delude with false pretences' (*OED*).

31 'dodge': 'a shifty trick' (*OED*).

32 The dingo (Australian native dog) was unknown in Tasmania; *AND*'s first citation of 'dingo' as a 'brute' is 1865. The earliest citation for Tasmanian Tiger (Thylacine) is J. Bonwick, *Geography of Australia and New Zealand*, third edition, 1855 (*AND*).

33 'snug': 'drunk', cf. 'Euphemistic comfortable' (Partridge, *Underworld*). 'Peep': 'a surreptitious, furtive or peering glance' (*OED*).

34 'Centaurs': presumably, Centaurus, one of the largest constellations visible, lying in the third quadrant of the southern hemisphere, between latitudes +25° and -90°; containing eleven stars, the brightest being Alpha Centauri; catalogued by Greek astronomer Ptolemy in the second century CE.

35 The constable who is 'initiated' in illegal practices.

36 'bobbery': 'a noise, disturbance; a quarrel, dispute' (*Dialect*), i.e. 'for all your fine to-do'. The irony here is that Maida refuses to speak at all.

37 CWL gives a precise number here and it's unlikely she counted public houses herself. Through her sister-in-law (Mrs Medland) and friend, Miss Dowbiggin, CWL had connections to the Dorcas Society, a benevolent society for the relief of 'married women during the time of their confinement' and 'to extend relief to the poor' as funds permitted (Dorcas Society, UTAS, University Archive, Ms RS1). Perhaps such information circulated among members. It is more likely, though, that CWL simply consulted a publication such as *Hobart Town General Guide*, where licensed publicans and 183 public houses are listed by name (127–30); see Ch. 20, n. 1.

38 'spreed' from 'spree': an 'occasion or spell of noisy enjoyment (freq. accompanied by drinking)' (*OED*).

39 'touch up the chap here': 'to get by underhand means' (*OED*), i.e. to get alcohol illegally.

40 'start ginger': as in 'ginger up, esp. horse, by enlivening' (*Routledge Dict. Hist. Slang*); 'low'; fig. 'to spice up . . . to put mettle or spirit into' (*OED*).

41 'reserve her', i.e. would arrange for Maida to be held at the depot for Mr Evelyn's employment; as it turns out, convicts are not permitted to be reserved. See Ch. 31.

42 Numbers 12: 5 Miriam and Aaron spoke against the marriage of Moses to an Ethiopian woman, thus, angering God who appeared in the form of a cloud. When the cloud departed, 'Miriam became as leprous, white as snow'. Gehazi, the servant of Elisha, was similarly punished, but for greed (2 Kings 5: 27).

43 Allusion to Job 6: 26, 'Do ye imagine to reprove words, and the speeches of one that is desperate, which are as wind?' Rev. Herbert argues against punishment for Maida's 'supercilious speeches'.

Chapter 28

1 'conning': 'to get to know, study or learn, esp. by repetition; hence in wider sense, to pore over, peruse . . . to inspect, scan, examine' (*OED*).

2 'cynosure': fig., 'something that serves for guidance or direction'; 'something that attracts attention by its brilliancy or beauty' (*OED*).

3 'puling': 'crying piteously or weakly, as a child; whining, feebly waiting' (*OED*).

4 An allusion to Asclepius' staff, a single snake entwined around his staff, regarded as the symbol of medicine. Modern physicians have usually adopted the caduceus (two snakes intertwined around a staff) as the ancient symbol of their profession. But the caduceus is a symbol of Hermes, the Roman Mercury, and usually linked with commerce.

5 'phthisis': 'a progressive wasting disease; spec. pulmonary consumption' (*OED*).

6 'frettin': 'To distress oneself with constant thoughts of regret or discontent; to vex oneself, chafe, worry. Often with additional notion of giving querulous and peevish expression to these feelings' (*OED*). In this context, with a pathological sense; see later descriptions. 'Schemin'': i.e. convicts who schemed or plotted to go to the Female Hospital in order to avoid work or for some other advantage.

7 Words by Isaac Watts (1674–1748), English theologian, hymnist and logician.

8 Matthew 13: 45-46 tells the parable of the pearl of great price.

9 'bantling': 'a child, a baby' (*Dialect*).

10 'famous': in this sense of 'not known for', rather than renowned', neither fig. nor ironic, not generally attested; *OED* gives 'famous' meaning 'that is a matter of common talk' as obscure, with the last citation at 1724-44.

11 'blister': 'In the treatment of inflammation, Blistering plasters act more rapidly; they consist of powdered cantharides . . . rubbed with wax or fat, and spread on linen, leather, or oiled muslin. Well-made ordinary emplastrum cantharidum, in pieces as large as a franc or a dollar, is fastened onto the skin, and in twenty-four hours a vesicle [lister] forms under it; this is to be punctured, and a piece of wadding applied over it; this dries on and becomes detached in three or four days, at which time the detached layer of the epidermis has been regenerated . . .' (Billroth, 389).

12 Psalms 103: 14, 'He knoweth our frame; he remembereth that we are dust.'

13 'sperm-plaister': a plaster to which spermaceti, the fatty substance found in the head of the sperm whale, has been applied for medicinal purposes.

14 From 'Against Quarrelling and Fighting' in *Divine Songs for the Use of Children* (1715) by Issac Watts (1674–1748), see n. 7.

15 'jade': 'an epithet applied to a woman . . . malicious, tricky, untrustworthy' (*Dict. Slang and Colloq. Eng.*).

16 Nurse's mispronunciation of 'perquisite', any 'casual emolument in addition to salary or wages' (*OED*); in this case, any tips or extras Nurse can take from patients or their benefactors.

17 An allusion to Matthew 15: 22 and the woman of Canaan.

18 An allusion to Psalm 102, 'He will regard the prayer of the destitute / and not despise their prayer.'

19 From 'The Blessed Hope', a hymn written by Rev. August Toplady (1740–1778).

20 'coney': a rabbit; 'now chiefly regional' (*OED*).

Chapter 29

1 Port Arthur Penal Settlement—named in honour of Lieutenant-Governor George Arthur, who described it as 'a natural penitentiary'—began in 1830 as a punishment-oriented timber station; developing as the primary source of secondary punishment, replacing Macquarie Harbour and Maria Island. With the progressive addition of further industries, tailored for heavy and light labour, Port Arthur held a key position within the colony's judicial system until its closure in 1877. The settlement achieved prominence under the regimented governance of Captain Charles O'Hara Booth (1833–44), during whose command, convicts experienced a system of administration based on corporal punishment. Changes in English penology had seen the 1842 completion of Pentonville Prison, marking a shift in the treatment of refractory convicts as emphasis moved from punishment and reform through physical subjugation, to psychological control. This was reflected at Port Arthur in the 1848 cessation of flogging and the construction of the Separate Prison in 1850. With the end of transportation in 1853, the number of convicts at Port Arthur began to decline. From a high of 1200 during 1846, the 1870s population lingered at around 500. (*Comp. to Tas. Hist.*) CWL visited Port Arthur in November 1851 with friends, Rev. T. B. Garlick and his wife.

2 'sine qua non': 'indispensable, absolutely necessary or essential' (*OED*).

3 'their way to California', i.e. on their way to freedom and, presumably, the goldfields that had been opened up on the west coast of North America in 1848.

4 'overhauled the Bishop's frigate': 'to take, to come up with, to gain upon' (*OED*).

5 'strike the darbies off': to 'take off the handcuffs; occas. fetters (slang)' (*OED*).

6 'take the Queen's money to some purpose': i.e. a man joins the Army or Navy for a purpose, to do a job, in this case, guarding convicts.

7 Louisa Ferres: see Ch. 22, n. 15. A case of attempted murder said to be 'diabolical', *Courier*, 1 May 1852, 2.

8 An allusion to Matthew 23: 27, where Christ accuses the scribes and Pharisees of hypocrisy: 'ye are like unto whited sepulchres, which indeed appear beautiful outward, but are within full of dead men's bones, and of all uncleanness.'

9 Perhaps an epithet for the novel's Sir William Denman, a version of Sir William Denison (Lieutenant-Governor, 1847–53); see Ch. 17, n. 4; or at least the suggestion that reform of the penal system is 'devilish' because stymied by 'government'.

10 'battledore and shuttlecock': 'The game of battledore and shuttlecock' (*OED*); here used figuratively to mean tossing an issue from one part of government to another without finding a solution.

11 'shuttlecock': 'An instrument like a small racket used in playing with a shuttlecock 1598.'

12 Perhaps an allusion to Ecclesiastes 1: 15, 'That which is crooked cannot be made straight: and that which is wanting cannot be numbered.' 'Colonel Arthur' here is Lieutenant-Governor George Arthur.

13 Genesis 45–47 tells the story of Joseph's conducting his brethren to the land of Goshen, a fertile part of Egypt, and their prosperous life during a period of famine.

14 A reference to the infamous Black Line campaign devised by Lieutenant-Governor Arthur 'for the purpose of capturing the hostile tribes' (Robson, 218). Beginning in October 1830, it continued for about seven weeks and was judged a 'catastrophic failure' in military terms. (Robson, 220). Lyndall Ryan contests Robson's account of the Black Line as a military operation by identifying this attempt at systematic genocide as integral to systemic British imperialism. The 'failure' of the program evidences the success of Indigenous resistance. See Ryan, 'The Black Line in Van Diemen's Land: Success or Failure?' The standard account of this episode is now Henry Reynolds, *The Forgotten War* (Sydney: UNSW Press, 2013).

15 In 1829 Lieutenant-Governor Arthur estimated 'there could not be above 2000 [Aborigines] left in the colony' (Robson, 215). In 1834 George Augustus Robinson took most of last remaining Aborigines to Flinders Island in Bass Strait; by 1843 only 54 were alive. Three years later, the survivors were settled at Oyster Cove in the D'Entrecasteaux Channel. See Reynolds, *The Forgotten War*, Chs 1–2, in the context of Indigenous survival in Tasmania.

16 Genesis 9: 6, 'by man shall his blood be shed: for in the image of God made he man'.

17 'Of convict clothing: black and yellow' (*AND*). 'This "magpie suit" is intended for chain gangs and doubly convicted prisoners, and is ordered by government as a badge of the deeper disgrace. It is composed of black and yellow cloth, of the same quality as the grey' (*AND*). 'snob': 'a shoemaker,' 'an inferior' (*Dict. Slang & Colloq. Eng.*); 'dial. Or colloq. A shoemaker or cobbler'; 'one having no pretensions to rank or gentility' (*OED*).

18 '*bon père* Raffre': from Anne Tuttle Jones Bullard, *Little Aimee, the Persecuted Child to which is added The Frightful Story, by the author of Louisa Ralston, The Stanwood Family, etc.* (Cincinnati: Truman, Smith & Company, 1833), 16.

19 'diluent': 'That which dilutes, dissolves or makes more fluid' (*OED*).

20 Trumpeter is a species of fish common in Tasmanian waters; it is now called the stripy trumpeter and makes delicious eating.

21 Psalm 49: 7–8, 'None of them can by any means redeem his brother, no give to God a ransom for him: / (For the redemption of their soul is precious, and it ceaseth for ever)'.

22 'Foraging in my paddock': 'To hunt or search about diligently'; 'To procure; to purloin, steal' (*Dialect*); here, a good-natured exclamation.

23 B. O.: Board of Ordinance, which issued equipment of all kinds to government agencies; O.P.S.O. see Ch. 26.

Chapter 30

1 Conflation of Christ's prayer—knowing what will come—in the Garden of Gethsemane (Mark 14: 36, 'not what I will, but what thou wilt') and the Lord's Prayer ('Thy will be done').

2 From the Lord's Prayer.

3 'smally': an unusual adverbial formation: 'sparsely, scantily' (*OED*).

4 'Elysian': the place where, in Greek mythology, those favoured by the gods enjoyed a full and pleasant life after death.

5 'Phyllis': 'a generic proper name in pastoral poetry for a comely rustic maiden, or for a sweetheart' (*OED*).

6 Now written Eaglehawk Neck, the narrow isthmus of land leading to the Tasman Peninsula.

7 Matthew 11: 28.

8 Proverbs 16: 6, 'By mercy and truth iniquity is purged; and by the fear of the Lord men depart from evil.'

9 Luke 15: 18, 'and will say unto him, Father, I have sinned against heaven, and before thee.'

10 Point Puer was 'the first British purpose-built reforming institution for criminal boys' (*Comp. to Tas. Hist.*); essentially used as a prison for convict boys from 1833–49, when it housed 162 boys.

Chapter 31

1 Isaiah 1: 19–20 'If ye be willing and obedient, ye shall eat the good of the land: But if ye refuse and rebel, ye shall be devoured with the sword: for the mouth of the Lord hath spoken it.'

2 'The Lord is my shepherd; I shall not want.
He maketh me to lie down in green pastures: he leadeth me beside the still waters.
He restoreth my soul: he leadeth me in the paths of righteousness for his name's sake.
Yea, though I walk through the valley of the shadow of death, I will fear no evil: for thou art with me; thy rod and thy staff they comfort me.
Thou preparest a table before me in the presence of mine enemies: thou anointest my head with oil; my cup runneth over.
Surely goodness and mercy shall follow me all the days of my life: and I will dwell in the house of the Lord for ever.'

3 'quinine': 'employed in treatment of malaria and (in early use) as a general febrifuge and tonic' (*OED*).

4 'gibbered': 'to speak rapidly and inarticulately; to chatter' (*OED*).
5 'guana': 'goanna' (*AND*).
6 'rangers': abbreviation of 'bushrangers'.

Chapter 32

1 Matthew 28: 20.
2 Psalm 104: 43.
3 James 5: 11.
4 'cerements': 'waxed wrappings for the dead; grave clothes generally' (*OED*).
5 John 11: 25.
6 Revelation 14: 13.
7 Job 3: 17, 20, 'There the prisoners rest together; they hear not the voice of the oppressor.'

Chapter 33

1 Agrippa II (d. 100 CE), last of the Herods, made this remark upon hearing Paul's account of his conversion and subsequent career, although he still delivered him up from transportation to Rome. See Acts 26: 28.

Chapter 34

1 In CWL's time, a farming district on the eastern side of the Derwent River but now part of the Hobart metropolitan area. In 1852, Rev. W. W. F. Murray was chaplain of St Matthew's, Clarence Plains, with a stipend of 200 pounds and 30 pounds for 'glebe and forage.'
2 'Bishopsbourne,' the Church of England college, near Cressy. See Ch. 17. The first warden was Rev. Gell, who resigned in 1848 when the college had gone into decline. Gell had several successors (Revs Cox, Windsor and Filleul), one of whom may have been the model for Rev. Walkden. By 1852, Rev. Samuel B. Windsor, MA was surrogate chaplain at Bishopsbourne (*Hobart Town Directory*, 108); Mr J. Helder Wedge is listed at Christ's College, Bishopsbourne (106), having been appointed Warden.
3 Evidently, from 'strategy', meaning 'skill in devising expedients' (*OED*) and referring to Uncle Ev's skilfully leaving the room.

Chapter 36

1 'cant': 'affected or unreal phraseology; esp. language (or action) implying goodness or piety that does not exist' (*OED*).
2 Matthew 7: 14, 'Because strait is the gate, and narrow is the way, which leadeth unto life, and few there be that find it.'
3 2 Timothy 4: 7, 'I have finished my course, I have kept the faith.'
4 See Acts 22: 6–7 and the account of Saul's (St Paul) conversion.
5 'Pish': 'expressing contempt, impatience or disgust' (*OED*).
6 'apostrophe': 'an exclamatory address' (*OED*).
7 'stark': 'rigid in death'; 'starken' = 'to stiffen' (*Dialect*). Hence to produce a horrible death mask.

8 'signalised': 'to make signals to; to communicate with by means of a signal' (*OED*).

9 i.e. a passenger bringing ill luck from Jonah, 'Hebrew prophet . . . Hence Jonah v. trans. to bring ill luck to' (*OED*). See Jonah 1: 4.

10 'rapture': 'the act of conveying a person from one place to another, esp. to heaven' (*OED*)

Chapter 37

1 Ezekiel 7: 6.

2 'canaries': i.e. yellow-clad convicts in a road gang.

3 'take shy': 'to take a sudden fright or aversion; to make a difficulty, "boggle" about doing something' (*OED*). Cf. Ch. 27.

4 'bulls-eye': 'a small circular opening or window' (*OED*).

5 'famous': 'an emphatic expression of approval' (*OED*). Cf. Chs. 27 and 28.

6 'loured', from 'lour': 'to frown, scowl; to look angry or sullen' (*OED*).

7 'Care comes too late . . .': from *Lyra Australis*, 'Blanche', Ch. 3, 185.

Bibliography

Primary sources: company records

Angus & Robertson. Correspondence. 24 April 1987–23 March 1989. Private Hands.

Ingram, Alison. Compiler. *Index to the Archives of Richard Bentley & Son 1829–1898*. Cambridge: Chadwyck-Healey; Teaneck: Somerset House. 1977.

Turner, Michael L. *Index and Guide to the Lists and Publications of Richard Bentley & Son 1829–1898*. Bishops Stortford: Chadwyck-Healey, 1975.

A List of the Principal Publications Issued from New Burlington Street During the Year 1859. London: Richard Bentley & Son, 1905.

A List of the Principal Publications Issued from New Burlington Street During the Year 1886. London: Richard Bentley & Son, 1920.

A List of Principal Publications from New Burlington Street During the Year 1888. London: Richard Bentley & Son, 1917.

Publications Issued from New Burlington Street, during the last three months of the year 1829. London: Richard Bentley & Son, 1893. https://bit.ly/2EQmHVh.

TAHO NS2849/1/1 *Walch's Literary Intelligencer*, March 1860.

TAHO NS2849/1/1 *Walch's Literary Intelligencer*, May 1860.

TAHO NS2849/1/22 *Walch's Literary Intelligencer*, December 1901.

TAHO NS2849/1/26 *Walch's Literary Intelligencer. Jubilee* Number. No. 608, May 1909.

TAHO NS2855/1/1 Letterbook No. 9, November 1869.

TAHO NS2857/1/4 Letters from the London Office. Letters 294–347. 01 Jan 1897-31 Dec 1897.

TAHO NS2857/1/6 Letters from the London Office. Letters 400–450, 01 Jan 1899- 31 Dec 1899.

TAHO NS2864/1/1 Walch's Circulating Library. Register. January 1846–December 1851.

TAHO NS369/1/26 *The Story of the Life of Charles Edward Walch with a Selection of His Writings*. Printed for Private Circulation. Hobart: Walch & Sons, 1908.

Primary sources: private

TAHO NS690/1/98. W. H. Hudspeth's Historical Files. Notes on 'Broad Arrow' by Olina [*sic*] Keese.

State Library of Victoria. MS9124. *The Journal of Mary Isabella Cameron 1847*. 'Written on board the Good Ship Tasmania, being a narrative of facts, which occurred on the occasion of her visiting Van Diemen's Land. October, 1847.'

State Library of Victoria. MSB454. Mary Isabella Cameron. 'Pages from the VDL Journal 3A-11.'

University [of Tasmania] Archives, RS131/16. Memories of S. B. Emmett (son of H. I. Emmett), who arrived as baby with his father by *Regalia* in 1819, as written down by J. B. Walker, 7 August 1892 (Inc. memories of aborigines, the old wharf, early settlers' homes). (1 mss. 7pp. plus letter).

Nineteenth-century non-fiction

Accounts and Papers of the House of Commons, 1852–3 to 1868–69. London: House of Commons, 1870.

A Catalogue of Books Contain in J. W. H. Walch's Derwent Circulating Library Wellington Bridge. Hobart: n. publ.; printed William Gore Elliston, 1846.

A Catalogue of Books in Various Branches of Literature Direct from Mudie's Select London Library, also Magazines and Reviews Contained in W. Westcott's Circulating Library. Hobart Town: no publ., printed by W[illia]m Fletcher 1871. http://bit.ly/2H7ZfUb.

Arnold, Thomas. *Passages in a Wandering Life*. London: Edward Arnold, 1900.

Backhouse, James. *Narrative of a Visit to the Australian Colonies*. London: Hamilton, Adams, 1843.

Bertram, James. Ed. *New Zealand Letters of Thomas Arnold the Younger with further letters from Van Diemen's Land and Letters of Arthur Hugh Clough*. London & Wellington: University of Auckland, 1966.

Bischoff, James. *Sketch of the History of Van Diemen's Land, illustrat by a map of the island, and an account of the Van Diemen's Land Company*. London: John Richardson, 1832.

Catalogue of Books in the Tasmanian Public Library. Samuel Hannaford [Compiler]. Hobart Town: James Barnard, Govt. Printer, 1870. http://handle.slv.vic.gov.au/10381/200582.

Catalogue of the Library of the Hobart Mechanics' Institute. Hobart Town: no publ., printed by William Fletcher, 1860. http://handle.slv.vic.gov.au/10381/200102.

Cave, Kathryn. Ed. *The Diary of Joseph Farington*. Vol. 10, July 1809–December 1810. New Haven and London: Yale University Press, 1982.

Diaries of Caroline Yarde Scobell. 1845–1846,.AMS5683 [n.d.]. East Essex Records Office. https://bit.ly/2Piwg30.

Fenton, James. *A History of Tasmania From its Discovery in 1642 to the Present Time*. Hobart: J Walch and Sons, 1884.

Hobart Town Directory and General Guide. Hobart Town: Moore, 1852. https://stors.tas.gov.au/AUTAS001136438959.

Leakey, Emily P. *Clear Shining Light: A Memoir of Caroline W. Leakey*. By her sister Emily. London: John F. Shaw, 1882.

Meredith, Mrs Charles [Louisa Anne Meredith]. *My Home in Tasmania, During a Residence of Nine Years*. London: John Murray, 1852.

Melville, Henry. *The History of Van Diemen's Land from the year 1824 to 1835, inclusive: during the administration of Lieutenant-Governor George Arthur*. Ed George Mackaness. Sydney: Review Publications, 1978. [First published as *The History of the island of Van Diemen's Land from the year 1824 to 1835: inclusive, to which is added a few words on prison discipline*. London: Elder & Smith, 1835.]

Report of the Commissioner of Inquiry, on the judicial establishments of New South Wales, and Van Diemen's Land: ordered, by the House of Commons, to be printed, 21 February 1823. John Thomas Bigge. London: House of Commons, 1823.

Report from the Select Committee of the House of Commons on Transportation Together with a Letter from the Archbishop of Dublin on the Same Subject and Notes. Sir William Molesworth, Bart. London: Henry Hooper, 1838. Includes 'Minutes of Evidence, Appendix, and Index.' Part 1. Evidence of James Mudie.

Morgan, John. Compiler. *The Licensed Victuallers Directory for the Year 1847*. Campbell Street, Hobart: J. Burnet, 1847.

Mitchel, John. *Jail Journal: Commenced on board the 'Shearwater' steamer, in Dublin Bay, continued at Spike Island, on board the 'Scourge' war steamer, on board the 'Dromedary' hulk, Bermuda, on board the 'Neptune' convict ship at Pernambuco, at the Cape of Good Hope (during the anti-convict rebellion), at Van Diemen's Land, at Sydney, at Tahiti, at San Francisco, at Greytown and concluding at no. 3 pier, North River, New York: with an introductory narrative of transactions in Ireland*. Dublin: M. H. Gill, 1913.

Nixon, Francis [Bishop]. *The Cruise of the 'Beacon': a Narrative of a visit to the Islands in Bass's Straits* [sic]. London: Bell & Daldy, 1857.

Penal Servitude Act, 1857. Ch 3 [. . .] in lieu of Transportation. https://bit.ly/2AnrOHS

Roth, H. (Henry Ling), Marion E. Butler, James Backhouse Walker, J. G. Garson (John George). *The Aborigines of Tasmania*. Halifax: F. King & Sons, 1899. https://bit.ly/2CAdei4.

Stoney, H[enry] Butler. *A Year in Tasmania: including some months' residence in the capital with a descriptive tour through the island, from Macquarie Harbour to Circular Head and a short notice on the colony in 1853*. Hobart: W. Fletcher, 1854.

TAHO G01/97, 147-49. 'Order-in-Council 8 September 1855 approving replace of the name "Van Diemen's Land" by "Tasmania" as the name of the Colony'. Proclaimed 1856.

'The Rev'd John Rashdall, A.M.' Online Collection entry. http://bit.ly/2qEUEOP.

Vaux. James Hardy. *Memoirs of James Hardy Vaux. Written by Himself.* [Includes Vaux's vocabulary of Flash talk]. London: Clowes, 1819. https://bit.ly/2CXyhvZ.

— — —. *The Memoirs of James Hardy Vaux: including his vocabulary of the Flash language*. Ed and introduction, Noel McLachlan. London: Heinemann, 1964.

West, John. *The History of Tasmania*. Ed. A.G.L. Shaw. Sydney: Angus and Robertson, 1971; first published 1852.

Walker, James Backhouse. *Papers on Tasmania. Papers Presented to the Royal Society*. Hobart: William Grahame, Government Printer, 1884–96.

— — —'List of books relating to Tasmania.' In James Fenton *A History of Tasmania From its Discovery in 1642 to the Present Time*. Hobart: J Walch and Sons, 1884.

Walker's Pronouncing Dictionary of the English Language. Boston: Charles Ewer, 1828.

Nineteenth-century fiction and poetry

Bullard, Anne Tuttle Jones. *Little Aimee, the Persecuted Child* to which is added *The Frightful Story*, by the author of *Louisa Ralston, The Stanwood Family*, etc. Cincinnati: Truman, Smith & Company, 1833.

Clarke, Marcus. *His Natural Life*. Ed. Lurline Stuart. The Academy Edition of Australian Literature. St Lucia: University of Queensland Press, 2001.

Keese, Oliné. [Caroline Woolmer Leakey]. *The Broad Arrow; Being Passages from the History of Maida Gwynnham, a Lifer*. London: Richard Bentley & Son, 1859; Hobart: J. Walch & Sons, 1860.

— — —. [Caroline Woolmer Leakey]. *The Broad Arrow; Being Passager from the History of Maida Gwynnham, a Lifer*. London: Richard Bentley & Son, 1887.

— — —. [Caroline Woolmer Leakey]. *The Broad Arrow; Being Passages from the History of Maida Gwynnham, a Lifer*. Revised edn. Sydney Electronic Text and Imaging Service. SETIS. 1997. https://bit.ly/2PNVhjD.

Leakey, Caroline W. *Lyra Australis; or, Attempts to Sing in a Strange Land*. London: Bickers and Bush, 1854; Hobart: Walch & Sons, 1854.

Martin, Catherine. *An Australian Girl*. Ed. Graham Tulloch. Intro. Amanda Nettlebeck. Oxford World Classics Series. Oxford: Oxford University Press [1892] 1999.

— — — *The Silent Sea*. Ed. Rosemary Foxton. Colonial Texts Series. Sydney: UNSW Press, [1892] 1995.

Reade, Charles. *'It is Never Too Late to Mend' A Matter-of-Fact Romance*. London: The Daily Telegraph, n.d. [1856]).

Reynolds, George W. M. *Mysteries of London*. 8 Vols. London: Dicks, 1849–56. https://bit.ly/2yBWmET.

Rowcroft, Charles. *The Bushranger of Van Diemen's Land*. London: Elder & Smith, 1846.

Savery, Henry. *The Hermit in Van Diemen's Land*. Ed. Cecil Hadgraft and notes by Margriet Roe. St Lucia: University of Queensland Press, 1964. [First published as by 'Simon Stukeley'. *Colonial Times of Hobart Town*. 5 Jun 1829–25 Dec 1829.]

Scott, Walter. *Ivanhoe*. Ed. Graham Tulloch. The Edinburgh Edition of the Waverley Novels. N.p.: Edinburgh University Press. [1820] 1998.

Spence, Catherine Helen. *Clara Morison: a tale of South Australia during the gold fever*. Susan Magarey. Intro. Netley, S.A.: Wakefield Press, 1986. [First published London: John Parker, 1854]

Tucker, James. [Giacomo di Rosenberg.] *Ralph Rashleigh or The Life of an Exile*. Ed. Colin Roderick. Sydney & London: Angus and Robertson, 1952.

Winstanley, Eliza. *For Her Natural Life. A Tale of the 1830s*. Dicks' English Novels No. 73. London. 1860, 1876.

Woodrooffe. Anne Cox. *Shades of Character; or, Mental and Moral Delineations; Designed to Promote the Formation of the Female Character on the Basis of Christian Principle*. London: Hatchard & Son, 1845.

Newspapers, periodicals and journals

Banner (Melb.), 17 March 1854.

The Athenaeum, no. 1644, 20 April 1859.

The Australasian, 5 February 1887.

Colonial Times, 21 January 1831, 8 February 1850, 24 July 1852.

Cornwall Chronicle, 29 February 1860, 31 March 1860.

The Courier [Hobart], 9 October 1847, 29 Jan 1848, 1 May 1852, 24 July 1852.

The Critic, 2 April 1859.

The Hobart Town Courier and Gazette, 5 January 1848.

Launceston Examiner, 10 May 1887, 12 May 1887.

The Literary Gazette: a Weekly Journal of Literature, Science, Art and General Information, 21 May 1859.

The Mercury [Hobart], 11 April 1871, 24 January 1887, 27 January 1879, 30 July 1988, 23 November 1864.

The Publisher, 18 July 1887.

Spectator, 14 May 1859.

Sydney Record, 20 January 1844.

Reference works

Athenaeum Title Record. https://bit.ly/2PiI8Sw.

Australian Convict Sites. World Heritage Nomination. Canberra: Department of the Environment, Water, Heritage and the Arts. 2008.

AustLit. Electronic Resource. The Australian Literature Resource. St Lucia: AustLit, 2010. https://bit.ly/2Pej0fS.

Australian National Dictionary. Ed. W. S. Ransom. Melbourne: Oxford University Press, 1988. [*AND*]

—— ——. Ed. Bruce Moore, 2nd edn. South Melbourne: Oxford University Press, 2016.

Billroth, Theodore. *General Surgical Pathology and Therapeutics*. The Classics of Medicine Library. New York: Griffon Editions, 1987; first published New York: Appleton, 1871. [Billroth]

The Feminist Companion to Literature in English. Virginia Blain, Patricia Clements and Isobel Grundy. Eds. London: Batsford, 1990.

Brewer, Cobham, E. *The Dictionary of Phrase and Fable*. New York: Avenel, 1978. [*Brewer's*]

'Champ, William (1808–1892).' John V. Barry. *Australian Dictionary of Biography*. Vol. 3. Melbourne: Melbourne University Press, 1969. https://bit.ly/2J9t4kN.

Companion to Tasmanian History. Ed. Alison Alexander. Hobart: Centre for Tasmanian Historical Studies, University of Tasmania, 2005. Online Resource. http://www.utas.edu.au/library/companion_to_tasmanian_history. [*Comp. to Tas. Hist.*]

A Dictionary of Critical Theory. Ed. Ian Buchanan. Online Resource. Oxford: Oxford University Press, 2010.

A Dictionary of the English Language: in which The Words are deduced from their originals . . . By Samuel Johnson. Vol I & II. London: P. & J. Knapton, T. & T. Longman, C. Hitch and L. Hawes, A. Millar and R. & J. Dodsley, 1755.

'Eardley-Wilmot, John Eardley (1783–1847)'. Michael Roe. *Australian Dictionary of Biography*. Vol. 1. Melbourne: Melbourne University Press, 1966. https://bit.ly/2OJFSVa.

English Dialect Dictionary: Being the complete vocabulary of all dialect words still in use, or known to have been in use during the last two hundred years; founded on the publications of the English dialect society and on a large amount of material never before printed. Ed. Joseph Wright. Vols I–VI (Oxford nd New York: Henry Frowde and G P Putnam's Sons: 1905). [*Dialect*]

Farmer, John S. and W. E. Henley. *A Dictionary of Slang and Colloquial English*. London: Routledge, 1905. https://bit.ly/2q5o1cv.

Ferguson, John Alexander. *Bibliography of Australia*. Vol. 1 1784–1830. Sydney and London: Angus & Robertson, 1941.

—— ——. *Bibliography of Australia*. Vol. 4, 1846–1850. Sydney and London: Angus & Robertson, 1965.

Greetham, D. C. *Textual Scholarship. An Introduction*. Garland Reference Library of the Humanities. Vol. 1417. New York and London: Garland, 1994.

Grieve, Mrs M. *A Modern Herbal*. Intro. Mrs F. C. Leyel. Vol. 2. London: Jonathan Cape, 1931.

Holy Bible. Reference Edition. King James Version New Jersey: Thomas Nelson, 1972.

Horner, J. C. 'Leakey, Caroline Woolmer (1827–1881)'. *Australian Dictionary of Biography*. Vol. 5. Melbourne: Melbourne University Press, 1974. 71–2. https://bit.ly/2RadwQN.

Jennings, James. *Observations on Some of The Dialects in The West of England - Somerset Particularly*. London: n. publ., 1825. https://bit.ly/2OFKzPD. [Jennings]

Laugesen, Amanda. *Convict words: Language in Early Colonial Australia*. Melbourne: Oxford University Press, 2002.

'Massina, Alfred Henry (1834–1917)'. Frank Strahan. *Australian Dictionary of Biography*. Vol. 5. Melbourne: Melbourne University Press, 1974. https://bit.ly/2q3NOSa.

Morris Miller, E. *Australian Literature From its Beginnings to 1935*. 2 vols. Melbourne: Melbourne University Press, 1940.

O'Donoghue, F. M. 'Leakey, James (1775–1865)'. Rev. V. Remington, H. C. G. Matthew and Brian Harrison. Eds. *Oxford Dictionary of National Biography*. Oxford: Oxford University Press, 2004. Online edn. Lawrence Goldman. Ed. https://bit.ly/2CXTiqh.

Oxford Classical Dictionary. Eds Simon Hornblower and Anthony Spawforth. 3rd edn. Oxford: Oxford University Press, 1996.

Oxford Companion to Art. Ed. Harold Osborne. Oxford: Oxford University Press, 1970.

Oxford Companion to the Book. Electronic Resource. Eds Michael F. Suarez and H.R. Woudhuysen. Oxford & New York: Oxford University Press, 2010.

Oxford Companion to English Literature. Ed. Margaret Drabble. Oxford: Oxford University Press, 1985.

Oxford Companion to German Literature. 3rd edn, Eds. Henry Garland and Mary Garland. Oxford: Oxford University Press, 1997.

Oxford Companion to Music. Ed. Percy A. Scholes. Oxford: Oxford University Press, 1970,1975.

Oxford English Dictionary Online. Electronic Resource. Oxford University Press. 2000. https://bit.ly/2OIiffF.

Partridge, Eric. *Dictionary of Slang and Unconventional English*. London: George Routledge & Sons, 1937. [Partridge, *Slang and Unconventional*]

Partridge, Eric. *A Dictionary of the Underworld, British and American*. 3rd edn London: Routledge & Kegan Paul, 1949, 1968. [Partridge, *Underworld*]

—— —— *Dictionary of slang and unconventional English : colloquialisms and catch-phrases, solecisms and catachreses, nicknames, vulgarisms and such Americanisms as have been naturalized. (With supp. material as Addenda.)* 6th edn. London: Routledge, 1967.

Partridge, Eric. *The Penguin Dictionary of Historical Slang*. Abridged by Jacqueline Simpson. London: Penguin, 1972. [Partridge, *Historical Slang*]

'Savery, Henry (1791–1842)'. Cecil Hadcraft. *Australian Dictionary of Biography*. Vol. 2. Melbourne: Melbourne University Press, 1967. https://bit.ly/2q3Jh2e.

The Shorter Oxford English Dictionary on Historical Principles. 2 vols. 3rd edn Oxford: Clarendon Press, 1933, 1984.

Secondary sources

Adelaide, Debra. Ed. *A Bright and Fiery Troop: Australian Women Writers of the Nineteenth Century*. Ringwood, Vic.: Penguin, 1988.

Adkins, Keith. 'Books, Libraries and Reading in Colonial Tasmania'. *Tasmanian Historical Research Association, Papers and Proceedings* [*THRA P&P*] 53.3 (2005): 158–69.

Alexander, Alison. *Obliged to Submit: Wives and Mistresses of Colonial Governors*. Hobart, Tas.: Montpelier, 1999.

Anon. 'From the Past: The Australian Twang'. *Ozwords*. 4.1 (1998): 6. The Australian National Dictionary Centre. http://andc.anu.edu.au/publications/ozwords.

Baker, Sidney J. *The Australian language: an examination of the English language and English speech as used in Australia, from convict days to the present, with special reference to the growth of indigenous idiom and its use by Australian writers*. Melbourne: Sun Books, 1970.

Bode, Katherine. '"Sidelines" and Tradelines: Publishing the Australian Novel, 1860-1899'. *Book History* 15 (2012): 93–122.

Bolger, Peter. *History of Hobart Town*. Canberra: Australian National University Press, 1973.

Brand, Ian. *The Convict Probation System: Van Diemen's Land 1839–1854*. Hobart: Blubber Head Press, 1990.

—— ——. *Port Arthur 1830–77*. Launceston: Regal, n.d.

Bradstock, Margaret. 'Unspoken Thoughts: A Reassessment of Ada Cambridge'. *Australian Literary Studies* 14.1 (1989): 51–65.

Buzzetti, Dino and Jerome McGann. 'Critical Editing in a Digital Horizon'. In Lou Burnard, Katherine O'Brien O'Keeffe, John Unsworth. Eds. *Electronic Textual Editing*. New York: The Modern Language Association, 2006. 53–73.

Clarke, Patricia. *Pen Portraits: Women Writers and Journalists in Nineteenth Century Australia*. Sydney, London, New York: Allen & Unwin, 1988.

Daniels, Kay. *Convict Women*. St Leonards: Allen & Unwin, 1998.

Colvin, Ian. 'Rescue Mission for Lost Literary Gem. *Mercury*, 30 July 1988

Dixon, Miriam. *The Real Matilda. Women and Identity in Australia 1788-1975*. Ringwood, Vic.: Penguin, 1976.

Dixon, Robert. Rev. of *Gertrude, the Emigrant; A Tale of Colonial Life* by Louisa Atkinson. Elizabeth Lawson. Ed. *Coppertales: a Journal of Rural Art* 6 (2000): 112–15.

Docker, John, Drusilla Modjeska and Susan Dermody. Eds. *Nellie Melba, Ginger Meggs and Friends: Essays in Australian Cultural History*. Malmsbury, Victoria: Kibble Books, 1982.

Eggert, Paul. *Biography of a Book. Henry Lawson's While the Billy Boils*. Sydney: Sydney University Press; Philadelphia: Pennsylvania State University Press, 2013.

—— ——. 'Australian Classics and the Price of Books: the Puzzle of the 1890s'. *JASAL Special Issue 2008: The Colonial* Present. Gillian Whitlock. Ed. (2008): 140–41. https://bit.ly/2PMIJZN.

—— ——. 'Changing Literary Tastes and the Blue Pencil: In-house Editing and Abridgement of Australian Colonial Novels at the House of Bentley in London'. Forthcoming.

Elliott, Brian. *Marcus Clarke*. Oxford: At the Clarendon Press, 1958.

—— ——. *The Landscape of Australian Poetry*. Melbourne: F. W. Cheshire, 1967.

Franklin, Miles . *Laughter, Not For a Cage*. Sydney: Angus & Robertson, 1956.

Frost, Lucy. Ed. *A Face in the Glass: the Journal and Life of Annie Dawbin Baxter*. Port Melbourne: Heinemann, 1992.

Frow, John. 'In the Penal Colony.' *Australian Humanities Review*. April-June 1999. https://bit.ly/2q65BIJ.

Giordano, Margaret and Don Norman. *Tasmanian Literary Landmarks*. Hobart: Shearwater Press, 1984.

Gettman, Royal A. *A Victorian Publisher. A Study of The Bentley Papers*. Cambridge: Cambridge University Press, 1960.

Hergenhan, L.T. '*The Broad Arrow*: An Early Novel of the Convict System' *Southerly* 36.2 (1976): 141–59.

—— —— *Unnatural Lives: Studies in Australian Fiction about Convicts, from James Tucker to Patrick White*. St Lucia: University of Queensland Press, 1983.

Howell, P. A. *Thomas Arnold the Younger in Van Diemen's Land*. Hobart: Tasmanian Historical Research Association, 1964.

Hirst, Warwick. *Great convict Escapes in Colonial Australia*. Rev. edn. East Roseville: Kangaroo Press, 2003.

Hughes, Robert. *The Fatal Shore: the Epic of Australia's Founding*. London: Harvill, 1987.

Johnston, Judith. *Anna Jameson: Victorian, Feminist, Woman of Letters*. Aldershot and Brookfield: Scolar Press, 1997.

Jordan, Richard and Peter Pierce. Eds. *The Poets' Discovery. Nineteenth-Century Australia in Verse*. Melbourne: Melbourne University Press, 1990.

Jordens, Anne-Marie. 'Marcus Clarke's Library.' *Australian Literary Studies* 1.4 (1976): 399–412.

Kirsop, Wallace. 'Selling Books at Auction in 19th Century Australia.' *Journal of the Royal Australian Historical Society*, 95.2 (2009): 198–214.

Knight, Stephen. 'Textual Variants, Textual Variance.' *Southern Review* 16.1 (1983): 44–54,

—— ——. *The Mysteries of the Cities. Urban Fiction in the Nineteenth Century*. Jefferson & London: McFarland, 2012.

Kristeva, Julia. *Desire in Language. A Semiotic Approach to Literature and Art*. Ed. Leon S. Roudiez. Oxford: Basil Blackwell, 1980.

—— ——. *A Revolution in Poetic Language*. New York: Columbia University Press, 1984.

Long, Chris. *Tasmanian Photographers 1840-1940: a Directory*. Hobart, Tas.: Tasmanian Historical Research Association; Tasmanian Museum and Art Gallery, 1995.

Lukács, György. *The Historical Novel*. Translated by Hannah and Stanley Mitchell. London: Merlin Press, 1962; 1955.

Martin, Susan K. 'She'll Rewrite Mate? Nineteenth-century Australian Women's Fiction and the Trials of Reprinting.' *Australian Women's Book Review* 3.3 (1991): 12–14.

Maxwell-Stewart, Hamish. *Closing Hell's Gates. Death of a Convict Station*. Crow's Nest: Allen & Unwin, 2008. E-book.

McCann, Andrew. *Marcus Clarke's Bohemia: Literature and Modernity in Colonial Melbourne*. Carlton: Melbourne University Press, 2004. https://bit.ly/2PKVm7S.

McDermott, John Francis. 'Mrs. Trollope's Illustrator: August Hervieu in America (1827-1831).' *Gazette des Beaux-Arts* 51 (March 1958): 169-190.

McKeon, Michael. *The Origins of the English Novel*. Baltimore: Johns Hopkins Press, c. 1987.

—— ——. Ed. *Theory of the Novel. A Historical Approach*. Baltimore: Johns Hopkins Press, 2000.

McLaren, Ian. *Marcus Clarke, an Annotated Bibliography*. Melbourne: Library Council of Victoria, 1982.

Mead, Jenna. '(Re)producing Caroline Leakey's *The Broad Arrow*.' *Meridian* 10.1(1991): 81–8.

—— —— 'Caroline Leakey: Body and Authorship.' *a/b: Auto/Biography Studies* Special Issue: Feminist Biography 8.2 (Fall 1993): 198–216.

—— —— 'Caroline Leakey, Oliné Keese and Bio/discourse.' *Australian Feminist Studies* 20 (Summer 1994): 53–76.

—— —— 'Caroline Leakey.' *Dictionary of Literary Biography*. Vol. 230 Australian Literature 17-88-1914, first series. Selina Samuels, ed. Detroit, London: The Gale Group, 2001): 245–53.

Moore, Bruce. 'The Dialect Evidence.' *Australian Journal of Linguistics* 24.1 (2004): 22–3.

Moretti, Franco. *The Way of The World: The Bildungsroman in European Culture*. London: Verso, 2000; 1987.

Morris Miller, E. 'Australia's First Two Novels: Origins and Backgrounds.' *Proceedings of the Tasmanian Historical Research* Association. (PTHRA). 6 (1957): 37–65.

Oats, William Nicolle. *A Question of Survival: Quakers in Australia in the Nineteenth Century*. St Lucia: University of Queensland Press, 1985.

Peoples, Sharon. 'Dress, Reform and Masculinity in Australia.' *Grainger Studies. An Interdisciplinary Journal* 1 (2011): 115–35.

Petrow, Stefan. 'The Life and Death of the Hobart Town Mechanics' Institute.' *THRA P & P*, 40.1 (1993): 7–18.

Pierce, Peter. *The Country of Lost Children. An Australian Anxiety*. Cambridge & Melbourne: Cambridge University Press, 1999.

—— ——. *Australian Melodramas: Thomas Keneally's Fiction*. St Lucia, Qld: University of Queensland Press, 1995).

Poole, Joan. 'The Broad Arrow: a Re-appraisal.' *Southerly* 2 (1966): 117-124.

Reynolds, Henry. *This Whispering in Our Hearts*. St Leonards: Allen & Unwin, 1998.

Robson, Lloyd. *A History of Tasmania*. Vol. 1 'Van Diemen's Land from Earliest Times to 1855.' Part IV 'From Denison to Self-Government.' Melbourne: Oxford University Press, 1983, 1992.

Roe, Michael. 'Mary Leman Grimstone (1800–1850?): For Women's Rights and Tasmanian Patriotism.' *THRA Papers and Proceedings* 36.1 (1989): 9–25.

—— ——. 'Historical Background: Clarke and Convictism.' In Lurline Stuart, ed., *His Natural Life*.

Rukavina, Alison. *The Development of the International Book Trade, 1870-1895*. Basingstoke. Palgrave Macmillan, 2010. https://bit.ly/2PPY8bJ.

Russell, Penny. *Savage or Civilised? Manners in Colonial Society*. Sydney: University of New South Wales Press, 2010.

Scheckter, John. 'The Broad Arrow: Conventions, Convictions, and Convicts.' *Antipodes* 1.2 (1987): 89–91.

Sorell, Jane. *Governor, William and Julia Sorell (Three Generations in Van Diemen's Land)*. Eastlands: Citizen's Advice Bureau, n.d.

Sussex, Lucy. 'Mrs Henry Wood and Her Memorials.' *Women's Writing* 15.2 (2008): 157–68. https://bit.ly/2R4CmkT.

Tardif, Phillip. *Notorious Strumpets and Dangerous Girls: Convict Women in Van Diemen's Land 1803-29*. North Ryde: Collins/Angus & Robertson, 1990.

Trevelyan, J. P. *The Life of Mrs Humphry Ward by her Daughter*. London: Constable, 1923.

Trigg, Stephanie. 'The Politics of Editing Medieval Texts: Knight's Quest and Love's Complaint.' *BSANZ Bulletin* 9.1 (1885): 15–22.

Walker, Shirley. '"Wild and Wilful" Women: Caroline Leakey and *The Broad Arrow*.' In *A Bright and Fiery Troop: Australian Women Writers of the Nineteenth Century*. 85–99. Ed. by Debra Adelaide. Ringwood, Vic.: Penguin, 1988.

Watson, Kate. *Women Writing Crime, 1860-1880. Fourteen British, American and Australian Women Authors*. Jefferson, NC: McFarland, 2012.

Webby, Elizabeth. 'Literature and the Reading Public in Australia 1800-1850: A Study of the Growth and Differentiation of a Colonial Literary Culture during the earlier Nineteenth Century.' Ph.D Thesis. University of Sydney. 1971.

—— ——. 'Fiction, Readers and Libraries in Early Colonial New South Wales and Van Diemen's Land.' In David Garrioch, Meredith Sherlock, Ian Morrison, Brian McMullin and Harold Love. Eds. *The Culture of the Book: Essays from Two Hemispheres in Honour of Wallace Kirsop*. Melbourne: Bibliographical Society of Australia and New Zealand, 1999). 366–73.

—— ——. 'Reading in Colonial Australia: The 2011 John Alexander Ferguson Memorial Lecture.'
    Journal of the Royal Australian Historical Society, 97.2 (2011): 119–35.
Williams, Raymond. *Marxism and Literature*. Oxford: Oxford University Press, 1977.
Winter, Gillian. '"We speak that we do know, and testify that we have seen:" Caroline Leakey's
    Tasmanian Experiences and Her Novel *The Broad Arrow*.' *Tasmanian Historical Research Association
    Papers and Proceedings* 40.4 (1993): 133–53.

www.ingramcontent.com/pod-product-compliance
Lightning Source LLC
Chambersburg PA
CBHW081226020726
47503CB00011B/2925